DEEP KISS
OF
WINTER

Kresley Cole
&
Gena Showalter

POCKET STAR BOOKS

New York   London   Toronto   Sydney

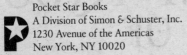

Pocket Star Books
A Division of Simon & Schuster, Inc.
1230 Avenue of the Americas
New York, NY 10020

This book is a work of fiction. Names, characters, places, and incidents either are products of the author's imagination or are used fictitiously. Any resemblance to actual events or locales or persons, living or dead, is entirely coincidental.

Untouchable copyright © 2009 by Kresley Cole
Tempt Me Eternally copyright © 2009 by Gena Showalter

All rights reserved, including the right to reproduce this book or portions thereof in any form whatsoever. For information address Pocket Books Subsidiary Rights Department, 1230 Avenue of the Americas, New York, NY 10020

First Pocket Star Books paperback edition January 2011

POCKET STAR BOOKS and colophon are registered trademarks of Simon & Schuster, Inc.

For information about special discounts for bulk purchases, please contact Simon & Schuster Special Sales at 1-866-506-1949 or business@simonandschuster.com.

The Simon & Schuster Speakers Bureau can bring authors to your live event. For more information or to book an event contact the Simon & Schuster Speakers Bureau at 1-866-248-3049 or visit our website at www.simonspeakers.com.

Cover design by Lisa Litwack
Cover art by Craig White

Manufactured in the United States of America

10   9   8   7   6   5   4   3   2   1

ISBN 978-1-4516-0005-6
ISBN 978-1-4391-6685-7 (ebook)

CONTENTS

Untouchable

Kresley Cole

Dedicated to Lauren McKenna and Gena Showalter, two incredible ladies and unstoppable forces of nature, for a thousand reasons why (and not just because my fabulous editor put me in a book with my favorite author).

ACKNOWLEDGMENTS

Much love to all my fellow rabid Showalter fans, for sharing a boundless admiration and warm affection for all things Gena. To those of you about to be initiated: Yes, we have T-shirts and we meet in the bar.

And thank you to Swede, for your wintry insights and nonstop support. You didn't have to drag me over the finish line on this one, but it means a lot to me that you were ready to.

GLOSSARY OF TERMS FROM

The Living Book of Lore

THE LORE

". . . and those sentient creatures that are not human shall be united in one stratum, coexisting with, yet secret from, man's."

- Most are immortal and can regenerate from injuries. The stronger breeds can only be killed by mystical fire or beheading.
- Their eyes change to a breed-specific color with intense emotion.

THE VALKYRIE

"When a maiden warrior screams for courage as she dies in battle, Wóden and Freya heed her call. The two gods give up lightning to strike her, rescuing her to their hall, and preserving her courage forever in the form of the maiden's immortal Valkyrie daughter."

- Take sustenance from the electrical energy of the earth, sharing it in one collective power, and give it back with their emotions in the form of lightning.

- Possess preternatural strength and speed.
- Without training, most can be mesmerized by shining objects and jewels.

THE VAMPIRES

- Two warring factions, the Horde and the Forbearer Army.
- Each vampire seeks his *Bride*, his eternal wife, and walks as the living dead until he finds her.
- A Bride will render his body fully alive, giving him breath and making his heart beat, a process known as *blooding*.
- *Tracing* is teleporting, the vampires' means of travel. A vampire can only trace to destinations he's previously been or to those he can see.
- *The Fallen* are vampires who have killed by drinking a victim to death. Distinguished by their red eyes.

THE HORDE

> *"In the first chaos of the Lore, a brotherhood of vampires dominated by relying on their cold nature, worship of logic, and absence of mercy. They sprang from the harsh steppes of Dacia and migrated to Russia, though some say a secret enclave, the Daci, live in Dacia still."*

- The Fallen comprise their ranks.

THE FORBEARERS

". . . his crown stolen, Kristoff, the rightful Horde king, stalked the battlefields of antiquity seeking the strongest, most valiant human warriors as they died, earning him the name of Gravewalker. He offered eternal life in exchange for eternal fealty to him and his growing army."

- An army of vampires consisting of turned humans, who do not drink blood directly from the flesh.
- Kristoff was raised as a human and then lived among them. He and his army know little of the Lore.

THE NOBLE FEY OF DRAISKULIA

"A warrior nobility who ruled over all the demon serfs in their realm."

- Were *Féodals*, an ancient term for feudal overlords, which became shortened to *Fey*.
- Masters in the art of poisons.
- Males prefer to be called Drais.
- Over time, divided into numerous subsets, including fire, ice, and forest fey.

THE TURNING

"Only through death can one become an 'other.'"

- Some beings, such as the Lykae, vampires, and demons, can turn a human or even other Lore creatures into their kind through differing means, but the catalyst for change is always death, and success is not guaranteed.

THE ACCESSION

"And a time shall come to pass when all immortal beings in the Lore, from the Valkyrie, vampire, Lykae, and demon factions to the witches, shifters, fey, and sirens . . . must fight and destroy each other."

- A kind of mystical checks-and-balances system for an ever-growing population of immortals.
- Occurs every five hundred years. Or right now . . .

"They say I'm as fickle as winter, as shy as frost, and as indifferent as a blizzard. It's rumored my body is pure as driven snow. Nobody imagines that I might be full of fire."

—DANIELA THE ICE MAIDEN,
VALKYRIE AND RIGHTFUL
QUEEN OF THE *ICERE*,
THE FEY OF THE FROZEN NORTH

"Women are like bottles of liquor. They should be sampled, savored, then discarded. Matrimony is for men who can't handle their liquor."

—MURDOCH WROTH,
EIGHTEENTH-CENTURY WARLORD,
MODERN VAMPIRE SOLDIER

ONE

"She's . . . near."

At his brother's weak and broken words, Murdoch Wroth's eyes narrowed in anger toward the one who'd brought the proud Nikolai so low.

Myst the Coveted, a female immortal with a vicious heart.

And Nikolai's fated Bride.

"How can you tell?" Murdoch asked.

"Because I can *feel* her," Nikolai said.

Murdoch adjusted Nikolai's arm, which he'd slung across his shoulders to help his brother walk as they searched. The humans milling all around them merely assumed Nikolai was another drunk.

Proud Nikolai. He was exhausted from consuming too little blood, his body racked with never-ending need for a mad Valkyrie who delighted in his pain. Nikolai had lost weight, his face turning gaunt, his muscles flagging.

"Murdoch, when I find her . . . I want you to trace from here."

He shook his head. "I'll stay until you've secured her—"

"No. Don't want you to . . . see me." Nikolai's weary gaze darted away from Murdoch's. "I will lose control."

Which would shame his stalwart older brother as little else could.

Murdoch couldn't imagine how Nikolai would react when he found Myst. Five years ago, she had *blooded* Nikolai, as only a Bride could, bringing to life his dead vampire's body. She'd made him breathe, made his heart beat, and stoked his newly reawakened lust with no intention of slaking it.

That same night, another Valkyrie had shot him through with arrows and still another had mocked his desires. Myst had fled with the two, dooming Nikolai.

A blooded vampire could only take release for the first time while touching his Bride in some way. If she wasn't available, then he would remain in a state of constant sexual readiness, aching indefinitely.

Which she well knew.

"Promise me you'll leave," Nikolai grated.

At length, Murdoch said, "I will." If Myst was indeed here tonight, it would make sense that there'd be more Valkyrie out on these very streets. More of their deceiving, manipulative, violent kind. "But only to find another one," he added.

He could capture one and interrogate her about the Lore, the world of not-so-mythical beings he and his brother were now a part of.

Murdoch's knowledge of the Lore was as limited as that of any of the vampires in their warrior order of Forbearers. Their army consisted mostly of turned humans, and the Lore creatures kept their secrets well guarded from them.

"Don't underestimate the Valkyrie as I did," Nikolai rasped. "Else suffer as I have."

He suffered because fate had forced this blooding on Nikolai. *As if Nikolai needed another burden.*

The blooding process was what Murdoch detested most about being a vampire, even more than never seeing the sun again.

Though he'd once been a rake, bedding a new woman each night, Murdoch hoped it never happened to him. To be mystically tied to a single woman sounded hellish, especially to a woman he didn't choose, and one who could spurn him, as Myst had Nikolai.

The pain had rendered his brother nearly mindless in his pursuit of her. Nikolai wanted retribution, but Murdoch suspected he also simply wanted *her.* Even after all that she'd done to him.

"Where will you take her this night?" Murdoch asked. "The mill?" They'd secured an old renovated sugar mill outside the city, staying there instead of the Forbearer castle while they'd scoured these streets.

Nikolai shook his head.

"Then back to the castle?"

When Nikolai didn't answer, Murdoch said, "You wouldn't take her to *Blachmount*?" The ancient

Wroth estate—where most of their family had died in a single night of sickness and murder. "Why?"

"Because that's where my Bride belongs."

Before Murdoch could question his meaning, Nikolai went still, his eyes briefly sliding shut. Then his head swung up toward a rooftop. "It's her."

Above them, a redhead stood frozen, her lips parting in shock.

Murdoch had only briefly seen her all those years before, and now he studied the details of her Valkyrie appearance. She had delicate fey features—pointed ears and high cheekbones—but he also spied the tell-tale claws and small fangs.

At the sight of her, Nikolai stood fully, no longer needing Murdoch's aid. *"My Myst."*

Her face paled, no doubt at the sight of Nikolai, who now looked like the monster she'd sought to make him. His irises had turned completely black, his fangs descending in his mouth, dripping from thirst.

Her horrified expression almost made Murdoch pity her, but she deserved no mercy. Which was good, because Nikolai would show her none this night.

Their pursuit of half a decade was . . . *over*. At last.

Just as Nikolai tensed to trace to her, Murdoch slapped him on the back, then teleported away as he'd promised, disappearing so quickly he went unnoticed in the morass of drunken tourists. Even if they had seen him vanish, the humans would think they'd imagined it.

Murdoch materialized in a back alley several blocks away, then walked to the Quarter's main thoroughfare, Bourbon Street. As he moved among the crowds, a warm breeze tripped down the street, dissipating the swampy haze and the fumes from food vendor stands.

Warm. In February. Good hunting weather.

Yes, Nikolai would be merciless tonight, as would Murdoch. Now all he needed was to find his prey.

The hunt is on.

I'm being followed.

Daniela the Ice Maiden furtively glanced over her shoulder once more. Again she spied nothing out of the ordinary—tourists milling, witches catcalling to human males—but Danii couldn't shake the feeling that she was being stalked.

Which begged the question: what creature would be stupid enough to court a Valkyrie's wrath?

Maybe she was just spooked by Nïx's cryptic remarks tonight. Nucking Futs Nïx, her half sister and the Valkyrie soothsayer, often made off-the-wall predictions. But this one continued to replay in Danii's mind.

"Sad, sad Daniela, the broken doll who wants to be fixed. Tonight she might."

Because of Danii's pale, freezing skin—she was part Icere—she was often likened to a porcelain doll. Well, because of her icy skin and because of what would happen to her if she grew overheated. . . .

But a *broken* doll? What did that mean? And fixed—for good, for bad? *What* precisely would be fixed?

She'd told Nïx, "I can't imagine what you're talking about. I'm not broken"—*my lonely existence makes me want to tear my hair out*—"and I don't know how I could be 'fixed.'"

Perhaps by being able to finally touch another? To feel a man's skin against her own without being burned, instead of constantly fantasizing about it?

I would give anything.

Yet the only males on earth who could touch her were the Icere. Regrettably, they also happened to want her dead.

Which meant the closest she'd ever get to having sex would be reading about it in the many tomes of erotica she kept hidden in her room or by indulging in her rich fantasy life. Which also meant she was probably the world's oldest virgin. Merely awaiting confirmation from Guinness.

And people wonder why I prefer fantasy to reality.

Her ears twitched with awareness. No, she wasn't simply spooked; *something* was happening. Her senses were alert.

Hastening her pace, she carefully wound around the people on the street, negotiating the ninety-eight-point-six degree gauntlet. Even the briefest contact with another's skin would burn her. A conundrum, because she kept cool by baring *lots* of hers.

When her frosty breath fogged in the warm night

air, she just stifled the urge to scream, and peeked over her shoulder once more.

This time she spotted a towering male, far behind her. He was striking, looked to be mid-thirties. But there was something unusual about him.

Was he even human? New Orleans was chock-full of Lore beings. He could be an immortal, maybe even the one trailing her.

At that moment, he wasn't looking in her direction, so she took the opportunity to duck into an alley beside a hotel. Leaping up four stories to the hotel's flat roof, she crossed to a low ledge wall overlooking the street, then crouched between two flags—one had a fleur-de-lis covered in beads, and the other said *Pardi Gras!*

Tilting her head, she studied the male below. He had longish dark brown hair, cut negligently, with a lock falling over his forehead. His face was fantasy-worthy, with a strong, masculine jaw and chin.

He wore tasteful clothes, a black button-down and jeans with a jacket that made her feel warm just looking at it. She herself was wearing the thinnest backless dress she could find.

He strode with an air of confidence. The male was gorgeous—and he knew it. How could he not, with the women gaping at him? Then she frowned. He seemed oblivious to the prancing coeds in low-cut tops angling for his attention.

His body was big, muscular in a way that hinted at immortal, but what he was exactly eluded her.

Considering his size, he was probably a demon, or even a Lykae—those animals had begun prowling the Valkyries' turf as bold as they pleased.

Or could he be . . . a vampire?

She trained her gaze on his chest, watching for the rise and fall of breaths. Seconds passed. Historically, the vampires had shunned Louisiana. Yet on this night her Valkyrie coven had heard that members of both warring vampire armies, the Horde and the Forbearers, could be out in the Quarter.

What they didn't know was why.

His chest is still. Bingo. Vamp.

Since his eyes were a normal gray and clear—not crazed and red with bloodlust—that meant he was a Forbearer, one of an army who didn't drink blood straight from the flesh.

Vampires who didn't kill. At least, that was their mission statement.

The Lore was still waiting to see how that worked out for them.

Though Danii knew she needed to report back on this sighting, she couldn't take her gaze off him. What was it about this vampire? She was aware of only two Valkyrie who'd ever been with his kind. One still lived. Danii knew the danger; so why this attraction?

Yes, he was breathtakingly cocky, with his leading-man face and broad shoulders, but she'd never been so absorbed by a male. Not a real one, anyway.

Broken-doll Daniela . . . *wanted.* Him. A vampire.

When he was almost directly below her, she noticed that he seemed burdened, preoccupied even. Hardly the expression of someone who'd been stalking her.

But if he hadn't been, then who—

The unmistakable twang of bowstrings sounded behind her.

She dove for cover, and a swarm of arrows sliced the air where she'd been standing. A second volley skittered against the brick where her head had just been, ricocheting off the low ledge wall.

She recognized the creosote-like scent of the arrowheads. Poison on the tips, *fire* poison. Which could only kill ice creatures like her. *Oh, gods.*

Without looking back, she vaulted over the side of the roof. When she landed in the alley below, she tore off at a sprint.

The bows, the poisoned arrow-heads—this wasn't a Lykae threat. Not a vampire attacking.

Icere assassins were hunting her. *My mother's people.* How had they found her?

No choice but to flee, knew she couldn't remain to fight. These assassins traveled in bands, and the number of arrows indicated at least half a dozen men.

Even as she raced directly toward the mortal gauntlet, her mind rebelled. She hadn't seen another of her kind in centuries. *I thought I'd be safe from them here.*

Her only hope was to outrun them, yet she knew how fast they would be. Like her, they were born of the fey—

She dashed right in front of the vampire, nearly knocking him over.

Two

Murdoch had just rubbed the back of his neck, then peered upward, convinced he was being watched.

He'd spied nothing, started on his way again . . . and almost ran over a small blonde in a skimpy backless dress.

With lightning speed, she darted in front of him, sparing him the briefest glance. He caught a glimpse of high cheekbones and alarmed silvery eyes before she sped across the main thoroughfare toward another alley. A pointed ear had peeked out through the wild spill of her long fair hair.

Pointed ears, silver irises, running too fast to be a human.

An immortal—possibly one of *them*.

That glimpse of her was all it took, and the chase was on. He hurriedly followed her into the alley, then traced, vanishing and materializing ever closer to her.

Though small, she was swift as she navigated through a maze of shadowy blocks, heading toward the river. He was barely gaining on her.

What kind of being could run as fast as a vampire could trace?

As he neared, he made out finer details of her appearance. Her legs were taut and shapely under her short dress. Her bared back and arms were slim. She wore silver bands above her elbows, and elaborate braids threaded her long hair.

She seemed foreign, unusual. Like women from faraway lands in olden times. *I can't wait to get a better look from the front.*

That thought threw him. Since the night he'd been turned into a vampire three hundred years ago, he'd had no interest in women, no need for them, just as he never reacted to the scent or sight of food.

Why would I give a damn about what her front looks like? He would wrest information from her. He could do little else.

His body was deadened. And he preferred it that way.

Just then, she glanced over her shoulder as she ran, and he caught sight of her elven face once again.

Those pointed ears . . . several factions in the Lore had them, at least that he knew of. Valkyrie were among them. He was becoming more and more convinced he'd found his quarry.

But she seemed to have lost sight of him altogether, focusing in another direction.

With each minute that passed, they traveled deeper into a decaying labyrinth of abandoned warehouses and stacks of railcars.

Finally she was slowing. She stumbled in a puddle, then tripped on the corner of a shipping pallet.

He stopped tracing and began running toward her. He was close enough to hear her heart drumming, her gasping breaths.

The Valkyries his brother had once encountered had known no fear of vampires. Maybe in the last five years they'd learned they had reason to flee from one. The thought made him pursue her with even more excitement. His vampire instincts rushed to the fore. The thrill of the chase overwhelmed him, and Murdoch played with her, letting her lope until she tired.

Just as he decided to end this, he turned a corner after her, running into a four-way crossing.

There was no sign of her.

Only silence.

Danii crouched on the second floor of a storm-ravaged warehouse, struggling to catch her breath and shuddering from heat.

She still couldn't believe the Icere were here. She'd thought she was safe living in such a warm climate, believing they'd never look for her this close to the equator.

Like the Icere, Danii didn't sweat. Unlike them, she could go into thermal shock if she grew overheated. But she was more accustomed to the temperature here than they were. And she knew every twist and turn of these downtown streets. As long as she didn't catch a fire arrow, she could handle the Icere.

The vampire was another matter entirely. When

she'd seen him tracing after her, she'd gaped in disbelief that yet another pursuer had joined the chase.

A clear-eyed vampire, a true Forbearer.

Though hidden, she could still see him from this vantage. With a narrowed gaze, he turned in circles below, determining her direction.

Any superficial and misguided attraction she'd felt for him was drowned out by annoyance. If this male would just move on, the Icere likely wouldn't find her here.

Otherwise, he was going to get her killed.

The assassins would separate to trap her, driving her with the threat of those poisoned arrows. They wouldn't lob their notorious ice grenades at her—they'd lose valuable cold and she'd simply take the impact with a smile on her face as she soaked the chill into herself.

But those arrows . . .

Tipped with a poison that ravaged through an ice being's veins like liquid fire.

I would know. This wasn't the first time a faraway Icere king had dispatched killers after Danii, the rightful Icere queen. . . .

Instead of leaving, the vampire called out in a deep voice, "I know you're here." His words were thickly accented. Russian? Perhaps Estonian. "You're a Valkyrie, are you not?" He stilled, listening for her. "If so, you'll want to know that my brother just captured Myst the Coveted."

Myst. Danii loved all her half sisters equally, but she *owed* Myst.

Wait . . . a Forbearer's *brother* had taken her? There was one Forbearer—an Estonian—who wanted Myst above all others: Nikolai Wroth, the Overlord. He'd done Myst wrong, but then she had definitely retaliated.

And the Overlord had brothers.

Danii had to find out what had happened to her sister. If Nikolai alone had her, then Myst probably wouldn't be in danger, since she was his Bride. But if Nikolai had surrendered her to the Forbearer king . . .

I have to know. Danii could trap the male below in a cocoon of crushing ice, then question him, but how much more cold—and time—could she stand to lose?

"Why do you cower?" Anger blazed off him. "A true Valkyrie would face me."

True Valkyrie? His taunt struck home, like a jab at an exposed nerve. She wanted nothing more than to be like her half sisters. To enjoy all the things they took for granted. *Broken doll* . . . She rose unsteadily, crossed to a gap in the wall, then stepped out.

At once, his gaze locked on her, following her down. His lips parted, revealing barely visible fangs, but he made no move to close the thirty or so feet between them.

Had she truly thought the gray of his eyes was normal? Recognition seemed to flare in them. *Recognition?* But how? She'd never seen him before—she'd definitely have remembered.

His gaze was focused . . . *predatory*. Then his irises turned black. Black in a vampire meant intense emotion. Yet his earlier fury seemed to be fading.

As they stared at each other, all other sounds—the eerie thrum of barges churning the river, the distant screech of streetcars—were drowned out.

"My brother warned me that your kind are vicious." His voice went even lower as he frowned. "I cannot see you as so."

"Where is my sister, vampire?"

"I can take you to her, Valkyrie."

I'll bet. Yes, the male before her was a Forbearer, which meant that he was clueless among the Lore.

He'd have no idea how dangerous Danii in particular could be.

THREE

A living, breathing Valkyrie stood before him. And she was so stunningly beautiful. . . .

Murdoch's view of her front had proved far more rewarding than he'd imagined.

He shook himself. Was she one of those who'd shot Nikolai? Had she been there to laugh at the idea of his brother's agony?

For some reason, he couldn't imagine her like that. He knew she was an enemy—one among an army of females who sought the annihilation of all vampires—and Nikolai had just warned him not to underestimate them. But this one looked even more fragile than Myst.

Though her features and lithe body were perfection, her blond locks were tangled around her pointed ears, and dust smudged her cheeks. Her face was feverishly red, and she was subtly swaying on her feet. She looked sad and miserable.

And spooked.

Chasing a female who feared him sat ill. Nikolai had sworn they were taunting, sadistic warriors. Yet this creature had hidden from him—after fleeing as if her life depended on it.

"Listen, Valkyrie, I don't want to hurt you. I just have some questions for you to answer."

She raised her hand, but lifted no weapon. Instead, she flattened her palm just below her lips as if to blow a kiss good-bye. The breath that left her mouth looked like a cloud of frost, surging forward, surrounding him.

Ice flash-froze around his boots. He couldn't move his legs. Couldn't break free. *"What the hell is this?"* Her breath continued to surround him, ice growing up past his knees, climbing to his thighs.

Then she coughed, bending over and rocking on her feet. The buildup stopped, leaving him fettered by this bizarre binding.

He strained against the ice, which seemed stronger than any he'd ever known, but he was unable to break free or trace from it. "Take—this—away."

She stalked closer. "Who has Myst now? Nikolai or the Forbearer king?"

"How do you know my brother's name?"

"Nikolai or the king?"

He spied the points of her ears twitching, and her gaze darted past him. Just as she *hissed* at something behind him, he heard movement and twisted his upper body around.

There stood half a dozen men, large Viking-looking warriors, with swords at their sides and arrows already nocked to the strings of their raised bows.

Their breaths smoked in the warm night air and their ears were pointed.

She hasn't been fleeing from me—

Arrows darkened the air around him, whizzing past his head. They'd aimed for her.

But somehow she was twisting to dodge the onslaught. Whirling around in the air, she turned to dart into another alley, her speed incomprehensible.

Then she was gone.

His hands shot down to claw his legs free, his fingers swiftly going numb. Just as the males behind him ran after her, Murdoch heard more fighting.

There are two groups. They're organized, flushing her out. Can't get this fucking ice off me.

Suddenly, her small body came flying out of the intersecting alley before him.

Thrown. She'd been *thrown.*

The force of her landing sent her skidding across the pavement. As she stabbed her claws against the bricks to right herself, a cloud of arrows followed her. The momentum took her out of his field of vision.

Then an unfamiliar scent swept him up. Though his instinct told him it was blood, his mind rebelled.

Never had it smelled so exquisite. So irresistible.

At last Murdoch broke free, tracing to intercept her. When he reappeared, his every muscle tensed in an instant.

The scent had been blood—*hers*. She was kneeling in a pool of it, her chest full of arrows. One of the males was holding her up by her hair, speaking in some foreign tongue. In his other hand, he held a glowing red blade.

She gazed up at Murdoch as crimson streams snaked from her wounds to the dirty street.

They'd done this to her?

What had you been about to do to her? His vampire nature warred with memories of the man he'd been. . . .

—*I would never have hurt her.*

—*She was* my *prey. They stole her from me. My prize.*

Just . . . *mine.*

At the thought of those men loosing their arrows at her, the idea of her pain and fear, rage erupted in him. The need to protect her, to destroy those who sought to harm her, burned within him.

Mine.

Two realizations struck him.

This strange female belonged to him alone. And these killers would die before they relinquished her.

Her gaze held Murdoch's, and she weakly extended her small hand. With tears running from her silvery eyes, she spoke, a whisper directed to him, loud above all sounds.

"*Mercy.*"

FOUR

Will he help me? Emotions warred on the vampire's face. Danii saw them with her vision flickering.

The poison was taking hold, leaching away her precious reserves of cold.

So hot . . . felt like she was cooking from the inside.

When she'd faced him earlier, he'd been filled with anger. Now his brows had drawn together at the sight of her injuries.

He grated, "Mercy?" Then something seemed to . . . snap. His fists clenched, and he bared his sharpened fangs. His body appeared to get even bigger. "I'm going to give you their heads, female."

Why would he? And *how*?

The vampire didn't understand how deadly these Icere were. They were expert bowmen, their fey speed unmatched in the Lore. And there were too many of them. At least eight stood between the vampire and her. They were already building ice grenades in their palms.

With an unholy roar, the vampire charged, half

tracing, half sprinting. Five of the Icere rushed to intercept him, lobbing grenades with lethal speed. But he dodged each volley, and the ice the warriors had just surrendered exploded all around him in the alley.

Like some living thing, a freezing glaze crawled over the battered brick walls, skittering all the way up to the fire escapes, coating the street.

The vampire clashed with the wall of Icere, battling his way to her, slashing through the warriors with a startling brutality. When he snatched one's jugular and blood arced out like a fountain in the night, her Iceren captor began to drag her away by her hair.

The poison had weakened her, but she still fought him. Her claws sank into his arm and tore, rending skin and bone, all but severing it.

He yelled in pain and dropped her hair to take his knife in his good hand, shoving it against her neck. The blade's heat seared her skin, and a scream erupted from her chest.

In answer, a savage bellow sounded; she and her captor looked up just in time to see the vampire flying at him.

One second the knife was at her throat. In the next, the vampire had wrenched the Iceren's head free.

The others took up their bows and charged him as one, the sound of their bowstrings louder than their footfalls. The impact of the arrows slammed the vampire against a glazed wall, shattering the ice.

He roared with fury, his arms twisting back to

pull the arrows free. Just as he tore all but one of them from his body, the Icere were upon him.

She could see him grappling again and again to get to her, yet they kept hold of him, preventing him from tracing.

Danii tried to crawl away from the skirmish, but the arrows jutting from her chest made movement impossible, and the poison was too strong. If she didn't get them out soon . . .

Thermal shock. A nightmare way to die. She was about to be executed, and for no reason. She didn't want her crown, only wanted to be left in peace—

Her would-be savior stumbled. From the ice coating the street? No, he seemed to be fighting some inner possession.

What's wrong with him? I can't think . . .

One Iceren punched the end of the remaining arrow until it pierced through the vampire's torso. He tore it from himself, but another's sword slashed his leg. Blood poured from his wounds.

There're too many of them.

As if he read her thoughts, the vampire caught her gaze. A last look for both of them?

"Touch their skin," she cried.

Though clearly confused by her words, he grasped one around the neck under the male's collar. The Iceren bellowed in pain.

The vampire's lips curled at the sound. Baring his wicked fangs, he laid his palm on another's face. A hand-shaped brand pressed into the Iceren's skin.

Seeming fresh to the fray, the vampire grew even

stronger—and more vicious, appearing intent on making it *hurt* as he dispatched them.

Soon scattered limbs littered the alley at gruesome angles. He easily separated heads from savaged necks, yelling as if with pleasure as the blood flowed.

Yet he never bit them. She saw he truly did forbear, and still he was somehow defeating them, sustaining injuries he didn't seem to feel, wound after wound that barely slowed him.

As he faced off against the last one standing, she wondered how much of the blood covering him was his own.

But one of the Iceren the vampire had felled wasn't dead. He'd clamped his neck, stemming the rush of blood. Unseen behind the vampire, he struggled to his feet and silently collected his sword.

"Look out!"

At her warning, he twisted around. The one he'd been fighting tackled him in a wrestler's grip from behind, holding him for the one with the sword.

Oh, no, no . . . She'd be damned if she'd let this warrior vampire die.

A weapon, she needed a weapon. Her gaze fell to her chest, to the six arrows riddling it.

Was she strong enough to do this?

She gritted her teeth and fisted one of the bloody arrow shafts. Choking back a scream, she wrested it from her body.

The pain made her vision waver, her muscles going limp. *No! Fight!*

Holding the feathered end, she threw it like a knife. It skewered the swordsman's neck.

The last thing she saw was the vampire snapping his head back to smash the face of the one holding him, breaking free to snatch up a sword.

When she forced her lids open once more, he was staggering toward her, his fangs still bared, his eyes black amid the blood covering his face. He'd savaged them and now was stalking closer to her.

Yet she was unafraid. He'd told her he was going to give her their heads.

And he had.

Dropping to his knees beside her, he reached for her wrist. She shrank from him, but not quickly enough to prevent contact. When she cried out, he jerked his hand away, gaping at the burn mark he'd left on her skin.

"No . . . can't be." His tone was rough, almost snarling. "You're like them? But you're a Valkyrie!"

She blinked up at him. "Part . . . ice fey."

In that growl of a voice, he repeated, "You're *like them.*" The big male was so unsure, so confounded by her nature. "I'll burn you?"

She nodded weakly.

"Is there no way I can touch you?"

"N-Never."

"Who can tend to you, then? Do you live in New Orleans? With other Valkyrie?"

"They'll kill you." If the vampire brought her to her coven, her sisters would behead him on sight and ask questions later.

Besides, she didn't have that kind of time.

If this vampire didn't save her . . .

I'm going to shatter like ice.

FIVE

With effort, the female whispered, "You . . . help me."

"How? When I'll burn you?" *Can't comprehend this. She's blooded me, this odd little creature whose skin can't be touched.*

No, she couldn't be his Bride. He couldn't be blooded. But his breaths mocked him, his thundering heart a constant reminder.

When his heart had first beat in the midst of the fight, it had sounded like an explosion, stunning him and nearly costing him his life. He'd inhaled, shuddering as air flooded his untried lungs, filling him with renewed strength.

Even now he was dizzy from his injuries, but his body still felt strong.

"I'll try to find Nikolai—Myst will be with him. She'll better know what to do."

His brother had described what happened when he'd been blooded, so Murdoch knew what to expect physically. But Nikolai had neglected to tell him that instinct, raw and bare, would take over.

"You, *please.* Arrows poison to me. No time."

Poison? No, she couldn't die like this. If she was a Valkyrie, then she was immortal.

But what did he know? He also hadn't thought a Valkyrie could be burned by his touch.

He ripped away the bottom of his shirt and wrapped his hands, then gently scooped her into his arms. Though their skin never touched, the movement jostled the arrows, making her whimper in pain.

He clenched his jaw, wanting to slaughter those fucks all over again, to punish them slowly. "Why trust *me* with this?" he snapped. Why did she want him to care for her? Why would she think him capable of it?

She tried to focus on his face, her silvery eyes going blank. "I . . . don't know why."

"You'll probably regret trusting me with your life."

In answer, she went limp, helpless in his arms.

Lord Jádian the Cold, general of the Icere, had watched the conflict impassively from his vantage in a warehouse above the street.

In his long life, he'd fought against vampires countless times, and he had the scars to prove it. But the one below had been stronger, faster. Now it crouched over Daniela the Ice Maiden. Crouched protectively. An unlikely ally for the female?

After tonight, there was no doubt that Daniela was Icere; it was bred into every line of her.

But she was also fierce like the Valkyrie—she'd wrenched a fire arrow from her own chest to cast at her enemy. He knew exactly how powerful that poison was, had harvested it himself from a fire demoness's horns.

Yes, Daniela was strong. As her mother Queen Svana had been.

When the vampire below disappeared with her, Jádian leapt down to collect the fire blade. It wouldn't do to lose it—the same knife had been used to take Svana the Great's head.

Jádian planned to wield it again.

He turned from the carnage, ignoring the low creatures that had already begun feeding on his fallen comrades. He walked on with the knowledge that Daniela was a threat that could no longer be ignored.

Just as Danii dimly perceived a bed beneath her, pain exploded in her chest. She woke to her own screaming, writhing in agony, bucking away from the source.

"Easy, girl," the vampire's deep voice intoned. "Have to get this dress off you."

She cracked open her lids, found herself on a mattress on the floor in some dark-paneled room. The vampire was surveying her with eyes the color of obsidian, a knife in one of his gloved hands.

He'd put gloves on? *Good vampire.* "In Kristoff's castle?"

"How did you—? No, we're not there." He finished slashing away the rest of her dress, leaving her in panties. He'd already removed her boots. "We're in a mill outside New Orleans."

He set aside the knife, seeming more uncomfortable with her nudity than she was. With a swallow, he wrapped his fist around an arrow just above her breast. He used his other hand to press her shoulder into the mattress. "We'll count to three."

She met his eyes and nodded. His gaze was frenzied, yet it comforted her. Never looking away, she gritted her teeth.

"One . . . two—"

Yank.

She choked on a scream, and lightning exploded just outside the house. His eyes darted around uneasily as he tossed the arrow to the floor.

Between panting breaths, she cried, "Remind me . . . to teach you . . . to count."

"Are you ready for another?"

Was she? How much more pain could she take?

"Think of something else, girl." He clutched another arrow. "Or tell me your name."

Another yank, another scream swallowed. Outside, lightning flashed once more, and thunder rocked the roof timbers.

He warily gazed upward before his attention settled on another arrow. As he worked the next shaft free—this one was lodged in her sternum— she clenched her fists into the sheets, fighting not to twist from him. The arrowhead grated against bone as it finally gave way.

"Your name," he demanded.

She gasped out, "Daniela."

"Daniela." He gave a tight nod. "Beautiful name for a beautiful girl."

She choked on a hysterical laugh, sending her into a wet coughing fit. Blood bubbled from her mouth when she uttered, "Beautiful . . . kidding?"

His expression darkened. "I only meant that you're lovely in form, or you would be—never mind."

"You're . . . *skeevy*."

He gazed away, looking like he was mentally cursing himself.

After such a long life, she was going to die of poison in the care of a crazed, skeevy vampire who couldn't count.

"My name is Murdoch Wroth."

"I know." He was brother to Nikolai, which meant he was one of the Wroths, four Estonian warlords famous in their time for their ruthless defense of their country. Five years ago, the Valkyrie had learned from Myst that two of the brothers had been turned to vampires. Nikolai and . . . *Murdoch*.

"How could you know my name?"

She tried to shrug, but only grimaced.

He let it drop. "Two more to go. Who were those men who did this to you?"

"You wouldn't know them—"

Yank. Her vision began to flicker again.

"Stay with me." Had he smoothed a gloved hand over her hair? "Only one left," he said, then added in a murmur, *"Brave girl."*

For some reason, she felt a rush of pride that he saw her as brave. She'd been weakened for so long, exiled from the very ice that made her stronger.

She struggled to remain conscious, wavering in and out.

"Will more of them be coming for you?" he asked.

"They always do. Sooner or later."

"Why would they want to kill you?"

She mumbled, "I was born."

"What does that mean?"

"Can't tell you . . . 'bout the Lore."

"Because I'm a Forbearer?" This plainly infuriated him. "You think Myst won't be telling Nikolai your secrets?"

"You think . . . they'll be *talking* tonight?"

He frowned as if she was confusing him, or more like she was *throwing* him. "Last arrow."

This one was wedged under her collarbone, refusing to come out. "Almost finished, sweet." He pinned her to the mattress, twisting and pulling as she bit back a shriek. "Just hold on."

Finally, it gave way in a rush of blood. "There." He threw it aside. "Now what do I do?"

She lay stunned, panting raggedly. *Too late. . . .*

Even with the arrows removed, too much poison remained inside her. She started convulsing from the heat, couldn't stop.

"Daniela, tell me!"

In her two thousand years of living, she'd never been this hot. Ah, gods, thermal shock.

Death by shattering. Just as she'd been warned as a girl. *Porcelain doll.* The starkest fear she'd ever known welled inside her.

She weakly grabbed his shirt. "Shock. Put me in . . . ice bath."

"Shock—what do you mean?"

"'Bout to . . . die."

Six

Murdoch swooped her up so fast his wounded leg almost gave way. In a flash, he traced her to the bathroom.

Inside, he began running a cold bath. Once he'd settled her in the large tub, he traced to a gas station, returning a few moments later with stolen bags of ice.

As he ripped open the bags to dump their contents into the water, he muttered, "This feels wrong to me. Goes against everything I know."

Because she was like nothing he'd ever known.

Am I truly covering a half-naked, critically injured female with ice?

But when she was up to her neck in it, she sighed in relief. The cold wasn't bracing or painful to her—it was clearly soothing, making her drowsy.

Her shuddering lessened, and her expression calmed.

When the fear in her eyes ebbed . . . He didn't even want to think about the relief he felt to see that. "Are you still in danger from the poison?"

"Nothing else can be done." She frowned, her gaze unfocused. "You're injured."

"It's nothing," he gruffly replied.

"Take care of yourself, vampire—" Her lids fluttered, and then she was out.

Sleeping. In ice.

He couldn't reconcile this coldness in her. She was like nothing he'd ever dreamed.

But it didn't matter if he understood her. Even if she appeared more comfortable, she wasn't out of danger. Her face was still flushed angrily. If cold was good for her, then she needed more of it.

He traced to the thermostat, turning on the air-conditioning full force. Though he didn't want to leave her—not to drink from the supply of blood he kept in the kitchen, nor to bandage his own wounds—he traced for more ice, stuffing the freezer full.

That task completed, he watched over her, beginning the most anxious vigil he'd held since the night his entire family had died, one by one.

As he paced the spacious bathroom, he couldn't take his gaze off her. Though Daniela had found him *skeevy* for remarking on her looks, he could see past her injuries. She was lovely, no doubt of it.

She had long flaxen hair, spreading past her shoulders and down to cover her breasts. Her lips were softly plump, parted around her shallow breaths. *Lush lips.* He imagined pressing his own over them, then teasing her tongue with his.

With a start, he realized he was growing hard for her. He groaned. *My first erection in three hundred years.* The erection he'd been hoping to avoid. *Christ, I am truly blooded?*

By a . . . Valkyrie.

They were warlike, many rumored to be half crazed. To be tied forever to a woman like that—and one he could never touch? *A living hell.*

No, surely there had to be a way for him to touch her, to claim her. Or would this one leave him in agony as Myst had Nikolai?

He crossed to the tub, crouching beside her, his injured leg screaming in protest. Ignoring that wound, he took her hand in his gloved ones, examining it. *So delicate.* But he'd seen her fragile-looking claws slash through a male's bone this night.

He released her hand to cup icy water and pour it over her hair, smoothing blood from the strands. Then he clumsily unthreaded her braids and rinsed them.

Why this care? Because it kept his mind off his fear for her—and his apprehension about his future. So he continued to run ice over the bruises on her shoulders and arms. Gradually, the hectic red of her face diminished, leaving pale, alabaster skin. Her breaths started to smoke.

As her wounds began to close seamlessly, his own pain increased. He'd been losing blood from his many injuries, didn't know how he could still be conscious.

Before, he'd been too concerned with keeping her alive to think about much of anything else. Now he became acutely aware that her blood was all over him, marking his bed and the arrows on the floor.

The scent was like nothing he'd ever known.

Thirst lashed him like a whip. His shaft shot harder. *Damn it, ignore it.*

His gaze trailed the lines of her jaw, her dainty pointed ears, her neck. Drinking straight from the flesh was against the laws of his order, because living blood carried the victim's memories, which in turn maddened vampires. Their enemies in the Horde, the Fallen, had all gone red-eyed with insanity.

What if he lost control and bit her? Every male in his order feared becoming one of the Fallen. Murdoch was no different, but breaking that law had never even been a consideration for him. He'd never understood the temptation.

Until now. *Am I going to make it to dawn without taking her neck?* He had to.

The damage I would do to her . . . Earlier, her wrist had all but sizzled beneath his palm. What would happen to her tender neck under his fangs and lips as he pinned her down?

Would he burn her as he licked her flesh in ecstasy?

Tearing his eyes away, he shot to his feet, tracing to the bedroom. He scooped up the arrows and stained bedding and pitched them outside. While he was there, he shed his torn jacket.

Then he traced to the refrigerator, pouring a cup of blood. Though he was depleted from his injuries, when he tried to drink, it tasted like dirt. He forced himself to swallow.

Damn it, get the cup down. Ignore this lust, blood and otherwise.

After managing barely half of the contents, he

returned, gazing down at her face. She lay so still, her blond-tipped lashes a sweep against her pale cheeks.

The mere idea of hurting her sent him reeling. He needed to *protect* her.

Without opening her eyes, she whispered on a frosty breath, "Murdoch?"

"Do you need more ice?" he quickly asked. Most of it had melted, but the wounds that had marred her chest were practically healed.

She shook her head.

"Do you want to get out of the water?"

In answer, she lifted her arms to him. He frowned. *So trusting, so vulnerable.*

He gathered her against his chest, then traced her back to his bed. Still holding her, he grabbed a towel for her to lie on.

Her breasts moved against his arm as he laid her down, and his cock shot even harder. For three hundred years, Murdoch had had no interest in women's breasts.

Now he nearly growled with pleasure.

Drawing back, he saw that her eyes were open, half-lidded. Gone was the silver. They were an aquamarine almost too vivid to be real.

"When I slept, I didn't dream of them. I dreamed of you." She sounded delirious. "Vampire, are you going to stay with me?"

He'd wanted to capture a Valkyrie and get her to talk. Why not now? "Yes, I'll stay with you."

This seemed to comfort her, and her eyes slid closed again, but he knew she was still awake.

"Daniela? Who were the men who attacked you?" He recalled the blade and the male's intoned words that had sounded like a sentencing. Tonight's attack had been an assassination attempt.

"The Icere, the fey of the north."

"Why did they want to hurt you?"

She shrugged. "Wasn't the first time. I stay on the move. Just two centuries ago, he sent a troop, but I was able to get away."

"Who sent them?" She was more than two hundred years old?

"Their king, Sigmund. This time they surprised me. 'Cause I was distracted."

"What distracted you?"

She grinned but said nothing.

"Why do they want you dead? Daniela?" When she pressed her lips together, he knew she wouldn't tell him more about this subject, so he decided to move on to a new one.

Nikolai had described the other Valkyrie he'd encountered. One had had skin that *glowed*, and one had been a supernatural archer. This female was some kind of ice creature. Perhaps all the Valkyrie had overarching similarities, but they could be born of different species.

"Daniela, your sister Myst is not cold like you. Why?"

Without opening her eyes, she murmured, "We share a set of parents. But one of our mothers is different."

"One of your mothers? An adoptive mother?"

"No. Have three parents."

She's delirious. Or was she? One thing he'd learned about the Lore was that nothing made sense to him. The laws of the Lore defied the laws of nature.

"How is that possible?" When she seemed to be going back under, he gave her shoulder a gentle shake.

Her blond brows drew together. "Wóden and Freya struck my mother with lightning to bring her back to life. I was in the lightning. The three are my parents."

No, she's definitely delirious.

"Myst was born of Wóden, Freya, and a human Pict."

Picts? They'd lived centuries ago. "How old are you?"

"Two thousand or so."

"Two *thousand*."

"'m a Pisces."

"I see. Why did you want to know whether Myst was with Kristoff or Nikolai?"

She softly answered, "Myst likes Nikolai. If he's nice tonight, he's going to be plus-one with a Valkyrie."

"Nice tonight?" he repeated. Murdoch suspected his brother would be many things with Myst. *Nice* was not among the possibilities. Feeling an unaccountable flare of guilt, he traced to the kitchen, returning with a glass of water for Daniela. He lifted it to her lips, but she turned her head away.

"Don't drink."

"It's just water."

"Don't drink anything."

"I suppose you don't eat either."

"Un-unh."

If *any* of this was true. . . . He needed to talk to Nikolai—

"Murdoch?" Her eyes were open once more, and they were focused on his mouth. "You have the most kissable lips I've ever seen."

He swallowed. "And would you like to kiss me? If you could?"

"If I started . . . I don't think I'd ever stop." Her words were throaty, so damned enticing. She wasn't a warrior, she was a *temptress*.

And a lesser man could get snared if he wasn't careful.

Her lids slid closed again. She seemed to be in that delirious state where the mind didn't want to cede to oblivion.

She eased her arm over her head, those sexy bracelets clanking, and the damp locks covering her chest fell away, revealing her perfect breasts.

They were little, but high and so plump that he ached to sink his fangs into one. Instead, he dug a fang into his bottom lip. He imagined the blood seeping on his tongue was hers.

He pictured how her breasts would bounce as he fucked her.

These lustful thoughts were so unfamiliar, so futile. She would never be beneath him. He angrily palmed his erection behind his jeans, which he knew was a risk, because the worse his arousal grew, the worse it would stay—if he couldn't get her to relieve him of it.

Just this once, he would need her to break the seal. Then he could go on his way, satisfying himself with others.

In his human life, he'd had women falling all over themselves to attract his notice. Whenever he hadn't been on the battlefield, he'd been cradled between a woman's thighs, and had grown notorious for his skills in bed. But if none of the tricks he'd learned would work on Daniela, then how could he seduce her to ease him of this burden—

"Murdoch," she sleepily sighed, "my panties are wet."

A shaky exhalation of breath. "Are they, then?" Had his voice broken?

She wriggled her hips as if she wanted them off her. With a hard swallow, he reached forward and dragged the scrap of lace down, revealing silky blond curls. Another groan, another coarse swipe over his shaft.

Too much temptation. He was about to fall on her, to mount the soft body naked before him.

Three centuries he'd been denied this. His fangs were throbbing along with his cock. He wanted to bury anything he could inside her.

With a sharp shake of his head, he snatched up a sheet to toss over her. When it glided across her nipples, they budded against it. He studied the ceiling, desperate *not* to see the way her nipples strained into the material. Then he sank into the room's one chair, but just as abruptly shot to his feet to pace again. He itched to stroke her, to explore the dream woman in his bed.

Fight the arousal. Resist it—

She kicked off the sheet. He rushed to draw it back up to her neck. "Keep this here, Valkyrie."

More restless pacing. With a huff, she kicked the sheet away once more. God, could she be any lovelier?

He ran his hand over his mouth. "Damn it, Daniela. It might be a fraction warmer, but it's a world safer for you." Had he drawn up the sheet more slowly, skimming it across her nipples on purpose?

Yet again, she rid herself of the sheet, but this time she drew one knee up. He saw her sex parted and nearly went to his knees.

Never to taste her there? Fury suffused him. Never to see those blond curls damp from his mouth or wet with his seed?

Never to claim his Bride. Why the fuck had *she* blooded him then?

He traced to the bathroom, stripped, then stepped under a cold shower. He scrubbed his body with no care for his many wounds.

This blooding business was the most ridiculous rot Murdoch had ever heard of. A woman had to bring him to life, and then he was expected to be bound to that one female—not for a year or a decade. Not even for a mortal's married lifetime.

For *eternity.*

He'd had no choice in the matter, none whatsoever in the choosing of the female. What if he didn't like delicate-looking blondes? As a mortal, he'd been attracted to buxom barmaids, and milkmaids, and kitchen maids, and the occasional shepherdess—robust women with hearty carnal appetites.

For his Bride, he'd gotten Daniela, the exquisitely fine but untouchable Valkyrie.

As he ran the soap down his torso, his hand brushed his rampant cock. Unremembered pleasure shot through him like an electric current. He was as hard as he'd ever been, aching to come.

When he gripped his shaft in his fist, a strangled sound of need burst from his chest. He gave a stroke up to the crown and back. Felt so good, he had to do it again, and again.

Masturbating for the first time in centuries.

His eyes slid shut when he perceived his semen welling. In a rational part of his mind, he knew it couldn't go further without her; she had to unleash this within him.

Resentment warred with his ecstasy—if she left him like this, he would be crippled by this lust. But everything else within was greedy for the pleasure.

Uncaring, lost, he thrust hard into his fist.

SEVEN

When Danii woke to the drum of an air conditioner chugging full blast, she found herself alone—and naked.

As she blinked in the shade-darkened room, foggy memories from the night before began to surface. She remembered the vampire's savagery in the fight. She recalled him later gazing down at her in the bathtub with his brows drawn, his face pale from blood loss. How doggedly he'd kept watch over her.

But after that, *nothing*. Once the poison had begun working its way from her system, she'd blanked.

So . . . naked? She was certain he'd put her in the tub with her panties on. Now he'd seen her completely unclothed.

Had he liked what he'd seen? No, as an unblooded vampire, he'd have no interest.

A cursory survey of her body revealed a mass of twinges, but her wounds had mended for the most part, leaving only a closing tear just below her collarbone. Her temperature was still high, but would gradually drop each day.

She inspected her wrist where he'd grabbed her. The burn had healed as well.

Even after all these centuries, she was surprised by the degree of pain involved with skin to skin contact. For some reason, it was always the worst. She could skirt a car exhaust and only suffer a lingering sting.

But another's skin against hers was like fire. . . .

She gazed around the spartan room. Considering the still unpacked duffel bag and sparse furnishings—a lounge chair, a desk, and the mattress—this definitely wasn't a permanent home.

Danii knew the Forbearers lived in the sinister Mount Oblak castle. So what was he doing here?

Over the drone of the air conditioner, she heard the shower going. The vampire hadn't left her? She recalled the injuries he'd sustained taking out *eight* of those Icere bastards, remembering that he'd been hurt much worse than she'd initially thought. She didn't know how he'd still been standing, much less how he'd cared for her.

If not for him, she would have died. The poison would have taken hold until even her immortality couldn't have saved her. *He* had saved her.

She grinned. No longer did she think him skeevy.

When blood had been everywhere and Danii helpless before him, Murdoch hadn't even tried to drink from her. And Valkyrie blood was supposed to be irresistible to vampires. Myst had confided to Danii that she'd given a drop to Nikolai the Overlord five years ago, and he'd been *wild* for it.

Oh, Myst . . . What should Danii do about her sister's abduction? Myst, who'd once done her a favor so great that she could never repay it.

The answer seemed obvious. Call Nïx and tell her to launch a search and a war if need be. Murdoch had a satellite phone on his desk.

But earlier, he'd said he could take Danii to her sister—because Myst would be with Nikolai. So the two of them *were* together.

Likely only the two of them. Making up for lost time.

If Danii called the coven about this, she'd unleash

a shrieking battle contingent to bust down the door of the vampire's love nest.

What would her sister want her to do? The facts: Myst was a master manipulator and enchantress. No Valkyrie was better at getting men to do her bidding. She could handle Nikolai.

Another fact: At the news that Forbearer vamps had been spotted in the city, Myst had been excited, her green eyes alight. Before setting out to *hunt* them, she'd checked and rechecked her hair.

Myst, it seemed, was already half in love with Nikolai. And if Nikolai was a fraction as thoughtful and gentle as his brother . . .

I'll get more information from Murdoch before I make a move.

With that decided, Danii rose from the mattress on the floor—typical vampire, craving to sleep as low to the ground as possible—and crossed to his closet.

Contrary to popular belief, she wasn't shy, but she still rooted through his duffel bag for something to wear. She and Murdoch had serious things to discuss, their siblings' situation, for one, and she didn't want to do it naked.

Even if he would have no interest in her that way.

She grabbed a black T-shirt and dragged it on, though it swallowed her, then explored his room. As she rummaged through his things, she found his wallet. She'd known who he was, but it was still a shock to see credit cards in the name of a warlord who'd "perished" in the Great Northern War three hundred years ago.

Likewise, seeing his sword belt lying next to his satellite phone was a jolt.

Danii knew much about him and his three brothers; most of the Lore did. The Valkyrie had had a correspondent in the field to cover the war, and she'd reported back on all the Wroths' heroic—and ruthless—deeds as they'd defended Estonia against the Russians. The four had been so merciless that even the creatures of the Lore had started paying attention.

She recalled that the Wroths all differed drastically in personality. Nikolai was the self-sacrificing general, Sebastian the quiet warrior-scholar, Conrad the mysterious one.

And Murdoch? Well, he was the ladies' man, a practiced seducer.

Or he *had* been, but no longer, now that he was an unblooded vampire. What a waste. The world just didn't have enough broad-shouldered seducers with piercing gray eyes.

She sighed, predicting that this male would star in all her future fantasies. Yes, Danii had a rich and complex fantasy life. While all her sisters were preoccupied with their latest lovers or intrigues, she listened and watched. Daniela the Watcher, observing and imagining. Forever a spectator.

But not tonight. She finally had a secret. She thought . . . she thought she might be growing infatuated with the vampire, even though her kind had a bitter history with his.

Wars, deceptions, atrocities.

Aside from Myst, the only other Valkyrie who'd been with a vampire had borne him a child—then died of sorrow shortly after.

Danii could lie to herself and say that Murdoch made it easy to forget he was a vampire. Yet in truth, she was aware of that every second with him.

She simply didn't give a damn what he was. For two thousand years, the Icere had tried to destroy her, either outright with attempts to execute her or with bounty hunters insinuating themselves into her life. She'd never met an Icere male that she trusted enough to be with.

Two millennia of stark loneliness did not a discerning Valkyrie make.

The broken doll wanted to be fixed. And somehow, she knew Murdoch was part of her journey. Even the fact that he was a vampire wouldn't sway her.

What he is *can't compete with the possibility of what he* could *be—*

She heard a stifled groan from the shower. *Ah, gods, he's still hurt.* She dropped the wallet, racing for him.

Just inside the bathroom, she stopped short. There was no steam, so she could see straight into the tiled shower stall above the half wall screening it—could see cold water sluicing over his broad chest, drops trickling over the indentations of his rock-hard torso.

Her lips parted, and her claws curled with desire. Her half sister Regin liked her men young, dumb, and hung, as she put it. Danii now knew her type: vampire with an Adonis physique. And she didn't say that lightly. She knew Adonis well.

Murdoch was leaning back, staring up at the ceiling, one brawny arm flexing as he washed himself. Stubble shadowed his lean cheeks.

She could see the trail of hair descending from his navel, but not where it ended because of the half wall.

Her ears were twitching. A warning? But why? "Murdoch, are you hurt?"

His arm stilled. When he met her eyes, she saw that his irises were black, burning with some hidden emotion. His gaze dipped.

Why is he surveying my body? Stingy about his shirt? "I borrowed this. Hope you don't mind."

He didn't answer.

"Okay, then," she said absently, distracted by the broad expanse of his chest. He had a few battle wounds from the Icere and a couple of old scars—not unexpected, since he'd been a warrior as a mortal, too. But his skin was surprisingly tanned.

Gods, she wanted to sweep her palms over those sculpted planes. She gazed at him greedily, taking in details—this would make choice fantasy fodder.

Wait. Had his chest just risen with a . . . breath? No, it couldn't be.

Her ears twitched again, and even over the sound of the water, she heard his heart beating, strong and fast. Her mind could scarcely comprehend this. He'd been unblooded before, but now . . .

"Wh-what's happened?"

In a husky voice, he said, "Come see."

As she blankly moved to the edge of the stall, he pressed his hands against the walls to lean forward, his chiseled muscles bunching and taut—

His engorged shaft extended straight out from his body. She gaped at his size. He was *glorious*.

And he hadn't been *washing* himself as his strong arm flexed.

"*I* blooded you?" If so, that would mean his erection was for her, and her alone. In answer to that hardness, her sex grew moist for it. Any lingering aches from her injuries were fading, no match for her mounting desire.

"You're . . . my *Bride*."

He sounded angered by the fact. Maybe his need was making his tone sharp? Of course, that was it. What vampire wouldn't want to be blooded?

"Do you know what's happening?" she asked.

He gave a curt nod, leaning against the back wall again, under the water. "Some. From my brother."

"When did you realize this?"

"During the fight."

Poor vampire, how long had he been like this? He already appeared on the verge of coming, his shaft visibly pulsing. His sac looked laden, as if it ached. She wanted to cup it with both hands.

"God, I can *feel* your eyes on me." His erection jerked, straining forward into the shower's spray. He tilted his hips until his shaft hit a hard jet of water, which, judging by his slack-jawed expression, felt *incredible*.

She swallowed. "D-do you know what needs to happen now?"

He choked out the words, "Been trying."

"For how long?"

He groaned, *"Hours . . ."*

If everything she'd heard about their kind was true, why hadn't he been on top of her, releasing the pressure he was feeling?

He was hurting—so she wouldn't have to. A pang squeezed her heart.

But if he hadn't been able to achieve his release by now, he was definitely going to have to touch her. She already dreaded that grueling pain.

No, there must be some way around that. Maybe he could touch her hair?

If so, then game *on*. They'd figure something out. And then she would have a memory to replace the one of the last time she'd been naked with a man. She shook herself, ruthlessly pushing that thought away.

Excitement began overwhelming her dread. A flesh-and-blood male wanted her. He knew her nature, and he still would need to be near her.

Around her sisters, Danii acted as if she couldn't care less that she was untouched. She assumed her ice queen persona, donning a cold cloak of indifference whenever they gossiped about their bed partners.

In truth, Danii was desperate for contact. At the very least, she yearned for companionship.

This god of a male was linked to her by fate.

*I lived through the night, and a gorgeous, virile
immortal needs me.*

Sad, sad Daniela just got happy, happy.

Murdoch's body was tensed to spring for her if she
chose to run.

Valkyrie hated his kind. This one would not be
pleased by this development.

He racked his brain for what to say to her. Normally, he would just take her hand and drag her into
the shower for a deep kiss until she'd gone weak-
kneed and mindless. In the past, he'd controlled situations with women. *I lead, and they follow.*

How to get her from here to his bed? "Dan-
iela . . . I . . . you *have* blooded me." Even to himself,
he sounded accusing.

"You don't sound too thrilled about that."

"Because I'm *not.*" *Damn it, where's my smoothness?* He'd never in memory said the wrong thing to
women, had always been able to sense exactly what
they wanted to hear.

I have no idea what this one wants to hear.

Her expression was inscrutable. At one instant
she looked shy and vulnerable, at another *ravenous.*
He couldn't read her, could hardly think.

Would she run? If so, what would he do?

He tried to moderate his tone. "I wouldn't have
chosen to involve you in this, but I have had no control over it." Still his anger thrummed in his words.

She blinked at him. "Lines like this got you laid
as a human?"

"Yes. No." He scowled.

"I'm going to give you the benefit of the doubt and assume that your brain is scrambled right about now, and I'm probably the first female you've ever encountered that you don't know what to do with. I'm familiar with your reputation, Murdoch."

"How? I don't—"

"Let's talk *after* there's no chance of you blowing this with me." When had the Valkyrie's voice grown so sultry? "So, do you want to go see if we can't work *that*"—she pointed at his erection—"out?"

His jaw slackened. "You will stay until I can spend?" *Say yes. . . . Say yes . . .*

Her gaze was lascivious, dancing over his body, all traces of the shy Valkyrie gone. "Wouldn't miss it for the world."

When she tossed him a towel and turned toward his bedroom, the legendary Murdoch Wroth dumbly followed, tripping over his own feet.

Eight

Any self-respecting Valkyrie would be figuring out how to kill the vampire. Being a Bride was considered shameful, unless you murdered the offending leech—which was the usual protocol.

But Danii? She was exaggerating the swish of her

hips as the newly blooded vampire followed her to his bed.

Playing with fire. It had a totally new meaning for Danii.

In a husky rasp from directly behind her, he said, "I thought you would run from me." His voice was just at her ear, giving her delicious shivers. He was so close she thought his erection would prod her, but he'd slung the towel around his waist.

"Uh-uh." She knelt on his bed, then curled her forefinger in invitation.

At once, he dropped to his knees before her, running his gaze over her.

Danii wasn't shy, didn't know many immortals who were. And considering how long she'd been waiting for a night like this—*fantasizing* about it—she'd be damned if she let her lack of expertise detract from the experience.

Yet even now, *he* didn't know how to proceed. "I want to seduce you . . . but I can't kiss you . . . can't stroke you."

She'd stumped a living legend. Danii was just contrary enough to be gratified by this. "There's no need to seduce me. I've already signed my name on your roster."

He frowned at that, then said, "But there must be a way for me to have you."

She shook her head sadly. She'd consulted the witches and had been told that one of them might be able to help once she came into her powers, which could take hundreds of years. She'd begged the Valkyrie soothsayer Nïx to foresee a way around this curse of coldness. Nïx had told her to simply accept herself and everything would work out.

That'd been eight centuries ago.

Suspicion tinged his expression. "If there was a way, would you tell me?"

She shook her head. "Wouldn't have to. You'd already be inside me."

His lips parted, displaying his white teeth and fangs. "Another Valkyrie teasing a vampire."

"No, I'm not teasing. I'm just *imagining* it."

At that, his shaft jerked between them, distending against the towel.

"Looks like it wants attention." She didn't ogle penises in person every day, not even every decade. "The towel off, please. I'd like to see it." Up close and at her leisure.

He raised his brows, but did reach for the towel. Once he bared himself, Danii's gaze descended along the trail of crisp black hair that led to the base of his erection. His thick length jutted boldly from his body, the crown swollen and taut. Perfection. "Will you stroke it in front of me, vampire?"

At her words, he made a guttural sound, and a drop of moisture beaded on the head.

She stared as he cupped his shaft in his palm, holding her breath as he slowly closed his fingers over it.

Finally he gave it a stroke. The sight made her go soft, her sex getting even wetter. Her nipples stiffened beneath his T-shirt. And he noticed.

"Show me your breasts." When she pulled off her

borrowed shirt, he inhaled sharply. "So beautiful."
He reached his free hand forward to touch one, but
she flinched before he could. With a curse, he closed
his hand and drew it back. "Too easy to forget."

"You can't forget, vampire. If we must touch, it's
got to be brief. Otherwise . . ."

He dragged his gaze from her chest to her face.
"Don't want to hurt you."

Tenderness bloomed anew within her, along with
the strongest desire she'd ever felt. "I believe that."

"You'll touch them for me."

It wasn't a question. Powerless to deny him, she
raised her hands to her breasts. As she petted them,
pressing them together, his eyes grew even more
excited, frenzied even.

"That's it, Daniela."

She knew her breasts were small, but right now
they felt heavy, lush. When he stared at the peaks
and ran his tongue over one of his fangs, she gave a
little moan.

"Let me see you play with your nipples."

Danii had *lots* of experience touching herself. She
brushed her thumbs over them again and again until
they puckered tight.

"Daniela!" His fist moved faster. "Spread your
knees." Once she did, he commanded, "Touch your
sex."

Without hesitation, she slid her hand down her
belly, slipping a finger to her folds.

His breaths were coming more quickly. "Are you
wet?"

"Very," she murmured.

Another groan. "I wish I could taste you, lick you." His voice had grown huskier. "Show me where you'd want me to kiss you."

Getting caught up, she spread her knees even wider, then circled a finger over her clitoris. "Here."

"Slower. Rub it slower."

She lazily flicked, gasping, "Like this?"

"Ah, God, yes!" His eyes were awash in black as he stared, his fist pumping faster.

"What would you want me to do to you?" What would a master seducer like?

With his free hand, he drew the pad of his forefinger along the sensitive slit in the crown. "You'd run your tongue over me here." When more drops of moisture slicked the swollen head, he spread them around with his thumb. "Tasting me, before you sucked my shaft between your lips."

The idea that he wanted her to know his taste made her mouth water. She yearned to lick him there, then to take that broad crown into her mouth, suckling it so deep. . . .

When her tongue dabbed at her lip, he groaned, "Almost don't want to know what you're thinking."

He seemed to be going out of his head with lust, stroking himself over and over. Gaze locked on her busy fingers, he fondled his heavy testicles with his other hand. When his brawny chest heaved with exertion, sweat lovingly trailed over the rises and falls of his bulging muscles—the most erotic scene she'd ever witnessed. He switched hands as one arm grew weak.

UNTOUCHABLE ❧ 63

Visibly frustrated, he reached out. "Just want to touch your hair." She held herself still for him, and he wrapped a long strand around his palm. Bringing it to his face, he inhaled deeply. "Your scent drives me mad." He made hoarse sounds of pain, but he still couldn't come.

Daniela didn't want to see him suffer. And he was in agony, stroking so fast she could barely see his hand. "You're going to hurt yourself." She knew that the more she healed, the colder she would become. Right now, his touch wouldn't be as excruciating as usual. "You have to touch me, vampire."

He shook his head. "Lie back and open your thighs. I'm *close*. If you come for me . . ."

The Valkyrie nodded, then lay back, wantonly spreading her glistening sex.

He would give *anything* to feed his cock inside it. Anything.

When she undulated her hips, he could see how ready she was. Her abandon aroused him like nothing ever had.

For hours, he'd been kept on edge. *Now to see this?* "Need inside you so bad, Valkyrie."

Her lids went heavy and she panted, those tight breasts bobbing.

"Bury myself so deep in you," he grated. "Fill you with my seed. . . . I wouldn't stop until you begged me." When he cupped and tugged his sac, she masturbated faster.

"Inside. Slip your finger inside." Once she did,

he leaned down to rasp right at her ear, "*Fuck your-self with it.*" He drew back to watch. "Does that feel good?"

"Ah, yes!"

"Then another finger inside."

Her voice was so sexy as she cried, "I'm about to . . . *come.*" Lightning bombarded the mill.

"Thrust faster, harder. Don't stop till I tell you."

As she began to climax, she arched her back, crying out. Her thighs fell open in utter surrender.

Eyes riveted to her sex, he gnashed his teeth, tortured with need. He helplessly fucked his fist as her orgasm went on and on. Her head thrashed on the bed, her body writhing to the motion of her fingers.

He still hadn't told her to stop, wouldn't. He was tormented; so would she be.

"Murdoch, I can't take more!" Finally, she curled on her side, still trembling, her hands between her thighs.

When the tremors eventually relented, Danii gazed up at him. During her pleasure, she'd heard him growl in pain. Now he was in even more misery.

"Vampire, just touch me!"

"Don't want to hurt you."

"Kiss my breasts." She went up on her knees, cupping her breasts to him in offer. "Put your lips on my nipple."

"Valkyrie," he bit out in defeat. He leaned down, about to press his mouth to her flesh.

She steeled herself against the coming pain—

With a ragged groan, he pulled back, forcefully shaking his head.

No. No more of this. Her hand shot out and covered his fist around his shaft. She cried out, and he jerked from the shock of cold.

The contact was scorching, a firebrand against her, even as he grated, *"Cold . . . so cold!"*

Tears welled. "Don't stop, Murdoch!" Keeping her hand on him took every ounce of will, like holding her hand to a flame.

Burning, burning, her skin seared. *Pain, dizzying . . .*

"Going to come!" His tone was awed as he began to ejaculate. "Ah, God, finally! Daniela. . . ."

Through tears, she watched him bucking into their hands, his every muscle strained in anguish. His expression was agonized, those fangs sharp and glinting.

When his seed erupted from him, he yelled to the ceiling. His massive body in throes, he came onto the bed, pumping out his jets of semen so hard she could feel them.

NINE

They lay back, both gulping breaths.

Murdoch was struggling to recover from the

most pleasure he'd ever experienced—and the hardest, most powerful ejaculation he'd ever imagined.

The release had been mind-numbing, but perhaps *all* immortal sex was better. If one had stronger senses, then why wouldn't sex be heightened as well?

With one need met, another instantly screamed within him. He'd lost blood the night before and hadn't come close to replacing it. He could still smell hers all around them.

Ignore it. He turned to her. She was cradling her burned hand, her eyes still wet.

When their skin had made contact, hers had felt like ice, definitely uncomfortable to him. His skin had made her *cry.* Yet earlier, when he'd been tearing poisoned arrows from her flesh, there'd been no tears.

"Let me see it," he grated.

She reluctantly showed him her blistered palm, and he winced, guilt assailing him. He rose to get ice for her, but was so unsteady he wondered if he could even trace to the kitchen. With effort, he made it to the refrigerator, saw the containers of blood there.

So thirsty. . . . He felt a mad urge to annihilate his supply. *Just get her the ice. She's burned because of you.*

Ice. Before now, he'd never much thought about it. Yet it had been his Bride's salvation. What would have happened if he hadn't gotten her cooled last night? Would an immortal like her truly have died?

Returning with a paper towel filled with ice cubes, he handed it to her, careful not to make contact—or to glance at her neck.

She closed her hand around a couple of cubes and sighed in relief. After a few moments, she peeked up under her lashes at him. "So what happens with us now?" *The shy Valkyrie was back?*

"You tell me."

"This is out of the realm of my experience." As her pain faded, her expression showed hints of excitement. She looked optimistic. No doubt, she thought they were embarking on something. Females always had in the past. No matter how much he warned them that he would never settle down.

Embarking with Daniela—a woman he could never bed? *I'd be consigning myself to misery.*

He just needed time to *think* about all this. He rose and yanked on his jeans, grimacing as the material scraped over his abused shaft.

She must have sensed his tension, because she dropped the ice and defensively bundled the sheet to cover herself. After a few moments, she said, "You've lost a lot of blood."

"I'll be fine. Been in worse shape."

"I expect so, since you died and all."

He turned to her. "And you know how I came to be like this?" When she nodded, he said, "Tell me, then."

"King Kristoff found you dying on a battlefield. He gave you a choice of fealty to him and eternal life—or death. That's what Kristoff does, what he's always done."

Fealty or death. Murdoch remembered that night as if it were yesterday. Kristoff had found Nikolai first, in a pool of his own congealing blood. But Nikolai hadn't feared death, so he'd negotiated with Kristoff before he would accept the king's offer.

He'd demanded to be a general in the Forbearer army, refusing to take orders from anyone but Kristoff himself. And he'd wanted Murdoch and any trusted comrades with mortal wounds turned as well.

Nikolai had also demanded the span of a human's lifetime to watch over their four younger sisters, their two younger brothers, and their father.

They'd all been dead in a matter of weeks.

Murdoch ran his hands through his hair. "Tell me how you knew who I was."

"The Valkyrie heard Forbearers were going to be out in the city. When you told me your brother had captured Myst, I put it together. He's the Forbearer most likely to search for her."

Now that Murdoch had experienced for mere hours the hell that Nikolai had endured for *years*, he was furious anew with Myst. Daniela's *sister*. "Shouldn't he have searched for Myst?"

When Daniela nodded blithely, he frowned. "And shouldn't you be demanding that Nikolai free her?"

She gave him a vulnerable grin. "If Nikolai is half as sensual as you are, I wouldn't be doing her any favors to get her freed. I'm sure they've come to an *understanding* by now."

The Valkyrie was throwing him. Again. *Too much to take in.* A new Bride. A hunger like he'd never known . . .

He gazed at her neck once more. Her skin was pale, smooth, begging for his fangs.

"Besides, the more I think about it," she continued, "the more I realize you should probably be rescuing your brother from her. She's going to twist him inside out."

Murdoch shook himself. "She's *already* done that. She tormented him for five years." His anger was growing, matching his thirst and exhaustion. "I barely got through a few hours of needing to come— imagine half a decade!"

Her pleased mien faded. "He deserved nothing less."

Murdoch traced directly in front of her, staring down. In a menacing tone, he said, "Did he? To be shot up, then left crippled by his Bride?"

She rolled her eyes at him, possibly the first woman ever to do so. "Either you don't know all the facts or you're ignoring them. On the night that Myst left Nikolai, he was about to *torture* her for information in Mount Oblak's dungeon. Our sisters rescued her from that fate, and they wanted to kill Nikolai, but Myst left him alive. Your brother owes her his life."

"Watch what you say, *plika*."

"Chit? You called me a chit?"

Figured she'd know Estonian.

Her own ire clearly mounting, she said, "And what'll happen if the *plika* doesn't watch what she says? Will you hurt me, your one and only Bride?"

"You think I'm bound by this? Bound to you?"

Even as he sneered the words, he had to resist that unbearable pull toward her. *Resent it.* "You think that I'll follow you around like a dog as you scorn me?" His eyes kept straying to her neck. Would she notice?

"Scorning you hadn't even been in the decision tree for me, but now that you bring it up, it makes total sense, especially considering the repercussions otherwise," she said. Yet then she frowned. "Wait a second. I see what you're doing. Trying to scare me off."

She rose, tucking the sheet around her like a towel. "Look, I'm as freaked out about this as you are. But the fact is that I . . . *liked* you, up until five minutes ago, and I wanted to see you again—even though I'd be risking ridicule at best and ostracism at worst." She took a step closer to him, that vulnerability in her expression. "I'm sure this is all overwhelming for you. One minute you're going about your business, and the next you're blooded with a Bride—"

"One I didn't *choose*." He was taking his frustration out on her, and he couldn't seem to stop. "I didn't manage monogamy as a human, though I could have wed my pick of the most ravishing women in my country. How do you think I'll fare with a female I can't touch?" Especially now that he could have others.

Her eyes narrowed, and lightning struck outside. "Monogamy? I'm not angling for a wedding!" All shades of that previous vulnerability were gone, replaced by haughtiness. "And if you don't think I can hold my own against all those eighteenth-century mortals you were out tagging, then you're a fool, Casanova." At his expression, she added, "Oh, yes, I know all about you."

He went still. "What are you talking about?"

"I was alive back then. And all the Lore heard about the ruthless warlord brothers from Estonia. The general, the scholar, the enigma, and . . . the *manwhore*."

He clenched his jaw at the thought of having his life analyzed, especially by creatures he didn't even understand. The Forbearers could garner little information on Lore beings—their lives held secret—and yet they'd been actively following his own exploits?

"A manwhore?" Was that all he'd been remembered as? "Maybe I left behind the women I'd enjoyed because I didn't want to deal with *exactly this*." Even now he wanted to end this argument by kissing her and taking her to bed, which confused him even more. "It doesn't take a genius to figure out that the hour we just shared was the best we ever will—it's all going to go downhill from there."

"You don't have the sense to realize you were blooded by one of the only Valkyrie who would accept a vampire in her bed."

"To do precisely *what* there? Freeze?"

In a flash, she drew back her blistered hand to slap him.

"Do it, ice queen. And feel the sting with me."

Lightning struck again as she lowered her hand. "You're not worth it, leech," she said, but he was scarcely listening. Below her collarbone, a small line of blood had just risen from the last remnant of her wounds.

That stark red against her alabaster skin called to him, made him imagine following the trail with his tongue, then pinning her down to suck from her breast.

Already the scent was all around him. And now to *see* it?

Don't look at it.

How the hell had Nikolai restrained himself from biting Myst all those years ago?

Murdoch's hands fisted as he struggled not to fall upon Daniela. He'd been able to resist touching her when under the most painful pressure he'd ever dreamed of.

But I'm not going to be able to deny this call. . . .

Ten

How can this be happening? They'd been doing so well. Fantasy made reality . . . somewhat.

But now the vampire's eyes had flooded black again. So he was as angry as she was?

Danii turned from him to snag the T-shirt, donning it as she dropped the sheet. When she met his gaze, he appeared even more incensed than before.

"Obviously, I need to leave," she said, while thinking, *Tell me I'm your Bride, and that I will be staying. Be an arrogant, possessive Neanderthal vampire!*

She wanted him to simply inform her that he would never let her go and she would just have to accept that, or whatever domineering misguided tripe these manly men always said. *To women that aren't me.*

This one wouldn't even look at her. "You need to go. *Now.*"

Kicking me to the curb. She didn't know how much more of this her ego could take. Leeches were detested by most Valkyrie—by most of the Lore— yet Danii had been ready to offer this one more. *He has no idea what I'd been willing to risk for him.* "I'm a bit perplexed here. Most vampires refuse to be separated from their Brides, yet you can't get rid of me fast enough."

Because he no longer needed her. Danii had helped give him his initial release, her Bride's duty done, and now he could be with other females. She was expendable.

But one day he would realize what he'd lost—a frigid, broken female he could never claim, and one with skin issues—and then he'd be sorry.

When her bottom lip trembled, she cursed herself bitterly. *Don't you cry in front of him!*

"I thought you were going."

Exasperation drowned out the urge to cry. Exactly *how* was she supposed to leave? She didn't have a car here, didn't even know where they were. "No."

"What?"

"Not until you tell me why you're so intent on getting rid of me."

His gaze was transfixed on her neck, his voice a snarl as he said, "I'm about to throw you to the ground. Take your blood in a frenzy."

"B-but your kind doesn't bite." Her lips parted, and she backed away with real fear. "I'm not strong yet, Murdoch. If you did that, you could kill me."

His eyes went wide, then narrowed. Yet he'd still begun striding toward her. She backed to the wall.

Can I spare enough cold to stop him? With a grimace, she started building ice in her palm, planning to trap him as she had before.

When he was just before her, he shook his head, his entire body going off balance. With a last look at her face, he snapped, "Leave here. Before I return for you."

Then he vanished.

How much time had passed since he'd left her, Murdoch didn't know.

Hours, it seemed. But only now was the ravening frenzy subsiding.

After leaving Daniela, he'd traced to his rooms at Mount Oblak, Kristoff's castle, then attacked his supply of blood like an animal.

Now crimson was everywhere. He stared at the smeared floor and counter. *My God, what would I have done to her?*

He was still astounded that he'd been able to

keep from touching those luscious breasts of hers—
yet he couldn't deny himself her neck?

Once he'd caught his breath, he rinsed his body
in the shower, then redressed. Having managed
some level of sanity, he decided to go to Blachmount.

Returning to the time-ravaged manor was always
uncomfortable—almost all of Murdoch's family had
died within those walls—but he needed to talk to
Nikolai.

He traced to Blachmount's great room downstairs, listening for the sounds of fighting. Or otherwise. The manor was silent. Frowning, he traced
to the master chambers, and was stunned by what
he saw.

Nikolai and Myst were sleeping together peacefully in the bed. Nikolai had his arms wrapped possessively around the Valkyrie, and she was clutching
his chest.

Contentment suffused Nikolai's face, his visage
markedly changed from the strain of the last several
years. He was still pale, still gaunt, but his face . . .

Just as Daniela had predicted, Nikolai and Myst
had come to some kind of understanding.

*I wonder if Nikolai takes it for granted that he can
hold his Bride?* With a start, Murdoch realized that,
for the first time, he was jealous of Nikolai. Which
shamed him.

He knew of no one who deserved this peace more
than his brother.

Seeing them like this eased much of his animosity toward Myst. No matter what had happened

in the past, at this moment she was giving Nikolai pleasure.

Murdoch shook his head, no longer surprised that his brother had taken Myst here. Nikolai always came to Blachmount when he missed their family.

With this woman, he was planning to start a new one.

Murdoch tried to imagine what it would be like to have a female belong to him alone, above all others . . . and couldn't. It wasn't meant to be for him. He'd driven his own Bride away. Only now did Murdoch recognize that he'd taken his anger toward Myst—and his frustration over the blooding—out on Daniela. Who'd done nothing to deserve his ire; indeed, just the opposite.

But it didn't matter *how* he'd driven her away. Only that he had. This way was best. He'd just end up hurting her, had almost *bitten* her.

Even after his brother's five years of torture, Nikolai hadn't succumbed to bloodlust and bitten Myst. Her neck was unmarked.

At that moment, Nikolai drew his brows together and tightened his arms around his Bride. Though he slept, Nikolai still sensed another's presence.

So Murdoch traced back to the mill. He held his breath as he materialized, not sure if he hoped Daniela would still be there or not.

Empty. He ignored his baffling disappointment. *What'd you expect?* He'd threatened her, insulted her—

He spotted a piece of paper on his desk. Tripping

in his haste to reach it, he snapped the note up and read:

> Vampire,
> At some time in the future, you're
> really going to want my number.
> So I thought I would give you this:
> 867-5309.
> XOXO,
> Daniela, the Ice Queen

The words were embellished with whimsical hearts. *I haven't blown it.* Relief sailed through him, so strong he sagged onto his mattress.

She'll see me again. He ignored the part of him that was filled with foreboding, the part still warning that she'd be safer if she didn't.

When he felt the afternoon sun's heavy reach over the earth, his lids grew heavy. Exhaustion caught up with him and, with her note clutched in his fist, he slept.

ELEVEN

The cracked vinyl of the truck bench stuck to Danii's heated thighs, disgusting her even further.

Her hands were clenched and a steady stream

of lightning trailed her as she and Farmer Ted bounced along a pitted road, closing in on Val Hall, the manor that housed the New Orleans coven of Valkyrie.

Earlier, once she'd trudged *a mile* from the mill, in the heat of a Louisiana noonday sun, she'd eventually stumbled onto a desolate county highway—and an old farmer driving by in an even older truck.

After dashing in front of him in the road, begging for a ride, she'd promptly deduced that Farmer Ted was a man of *no* words, communicating solely by strategic spitting of his tobacco chew.

With one healthy splat out of his truck window, he'd agreed to drop her near home. At least, she'd translated that as an agreement. Before he could argue—that would just get untidy—she'd clambered into the cab. The one without air-conditioning that reeked of taxidermy and Levi Garrett tobacco.

If Valkyrie ate, Danii would be vomiting right now.

All because of that vampire. The only thing getting her through this ordeal was the belief that Murdoch would regret what he'd done.

And the fact that she'd left him a special number for when he returned.

The second he'd vanished, she'd rushed to the mill's garage, agreeing that she needed to leave, stat. *Rule to live by: If a vampire warns you he's coming back to attack and possibly kill you, then you listen.*

Inside, she'd found a classic Porsche, refurbished and lovely, with a new Maserati Spyder beside it. She'd been eager to steal and trash either one, already planning to return the vehicle with a UV bulb in the overhead light. But she couldn't find the keys.

She'd tried to call for help on his sat-phone, but the service was code-locked.

Rather than stay and wait like an unwitting bag of O positive, she'd scribbled her note and set out in her bloody boots, wearing damp underwear, the vamp's T-shirt, and a cloak of rage that only a two-thousand-year-old Valkyrie could pull off.

For so long, those in the Lore had noted the differences between Danii and her sisters—including Danii. But in truth, she had just as many Valkyrie traits as she had Icere.

Most notably, Danii possessed the Valkyrie's notorious pride and need for retribution. Like her sisters, if she was wronged, then gods help the subject of her wrath.

I've so been wronged. By the first vampire in history *not* to want his Bride. She didn't know if that said something about him—or about her. If anyone found out she'd been cast away by a Forbearer, she would never live it down. Her only hope was that no one ever discovered her disgraceful morning.

To add insult to injury, she'd also remembered him *interrogating* her. While she'd been filled with poison, he'd been filled with questions.

Her supposed white knight had taken advantage of her, and she couldn't recall how much she'd told him. Surely she hadn't revealed any critical secrets or weaknesses. . . .

Stop thinking about him. You have things to do. Like fleeing the city.

Since none of the assassins from last night would be reporting back, King Sigmund would soon send another Icere contingent. He wouldn't stop until he'd killed her.

Just as he'd murdered the true queen of the Iceren, Svana the Great, Danii's mother.

Danii had to get home and pack, but she grew weary merely thinking about returning to Val Hall, weak and shamed, a vampire informer. Via Farmer Ted. How could she face her sisters now?

Myst was *still* getting razzed for hooking up with Nikolai five years ago, even by other Lore factions. Having the aggressively omnisexual nymphs ridicule one's choice of lover was about as low as one could get. Mysty the Vampire Layer was the butt of many a joke.

Who was worse? Myst, who'd dabbled with a vampire, or Danii, who'd dabbled and had desperately wanted more?

Murdoch dreamed.

Sometimes he dreamed of the sun, sometimes of old battles. Now he dreamed of his father, of walking in on him wet-eyed, clutching a portrait of Murdoch's mother on the fifth anniversary of her death.

Murdoch had loved his mother, though she'd

been zealously religious, and he'd grieved her loss, but his father had been left a broken shell of a man.

At first, Murdoch had pitied him. Then he'd scorned the father who had scant time for his family, who'd all but orphaned his four young daughters with his neglect.

By this time, Murdoch had been enjoying women for years, knew that they were always about when he needed one. His father could have enjoyed the same—as a wealthy aristocrat, he could easily have found a woman to replace his departed wife.

"Get another one," Murdoch had finally demanded, unable to comprehend what kind of hold the woman had over him. His father had refused to move on, obsessed with her.

A woman's death had *broken* a strong man. . . .

The dream began to change. Murdoch found himself with Daniela in a strange room made of ice walls. But he felt no chill from it, no discomfort.

He placed his palms on either side of her ethereal face—without giving her pain. When his thumbs brushed her delicate cheekbones, she smiled up at him, but her countenance was different. Everything about her had changed.

Wisping ice crystals had formed in half-moon shapes at her temples. More crystals spiked her lashes and tangled in her wild, shimmery hair. Her skin was even paler, her lips tinged with blue. Delicate cobalt-colored designs laced around her wrists and descended over her hands. In his dream, he knew they ran across her lower back as well.

Her eyes seemed to be filled with an ancient knowing, and they glowed as if banked with a blue fire.

She looked otherworldly. Like a completely alien being. *She is otherworldly.* . . .

"Do you want me?" she whispered on a frosty breath, leading him to a bed in the center of the room.

He'd never wanted anyone more. "I have to have you."

"Then take me, Murdoch."

He was about to give her his standard warning, that this was only for a night. He wouldn't be interested in more. But she pressed her chill lips to his, stunning him with the cold—and with the pleasure. Perfection. Delicious.

He lost track of what he'd been about to say.

As they kissed, he slipped her skimpy dress from her, then pressed her back on the bed. He tugged her panties down, left her heels on.

Sweeping his hands up her thighs, he spread her legs. Now that he could, he made a feast of her body for hours, licking her in secret places. Instead of her own fingers delving into her sex, his now thrust inside her.

He tormented her, first keeping her from coming, then forcing her to, over and over.

In his dream, he knew she'd never been with another man. He painstakingly prepared her body for his, determined to spare her pain as he claimed her virginity.

When he'd been human, he'd never been interested in virgins. Back then, much was taboo in his conservative country. Deflowering a maid one never intended to marry was virtually blasphemous.

So why was he continuing with Daniela, positioning his hips between her pale thighs? Why was he kissing her soft breasts, rubbing his face against them, sucking on those stiff nipples? Did he want to be bound to her? *One woman.* For more than even a mortal lifetime. Possibly *forever.*

These thoughts left him when the head of his cock found her wetness.

She softly cried, "*Murdoch . . .*" Lightning fractured the night, the thunder booming all around them.

With a groan, he slowly rolled his hips up, pressing the crown inside her untried body . . . *the tightness, the connection.*

When she gasped in his ear and made little whimpers of pleasure, he ran his mouth against her neck, licking her sweet skin, knowing he'd take her blood this night.

He rode her harder, faster, shocked when she met his frantic thrusts with a hidden strength. She dug her heels in to lift her hips, seating him even deeper inside her.

She told him she was about to come, and he was desperate to feel it.

Her sheath began squeezing his throbbing cock, and the power of her orgasm sent his seed climbing. The pressure would soon make him mindless. His cock ached; his fangs ached. No amount of will could prevent him from bucking his hips to lose his semen . . . or from piercing her neck.

With a yell, he sank his fangs into her tender flesh. And it was like coming home.

"Murdoch!"

He *felt* her crying out as her blood filled his mouth, coursing through every cell in his body.

Connection.

As the overwhelming urge to come inside her grew, he slammed his body between her legs. Growling against her neck, he began to ejaculate, spending so hard he knew she felt it inside her. Still sucking her blood, he flooded her womb.

Once he was spent at last, he collapsed atop her, releasing his bite. Afterward, as their hearts pounded, he couldn't seem to stop kissing her neck and murmuring praise in her ear. This new bond between them was like nothing he'd ever known.

Yet she began fading, disappearing from him.

"Murdoch, what's happening?" The fear in her eyes was like the night before—stark, filling him with dread.

"No! Daniela, don't go. . . ."

A strange voice in his mind whispered, *"How badly do you want her? What would you sacrifice?"*

He woke to his own yelling, tracing to his feet. With her number still in his hand, he snatched up the phone, staring at one, then the other as he caught his breath.

He shook his head hard. What the hell was this? Like a spell on him, making him behave in ways he normally wouldn't.

Calm yourself. Think this through. You have blood-lust for her.

He couldn't control it. He acknowledged that. Yet he kept remembering his brother's contentment. Murdoch's mind seized on the rightness of being with Daniela in his dream.

Think, just think. . . . As he debated, he stalled, tracing to the kitchen to drink blood, though he had no appetite, then showering. He took time selecting which clothes he'd wear for the night—in case he decided to meet her again.

In the end, Murdoch found it impossible not to call her. *To hell with it.*

He was strangely nervous as he picked up the phone. After all, he'd never contacted a woman for an assignation. They'd always come to him.

He'd have to smooth-talk Daniela, since he'd left it so badly today. That wouldn't be a problem. He'd been called silver-tongued by more than one lover in the past.

Eight-six-seven-five-three-oh-nine—

"Kristoff wishes to see you," a male said from behind him.

He hastily disconnected the call, then cast a scowl over his shoulder. Lukyan, a Russian For-bearer, leaned negligently against the doorframe.

Murdoch didn't trust the former Cossack. Not bothering to hide his irritation, he said, "Can't it wait?"

"It's about your brother. You're to go to Blach-mount."

"*What* about him?"

Lukyan's expression was studiously blank. "He's probably about to be executed."

TWELVE

Danii had gotten into Val Hall undetected. *Now I just have to get my things and get out.*

Although a couple dozen Valkyrie lived here at any time, the manor was quiet this morning. Most were nocturnal, as was Danii usually—it was cooler that way.

Nïx, the one half sister she wanted to see, was nowhere to be found.

Upstairs, Danii passed the most shaded chamber in Val Hall, belonging to Emmaline, her beloved niece. But she knew Emma would be asleep as well. It was day, and Emma was vampire. Or half one. No one knew who her vampire father was, and that information wasn't likely forthcoming, since her Valkyrie mother had died of sorrow decades ago.

Gentle Emma was the single vampire the Valkyrie accepted. Though a blood drinker, she was so timid that she made it easy to overlook the vampirism.

Emma was the exception; Murdoch was the rule. *Just accept it. He almost bit you. . . .*

Danii reached her room, which was basically a

giant freezer, and pushed open the heavy insulated door. A blast of arctic air and the comforting drone of refrigeration met her.

She lived at Val Hall year-round. But in the summer, even the meat locker—as her sisters called her room—was barely adequate for her needs.

There simply was no call for hundred-degree days.

Closing the door behind her, she gazed around the spacious area. She'd decorated it with frost, glazing the walls with it. Icicles dripped from the blades of the ceiling fan. Valances of ice capped her windows.

She couldn't say she loved it here, but she'd adapted to life with her coven. Others could tolerate hours in the snow, but would seek a hearth at the end of the day. Danii was the same way with heat, except she sought the comfort of her meat locker.

Her slushy waterbed was filled with saltwater, which lowered the freezing point to below thirty-two degrees. Above her bathtub was an ice maker, and beside it hung an Epsom salt dispenser. On occasion, she had to add salt to the water so that *she* didn't freeze it.

Her ice-proofed computer was a military-spec laptop with a magnesium chassis and a sealed keyboard.

Yes, she'd adapted. And she'd felt some security living in such a warm climate. *I thought I was safe from Sigmund here.* It should've been the last place the Icere would look.

The attack was another reason Danii was avoiding her sisters. If she told them about last night, they would insist on her staying—and them fighting. But the Icere were an enemy the Valkyrie didn't need.

And one they could never find to defeat.

When Danii had been a girl of seven, her mother Svana had journeyed to Icergard, the Icere castle, to reclaim her crown from the vicious Sigmund. Danii's memories of this time were indistinct after the passage of so many years, but she remembered her mother saying, "If I don't return to you here, you must promise me, love, never to follow me. Never, never go to Icergard." She'd made Danii vow it.

Svana had never returned. Before she'd even made it to the castle, Sigmund had assassinated her—the mother who'd refused to linger endlessly in peace with her young daughter in the godplane of Valhalla.

Once Danii had grown old enough to leave Valhalla herself, he'd dispatched killers after her to prevent her from ever challenging his reign. As if she ever would.

Over the centuries, she'd considered breaking her vow to her mother, but only to gather her sisters and strike back at Sigmund, freeing herself from his threat. Yet even if the Valkyrie could find Icergard—rumored to be hidden within the Arctic Circle beneath a dome of ice—they could never attack the castle without getting slaughtered.

Sigmund was perfectly protected from the Valkyrie, inadvertently utilizing their greatest weakness as his defense.

Diamonds. Svana had told her they dotted the walls and perimeter fences. Though Danii was immune, most Valkyrie could be mesmerized by them.

With a sigh, she rose. She needed to pack, and then she needed to find Nïx to ask the half mad soothsayer about three things:

Myst.

Exactly *what* was supposed to have been fixed the night before.

And where Danii should flee before the next wave of Icere arrived.

There were eleven other Valkyrie covens around the world that Danii could choose from.

The latitude of the Seattle coven had always intrigued her. And then there was the one in New Zealand. Fall approached down there.

Yet as ever, Danii hated to leave her own coven. Valkyrie visited others, but they always returned to their primary coven, like preferring an immediate family over an extended one.

Plus, the New Orleans Valkyrie had plagued the others with practical jokes, which might make it awkward for Danii to pop in.

She could just see herself telling the Seattle Valkyrie, "I had nothing to do with signing you up for the emu farming franchise. And I am sorry twenty of them were released in your pool house, startling your harem of cabana demons. See Nïx."

Tonight, the wily soothsayer would likely be downtown in the Vieux Carré. So Danii would be trolling Bourbon Street yet again. Her only consolation was that she wouldn't run into Murdoch.

He and his brother had only been in New Orleans to find Myst. Good riddance.

Damn it, why did never seeing him again matter to her?

Because he saved your life and surprised you repeatedly. And she'd *enjoyed* him, had liked what they'd done together. It was the first time she'd had an orgasm with someone else in the room. She grew aroused just recalling how he'd worked the seed free from his shaft. He'd been naked in bed with her, his mighty chest heaving, yelling out as he came.

And now he was free to use those sensual lips to kiss another woman, could use that magnificent body to pleasure others. She glanced at her claws. They'd straightened with aggression.

Stop thinking about him, she told herself firmly as she crossed to one of the windows, brushing away a layer of frost. As her gaze flickered over the lightning-scorched trees in the yard, a sense of melancholy fell over her. *I don't want to leave.*

In the window glass, Danii spied her reflection. She was exhausted, which meant there was a reddish tinge to her lips and under her eyes, instead of the blue that should be there. Her face was pinched.

She *looked* miserable. Tally yet another reason why the vampire hadn't wanted to have anything to do with her. Well, other than biting and possibly killing her.

She glared down at her pale, icy skin. Never to be

touched. Never without pain. Danii was stuck in this body, stuck in this rut.

Most of her half sisters were fiercely independent—many were legendary warriors or love-'em-and-leave-'em jet-setters. Danii was just . . . Danii. And she could admit she'd longed for a male of her own, maybe to make a home with. A male who would always clasp her in his arms when she ran for him.

I'm the Valkyrie who most wants to be held—and I never can be. At the thought, she felt her bottom lip trembling. *I'd rather not have had a glimpse of what I've been missing.*

She dropped her head into her hands and wept, her freezing tears making her want to scream.

THIRTEEN

Tonight Murdoch might be forced to kill his king.

He had sworn fealty to Kristoff and his Forbearer order, but he was loyal to Nikolai above all others.

After Lukyan left, Murdoch quickly stuffed Daniela's note in his pocket—and donned his sword. He would strike down Kristoff in a heartbeat if his brother was in danger.

When he traced to the great room in Blachmount, Kristoff intoned, "Sit, Murdoch."

Kristoff was at the head of the timeworn table, flanked by four Forbearer elders from Russia, some of the first ones he'd turned—his own countrymen.

Within their order was a tense alliance between the Russians and Estonians. Kristoff thought the realm of the Lore superseded human concerns and wars. But history was difficult for Murdoch to forget. Russians had killed him and most of his family.

"I imagine Nikolai will be down shortly." Kristoff was analyzing him. Would he hear Murdoch's beating heart? And if he did, would he say anything about it?

The king often acted in ways that were incomprehensible to Murdoch. He'd demonstrated blistering wrath toward some subjects, and unexpected leniency to others.

Kristoff was a natural-born vampire, not a turned human, and was as shrewd as he was ruthless. As a boy, he'd had his crown stolen by his uncle, Demestriu, the current leader of the Horde. Kristoff had been smuggled out of the capital before Demestriu could assassinate him, then raised in hiding by humans.

Once Kristoff had grown old enough to seek his birthright, he'd had no army, so he'd started *making* one, siring troops of turned human warriors.

Murdoch sat down uneasily. "What are we doing here?"

"Questioning your brother," Kristoff said. "About his crime."

Striving to make his tone level, he asked, "What crime would that be?"

"One of the worst."

The worst crimes in their order were treason and drinking living blood straight from the flesh.

There'd been no treason. Though Murdoch didn't particularly care about Kristoff's cause—he'd agreed to join the king's army because he'd wanted to live—Nikolai had always fervently believed in what the Forbearers stood for.

And drinking living blood? When Murdoch had seen Nikolai earlier, he'd been content, but he'd still been pallid, still lean. His eyes had been closed, so Murdoch hadn't been able to tell if they were red.

"My liege, you know Nikolai," Murdoch said. "He's a loyal soldier." Besides, Nikolai would've told Murdoch if he'd planned anything.

"Exactly."

Murdoch fell silent at that, knowing from experience that Kristoff would say no more. As a natural-born vampire, Kristoff was unable to lie, so instead he often ignored questions and answered others cryptically.

As they waited for Nikolai, Murdoch restlessly glanced around the decaying room. So many memories haunted this place. Here Nikolai had made the fateful decision to try to turn all of their dying family.

Murdoch remembered that time as if it were yesterday.

After he and Nikolai had risen from the dead, they'd traced home and had found their sisters and father dying of plague. Sebastian and Conrad had been stabbed through by Russian marauders and barely clung to life.

All in this room . . . How the girls had wept when they'd comprehended that they were dying. How filled with rage Sebastian and Conrad had been to be turned into vampires against their will—

Nikolai suddenly materialized. He was black-eyed with fury, his fangs dripping. He must have sensed intruders, and thought them a threat to Myst.

"Wroth, I pity the being who wishes to harm your Bride," Kristoff said.

Murdoch nearly whistled out a breath at Nikolai's appearance. His face had been beaten. His clothing was filthy, his shirt tattered and marked with blood.

Nikolai seemed to be grappling for control. "I would not wish to attend you in such a condition. I'll go wash and change—"

"No, we know you are eager to get back to her for the remains of the night," Kristoff said, then added in a proud tone, "Congratulations, Wroth. You've now been blooded *and* claimed your Bride." He studied him. "Recently. Though it appears she didn't acquiesce to you."

Did Kristoff think *Myst* had fought Nikolai? What the hell had happened to his brother since earlier this day? If Nikolai had been content earlier, now he looked *determined*.

"I'd like to meet her," Kristoff said.

"She is resting."

Murdoch thought he heard her in the bath

upstairs. Leisurely bathing? If they'd fought, then why was she not fleeing Nikolai?

Kristoff said, "I suppose she would be resting. In fact, we'd wonder if she weren't."

Two of the elders snickered until Nikolai shot them a quelling scowl.

Kristoff steepled his fingers. "And you drank her blood this night?"

Deny it, Nikolai.

"Did you take her flesh as you did so?"

No, steady Nikolai would never commit this crime, the one punishable by death. Should Kristoff decree it, Nikolai would be chained in an open field until the sun burned him to ash.

When Nikolai's eyes narrowed, Murdoch's hand slipped to his sword hilt. Five against him and Nikolai. Likely the brothers wouldn't make it out of Blachmount alive.

How fitting.

Nikolai's shoulders went back. "I did."

No, brother. . . . He *hadn't* restrained himself. But why were his eyes clear?

Kristoff ordered, "Take off your shirt."

Murdoch caught Nikolai's glance, tensing to fight, but Kristoff said, "Stand down, Murdoch, no one's dying tonight."

A lashing then? Nikolai removed the shirt, too proud for his own good. His gaze darted to the stairs; even now he worried for his Bride.

"Toss it on the table."

Frowning, Nikolai did. Murdoch caught the scent

just as the other elders did. Kristoff had detected traces of Myst's blood, and now they all did as well. Like the others, Murdoch's hands went white on the table, but for a different reason.

Murdoch was reminded anew of Daniela's blood—and of his dream, recalling how he'd pierced the supple flesh of her neck, sucking from her.... "And what was it like?" he absently asked, his voice hoarse.

Nikolai didn't answer. Then Kristoff raised his brow in a wordless command.

After a hesitation, Nikolai grated, "There is no description strong enough."

Murdoch barely suppressed a groan and was surprised that no one noticed the hectic drum of his heart.

"How did she feel about your bite?" Kristoff asked.

Again Nikolai was silent.

Kristoff's stare was unflinching. "You resist answering your king on the heels of confessing to our most reviled crime?"

Nikolai resisted because he'd accepted Myst as his. As his *family*. Wroths protected their family's honor.

Answer him, Nikolai—you can't protect her if you're dead.

Nikolai must have been thinking the same thing. Though distinctly unwilling, he bit out, "She found extreme pleasure from it."

She'd *liked* being bitten?

Kristoff relaxed back in his chair, his demeanor pleased. He asked those at the table, "Do you think I should forgive Wroth his transgression? For which one of us could have resisted the temptation when she was our Bride and her exquisite blood called?" The king stared at the shredded garment marked by a Valkyrie's blood.

Murdoch masked his shock. For centuries, this had been law. Forbearing from drinking the flesh was how they'd earned their name. Was this a license to drink from one's Bride?

"Continue as you were," Kristoff told Nikolai. "But if your eyes turn red, know that we will destroy you."

Nikolai is free to drink his Bride, to take her blood at his leisure. Murdoch envied him. Again.

Nikolai was stunned as well, but recovered enough to say, "I was coming to Mount Oblak tonight to tell you that Ivo was spotted in New Orleans."

Ivo the Cruel was a leader in the Horde, and their armies had battled in the past. In fact, Mount Oblak had once been his holding.

"He's looking for someone," Nikolai said. "I suspect it could be Myst."

That made sense. She'd been Ivo's prisoner, had already been in his dungeon when the Forbearers had taken the castle.

Nikolai ran a hand over his face, his concern evident. "I need to go—"

"We'll take care of it," Murdoch interrupted sharply. "For God's sake, you stay here and . . . enjoy . . . everything." *Everything I can't.*

Kristoff returned his attention to Nikolai, eyeing him shrewdly. "Find out as much as you can from her. And you will tell us if the memories follow the blood."

After a short nod, Nikolai traced from the room.

His brother hadn't just been spared, he'd as much as had a slap on the back from Kristoff. The king was no doubt thinking of an alliance with the Valkyrie.

And I have a Valkyrie Bride. But Murdoch could never drink her anyway, was a danger to her.

If Nikolai had succumbed, knowing he was breaking the laws of their order, then Murdoch didn't stand a chance of controlling himself with Daniela. And she would find no pleasure in it, had told him she could die from it.

Kristoff stood. "Now, which of you will volunteer to accompany Murdoch to New Orleans where this coven full of Valkyrie is located?"

They all shot to their feet.

One asked, "Does this mean we can drink from our Brides? Without repercussions?"

"Only if they're immortal and can't be killed from blood loss. I believe that's why Nikolai's eyes are still clear," Kristoff said absently, his gaze focused on Murdoch. "A word," Kristoff told him, ushering him aside. "You are charged with protecting Myst the Coveted. This match between her and your brother is critical. Scour the city for Ivo until the sun drives you back."

In the past, Murdoch had searched those city streets for his brother's sake. Now he would do the same for Myst, a female he'd hated for years. "And when I find him?"

"Take him out."

"Gladly."

"Is there anything you'd like to tell me, Murdoch?"

"My liege?"

"Your heart beats," Kristoff observed. "Don't worry, the others won't notice. Turned humans rarely think to listen for it. When did this happen?"

"Last night."

"A mere five years after your brother. While I've waited millennia." Did Kristoff envy them?

Doubtless. The natural-born vampires had the same pressing drive to find their mates. They were born fully alive, growing much like mortals, until they neared the age when they froze into their immortality. Then with each day, their hearts would beat less, their breaths—and sexual need—gradually diminishing to nothing until they could become blooded.

Just like the Forbearers, the natural-born vampires knew exactly what they were missing. . . .

"Is your Bride by any chance a Valkyrie?"

When Murdoch hesitated, Kristoff's eyes flooded black with anger. "Need I remind you that I'm your king? And I've just shown mercy to your brother."

"She is a Valkyrie."

"Have you been able to learn anything about the Lore from her?"

"I'll be able to find out more in the future," he said, hedging for some reason.

"The future? She's a Valkyrie—the odds are against her wanting anything to do with you."

Murdoch's shoulders straightened. "She told me

she wanted to see me again." *Before* he'd threatened to bite her. But she'd still left her number. "She even gave me her contact information." He pulled the note from his pocket, displaying it.

Kristoff raised a brow at the *X*s and *O*s, the puffy hearts. "Call her," he challenged.

Murdoch took his sat-phone from his jacket, then dialed the number. It rang several times.

"Hmm. Not waiting by the phone for your call?"

Murdoch heard a voice-answering service clicking on. Kristoff did as well and said, "Probably in the shower, then?"

"Of course."

But a woman's voice said, "If you've reached this message and you weren't trying to contact Regin the Radiant"—

Regin?

—"then I know three things about you. One of my half sisters just tooled your ass and never wants to see you again. B. You're pop-culturally illiterate not to know that this number is a song. And three, you'll never tell another male about this humiliating prank, so the number trick can be continued indefinitely. If, however, you called for *moi*, then say something to amuse me after the beep."

Murdoch's anger was boiling. Just as he was about to unleash his wrath in a message, a computerized voice said, "Mailbox is full."

That little witch . . .

"I understand you had a reputation for being popular with women," Kristoff said as he collected

Nikolai's bloody shirt from the table. "You'd better recognize that a Valkyrie is not exactly your typical woman."

FOURTEEN

"Forbearer scum."

"Ignorance is bliss, leech."

"Go sun yourself."

Being met with insults was the only way Murdoch and his men could determine that they'd even approached Lore beings in their search of the Quarter.

Hours ago, Murdoch had mapped out the rest of the city for the other Forbearers, and then they'd split up, each elder with two men under him. Murdoch had taken his old friend Rurik, an Estonian who'd served under him in the war, and they'd been stuck with Lukyan, the hotheaded Russian. Kristoff could insist that the former political alliances of his soldiers had been nullified by those of the Lore, but the wily king always put a Russian with Estonians, and vice versa.

Over the course of the night, Murdoch had grown better able to recognize the Lore beings— they seemed more adroit, more suspicious, and often more drunken than the humans—but he still didn't know what they *were*.

And not one of them would offer information. The females hadn't given him enough time to charm them. The males had looked ready to fight on sight.

The closest he'd gotten was with a scantily clad female who'd painted her skin with leaf designs. She'd at least given him a few moments to state his introduction and questions, not that she'd *listened*. She'd merely been ogling him while nodding dimly and murmuring, "Uh-huh, baby boy, you keep talking, Trixie's lis'ning."

She'd kept this up until another female, dressed and painted like her, came charging between them to harangue the first one. "He's a *vampire*. You really are a ho-hum whoreslut of a nymph, aren't you?"

"No, you are!"

Then they'd lunged at each other, deep-kissing as they went tumbling to the ground.

All in all, the Forbearers had learned nothing about Ivo's whereabouts.

Now, as midnight neared, Rurik, Lukyan, and Murdoch stood on a balcony overlooking the crowd. The other two were arguing over various topics, while Murdoch was silent in thought, mired in unease over Daniela.

Of course, he knew *why* she'd played the prank on him. And he knew why it would be best if he never saw her again. So why did he feel this urgency to find her? He craved the sight of her, needed to have her scent fresh in his mind.

This eve, he'd seen pretty women, but he had

no interest in them. Though he knew so little about Daniela, the blooding made him think of her constantly.

It forced him to recall her vulnerability when she'd said she wanted to see him again. It made him remember with a disturbing tenderness the way she'd lifted her arms to him so trustingly.

As a mortal, he'd had a happy-go-lucky personality. Women had trusted him with their pleasure but little else. Yet Daniela had believed in *him* to remove the arrows in time to save her life.

Tomorrow night, he could go to Blachmount and ask Myst how to contact her sister. But then, Myst might refuse to divulge that information. If all else failed, he supposed he could try to find the Valkyrie coven, despite Daniela's warning that they'd kill him on sight.

Another source of his unease? He couldn't stop mulling over how the Wroth brothers had gone down in Lore history for their deeds, or misdeeds. After the continuous battles and hardships they'd all suffered, Nikolai had been remembered as the self-sacrificing general, and Murdoch had been classed as the manwhore?

He also suspected that this bothered him solely because that was how Daniela saw him—

"What say you, Murdoch?" Rurik asked.

"What? I didn't hear you."

"We were speaking of Brides and Valkyries."

Murdoch almost coughed. "Were you, then?"

Rurik's scarred face creased into a frown. *He can*

tell something is going on with me—has known me for centuries. Rurik had been one of five dying war compatriots who'd accepted that fateful deal Nikolai had brokered with Kristoff.

But cunning Kristoff knew that these men were loyal to Nikolai and Murdoch, and always would be. Demonstrating his shrewdness yet again, Kristoff had dispatched the other four—Kalev, Demyan, Markov, and Aleksander—in separate directions on the continent to search for the Daci, a rumored hidden enclave of natural-born vampires.

Rurik alone remained, and only because of his weakness: an uncontrollable temper when in conflict. Not the best trait for a potential ambassador.

"I heard at Mount Oblak that Nikolai's Bride was fine beyond words," Lukyan said. He was a bold and skilled fighter—as a Don Cossack, Lukyan had been bred for war—but Murdoch didn't trust him. There was something off about him, even beyond the fact that he'd died on the other side of the same battlefield Murdoch had perished on. "You saw her. Is she that beautiful, then?"

"She is." *But not more so than Daniela.*

"I haven't really *looked* at a woman in so long." Rurik's gaze fell to the street below. In his human life, he'd been a simple farmer, a gentle giant, until he'd gone into battle; then he would go berserk. He didn't wield a sword—he carried a war hammer.

Rurik's father had often liked to say that the men in their family were descended from berserkrs. After Rurik had been turned into a vampire and learned this new world existed, he'd had to wonder, *literally descended from berserkrs?*

"Wouldn't matter if you'd looked at women, you'd only see half of them," Lukyan said with a smirk.

Rurik had the war wounds to show for his rages. He walked with a marked limp and was missing an eye under his rakish patch. Ignoring the Cossack's comment, he said, "Have females been showing this much skin the whole time?"

Murdoch understood his comrade's puzzlement. He himself had been disinterested in women to the point of oblivion. Until the Valkyrie.

"Christ, look at that one," Rurik said in an awed tone. Murdoch remembered that even before he'd lost his eye, Rurik had been unlucky with women. He wondered if Rurik remembered that.

With a leer, Lukyan said, "Maybe she's the one who'll tempt me back to life."

Pinpricks skittered along the back of Murdoch's neck as he turned to the object of their attention.

Daniela. Just there.

The gnawing ache he'd been experiencing redoubled at the sight of her.

She was strolling the street below them, her white-blond hair swaying about her shoulders with each of her graceful steps. She wore a wrap of black silk around her hips, with a thin swath of the material climbing up over one breast, around her neck, and down over the other.

Could she have revealed more of her perfect

flesh? Her back and arms were bare, as was a good bit of her chest and flat belly. The only jewelry adorning her were those exotic armbands. A satchel was slung over her shoulder.

Damn her, she was noticeably braless. And now he stood spellbound by how her high breasts bobbed as she nimbly wound through the crowd.

She seemed oblivious to the men she left ruined in her wake. They froze, gaping after her as if they loved her and would do anything for her.

When one male spoke to her and she smiled up at him, Murdoch's fangs sharpened. The blooding at work again?

He shook himself, disconcerted by the violent drives racking him. *Get control.*

"She's got to be an immortal." Rurik's voice was rough with appreciation, and Murdoch had to check an impulse to hurt his old friend. "Do you think her blood would be like that of Nikolai's female?"

It would be, God help me, it would be. . . .

Lukyan said, "Bedding an immortal. Can you imagine how much experience that one has?"

Can't rip out his throat. Murdoch wanted to bare his fangs at them, to growl that she was his. But it would only make Lukyan more determined to meet her.

What if Daniela blooded one of these vampires? Was that even possible? He had to get them away from her.

"Back to work," he ordered them. "I'm starting

at the head of the street. You two come from the other end. We'll cover more ground."

Once they'd reluctantly traced away, with lingering looks that almost got them killed, Murdoch descended to the street, then strode toward her.

What the hell was she doing out here alone? There could be more of the Icere out in this city. To risk her safety like this . . .

Without warning, a memory arose. "I don't understand why men get so jealous over possessions, or over their women," he'd once told his father.

His father had seemed deeply disappointed when he'd answered, "Son, that's because you've never cared about anything enough to fight for it—or to fear losing it."

FIFTEEN

"Oh, no, no. This isn't happening," Danii muttered as she jogged backward three steps, then whirled around in the opposite direction from the vampire intently approaching her.

It's him! Earlier when she'd reached the Quarter, she'd asked around for Nïx, but instead had found out that Forbearers, led by a very big and handsome vamp, were going door to door, canvassing the streets for someone.

She'd joked to herself that maybe it was Murdoch out seeking her—laugh, laugh—to abjectly apologize. Had she been not far off the mark?

Or maybe he still wanted to throw her down and drink her.

"Wait, Daniela!"

When he traced in front of her, she halted with her palm raised to her lips. "Come any closer, and I'll fill your lungs with ice."

"I don't want to hurt you."

"No? You were going to bite me earlier."

He didn't deny it, just gave a curt nod.

"So what's different now?"

"I've replenished the blood I've lost. And I'm not surrounded by the scent of yours."

"Sounds like you're trying to make *your* loss of control *my* fault."

"No, it was solely mine."

"If not to bite me, then what do you want?"

He didn't seem to know how to answer that. At length, he said, "Just to talk to you."

"Is that why you and your henchmen were looking for me?" Predictably, he'd need to see his Bride.

He ran his palm over the back of his neck. "We . . . weren't . . ."

"You're *not* looking for me." *How embarrassing.* "Then who?"

"We seek Ivo the Cruel."

A Horde baddie. "Good luck with that," she said between gritted teeth, turning to leave.

He followed her. "You know of him?"

"Of course I do. I'm not the one batting for Team Oblivious like you are." She snapped her fingers and made a face of realization. "Oh, but wait, you're no longer quite so clueless since you *grilled me last night.*" Again he didn't deny it. "Did you tell all the Forbearers about what I said when I was delirious?"

"I've told no one," he said, his handsome face darkening into a scowl. "What in the hell are you doing out here alone?"

"I'm looking for someone myself."

"Who?" When she didn't answer, he said, "You should be where it's safe. There could be more Icere."

Like he cared. She picked up her pace, refusing to spare him a glance—and failing. He seemed to be puzzling over what to say to her.

Finally he decided on: "You gave me the wrong number."

He called? Her immediate high promptly nose-dived. Of course, he'd only called for help with Ivo. "You have a lot of nerve bringing that up."

"Why would you do that?"

"For—fun." *To get your hopes up and then have them dashed. Like mine continue to be.*

She reminded herself that any "hopes" she might have had about him were firmly in the tense that was past. "And for the record, I wasn't seeking to wed you, vampire"—*I might have been right after we came together*—"and I wasn't even looking for an exclusive relationship." Unless he'd been interested in one. With that, she stormed off.

He was right behind her. "Where are you going?

Why won't you give me two seconds of your time?"

I don't think my battered ego can take it. Like her body, it hadn't quite recovered.

"You've easily forgotten that I saved your life last night!"

She rounded on him. "Which wouldn't have needed saving if you would've just shut up and moved on!"

He didn't even seem to be listening—instead his gaze raked over her, from her chest to her uncovered navel. "What are you wearing?" he grated. "For someone whose skin is in danger of being burnt, you show enough of it."

Too late, he was acting like a domineering vampire with a Bride he considered worth having. "Because otherwise I'd burn up!" She wished she could criticize his clothing, but he looked irritatingly GQ in his tailored slacks and expensive shirt. His black cashmere jacket fit his broad shoulders to perfection.

Normally, she'd have been ecstatic to be seen with such a man.

"Then why do you live in this warm city?" he asked.

"Because this is where my coven is. For now."

"For now? Is it moving?"

She narrowed her eyes up at him. "Don't you have someone to be searching for? I'm sure you need to catch up with all the other little Forbearers."

He cocked a brow at that. "We've split up. You could help me."

"Oh, that's rich. The last time I 'helped' you, I got nothing but a burned hand and a death threat."

He closed in on her, forcing her to back up until she met a shop window. Looming over her, his voice a husky rasp, he said, "Is that all you got out of it, *kallim?*"

Kallim meant "darling." *Woo-hoo, a step up from "chit."* "Does this usually work on women?" Somehow she managed to be cold and unaffected. Or to look it. She hoped. "The threatening and then the full-court press?"

He exhaled. "I regret how today ended."

"Just as you predicted, it all went downhill from that one good hour." Where she'd made contact with the window, ice crystals fanned out on the glass, outlining her bare shoulder and upper arm with frost.

He noticed and said, "I'm glad you're, uh, cooling." Then he bit his lip, looking like he was inwardly kicking himself.

"I see why you were so popular with the ladies, Murdoch Suavé. With lines like that, how could you not be?"

"Murdoch Suavé?" With a shake of his head, he said, "We're looking for Ivo because he might be a danger to Myst."

Ivo could be. If the creep was in town, he'd probably be looking for his former captive.

"I've been ordered to protect her," Murdoch added.

"Protect Myst? This is a considerable change from"—she imitated his low, accented voice—"Myst is Nikolai's enemy! We hate Myst! She's *mean.*"

His lips quirked, which seemed to surprise him,

then he resumed his scowl. "They have come to an ... understanding."

"Told you. So what do you need my help for?"

"My men and I can't get any leads. I've tried to question beings from the Lore—"

"But no one will speak to any of you. The rookies keep striking out?"

His glower deepened at her comment. "Finding Ivo is critical to me, Daniela. My brother would be destroyed if anything happened to Myst. The blooding is making him fall for her."

"That's not what the blooding does, you oaf!"

His expression indicated that he'd never in his life been called an oaf.

"The blooding doesn't *make* you fall for your Bride. All it does is indicate who you'd be most likely to have a successful relationship with—biologically and emotionally. That doesn't mean you're *capable* of a relationship," she said with a pointed glance at him. "Look, if Nikolai's falling, then it's just love. Real simple."

"I don't believe that. Then have you ever seen a fated pairing that didn't work out?"

"Oh, it happens." *To my mother for one.* Svana and Sigmund had been fated mates, and a much-celebrated love match. She'd taken him as her husband and prince consort. Then he'd stolen her crown and murdered her. Danii shook herself. "Now, if you don't mind, I have things to do."

"You wouldn't help me to help your sister?"

Danii stilled. *I owe Myst.* Unbidden, a memory washed over her.

Centuries ago, Danii had been captured by a sadistic Roman senator. He'd kept her among his slaves, bringing her out of her sweltering prison cell just to *play* with her, burning her naked skin with his touch.

She'd remained a virgin only because he'd intended to offer her to the Emperor, due to visit that season. Before he'd arrived, Myst had seduced her way past the senator's legions of guards, then killed him.

"I want to help her," Danii finally said. "But I won't work with you."

"Why not? You can't go about alone on these streets. The Icere could return."

"I've got a couple of days before they can get this far south. Besides, who's more dangerous to me? Them? Or the vampire who was about to attack me just hours ago?"

"Damn it, I told you why—"

"Have you ever bitten anyone before?"

"You know I haven't. My eyes are clear."

She shrugged. Actually, the Forbearers had it wrong. Vampires only turned red-eyed when they *killed* as they drank.

"We've pledged to our order that we would never take blood from the flesh."

"What would happen if you did?"

His brows drew together. "We . . . well, after tonight, it's *complicated*. But I vow to you I won't bite you. Just help me."

Danii hesitated. She was a skilled fighter, as were most Valkyrie, but because she risked overheating, she could seldom go into a protracted conflict here in southern Louisiana. And her special talents—conjuring blizzards as battle offense and frostbiting enemy armies—had been relegated to the past.

Since the coven had moved here seven decades ago, she'd felt . . . *underutilized*. Finally she would have a chance to assist her sisters in a meaningful way.

And she could do damage control. If he hadn't told anyone about what she'd divulged last night, then she could extract a vow from him never to do so!

Yet she feared there was nothing so noble ultimately steering her decision.

Sad, sad Daniela . . . so lonely and lame that she still yearned to be around the vampire.

No! Remember Farmer Ted, Danii!

In the end, it wasn't what Murdoch said that convinced her, but what he did. When three trashed frat boys leered at her as they passed, Murdoch's fists clenched.

He did feel *something* for her. Perhaps he did truly like her, but was afraid to settle down after so many centuries alone. Maybe he had bachelor's panic.

Maybe it's him, not me. "I'll help you, on three conditions."

"Let's hear them."

"You protect me if we encounter any more Icere—"

"Of course. I will protect you from any threat."

"Hold on there, I don't need your help with anyone but them. Second condition: you'll answer any questions I ask you. And third, you'll vow never to tell another about anything you learn tonight—or learned this morning. Or anything about me."

Seeing he was about to balk, she said, "I'm risking a lot by being seen with you. I could search on my own. And I would, if I thought you wouldn't follow me."

"Daniela, that's not—"

She turned to walk on.

He grated, *"Agreed."*

She faced him once more. "And if you even peek at my neck, I *will* go cryo on you."

Sixteen

Yet another female cajoled to do my bidding, Murdoch thought as they started out. He hadn't lost his skills.

"Where do we go first?" he asked, trying to tone down the smugness in his voice. *I control situations with women.* Just as it had always been. Which sometimes made for boring fare since he was never surprised, but that was unavoidable.

"We're off to a bar, a few blocks east on Bourbon. I know a demon. If we don't have any luck, then we can stop by a store that caters to Loreans."

"Very well." Now that he'd received the promise of her help, Daniela had become a means to an end. He would be staunchly focused on what he needed to do.

But, God, her hair smelled so damned good,

giving him a shot of her scent each time her braids played about her bare shoulders. . . .

As they meandered through the crowd, humans kept looking at her, some more intently than others. He felt his fangs sharpening.

Did that fuck just ogle her br—

"You're going to have to cut that out, vampire."

His head whipped forward. "Cut what out?"

"Baring your fangs anytime a mortal checks me out." Now *she* sounded smug.

"I was *not* baring my fangs." He might have been baring his fangs. "Daniela, you'll find that I'm far from a jealous person."

"Uh-huh."

"Maybe I'm just concerned that you'll get burned. Since you're displaying so much skin." *That I can't touch.* He had to stifle the impulse to drape his jacket over her to protect her from injury—and lecherous gazes. "You're not nervous about making contact?" He thought *he* was more anxious about it than she was.

"I've threaded through the ninety-eight-point-six degree gauntlet many a time. Have you forgotten how fast I am?"

He hadn't. Still, for the next several minutes, if he spotted any passersby more intoxicated than others, he ran interference for her. When he almost grabbed her elbow once to steer her out of the way, she warned, "Ah-ah."

He ground his teeth in frustration, then said, "I'll return directly." He traced to Mount Oblak, snagged a pair of thick gloves, then traced back so fast that she'd hardly had time to react to his disappearance.

When he held up his gloves, she said, "That's just weird."

"It's convenient." He drew them on.

"You would still have to be extremely careful with me, and I'd need to know how thick those were—"

He placed his palm flat on the small of her back, his hand nearly spanning it. "They're as thick as the ones from last night. I didn't burn you then."

She stiffened, but after a few moments, she allowed it, continuing along the street.

Even with such an innocuous touch, he found himself hardening for her, his second erection in centuries. Though his glove and her dress separated their skin, he could still feel her moving beneath his hand, her shapely hips swishing.

For many minutes as they walked, she was silent, seeming deep in thought. Had he made a mistake by tracing, reminding her what he was?

She'd wanted to be able to question him, but hadn't. So he said, "I went back to the alley where we fought last night. What happened to the bodies?"

She frowned. "They were probably eaten. By low creatures."

"By dogs? By rats?"

She gave him a cryptic smile. "Nothing so *generic*."

"And you won't specify what kinds of creatures? Come on, this is ridiculous," he said. "Do you think Myst won't tell Nikolai everything? So many beings in the Lore can't all keep such secrets."

"Humans think we're myths. Enough said."

A dead end. He let that drop. Yes, he'd succeeded in getting her to help him tonight, but he'd begun to suspect that this situation might not be precisely under his control.

Finally, she glanced up at him. "You said you were ordered to protect Myst. By whom?"

"By King Kristoff himself." *But I'd do it anyway.* Murdoch recalled the expression on Nikolai's face when he'd been grilled by Kristoff about Myst. Loyal, steadfast Nikolai had disobeyed his king, and looked as if he'd do it again for that woman. If she were killed, Nikolai would be as doomed as their father had been.

"Forced to protect her. That must grate."

"Grate? I was angry with her . . ." At Daniela's raised brows, he admitted, "I was furious for what she did to Nikolai. It's hard to see someone you care about and respect in misery, and Nikolai suffered as you can't understand. If anyone deserves happiness, it's him."

"Why?"

"He carries the weight of the world on his shoulders, guilt as you wouldn't believe."

"For what?" she asked, but he hesitated to answer. "Already breaking the terms of our deal?"

Murdoch scowled. "Nikolai believes he failed his country."

"There's got to be more than that."

"There . . . is." He exhaled. "Does the Lore know what happened to other members of my family?" When she shook her head, he said, "Nikolai tried to save their lives with his 'tainted' blood. He feels guilt for both succeeding and failing at that."

"How did he succeed *and* fail?"

"Daniela, this is a difficult subject."

"You have no idea what a good listener I am."

He looked down at her eyes. So vividly blue. As they'd been in his dream. He found himself recounting how he and Nikolai had returned home to watch over their family but had found them all dying, and in unimaginable pain. He told her how they'd fed blood to his brothers and sisters, his father.

Though Murdoch had never revealed to another living soul the details, the words fell from his lips as if she'd drawn them from him. "Most were out of their heads, but my brother Sebastian was awake, aware. He even figured out what we'd become and demanded that they be allowed to die in peace." At the memory, Murdoch ran his hand over his forehead. "Sebastian was particularly close to the girls, a kind of substitute father, and he hated Nikolai and me for trying to turn them. Even more so when only he and Conrad rose from the dead."

"What happened once they woke?" Daniela asked, her tone softer.

"Sebastian tried to kill Nikolai. And Conrad . . . when he comprehended what had been done to him, he went mad, bellowing as if in unbearable pain, and ran into the night. We haven't seen either of them in three centuries."

"Do you believe your brothers are still alive?"

"I have to," he answered, then waited for her to

ask another question. Again, she remained silent, contemplative, so he said, "I was thinking about your enemies. If a king wants to kill you simply because you were born, then your very life is a threat. Which means that you're an heir. A royal one."

She shrugged. "You got me."

"What title do you possess?"

"I thought you knew. You called me an ice queen earlier today."

"A . . . queen." And if her delirious ramblings were to be believed, then she was also the daughter of gods.

"Yes, of the Icere," she said. "From a long line of Winter Queens."

"But Sigmund usurped your throne?"

She stiffened beneath his palm again. "You *did* get me to talk last night."

"Why don't you rebel and get your kingdom back? Gather the Icere to follow you?"

"It's not that simple. Sigmund is very powerful."

"There are none here to help you against him?" When she shook her head, he said, "I have a hard time believing that every last one of the Icere is united against you."

"New Orleans isn't exactly a coldbed of Icere."

"You're here."

He thought he heard her mutter, *"Not for long."*

"Is Sigmund any relation to you?"

"Not by blood," she said. "He was my mother's prince consort. I wasn't born until after his men had mortally wounded her."

"Do you know how crazy that sounds?"

"Welcome to the Lore. Little makes sense. Rules are fluid. Just when you think you've got it all figured out, you hear about a vampire unaffected by the sun, a mute Siren, or a chaste nymph."

"So there's no one here like you?" he asked.

"Are you trying to plan a coup for me, or attempting to find out if I have a boyfriend?"

He grated, "Do you?"

"Why would you care?"

"I'm curious. You don't strike me as the disloyal type, and you were just in my bed. Eagerly."

"Hey, now." She peered around and made a dampening motion with her hands. "Not so loud, vampire. Let's not expedite the death of Danii's respect in the Lore."

"Earlier, you weren't too concerned about this, not when you were telling me that you wanted to see me again," he said, then added for good measure, "And that I have kissable lips."

"I said that before I concluded the risk-benefit ratio was one hundred percent risk and none-point-none percent benefit." She cast him a glare. "And I *really* wouldn't keep reminding me of all you learned last night and this morning."

"None-point-none?"

"Exactly. Unless threatening to drain me was your way of asking for more."

He wanted to tell her that the threat had been groundless, that he'd never hurt her like that. But the way he'd been feeling at that critical moment . . . ? It'd be a lie.

"Look at your vexed expression! Don't worry, Casanova, I didn't exactly take your behavior as an invitation. You made it very clear how you felt."

"I just didn't want to be blooded."

"Most vampires long for it to happen to them," she pointed out.

"Why? For the strength?"

"Sure. But also because immortality is lonely." Another display of that shocking vulnerability in a warrioress.

"Daniela, who were you searching for earlier?"

"You wouldn't know her."

Not a man. Relief? "And you're not going to tell me more about her." When she shook her head, he asked, "What happens in a couple of days when the Icere return? Will you and your sisters attack them?"

"No."

"Are you just going to wait until they take another shot at you? I thought the Valkyrie considered themselves the top of the Lore food chain. Have you never launched an assault, or sent assassins back to kill him?"

"There's something about their castle that repels my kind." At his questioning look, she said, "I won't reveal more. Besides, we can't find the Icere kingdom." She obviously hated to say *king*dom. "No one can, not even through scrying. You know, considering you washed your hands of me, you're awfully concerned about the Icere."

"Yes, because no matter what happened afterward with us, twenty-four hours ago I was plucking their arrows out of your body."

When her hand flittered about her chest at the painful reminder, he gentled his tone. "What would have happened if you hadn't gotten cooled?"

She cast him a begrudging expression as if she supposed she owed him the answer to this. "Thermal shock. At some point, the rapid temperature change would basically make me shatter."

"*Shatter.*" His voice sounded astonished even to himself. "How's that possible?"

"If glass is heated evenly, it just gets hot. But when it's heated unevenly, it cracks. Well, I don't heat evenly."

"All Icere are susceptible to this?"

"No. Like them, I have freezing skin. But because I'm part Valkyrie, my blood is a fraction warmer than theirs."

He slowed. "If you're at risk like that, why would you ever be out here alone?"

SEVENTEEN

Because I don't fit in with my half sisters. Because, in lieu of true companionship, I'd rather be alone, so I can get lost in my fantasy world, dreaming about sex and snow. Maybe even sex in the snow. . . .

"The arrows are what made me so heated," she finally said, relieved that they'd almost reached their destination. "Take away the poison, and I would have survived. I can usually handle myself just fine."

"Usually? Have you gone into shock before?"

"No. Last night was the closest I've been."

"Then how do you know what will happen?"

"I was warned." *Danii, your face is red!* Svana had cried again and again. *You've been playing with your sisters too long. You know what your godparents said about getting too hot. . . .*

"Warned? By your parents?"

"Murdoch, I appreciate your candor about your family." An understatement. His tale had moved her in unexpected ways. "But I won't share it about mine." When he opened his mouth to ask more, she said, "Besides, we're here." With a negligent wave of her hand, she indicated their first stop, Jean Lafitte's.

Though on Bourbon, the tavern was situated at the opposite end from all the hustle and bustle, so it was more like a normal bar without the artificially inflated Bourbon Street buoyancy.

One of the Valkyrie's allies, a storm demon named Deshazior, hung out here whenever he was in town. Fitting, since he was a former pirate. Of course, he'd been hanging out in this building since the infamous Lafitte brothers had run a smithy in it.

Pausing outside the closest set of double doors, Danii told Murdoch, "You should wait here."

"Why?"

"Because my contact and his crew will want to kill you, and also, I might have to flirt with him."

The garrulous Deshazior had a known weakness for Valkyrie—and a lot of Valkyrie had known weaknesses for him.

Desh had even propositioned Danii, solemnly telling her in his briny accent, "I'd risk freezin' off my bollocks to claim yer maidenhead."

"You think I'll be jealous?" Murdoch's tone was disbelieving. "I believe I can handle it."

So arrogant, so dismissive. *Ego takes another hit. Round four, ding ding.*

With that, he guided her inside. As they entered, cigarette smoke wafted around them. Nick Cave's "People Ain't No Good" crooned from the jukebox. Drunk, glum mortals stared into their drinks.

Murdoch muttered, "This is a human bar. I thought you mentioned a *demon*."

"I know where Loreans loiter, okay?"

She swiftly spotted Desh. He was hard to miss, since he stood seven feet tall. And since he sported large, forward-pointing horns. "See that big guy with the horns—"

"He goes out like that?" Murdoch snapped under his breath. "With them uncovered for everyone to see?"

"Yes, whenever he likes. Humans think Deshazior and his crew are in costume. The demons draw straws to see who gets to wear that." She pointed out a sulky-looking demon wearing a neon pink T-shirt that read: *"Big Easy Movie Casting! We arrive in costume!"*

Humans asked them about prosthetics in cosplay, autographs, and movie release dates—not about their blatant protrusions.

Desh turned then, spotting her. "Ah, if it ain't the fair Lady Daniela," he called. He caught sight of Murdoch behind her and immediately tensed. "With a blightin' vampire. Ye'll be tellin' me why me and my boys won't be evisceratin' the leech."

Murdoch watched as Daniela's friendly demeanor turned cold in a flash. "Because I'll turn your blood to slush if you do," she said, raising her palm to her lips.

She was so small compared to the hulking demon, but Deshazior held up his hands in surrender.

"Now, now, beauty. No need to be freezin' an ole demon like me. It hurts." When she dropped her hand, he added in a mutter, "Ladies goin' with vampires? City's gone to hell whilst I've been away."

"I'm not *going with* him. We're in an unlikely alliance on a dangerous mission to help Lorekind. An alliance with an expy date of . . . oh, dawn."

"This one's lookin' at ye like yer together," the demon said. "All possessive-like."

That noticeable?

"And how am I looking at him?" Daniela asked in an innocent tone.

"Like ye'd be well rid o' him," Deshazior said with a chuckle. "So what can I do for ye, luv?"

"Have you seen Nïx?"

Who was that? And why was Daniela seeking her?

One of the demons with Deshazior said, "Nïx is out tonight?" He anxiously smoothed a palm over each of his horns and straightened his collar.

"I guess that answers that question," Daniela said with a sigh. "I'm also looking for Ivo the Cruel."

A flicker arose in Deshazior's eyes as he said, "Aside from the one loomin' over ye just now, I haven't seen any vamps."

He's lying.

"That's a shame." Daniela pouted, traipsing closer to him. "I thought I could count on you for information." She reached up and ran the back of one claw along his right horn. At once, Deshazior's muscles tensed. The other demons gasped and groaned.

Murdoch didn't see why her behavior would elicit a response like that, but their eyes were spellbound by her stroking claw.

Deshazior had begun quaking. "Givin' me fits, Valkyrie!"

"A word alone," Daniela purred. "Outside."

With a defeated exhalation, the demon followed them out, mumbling about teasing Valkyries and "horn jobs."

Once the three were out on the street, Deshazior glowered at Murdoch. Then, after an uneasy glance back at his crew inside, he muttered to Danii, "Ivo's here in the city. I don't know where, but watch yer-self. He's got some on his side that even I wouldn't tangle with."

"How do you mean?" Murdoch said.

Deshazior ignored him. "And if ye've need of a partnership to save Lorekind, I'm yer demon." He thumped his colossal chest. "No need to sully yerself with the likes of him."

Murdoch eased his lips back from his fangs.

"I appreciate the offer," Daniela said. "But I can make it a night. Will you leave word at the coven if you spot them?"

"Aye—" Suddenly the demon began disappearing, as if he were involuntarily tracing. "Damn it! A swimbo calls."

"What the hell is a swimbo?" Murdoch asked; they *both* ignored him.

The demon gazed down at Daniela as he began to fade. "Remember, ice maiden," he murmured intently, "my other offer still stands as well."

The vampire was in front of Desh in an instant. "Whatever you offered, she's not interested." But the demon was already gone.

Murdoch turned to her. "What was that?"

"I told you I might have to flirt to get some infor-mation. Now will you admit you're jealous, vampire?"

He surprised her by answering, "Yes." Just when she felt a flare of pleasure, he doused it by adding, "Though I'll be damned if I know why."

"You truly just said that?" She glared at the sky, imploring it for patience before facing him again. "Maybe because I'm cute and intelligent and I was in your bed last night, and because—oh, I don't know—I'm your Bride."

"What was the demon's offer?"

"That's between me and him."

"Is he your type, then? Really? You like behorned demons who growl *yar!* after every bloody sentence? I thought you'd be more discerning."

"And I thought you were supposed to be seductive and charming. You're just insulting, gruff, and brooding."

"With *you*." He took a step closer, frustration in his expression.

"What's that supposed to mean?"

"I don't know. I've never been jealous before. And I've never been clumsy with words around women." At that moment, a pair of name-tagged conventioneers ogled her, earning a killing look from Murdoch. When they hurried on, he said, "This is *not* my typical behavior." He exhaled. "And I can't control it."

He looked defeated, like he couldn't reason out this situation and might just stop trying to. "Valkyrie, I've never been more at odds with myself in my entire existence."

She almost felt sorry for him, and gentled her tone. "Maybe I'm getting under your skin."

He muttered, "Like a thorn."

Danii was just contrary enough to be pleased by this. "Every thorn has its rose, vampire."

Eighteen

With that, the Valkyrie sauntered back up Bourbon, drawing slack-jawed stares from more men than he could bare his fangs at.

Murdoch followed, dimly aware that this might be the longest conversation he'd ever had with a woman.

The steady stream of them in his mortal life meant that he'd never had to spend a lot of time *talking* to any single female. In fact, he'd long felt as if he spoke two languages: one he used with men and the other with women.

The former was direct, used to convey information. The latter was laden with innuendo and flirtation, and consisted of little more than compliments.

With Daniela, he seemed to have forgotten the woman language. Maybe he was just out of practice. Didn't matter anyway, since she was having none of it, probably didn't even speak it.

When he caught up with her, he said, "Now we go to the store?"

She nodded. "It's back up Bourbon for a few wild and woolly blocks, then west a couple more."

Up ahead, the crowd had burgeoned as the night

wore on. Each bar they passed had begun blaring its own style of music. "Then we have some time to kill. You might as well tell me what a swimbo is. And who's Nïx?"

"Might I?" she said, and that was *all* she said.

He took another tack. "Deshazior called you 'ice maiden.'"

"That's one of my names. Along with 'ice queen.' Which you like calling me when you're being unpleasant."

"You aren't . . . are you a virgin?"

She gazed away. "Why do you sound so dismayed by this?"

Because you were a virgin in my dream. "Because you've lived a long time. Surely in all those years, you've found one of your own species to be with."

"*Species*, Murdoch Suavé? Really?"

He could have phrased that better. But he was a shade shocked that he could be walking next to a two-thousand-year-old virgin. "Answer me. Has no man ever claimed you?"

"Only another within my own kind can touch me without hurting me. And yet they've been trying to kill me since I first left Valhalla," she said. "You put it together."

God, she's never known a man.

Whatever she saw in his expression made her glare. "Don't you dare pity me, Murdoch."

"Have you sought help for this . . . coldness?" he asked, squiring her well away from a performing fire breather.

"You make it sound like a condition! But, yes, for your information, I've gone to the House of Witches, to wizards, and even to the patron goddess of impossible things. So far, the best I've been offered were incomplete spells—like a hex that would prevent me from feeling pain, even though my skin would still burn, or vice versa."

"And the goddess?"

"She gave me a pair of bowling shoes."

"Bowling shoes?"

Suddenly plastic beads rained down on them, tossed by topless—male and female—tourists on a balcony to their left. Without missing a beat, Daniela cast the strands to another group on a balcony directly to their right. "Yes, bowling couture. Don't ask me why."

"There's got to be a way, some other power in the Lore—"

"I've been to all the reliable, vetted mystical sources I know of. Unreliable sources would extract too high a penalty."

"What does that mean?"

"I could go to a Lore bazaar where magics are peddled, but would probably end up worse than I am."

"Worse off?"

"Magic dispensed by the wrong hands begs for cosmic justice, and it's usually in the form of a paradox. So if I hired some random practitioner for this, I might become touchable—by, for instance, growing scales. And then no one would *want* to touch me."

"I see." Fables held the same. Like the dying man who journeyed to a mystic for a cure, but perished in a freak accident on the way home.

"This is just something I have to live with," she finished with a shrug, as if she'd long since accepted this reality, but he sensed that nothing could be further from the truth. "I'm the one virgin you won't be adding to your collection."

"I've never had one before." But he longed to now. *To claim Daniela . . . to show her what sex can be like.*

To see that vulnerability in her eyes just as he entered her.

This plainly surprised her. "Am I supposed to believe that?"

"In my time, taking a virgin meant one risked a sword-point wedding." *Beget no bastards, deflower no maids.* As long as he'd followed those two simple rules, he'd always gotten to do as he pleased.

"I thought guys like you were forever on the hunt for the next rascally cherry to subdue."

"Women always think men bed virgins because of the conquest."

"You're saying that has nothing to do with it?"

"No. The conquest is definitely a part. But I believe the truth runs deeper: Men like virgins because women always remember their first lover. Men want to be remembered sexually."

"So if you didn't enjoy any virgins, did you not want to be remembered?"

He closed in on her, backing her up against the

wall of a closed bistro. Resting his hand beside her head, he murmured, "I had no such fears or desires. I always knew I'd be remembered—not as the first, but as the *best*."

In a clear attempt to disguise how curious she was, Daniela said, "And how does one get to be the best? I mean, aside from the obvious answer of *practice*."

In his mortal life, he'd been considerate in bed. He'd made sure he brought great pleasure to every woman he'd been with. This wasn't out of self-lessness. Quite the opposite. At an early age, he'd learned that the more word got around that he was a skilled lover, the more women dallied with him.

He'd had an agenda going into each encounter. He'd been painstaking, his actions measured—and he'd never, never lost control.

Now he inched closer to the Valkyrie. "I was generous with my attentions. And I was always in complete control of myself, able to go as long as I needed to go . . ."

"In order to be generous," she finished for him in a breathy voice. "You must have been devoted to women."

"I was." To *women*, yes, though never to one. "But that's not *all*. I—" He stopped.

"What? What were you going to say?"

"I don't want you to think . . ." He trailed off, running his fingers through his dark hair. "Damn it, I fought just as hard as my brothers in the war."

"Murdoch, sometimes history isn't kind—"

"I don't want *you* to believe that I shirked my

duties. I dug in just as doggedly to protect our people. And I always came through when it counted. The only difference between me and my brothers is what we did in the downtime between conflicts. Sebastian spent his time reading, Conrad disappeared for reasons unknown, Nikolai paced his tent with the weight of the world on his shoulders. I was carefree. . . ."

"And you enjoyed women," she said. "Why do you care what I think about you?"

Why? He had no good answer for that. *Because the blooding tells me to.* Everything he'd been thinking and feeling tonight was dictated by it.

That had to be what was happening to him. Or else he was a masochist about to get attached to a woman he could never touch.

ΠINETEEN

"I'll tell you why if you reveal the demon's offer to you," Murdoch said.

"No, thanks, vampire, I gave you a surplus of information last night," Danii said tersely, still annoyed that he'd interrogated her.

"You did tell me much," he said. "But I believe little of it."

"Is that right?"

"You said you didn't eat."

She raised her brows.

"*Can* you?"

She shrugged. Valkyries *could,* but since they took nourishment from the electrical energy of the earth, they didn't need to. Besides, refraining from eating was a sort of inherent birth control. Her kind had no courses and were infertile unless they "ate of the earth."

"You told me you were two thousand years old," he said, keeping his gloved hand on her lower back—and keeping pedestrians *away*. Since he'd learned about the threat of thermal shock, he seemed to be continually checking on how warm she'd become, monitoring her to see if her breaths were smoking.

His attention was flattering, softening some of her anger. "Two thousand is roughly my age."

"And two of your *three* parents are gods?"

She gave him a pointedly blank expression, which she could tell irritated him.

"Then why would they let you get hurt?"

"Because they're asleep."

"Gods . . . sleep?"

"To conserve power. They derive strength from worshippers. And when was the last time you passed a temple dedicated to Freya?"

He deftly drew her out of the way when a full go-cup dropped from a balcony above, then said, "The one thing I believed without question? You told me that if you started kissing me"—his shoulders went back, cocky grin in place—"you didn't think you'd be able to stop."

Could he be any more handsome? Though her attraction to the vampire was wrong on so many levels, it remained as fierce as ever.

All night, Danii had been drawn to him. Not surprisingly. Every time she regarded those broad shoulders and steely gray eyes, she recalled their time in his bed. Whenever that lock of hair fell over his forehead, she'd just stopped herself from sighing.

Though she was an ice queen, acting coldly uninterested with him was becoming more difficult. And coldly uninterested was her shtick!

When he'd said he'd been the best lover . . . ? Gods help her, she'd *believed* him.

But she'd also been anxious about him possibly biting her. She didn't think she'd ever forget the look in his eyes this morning. "We'll never find out about the kissing, will we?"

His brows drew together, as if she'd uttered something monumental. "No. We won't, then. Ever." They walked on in awkward silence until she directed him off Bourbon.

"What's this store like?" he asked.

"It's owned by a purported voodoo priestess named Loa." Her very name meant *voodoo spirit*.

"Loa is a *female* shop owner?"

When Danii nodded, he perked up. And considering what Loa looked like, Danii mused that this might be a bad idea.

But Nïx often dropped by there, and even if Loa knew nothing—doubtful—any of her patrons might have information.

"Does she have powers?" he asked.

Just as they reached the shop, Danii drawled, "You have no idea."

On the door hung a sign with the universal symbol of the Lore, recognized by all Lorekind—except for the Forbearers. Beside it was a sticker with the word *Vampires* overlaid with a cross bar. Beneath that were the lines, *"No shirt, no soul, no service. We use UV protection."*

Murdoch frowned. "UV protection? Is that a joke?"

She shook her head. "It's candlelit inside, but along the ceiling are UV lights that can be turned on with a panic button—a fail-safe vampire security system." The Valkyries had wanted a similar setup for Val Hall, but their shrieks would just have shattered the bulbs.

As unabashed as ever, Murdoch shrugged and opened the door for Danii.

"Are you sure you want to go in?"

"You said the owner of this place is a woman? Well, I have a way with women. No panic buttons will be pushed tonight."

She rolled her eyes, then entered, with him closely following.

The front of the shop was a typical tacky tourist haunt, with preserved gator heads and fake gris-gris bags made in China.

But, like many of the Loreans in the Big Easy, Danii knew there was a back room. Inside those walls was everything from demon-size condoms and non-acetone horn polish to intoxispell hangover relief and ghoul blood remover.

As expected, candles lit the darkened shop, the bulbs above unused. For now. A lazy, old-fashioned fan buzzed softly, making the candle flames dance.

"Does that UV really work?" he asked with a glance at the ceiling.

"Oh, yeah. I was going to swap out the over-head light in your Porsche with one before I left town."

"Left New Orleans? Where are you going?"

Loa sauntered out from the back room, saving Danii from answering. As usual, the sight of Loa made Danii scowl. Gifted with flawless café-au-lait skin and a brick-house body, she spoke with a lilting island accent that men found sexy as hell.

Would Murdoch?

Tonight she was wearing an impeccably fitted red silk dress that highlighted her every abundant curve.

Murdoch gave Loa an appreciative glance, but so far he hadn't looked like a slavering cartoon wolf in a zoot suit.

Loa was an enigma. She'd come here—to a town filled with immortals at the most tumultuous time in the Lore—as if she wanted to be first in line for the unrest and war of the Accession.

When Loa had taken over the shop for her grand-mother, Loa Senior, a voodoo high priestess, she'd assumed her new role almost *too* well.

Danii recalled telling her at her first open house, "There's something puzzling about this island vibe you've got going. Loa Senior told me her grand-daughter was raised in a ritzy suburb outside Parsip-pany and graduated from Notre Dame. So how'd you get the Caribbean accent?"

Loa had narrowed her bright amber eyes and answered, "Loa Senior tells tales to impress a Val-kyrie." Then she'd added under her breath, "Don't try to stuff me into one of your little mental boxes. I won't fit—any more than you would."

"Well, Valkyrie," she said now, making the word sound like *Va-kree.* "Slumming with vampires, I see. If your sisters found out . . ."

"They won't. Because you won't tell them if you want to stay in business."

"What are you thinking, bringing a vampire into my shop? Can you not read the signs?"

Loa's attitude rankled. Her red, curve-hugging dress rankled. "Probably not as well as you can, since I don't have a fancy college degree from Notre Dame."

Between gritted teeth, Loa said, "Damn you, I did not go to Notre Dame."

"Go Fighting Irish, rah-rah."

"I'm Murdoch Wroth, of the Forbearer order," the vampire interjected smoothly, extending his hand. Loa offered her own out of habit, then clearly thought better of it, but he'd already leaned down and kissed the back of it. "And you must be the *incomparable* Loa."

Could his deep voice be any sexier? It reminded Danii of how he'd sounded in bed this morning.

Loa gazed up at the vampire, looking a bit thunderstruck. "Murdoch Wroth? Aren't you one of the legendary Wroth brothers?"

"One and the same." He cast Danii a superior grin.

"If I recall, you were the wicked, bed-hopping one."

Danii thought a muscle ticked in his jaw, but he was all polished composure as he said, "Only when around women as lovely as you."

Loa actually tittered. "Well, I *suppose* if your eyes are clear, I could make an exception to my no-vampire rule."

"Thank you. It's a pleasure to meet such a beautiful proprietress."

I'm going to be sick. Except I don't eat.

"And I can hear that you've been blooded," Loa said. "Surely not by the ice maiden?"

"Yes, by her," he answered in a noncommittal tone.

Loa smiled. She should. Vampires simply didn't flirt like this once they'd been blooded. At least, not with anyone but their Brides.

"What a rogue this one is, ice maiden. You'll never tame him, child."

"Don't want to."

"So you won't mind if I put you two in Loa's betting book? The notorious rake blooded by the ice queen—but how long can her frozen clutches keep him from straying?"

Knowing Loa would do it regardless, Danii

affected an unconcerned demeanor. "Knock yourself out." *Cold as a block of ice.*

"I suspect we'll soon be calling you the For-bearer's forsaken one—"

"Can we just get to what we came here for?" Danii interrupted sharply, her cold façade cracking.

"Ah, yes," Murdoch said. "Loa, have you heard any information about Ivo the Cruel?"

Loa turned to Danii. "Why ask me?"

"Ivo's in the city."

Her lips parted, her amber eyes excited, glowing in the candlelight. "Vampires overrunning us, Lykae hunting these very streets. . . . It's the Accession. Finally!"

"And you sound like you're *looking forward* to it?" Danii demanded. "What? Do you want to have an Accession sale or something?"

"Some people benefit. People like me."

"Alumni, rah?"

"Ladies." Murdoch seemed to find Danii's surly behavior amusing. If she were surly, it was only because the air was hot in here. Danii always got irritable when hot.

"This makes sense," Loa said. "I'd heard Lothaire is here, and he often travels with Ivo."

At the mention of Lothaire, Danii stifled a shud-der. Ivo was an evil, sociopathic fiend, but he was at least manageable.

Lothaire, the Enemy of Old, was incomprehensi-ble. No one knew what he wanted, and no one could predict what he'd do next.

"You know where they might be?" Danii asked.

"They're definitely staying in the area."

"How do you know?"

"Because Lothaire has been seen night after night," Loa replied. "There are kobolds camping in the sewers by the river. Ask some of them."

"I'll do that. Have you seen Nïx?"

"Aye, she came round and bought . . . She made a purchase. But I don't know where she went. Now, back to you, Murdoch." Loa leaned over the counter onto her elbows, displaying more cleavage than Danii could manage with a thousand water bras.

When he raised his brows in admiration, Danii stormed from the shop. "Going to make a call outside." She refused to watch any more of this. After Lafitte's, she'd gotten her hopes up about the vampire, again, only to have them dashed now. *Do I need to see a neon sign flashing* THIS GUY'S A PLAYER?

"Directly outside, Daniela," he ordered, surprising her that he'd even been aware she was leaving—and making her bristle at his commanding tone.

On the street, fog from the river was stealing over the Quarter, wrapping it in haze. She took a deep breath of low-tide air to calm herself and debated ringing up Nïx. Usually calls were reserved for emergencies, because you never knew when a Valkyrie might need silence for stalking something.

Deciding this was an emergency, Danii pulled her sat-phone from her satchel, then dialed Nïx's number.

And heard Nïx's Crazy Frog ring tone going off in the next alley over.

TWENTY

"I am astonished she's even talking to you," Loa said after Daniela had walked out, her tone turning decidedly neutral.

Murdoch narrowed his eyes. She'd been flirting for the Valkyrie's benefit? "Why give Daniela such a hard time?"

"Ooh, the vampire doesn't like Loa toying with his Bride."

"Answer me."

"Because she wants to be treated like other Valkyrie, and that's how I treat them," the priestess said. "Want some advice?" When he grudgingly nodded, she said, "Watch for her claws curling, vampire. In a Valkyrie, that means she needs a male to sink them into."

Daniela, with her claws sunk in my back as I took her—

"Oh, and here. These are on sale," Loa said as she bent down behind the counter. "For the ice maiden." She tossed him a pair of gloves. "Tell her I said to handle you with care. . . ."

When Murdoch left Loa's, he wore a victorious grin. He'd purchased the gloves and had garnered a secret about the Valkyrie that could be very helpful to him.

But by the time Murdoch emerged to the now foggy street, Daniela was gone.

He started back toward the main thoroughfare. After several moments, he spied Lukyan at a distance, still intently prowling the streets for Ivo. The Cossack always seemed to be devoid of fear, almost as if he had a death wish. Vigilant Rurik traced on the roofs above him.

Yet there was no sign of Daniela.

Danii rushed to the sound, peering down the stygian alley. Finally, she spotted the soothsayer, talking to some figure in the shadows.

"Nïx!" By the time Danii reached her, the figure had hastened away. "Who were you talking to?"

"Hmmm?" Nïx's raven-black hair was wild, her golden eyes vacant as usual—she often saw the future more clearly than the present—but she also looked frazzled and tired. Though she wore an immaculate white dress, her hands were filthy.

"And why are you so dirty?" Danii asked her.

"*I'm* dirty? You're the one getting busy with a leech. You naughty, freaky minx."

"Answer the question," Danii gritted out. "Who was that?"

"Who was who?"

Typical Nïx—she could be playing innocent, or she truly could have forgotten who she'd just been talking to seconds before. "What are you doing here?"

She blinked at Danii. "Laying low like po-po?" At Danii's glare, Nïx's mien turned playful. "Trolling for some strange! No? Composing a tweet?"

"Nïx, are you following me?"

"Do I need to be?"

Danii inhaled for patience. "I was looking for you. I need to tell you about—"

"Myst. Don't concern yourself. She's taken care of. As for your next question, you should go somewhere that is not here." She gazed around as if they might be overheard, then loudly whispered, "There are dempires about."

"*Dempires?*" Danii had never, in her long life, heard the term.

"And Lykae all around as well." Nïx jerked her chin in the direction of the main drag.

Danii glanced over and spotted three Lykae walking by, twins and one more. All of them were striking examples of heart throbbing maleness, but then, Lykae often were.

Now they stopped, turned toward Danii and Nïx, and sniffed the air. All three tensed with awareness of other Loreans. A standoff. Danii drew ice into her palm.

Then Nïx wiggled her dirty fingers, beckoning them. Looking scarily crazed with her wild hair and unsettling eyes, she cooed, "Come, puppies. Come meet Destiny." Out of the corner of her mouth, Nïx stage-whispered, "Destiny is my fist's name."

When the trio spoke in Gaelic, and carried on, Nïx chuckled.

"What? What'd they say?"

"That we weren't worth the bother. That you're the frigid one and I'm crazy. Seems they've got our numbers!"

The frigid one. Lowly Lykae thought of her like that? *My ego's on life support. Prognosis grim.*

"We're eventually going to be allies with them, you know," Nïx said dimly. "In-laws, even."

Danii snorted. The Valkyrie considered the Lykae little better than animals. "You're joking, right?"

"Would I joke about something like this?"

"Emphatically, yes. Now tell me, why did you predict I'd get fixed last night?"

"I said you *might*. Look at the upside: you got to enjoy a male who wasn't an Icere bounty hunter and who didn't have designs to murder you. At least, not until he got peckish."

"Would Murdoch have hurt me? *Will* he?"

Nïx tilted her head in the direction of Loa's shop. "I used to be able to read him as easily as his brothers, like open books. But now I get little on him. I just see that you've got him confounded, not knowing up from down anymore. At three hundred years old, he'd thought he was quit of uncertainty like this."

"Wait, you said *brothers*? Does more than one live?"

"You'd better get back to the vampire, he's about to spot—"

"Daniela!" Murdoch's voice boomed down the alley.

Danii glanced over her shoulder at him, then

back, but Nïx had already vanished. *Damn it.* She swiftly hit redial on her phone, yet all was silence.

When Murdoch reached her, Danii saw genuine concern on his face. "Why did you leave?"

She hiked her shoulders. "I thought you'd be longer in there."

"Now who's jealous?"

"Hardly."

"I just wanted to prove that I'm not gruff and brooding," he said. "Or that I only am with you. And besides, I was just flirting to get information." When she still glared, he said, "Admit it, you were jealous."

"No, I'm *embarrassed*. Because everyone would expect you to be possessive and intent only on me. They're going to see this as a failing in *me*."

"You said the blooding didn't make one want his Bride."

"No, not if the Bride or mate or whatever was objectionable. But am I really that objectionable?"

His brows drew together. "You truly can't understand any hesitation on my part?"

He was making her feel like more of a freak than anyone had in two thousand years.

But that was a lie. There'd been the Roman. . . .

"Vampire, I think you're afraid to settle down—with anyone. You were single for years and celibate for three hundred more. And now you have bachelor's panic."

"I don't even know what you're talking about."

"BP? It's when a man irrationally fears a woman he especially likes. He gets *ascared* of said woman's toothbrush breaching the perimeter of his man cave, et cetera."

"Panic? I don't panic," he sneered the word. "Daniela, you can't be touched."

The frigid one. Enough of this. "No, you can't! Your heart's colder than mine. *You* are the untouchable one."

She turned from him, wanting away from this vampire with his unflinching honesty. Because it . . . hurt. *The life I have inside my head* . . .

Murdoch followed her. "Just because I'm not ready to blindly accept a Bride I hardly know—for eternity—makes me coldhearted? I'd say it makes me rational."

"Oh, so maybe it's not me, it's you? Make up your mind!"

"Even if you were all things perfect for me, I would resent this situation. The Forbearers have learned to fear bloodlust because it makes vampires crazed and out of control. But so does the blooding! Yet we're supposed to welcome it?" He hastened in front of her, blocking her way. "It's making me behave in ways I normally wouldn't. Would you wish this for yourself? To have your personality completely rewritten?"

"If I had your personality? Ab-so-lutely. Because here's the thing—you're not special anymore. You're not unique in the Lore. You're a leech who used to have it easy getting laid. And now, you're just *predictable*."

He advanced on her until she backed up against the wall of a building. "Just a manwhore, huh?" They were in each other's faces, her breaths smoking between them.

"That really bothers you?" They were fighting—she needed to stop glancing at his lips.

"Shouldn't it?"

When his gaze dropped to her breasts, transfixed as she panted, she demanded, "*What?* What do you want from me?"

He faced her with his eyes narrowed, turning that fierce obsidian color. "The same thing I wanted this morning." His voice grew husky. "To stop fighting with you and start kissing you."

She swayed on her feet. He'd wanted that? "But you can't."

He shook his head. "I can't smooth my fingers over the inside of your wrist." With his gloved hand, he lifted her hair. "I can't run my lips over your neck ... or suckle your breasts. And it's driving me mad."

He eased his body even closer to hers, resting his forearms against the wall on either side of her head. His mouth was right at her ear as he asked, "Am I too close? Does this hurt you?"

She felt his erection press against her belly and choked back a moan. "No, no. . . . But how do I know you won't bite me?"

"I won't. I swear it."

Just when she perceived his hips drawing back, and she knew he was about to thrust against her body, her ears twitched.

She shoved him away. "We've got company."

—❧✦❧—

Daniela had spotted something. "Grab that one!" she cried, pointing in the direction of a garbage heap down the alley.

Murdoch spied a gray-haired gnomelike being with a miniature cane and traced forward like a shot. But the creature was fast, scurrying from him. It took several minutes of cat-and-mouse before Murdoch caught it by the collar, lifting it up.

The little thing had red cheeks and a kindly appearance, but looked terrified.

"That's it!" Daniela called from a distance, hastening to catch up. "Now smack it around!"

He glanced back at her. "*Smack* it?"

Once she reached them, she jerked her chin at the gnome. When Murdoch turned back, it was twisting around to take a bite of his arm. Murdoch gave it a shake, and for the briefest instant, he thought he saw a reptilian-like visage flicker over its face. "Christ! What is this?"

"Can't tell him, Lady Daniela?" it said. "He's a Forbearer leech. But you might tell all if you became a vampire's whore, like the Coveted One? How far you Valkyrie fall!"

Daniela strode forward and slapped it, stifling a wince at the contact.

The creature growled, then locked its eyes on Murdoch. "What are you doing with a cold bitch like this one?" it asked, becoming the first being to question why *Murdoch* was with *her*.

Now Murdoch cuffed it.

"Where is Ivo the Cruel, kobold?" Daniela asked.

Kobold? As Loa had spoken of.

"Why should I tell you?"

She lowered her voice, looking sinister when she said, "Because if you don't, I'm going to freeze you solid, then chip away your flesh with your own little cane."

The kobold swallowed. "I-I might have seen Ivo and Lothaire about earlier."

"Where are they staying?"

When it hesitated, Murdoch gave it another violent shake.

"Outside the parish! In the bayou. Near Val Hall."

"Near Val Hall?" Daniela repeated in amazement. "Have they no fear?"

"They're *different*," the kobold said. "You can't fight them." The same thing Deshazior had told them.

"How do you know this?" she asked.

"Heard it from a rat demon who heard it from one of the crocodilae shifters. That's all I know—vow it to the Lore!"

"Toss him," Daniela said. "Hard."

Murdoch flung the kobold back into the garbage heap, and it skulked away with a gurgling hiss.

"Okay, vampire, you have plenty to go on now," she said, still catching her breath from her earlier sprint. "Dawn's only a couple of hours away, so I think this is where we . . ." She trailed off when she saw him frowning at her. "What?"

"Are you hot?"

"No, I'll manage," she said, but her skin was reddened, her face pinched.

He swallowed. "Daniela, your breaths aren't smoking."

TWENTY-ONE

The vampire stared down at her with alarmed eyes.

"I'll be fine," she assured him, but she was still hot from the night before and had exerted herself too much keeping up with Murdoch's chase. "It's . . . nothing." *If* she could get back to the meat locker quickly enough. *How many blocks is it to my car—*

He grabbed her hand. "What are you doing?" she demanded.

"You'll see."

Suddenly she was in a cold, dark room. *He traced me?* She'd never been traced when she was fully cognizant, and it made her dizzy, as if she'd just stepped off a pitching ship. She warily darted her eyes around them.

The heat and sounds of New Orleans were gone. She and the vampire now stood in what looked like an old-fashioned drawing room with sheet-draped furniture. Extensive marble floors conducted the chill until it seeped right into her bones. *Delicious.* "Where have you taken me?"

"A hunting lodge in Siberia."

"Siberia?" The very word connoted cold and made her toes curl with pleasure. "Why?"

"You were getting hot."

"It happens, you know. You didn't have to trace me out of Louisiana." She started toward one of the soaring windows, taking in details as she crossed the spacious interior.

She could tell that Murdoch wasn't actively living here, but the lodge was clean and in good repair. It was also *opulent*, with gilt walls and moldings inlaid with gems. Elaborate wood carvings adorned the doorways and the great hearth.

This place was a time capsule, like a tsar's hideaway preserved from hundreds of years ago. At the window, she gazed out, then inhaled sharply at the night scene.

"If you'd rather go . . ." he said from behind her.

Snow. Everywhere. Danii adored monochromatic landscapes, and here white fluff blanketed the grounds—as it *should*. "Is this property yours?"

"Yes, it's one of my war spoils."

Then this was a kindness, bringing her here. Maybe he'd been right before—maybe when it really counted, he came through. "There are so many trees," she said. Copses around the lodge led to the dense forest beyond. They were all coated with ice, their branches ponderous with it.

"Larch trees," he said. "One of the few kinds that will grow here."

In front of the manor, a lake lay frozen and glazed, reflecting the blue aurora borealis above.

Stunning. Without tearing her gaze away, she asked, "You've kept this since the war?"

"Surprisingly, there's not a large market for Siberian hunting lodges. I know, I scarcely understand it myself."

Her lips curled.

"My brothers and I divided anything we won. Nikolai needed no residence, because he would have Blachmount, the family manor. This property lay in the middle of nowhere, with lands all the way to the Arctic Ocean, yet the lodge was incongruously lavish. I wanted it," he ended with a shrug.

"Why is it so lavish?"

"It belonged to a baron. He owned a nearby diamond mine."

"Do you ever stay here?"

"Sometimes I come here to hunt in the winter," he said. "Lots of game, since we're at the edge of continuous permafrost. It stays frozen almost year-round, only thaws for a month or two in the summer."

She could tell he was already feeling the cold, though as an immortal, he could withstand some seriously harsh elements. The temperature here was getting to her as well, *invigorating* her, even as she felt herself relaxing from the stresses of the night.

Here there was no threat from the Icere. Or the vampire. For hours, she'd been both attracted to him yet fearful at the same time, but no longer.

He wouldn't be able to bite her here. She'd be too powerful.

"I haven't seen snow in decades." Were those

sideways icicles? Her heart sang—that meant some formidable storms blew here. "I can have ice, but never snow."

"You could visit cold climes."

"I'd almost rather not," she said. "Since it would be too hard to return."

"But now you *can't* return. You were leaving New Orleans tonight for good, weren't you?"

"My suitcases are in my car," she admitted, her mind working. Murdoch had taken her to the vastness of Siberia, which spanned a third of the northern hemisphere. She couldn't find a better place to disappear. Tracing vampires couldn't be followed. There'd be no travel arrangements for Icere assassins to unearth. No airports where she might run into Sigmund's spies.

And more, something about this place called to her. Breathing deeply of the crisp air, she said, "It's so lovely here." With the natural cold permeating every cell in her body, she felt better than she had in memory. She grew more confident, brazen even. At that moment, she decided that he didn't appreciate his Siberian paradise as much as he should. She would do a far better job of treasuring it.

Danii would be *staying*.

Now she just had to convince him. Should she prove unmoving and intractable as a glacier? Or should she dazzle him like a rare frost flower?

When she faced him, the look in his eyes made her decision easy. His gray irises were flickering with black, his mien showing hints of that possessiveness she'd detected earlier this eve.

I'll show him frigid. . . . "You know, vampire, nothing feels quite so decadent as snow against my bare skin," she murmured, slipping off her satchel. "And ice can be a wicked pleasure. If I'm . . . naked."

As she began unlacing her dress, he swallowed audibly. She could see his shaft thickening in his slacks. "You're getting hard. But then, you don't need me for that anymore."

He drew closer to her. "Maybe I want you for it. I'm hard—*for you*."

"Maybe you should have thought about that before you treated me so badly."

Again, he denied nothing, just gave a sharp nod.

"But perhaps there's a way you can make it up to me."

"Let's hear it."

She tilted her head. "Murdoch, do you spook easily?"

"I haven't been known to. . . ." He trailed off when she turned to the door, heading outside into the night, stripping as she went.

Twenty-two

All thoughts of *I lead and women follow* vanished when he tripped outside after her.

As her delighted laughter sounded in the distance, he realized he couldn't remember the last time he'd felt this much excitement.

Christ, when she'd begun removing her skimpy dress . . . exhilaration had spiked in him, not to mention arousal.

He was so very rarely surprised by women. Now he had no idea what she'd do next.

Soon he came upon her little boots, kicked off in the snow, and he gave a low groan. *Will she strip completely?* Each second, his shaft was getting hotter, even as the temperature dropped.

A dozen feet farther on, he saw her discarded dress. He scooped it up, bringing it to his face to inhale her cool scent. His heart—which had begun beating for her alone—was thundering.

When he reached her, she was lying back in a snowdrift, stretching with her arms above her head—in nothing more than a wisp of black silk panties. Her perfect breasts were uncovered, her nipples so stiff they looked like they ached.

His fingers went limp and he dropped her dress, hissing, "*Almighty.*"

She laughed anew at his reaction. Not surprisingly, she had a musical laugh.

His jaw clenched. *Where's my control now?* Seconds before, he'd found himself thinking, *I'd follow her anywhere.* "No compunction about being stripped in front of me?"

"Never. Besides, you've seen every inch of me." She seemed drunk from the snow, shoveling her fingers through it, bringing handfuls up to her lips to kiss.

He turned away from her, disconcerted by how much she affected him, by how her laughter seemed to make something twist in his chest. Determined not to even glance at her until he regained some equilibrium, he sat back against a frost-coated tree trunk.

"You're angry with me, vampire?" She was walking on her knees toward him.

Don't look at her. His hands were fists by his sides. "Not angry." *Bloody confused, exasperated.* "No, I'm—" He broke off when she was kneeling inches before him. In a strangled voice, he said, "What the hell is happening to you?"

Here in the cold, her appearance had begun to change. She was *transforming.*

Her hair had become laced with ice and lighter in color, so blond it was almost white. Shining tendrils were frozen in long streams, descending to cover her breasts or spreading out from her head as though whipped in the wind.

Her lashes were tipped with ice crystals, and more crystals formed semicircles around her eyes. Her lips were pale, bluish even, and were parted, but no smoke came from her breaths. Because they were freezing as well.

Delicate cobalt blue tracings swirled around her wrists in wispy patterns. Her eyes were bright beneath the aurora, a fiery blue matching that in the sky. They burned with an *ancient knowledge.*

Everything about this moment with her should feel foreign. But it . . . didn't. *I've dreamed of this.*

Would she think him mad if he told her he'd seen her like this in a vision?

He'd been hard for her before, but now he was throbbing. These changes attracted him fiercely. He feared he could go off right in his pants. *No, I never lose control.*

Keep telling yourself that, Murdoch.

"You like?" she murmured.

"What is this?"

"This is how I'm supposed to look. And how I'm supposed to feel."

The cold clearly aroused her. His greedy gaze took in her shallow breaths, her trembling lithe body. Her little claws had turned blue and were curling sharply.

I know what that means now. At the thought of her sinking those claws into his back as he plunged inside her, he had to stifle a groan.

Behind her, lightning speared through the aurora. "The lightning is *yours.*" He was surprised his voice was steady. Her gaze was mesmerizing.

She nodded. "Valkyrie give it off with emotion."

"I dreamed of you like this, Daniela." *Connection.*

When she cast him a doubting expression, he said, "Don't believe me? Those lines of blue trace along your lower back as well."

Her eyes widened. "What else did you dream?"

"I took your virginity," he blurted out.

She shivered. "And how did I react?"

"You wanted me to. You wanted . . . me." *You let*

me take your neck. His eyes fixed on her supple flesh, and his fangs ached for her. He raked his tongue along one of them for a shot of blood, pretended it was hers.

"Come closer, vampire."

In a flash, he was up on his knees before her.

Without removing his coat, she began unbuttoning the shirt underneath, spreading the edges. "Will you be too cold?"

"I can take it."

Once his chest was bared, she drew closer until her lips were less than an inch away from him. She eased down his torso like this, her breaths like little bites of frost, as if she were running an ice cube along his skin. He shivered—but not from cold.

As she made her way back up, she said, "Murdoch?"

"Uh?" was all he could manage.

She leaned up to whisper right at his ear, "You're going to let me stay in this place." When she nipped his earlobe with her teeth, his cock jerked in his pants, his sac tightening.

Wait, what had she just said?

She moved to his other ear. "Would you like to do that?" she breathed, making him shudder with want. "I'm going to install myself—a female—in one of your properties. And I'm going to decorate it as I see fit."

Can't . . . form . . . words.

"You want me to, don't you?" She slowly gazed up, looking at him from under a lock of shining, icy hair. She nibbled her plump lip, and he was finished, defeated. He watched, bewildered, as his gloved fingertips traced the crystals at her temple.

"Yes." *I can't believe I'm saying this.* "You can stay." He'd always wanted to discard females—not move them into his home.

He was dimly aware that the seducer was being seduced. The player had just gotten played.

Yet he was still in the game. "You'll stay here. But first we need to seal this deal, Valkyrie. And I know just how."

"Oh?"

He took out the gloves Loa had given him. "Put these on."

TWENTY-THREE

He bought me gloves? "What did you have in mind?" Danii asked as she gamely drew them on. For the first time in ages, she felt powerful. The ability to bring this massive warrior to his knees was heady.

"You'll see." His voice was rough with need, his expression one of single-minded intent.

With each second, she grew more aroused for him. Yet then the wind came up, and the snow-covered limbs raked the drafts. They soughed like music, like secrets. The sounds, the scents, teased her. Something within the dark depths of that cold beckoned. . . .

"Daniela?"

Murdoch competed with the pull. She faced him once more, gazing up into eyes grown black with desire.

Anticipation. Danii felt it, was getting caught up in it.

When he took a lock of her hair and used a curl to stroke her nipple, she gave a cry and arched her back. The cold amplified every whisper of touch—she needed more. "Put your hands on me, vampire."

He groaned, covering both of her breasts with his gloved palms, molding them, cupping as she panted. With a master's skill, he tormented the tips, puckering one, then the other. Once he'd made them throb, he placed a hand flat against her chest, pressing her back.

As she stretched out in the snow, he curled his fingers in her panties, dragging them from her. Yet then he merely gazed over her naked body for long moments, his shaft bulging.

She reached forward, stroking his erection through his pants as his head fell back. Eager to use her gloves, she murmured, "Take it out, Murdoch."

"It will freeze," he said, facing her.

"If it did, then I could suckle you at my leisure."

He groaned. "Would you?"

"For hours. But for now, I'll be sure to rub you really fast, keep it warm with friction."

With a hard shake of his head, he set her hand

away. "I want to see you come first. When you're like this. Want to see your face," he said, moving to kneel between her legs. "Daniela, put your arms over your head. Part your thighs for me."

Following his commands, she eased her arms back, then spread her legs.

"That's it," he rasped, his gaze riveted to her sex. He might as well have been petting her there, because her body responded.

When he licked his lips, looking desperate to taste her, her hips rolled. *What would his kiss be like? Would he be gentle with her? Or ravenous . . . ?*

"Wider," he grated, and she let her knees fall open. With a harsh groan, he lowered his head to run his face alongside her thigh, never touching her. But she could feel his breath, making her tremble.

Over and over his breaths trailed up and down her thighs as his gloved hands fondled her breasts. She was shameless, undulating for his mouth, nearly ready to endure the burn just for a brief touch of his tongue.

"I want to kiss you so much." His mouth was an inch from her sex, his fogging breaths tickling her clitoris. "Spread you before me and lick you till you scream for me."

"Murdoch," she moaned. "I can't take much more of this."

"Do you want me to make you come?" he asked, leaning up.

"Yes!"

"You told me the ice feels wicked against your skin." He reached to his side and plucked a long, thick icicle from a twig. "Were you hinting to me?"

His eyes were dark and fierce. Hers went wide. Ah, gods, did he plan to touch her with that?

She held her breath . . . until he grazed the smooth end over her cheek, making her shiver.

"It doesn't melt against your skin," he murmured, seeming fascinated as he traced it lower to her parted lips.

With her gaze holding his, her tongue darted out to lick the tip just before she sucked the phallus-shaped ice between her lips.

A strangled sound broke from his chest. *Heady power.*

When she relinquished it with a last darting lick, he skimmed it down her chest to the beginning swell of her breasts. They were heaving with excitement, her nipples begging for attention.

With the ice, he circled one taut peak, then the other, until her back was arching up to meet each frozen caress. *So sensual, so perfect.* "Yes, Murdoch . . . clever vampire." Now he was using his mind, delighting her by taking her here, pleasuring her body with the ice.

She swallowed when he trailed it along her torso, past her navel. He repeatedly teased it just above her curls, making her undulate for it, sometimes holding it just out of reach to play with her. "Do you want this?"

"Yes!"

"How badly?" He smoothed the edge of the ice down until it was just against her aching clitoris.

"Please, please . . ." When he began lazily rolling it over the bud, she gasped, then moaned low.

"My female likes this." His smoldering gaze was rapt on his ministrations.

"Ah, gods, yes!" Again and again, he worked it back and forth, sending her closer each time. Between ragged breaths, she said, "More, Murdoch."

He skimmed her slick opening, making her cry out with bliss. Lightning streaked across the sky.

Their gazes met; his held a question. "Yes, do it! Inside me . . ."

Then . . . he slipped it into her wetness. She arched her back, moaning with abandon. *Cold. Exquisite.*

Emboldened by her response, he began languidly thrusting the phallus inside her sheath.

Her gloved hands dug into the snow, her head thrashing. She'd never been brought to come by another.

I'm about to be.

He'd meant to tease her. To send her out of her mind with pleasure.

But now *his* mind was in turmoil, his shaft rampant in his pants, about to erupt.

"Don't stop . . ." When she rolled up her hips to drive the ice deeper, his own hips bucked uncontrollably in response.

Sex.. Want sex. Want to plunge hard into her. He needed to replace the ice with his cock so badly he thought he'd go mad.

"Murdoch," she moaned. "I'm coming!" As she climaxed, her body writhed in a wanton display—and he felt the beginning tremors in his shaft.

Her cries made him frenzied. Now, for the first time, this encounter wouldn't be about building his reputation so he could secure pleasure for himself.

This was going to be rough and unplanned and dirty. Because he was about to spill in his pants.

As soon as she pushed his hand away, spent, he said, "You're going to make me come, Bride." He tore open his zipper, took his cock in hand, and almost went off. He had to squeeze down tight on the head to stop his seed. "Do you want to?"

She breathed, "Oh, yes."

"Then stroke it." He didn't recognize his own snarling voice.

As he held on to the head, she cupped the shaft in her fingers, running her fist up and back.

"Ah, God, again!"

On her second stroke, he widened his knees, thrusting up to her grip. His balls drew tight, readying, swelling. *"That's it. . . ."*

On the third stroke, he removed his hand.

At once, he began ejaculating in her fist, the crown of his cock steaming with hot seed. *So fucking good . . . feels . . .* A brutal groan broke from his chest as he watched her milking him steadily, pumping his semen out into the snow, again and again.

Once she'd wrung him dry, he collapsed onto his back, hurriedly tucking his rapidly cooling shaft back in his pants.

Unable to help himself, he turned on his side to stare at her. Daniela the Ice Maiden had so much fire . . .

A man could get burned.

If I'm not wary, I'm going to become dangerously obsessed with a woman.

He'd bragged to her that sexually he'd been able to last as long as he pleased—because he always had been. Yet within hours of his boast, he'd almost come in his pants. He'd told her that he never lost control—she'd made him *totally fucking lose control.*

She was smiling, glancing up from under her icy lashes. "You should probably go get my things before dawn breaks in New Orleans. I left two suitcases in my car. It's a red X6, parked near the corner of Dauphine and St. Philip." She had that optimistic air about her again, her eyes glittering like the crystals on her face.

Her expression reminded him of the hopeful one she'd evinced their first morning together. He stiffened, reacting to it as poorly as he had then.

She noticed his sudden tension. "Murdoch, we had an agreement."

How did she turn this around on me? He felt like scratching his head in bafflement. *I control situations with women.* "And how are you to stay here?"

"You know I don't eat. I don't need or want heat. This is ideal for my needs," she said, her tone growing absent. She seemed distracted, her gaze fixed on the drifts in the distance.

"Fine, suit yourself." He stood, buttoning his shirt. "Though I don't know when you think I'll be able to return."

She blinked up at him. He thought he spied a brief flash of hurt in her eyes, but it vanished so swiftly he decided he imagined it—especially when she said, "Vampire, after you fetch my stuff, I'm not asking you to return at all."

With a scowl, he traced back to the Quarter and found her car just where she'd said it'd be. He traced inside to grab her bags.

Back out on the street, holding two suitcases, he thought to himself: *My God, what have I done?*

TWENTY-FOUR

While he went to collect her things, Danii slipped on her dress, then explored her new hideout.

Murdoch had modernized the lodge to a degree. There was running water, lighting, plumbing, and a fairly new generator. She found bedding and towels.

In every spacious room, the timeless sculptures, decorations, and brickwork had proved impervious to cold. Which meant this place was perfect for her.

She was a nester. Her star sign decreed nesting, and she was helpless to resist.

The first thing it needed was . . . ice.

When he returned with her bags, Murdoch gruffly showed her to a guest room, acting like he'd made a huge concession by letting her stay. But he also appeared a bit wild-eyed as he glanced from her to the suitcases and back. She supposed BP would be worse in him since he'd been single for so long.

"Do you have something in your bags to write my number on?" he asked her.

"Yes, but you can just tell me. I'll remember."

As soon as he uttered the last of the digits, he hastily said, "But keep in mind that I'll be *extremely* busy following our leads and hunting Ivo."

She gave him her best ice queen impression. "Of course, I understand." But did she? If she were honest, she would acknowledge that deep down, she'd hoped to convince him to stay here with her.

Which regrettably hadn't panned out. But no matter what, she still had this prime place of safety to hide out for a time—and that's what really counted. If he didn't want to experience more of the exquisite pleasure they'd just shared, then it was his loss.

Which means it's mine as well—

"Good-bye, then," he said, tracing away before she could say anything else.

Once she was alone, she gave a casual shrug as if she wasn't hurt. But fooling him was easier than fooling herself. Ignoring the pang in her heart, she proceeded to decorate, figuring it would be many days before she saw him again. . . .

Hours later, she lay on the stripped bed in the master room, eschewing the smaller chamber he'd stuck her in. A delightfully chill wind blew, rushing in through the outer doors and windows—which she'd opened to the freezing night.

She was fatigued from her labors, but pleased with her progress. Icicles embellished all the woodwork and doorways, and ice sheets covered each of the walls.

Yet then she frowned. The glazed walls looked faceless, the flawless ice seeming barren to her.

Those unbroken sheets bothered her, like an off smell or a discordant sound would. And the irritation was sharp, as strong as the pull she'd been feeling to this place.

She rose and crossed to the bedroom window, looking at the dark woods surrounding the lodge, then back inside at the walls. Out, then in. *Wrong.*

Unable to stand it any longer, she fashioned a spear of ice, galvanizing it with layer after layer, honing it.

Once finished, she took her makeshift chisel to the wall, stabbing the glaze. Then again. And again, until peculiar markings began to take shape.

Murdoch would *not* return to Siberia. *I've made it seven days, I can make it seven more.*

He'd finished chasing his leads for the night, and

dawn was approaching—Lukyan and Rurik had already returned to Mount Oblak.

But it would be dark in Siberia.

Lulls in action were dangerous for Murdoch. They made the temptation to return to Daniela harder to resist.

No, he *refused*. Because of the blooding, he was just supposed to succumb? To tolerate this total loss of power? Welcome a complete personality rewrite?

He was determined not to go to her like some lovesick lad, especially since she obviously couldn't have cared less when he'd been about to leave that last night. And she hadn't called him once.

Part of him resented how easily she'd manipulated him. Another part resented her encroachment. But that didn't mean he had bachelor's panic, as she'd accused—which, he'd noted, handily placed all the blame on him for this, while ignoring the difficulties she presented as a Bride.

In any case, if a woman's toothbrush was this age's symbol of female encroachment, try two stuffed suitcases.

So for the last week, he'd kept himself occupied, endeavoring not to think of her at all. With Lukyan and Rurik, he'd been following the leads she'd helped generate, closing in on Ivo with each one. He'd tried repeatedly to see Nikolai, but his brother was usually ... engaged with Myst.

During this time, Murdoch went to bed exhausted every day, hoping that he wouldn't dream of Daniela. But he always did. And each time, that strange voice asked: *What would you sacrifice? What would you do for her?*

He glanced at the lightening sky once more, feeling nearly powerless not to return to her, to check on how she was settling in, to see if he'd imagined the blue of her eyes or her crisp, clean scent.

In his homeland, the fall came with a pounding rain, scouring the countryside. Then one morning the rain would be gone, and they would wake to a white landscape. The air would be briskly clean, carrying the slight tang of the nearby northern seas.

Daniela smelled like those rare mornings. The ones he had never forgotten.

Wait—maybe she hadn't been able to recall his number. What if she'd wanted to contact him but couldn't? He should go just to check on her. Yes, to make sure she had everything she needed. He traced back to the lodge.

Murdoch's jaw went slack at the scene that greeted him.

The windows were all open and ice was . . . everywhere. She'd spun it all over the manor like a spider spins a web.

He'd been raised on the Baltic in the seventeen hundreds. Keeping a home warm had been paramount. Yet now ice arched in the doorways, rounding out the square doorjambs. Icicles dangled from the ceiling and descended from the windows like curtains. The walls were covered in a white glaze, and she'd carved primitive-looking symbols into the ice.

She had no right. Bachelors panicked over a toothbrush? Try having an otherworldly *female* leave a permanent ice storm in one's *hunting lodge*.

Who *wouldn't* panic?

And she was nowhere to be found. As he stalked from one empty room to the next, the level of disappointment he felt both staggered and perplexed him.

When he reached his bedroom, he saw that she'd been sleeping there—she'd stripped the bed of all its blankets. Why would she stay here and not in the room where he'd initially put her bags?

She's been sleeping in my bed? That knowledge did something to him, touching some dark, primal drive within him. The thought of keeping his female protected within his property, in a stronghold won by his sword . . . *aroused* him.

Sleeping in my *bed.*

He gave himself a shake, then turned to one of her unpacked suitcases, finding a couple of erotic novels with titles that had him raising his brows and a collection of lingerie he'd be imagining on her for years to come. He picked up one of her silk nightgowns, inhaling her scent.

Not surprising, he grew hard as rock. But his fangs also sharpened. Why was she the only one who tempted him to drink from the flesh? He'd never been tempted before her and hadn't had the slightest urge all week until now.

Setting the gown away, he opened the second bag. It was filled with containers of *salt*. What could she need so much of it for?

He crossed to the dresser. Atop it sat her sat-phone, which he checked in case she'd been unable to contact him. Not a chance—fully charged, the ringer muted, the screen displaying numerous missed calls. He scrolled through her contacts, finding his number saved as VAMP PHONE. She could've called, but hadn't.

Tethered to the phone was a rugged-looking laptop, apparently ice-proof. At times, the world of the Lore proved boggling for him; the idea of internet capability in this lodge ranked right up there with the notion of an otherworldly ice being inhabiting it.

Once he entered the bathroom, he discovered what she used the salt for. A container was opened beside the old fashioned bathing tub. Daniela needed salt so she wouldn't freeze her bathwater. He dimly thought, *No wonder she smells like the sea.*

This was too bizarre to be believed. . . .

The north wind gusted through the window, blowing snow inside. Without thought, he rushed forward to close the window, but it was frozen open.

He stared out into the harsh, wintry night. She was out there, somewhere, the little Bride he could never touch. Everything about her, about this situation, was unfathomable to him.

And all the ice was a blatant reminder that he could never drink her. *You have bloodlust for her. Leave this place.*

His chest felt like it had a band tightening around

it. He traced away, out of breath and mystified by the female living in his manor.

I'll be damned if I ever return.

Twenty-Five

Murdoch glanced at his watch yet again.

The night was waning, and still he waited on Rurik and Lukyan. They were to meet here in the Quarter to investigate a new lead, and it wasn't like Rurik to be late.

Lulls in action were *still* dangerous for Murdoch—even after his ill-fated trip to the lodge a week ago. Yet he was determined to fight the unnatural pull toward Daniela. Yes, he'd experienced mind-blowing pleasure with her. But that just brought into relief how much he missed sex. The driving need, sweaty bodies writhing, hips pumping. And kissing. God, he missed kissing.

No, there was no future with her. Monogamy was not his way. He'd seen it destroy better men than he was.

And she iced my goddamned lodge.

After leaving Rurik another message, Murdoch leaned against a light post. He caught the eye of an attractive brunette in a low-cut top. She cast him a lascivious smile, but all he could think was that she wasn't a fraction as comely as Daniela. He turned away.

In fact, over the last two weeks, he'd compared all women to Daniela, and without exception, they were all lacking.

But at least they could potentially be touched.

When his gaze wandered back over the female, she stared at him with undisguised interest. No, he hadn't wanted to be blooded, but now that he was, he might as well enjoy it.

He knew from experience that he could have that woman with little more than a crook of his finger. Old habits rose to the fore, even as he told himself he didn't have time for this. He needed to give his undivided focus to finding Ivo.

But without Rurik and Lukyan, Murdoch could do nothing but wait, and he needed to slip the leash Daniela had put on him.

If he could blunt this need, he'd be more focused, more effective. A tall brunette seemed just the thing. . . .

"May I wear it, mama?" Danii asked. Svana had just taken her crown out of safekeeping for her upcoming trip. As ever, Danii was fascinated with it.

"Just for a bit, dearling," Svana told her as she placed the band of ice and diamonds atop her braided hair. Jewels dropped down over her forehead. "There. My little winter princess."

"I want to show the other Valkyrie."

"But they would be spellbound."

"I'm not."

"No, daughter." Svana smiled as she adjusted the crown, but it was too large. "Because our kind comes from a land of diamonds and ice."

"Is that where you're going now?"

Her beautiful face had grown grave. "Yes."

"When will you come back?"

Svana knelt before her. "Daniela, I might not make it back."

"Then why do you have to go there?" Danii asked, beginning to cry. "Just stay with me."

"I must reclaim my throne. I'm a queen from a long line of queens. And one day you will be, too."

"How will I find you?"

"If I don't return to you here, you must promise me, my love, never to follow me. Never, never go to Icergard. Not until you're shown the way. . . ."

Danii shot up in bed, awake in an instant. *My gods.* She'd just recollected more of that fateful day when her mother had left her. *Not until I'm shown the way?*

Who exactly would be directing Danii to Icergard? And why was she only just remembering this?

The dream had been so realistic, she could almost feel the weight of that crown on her head. Svana had worn it when she'd gone to meet her destiny, even knowing she'd likely die. How brave she'd been.

Danii rose, feeling a pleasant jolt as her bare feet met the freezing marble, then crossed to the open window. The north wind blew with a proud gust as if embracing her. She closed her eyes, swaying with it.

The vampire—who had yet to return—had talked of dreams. Now she'd been awash in reverie each night. Was it the cold or this particular place that drew forth her memories and dreams?

She loved it here. The frigid winds affected her like adrenaline, each flake of snow a balm on her soul. For two weeks, she'd indulged in ice hunts, followed whispers, explored the countryside. And she'd continued to carve arcane symbols into any ice face she'd come across.

The markings were simple in form, like the inscriptions on ancient rune stones from northern lands. She didn't think she'd ever seen these designs before, and had no idea how she knew them.

Eventually, she'd begun creating her own ice tablets to carve on, some as large as a table, later placing them in different parts of the forest and snowdrifts, settling them just so. She didn't know why she did this, just felt compelled to.

With each day here she was growing stronger, thinking more about this puzzling new pastime—and less about the vampire. *Yes. Some minutes less than others.* At first, she'd wondered if her carving was merely a desperate bid for distraction, like a Valkyrie/Icere equivalent of downing a gallon of Häagen-Dazs.

But she'd concluded it must be more, because the compulsion intensified—even as her desire for him should've begun dwindling. . . .

Murdoch kissed three different women that night.

Mere minutes after spotting that first brunette, he'd found himself with her in an alley behind a bar, taking her lips with his own.

And still he'd thought of Daniela. Ultimately, he'd broken away with a muttered curse. "Sorry, sweet. Have to go."

She'd clung to him, begging him not to stop. What should have excited him had wilted any arousal he might have managed by imagining it was Daniela he kissed.

The second woman had been passable, but there'd been no distinct intelligence shining in her eyes. So different from his Bride. He admired Daniela's tricky mind, liked the way he could rarely read her expressions.

The third smelled of cloying perfume and whatever she'd dined on earlier. Such a contrast to Daniela's clean scent. . . .

Now as he thought back, he realized that not one of the three had tempted him to take her neck. Another reason he needed to stay away from Daniela. *Easier said than done.* He felt as if he was waging a losing battle, and in his life, he'd bloody had enough of those.

He'd died in one.

Why fight this? It would *have* to be easier to resist drinking her than to go without seeing her face again—which was proving impossible. . . .

He pictured his Bride sleeping in his bed, as if she were awaiting him. If he were going to settle down, why not with the most exquisite, intelligent female he'd ever known? Even if she was an ice being. He recalled the supernatural scene that had greeted him at the lodge and came to a determination.

It'd never be dull with her.

Could the reason he'd never committed to a woman be that he'd been waiting for her all his life? He glanced at the sky. Dawn was only a couple of hours away. Too late to do much here. But it would be dark in Siberia.

Why not try this out? *If I'm ever tempted to drink from her, I'll trace away.* At least then he'd know.

With that conclusion, he almost wished he hadn't pursued those other women. He thought he might be feeling . . . *guilt.* Him.

He spied a flower street vendor on the next corner over. Murdoch knew women—they loved flowers. He snatched up a bouquet of roses, tossed a twenty to the half-asleep vendor, then traced to Daniela.

Again, she wasn't inside. When he heard the front door creaking open, he traced downstairs with the bouquet behind his back. "Daniela?"

Her lips were even bluer than before, her skin pale as milk. She had twigs in her icy hair.

God, she's lovely beyond words. He cast about for a compliment and came up empty. *What's new?*

She gazed at him, not with the excitement he'd anticipated, but with measured curiosity.

"Where were you?" he asked.

"Just got back from a walk."

She was barefoot in a halter top and shorts. He wondered if he'd ever get used to seeing so much of her perfect body exposed to the elements. "I hadn't heard from you. Wanted to make sure you're settling in."

She shrugged, turning toward the stairs.

He followed her up. "I am just stopping by. To check on you."

"You kind of said that already. And as you can see, I'm doing great."

"You've been busy here," he said when they reached his room. Since he'd been here last, she'd added to those carved designs in the glazes that coated the walls. More snow had accumulated. "Busy *decorating*."

Again, he felt that sense of encroachment. But when he didn't feel the accompanying resentment, he figured he'd become inured to it. "Those symbols you carve—what do they mean?"

"I'm not sure." Her eyes darted around the room. "Just stuff I made up."

For some reason, at that moment, both of their gazes fell on the bed. His voice was rough when he said, "Why are you sleeping in here?"

"My room faced south. In here, the north wind blows right in."

Sleeping in my bed. He grew aroused at the idea once more. He might not be able to claim her, but there were other benefits. Reminded of that, he offered her the flowers.

Her gaze flicked over them. "A bouquet? Like in the days of old?"

"I thought that bringing flowers to a woman one desires was a timeless gesture."

"The timing was fine." She canted her head to the side. Had her ears twitched? "But your supposition about the woman was off."

Is she studying my face? Could she tell he'd kissed other women? "What do you mean?"

In answer, she wiggled her fingers, motioning for the flowers. The moment he handed them to her, they began to wither. As he stared, they blackened and died.

He ran his gloved hand over the back of his neck. "Glad I didn't get you a kitten."

She tossed them into the unused fireplace. "You have to understand that I'm not like the women you knew. This world is not like you thought. Everything has changed for you. And you can't apply your human expectations to it."

"Then tell me about this world. Teach me."

"Would you like me to give you a lesson right now?"

"Yes. Absolutely."

"Valkyrie have a superhuman sense of smell. Not as strong as Lykae or demons. Maybe not even as strong as vampires. But enough so I can smell the women you've been with."

Ah, Christ.

TWENTY-SIX

Danii smelled women's perfumes. *Plural.* She could tell he'd been close enough to them to pick up their scents, but she couldn't detect exactly what he'd been doing with them.

At her words, he'd gone still, his eyes narrowing. Now he shrugged, and any hint of guilt she might have imagined was gone, replaced by nonchalance. "I kissed . . . a couple of women."

Her claws straightened with jealousy.

"Just wanted to see what it'd be like. After so long."

Lightning flashed outside. His cavalier manner infuriated her. "Did you do more?"

"Daniela, you're making an issue out of something trivial. The women were humans, and I *only* kissed them."

"Trivial? Did you just happen to know these mortals? Or were they tramps you picked up while you were supposed to be searching for Ivo?"

At his expression, she grew queasy. *Bingo.* She could just see him lustily making out with skanks in some alley in the Quarter.

I've always ridiculed tourists who did that.

There were so few secrets within the Lore. Gossipers abounded. Everyone would know Murdoch had spurned Danii to be with other women. And it was bad enough for a Bride to be forsaken by a leech, but it was entirely humiliating to be passed over for mortals.

"We never made a commitment to each other," he finally said. When lightning flashed again, he scrubbed his palm over his mouth. "You simply *informed* me that you'd be staying here. And

I haven't kissed a woman in three hundred god-damned years."

"Then why didn't you do more with them?"

He exhaled wearily. "They left me cold—"

"Cold?" she cried, a hysterical note to her voice. "I'm so glad I made you swear not to tell anyone anything about me, not that they won't all know now. I hope you put money against us in Loa's betting book."

"We aren't wed." His own ire spiked. "I made you no promises. You have no call to be angry with me."

"I'm angry because you've finally seen what's been just before you all along. But you've seen it too late."

"Too late? Again, I only kissed them. I came *here* tonight, to be with you, even though I had those women begging me for more."

Begging him? Was he that good a kisser? She shook herself—she'd never know. "And yet you chose to come here and be with me, a female who *can't* give you more. I find that difficult to believe!"

"Believe it, ice queen. You've broken me—I want no other!"

"And that makes you *broken*?" She gave a cry. "Gods, I am so sick of you!"

"Sick of me? When I admit that I chose you above others? Your timing is ridiculous."

"Because I don't buy this! If you think you're broken, then you're going to want to get fixed. Not to wallow in your brokenness. Trust me, I know this!" *Sad, sad Daniela . . .*

"So now you've got me all figured out, when you've known me for a couple of weeks? Ah, that's right, I'm merely a manwhore and nothing more."

"I've only known you a short while, but I know men. I've witnessed the entire spans of their lives. You're not a man who won't deign to commit. You're a coward who's *afraid* to."

"Coward?" Though he sneered the word, Danii saw a flicker of some emotion in his eyes. She'd hit a nerve.

"A *selfish* coward! You expect me to just be waiting here, standing by for whenever you decide you want more from me?"

"You *are* just waiting here, Valkyrie."

At that, she began building ice in her palm, and he eyed it with contempt. "Leave here, vampire. And don't come back!"

"This is my house!"

"Does this look like *your* house any longer?" A gust of flurries blew in the window to punctuate her words.

"Fine. Have it! Consider it a gift for a couple of pleasurable nights."

With a bitter curse, Murdoch traced from the lodge. He returned to his meeting place in case Rurik showed—

And found himself surrounded by beings.

They looked like demons, but they had red eyes like Fallen vampires. They were immense and carried medieval weapons, cudgels and maces.

Behind them stood Ivo, his bald head gleaming. Just five years ago, they'd met on a battlefield. *Finally, I've found this prick.*

"We seek the halfling," Ivo said. "If you have information about her, we might spare your life."

Halfling? "I wouldn't tell you anything, even if I knew what you were talking about."

In a bored tone, Ivo commanded, "Then kill him."

Murdoch drew his sword in a flash, swung it at the closest demon. The male laughed as he easily dodged the blow.

The speed was inconceivable. *You can't fight these beings.* Just as he'd been told.

Before Murdoch could retreat, they were upon him, preventing him from tracing. A cudgel caught him across the face, tearing and crushing at the same time. Blood sprayed.

A blow to his leg bludgeoned his femur, sending him to his knees. Another shattered his arm.

The strength . . . *monstrous.* A studded mace hit him directly in the chest, embedding in his sternum. *Can't breathe, can't . . .*

Against his will, his blood-drenched eyes closed. Realization dawned. *I'm about to die.* And all he could think about was how he wanted to see Daniela just one last time.

Ivo ordered, "Take his head—"

A roar sounded. Murdoch struggled just to crack open his lids. *Rurik and Lukyan, here? They must've been trailing Ivo earlier.*

As the two charged into the fight, Murdoch

tried to warn them, but couldn't speak. *Jaw not working?*

Rurik went fully berserk, wildly swinging his battle hammer. Lukyan wielded his two swords, looking as if he hungered for death—and planned to take with him as many as possible.

But when Rurik received a hit that felled even his giant frame, Lukyan muttered, "Fuck this." Then he traced away.

TWENTY-SEVEN

I'm going to miss it here. But Danii knew she couldn't stay.

She'd be relinquishing the vampire's gift for two nights of pleasure.

How could she even be surprised that he'd remained away? After all, he was probably busy mugging with mortals in back alleys. Which left Danii to be the Forbearer's forsaken one.

She reminded herself yet again that she'd dodged a bullet with Murdoch. This could have been much worse. Anything between them could never have worked out. If she threw all in with him and then got jilted, people would ask, "What was she thinking, to make a grab at a rake like that? With no warm bed to offer him?"

She sighed. Damn it, she'd liked him—and she'd liked it *here*.

The pressure to carve had continued to grow within her, as if she were nearing some goal and gaining momentum. It was satisfying to her, and brought into stark relief exactly how little in her life had contented her before.

Her mother had told Danii that she descended from the line of the Winter Queens, but Danii had never felt a connection to that ancestry. She felt more Valkyrie than ice fey. Of course, she didn't fit in with the Valkyrie either. *Sad, sad Daniela.*

Were these symbols the very first tie to her heritage? Why was she only now seeing them?

Didn't matter. Her time here had ended.

If she remained, she'd get too attached to the lodge. The longer she stayed, the longer she'd want to. And she could just see Murdoch bringing another woman here in a few years and finding Danii still inside, putzing around in her nightgown, muttering, "Oh, hai. Don't mind me."

Danii had determined and finally accepted that Murdoch equaled misery. Unfortunately, she'd concluded this *after* she'd begun falling for him.

Time to leave.

Now I just need to find a ride.

"You should see the other guy," Murdoch grated from his bed.

Nikolai had already been pale when he traced into the room at Mount Oblak. Seeing Murdoch like this made even more blood drain from his face.

He knew how bad he looked. A metal brace was screwed into his leg to stabilize his crushed femur. One arm was immobilized in a cast, and bandages swathed more of his body than not. His face was lacerated from the corner of his mouth to his ear, held together only by stitches. All in all, he was lucky to be alive.

No. Not *lucky*.

Murdoch and Rurik lived only because Lukyan had returned directly with a full battle contingent. It turned out that Lukyan didn't like to merely fight— he liked *to win*.

Nikolai finally found his voice. "What has happened to you?"

"I was about to ask you the same. My God, Nikolai, you look worse than I do." His brother was always so stoical, always sure of his actions.

So what the hell was going on?

Nikolai's eyes grew dark before he glanced away. "We'll talk of my problems later. Who did this to you?"

Murdoch let the subject go for now. "Ivo has demons. Demons turned vampires. They are strong— you can't imagine it. He is looking for someone, but I don't think it's your Bride. They mentioned something about a 'halfling.'"

"How many?"

"There were three demonic vampires in his party, other vampires as well. We took down two of the demons, but one remains." Murdoch glanced behind him. "Where's your Bride?"

Nikolai hesitated. "She's at Blachmount. We're . . . I'm . . ." He ran his hand over his haggard face, then said in a rush, "Ever since I tasted Myst's blood, I've been dreaming her memories. . . ."

It was all Murdoch could do to mask his shock as Nikolai continued talking, the words spilling out. So the memories *had* followed the blood. Why weren't his eyes red? Would Nikolai confess this to Kristoff?

Through these dreams, Nikolai had learned that in the past Myst had been a calculating femme fatale who'd used and discarded lovers without mercy. She'd been bent on tricking Nikolai, acting as if she wanted more with him, when she'd actually had ulterior motives.

Before Murdoch could even formulate a response to this, Nikolai delivered yet another bombshell. He'd come into possession of an enchanted chain— that *controlled* Myst. By owning the chain, Nikolai could make her do whatever he pleased.

This was their *understanding*? Some kind of enthrallment?

Long moments of silence passed before Murdoch said incredulously, "You took away the free will of a creature who has had it for upward of two thousand years. A good wager says she's going to want it back." Nikolai had dealt with war, plague, and famine all in one decade. He'd lost most of his family. And yet he'd always acted honorably. Until now.

It figured that it'd take a woman to break him.

"No, you don't understand," Nikolai said. "She's callous. Incapable of love. It eats at me, her deception, because it's the only thing that makes sense." More to himself, he muttered, "Why else would she want me?"

Murdoch weakly grabbed his brother's wrist. "All these years, I've seen you continually choose the best, most rational course, even if it's the most difficult. I've been proud to follow your leadership because you've acted with courage and always— always—with rationality," he grated, stopping for a ragged breath. "I never thought I would have to inform you that your reason and judgment have failed you, Nikolai. If she's as bad as you say, then you have to . . . I don't know, just help her change, but you can't *order* this. Get back to her. Explain your fears to her."

"I don't think I can. You saw her, Murdoch. Why would she so quickly acquiesce?"

"Why don't you just ask her?"

His brother's expression said it all. He didn't want her to know how desperately he needed her.

"And about the other men," Murdoch said. "This isn't the seventeen hundreds anymore. This isn't even the same plane. She's an immortal, not an eighteen-year-old blushing bride straight from a convent. She can't change these things, so if you want her, you have to adjust."

If her skin can't be touched, you have to adjust. . . .

Nikolai ran a hand over his face and snapped, "When did you get so bloody understanding?"

Since I met Daniela. Since I nearly died. Murdoch shrugged, then stifled a wince at the pain in his chest.

"I had someone explain a few rules of the Lore to me and learned that we can't apply our human expectations to the beings within it." *Some men's Brides are untouchable.*

"Who told you this?"

I can't tell you. I took a vow.

Nikolai didn't press for an answer. "Will you be all right?" he asked.

"That's the thing about being immortal. It'll always look worse than it is."

Nikolai attempted a grin—and failed.

"Good luck, brother," Murdoch said. As soon as Nikolai left, he lay back, weak from hiding how much pain he was in, and still astounded by what he'd just seen. *First my father, then Nikolai, now . . . me.* Was it Murdoch's inescapable fate to become obsessed with one woman?

After witnessing his brother like this, he came to a conclusion. Murdoch was *already* ruined without Daniela regardless.

I'll be broken if I lose her in the future—or if I lose her now.

Now that this realization had struck him, Murdoch was oddly resigned to it. *It's too late for me.*

"I'm besotted with her." He gave a laugh, then grimaced as his wounds punished him for it. At least now he knew.

For the first time in weeks, he felt optimistic about his future. All he had to do was convince her to forgive him. Though he'd proved he was in no way silver-tongued with her, he would somehow figure out a way to persuade her. He always came through when it really counted.

He craved seeing Daniela again and was eager to get this sorted out between them, but he was still too weak, and he didn't want her to see him like this.

Kristoff had put him on two weeks' leave, so Murdoch could wait another day or two.

After all, he knew exactly where she'd be.

Twenty-Eight

Danii's ear twitched a split second before she heard the masculine demand: "Where the hell are you going?"

So the vampire's returned. "Away," she said as she zipped up her second suitcase.

"You were just going to disappear without a word?"

"I'll bet you've *never* done that to a woman. Besides, I didn't figure you'd even notice I was gone. Thought you'd be busy trolling for humans."

"I haven't looked at another woman since—"

"Anyway, I wrote you a note on the dresser," Danii interrupted, uninterested in whatever he'd come to say.

He snatched up the paper where she'd written: *Murdoch, it's been real. Daniela.*

"How were you going to leave?"

"I have ways." *Ways* being the one Sno-Cat operator in Russia who would journey to this place, the one due to arrive in an hour.

Murdoch crumpled the note in his fist. "How would I have been able to find you?"

She paused in her packing, briefly glancing up at him. "I guess you *wouldn't*."

Then she frowned. Though he always dressed well, tonight he seemed to have taken great care with his clothes. He wore an expensive sweater and luxe overcoat. His boots had been polished.

She sported a miniskirt and a camisole. With no shoes. "Why are you all dressed up?" she asked irritably.

"This night is important to me." He was moving stiffly, and stood at an odd angle to her, keeping half of his face in shadow. "I need to tell you something."

And I need to see why you're not showing me the other side of your face. She moved to get a better look at him. *Stitches?* His face had been cut up, and yet he'd still tried to shave. What was so important? "Murdoch, what happened to you?"

"I almost got killed by a few half-demon, half-vampire beings."

"There's no such thing." She waved his words away. "It's one of the rare 'myths' in the Lore that's actually false."

"They had horns and fangs and were stronger than any vampires I've ever fought. They also had *red* eyes."

All Fallen vampires had red eyes, but very few species of demons did. There'd been rumors of Ivo plotting something major. Had he conceived of a way to turn demons into vampires?

"Remember when Deshazior and the kobold said they were different and unfightable?" Murdoch said. "Well, they are."

She had to contact Nïx about this. *Wait* . . . Her sister had mentioned *dempires* the last time they'd spoken. *Demon vampires.* Nïx already knew.

Murdoch began pacing, stabbing his fingers through his hair, his energy seeming to take up the entire room. But he was limping. And she thought she heard a barely perceptible squeak. A leg brace? Whatever he'd tangled with had inflicted some serious damage.

"Daniela, I think I know why I'm like this around you. Why I'm always at a loss for words and gruff. It's *you.*"

"Blaming much? *This* behavior used to impress the ladies? Really?" She turned back to her packing.

"That's what I'm trying to explain. I wasn't like this. I was smooth, compliments falling easily from my lips."

"Murdoch Suavé?" She knew he hated it when she called him that. "Then what's different now?"

"Now I fear that . . . I think that this . . . matters. You matter. To *me.*" He ran his hand over his forehead. "I feel a lot of pressure not to fuck this up with you."

"What do you want from me?"

"I don't know. A chance? To see where this leads."

She felt a spark of excitement at the idea, but mentally snuffed it. *Murdoch equals misery.* When would she finally accept that?

"Stay here, Daniela. With me."

She narrowed her eyes. "With you? Like living together?" Had his nod been the tiniest bit hesitant? "What's changed?"

"You said that I was afraid, and I think you were not . . . wrong."

She didn't reply, just raised her brows.

"I didn't see it before, didn't understand my reluctance. But when I was ambushed and believed I was going to die"—he stopped, meeting her gaze— "all I could think of was you."

Oh. She felt herself softening. *I've been thinking about you, too. No matter how hard I try not to.* If she hadn't had her carving, she'd have gone mad.

"And then a few days ago, I saw my brother. He's a wreck over Myst. I thought that I'd never seen a man so twisted inside over a woman. But I have. Our father was that way for our mother."

Murdoch resumed pacing. "He was obsessed with her. When she died, he never again laughed, never moved on. He used to sit in their room and stare at her portrait for hours. I think I feared something like that happening to me, if I sought more with you. But then I realized I'm more afraid of missing this with you."

A breath escaped her as she edged closer to him. *I want him. I want reality over fantasy.* "Murdoch, did you practice that speech?"

"Continually for the last two days."

No, remember Farmer Ted! Remember Loa's betting book! "Since we've been seeing each other, you've threatened me, frightened me, and put me in a position where I was forced to walk out into the heat of noonday to hitchhike in a hell vehicle that reeked of tobacco. When you went out trolling in the Quarter, you . . . hurt me," she said. "So you think long and hard about this. I saw your frustration when you wanted to bite me. I saw your hunger as you stared at my neck. And I've seen you clench your fists when you want to touch me."

Closing in on her, he asked in a husky voice, "And did you see nothing else, *kallim*?"

She swallowed, unable to look away from his intense gray eyes, already flickering black with emotion. "You can never touch my skin, never drink from me. I'm colder than I've ever been. The pain would be much worse for me, and for you as well."

"I understand."

"Murdoch, there's no magic that's going to change our situation, no way to circumvent it—not now, and potentially not ever. Do you think you can be satisfied with that?"

"Satisfied? Completely? No. But I think we can be happier together than apart."

If he had waxed rhapsodic about their chances, she probably would've run screaming. Instead, he'd been honest. And she agreed—she wouldn't be satisfied completely either.

"I'll give this a few months," she eventually said. "On two conditions."

"What are they?"

"Just as before, you can never tell anyone about me. Not until I'm ready."

"Why?"

Because I give this a one-in-fifty shot of working out. "Because I don't want to be the butt of jokes or the betrayed one on the betting books. And I don't want to be known as the Forbearer's forsaken one."

"You expect me to forsake you."

"Any reason why I shouldn't?"

"I'm not my history. At least, that's not all I am. Anymore." He frowned, as if he couldn't believe what he was saying.

"You've told me that you can't do monogamy."

"I'm going to. Do it. Now. But you must as well." When she gave him a "no kidding" expression, he gritted his teeth. Again, clearly not pleased with what he'd said.

"I won't be dissuaded from this condition. You must keep us a secret."

"My brothers will hear my heart beating. They'll know."

"Do you agree or not?"

Finally, he said, "I agree. And what's the second?"

"You have to vow never to bite me."

"I vow it."

Don't get too excited, Daniela!

He placed his gloved hands on the sides of her

face, gazing down at her. "Now, does this mean you've signed back up on my roster?"

Too late. "Did you practice that line as well?"

That lock of hair tumbled over his forehead. "Repeatedly."

TWENTY-NINE

"Come on in!" Danii called to the vampire pacing on shore. "The water's great."

Under the moonlight, Murdoch looked as if he were actually considering joining her as she swam amidst the ice floes. He was also probably regretting that he'd agreed to trace her to the northern limits of his property, which extended all the way to the Arctic Ocean.

Seconds after she'd seen the water, she'd been skinny-dipping in it.

Poor vampire, pacing at the very edge of the sea, wanting to follow her, his gorgeous face tense. Her heart tugged at the sight, just as it'd been doing daily for these last several weeks, ever since the night she and Murdoch had started living together.

After they'd paid off the irate Sno-Cat operator, of course.

"Maybe the water's a jot brisk," she teased. These closing months of winter had been particularly harsh, an idyll of blizzards and negative degrees for her—and of course virtually twenty-four hours of darkness for him.

Without complaint, he endured the cold to be with her. She slept during the brief murky daylight to spend more time with him. And when they hadn't been talking, learning more about each other, they'd been indulging in bouts of sensual—albeit inventive—bliss.

She'd never been happier.

"Out, Daniela," he called, still pacing. "You've been in long enough."

"If you don't come join me, a merman might get frisky with me!"

He stopped and canted his head, wondering if she was kidding, growing increasingly agitated.

"Oh, very well. I'll come in." She wanted to walk some of the way back to the lodge anyway, and needed to budget time for snowball fights—she might let him win one tonight. She loved playing in the snow with him. When he had all his cold-weather gear on, they could roll around without having their skin touch.

As she swam in, she called, "Trace and get me a towel?"

Obviously reluctant to leave her for even seconds, he disappeared, returning moments later with one. He met her at the shore, wrapping her in it. As he rubbed her dry, her eyes closed with pleasure, reminded anew of their earlier encounter. For hours, she'd teased him with ice cubes, running them all over his body, everywhere she wished she could lick him.

"You were kidding about the merman, right?" he said. "You'd never told me they existed."

"I haven't gotten to merfolk yet." Yes, Danii had relented, finally divulging the secrets of the Lore, once she'd sworn him to secrecy. She owed him her life and couldn't stand the thought of him out there engaging opponents that would try to kill him just for being a vampire—enemies with powers and weaknesses he wouldn't understand. "I've only covered the first two hundred or so beings, and there are more than can be catalogued. And that's just on this plane."

She'd outlined many of the larger factions, from the demon kingdoms called demonarchies to the history of the noble fey. "They were feudal lords called Féodals," she'd explained. "That's where they get the name. They hailed from the plane of Draiskulia, but once they came here, they became divided into different factions. Like the Icere." And she'd related humorous trivia: "Some demons, like Desh, can be involuntarily summoned by previous bed partners. They call those summoners swimbos—a play on She Who Must Be Obeyed. . . ."

"Merfolk," he repeated now, handing Danii her clothes. At times he seemed overwhelmed by all the Lorean histories and details. Admittedly, it was a lot to take in.

He'd probably learned the most via laptop, by following the web results and commentary on the Talisman's Hie, a sort of immortal *Amazing Race*, sponsored by Riora, the flighty Goddess of Impossibility. Entrants from all factions crossed the globe, competing for mystical prizes.

Through the results, he'd discovered that his brother Sebastian was indeed alive and well—because he was competing in it. "My brother's alive?" he'd said that day, shooting to his feet. Just before he'd swung Danii up in his arms, he'd abruptly dropped his outstretched hands, drawing back self-consciously. "Can you believe it? I have to let Nikolai . . ." He'd trailed off. "Why did you just go pale? Daniela, is Sebastian in danger?"

Regrettably, Sebastian was competing against Danii's half sister, Kaderin the Coldhearted, a vicious vampire assassin. "The rules state that the competitors can't kill each other until the final round," she'd said, not wanting to extinguish his hopes, but Kaderin had never lost a Hie. And this time they played for Thrane's Key, which unlocked a door *to the past*. Since Kaderin felt responsible for the deaths of two of her full-blood sisters, she'd be a ruthless menace in order to win that key.

When Murdoch had asked Danii if she could find out anything about this—like exactly why Sebastian would enter—she'd left a message with Nïx. Yet though Nïx was the most powerful oracle in the Lore, she was also forgetful, capricious, and notoriously bad at returning calls. . . .

Danii finished tugging her skirt up her thighs, then she glanced up—to find Murdoch's fierce gaze rapt on her body.

He took her shoulders in his gloved hands, staring down at her with his obsidian eyes reflecting moonlight. The breeze blew that unruly lock over his forehead. "You couldn't be lovelier," he rasped, the mere sound of his husky voice making her body go soft for him.

Her gaze dipped to his lips. The moment was ripe for a kiss. "Vampire, I would give anything to taste you right now." *Anything.* Though this time together had been almost perfect, frustration simmered just below the surface. With each day, she wondered how much longer they could go without real touching.

His hands tightened on her shoulders. "As would I."

She was fantasizing about wicked sex even more than she had *before* she'd met Murdoch. Danii envisioned suckling his thick length for hours. She imagined how it would feel plunging inside her. *What would it be like to have his scent all over me?*

Would his kiss make her breathless and weak-kneed, her toes and her claws curling?

As his gaze flicked from her eyes to her mouth, he grated, "Almost don't want to know what you're thinking right now." He broke away, turning from her with clenched fists—instead of claiming the kiss that should have been his due.

Yet another reminder that the broken doll was in no way fixed.

"We need to get back," he said. "I should check in at Mount Oblak."

"But you just went there two nights ago," she

reminded him. "You said you weren't going to be needed there as much." Now that there was no impending threat from the Horde.

In the past months, the vampire world had been rocked to its core. The Horde king Demestriu had been slain by Emmaline, Danii's lovable niece. Emma had discovered that he was her father, and then she'd somehow managed to defeat him in a fight to the death. Ivo, too, had been assassinated for seeking to wed Emma, the 'halfling.' Apparently Lachlain MacRieve, her new Lykae protector, had taken exception to that, because he'd released his savage inner werewolf, slaughtering Ivo and the remaining *dempire* as well.

"Is there some new threat?" Danii asked. "Or has Lothaire returned?" Rumor held that the Enemy of Old hadn't even remained on this plane.

"No, nothing like that, just the usual aggressing bands," Murdoch said. Without Demestriu to lead the Horde, their numbers had been divided into smaller, weaker factions, but they could still prove deadly. "It can't hurt to check in. I'm sure you want to carve, anyway." Had his tone been a shade brusque?

Maybe she was carving too much, but getting each symbol perfect felt so crucial. Sometimes she worked till her fingers bled. If Murdoch was there, he'd take her hands in his big gloved ones and ice her wounds.

The first time he'd found her like this, he'd demanded, "Daniela, why do this to yourself?"

How to explain the compulsion? *The Call of the*

Wild meets *Holiday on Ice*? "I feel antsy and full until I carve. It's like an instinct, or maybe some kind of genetic memory, passed down by blood. Kind of like how you might get my memories if you ever drank from me."

Always, Danii pondered the mystery of who would lead her back to Icergard, a puzzle as yet unsolved. Could her carvings be some kind of clue?

Reminded of that, she said, "Yes, maybe I could work a little." Though she felt selfish on occasion, investigating her memories, this was her time. There was no one to keep secrets for or from, no one to *observe*, except her own determined expression in a mirrored glaze of ice.

The world was passing her by. One month, then another. . . .

"Very well." He took her shoulders once more to trace her back to the lodge. Before he left again, he said, "I might see Nikolai tonight. Have you thought about my request?" Murdoch had announced a couple of weeks ago, "Myst has consented to marry my brother. I want us to visit them." When Danii had hesitated, he'd said, "Just think about it."

He continued pressuring her to go public with their relationship. Though she was tempted, always something made her reluctant to take the leap. Now she told him simply, "It's not time yet."

"When will it be time?"

"You agreed to my condition. I'll tell you when I'm ready."

He gave her a tight nod. "I'll return when I can,"

he said, brushing a kiss over her hair, but the tension between them was thick.

Danii sighed when he left. Murdoch had once admitted to her that he'd never cared about anything very much. And that, other than defending his country, he'd committed to nothing. She couldn't shake the feeling that he hadn't committed to them.

Though she wanted to trust him, he had been a player. *Once a rogue, always a rogue, right?* Especially since she was unable to fulfill not just one, but two of his most basic needs.

Sometimes, even though he knew how badly his bite would hurt, he still stared at her neck. Each time she got an unpleasant feverish tremor, like she supposed others might have chills. . . .

Yes, the world was passing her by—but the pressures were escalating. Each denial made them hunger for each other even more.

They knew pleasure, but were never completely sated, and the frustration built and built, like a volcano that vented steam but would inevitably erupt.

Thirty

Jádian the Cold climbed the stairs past the guards he'd killed, stealing toward King Sigmund's tower chamber.

Though he found it distasteful to dispatch his own kind, Jádian had done it without mercy. He had to act quickly. The Valkyrie's time was nigh.

"Any word on where that little bitch is?" the king demanded as Jádian entered, not even glancing away from his glazed window. "I thought you were closing in on the Valkyrie."

"Yes, I know precisely where she will be." Eventually she would come to him. Each month, she neared, without even knowing it.

Sigmund whirled around. "Then why does she yet live?" he bellowed, slamming his staff into the floor, sending up shards of ice.

Jádian slowly unsheathed the fire blade that had slain Sigmund's queen, relishing the fear dawning in the king's eyes. Jádian had been awaiting this sight since Sigmund had stolen a throne that didn't belong to him, and plunged the Icere into a needless war with the fire demonarchy.

The war in which Jádian's own pregnant wife, Karilina, had perished. "Daniela lives, because it's your death that comes next."

Like a shot, Jádian lunged for him, forcing a hand over Sigmund's mouth as he sank the blade into his heart—Jádian needed him quiet to savor the hiss of burning skin and the futile flailing of the king.

Blood sprayed, wetting Jádian's hair and face. When he yanked the knife free, Sigmund lived still, even as Jádian began slicing through the skin and bone of his neck.

By the time he had Sigmund's head, Jádian was covered in gore, but his heart was calm.

He turned to the south. Now, *now* was the Valkyrie's time.

If Daniela keeps up this carving, her hands will bleed.

Did she not think about what the sight and scent of her blood did to him each time?

As Murdoch watched her, he wondered yet again what could force her to work like this. Her elven face was tense with focus, her blue-tinged lips pressed together.

Over the previous winter, she'd seemed to be rediscovering herself, exploring those elemental instincts she could scarcely explain to him—or to herself. Yet then had come the summer. What had started as a dark and cold paradise for them turned sunny and mild. Their contentment had melted away as surely as her ice.

For those months, there'd been continual sniping between them. Any accidental contact could set either of them off. But she'd refused to leave the lodge for a colder clime, as if those genetic memories of hers had ended in a cliffhanger and she wouldn't leave the book behind.

Now, fall was upon them at last. *But we still aren't like we used to be. . . .*

Despite the strain between Murdoch and his Bride, things had begun to look up for the Wroth family.

Nikolai had wedded Myst, once she'd forgiven

him for using that enchanted chain against her. Nikolai had ultimately realized that he'd misunderstood Myst's memories, discovering that she'd been more Fury than femme fatale, using her wiles to seduce evildoers to their downfall. Then he'd had some apologizing to do.

Sebastian had somehow won both the Talisman's Hie *and* Kaderin, the deadly little assassin who'd actually been dispatched to execute him.

Though his brothers' Brides were half sisters, they were as different as day and night. One was a bold redhead, legendary for her beauty. The other was a golden-skinned killer with a predilection for stringing up vampire fangs as trophies.

Mine is an ethereal ice queen. Exquisite and always just out of reach. . . .

Murdoch and Nikolai had at last reconciled with Sebastian. Naturally, now that the three brothers were speaking again, their conversations turned to Conrad—how to locate him, where he'd last been seen. They'd all begun searching and had unearthed some leads, though they chose not to believe the rumors that Conrad was a Fallen, red-eyed assassin who drank all his victims.

They were close to finding him. Murdoch could *feel* it. Yes, things were finally looking up for the brothers.

But between him and Daniela . . . Even though they found ways to pleasure each other, Murdoch was continually tormented by how soft her skin looked. He'd never been one for open displays of affection, had never felt any sort of romantic attachment before. Now he found himself checking impulse after impulse to simply stroke her cheek or run his palm down her arm.

And to kiss her—Christ, he wanted that so much.

She felt the yearning, too. He often found her dreamily gazing at his lips while running her fingertips over her own.

Sometimes he unreasonably felt as if fate was punishing him with her for all his previous sins. Never to hold her; always to suffer this need—and to bear the knowledge that it would forever go unslaked.

If "faint heart never won fair lady," then the opposite should hold true. Murdoch had meant it when he'd said he would do anything to have her— anything but risk her safety. He needed gates to storm, an enemy to fight and defeat. Instead, he could do nothing but covet what was already his. . . .

At that moment she nicked her forefinger. Rich blood beaded, and he clenched his jaw at the scent. *Never to drink her, though I dream of it more and more.*

On occasion, she'd caught him staring at the alabaster skin of her neck, but she still stayed with him. Which meant she trusted him not to hurt her.

His gaze fixed on the small welling of crimson. With each day, he wondered how much he trusted himself.

"*Nïx, is that really you?*" Danii cried. When her phone had rung, she'd expected Murdoch or even Myst again.

"In the telephonic flesh," the soothsayer replied.
"I've called you repeatedly!"

"Then I must've not wanted to talk to you."

Danii pursed her lips. "What are you doing?"

"Just *chillin'* since you gave us the *cold shoulder*—
huzzah! Somebody stop me! How's the vamp? Too
hot to handle? Because I could do this all day!"

"Ha-ha." Today Nïx was playful. Which unfortunately meant she'd probably be forgetful as well.
"And I'm not giving you the cold shoulder. You knew
why I had to go."

"Did I? Guess I forgot. Mental note: stop telling
people that Danii's gone missing. Cease hinting feral
koi to blame."

Danii sighed. Nïx could be incredibly useful.
And incredibly frustrating. "What's that noise in the
background?"

"Your room. No one can figure out how to turn
off the freezer."

Danii swallowed. "Why would you want to turn
it off?" *All my ice!*

"Because Soloflex and litter-box storage wait for
no one?"

"You're acting like I'm never coming back."

"Are you?" Nïx asked.

"You tell me, soothsayer," Danii said, but her
words were breaking up. Nïx's call waiting kept
clicking.

"Who keeps calling you?"

"Not the same person. All different. Everyone
wants a piece of Nïxie," she said, a hint of weariness

in her tone. "Lemme block them. There. Speaking of calls, Myst said she's tried to contact you several times."

Danii hadn't picked up. "Look, I know what she'll say to me—that I can't possibly keep Murdoch from straying and we'll never work out in the long run." *Pressure building . . . time passing.*

Instead of arguing that point and reassuring her, Nïx only made a noncommittal sound.

"How is Myst, anyway?" Danii asked.

"Even more insufferably ravishing, with the glow of a female who's well loved," Nïx answered. "Married life suits her."

I want to be well loved. Would kill to be. Instead, Danii lived in an increasingly untenable situation, blinders firmly on as she strove to build a life with him. *Like building a house of tinder atop a powder keg.*

And Murdoch had never mentioned marriage.

"Don't forget fierce Kaderin!" Nïx added. "Sebastian's turned her into an amorous Kiddy Kad. So, Kaderin and Myst are both freaky, naughty minxes who get it on with vampires. Just like you, Danii! They both wear their bites proudly, bragging to everyone how orgasmic it feels."

"Orgasmic?" Great, yet another thing to fantasize about with Murdoch. "They, uh, like it?"

"I know, *right*! The coven considers them bite bores. But Sebastian did use Thrane's key to whisk Kad's two sisters back to the future, and he saved Kad's life. Plus, Nikolai tried to sacrifice his life for

Myst's. Not that she'd needed him to. So some Valkyries have stopped overtly plotting to massacre the
two brothers. Though Murdoch and Conrad are still
fair game," she concluded brightly.

"Conrad? I knew he was alive!" Danii said in a
rush. "Are the rumors true—is he Fallen? Will they
ever find him?"

"He lives. Dunno if he's Fallen. And yes, eventually the brothers will locate him. I've been helping
Nikolai, you know."

And *only* Nikolai. Nïx refused to meet with
Murdoch or Sebastian. "I know you have. Murdoch
keeps me up to date about everything."

"Indeed? Did he tell you that the Goddess of
Impossibility gifted Sebastian with another turn of
Thrane's Key? So he could go back in time and bring
his own sisters and family forward? Obviously Riora
grew quite enamored of the studly scholar."

Murdoch hadn't told her that. *But why?* This was
huge! Instead of answering Nïx, Danii demanded,
"Why are you meddling in this? You don't even
really like vampires."

"How can you say that?" Nïx asked in a scandal-
ized tone. "I have *never* in my life meddled."

Danii gave a harsh laugh. "You even got the
House of Witches to sell Nikolai, a vampire, mystical goods." If Conrad was indeed Fallen, the brothers planned to capture him to keep him from killing
again. Nikolai's first purchase had been unbreakable manacles that prevented the wearer from
tracing.

"*Gold* got those mercenaries to sell to him," Nïx countered. "I merely brokered the deal. Would you rather I not help? Hmm. You seem irritable. Usually when I speak to shacked-up Valks, they sound cheerier."

"Bet they can make skin-to-skin contact with their co-shackers."

"Is that the only reason for trouble in paradise? Tell, Nixie, tell. You know I'll just forget."

"I think he's . . . avoiding me. He spends night after night away, following leads about Conrad. That's where he is tonight."

"Do you think he would avoid you if you two could touch?"

"No, I don't. This situation has to be tormenting for him." *Because it is for me.*

"I was thinking about Mariketa the Awaited," Nïx said. "She's finally begun to come into her powers. In another fifty years, she might be able to help you."

"Truly?" Mariketa was supposed to be the most powerful witch ever born to the House of Witches. "I've been waiting for this since she was a girl!" No one in the Lore had known how long they'd be *awaiting* Mariketa to attain her full strength, which could've taken anywhere from years to millennia.

"Mariketa's taking deposits, escrowed of course. You could sign up on her waiting list."

Danii *could*, and until the time came, maybe another less-powerful witch could put her and Murdoch to sleep, hibernating like Wóden and Freya.

When Danii and Murdoch woke, they'd be able to be together.

Yet she almost didn't want to tell Murdoch about this idea. Fifty years would still sound like an age to him. Besides, it was in no way certain.

"I don't suppose you know of any way that might predate the fifty-year wait?" Danii was aware of other immortal competitions with outrageous prizes, as well as those extensive Lore bazaars where magics were peddled. Both tended to be held around the Accession.

Could there finally be a magic out there that would allow her and Murdoch to touch? Without exacting a devastating—and potentially scaly—penalty?

"I'll have to see into the future on that and get back to you," Nïx said. "But for now, let's *gossip!*"

For half an hour, Nïx filled her in on Lorean current events, such as the marriage between Emma and Lachlain MacRieve, her werewolf protector. "Told you so about Lykae inlaws," Nïx chirped.

And she related how Kaderin had set about acclimating her medieval sisters to this time: "Video games can be deeply enlightening to the uninitiated."

"What about Regin?" Danii asked. "Surely, she's drummed up some kind of trouble." Regin the Radiant was the coven's resident prankster, hopelessly immature and proud of it. Her "superhero identity" was The Fellatrix, and she was prone to snicker and say things like "The song 'Come On Eileen' doesn't have a comma after *on*. . . ."

"She's been skirting nuclear meltdown since her b.f.f. Lucia went scarce without her."

Surprisingly, brash Regin and level-headed Lucia the Huntress were inseparable best friends. Her past shrouded in mystery, Lucia was an archer who'd been cursed to feel indescribable pain if she missed a shot. At least, that was one of her curses. "Why would Lucia do that?"

"She's gone on walkabout, with her own Lykae admirer hot on her heels. . . ."

While she and Nïx gabbed, Danii endeavored to explain her obsessive carving and the arcane symbols, but the soothsayer revealed nothing, saying only, "Your ways are not like our earth ways."

"Oh!" Nïx suddenly exclaimed. "I almost forgot, I'm sending you a pressy."

"When?" Danii liked gifts! As did every Valkyrie. "How will you know where to send it?"

"As if I don't know exactly where you are! Now, I must go. I have mayhem down at five o'clock and *Survivor* at eight."

"Will you tell everyone that I said hi, and not to steal the clothes I left behind?"

"The second of those requests has already been rendered moot. Literally a free-for-all."

"Nïx!"

"One last thing, do you remember those pesky dempires?"

"Do I ever," Danii said. Murdoch had barely survived his encounter with them. "Want to say you told me so about them as well?"

"No, no, I just wanted you to know that they're mewling creampuffs compared to Conrad Wroth. And when I said that his brothers would eventually locate him? Eventually is *tonight. Ciao!*" Click.

THIRTY-ONE

Murdoch and Nikolai entered Erol's—a ramshackle bayou tavern that catered solely to Loreans—with Sebastian due to meet them any minute.

A contact had told Nikolai that Conrad was within this bar on this very night, and had been returning here repeatedly.

As if to draw his brothers out.

In the past, Conrad had wanted to kill Murdoch and Nikolai, had hated them for turning him, even more than Sebastian had. Did Conrad still want to? They'd soon see.

Murdoch scanned the interior of the dimly-lit tavern—

He's . . . here. "In the back," he muttered to Nikolai. Conrad sat at a table in the shadows, clasping his head as if it pounded. *Our brother. Just here. After so long.*

"He's wearing sunglasses?" Nikolai muttered back.

To hide his red eyes? *Christ, don't let it be.*

Conrad must've sensed them. He lowered his hand and raised his head to face them. At once, he drew his lips back, baring his fangs menacingly.

A standoff. Patrons noticed the sudden tension and fell silent. One look at Conrad and they exited in a hurry. The place emptied, right down to the bartender.

Quiet reigned. Murdoch said nothing, dumbstruck to see his brother after all this time, to find him alive. Nikolai was speechless as well.

Sebastian entered then, his countenance grave. He crossed to his brothers, standing with them in a united front.

Murdoch gave Sebastian a quick nod, gratified once again that he'd allied with them. *The first time in centuries the four of us have been in the same room.*

Conrad drew down his sunglasses, revealing eyes as red as blood. Murdoch's lips parted, and Sebastian muttered a curse. Nikolai winced, but he squared his shoulders, and the three strode forward—

With uncanny speed, Conrad lunged from his seat. In one astonishing move, he vaulted over the table at them and struck Sebastian with a skullcracking blow, sending him hurtling into a wall.

Before Murdoch and Nikolai could react, Conrad snatched them by their throats, one in each hand as they fought to free themselves.

"Three hundred years of this," Conrad hissed, his red eyes blazing with hate.

Then all hell broke loose.

⟶•❊❊•⟵

Pace forward . . . and back. Sit. Carve on tablet for huff-ish moments. Rise and repeat—

The phone rang. Danii dove for it, answering in a rush, "Murdoch, is that you?"

"We have Conrad," he said, his voice rough. "He's . . . Fallen."

"Oh, Murdoch, I'm so sorry." Danii's heart hurt for him. She knew how much Murdoch cared for his brother, how devastating this was to him.

"He was an assassin, but he drank all of his hundreds, or even thousands, of victims. He took all their memories—and their strength."

"Is he crazed?" she asked, though she knew the answer.

"He nearly totaled Nikolai's car. From *the inside.* We barely captured him, and only because the Lykae Bowen MacRieve showed up and helped take him down. By swinging a bar rail into Conrad's face."

"Are you safe? Were you hurt?"

"Let's just say we're all glad to be immortal," he muttered, then added, "We've got Conrad locked up on a property outside of town, a place called Elancourt."

"I know of it." Elancourt wasn't far from Val Hall and had always struck Danii as creepy. Surely the decrepit gothic manor there wasn't even livable. "Why would you put him there?"

"Nïx advised Nikolai to."

What does she have up her sleeve with this?

"It's going to take a lot of work for the three of us to make it comfortable for Conrad."

More time away. *Avoiding me.*

"But it's hidden," he reminded her, which was important considering what they were doing. One of the primary rules of the Forbearer order was to kill Fallen vampires—without mercy.

To harbor one would be considered treason, punishable by death.

"What's the plan now?" she asked.

"We'll keep him here, try to rehabilitate him with a potion from the witches. Basically do everything in our power to save him. If we can keep him from killing, this might work."

The common wisdom was that the Fallen couldn't be brought back. They couldn't be rehabbed. "What if he's beyond saving?" she asked quietly, wishing she could spare him the inevitable failure.

"We might have other options," Murdoch said cryptically.

Reminded of what Nïx had revealed, Danii asked, "Like using Thrane's Key? Why didn't you tell me Sebastian had it?"

"I take it Nïx finally called you." He exhaled. "Danii, it wasn't my secret to tell. I keep Sebastian's, just as I keep yours."

"Will you use the Key?"

"We plan to in time," he said. "But it was meant to retrieve *all* our family. If we bring Conrad back from the past with them, his present self would fade. We'd wipe out three hundred years of his life. At the very least, we want to get him well enough to make the decision. We won't make this one for him. Not like last time."

"I see," she murmured, disappointed that he hadn't confided something so major—even as she knew that Murdoch couldn't exactly ask Sebastian to let Danii in on the secret. Because Sebastian didn't know about her.

In a distracted tone, he said, "Look, when we finish up with Conrad, you and I should visit Riora. Maybe we could get her to help us—we're in an impossible situation, right?"

He doesn't even realize how hurtful that is to me.

And he also didn't realize that Riora was the flighty goddess who'd given Danii the bowling shoes. . . .

Thirty-two

"Leave me!" Conrad bellowed, straining against his bonds so hard the manacles cut into his wrists.

Murdoch was baffled by this sudden change in his brother after two weeks of gradual—some would say plodding—improvement. He hesitated, contemplating whether he should try again to reach him, or to leave.

When blood began dripping down Conrad's wrists, Murdoch stood. "Things are heating up overseas," he finally said, "and none of us will be back until late tomorrow." Kristoff had warned that a league of Horde vampires might attack Mount Oblak soon. "Do you want to drink before I go?"

"Get out of my sight!"

"Conrad, calm yourself," Murdoch said, to little effect. Damn it, he'd thought they'd been making such progress with him. They'd gotten him to drink from a cup without spitting blood in their faces and even to shower. Lately, he'd had long spells of lucidity where he'd engaged the brothers in conversation.

But Conrad was still hallucinating, seeing scenes from all those memories he'd harvested, and more recently—an invisible "ghost woman," who he believed lived in Elancourt with him.

Then today had come this inexplicable setback. All Murdoch had done was try to talk to him about finding his own Bride, about all the benefits inherent in that—because the brothers had discovered that Conrad . . . had never been with a woman.

And they'd at last determined why he'd gone mad from the turning. Unbeknownst to the entire family, Conrad had been a vampire hunter for more than half his mortal life, had even secretly joined a *monastic* order sworn to wipe out the species. He'd given up everything—his freedom, his future, women—for this cause.

Then Murdoch and Nikolai had turned him into his starkest nightmare. No wonder he still struggled.

When Conrad began rocking on the bed in a snarling fury, Murdoch murmured, "I'm leaving," then traced downstairs. Christ, this was a piss day. Had he actually once lamented that life was too boring? Now it seemed a thousand demands were converging on him.

He couldn't reach Conrad.

Kristoff prepared for war. The three Wroth brothers were to be ready and on call, yet Murdoch couldn't shake the feeling that their king had become suspicious of what they'd been doing in their downtime.

And Daniela . . . Murdoch knew he'd been neglecting her. First he'd had to find Conrad, then capture him. Now Murdoch was investigating his brother's past for anything that might help him recover. Remarkably, Murdoch had yet to learn of a single instance when Conrad had slain an innocent.

But how many times had Murdoch told Daniela he'd be back at the lodge by a certain time, but then Conrad attempted an escape or went into a rage? Murdoch would call to explain, and oftentimes she wouldn't even answer. Would she tonight? He dialed her number. "Pick up, Danii," he muttered. No answer. He tried her again.

Murdoch was growing so weary of his double life. *Can't talk about my Bride, can't bloody touch her.* Even as part of him yearned to be near her, another part of him was growing to hate the temptation that was never satisfied. Having his lips a breath away from her flesh and being denied a taste . . . He didn't know how much longer he could hold on.

Where the hell is she?

He could simply trace to the lodge, but she might

be out, anywhere within that vast forest. Besides, he'd planned to follow leads this eve.

Yet if he were honest, he'd admit he was reluctant to return to their freezing home. Earlier when he'd left, the first Siberian blizzard of the season had just begun raging, delighting her, and dismaying him. Tonight there would be no warm hearth, no warm wife to gather close to him. No warm body to lose himself in. . . .

No answer. His fist shot out, slamming into the crumbling plaster wall.

Long hours passed before Murdoch returned to Daniela, and he arrived even later than he'd intended to. Surprisingly, she wasn't at work on her ice tablet—it sat idle against the wall. Nor was she outside.

He found her in bed, dressed in a wispy black gown with her hair loose. The ice crystals around her eyes glinted in the room's dimmed light. *She's so beautiful.*

"It's late," she quietly said.

"I tried to call you earlier, but you didn't answer. I had some things to look into."

"Murdoch, if I didn't know better, I'd swear you were looking for excuses to be away from me."

"You know how important this is to us," he hedged. "And we're running out of time. I'm asking for you to be understanding about this, and for your patience with me."

But she was still upset, lightning streaking outside. Luckily, he'd had the foresight a few nights ago to buy a get-out-of-jail-free card, an emerald comb he'd kept in his pocket for just such a time as this. "Just to show you that I've been thinking about you, I got you a surprise."

"A gift for me?" Her eyes instantly grew bright. "I love gifts!"

Grinning, he made a mental note always to have one of these on hand and dug into his coat pocket. *Empty.* "It's . . . not here?"

She cast him a sad, crestfallen look that seemed to rip into his chest. "That's fine. You didn't need to get me anything."

A piss day. "Damn it! It was an emerald comb. I just bought it the other night for your hair." He checked all his pockets, then tore through his things. Nothing.

He must have evinced his disappointment, because she sighed, and her tone softened. "We'll find it later, Murdoch. But for now, you look exhausted. Why don't you come to bed?" She patted the spot beside her, glancing up at him from under her icy lashes.

Undone. Just like that, he grew hard for her. "You don't have to ask me twice."

Ignoring the cold, he stripped off his clothes—everything but his gloves—as she pulled off her gown. Once he joined her in bed, he snagged a blanket. She nibbled her lip, her eyes excited, knowing what he wanted to do.

"Lie back."

As she reclined, he drew the blanket over her,

covering up to her breasts. Barrier in place, he eased above her, settling between her legs. He rested his upper body on his elbows, leaving his gloved palms free to fondle her luscious little breasts.

With his face buried in the flaxen hair spread over her pillow, he rocked his shaft against her, shuddering with pleasure.

This was his favorite position with her. At least like this, he could imagine he was actually inside her. And it made him recall his recurring dream of drinking her. The more tense their situation became, the more he dreamed of it. Now as he moved over her, he dragged his tongue across one of his sharpening fangs for a shot of blood, pretending it was hers, pretending he was truly taking her.

When he rolled his hips again, she wriggled her own, putting his shaft in just the right spot. "There, *kallim?*" he grated with another thrust.

"Ah, *yes,*" she moaned, letting him know he'd rubbed directly over her clitoris.

Squeezing her breasts, he ground against her there, making her cry, "More!" He gave her more, harder and harder. As her moans grew louder, she writhed wildly, meeting him.

"Come for me," he rasped desperately, about to spill on her.

She arched her back, her body tensing beneath him as she neared her peak.

Suddenly he felt his ankle brush hers, skin to freezing skin. *The blanket rode up?* His eyes went wide, just as she cried out in agony.

"Murdoch, no!" She shoved him off her, scrambling away.

There she sat on one side of the bed, quivering with pain, while he moved to the other, sitting with his head in his hands. "Christ, I didn't mean to hurt you."

"W-we have to be more careful."

"Damn it! I need to touch you, or I'll go mad!"

She whispered, "Do you think this is any easier for me?"

He raised his head, staring at the wall as he said, "I want to make this better, I want to fix this for us. And I can't. There's nothing I can do."

He heard her pull on her gown before she walked on her knees toward him. "Murdoch, there might be a way. I didn't want to say anything because it's so uncertain, but there's a witch who is coming into her powers. The strongest one. In a mere fifty years, she could find the answer for us."

"A *mere* fifty years? Half a century of this?"

"We could get one of them to cast a spell and make us sleep, or—"

"Sleep? You mean hibernate?" He shot to his feet, yanking on his pants as he whirled around to face her. "Like goddamn animals? You expect me to lose five decades of my life?" he demanded, his frustration goading him. "Maybe this wasn't meant to be." As soon as the word left his lips, he regretted them.

But when she blinked at him as if he'd spoken blasphemy, his temper flared hotter. *As if she's never thought that.*

"Not meant to be?"

"What? You've never considered bailing on me?"

"No. I haven't."

"When we are together, all we do is fight. It just wasn't this hard . . ." He trailed off.

She stood as well, moving to face him. "What? What were you going to say?"

"Nothing."

"It just wasn't this hard with other women?" When he didn't deny it, her lips parted. "I am so sick of you talking about your past conquests!"

"I can't do this anymore!" He kicked her latest ice tablet, shattering it.

She stood motionless, her eyes growing silver with hurt and confusion. A tear spilled, then another, each one a knife to his heart.

He wanted to comfort her, to take her in his arms and ease that confusion. Then he remembered he *couldn't*.

"If you don't think fighting for us is worth the trouble," she murmured, "then I'm not going to bother either." She strode from the room, down the stairs, then out into the night.

He gave a vile curse, fighting the impulse to go after her. He was still angry, still exhausted. They would only fight more.

So he dressed, then traced to Mount Oblak, seeking one of his brothers or Rurik. He needed to talk with someone, to unburden himself. But never to speak about Daniela. No, never about her. What would he say anyway? "*Just looking at her wrecks me.*

人

I'm tempted every second by something that's dazzling and perfect—and always just out of reach."

Though his brothers weren't there, he found Rurik, Lukyan, and a few others gambling in the castle's common area.

"Murdoch, join us!" Rurik called. "Have a drink."

Lukyan gave a snide laugh. "He won't."

Clearly nothing had changed between Murdoch and him since the demon attack. Worse, Lukyan was right—Murdoch had been just about to decline. When had he become so domesticated? So *predictably* domesticated.

Why not stay here? He resented another night of not having her, resented the strife between them that had no end in sight. A stiff whiskey seemed just the thing.

He took off his gloves and settled in front of the great hearth fire, rebelliously basking in its warmth.

Numb the ache. One shot down.

Blunt the need. Then another.

THIRTY-THREE

Danii marched straight out into the blizzard. All around her, snowdrifts crested and furrowed, illustrating the path of the gusts.

With her gown whipping about her thighs, she

sniffled, running her forearm over her teary eyes. She hadn't expected things to be easy between her and Murdoch, but she'd thought the prize was worth the fight.

Maybe he was right. *Maybe I* should *bail.* She'd never considered it before. Not until he'd all but dared her to. Another swipe over her eyes.

Murdoch equals misery. They would just keep hurting each other. Where was the limit? *When do you give up on someone you love?*

Ah, gods, she did love him. With all her heart.

Though the Valkyrie didn't have "fated mates" per se, they believed that one would know her partner when she realized she would always run to get into his arms.

If he came back now, I'd run right to him.

Which meant there'd be no bailing for Danii, not yet—

Her ears twitched. Even over the wind, she heard something moving behind her. Danii sensed she was being followed, but for some reason she didn't believe it was Murdoch.

Then who the devil would be out here?

When a footstep crunched in the snow, she whirled around, spied a male in the icy shadows. His breaths didn't smoke. He had pointed ears.

An Iceren. No, not again! Her eyes darted, scanning for the rest of the assassins in the blustery night. She'd been unwary; now she would pay for it.

And all she could think of was how she'd left things with Murdoch.

Yet the male raised his palms. "My name is Jádian the Cold." His voice was deep-toned, raspy.

"How did you find me?"

"Actually, you found us. The cryomancy symbols you've been carving were about to unlock a portal. We learned you were nearing and merely awaited."

Cryomancy? Portal symbols? "Now you've come to kill me?"

"Not in the least. I mean you no harm."

She gave a bitter laugh. "Where's the rest of your battalion to back you up?"

"I've come alone."

"Your mistake. Since the last batch you bastards sent didn't fare so well."

"They were sent by Sigmund—before I assassinated him."

"He was . . . killed? By you?"

This Jádian nodded. "I was a general in his army and led a coup against him."

"Wh-why?"

"Because our people want their true queen back."

Had he just said *our* people? True queen? *Stay standing.* "Why now?"

"First I had to find you. Then I had to determine whether you were strong enough to rule. To make sure you were worthy to be Svana's heir. You are."

"This could be a trick, a way to take me prisoner."

He frowned. "Nïx didn't tell you about me?"

Was this Icere male the "pressy" coming her way? The one Nïx had mentioned directly after

Danii had tried to explain the symbols and carving? "Uh, not in so many words."

"She told me she would."

He and Nïx had been *talking*?

"But then, your sister also said you'd be more accurate with your cryomancy."

"What does that mean?" Danii demanded.

"You're one symbol off from creating a portal into our realm. But yours would have opened two hundred miles south of Icergard, amid the White Death—a frozen wasteland that even you would have difficulty crossing."

"Then how did you find me?"

"One of your symbols was shattered tonight. It sounded like a cannon blast through the castle, and was a beacon for me."

When Murdoch kicked my tablet. . . .

"I opened my own portal directly to you here." He pointed in the distance, to an oval of diffused air that rebuffed the driving snow.

She shook her head irritably. "My shoddy cryomancy notwithstanding, this doesn't make sense. Why would they want me? My mother was reviled for attempting to kill Sigmund."

"Not reviled, *revered*. But the Icere were too fearful of Sigmund to rebel. Especially once Queen Svana was gone and they knew of no one to replace her. They have a holiday in Svana's name now."

"Oh." Such a queenly answer. But to be fair, this was *staggering*. "Wait. They knew of no one to replace her?"

"It was forbidden to speak your name. After a few centuries, new generations didn't even know it." He stepped closer to her, now mere feet away. "But they do now. And they await you."

"Jádian, there have been too many years of suspicion and running. If our positions were reversed, you wouldn't just blindly accept my word," she said. Yet even as she spoke, she realized she did believe him.

Danii knew men. And this one was telling the truth. Her previously twitching ears were still.

"You should contact Nïx if you have doubts," he said. "Until then . . ." He pulled something from his vest.

"Oh, gods," Danii breathed. *My mother's crown.* With shaking hands, she accepted the piece from him, staring down at it through watering eyes.

And as she held the crown, cold and right in her hands, fresh memories of the day her mother left finally surfaced.

"Never, never go to Icergard. Not until you're shown the way."

"Who will show me, mama?" Danii cried. *"When?"*

"When the time is right, you'll show yourself."

"How? How will I know?"

"You already know the way, my darling. You just haven't remembered it yet. . . ."

Danii exhaled a stunned breath. She'd been making her own way to Icergard, because the time was right. All of this was . . . real. Danii felt it, down to her bones, as pure as a chill. All those years of fearing the Icere soldiers and spies were over.

She could have a normal life. No more assassination attempts! She could be with her own kind. This was the solution to all her problems.

So why was she suddenly so depressed?

Because her first thought was that she couldn't wait to tell Murdoch. And because this new life didn't have a surly vampire in it.

"Jádian, this is a lot to take in."

He drew nearer. "You only need accept what's yours." The corners of his lips curled, disconcerting her. "What's been yours for so long."

Is he flirting with me? Brain overload. *I can't believe I'm in my nightgown. . . .*

Jádian was kind of *sexy*. He stood as tall as Murdoch and had intense blue eyes, the color of glacial ice. Berserkr ravels tangled in his thick blond hair. His sleeveless shirt displayed muscular arms and the cobalt tracings of the Icere. But whereas her markings were delicate, his were wide and bold, designed to attract females like her.

And still, for Danii, the vampire won hands down. "Um, let me think about it," she said. "You can just make another portal here, right? Let's meet at the same time tomorrow night."

She turned to go—and felt fingers close around her bare arm. She stiffened. A split second later, comprehension hit her and she gasped.

No pain. She turned back.

Again that sensual curling of his lips. "Maybe I need to explain the other benefits of coming back with me."

Jádian was *very* sexy. "You're, uh, really devoted to your people. You'll resort to flirting to get me to return."

"There's no hardship."

"I'm not . . . yours or anything?" Could she be a vampire's Bride *and* a noble fey's lady?

"I'm not a big believer in fated mates." Had a shadow of some emotion flickered in his blue eyes? "But I could kiss you to better tell."

"K-kiss me?" She'd never been kissed. Her curiosity prodded her. Her head spun. What about Murdoch? Gods, she loved that vampire.

But he doesn't even want to fight for me.

Jádian took the matter out of her hands. "I think my queen would like a kiss," he murmured, leaning down to her.

Danii tensed when his lips touched hers. She couldn't help the defensive reaction. Yet again there was no pain. Instead she felt the firmness of his lips, the delicious brush of his tongue.

So this is kissing. If only she could do this with Murdoch, she'd never stop. . . .

Thirty-four

"Murdoch used to say that women are like bottles of liquor—sample them, savor them, then discard them," Rurik drunkenly declared, his eye patch crooked.

More vampires had joined in the gaming, and they all laughed. Yet Rurik's words sounded hollow to Murdoch, hollow like the ache in his chest. *What a slavering jackass I used to be.*

He remembered other men slapping him on the back over his conquests. They'd been so envious of his success with women. He no longer shared their definition of success.

Rurik quieted his tone, skewering Murdoch with a look. "I wonder if he still feels the same way."

He's aware that my heart's beating. At length, Murdoch answered, "Until you meet the one woman who's meant to be yours. Then you hold on and never let go."

How well was he holding on to Daniela? *I'm driving her away.*

She'd been so vulnerable when she suggested they sleep through five decades. And he'd been so busy raging over the unfairness of their situation that never once had it registered what *she* had just offered to do for them—sacrifice fifty years of her own life.

He hadn't thanked her for her offer. He'd ridiculed her for it.

I've been such a fool. What the fuck was fifty years if they were together? *She's my life now.*

Clarity. His brother Nikolai had told him that love would feel different from anything he'd ever known. Murdoch concluded he was right.

I'm in love with her.

He pushed away the bottle. *Go to her . . . apologize.* He'd left her crying. He'd been such an ass, like the old selfish Murdoch who'd boasted about women being as expendable as liquor.

With that thought, the truth sank in. *I'm not worth her tears.*

But he *could* be.

He stood unsteadily, donning his coat and the obligatory gloves, then traced to the lodge. When he didn't find her inside, he started out into the still-raging blizzard, following her fading tracks.

Finally, he caught sight of movement among the thick drifts. Just as he was about to trace to her, he spotted something that defied belief. He stared in drunken shock, squinting through the flurries.

There was another male, one who looked to be of her kind, with Nordic coloring and pointed ears. He was easily as tall as Murdoch.

And Daniela was up on her toes . . . kissing him.

Can't be real. I'm drunk. Can't see through the blizzard. Somehow she was withstanding the male's touch, receiving his kiss. The bastard grasped her bare upper arms—with his ungloved hands. Murdoch gnashed his teeth. *Skin to skin.*

A jealous rage ripped through him. All the frustration he'd grappled with for months roared to life. His fangs went sharp with aggression, his heart pumping with wrath. Just when he realized he loved her, she would betray him?

The words from his dreams echoed in his mind: *How badly do you want her? What would you sacrifice?*

Anything, he'd do anything. . . .

Didn't she know that she belonged to him? *After tonight, she will.*

This is nice, Danii thought. *But it's not as I imagined it.*

There was no loss of control or breathless wonder. No weakening of her knees. No *lust.*

Because it wasn't Murdoch.

Just as she began to pull back from Jádian, her ears twitched. Something was wrong—

Jádian went flying away from her into a tree. She blinked, struggling to get her bearings. Murdoch? *He's back!*

And he was seething, staring at Jádian with deadly intent, his eyes flooding black.

"No, Murdoch!" she cried. "This is Lord Jádian. He's come to offer me my crown! He's killed Sigmund. Murdoch, are you hearing me?"

Nothing.

"Are you drunk?"

Finally he spoke. To *Jádian.* "You dare touch my woman?" He launched himself at the Iceren, who eagerly met him. They clashed in the snow and howling winds, throwing punches.

Jádian was fast, skilled, and in his element, but against Murdoch's tracing and palpable fury he was no match. Until Jádian raised ice in his palm. . . .

Oh, gods, Murdoch. "Stop! Both of you, stop fighting now!"

Jádian immediately dropped his hands. *Following the order?* He gritted his teeth just before Murdoch roared and swung his fist, connecting with Jádian's temple like an anvil hit. Jádian staggered.

She rushed between them. "Jádian! Are you all right?" Never taking his eyes from Murdoch, he nodded. "Stay here, please." To Murdoch, she said, "Vampire, come inside with me. *Now!*"

She couldn't believe she was talking like this to the drunk, infuriated vampire who'd just caught his Bride kissing a strange male. Yet when she strode toward the lodge, Murdoch did follow her, though he seemed to be getting more and more enraged with each step.

Once they were inside, she said, "This is not as bad as it looked."

"He *kissed* you," Murdoch grated, his eyes wild. "He took what doesn't belong to him."

"What are you talking about?"

"Your first kiss—it was mine to give you one day. But you let him."

"I just wanted to see what it'd be like," she said, repeating his words from all those months ago. "It's *trivial*, especially compared to what has happened tonight. Jádian has come to take me back to Icergard, to my people. They want to offer me my throne."

"And *Jádian*"—he sneered the name—"had to kiss you to extend the fucking invitation?"

"You have a lot of nerve to blame me for kissing another, since you did it to me."

"*Before* we'd become committed."

"Committed?" she cried. "You don't even know the meaning of the word! You leave me here, avoiding me, and when you do return, you're distant and preoccupied."

"You let him touch you!"

"I did, and it was nice. *More* than nice!" she added the lie. "But maybe you're too drunk to notice that I was pulling away from him—because of you. I chose you, over a male I can touch! And now I see that I chose poorly. Luckily, I can rectify the situation." She held up her crown, clenched in her fist. "I'm going to Icergard with him."

Something in Murdoch seemed to snap. "No, Daniela, you're not." He stalked closer to her. "You're going to stay with me—because you are *mine*." Finally he was behaving like the domineering vampire. "My woman to possess, to kiss, to drink." As he stared down at her, his irises were black as night and just as fathomless.

Wait . . . to drink? "No, no. Don't, Murdoch!" But she was caught, mesmerized by the desire in his eyes. "Ah, gods . . ." When his gaze dropped to her neck, she knew he was going to do it.

So why am I not fighting him?

His gloved hands clamped her shoulders, squeezing them as he held her in place. His parted lips covered her neck, seeking. . . .

Just as she cried out, he groaned and bit down. She flailed, but he held her tight. Pain seared her skin, his fangs like two brands shoved into her neck, his tongue like a flame.

Thirty-Five

Murdoch fell upon her, pressing her into the wall as he sank his fangs deeper into the sweet flesh of her neck. The cold pained him, so badly he nearly released her, but soon blood wet his mouth. The taste . . . He growled against her, the pleasure was so intense.

Finally, she's in my arms. At last, I can hold her, taste her.

Couldn't believe he was doing this, needed to pull away. *I'm taking too much.*

He could *feel* her cries against him. When she screamed, he somehow released her, stumbling back. "Oh, God, Daniela!" He stared in horror at her ravaged neck, her tender skin burned.

As she backed away from him, her silver eyes welled with tears. "How could you, Murdoch?" Her pupils were huge with shock. "You *vowed* to me."

Between heaving breaths, he rasped, "Daniela, I don't know what happened."

"You lost control. And you'll do it again."

He wanted to deny it. *Christ help me, I can't.* His expression must have betrayed his thoughts.

Her tears spilled, her face paler from blood loss. "Now you're the second man who's touched me against my will." Her words were growing weaker, indistinct.

He grated in confusion, "The second?"

"I'm leaving, and I never want to see your face again as long as I live."

Jádian rushed into the lodge then, his watchful gaze taking in the scene. "You *bit* her?" He looked at Murdoch like he was scum, like he was a monster. "I will slaughter you for harming my queen."

"N-no," Daniela said through her tears, tugging on his arm. "I just want to go."

Go, with that male, away from Murdoch. Forever. "Don't you leave me!" he bellowed.

In answer, she put the back of her hand against her mouth and sobbed. Unsteady, crying freely, Daniela turned to the door without a glance back. When Murdoch charged after her, Jádian stood in his way. Murdoch tensed, about to attack him once more—

Daniela's legs gave way, her body crumpling. In a flash, Jádian swung around and caught her up against him. "Queen Daniela?" Then his eyes narrowed. "Blood loss."

"Give her to me," Murdoch grated with outstretched hands, "or I'll kill you so slowly."

"So you can drain more of her?" Jádian shifted

Daniela into one arm; with his other, he hurled a handful of ice at Murdoch.

The hit connected with his chest like a freight train, sending Murdoch crashing into a wall. His skin began to freeze, trapping him in place.

He thrashed to break free, but the ice was too strong. "Don't you dare take her! She can't see that this is a trick—"

With Daniela still in his arms, Jádian loomed over Murdoch. "There is no trick. I've eliminated any threat against her. Her sister even told me how to find her, because she wants Daniela to be with her own kind."

"Then where the fuck were you for the last two thousand years?"

Jádian didn't answer the question, just said, "I will leave you alive, but only because that was her will."

"Give her time to wake, so I can talk to her—"

"You believe you can convince her to stay with you? You attacked her. Look at her neck. *Remember* this sight. This is what you are to her—pain."

"No . . . no . . ."

"I'm taking her to where she can be content, vampire. Where she will be safe."

"Like her mother?"

"Her mother didn't have *me* to protect her." With a wave of the male's hand, the ice began to build up over Murdoch's torso, crushing him. Higher and higher, climbing up over his chin.

Powerless to do more than watch them leave,

Murdoch had time for a last breath—and used it to bellow her name. But they were already gone.

Ice swallowed him, cutting off his air. Soon blackness followed. And in that time, he dreamed Daniela's memories, taken from her blood.

Unable to wake, his clenched fists frozen, Murdoch watched as a Roman senator took her from a cage so he could run his fingertips over her delicate skin, fascinated by how it burned.

Murdoch *felt* her pain, her revulsion.

How long she'd been trapped in that hell, he couldn't determine. But he experienced her relief when Myst—the female Murdoch had hated for so long—and two other sisters had come for her. Myst had saved her life and murdered the Roman.

Why had Daniela never told Murdoch about any of this? About being a captive? Rage consumed him for the long-dead Roman who'd tortured her.

And yet Murdoch had hurt her just as badly, if not worse. After all, she'd trusted him.

Daniela thinks of me as she does that monster.

And she should. *The look in her eyes when I released her neck. . . .*

When the ice had melted enough to be broken and he regained consciousness, his driving need to go after her was extinguished.

Who the hell was he to take her away from her fate? From her own kind?

Her whole life had been made better, fixed. Part of him still wanted to believe that she'd been tricked, that she would need him to save her . . . but the disgust shown by Jádian had been real. And he could easily have killed Murdoch.

As much as it enraged him to recall how Jádian had kissed Daniela, Murdoch knew they looked right together.

She's gone.

For hours, he mindlessly roamed the too-quiet lodge, cursing bitterly, ignoring his brothers' calls. Even as Daniela's blood still thrummed in his veins, his chest felt empty, aching for her.

I've lost her. The look in her eyes . . .

Murdoch punched the wall. The pain briefly diverted his attention from the hollowness in his chest.

So this is love.

He'd lost the one woman he'd ever loved. No, not *lost.* He'd driven her away with his selfishness and neglect. With his broken vows and attack.

Now that he could think about the night with a clearer head, he remembered that she *had* been pulling away from Jádian. *Because of me.*

Murdoch had never understood Conrad's madness. Now he did. There were some things the mind was not made to handle, differing in each person.

I'm not made to live without Daniela.

The phone rang yet again. There'd been talk of an upcoming battle. Maybe that was exactly what Murdoch needed. To fight. To be a vampire. To kill and destroy and not think about how Daniela would be happier away from him.

He answered the phone.

"We go to war," Nikolai said.

Perfect.

THIRTY-SIX

So this is Icergard, Danii thought as Jádian gave her the grand tour of the castle the next day. *I'm definitely getting a Fortress of Solitude vibe.*

When she'd awakened, sharp-eared Icere maids had smiled shyly as they laid out a gown of the softest silk Danii had ever imagined, along with Svana's crown.

A fire had burned in a hearth of ice—a blue fire that emanated *cold*.

Which was just *cool*.

Last night, it had been late here when Jádian had sneaked her into her new royal chambers. He'd thought it "politically unwise" for the Icere to see their new queen's face wet from tears, her body lifeless, with her neck bearing the unmistakable mark of a vampire.

"As in most factions of the Lore, vampires are feared and hated here," he'd explained.

Without wonder. She still couldn't believe that Murdoch had bitten her. "What did you do to him?" she'd asked.

"I left him in ice. I would have killed him, but you ordered me not to fight."

"And you follow my orders?"

"You're my queen," he'd said simply. "One who'll be crowned in three days, if that's acceptable to you."

"It is. But what are the Icere going to think of me?"

"They're going to love you as they did your mother. . . ."

Now, as he showed her around, she tried to concentrate on what he was saying, but her mind was troubled over the events of the night. Murdoch's bite had been the worst pain she'd ever experienced, and yet she'd felt some kind of connection to him.

He'd taken her blood, lots of it. Would he dream her memories? At the idea, embarrassment suffused her. Would he know how lonely she'd been?

Gradually, her neck had healed, but she was still uneasy, fretful. Guilt weighed on her. She didn't believe she'd brought on the attack—or that she'd deserved it in any way. But she still felt complicity, because she hadn't repelled him.

She could have frozen Murdoch, could have blasted him with the fury of that blizzard. Instead, a fatalism had swept over her, as if she'd been *waiting forever* for his bite.

Myst had taken pleasure from it, as had Kaderin. It'd been a nightmare for Daniela—

"Do you regret coming here?" Jádian asked, rousing her from her thoughts. He was gazing straight ahead, his face impassive, but she could sense his tension.

"No, not at all."

"You are quiet."

"Uh, I'm just amazed by what I'm seeing." In truth, Castle Icergard was an engineering marvel. Built beneath an invisible dome of ice, the structure was bricked with baguette-cut diamonds—each half a foot long. The prisms at the ends of the diamonds glinted unrelentingly, like a Valkyrie's worst nightmare. *Good thing I'm immune.* "It's remarkable," she added.

"It's . . . home," Jádian said simply.

Inside the castle, elaborate designs were carved into all the walls, with smaller diamonds embedded throughout. Thin sheets of polished and etched ice comprised the windows. Chandeliers of ice hung from the great-hall ceiling, their lights that cold blue fire, shimmering like the aurora borealis dancing in the night sky.

The more Danii saw, the more she loved it here. *Ice, ice, and would you like some ice with that ice?* Here, plants grew from it. The people held it sacred, just as other cultures worshipped the sun or the earth as life-giving.

Earlier, any of the Icere they'd come upon had been reserved, but as word got around that Danii was personable, more approached her.

A female even asked her to bless her baby girl. Danii swallowed nervously as she gathered the babe in her arms. She'd never in her life held one.

The mother said, "Welcome home, Queen Daniela."

As Danii traced the backs of her fingers over the baby's soft cheek, tears welled.

This is where I belong. Where she'd always belonged.

I am *home.*

The cell door slammed behind Murdoch, Nikolai, and Sebastian.

"We're screwed," Sebastian muttered.

Murdoch did not disagree.

When the three had shown up at Mount Oblak ready to go to war, the king's guards had instead forced them into a barred suite.

These chambers were used for political prisoners. Here were facilities, a shower. Yet no one could trace inside or out, and the walls and door were mystically reinforced.

Luckily, the three brothers hadn't been taken to the dungeons below, filled with Ivo's old torture devices. But then, Kristoff had made it clear he had no intention of torturing them.

Or freeing them—until they gave up Conrad. Which they would never do.

How long would the king keep them here? Weeks? Or more? At the thought of a protracted imprisonment, Murdoch swore under his breath. Though he had decided not to go after Daniela, his resolve hadn't lasted long. No matter what, he was deeply ashamed of hurting her, and wouldn't rest until he'd apologized to her.

Now he paced, barely listening to his brothers.

"We knew this might happen," Nikolai said. "A one-in-a-thousand chance."

"How did Kristoff find out?" Sebastian snapped.

"He has ways."

"Ways? As in Lukyan or some other Russian," Sebastian said. "When I find out who informed on us—"

"You'll do what?" Nikolai demanded. "We're the ones at fault here. *We* broke the law."

"But how can Kristoff expect us to give up our own brother?" Sebastian shook his head. "Conrad would be powerless against his men, unable to defend himself, unable to escape."

"We might as well swing the swords ourselves," Nikolai agreed. "But if we think Myst and Kaderin are going to just sit around and accept our capture, we're deluded."

"Kristoff must know they'll wage an attack," Sebastian said. "As soon as they find out what happened, they'll likely plot to take this castle and execute him."

When a chill night breeze sieved through the barred window, Murdoch crossed to it. He sucked in air, feeling hot, claustrophobic.

"Murdoch?" Nikolai said. "Are you even listening to us . . . ?"

How could I have bitten Daniela? When he loved her. And what was fifty years? He could wait an eternity. But he couldn't get to her to tell her this. Frustration strangled him like a noose.

In Murdoch's absence, would Lord Jádian continue kissing her? His fists clenched. *Kissing my Daniela.* When he punched the wall, he broke every bone in his hand, the protected stone mocking even his immortal strength.

Murdoch turned in time to see Nikolai and Sebastian share a glance. They had to know that he'd been blooded—even Conrad had heard Murdoch's heart beating—but they'd said nothing over the last several months. Probably because of all the secrets they'd been keeping, as well.

"What the hell is going on with you?" Sebastian said.

Murdoch knew he must be shocking them. For so long he'd been carefree. "Don't want to be here," he muttered. The need to talk to his brothers pressed on him, but he volunteered nothing, keeping at least one vow to Daniela.

Only now did he understand why she'd been so secretive about them. *I wouldn't have bet on a future with me either. Definitely wouldn't have advertised it.*

When dawn came, his brothers slept, but Murdoch dreaded dreaming about her, stealing more of her memories. Hour after hour, he paced, feeling a madness creeping over him. The bars were keeping him from her. Silently, he strained against them. *Want to be with her.* He couldn't budge them.

Eventually, exhaustion ruled and he passed out, unwillingly slipping into dreams. This time, he saw the reflection of a young girl—he knew it was Daniela—gazing back at him from a mirror.

A striking woman with the same unusual coloring as Daniela was behind her, fitting a crown atop her head. Her mother? They spoke to each other in a language that sounded similar to Icelandic, but he understood it. . . .

"*You already know the way,*" the mother said. "*You just haven't remembered it yet.*"

Then came a more recent memory: Daniela staring at her ice carvings, wondering, *Are these clues how to get to Icergard . . . ?*

Murdoch woke in a rush, shooting up from his cot in the middle of the day. "It's so bloody hot in here!" He yanked off his jacket in irritation.

When Nikolai rose to stoke the fire, Murdoch grated, "No, no fire! Put it out." He imagined frost. Blood served cold. For once, he craved being back amid the ice at the lodge.

Sebastian was awake as well and frowned at him. "It's actually cool."

"How can you say that?" he snapped, unable to contain his aggravation. Then he stilled. Were his breaths . . . smoking? He traced to the suite's bathroom, gazing in the mirror. His breaths didn't fog the glass. As Daniela's didn't. Blue tinged his lips and under his eyes.

My God. The reason he'd felt so hot—her blood was running through his veins.

Nikolai had told him that Myst's blood made him even stronger. Sebastian had said the same about drinking Kaderin's.

Why couldn't Daniela's make Murdoch more

like her? He gave a shout of laughter. *I've found a way to touch her!*

Then his heart sank. *Just when I've lost her.* He was trapped by his own king, by his loyalty to his brother. . . .

Another day dragged by, then two. As their imprisonment wore on, Murdoch began returning to his normal temperature, which maddened him even more. He couldn't lose this coldness—otherwise he'd have to hurt her again.

If he was ever freed from this bloody cell. And if she'd ever let him drink her.

"Nikolai! Where are you?"

Murdoch shot awake, his gaze darting. He could have sworn he'd heard Conrad—in Oblak—yelling for Nikolai. But all was quiet, his brothers still sleeping. He must've dreamed it. Strange, he usually dreamed of nothing but Daniela.

With a weary exhalation, he rose. *More than two weeks gone.* The brothers and their king were locked in a stalemate. Would they stay here indefinitely?

As he did every night, Murdoch tried and failed to drink enough to sustain his weight. Then he prowled from one wall to the next, deciphering more scenes from Daniela's life that he'd witnessed in sleep.

Her memories were becoming clearer to him. When he dreamed, he felt how lonely she'd been, how she'd tried not to nurse hope over Murdoch. *Once a rogue, always a rogue.*

He'd done so little to set her mind at ease, had

done nothing to make sure she understood her lone-liness was over. *I never told her I'm in love with her.* Instead, he'd voiced his doubts.

During one miserable day, he'd seen her mem-ory of that night with Jádian and had learned her thoughts as she'd kissed the Iceren.

She'd been thinking about Murdoch. Danii had chosen *him* over a male who could touch her, a nobleman of her own kind who could kiss her. She hadn't been thinking about bailing on Murdoch at all. At least not before he'd hurt her, *attacked* her.

This situation was intolerable. To be kept from Daniela now? Murdoch wanted her so much, he'd once actually considered betraying his brother—

"*Nikolai!*" The word boomed down the castle corridor, echoing.

Nikolai and Sebastian shot awake.

Dear God. "Was that . . . ?"

"Conrad," Nikolai said. "He's *here*."

Maybe I'm not home.

Danii sat upon her throne, among her own kind in a paradise of ice, and she was . . . bored.

Days ago, she'd been crowned with much fan-fare. The Icere had prepared banquets, carved sculp-tures in her honor, and played music. Plus, they'd declared a snow day at the castle—literally, it had fallen from the ceilings.

And since the festivities?

Jádian was a constant bodyguard, always nearby, always solemn. Most of the fey she'd met could be described as "serious." She'd figured this was an aftereffect of having an evil dictator ruling them for so long—but had learned this was just their nature.

Here, there were no practical jokes, no sisters bent on thieving her clothing. No gorgeous vampires to tackle into the snow.

Time seemed to be moving as slowly as the glaciers surrounding them. She wondered if it was possible to expire from boredom. *The study begins . . . now.*

To make matters worse, she missed Murdoch like an ache. Every day, she dwelled on what she could have done differently. *Perhaps I shouldn't have kissed another man? Just a thought.*

But that indiscretion hadn't mattered. She and Murdoch had already been finished. Danii had thought they would be together forever, but he hadn't agreed, hadn't believed that they were worth the fight—

With a sudden flush of guilt, she recognized that maybe she hadn't *truly* committed either. Hadn't she herself given them a one-in-fifty shot? She'd been betting against them from the beginning, might as well have gone and signed Loa's book. . . .

Across the throne room, Jádian turned to her with his brows raised. Since she'd arrived, she hadn't seen him smile once. There'd been no more flirting from him. She'd concluded that he *was* devoted to his people, had probably only kissed her to sway her to come to Icergard.

His name of Jádian the Cold was well earned. Thinking back over his fight with Murdoch, she recalled that Jádian's pulse had never gotten elevated.

He'd been indignant, ready to die for his queen. But he hadn't been ready to lose his temper for her.

Aside from being unemotional, he had a reputation for cold-blooded ruthlessness. Her ladies-in-waiting had told her how he'd blamed the death of his wife on Sigmund, conspiring relentlessly for years, only waiting for Daniela to be located before striking.

They'd also spoken of sordid rumors that Jádian had once kept a seductive fire demoness as his prisoner hidden in the dungeon....

He crossed to Danii then. "You are unhappy here." It wasn't a question, but he did sound disbelieving.

"I . . . it's been a big change."

"You'll grow accustomed." He was no-nonsense and logical to the point that most Valkyrie would deem him a buzz kill. But he was beloved by the orderly people here.

"Jádian, I was recalling our kiss."

He stiffened, as if he thought she'd want to resume some dalliance with him. "What of it?"

"You weren't thinking about me."

"And you were imagining that I was a vampire," he said with the tiniest hint of irritation, adding, "my queen."

Busted. It was too true. Though Jádian was as sigh-worthy a male as she had ever seen, she still longed to run her fingers through dark hair. She yearned to gaze up at gray eyes that turned black with lust. "Was it just a play to get me to return with you?"

He shrugged. "You needed to be here."

So their kiss hadn't even been real. Now her curiosity redoubled. What would a *real* one be like—

"And you need to accept that this is where you belong," he said.

Yes, no longer was she living in the sweltering heat of Louisiana, surrounded by people she couldn't touch. No longer was she in a relationship that was doomed by her very nature.

Here, the broken doll was all fixed. *And I'm miserable.*

Thirty-seven

"Nikolai!"

Stoic Nikolai looked flabbergasted. Then he shot to his feet, tracing to the cell door. "Conrad?" he called back.

"He's come *here*?" Sebastian bit out. "How did he get free from those manacles?"

Murdoch cursed under his breath. "Kristoff will take his head."

"If his guards don't," Nikolai said.

Conrad appeared outside their cell. Through the bars, they stared in bewilderment. Conrad had blood and mud splattered across his beaten face and matted in his hair. His red eyes glowed with menace. Gaping wounds covered him.

"What in the hell are you doing here?" Nikolai demanded. "And whose blood is that?"

Conrad studied the cell bars. "I don't have time for questions."

"You have to leave!" Murdoch said. "They'll execute you if they capture you."

He gave a rough laugh, clamping hold of the bars. "Defy them to do either." Gritting his teeth, he strained against them.

"Those are as protected as your chains were," Sebastian said. "The wood, the metal, and the stone surrounding them are all reinforced. You can't possibly—"

Conrad wrenched them wide, breaking the metal.

"My God," Nikolai murmured.

Conrad had gotten *stronger*?

"Need your help to find my Bride!" In a frenzy, Conrad yanked the wreckage free. "I'm not mad . . . but I need you to trace me to every cemetery in New Orleans. Do you know where they are?"

Nikolai gaped. "Your . . . Bride?"

"His heart beats," Murdoch said.

"Do you know where they are or not?" Conrad bellowed.

Nikolai nodded slowly. "I know all the cemeteries. Myst and I hunt ghouls there."

"Will you do this?"

"Conrad, just calm—"

"Fuck calm, Nikolai!"

"So this is Conrad Wroth," Kristoff said from behind him, surrounded by his personal guards.

Without turning, Conrad sneered, "The bloody *Russian*. What do you want?"

Kristoff seemed amused by this. "I'd known the Wroths were genetically incapable of fawning to a king, but a modicum of respect . . ." His demeanor was self-satisfied, almost like he'd planned this all along.

Conrad faced the natural-born vampire.

"You've taken out my entire castle guard," Kristoff said in a casual tone. "Something a Horde battalion couldn't do. My informants didn't tell me you were *this* strong." His pale eyes were expressionless, yet Murdoch knew he was calculating. "But then, you've been blooded."

"I don't have time for this!" Conrad snapped. "I'll kill you just to keep you from speaking."

The guards tensed, hands at their sword hilts.

"Kill me? You wouldn't know your Bride if not for me, if not for your brothers. You'd have been dead three hundred years ago."

"I've put that together!"

To Nikolai, Kristoff said, "He took out the guards without killing a single one—almost as if he was making a point. You were right. Conrad isn't lost." He cast Conrad a quizzical glance. "He's . . . quite a few things, but he's not irredeemable. And I can concede when I have made a mistake. Though you should have come to me instead of willfully breaking our laws."

Nikolai exhaled. "I couldn't take the risk that you would say no. He's my brother," he said simply.

Kristoff turned back to Conrad. "Swear fealty to me, and all of you leave today as allies. Otherwise we fight."

Conrad gritted his teeth, eyes darting, but eventually he grated, "I'll vow . . . that I'll never engage you or your army."

After an appraising look, Kristoff said, "It will do. For now." To the other three brothers, he added, "Take a week off. And do get your Brides to cease plotting my downfall."

When the king and his men disappeared, Nikolai said, "Conrad, you must tell me what's happened for me to help you. Who is your Bride?"

Conrad hastily said, "Néomi, this beautiful little dancer. Love her. So much it pains me. Have to find her."

We're free. I can go to Daniela at last, Murdoch thought, barely hearing what Conrad told them, something about cemeteries and resurrections— needing to listen for his Bride's heartbeats?

Sebastian said, "The ghost thing again," just as Murdoch muttered, "Con's thoroughly lost it."

Conrad snapped his fangs at them, his red eyes glowing. "This happened!"

"I don't know what outcome I'm hoping for," Sebastian began. "Either Conrad's irretrievably mad, or his Bride is a spirit from beyond whose corpse is lost. This seems like a lose-lose."

"He always did things differently," Murdoch said absently, scarcely believing the fact that Conrad had gotten loose—and been blooded—and that Murdoch and his other brothers were freed. All was right with Kristoff.

I can possibly win Daniela. And keep her. But first he had to find her. Murdoch dared a slap on Conrad's back, saying, "I would like to stay, but I have an emergency that's weeks overdue. Good luck, Con." With that, he traced from the castle.

He could think of only one person who'd know how to reach Daniela.

In the past, he'd gone by Val Hall to see where she had lived for the last seventy years—it was a haunting place protected by flying, spectral wraiths.

Now Murdoch returned there, ready to do battle with them in order to see Nïx the Ever-Knowing. The soothsayer had been helping everyone else.

Why not me?

THIRTY-EIGHT

"Because you bit her," Nïx told him before he'd spoken a word.

While he'd been wasting precious time determining how to evade the cloud of wraiths and storm Val Hall, they'd suddenly parted for Nïx as she'd casually strolled from the manor.

"That's why I won't tell you where it is," she

continued. She was chewing gum and wore a pink T-shirt that read: *Jedi Kitty.*

Taken aback, he said, "Nïx, I'm Murdoch Wroth. You've been working with my brother Nikolai, and I need—"

"I know who you are. And what you've done to poor Daniela. You've driven her straight into the arms of that hot-on-a-stick Jádian."

No, Daniela wasn't lost yet. She *couldn't* be. "Tell me how to get to her."

"Why should I?" the soothsayer asked in a mulish tone. "I like her with Jádian. He doesn't, oh, burn her cold skin as he drains her blood."

Murdoch flushed.

"Maybe you should do the selfless thing and let her go," Nïx said. "What if she can be happier there?"

"Maybe I should give her all the information she doesn't have yet, information she'll need to make this decision."

"What doesn't she know?"

"That I'm in love with her, and I'm willing to do whatever it takes to be with her." His father's words arose in his mind: *Son, you've never cared about anything enough to fight for it—or to fear losing it.* Though this might have been true then, now Murdoch was making up for three centuries of not caring.

"I never told her these things." Murdoch closed in on Nïx. "Valkyrie, I won't rest until I get the chance to."

She cast him an appraising glance, squinting as if he were a book she was trying to read in dim light.

He ran his palm over his face. "Look, I know you helped the Lykae Bowen several times. You've even assisted Nikolai. But you won't help me? Why, damn it?"

She blinked up at him. "Because I play favorites?"

He scowled. "Tell me anything. Anything at all."

"Anything? Okay—a lot of people have some serious money on the fact that you're a cad."

"No longer," he bit out. "Can't you see the future and know that I'm going to be good to her?"

She narrowed her eyes. After long moments, she said, "Huh. You remain eternally faithful to her. I did *not* see that one coming."

Irritation flared. Like he needed her to tell him that.

She shrugged. "I still won't help you find her. Even if I was moved to *deus ex* your *machina*, I refuse to portend for every Tom, Murdoch, and Harry. It cheapens the experience, and before long I'll have a reputation as a sooth-whore." She fogged her claws, then buffed them on her T-shirt. "Besides, you already know how to reach Daniela."

"How? Tell me!" From the memories?

The moment began to feel surreal, as if all of his life had been leading up to this. The world seemed to spin. He pictured Daniela carving tirelessly; he strained his memory to see precisely what she'd wrought—

"Fine, I will divulge one thing. . . ." Nïx said. "Danii's going to make Jádian her king. If she hasn't already."

Ah, Christ, no.

With that prediction, Nïx traipsed back past the wraiths—*handing them a lock of hair?*—leaving him with a knot of dread in his chest. What if Daniela had married Jádian?

Murdoch's fangs sharpened. *Then she'll become a widow.*

He traced back to Siberia to gear up at the lodge, dragging a backpack from a closet. When he turned around, Nikolai and Myst appeared in the room.

"So this is where you've been hiding out," Nikolai said. Then he frowned. "The last place I would've looked for you. Literally, the last of your properties we've tried over the months. Siberia, Murdoch? There's only one way it could make sense to live here."

Murdoch punched clothes and cold-weather gear into the pack. "I don't have time for this."

"Make time," Myst said. "We know you're with Danii."

"I'm *not* with her. That's the goddamned problem."

Whatever Myst saw in his expression made hers soften. "What are you planning?" she asked more gently. "To go to Icergard?"

"Yes."

"To bring her back?"

He said nothing, just continued to pack.

Her eyes went wide. "To live there? You won't survive it. The Icere lands make Siberia feel balmy."

Nikolai added, "It's dark now, but what will you do in the summer? At that latitude, it will be light twenty-four hours a day."

"I'll stay inside. In a coffin, if I have to."

"And Kristoff?" Nikolai asked. "You swore your fealty. And now that we're finally working on an alliance with the Valkyrie, you plan to desert the army? He'll be forced to kill you for that, especially on the heels of our last transgression."

"I know this! God, I know."

"You won't be able to see your family any longer." Nikolai moved in front of him. "Speaking of which, I know you're too preoccupied to ask, but Conrad is fine. I just left him. He was telling the truth about his Bride, Néomi. She's a comely little dancer who—if you can imagine this—adores him and calms him."

Murdoch slowed. "I am glad for that."

"How are you even going to get to this Icergard?" Nikolai said. "It's late fall in the Arctic. The temps could already be forty below. Damn it, Murdoch, *think* about that. If you spit, it will freeze before it hits the ground."

"No planes can fly there," Myst said. "Not even Lore planes."

He fastened up his pack. "I'll get as far north as I can, then trace the rest of the way."

"You can only trace as far as you can see," Nikolai said. "You better hope the visibility is good."

"We'll call Kaderin," Myst offered. "She'll be able to help with the logistics. She knows how to get to places better than anyone."

Murdoch shook his head. "I don't have time. And I think I know a way."

Daniela had been missing one cryomancy symbol, the one Murdoch had shattered. He would use her memories to recreate it.

Because he'd dreamed her meeting with Jádian and had heard their conversation, Murdoch was aware that her last symbol wasn't correct. He knew if he copied Daniela's work, the portal would open two hundred miles south of Icergard.

He also knew that Jádian doubted even Daniela could survive that cold wasteland—*the White Death*.

Murdoch shook his head hard, resolve like steel inside him. So he would have to trace a couple hundred miles north—quickly.

How bad can it be?

Murdoch had never comprehended what cold was.

An arctic blizzard raged around him, howling so loudly it pained his ears.

The visibility was maybe two feet, which meant he could trace no farther than that at a time. His muscles were weakening, flagging more with each brutal minute. He'd been forced to ditch his gear miles back.

Hour after hour dragged by. . . . *I've gotten turned around somehow.* His compass didn't work. There was no way to see the stars in this never-ending storm. *So confused.*

If he stopped, he would freeze here. But it wouldn't kill him. He'd live on, frozen and trapped, until someone dragged him to a warm place to thaw.

Yet even that horrific fate wasn't enough to keep him moving.

No, it wasn't until he thought about never seeing Daniela again that he gritted his teeth and pushed on. Envisioning her elven face kept him going—

Were there lights ahead in the distance? *Imagining it?* Struggling to make out the hazy sight, he pulled aside his face guard, taking off a frozen layer of skin with it. He staggered, feeling like acid had just doused his face.

Ignore the pain. How far was it to those lights? He teleported forward, but got no closer, forced back by some kind of invisible barrier. He tried once more. Nothing. He fought to get there, grappling to reach the lights, to reach *her*.

Toiling . . . over and over.

Ultimately, his strength ebbed to nothing, and he collapsed to his knees in the snow. A vicious gust roared over him, laying him out.

With his last ounce of will, he stretched a hand forward.

"Daniela . . ."

Thirty-nine

Danii sat on her throne, thinking about witches— and abdication.

I could meet with Mariketa the Awaited, bring her

a bucketful of softball-size diamonds, and ask her to put me on her list.

Even if Murdoch wasn't keen on waiting fifty years, reserving a spot couldn't hurt.

And Danii could return to Val Hall, now that she could live in New Orleans safe from assassins. She'd add some serious tonnage to her A/C and really get some cold cranking.

Maybe she could be happy there. It would be even harder staying in Louisiana so fresh from the cold. But fall had arrived there, at least.

Was she an idiot even to contemplate relinquishing her throne—and her new life, tucked away amid the freezing security of Icergard? Could she truly leave behind an ice world where she lived among her own kind, to seek a vampire she could never touch?

Over and over, Danii recalled the look in his eyes when he'd yelled for her to come back that night.

Yes. She would try once more to convince him that they could—

"My queen," one of her ladies-in-waiting said as she hastened into the throne room. "Come quickly. There's a *stranger* in Icergard. He crossed the White Death. . . ."

When Murdoch woke, he lay in a bed in a bizarre room of ice. Though it was lighter and quieter here out of the wind, the temperature wasn't warmer.

He was wearing new pants and a coat of sorts that kept him from freezing. Someone had cleaned him and bandaged his frostbitten hands. He must be within Icergard. Which meant *she* was near. *Have to get to her.* He labored to rise—

Jádian strode into the room. "So, it is you. Why have you come to our realm?" His expression betrayed no surprise, no emotion whatsoever.

This is the bastard who knows what it's like to kiss Daniela.

And I can't kill him. Yet.

Murdoch managed a sitting position. "I seek Daniela." His words were hoarse, his body still exhausted.

Jádian crossed his arms over his chest. "Why would I ever let one such as you near her?"

"I just need to speak to her. And then, if she still doesn't want to see me, I'll never bother her again." *What a lie—*

Daniela entered. And Murdoch sucked in a breath.

She was more stunning than he'd ever seen her, her body bedecked in diamonds. Her hair was wild beneath a band of ice and jewels—the crown from Daniela's memories, her mother's.

To see her again. These mere weeks had felt like eternity.

She looked dazed to find him here. Surely she had to know he'd come for her.

He couldn't read her expression. Was she not pleased at all to see him? Then his heart sank as comprehension took hold. *I'm too late.*

Oh, gods, Murdoch was *here.* He was wild-eyed, with his lips and hands frostbitten and his face abraded.

He'd crossed the White Death? *To come for me.*

Jádian was eerily calm. "I say we throw him back out and let the cold take him."

Pointedly ignoring that, she said, "Murdoch, how did you get here?"

"I followed your memories. But the portal was . . . off."

"My memories," she repeated softly. He had taken them from her blood. "Why have you come?"

"Can I talk to you? Alone. Please, Daniela, just a few minutes of your time."

"My queen, this is ridiculous," Jádian said. "Remember what he did to you last time?"

Murdoch cast him a killing look, then turned back to her. "I have an idea—there's a way we might be together."

"What? How?"

"When I drank from you before—"

"Why bring that up to me?" Her hand flittered to her neck at the reminder.

"Because now I know why it was so irresistible to me."

Jádian said, "Because you're a parasite."

"Jádian!"

"He plans to bite you again."

"Of course he doesn't. Murdoch, tell him."

"Daniela, speak with me alone." Somehow he managed to make it to his feet. "I swear I won't do anything to you that you don't agree to."

His words piqued her curiosity. He hadn't promised not to hurt her, not to bite her, yet she felt no threat from him. "Very well," she said, turning to Jádian with raised brows. After a hesitation, he turned for the door, stonily silent.

As soon as they were alone, Murdoch demanded, "Are you marrying him?"

"What? No!"

"Nïx told me you were."

"She must be confused then, or you misheard her. Now, tell me. What were you talking about?"

"Daniela, before I took your neck, I'd dreamed of doing it. More and more as we grew apart. Every night. Now I believe it's the way for us to be together."

"I don't understand."

"With your blood in my veins, everything felt warm to me. My brothers were chilled, but I couldn't stand to be near the fire. Your blood made me *cold*."

"That can't be right. I can't turn you into an Iceren."

"No, but I can pick up characteristics of your kind," Murdoch said.

"Do you have the skin markings, then? Are you unaffected by the sun?"

He shook his head. "There was a blue tinge under my eyes, but not the body markings. When I tested my skin in the sun, I still burned, even when I was immune to the cold."

"Immune? Then why are you freezing right now? How did you get frostbitten?"

He ran his bandaged hand over the back of his neck. "The effect only lasted a couple of days."

"So for this to work, I'd have to repeat that pain?"

"One last time. After that, as long as I drank every day or two, I'd never hurt you again. We could be together." His voice went lower, and his eyes flickered black. "In all ways."

Her mind was whirring. Yet then she recalled what had happened after the last bite. "But I-I went unconscious."

Looking shamefaced, he said, "I took too much. I wouldn't this time. I know I don't deserve your trust, but I'm asking for it anyway."

"Why should I do this?"

"Because I'm in love with you," he said—without a hint of hesitation.

Her lips parted and the world seemed to shift under her feet. After what he'd done to reach her, she had to believe he did. But to hear him say the words, with his eyes so intense and dark. . . .

Maybe the vampire *did* always come through in the end.

"And I think you love me, too." Hope tinged his words.

She turned away, breaking his searching gaze. "Maybe that doesn't matter," she said over her shoulder. "Maybe we're only fated to make each other miserable. You forget we'd fought before all this happened. You'd given up on us."

"No, just before I returned that night, I realized that fifty years was nothing if we could be together. I'd come back to tell you that. But then I saw you kissing Jádian . . ."

She faced him once more. "I'm sorry for that."

"It doesn't matter now," he said, but she could tell that she'd hurt him. "When I was in jail—"

"Jail?"

"That's why I wasn't here sooner—Kristoff imprisoned us at Mount Oblak for harboring Conrad. It's all worked out now, but we spent weeks inside. And while I was there, I determined that I would do anything to be with you. Desert my order. Live here in the cold in twenty-four hours of daylight."

"Murdoch, that's not the point. You're talking about biting me again, about more pain. And not just mine. I'm colder than I've ever been. It would hurt you too," she said, then added, "If this did work, you might be vulnerable to thermal shock, like me."

"I don't give a damn about that!" He crossed to her until they were toe to toe. "Please, Danii, I know I'm asking for a lot more than I deserve, but if you can endure this one last time . . . Just give me your trust."

Hadn't she said she'd give anything to know his taste? To touch her lips to his?

Before, even amidst the agony of his bite, she'd felt a connection to him.

I will trust him. Fantasy finally made reality. And reality sometimes took sacrifice.

Daniela bowed her head, then gazed up at him from under her lashes. And again, he was undone.

"I do trust you." She pulled her hair to the side, baring the pale column of her neck to him, inviting him.

"You won't regret this." But even as his fangs sharpened for her flesh, he hesitated. "I dread hurting you. When I think about how I took you last time . . ."

"I'm afraid I'll try to break away," she admitted. "Or that you will—from the cold."

Each would want to recoil. They'd have to force each other to hold on. "Hang on to me, *kallim*, because I'll be holding you tight. We do this now, and then we have forever."

She inhaled a steadying breath. "I'm ready."

What would you do for her . . . ? The scent of the supple skin he was about to taste proved too much temptation. He couldn't resist. He laid his bandaged palms on her hips and drew her closer.

Her hands rose to clasp his shoulders. "Do it," she whispered.

In a flash, he sank his fangs into her. This time he groaned—in pain. She was even icier than before.

Stabbing cold shot through him. The urge to release her screamed in him, but he held on, squeezing her hips. He felt her little blue claws digging into him as well.

Yet with each of his draws, the pain lessened. At the remembered sense of connection, his eyes slid closed in bliss.

Mine. Forever. Thoughts were a jumbled knot.

Slow . . . slow . . . Don't take too much this time. This is a gift. . . .

FORTY

By the time Murdoch released her, they were both out of breath. And Danii was crying.

"Christ, I tried not to take too much—"

"Y-you didn't." But it had still been excruciating.

He winced at her neck. "You're burned."

"It'll regenerate quickly with the cold. Did you even drink enough?" she asked, struggling to disguise how much pain she'd felt. "Do you think this will work?"

"The effect takes time."

"You're already better." With her blood accelerating his regeneration, he began healing almost at once, his battered lips and face soon returning to normal. He unwrapped the bandages from his hands as they mended and flexed his fingers.

But his breaths still fogged.

Minutes passed, then half an hour. She sank onto the bed, and he paced. Another hour had trudged by in anxious silence before he said, "Daniela, why didn't you tell me about the Roman?"

"You saw that?" At Murdoch's nod, she said, "He's in my past."

"You think of me as you do him."

She shook her head. "No, Murdoch. I was angry when I said that. Bewildered."

"But it's true that I took what didn't belong to me."

"We both felt the pull. I could have stopped you. And I've wondered again and again why I didn't. Now I think it was instinct telling both of us the way to be together. If . . ."

"If this works? It will." He ran his hand over his forehead. "Damn it, if you were brave and strong enough to withstand this—twice—it's got to work."

"Will you still want me if it doesn't?" she asked quietly.

Reaching for her, he cupped her waist between his hands to tug her to her feet, then gazed down at her with fierce eyes. "Look at me, Daniela. I'm in love with you," he grated. "I want you always, no matter what!"

"Murdoch, I . . . y-your breaths aren't visible." Was there the slightest blue tint under his eyes?

He frowned. "The temperature doesn't feel as cold in here. It's becoming *comfortable.*"

"Could this truly be working?" Her hand trembled wildly as she reached up to his face.

"Careful," he warned. "Maybe wait a little longer."

"I can't. I have to know." When she caressed his cheek, his eyes went heavy-lidded.

No pain. With a strangled cry, she sagged against him.

"Daniela, are you hurt?"

"I just can't believe this." Tears gathered and fell. She could be with him—Murdoch, the vampire she loved. After two millennia, her constant yearning would end at last.

"Please don't cry." With an audible swallow, he tentatively laid his palms against her face, brushing his thumbs over her tears. *No pain.*

For so long she'd felt lacking, and the answer had been within her, within them, all along. "I'm crying because I'm happy." She unbuttoned his jacket, pulling it off him to display the chest she'd imagined stroking. Then she placed her hands on him, finding his skin was the perfect temperature.

No pain. His muscles went rigid, tensing to her fingertips. She gave one exploring sweep, then another, until she was rubbing her palms all over him in delight. *Only pleasure.*

He was still caressing her cheeks. "You're so soft, Daniela. Softer than I ever imagined—and I imagined constantly." He tipped her face up. "I've got to kiss you."

"I'm yours to kiss. I'm yours."

His voice a husky rasp, he said, "You're about to be." He cast her a slow, possessive grin, flashing his fangs—no longer would she look at them with fear. They'd been the means to her and Murdoch's deliverance.

Then he leaned down. "Close your eyes."

She did. After the space of a heartbeat, she felt the lightest brush of his firm lips to hers. The barest contact sent tingles through her. Drawing her closer, pressing her body against him, he slanted his mouth over hers.

His kiss grew unyielding, intent, even as he gently coaxed her lips open so he could stroke a sensuous lick against her tongue. When she moaned, meeting him, lapping softly, he wrapped his arms tightly around her, as if he couldn't get close enough, as if he feared she'd get away.

She clutched his shoulders in turn. Their tongues tangled. Their breaths mingled and grew hectic.

Now *this* was a kiss—deep, frantic. What she'd long imagined. *Hearts thudding, bodies shaking.* She whimpered against his mouth as her knees went weak. But he held her steady and safe against his chest as he continued to plunder her mouth.

Too soon, he broke away, leaving her dazed and panting.

"I need to claim you." He pulled her hair to the side and skimmed his lips across the now healed skin where he'd bitten her.

She shivered violently, her nipples hardening in a rush.

"I never want to be apart from you again," he murmured. "Now I'll be able to stay with you here."

Oh, Murdoch, no. Should she lie to him, act as if that could possibly happen?

When he drew back to meet her eyes, she forced herself to smile, though she knew the Icere would never accept him. Vampires were despised here.

She should just enjoy this miracle. *Worry about what to do later.*

"What? Something's wrong."

"Uh-huh." Her hands dipped to his pants, untying the waist. "You're not naked enough," she said, working them past his protruding erection. When he stood unclothed before her, she gripped his gorgeous length.

He hissed in a breath; she gasped. She could perceive his shaft throbbing in her palm, could feel the texture of his smooth skin stretched taut over the veined ridges.

Against her sensitive fingers, it grew. . . .

So incredibly hard. Could she even take him? *We'll know soon enough.*

While she explored, he slipped the thin straps of her gown from her shoulders. Gathering the material in his fists, he skimmed it down her body. He paused just before he revealed her chest as if he wanted to prolong this moment.

At last, the silk inched past her erect nipples. He stared at her breasts as if he'd never seen them.

"Murdoch, please . . ."

Without warning, he gathered her in his arms, moving them to the bed so he could place her in his lap. Once he had her settled over his erection, he lifted a finger to circle her nipples—one, then the other, his gaze transfixed as the tips swelled to his touch. With a desperate groan, he pressed his lips against one breast, palming the other.

When she felt his tongue snake out over her nipple, her head lolled.

Again and again, he flicked the puckered bud. "Do you want me to suckle you?"

"Yes, oh, yes. . . ." She ran her fingers through his thick hair, cupping him to her.

He drew one of her nipples between his lips, sucking, licking, giving a harsh groan that vibrated into her breast.

"Oh, gods!" Lightning exploded outside. He knew what the lightning meant and drew even harder. Once her nipple was stiff and wet, he moved to the other, delivering the same attention. Then he gazed at them as if in awe.

"Vampire, no more teasing!"

Looking slightly dazed, he grinned. "My fire and ice Bride. Never shy about what she wants."

She shook her head. "Especially not when I've wanted it this long."

FORTY-ONE

Though they'd been together for months, Murdoch was anxious with Daniela, determined to make this perfect for her.

Since she'd waited more than twenty lifetimes for it.

And he'd noticed that she hadn't replied when he said he wanted to stay with her here. Maybe she still needed convincing? He was up to the task.

"If you knew how good you taste." He nuzzled

her ear, dimly marveling that her body didn't feel cold—because his was as well. "I can't wait to taste all of you."

She inhaled sharply, shivering against him.

His hand trailed from her breast down to her spread thighs, quaking in anticipation of feeling her flesh for the first time. Reaching under her dress, he tugged her silk panties to her knees. Then returned his hand . . .

His palm met damp curls. "*Almighty*," he rasped, as he cupped her slick sex. Gently, he slipped his forefinger between her folds and into her tight sheath, making her jerk in his arms. "Easy, baby," he murmured. "I've got you."

"Oh, gods, Murdoch!" Her curling claws bit into his shoulders, which only stoked his arousal, already nearing a fever pitch.

"So perfect. You feel so good." Needing to taste the wetness he was stroking, he withdrew his finger. Her lids went heavy as she watched him suck it between his lips, then shudder from how sweet she was.

"I need *more*." His voice broke low on the word.

Laying her back on the bed, he removed her panties and dress completely. When she was naked to his gaze, he stared at her, wanting to remember her like this forever.

She was a fantasy made flesh, her body arrayed with diamonds, her shining hair fanning out around her head. Her silver eyes glittered like the stones adorning her. *Mine*.

And I can touch every inch of her.

She was panting, her breasts quivering, the peaks pouting. He knelt before her on the bed and nipped each tip with his teeth, giving them each a short, hard suck. "Spread those pretty thighs for me."

As she did, he drew back to watch, exhaling a shaky breath. It took all the discipline he'd ever garnered to keep from falling upon her like an animal.

Her flesh was lush with arousal, misted wet. At the sight, his cock surged harder, hanging down between his legs like a steel rod. The crown dragged against the sheet as he bent down to her sex, inch by inch.

Whatever she saw in his expression made her murmur, "*Oh.* Murdoch. P-please go slow. At first."

"Trying to. Never wanted anything so bad in my life." With the first brush of his lips against her thigh, she tensed in reaction, as if she'd been burned. "Daniela?"

"No, no, keep going." She threaded her fingers though his hair, surrendering to his kiss.

"Do you want more?"

"Yes, more," she bit out, her voice throaty.

Good. Because I crave this—must have it. She whimpered when he used his thumbs to part her damp flesh. Then, at last, he pressed his mouth to her.

The first flick of his tongue against her made her moan. When she quivered for him, his cock jerked in answer, the head brushing the sheet.

How he'd dreamed of this. But nothing could

have prepared him for her maddening taste, the softness of her folds yielding to his mouth, the tight bud of her clitoris swelling under his tongue.

The act was beyond imagining and felt as if something right and natural was shifting into place. He was meant to bring her pleasure like this.

He spread her wide, fingering her as he licked and sucked, until she was wantonly rolling to his tongue. *No inhibitions.*

Her response had him rocking his shaft up and back, wetting the sheet with his precum. *I'm going to spend before I'm even inside her.*

But his eyes closed in bliss when she whispered, "Please, don't stop. . . ."

"*Never,*" he growled, setting upon her once more. Laying his hand over her flat belly, he pinned her in place, holding her fixed to his mouth as he suckled her clitoris between his lips.

"*Murdoch!*" At once, she began coming in a wet rush, her head thrashing.

Never releasing her, he watched as her back arched like a bow, her stiff nipples pointing to the ceiling. He groaned against her even as he sucked.

He wrung every last ounce of pleasure from her, and was still unwilling to give up this prize. Stifling growls, he licked her clean until she had to grip his face and draw him away.

When he finally rose up on his knees, he hissed a curse at how luscious she looked—her pleasured sex slick from her orgasm, her eyes glinting with passion, her hair wild.

"You'll make me lose my mind, Daniela." *My control as well . . . About to take her virginity like a rutting beast.*

"Would that be so bad?" she purred.

Have to be gentle with her. He'd had sex before, but now he wanted to make love to his woman. Was she ready for him? "How do you feel right now?" His voice was unrecognizable. *I can do this. I can hold on. Just a little longer.*

"Aching. Empty. Hungry."

He swallowed, and his voice broke low as he uttered, "H-hungry?"

FORTY-TWO

When Danii licked her lips and pressed him back on the bed, his expression wavered between excited—and agonized.

And the seducer might even be nervous.

Kneeling between his legs, her palms flat against his chest, she kissed down his torso, nuzzling the trail of crisp hair below his navel. "Remember when I said I'd do this at my leisure? For *hours*?" When she took him in hand, he bucked as if helpless not to.

"Hours? This might be over before it starts." His accent was thicker than she'd ever heard it. He was watching her as she gave her first seeking lick. "Dan-iela! Ah—"

Another lick silenced him. A third made him growl. Soon she was raining wet flicks over the slit, tasting him, just as he'd described all those nights ago. He was delicious, with a salty tang.

"Umm, I love your taste," she murmured in a delighted tone.

He cupped her head with shaking hands. "You want me to lose my mind for you? We're on our way."

"But Murdoch, I need more of this." Unable to stop herself, she continued her wet kiss, closing her lips over him. And while her mouth slid down his length, her fingers explored, hefting his sac, which seemed to madden him more.

"Ah, that's it, Danii. . . ."

Sucking hard, she darted her tongue all around until she'd built up a cold, freezing friction.

He groaned, "You're doing it so good, *kallim.*" Digging his heels into the bed, he let his knees fall open. "I'm close. Pull back."

She ran her cheek along his damp shaft. "Let me make you come," she said before she took him back between her lips.

He seemed to be struggling to keep his hips still. Hoarse groans erupted from his chest.

"Daniela, going to come in your mouth . . . if you don't stop." The big hands palming her head couldn't seem to decide if they wanted to draw her away or press her down.

"No!" He tried to pull back, but her claws were sunk in his ass, so he couldn't move without hurting her. *"Ah, baby, I can't hold on."*

She could feel his shaft thickening, straining as he began to ejaculate against her tongue.

She's done it—made me lose my fucking mind.

"Daniela!" he roared as he came into her hungry mouth.

His eyes rolled back in his head when she sucked him as if she were starved for him. As if she'd waited two thousand years just to swallow him down, over and over. . . .

Once she'd drained him dry, they both lay back on the bed, gasping, as they had that first night together. Only now could he reach over and hold her hand.

Recalling every wicked instant of what they'd just done had him rebounding in a rush. When he raised himself over her, Daniela's gaze dipped and her lips curled. "My man has talents."

But as he used his knees to spread her thighs, she tilted her head at him. "Murdoch, are you nervous?"

"I want this to be worth the wait."

"It already has been. Anything else is a bonus."

"I haven't done this for a while." He frowned. "Actually, I've never done this." When she quirked a brow, he said, "Claimed my virgin female for all time."

"Oh." She gave him that soft look from under her lashes, the one that made his heart twist in his chest.

"When I make you mine tonight, I'm never letting you go."

She gazed up at him with that exquisite elven face, mesmerizing him. "I never want you to."

He took himself in hand, positioning his cock at her slick entrance. The crown met her wetness, beckoning him inside. He wanted his shaft covered in it, wanted to stir himself in it.

As the head nudged inside, he stared down at her eyes. *"Ma armastan sind."*

Her eyes glinted at the words, and she whispered, "I love you, too."

Mounting her untried body, he inched inside, stretching her sheath. "Don't want to hurt you," he grated, fighting to go slow.

"It's not . . . too bad. Just keep going." She was clutching him to her, her curling claws holding him as if she'd never let go.

"You're so tight. Like a fist squeezing me." Once he'd seated his cock deep, he forced himself to go still, letting her grow accustomed. With untold will, he waited until she began undulating under him.

Only then did he draw his hips back, giving her a measured thrust. The pleasure was so intense that his vision wavered.

"Murdoch, yes!"

Another withdrawal, another pump of his hips that made her moan low. Once he began a rhythm, rocking between her thighs, he kissed her again, delving his tongue in time with his body.

The friction made it warmer, but it was still cold, and cold felt so damn *good.*

"Daniela, tell me that you're mine."

"I am *yours.* . . ."

Already, he didn't know how much longer he could last with her nipples rubbing against his chest. The drenched clench of her sex called for his seed, demanding. . . .

"I'll never get enough of you, *never,*" Murdoch rasped with his brows drawn.

His expression made Danii's heart squeeze, even as his determined thrusts were sending her closer to orgasm. His scent drove her wild; his strength captivated her.

As his body worked hers, magnificent taut cords of muscle stood in relief. The latent power of a male vampire. She desired that power, savored the way he toiled under her claws.

His arms bulged as he held himself up to alternately buck his hips hard, then languidly stir them. *Gods, the man knows how to move.*

Cupping her ass with his fingers splayed, he lifted her, wrenching her along his shaft.

"Murdoch!" she cried, already on the verge again.

He worked her up and down, harder and harder until her teeth clattered with each landing.

She wrapped her legs tight around his waist, which seemed to spur him. He went wild, possessively pinning her arms over her head, so that even more of their bodies could touch.

Surging over her, he rode her sheath in a frenzy. His face was an agonized mask, his body straining for her. "Come, *kallim*. Let me feel you."

At that moment, she wanted to give him anything he desired. She needed to surrender to him. Surrender everything to him.

"Take my blood," she managed to whisper.

"What?"

"Drink me."

"Ah, Daniela, you don't have to ask me twice. . . ." He licked her neck, then sank his fangs into her.

As he pierced her, Danii's eyes went wide, and she gave a shocked cry—she'd begun to come immediately. He must have felt her, because he gave a frenzied growl.

"Murdoch! Ah, yes!" As her orgasm ripped through her, his shaft thickened even more, swelling until he could barely move inside her.

Then he went motionless, snarling against her. Just when she felt the first lash of his semen, his hips began plunging like a piston, taking him to the very end.

As he drew her blood, he flooded her with seed. She felt every pumping jet, prolonging her own ecstasy.

With a final groan, he released his fangs, collapsing atop her, his breaths cooling against her new mark. With seeming great effort, he rolled off her, but only to enfold her in his arms.

She lay on his chest, skin to skin. He clutched her to him, pressing a kiss into her hair.

"That was worth my wait, vampire."

"I'm glad, Valkyrie. Because I'd have counted down eternity for that."

FORTY-THREE

"If I could kiss you, I don't think I'd ever stop," Daniela had told him all those months ago. Now they could and she didn't stop—for hours, they lazily kissed and touched.

So this is utter contentment. Murdoch had never known it before.

For the first time, he experienced the luxury of her smooth legs entwined with his. At last, he could trace all the cobalt markings on her skin that had always tantalized him. They'd discovered that the tips of her ears were ticklish—she'd been unaware. He reveled in her taste, her responsiveness, wanting to go to his knees in thanks for the Bride he'd been given.

He'd been trailing kisses along her delicate collarbone when she sighed, "Now I understand why my sisters enjoyed being bitten so much."

"You liked my bite, little Bride? You'll be able to endure it every other day?"

"I'll *demand* it every other hour. And I'll make sure you're properly exerted, so you'll be thirsty all the time."

Just getting better and better. "That won't be a problem."

"But Murdoch," she began, her tone uneasy, "about your living here. . . ."

He pulled back to meet her gaze, dread drumming in his chest.

"They'll never accept you," she said. "Not after what happened to my mother. They'll reason that if Sigmund could turn against his own queen, then a vampire surely could . . . and they were punished by Sigmund, every day."

"Daniela, you told me you were *mine.* I warned you I'd never let you go. But I won't ask you to give up your crown."

She grew still. "You won't?"

"No, but just as before, we'll have to find a way to be together, because you can't ask me to give you up either."

She seemed pleased ·by his answer. Had she expected him to demand she relinquish her throne? The old, selfish Murdoch would have. He would have believed it was her honor to be with him. Now he knew it was the other way around.

"Explain to me exactly what Nïx told you," Daniela said.

He scowled. "Still planning on marrying Jádian?"

"Murdoch!" She play-punched his arm, then seemed to get briefly distracted by the feel of his skin. "Now tell me."

So he did . . .

When he'd finished, she said, "You know, I

didn't need a soothsayer to convince me that you'd be true."

He gave a decisive nod. "My thoughts exactly."

"And I have an idea," she said. "A way we could be together—and do only as we please."

"No, no," Murdoch grated. "Not a chance. I can't let you do this for me. Daniela, I saw your memories. Your mother wanted this for you."

Danii shook her head firmly. "I think she'd want me to be happy. And this is the only way. Murdoch, if you saw my memories, did you not feel how long I've waited to be happy? A lonely life of service will *not* be forthcoming from me."

"I did feel it. But don't you even want to think about—"

"I have been thinking about this," she said, meeting his gaze. "And it's what I choose."

After long moments, he said, "I'm with you, Daniela. Whatever you want, I'll support you."

"Then let's get some clothes on, because what I want is to get this settled as soon as possible."

Once they'd dressed, she called for Jádian. When he arrived, she wasted no time. "I'm abdicating, and I want you to take over the throne. I'd like you to be king of the Icere."

Instead of jumping at the chance, Jádian almost seemed put out and kept glancing at the door.

Danii said, "You don't appear too happy about this."

"I had . . . other plans, once you got established

here," Jádian replied. "But I'll do my duty, if this is your will."

Jádian the Buzz Kill, all duty, no fun. "Yes, it is. But I have a few conditions. I want to visit whenever I like, come around for holidays and such, once I get the cryomancy down. And the Icere must always ally with the Valkyrie."

"Agreed. But I have some conditions as well," Jádian said. "If I die with no heir, you'll resume the throne. And you'll take with you your mother's crown."

"But it belongs here—it belongs to your future queen."

"I'll never take a *wife* to wear it."

Still waters run deep with the Iceren? "Then I can agree to that."

Jádian nodded to them, then strode to the door. As he left, she thought she heard him mutter a curse, demonstrating the most emotion she'd ever observed.

When they were alone, Murdoch pulled her back into his lap. "I think Jádian was a shade shocked at your offer."

"Well, Nïx did say that I would make him my king—so I did." Danii smiled brightly. "Now it seems I'm a woman of leisure."

Murdoch nipped the tip of her ticklish ear, making her laugh. "Good. Then you can take a day to marry me."

EPILOGUE

Christmas Eve
Blachmount Manor

The Wroth family—four couples brought together by the Accession, and in some cases by Nïx—had gathered to celebrate Murdoch and Daniela's marriage, the holidays, and the renovation of Blachmount.

Myst and Nikolai had completely restored the manor, and now it was lavishly decorated for the festivities.

While the brothers drank whiskey, the females gathered around an enormous table laden with food and drinks. But Myst and Néomi were the only ones with plates. *Myst eating?* There went the Valkyrie's inherent birth control.

Danii raised her brows, but Myst only shrugged. "What can I say? Nikolai's big on family. And I felt sorry for my poor biological clock, having to tick for millennia."

Kaderin received a questioning glance as well, but she held up her hands. "Don't look at me. I've got shite to do and no pity for clocks...."

When they convened by the fire to exchange gifts, naturally Danii and Murdoch took the chilly settee farthest away from the heat.

Murdoch gazed around again, still seeming stunned by the changes. "It looks just like home used to."

Nikolai took Myst's hand in his. "She wanted to keep it as close as possible to what I remembered," he said, looking like he was about to explode, he was so proud and satisfied.

All of the brothers gave that impression. Even Conrad, with his flame-red eyes. He was doing so well, seeming more of an eccentric than the madman Danii had expected, but he did appear to occasionally get lost in memory. Whenever he did, his new wife, Néomi, was there, gently tugging him back to the present.

Danii had liked Néomi immediately, though she was a bit puzzled about how the ballet dancer had gone from ghost to human to the more powerful phantom. Now Néomi was telekinetic, with the ability to become incorporeal and vanish at will.

Néomi wasn't spilling the details—even though she was visibly tipsy, speaking in a mix of her native French and English. *"Merry Noelle!"*

The atmosphere was cozy and domestic, and Danii relaxed, enjoying herself, savoring the time spent with her sisters and siblings-in-law. Murdoch drew Danii even closer into the chill of his arms until she all but sat on his lap. He rubbed his big, cold palm up and down her arm. With his other hand, he held hers.

Constant contact. Over the last few weeks, he'd barely kept his hands off her. She soaked up his affection as she would frost.

After Jádian's reluctant coronation, Danii and Murdoch had been married in a simple Lore ceremony. He'd been Catholic, and she was a pagan. Simple was best.

Since then, Danii hadn't had time for fantasies anymore. Her husband had proved deliciously insatiable. Each sunset, he would ease into her, waking her that way, drawing just enough blood to keep him cold. Though she always wanted him to drink more.

He'd taken the icy changes in himself in stride. And if she'd expected his brothers to be disappointed with this development, she would've been wrong. They'd easily accepted Murdoch's decision.

With much fanfare, the family began exchanging gifts. Murdoch had bought her an extravagant case to hold Svana's crown—and an emerald comb to replace the one that Néomi had admitted to stealing right out of his pocket at Elancourt.

Danii gifted him with her own creation: an intricately carved ring of ice for his forefinger, to wear as a type of cold monitor, until he got accustomed to his transformation. They didn't know if he could overheat, and she never wanted to find out.

Yet every present was upstaged by Sebastian and Kaderin's gift to the family. Thrane's Key.

At the sight of it, Danii stifled a shiver. She'd heard that the key didn't always do as one hoped, and it didn't always go back to the exact time one wished.

But Murdoch had such hopes of being reunited with his family. He'd told her his father would be so proud to see that Murdoch had given his heart completely.

She shook away her apprehension. This family was so formidable, fate should yield to it.

"We go back at the beginning of the new year?" Sebastian asked, wrapping his arm around Kaderin's shoulders. Danii curbed a smile when fierce Kaderin melted against him, half-lidded with happiness, all but purring. Danii made a mental note to razz her about that later.

"Yes, it's time," Nikolai said. "We've all gotten settled."

Conrad's red eyes grew blank, his fists balling as he went awash in a memory. But Néomi tenderly cupped the side of his face, tugging him back into the conversation.

"*Néomi?*" he rasped in confusion.

She smiled lovingly, with infinite patience. "*Écoute-le, mon coeur.*"

He gave her a nod, his red gaze filled with what could only be described as adoration.

"Are you ready to go back for your sisters?" Néomi asked him.

Conrad faced the others with a decisive nod. "I'm ready."

"Are we all agreed about this?" Nikolai asked. "I am most concerned about how the girls will do.

They were so young, and they'll be thrust into not only a completely different world of beings, but a completely different time."

Kaderin said, "My sisters are managing well— aside from the occasional slain toaster—and they were premedieval."

Myst said, "And look at how fabulous the girls' aunts will be with them. I can instruct them in high fashion, and Néomi can teach them to dance."

"*Bien sûr.*" Néomi nodded. "And I can go invisible and follow them to school, watching over them."

Kaderin said, "I can teach them how to fight."

"What can I teach them?" Daniela asked quietly.

Myst answered, "How to get exactly what they want when the odds are stacked against them. Oh, and how to reform rakes."

"*Rake.* Singular," Murdoch grated with a possessive squeeze of her knee, making them laugh.

The talk turned to reminiscing, and though Danii wanted to learn more about Murdoch's family, the fire was blazing.

The instant she even perceived being uncomfortable, Murdoch seized her hand, leading her to the balcony. He told the others, "We're going out for some cold air."

Outside, she said, "Thank you. It was getting warm."

He took her into his arms to give her some of his coolness, pressing her face into his chest. "For me, too, love."

"Doesn't it bother you?" she asked him. "Not to be able to sit with them around the fire?"

She gazed back at the scene, the family laughing around a hearth, holiday decorations glittering in the firelight. A Hallmark card. Except that a phantom, Valkyries, and vampires populated the portrait.

"Sitting around the fire, versus making love to my wife as soon as we can possibly ditch?" Cradling her face in his palms, he kissed her forehead, her lashes, the tip of her nose, and a corner of her lips. "Danii, I've never been more satisfied with my life, didn't know I could be."

Between his light kisses, she felt snow beginning to fall. She raised her face in delight, laughing softly.

When her gaze met his once more, his eyes had darkened to black. "I can't get enough of you, Valkyrie."

Her hands slipped up his chest to meet at his nape. "Then kiss me, vampire." *And don't ever stop. . . .*

TEMPT ME ETERNALLY

Gena Showalter

ACKNOWLEDGMENTS

Yes, Kresley Cole is in the dedication, but she also needs to be in the acknowledgments. That's how fabulous she is. Little girls are made of sugar and spice, but Kresley is made of glitter and rainbows. I heart you.

ONE

They were coming.

Warriors unlike any other. Monsters of unimaginable power. Otherworlders. Fierce creatures with the ability to look inside your soul, glimpse your greatest fear, and present it to you with an unrepentant smile.

Should've stayed home, Aleaha Love thought. *'Cause we're gonna get spanked. Hard. And not in a good way.* Instead, she'd answered her cell and her captain's call to action, and now found herself crouched in the middle of a gnarled forest, staring into a snow-laden clearing, moonlight shooting bright amber rays in every direction as flakes wafted in the breeze like fairy dust.

Though she wore white from head to toe, had a pyre-gun stretched forward, and was burrowed in a drift as cover, she felt exposed. Vulnerable. And yeah, damn cold.

What in the hell did I get myself into?

"Everyone in position?" a voice whispered from her headset.

A whisper, yeah, but it startled her. She managed to cut off a yelp, but couldn't stop tremors from sweeping through her. *Steady*. She'd never hear the end of it if she accidentally fired her weapon before the fight had even begun.

"Premature weapon ejaculation," they'd say with a chuckle, and she wouldn't be able to deny it.

One by one, twenty teammates uttered their assent. They had wicked cool nicknames like Hawk Eye and Ghost. Her turn, she said, "Lollipop, in place."

She rolled her eyes. "Dress her up and watch her play bad alien, delicious cop," the boys had laughed before giving her the stupid moniker her first day on the job. "Naughty lawbreakers will want to taste her, not outrun her."

That had been, what? Five weeks ago, she realized with a jolt. Oh, how life had changed since then. From hiding in the shadows, afraid of what she was, to working cases with New Chicago's elite team of smart-asses, content with her somewhat pampered existence. A pampered existence she didn't deserve and hadn't earned, but whatever. No guilt for her. Really.

"Need someone to snuggle against, Lolli?" a quiet, amused male voice asked. Devyn, supposedly a king of some sort and a self-proclaimed collector of women. He wasn't really a member of Alien Investigation and Removal but was a special contractor, as well as the man who'd once wired her gun to blow bubbles rather than fire at target practice.

Word on the street, he was more powerful than God and deadlier than the devil, though no one would tell her outright what he could do. He was an otherworlder, that much she knew. That, and most of AIR's flunkies kept their distance from him. They feared him, which only heightened Aleaha's need to keep her own secrets.

She, too, was different.

She didn't know whether she was human or alien. Or both. She didn't know whether there were others like her or not. She didn't know who her parents were or why they'd abandoned her on the dirty streets of the Southern District—a.k.a Whore's Corner—of New Chicago, and she didn't care. Not anymore. All she knew was that she could assume anyone's identity with only a touch. That person's face became hers; their height became hers; their body became hers.

For years, she'd lived in fear of being found out, of being hunted and tortured for her unnatural ability, afraid that everyone who looked at her saw the truth and knew she wasn't who she claimed to be. But she couldn't drop the mask. As herself, she was wanted for theft, assault against a police officer, and more theft. And then maybe kinda sorta murder. Not that she was culpable. He'd deserved it.

She'd rather lose a limb than spend any more time in jail.

Her fear of discovery was waning, though, and she was settling comfortably into her newest life as Macy Briggs. *Maybe one day I'll even be worthy of it.* Again, not that she felt guilty. *Really.*

But with Christmas only a few weeks away . . . ugh. Worst. Holiday. Ever. Her "friends" would bake Macy's favorite foods, not Aleaha's. They would give her gifts meant for Macy, and reminisce fondly about good ole days she knew nothing about, and she would have to smile through every minute of it. And yeah, okay. Fine. *Then* she would feel guilty.

"What, ignoring me?" Devyn said with another of those snarky laughs. "Wasn't like I was going to ask to feel you up or anything. I mean, I was just gonna surprise you with my handsiness."

God, she was on the job, yet she'd lost track of her thoughts. Mortifying. "Can you take nothing seriously?"

"Hello, have you met me? I take making out very seriously."

All the men on the line snorted in their attempts to muffle their laughter. They might be wary of him, but they couldn't help but enjoy his perverted sense of humor.

"Fuck you, Chuckles," she said, trying not to reveal *her* amusement. Irreverent bastard.

"Excellent. We're on the same page, because that's exactly what I'm trying to do to you."

Give herself to Devyn? Not in this lifetime, and not because he wasn't attractive. If anything, he was *too* attractive. Hell, he was total screw-like-an-animal perfection. Tall, with dark hair, wide amber eyes, and skin that glittered like a jewel; there was no one else like him. There *was* a recipe for his smile, though: wicked desire dipped in acid, wrapped in steel and sprinkled with candy. The recipe for his laughter? Well, that was wicked desire tossed in the gutter, wrung out in a whorehouse, and slathered with scented body lotion. Women threw themselves at him constantly, and he ate it up like they were his own personal smorgasbord.

They probably were. Thank God she wasn't in the market for a boyfriend. Or, rather, a lover, since that's all someone as fickle as Devyn could ever amount to. Macy—the real Macy—had been dating a piece of scum Aleaha was still trying to lose and she didn't have the time or patience to throw anyone else into the mix.

"Temper, temper," Jaxon Tremain chided. He was one of two agents who hung out with the sexy otherworlder, and the resident smoother. There was something unnaturally calming about his presence, as if he could slink inside a person's psyche and wash away her fears. "Would you kiss me with that mouth?"

"Funny," she said dryly.

She could hear the others chortling and snorting with more surprised amusement. Someone said, "Soliciting kisses from women, Jaxon? Mishka will kill you for that."

"If by *kill* you mean *seduce*, then yeah," Jaxon replied. "You're right."

Mishka was Jaxon's wife and a hired killer who possessed a robotic arm. Aleaha had only seen her once, but that had been enough to scare ten years off her life. Never had she seen eyes so cold or heard a voice so uncaring. Of course, the moment Mishka spied Jaxon, her entire demeanor had changed. So had Jaxon's, for that matter. Usually he was as conservative as a priest. One glance at Mishka, though, and he'd morphed into gutter man.

Aleaha had marveled at the change in him, a change she was witnessing once again. Empathetic as he was, perhaps he was veering onto the perverted track now to get her mind off the bloody massacre sure to begin. Apparently, though, she didn't need help today. She couldn't concentrate worth a damn. What was wrong with her?

"Well," Devyn said, drawing the spotlight back to him. As always. "Be a good lollipop and answer the man. Will you kiss him or not?"

"I could give you a list of all the things I'll never do to you with my mouth," she muttered. "How 'bout that?"

Devyn laughed, and, yep. It was wicked desire. "She reminds me of Mia when she talks like that. Tell us, Lolli, is that list for everyone or just Jaxon?"

"All right, team," Mia Snow herself interjected before Aleaha could reply. "Save it. You know I only want you to stun these men. Do not burn them. I repeat, do not burn them. An open wound will bleed and that will spread their infection. And believe me, I will kill every single one of you myself if that happens."

There was a moment of frightening silence. Infection. What a delightful reminder. Not only were the warriors coming here vicious, there was a possibility that they were bringing the plague with them.

"Good," Mia continued. "I've got your attention. Solar flare approaching in ten." She was inside a van about a mile away, watching the action on a night-vision monitor with a handful of backup agents. "Nine."

Aleaha tensed. A few months ago, a big case had busted wide open and AIR had learned that otherworlders were traveling to Earth through interworld wormholes that initiated with solar flares. Then, a few weeks after that, another case had come to light. Members of a race of aliens known as the Schön had descended, their bodies carriers of a virus that passed to humans through their blood and ejaculate. This virus turned men and women into cannibals. Their queen—or living host of this sickness—was on her way here, due to arrive in the near future.

Tonight, ten members of her horde were supposed to utilize one of those wormholes. Their purpose: to smooth the way for her. Which meant, destroying AIR.

"Six."

Shit. The countdown. Despite the frigid temperatures, sweat beaded on Aleaha's brow, dripping from the brim of the white cap she wore. *Stay calm. You have to stay calm.*

"Five."

Though her résumé claimed she'd worked as a cop for more than two years, this was actually *Aleaha*'s first mission.

What seemed forever ago but had only been a few months, she'd stumbled upon the body of a woman who'd been raped and killed in a back alley—a woman she'd recognized as Miss New Chicago's Finest in Uniform calendar girl, Macy Briggs.

She'd almost walked away. The higher the public profile, the more scrutiny she received. But . . .

Already tired of the adult-toy-store clerk identity she'd previously stolen, Aleaha had seized the chance to better herself, hiding the body and shifting so that she was an exact match to Macy's appearance, thereby claiming the woman's life as her own.

Only later had she learned that Macy had applied to AIR and been accepted. To back out would have looked suspicious and changing identities yet again hadn't appealed. So she'd done it. She'd attended that first day, then the next. And the next. They'd watched her suspiciously, as if they knew the truth, but they had never accused her and she'd realized she was probably paranoid. Soon they'd even relaxed, accepting her as one of their own. Now, here she was, done with trials and on mission one.

"—was actually your warm-up," Mia said, cutting into her thoughts. "Ten. Nine."

Shit. She'd missed the end of the first countdown? She was practically begging to be killed tonight.

"Seven. Six."

Oh, God. What if she did, in fact, die out here? What if she lost everything she'd worked so hard to gain? Her gun hand shook. *You have to stay calm, damn it.*

With bouts of extreme emotion, she shifted from one identity to another without any control.

"Four. Remember, guns set to stun and only stun."

Her pyre-gun was already dialed to the proper

setting, so she curled her index finger around the trigger and swallowed the hard lump in her throat. *Breathe in, breathe out. You do know how to fire a weapon, at least.* A skill she'd learned from her only true friend, Bride McKells. A vampire, and her champion. They'd been separated more than a decade ago, chased apart by cops who'd caught them breaking into homes for food, and Aleaha hadn't been able to find her since. She'd never stop looking, though.

"One."

All the air in Aleaha's lungs escaped on a sudden rush, hot and blistering, burning her throat and mouth. She tensed, waiting. Waiting. And then it happened. Overhead, the gloomy darkness gave way to sparkling orange-pink flickers. The wind picked up, swirling leaves and beating limbs against each other. Snow danced in every direction.

Then . . . nothing. It was almost disappointing. Almost.

The flickers died, leaving only the haze of stars. The wind quieted, leaving only the rasp of human breathing. Gradually, she relaxed. Maybe the Schön had decided to stay home. Maybe there'd be a party tonight rather than a war, and she wouldn't have to worry about—

"Commander?" someone asked.

"Hold," Mia replied. "Hold steady. We'll stay here all night if we have to."

Easy for her to say. She was nestled inside that warm van.

Several minutes ticked by in silence. Shudders

of cold began rocking through Aleaha, causing her teeth to chatter. This sucked. Much longer, and her gloved fingers would be frozen to her gun. If that happened, growing a penis would be easier than shooting. 'Cause, yeah, she could even become a man. And had, on several occasions. Hadn't been as fun as she'd assumed. Penises were weird. They were also—

One second the circular clearing was empty, the next it was bursting with hulking, black-clad warriors. And there were far more than the expected ten.

"What the hell?" someone barked.

Aleaha jolted in surprise, sizing the visitors up in one panicked flash: living weapons. They were tall, well-muscled and radiated absolute power and authority. In the traitorous moonlight and snow, she could see that their features were humanoid—if you didn't count their glowing, golden eyes, like twin suns crashing through daybreak.

"Fuck!" another of her teammates shouted. "They aren't Schön, they're Rakans! What do we do?"

Rakans? The peace-lovers? Couldn't be. There was no damn way these ready-for-combat warriors would be waving a white flag.

"Do not kill," Mia commanded. "I repeat, do not kill them. Continue with stun. I want to know why they're here. Now go, go, go."

Just as she was about to squeeze her gun's trigger, a honey-scented breeze wafted through the air, taunting, beckoning her to lassitude and . . . How odd. Her nipples were beading, but not from the cold. Moisture was dampening her panties, her skin tightening over her bones, and drugging heat pouring into her veins.

Surely not. Surely the scent was *not* arousing her. Yet . . .

Why shoot them when she could kiss them? Kiss them . . . yes . . . Naughty images saturated her mind. Images of naked, writhing bodies—one of them golden. Seeking, hungry mouths—one of them golden. Wandering, teasing hands—again, a pair was golden. Satisfaction was only a heartbeat away, the anticipation of pleasure a consuming ache. All she had to do was drop her weapon, stand, and strip.

Strip? Seriously? What the hell was wrong with her? Was she the only one feeling this way? Like her, no one else had moved.

"Beautiful," an agent said.

"Want," another moaned.

Apparently not.

The warriors remained unmoving, silent, as if they were disoriented and needed to sober.

"Why are you just lying there, lusting after them? Did you not hear me? I said stun them, damn it," the commander growled.

Forcing her mind to blank, one of the toughest things Aleaha had ever done, she hammered at the trigger with her index finger. Other agents followed suit, and multiple blue stun-beams erupted in the night, blending with hers and charting a direct course to the aliens.

Hit. Hit. Hit.

As the beams made contact, the Rakans were

rendered immobile, aware of their surroundings but now unable to move. But most remained untouched, their comrades having acted as their shields.

As though realizing what was happening, those men quickly gained their bearings and charged forward, successfully dodging the next round of rays.

Aleaha blinked in shock. Never in all her twenty-six years had she seen anyone move so swiftly. They moved so swiftly, in fact, that they left some kind of ethereal, ghostly outline of themselves behind. Their spirits? Those outlines then had to play catch-up with the tangible bodies, which created a dizzying blur of movement, light, and shadow.

"I'm down! I'm down!" someone cried. "Had the shit knocked out of me."

"I can't fucking freeze them," Devyn said. Odd. He had refused to bring a gun to this fight, the cocky bastard, so he wouldn't have been able to freeze them anyway.

After that, absolute chaos erupted. There were screams of pain, frantic footfalls, and humans collapsing. Aleaha pinched off a few more rounds. And, goddamn it, she missed every time.

She never missed. People who lived on the streets often depended on their aim for survival. She'd taught herself to hit whatever she aimed at—no matter what she was doing or what was going on around her. This was unacceptable.

Calm. Focus. She concentrated on the blurs as best she could, narrowing her eyes until she saw—

Squeeze.

This time, she hit a target dead-center. No, she realized a baffled moment later. She'd hit his spirit, that ghostly animation or whatever it was. Damn it! Unaffected, his body continued moving, darting from one place to another, felling one agent after another. And then, before her horrified gaze, the Rakans scattered in precise, measured increments. They weren't running away, but were encircling the entire AIR team and lethally closing in.

Caged, she thought. *We're being caged.* Despite the direness of their circumstances, the agents continued to fight, and Aleaha was utterly proud of them. Blue stun-beams glowed throughout the enclosure, lighting up the snowy night with majestic fury.

"Shit," someone said. "What the hell should we do? I can't see them anymore. I can't fucking see them!"

An agent ran over her, mowing right over her legs. No longer quite so proud, she popped to her feet, abandoning her cover in favor of protecting her limbs. Her knees knocked, but she managed to remain upright.

"Keep firing," Devyn commanded one and all. "Stay together, and for God's sake, stay calm."

He sounded so close that she turned her head— and found him standing right beside her.

"You okay, Lolli? You staying calm like I said?"

If her emotions wouldn't listen to her, perhaps they'd listen to him and calm. "Yeah." At the moment, she wasn't capable of saying more. Okay, so no. Her emotions wouldn't be listening to him, either. Fear still held her in a tight clasp, growing as another agent fell just in front of her. Much more, and she might lose her hold on Macy's image.

Jaxon sidled up to her other side, firing two guns at once, each pointed in a different direction. His green eyes were eerie in the darkness. Eerie but calming. Just being near him was like finding shelter in the midst of a raging storm. Finally, blessedly.

"Aim just ahead of the bodies," he instructed. "Or rather, ahead of the lights. It's the best way to lock on them."

Grunts, groans and screams filled her ears, louder by the second, distracting her. She pivoted and fired, pivoted and fired, trying to direct her beams in front of the blurs, just as Jaxon had said.

To her consternation, she only managed to nail one of the warriors. How many were out there, damn it? They seemed to be multiplying like flies.

"Help me!" an agent sobbed. "Please, help me."

Automatically, her gaze searched the night, the frenzied crowd. Before she found the beseeching male, one of the Rakans bypassed Aleaha's protective wall of testosterone and slammed into her, shoving her to the ground. She landed flat on her back, suddenly breathless and experiencing a moment of terror and anger, helplessness and courage.

As she raised her weapon to defend herself, she could feel her face and body beginning to change, the bones adjusting to accommodate a new form. No. No, no, no. When she changed involuntarily, she never knew who she would end up looking like.

The alien with glowing golden eyes leaned down,

not to strike her but to . . . kiss her? She struggled against him, and, yep, he opened his mouth to fit it over hers.

"Woman," he said, voice slightly slurred. "Mine." Just before contact, an azure shower of sparks exploded around him, framing his large body and freezing him in place. Panting, instantly comforted, Aleaha crawled backward, forcing her image to conform once again to Macy's.

Jaxon held out a hand to help her up, and Aleaha prayed he hadn't seen her mini-transformation.

"Thanks," she rasped, somehow finding her balance. She ripped off her headset and tossed it on the ground. No more distractions.

"These guys are Rakan," he said. "Don't worry if you were dripped on."

Until that moment, she'd forgotten about possible contamination. Shit. Rakan or Schön, she was going to be more careful. The few times she'd been sick, she'd unknowingly transformed into an ailing identity. Each experience had taught her that it's more fun to be stabbed than ill.

"On my signal," Jaxon told her, shooting around her, "I want you to run and lock yourself in one of the vans."

The vans, hidden as they were, would offer a reprieve from danger, injury and death.

"No," she said, surprising herself. She'd stay and she'd fight, even though the prospect terrified her. How could she live with herself if these men died and she'd done nothing to help? "I'm staying."

"Don't argue," Devyn snapped. "Women are always prettier when they agree."

Pig. "I need to stay." She wouldn't defile everything Macy had built with her own cowardice. "I *have* to sta— Ohmygod!" One of the aliens had just stepped into an agent. *Stepped into*. Like a demon intent on possession, the otherworlder's body had entered the human's, fusing them until only the human was visible.

There was a tormented scream. The agent spasmed, shaking and quaking as he raised his own gun to his temple and fired. Brain tissue sprayed, obscene against the snow, and Aleaha gaped in horror.

"Fuck," snarled Dallas Gutierrez, Mia's second in command, as he joined them. "They're motherfucking soul jumpers."

Soul jumpers. She didn't know what that meant exactly, and she didn't want to find out. Her hands shook as she increased the speed of her shots.

"I've controlled the energy of a Rakan before," Devyn said, his voice strained. "But I can't grasp on to a single energy molecule to control these guys."

"Unlike Eden, they weren't raised on Earth. Maybe that's the problem. But it doesn't matter. Surely they'll tire soon," Jaxon replied. "That kind of speed has to drain them."

Aleaha lost the thread of the conversation. Energy molecule? Eden? All she knew was that a few more minutes passed and the aliens *didn't* slow. Their unparalleled swiftness only seemed to increase, so much so that she had trouble fixing another target in her sights.

"Shit." Devyn slid a knife from his boot. "You were wrong, my friend, and we're out of time. They're coming for us next." He slapped the hilt of the knife into Aleaha's free hand, the silver tip gleaming in the moonlight. "Be ready, Lolli. Go for the jugular."

She gulped. The blade weighed less than her gun, but somehow felt all the more menacing. "O-okay."

Jaxon turned those eerie green eyes on her. "There's still time to run."

Sixteen Rakans remained standing and they continued to close their circle, hopping over fallen agents. There might as well have been a thousand. Not long before she, Devyn, Dallas, and Jaxon—who held the center of that circle—would be reached. But Jaxon was right. There was still time to escape. Not much, but enough.

"No." Determined, she shook her head. "I'm staying. We can win this." If not, if AIR fell, she'd fall, too. *For Macy.* Aleaha owed the woman that much.

She kept firing with one hand while gripping the hilt of the serrated knife with the other, trying to prepare herself for what she might have to do. She'd never used a knife on anyone but herself, and the thought of slicing into someone else's flesh . . . *You can do it.* A cornered animal did anything necessary to ensure survival.

Another agent placed a gun to his own temple and fired.

Yeah, she could do it.

"For all that's holy, Lolli," Devyn snapped. His

hard tone of voice made her blink. Especially since he'd used it twice in one night and that was twice more than ever before. Where was his dry sense of humor? Where were his dirty jokes? "The knife was supposed to scare you, not empower you. Hit the vans so we don't have to worry about you!"

"Stop worrying and do your job!"

"Go." This from Dallas. "Run."

"No!" Even as she spoke, strong fingers of compulsion and agreement stabbed their way into her mind. *Do what he says. Don't argue with him. Run.*

Aleaha was almost into the woods, sidestepping the Rakans as Dallas distracted them, before she realized what she was doing. She stopped short and frowned. What . . . why?

The answer hit her with the force of pyre-fire. Mind control.

Which agent was responsible? Devyn, Jaxon or Dallas? Didn't matter, she supposed, because they were all bastards. Somehow, someway, one of them had controlled her with a thought.

Scowling, she whipped around. Trees stretched on both sides, so close she had only to reach out to hug their trunks. Their twisted, snow-heavy limbs shuttered her line of vision, so she brushed them aside.

The sight she next drank in would haunt her for years to come.

Most of the agents were lying on the ground, some writhing and groaning sounds of impending death. Others were motionless in the blood splattered snow. Dallas, Devyn, and Jaxon were slashes of white in that violent nighttime canvas, the tallest of the Rakans stalking the outer edge of the circle. Other Rakans took turns taunting them with punches and kicks, each expertly evading the pyre-fire launched at them.

What can I do? What the hell can I do? "Stop," she called, hoping the distraction would give her friends some kind of opening to . . . what? Take off? Attack? "Stop!"

The stalking alien obeyed, stopping in a ray of moonlight, his gaze quickly finding her. Jolting her.

Aleaha trembled in shock, another honey-scented breeze suddenly enveloping her. Arousing her. *Kiss,* she thought again. The man was utterly and absolutely breathtaking. A hedonistic god fallen straight to Earth. Sensual, exotic, with kohl-rimmed eyes of gold, a strong nose, a square chin, and chiseled . . . everything.

He put Devyn to shame.

What little of his skin was visible glowed like liquid rays of sunlight poured over hot steel. His hair hung to his jawline, the same golden shade as his skin. He was mesmerizing, unimaginable power and dark savagery blanketing his expression. And God, he was a predator, the knowledge banked in every line of his big body. Yet he was also a being so beautiful, he lured with only a look. Probably snared women before they could snap out of his spell.

"Female," he said, his voice as mesmerizing as his face. How did he know English? In fact, how had the other, the one who'd tried to molest her?

"Oh, no, you don't," Dallas said, breaking through the circle and punching him in the jaw.

The Rakan's head whipped to the side. Quickly finding Aleaha's gaze again, he reached out, grabbed Dallas by the neck, and tossed him against a nearby tree. "Mine."

The force he used—amazing. The speed and agility—dumbfounding. Dallas slumped to the ground, unconscious. Jaxon roared, a wild sound, and attacked. The beast reached out yet again. This time, he slammed a ghostly hand inside the agent's chest cavity and twisted.

Jaxon crumpled and like Dallas, he didn't get up. Devyn watched it all, a hard smile on his face. A smile that promised death. But he didn't strike. No, he held up his hands in surrender.

Aleaha could barely believe her eyes. That wasn't like him. He'd rather be stabbed than lose a fight. Dear God. The situation must be grimmer than even she had realized.

Instinctively, she backed up, halting only when she considered a new possibility. Maybe, hopefully, he had a plan. Maybe he was pretending to surrender while giving Mia and crew time to get here. Yes, of course. But why hadn't help already arrived? They were supposed to swoop in if something like this happened, and close as they were, they should have been here by now.

The tall golden alien strode toward her, shoving his own men aside. With every step, he appeared more indomitable. Deadly. Her heart drummed erratically in her chest as he came closer . . . closer.

Do something! He was almost upon her. "Stop,"

she shouted again. *Good going. I'm sure he'll obey.* "Stay where you are." If Mia needed more time, it was up to Aleaha to stall this man.

Surprisingly, he stilled at the sound of her voice. Except for his eyes. Those trekked over her, hot and blistering, as if she were his property, already naked and begging for his touch. Goose bumps broke out over her skin; her mouth dried.

"One more step, and I'll shoot." Trembling, she raised her gun until she had a direct shot at his groin. Men tended to agree to anything when their dicks were threatened. "Let's talk about this. Maybe we can work something out. Why are you here? What do you want?" *Come on, Mia.*

Slowly he grinned, silently promising that he'd do whatever he wanted, whenever he wanted. Clearly there would be no chatting. Bastard. She squeezed the trigger. Just like the others had done, he darted away from the azure beam as if it were nothing more than a pesky insect.

A second later, he was in front of her, appearing in the blink of an eye and towering over her. She gasped in surprise as heat radiated off him and enveloped her. Heat and that honey smell. Her nipples beaded again, reaching for him, and her stomach fluttered. The need for him to strip her, to slide inside of her, was potent, heady, part of her wanting to drop to her knees and beg him for it.

Who are you? she wondered, dazed. In fact, the urges were so unlike her, common sense easily fought its way to the surface. *Kill him. Now. End this!* Mia had told them not to kill, yes, but Mia wasn't here. At this rate, Aleaha would be dead before backup arrived.

"I told you I'd shoot you, and I never lie." Of course, that was a lie. Her entire life was a lie. This, however, she would do. "I mean it! Back away or I start firing."

He remained in place. "Shooting has not been favorable for you so far, has it?"

"There's a first time for everything."

"I agree. Like the first time I disarm you."

Before she could act, he knocked the gun from her hand. It clattered to the ground, out of reach, and he purred silkily, all kinds of erotic in the undertones. "What do you plan to shoot me with, my female?"

Two

Instant, searing arousal. That's what Breean Nu, now leader of the Rakan army, had experienced when he first heard the woman's raspy voice drift through his fight-craze. When his gaze had landed on her, bathed in moonlight as she'd been, that arousal had only intensified and, foolishly, he'd lost sight of everything but her. Understandable, considering his past.

He'd seen, and he'd wanted. Desperately.

He'd whisked himself to her with every intention of claiming her as his own, for every warlord deserved a prize after a victory. He was a warlord, he had won, so *she* would be his prize. Even now, *especially* now, blood roared through him, hot, hungry. And not for more fighting. For every inch of her.

"Mine," he said again. The females of Raka had been decimated by plague after aliens began sneaking onto their planet several years ago. Those females had then begun to eat the men. Eat, as in meals. Having never encountered disease before, the Rakans had been at a loss, not knowing what to do or how to help. And then it had been too late. So many had died, hardly anyone had been left.

Trembling, his prize jerked her wrist from his hold and backed away from him. One step, two. Oh, there would be none of that. Too much did he enjoy being near her.

"Stop," he said, as she'd said to him a moment ago.

She raised her chin, stubborn, and kept moving. "Don't think so."

A refusal? From a war prize? He'd never owned one before, only knew that other soldiers on other planets often kept them as slaves. And slaves were to do as they were told. He would just have to instruct her.

Although, to be honest, Breean had never thought to find himself in this type of situation. He'd been a simple fisherman and Raka, as peaceful as the planet had been, had never had to utilize its royal army. Most citizens had obeyed the king without question, and otherworlders had never been allowed to enter their land. Until the Schön came in secret. Until the Schön destroyed them, infecting the women who then took out the soldiers and everyone else.

At the time, Breean had been living on the seas that cover most of Raka, the sole provider for his mother and sisters. He'd returned one day to find them dying, and thousands of others already dead, for once the females had lost their food supply, they'd turned on each other. So he'd gathered what uninfected survivors he could and they'd started fighting back, driving the Schön away.

The experience had changed them. They were not the innocent, naive men they'd once been. They were harder, meaner, utterly unforgiving. And that's the way they had to stay.

"I told you to stop, female." There was no room for compromise in his tone. "You will obey. I am your master."

"How cute. The big boy thinks he's in charge." She whipped out another pyre-gun from the holster at her side. He'd never actually seen one until tonight, but he'd seen pictures and knew what to expect from them. In the other hand, she held a knife. With knives, he was already intimately acquainted. "Now back off."

War prize or not, she should have responded to his scent by now. "Come to me," he said, just to see what she'd do. "Touch me." Since building his own army, he was used to having his every command obeyed.

She shook her head, continuing her slow backward journey. Her eyes were large, luminous, and crystalline, swirling with flecks of silver and cerulean. Underneath her cap, her hair was pale. Her nose was dainty, her cheeks rounded. But something about her was . . . wrong. The more he studied her, the more it seemed as if *another* face lurked underneath the first. A face with wider-set *green* eyes. A more aristocratic nose. Slimmer cheeks. *Dark* hair.

All together, that packaging was not as pretty. And yet it was more erotic, more sensual. The lips were more lush, redder, and made for sucking. The hair was silkier, and he could easily imagine the dark strands fisted in his hand while he pumped in and out of that delectable body.

She wasn't the reason for such strong, instantaneous fantasies, though. Any female would have triggered the same response. It had just been so long since he'd known pleasure, so damned long. He missed sex more than he would have missed an arm.

"Why are you looking at me like that?" she snarled. She glanced behind her as if searching for someone else. Her shoulders slouched in confusion when she spied no one. When she faced him, she must have realized he'd inched closer because she yelped. "Get back!"

Breean didn't know what to make of this woman. Not the dual faces, and certainly not the fact that she seemed to be immune to him in every way. Granted, he hadn't been around a woman in two years, but surely he was still capable of seducing one. And what had happened to his determination to force a slave to his will?

Drop the weapons and touch me, little human. Or was she alien? He frowned, not liking that he didn't know. Actually, there was a lot he didn't know and the answers were far more important than his hunger. "How did AIR know we were coming?" He'd visited several times in secret, hadn't talked to anyone, and had remained in the shadows. Still. They could have seen him, he supposed. But why not attack before now?

"They were good people," she said angrily, ignoring him, once again backing away. "You shouldn't have hurt them."

"*We* are good people." He stepped toward her just as slowly. "Those agents should not have tried to hurt *us*."

She swallowed. "Our guns were set on stun, not kill. You and yours, however, killed, so excuse me for not agreeing that you are good. And how many times do I have to say this? Don't you dare come any closer!"

"The warrior who killed those agents will be punished, believe me." In a movement so quick no eye could see it, Breean swooped in and slapped the second gun out of her hand. "Now, there will be no more shooting from you."

Shock settled over her lovely dual-features. He didn't give her time to threaten him with the knife. He simply snatched the blade out of her hand, studied its serrated tip in the moonlight, and sheathed it at his back. Could be useful.

Her mouth hung open in furious disbelief, revealing perfect white teeth that were a little sharper than those he'd seen from the other humans he'd encountered. Her kiss would have bite.

His cock twitched in reaction to the thought, and he frowned again. Biting was no longer allowed among his people. A rule he'd instigated and a rule he would keep. Always. Anything that drew blood, the liquid poison that could very well carry thousands upon thousands of diseases, was now forbidden. Disobeying meant death.

He watched as she tossed another glance over her shoulder.

"Are there more agents out there?" he asked.

"Of course not."

Which meant, yes, there were. With a tilt of his chin, he motioned for several of his soldiers to scour the area. Instantly they headed into the trees. Though they were dressed in black and clashed against the snowy backdrop, they moved liked midnight apparitions, barely noticeable.

"What is your name, female?"

Silent, she slid her gaze to the gun that lay several feet away on the ground. His remaining men stood in a semicircle around it, he noticed, arms crossed over their chests, waiting for his next order. The living agents sprawled behind them, already cuffed and gathered in an unconscious heap.

"I won't let you win," she said, ignoring him. Again.

"But I already have. Your brethren are defeated. You are the last one standing."

"That just means it's up to me to kick your ass."

"I'll let you do many things to my ass, female, but kicking it isn't one of them." He leaned into her, eating up the rest of the distance, in her face before she could blink. The fragrance of newly fallen snow and dark, mystic nights drifted from her, and he inhaled deeply, savoring. "I'll let you massage it. Caress it. Grip it while I pound inside of you."

Her cheeks colored prettily, and she growled, "What about rip it to shreds?"

If she was half as passionate in bed as she was now in the face of danger, she would burn him alive. And, oh, he wanted to be burned. "If you ask nicely, yes," he said honestly. "As long as you draw no blood."

"Fuck you."

"I hope so," he replied as his men returned, shaking their heads. No one was out there, and there was no sign of anyone having been there. He relaxed.

His female was still choking out a breath. "Never," she finally managed.

"Never is a long time. Perhaps we should negotiate."

No reply. Instead, a look of intense concentration claimed her features. Her eyes narrowed, the blue somehow darkening, becoming . . . golden? Impossible. Yet as he watched, her body seemed to grow taller and more muscled, her clothing ripping to accommodate the new bulk. Within moments she was his exact height, her features realigned to match his.

He was gazing at his own face, he realized, mouth falling open in shock. The green-eyed temptress was still underneath, still barely visible, but that didn't dampen the shock of seeing *himself* in place of the sweet-faced blonde.

"How did you do that? *What* did you do?"

She peered down at her hands. No—*his* hands. Turning them over, studying them. Big, golden, calloused. Reeling, he considered the rest of her. She no longer had breasts but was solid from head to toe. She even had a bulge between her—his—legs. A nice sized one, if he did say so himself.

"Will I be able to move like you, do you think?" she asked, more of herself than of him.

His voice. She did not merely look like him, she now spoke with his voice. How was any of this possible?

Breean reached out to touch that familiar visage. What would he feel? Warmth? Cold? Surely this was an illusion. But just as his hand was about to make contact, the . . . whatever she was disappeared and his hand swiped only air.

He blinked. Confusion, anger, and more of that shock pounded through him. He glanced left, then right, but saw only the sway of trees and the swirl of snowflakes.

Brow furrowed, he wheeled and confronted his men. "Where did she—I—go?" More to the point, *how* had she gone? If she had always been able to move as swiftly as him, why had she not done so before now? If she hadn't, and this was as new a development as her appearance . . . damn. She might posses *all* of his strengths now. "Did you see her?"

Expressions as baffled as his must be, they searched the clearing for some sign of her.

From the corner of his eye, Breean caught a blur of movement, a flash of white and gold. That blur paused directly in front of the first pyre-gun he'd liberated from the woman. A second later, her—damn it, *his*—image solidified. She wobbled on her feet as though dizzy, weariness glinting over her still-masculine features. A frown pulled at her brow while she rubbed her temple with one hand and snatched up the weapon with the other.

He pounded toward her, intent. Sensing him, she looked up. Their gazes locked, gold against gold—and, thankfully, that hint of ethereal green. Sweat beaded her forehead, and she was panting. With fright? Fatigue? Or with the thrill of the chase?

A moment later, she grinned. Thrill of the chase, definitely, for that grin did not belong to a frightened female but to a taunting agent. Surprisingly, that aroused him all the more, this new challenge of her.

He didn't whisk to her, but stopped, continuing to watch her, curious about what this human—alien—would do next. What race could assume another's appearance, as well as another's abilities?

She threw an I'm-the-boss look at his men and barked, "Stay where you are. This is between the woman and me."

They had been inching toward her with determined expressions, but now they froze in place.

"Which one is which?" one of the men asked, glancing between the two of them.

"Look at the clothing," someone said. "Hers is a different material and ripped."

"But what if even that is a trick?"

"Stay where you are," Breean told them, parroting the female. "I will handle her."

"*I* will handle her and the prisoners," she said as if she truly were him. That intense glaze of concentration fell over her, and once more she disappeared.

His eyes narrowed as he searched the field, trying to zero in on a blur . . . seeing nothing . . . nothing . . . there! She materialized in front of the sleeping agents and crouched.

Her back was to him, and she seemed to shrink before his eyes. Her short golden hair lengthened and paled, appearing exactly as before. One of her hands shot out, slapping a human across the face. Pause. Another slap. Pause. She leaned to the side, muttered something, and slapped a second agent.

Who was she hitting? Slight as her body now was, it still managed to block Breean's gaze. He was afraid to move, however. Afraid she'd change personas or leap into motion again. Afraid he'd lose her.

A second later, she shoved to her feet and faced him. Leveling two guns, she edged to the center of the clearing, her left shoulder toward him, her right shoulder toward his men.

When had she picked up the second gun?

"Why won't they wake up?" she demanded angrily.

As he soaked in her blue eyes and womanly form, relief was like a living entity inside him. Much as he liked himself, he didn't want to seduce himself. Well, not anymore. There'd been enough of that over the past two years to last a lifetime. "They are merely sleeping."

"You had better wake them up. Or, to answer your earlier question, I'll shoot you with *this*."

Fierce, passionate, and now protective. His admiration spiked, and yes, so did his desire, damn his hot-blooded nature. And damn his abstinence. Yet he couldn't deny that he was glad the first woman he'd stumbled upon was this one. Even though he could not control her, she was delectable. To have her the way he wanted her, he would have to calm her, something else he had no experience with.

"Be easy," he said. Surely that would work.

"Don't just stand there," she snapped. "Wake them."

Or not. "Your commands will continue to go unheeded." *That is not how you calm a female, I don't think.* It was just, Rakan females had striven to do all they could to satisfy those around them—before the disease, that is. They'd rarely argued and had never disobeyed. They'd accepted and they'd agreed, as though the need to please had been ingrained in them at birth.

This woman obviously bowed to no one. That should have angered him, or at the very least deterred him. Yet he could suddenly imagine being tied up, *dominated*, helpless to this female's pleasure as she ground herself on his cock.

Interesting, but not something he could allow.

There was just too much risk. To give up control was to invite bloodshed.

He stood there, unsure how to proceed. How *did* you calm a female you could not bend to your will, if silken commands failed? His men shifted uncomfortably, as if, like him, they were trying to decide what to do. They meant well, but he didn't want one of them to take her down or touch her in any way.

"Hold," he told them.

The woman's hand shook—what was her name? He found that he wanted to know as intently as he wanted to know what species she was. Which also happened to be as intently as he wanted to lick her until she came, starting with her breasts and working his way down.

"Didn't I tell you once before to get that look off your face?" she said breathlessly, then fired both guns simultaneously.

He easily leapt out of the way, the blue stun-beam sailing past him. As fast as he could move, the gun's rays were slow motion to him. But one of his men, Eton, did not see the approaching beam and was nailed, instantly freezing in place. The other warriors glanced to Breean, clearly angry that another of their brethren was immobilized and would have to be carried. They wanted to act.

"No," he said. "Mine." To her, he added, "What look?"

"Like you're going to eat me. I don't like it."

"The look will disappear, I'm sure, after I *have* eaten you." The good kind of eating, too. Not the kind his people had enjoyed, there at the end. He shuddered. "Do not worry, though. I promise not to use my teeth."

Scowling, she fired again, but once more he easily dodged. "Will you just be still already?" Her gaze circled the clearing and she pushed out a frustrated breath. "Come on," she muttered, though he didn't think she realized she'd said anything aloud.

There'd been no sign of anyone out there, but she obviously expected someone to show up and didn't like that they hadn't yet. Better they came here to fight amid nature than to fight amongst the innocents living in the city. He, too, would wait for them. Silver lining: another fight might help dull his arousal.

"What is your name, female?" he repeated, remaining on alert.

"Why did you come here?" she demanded, pretending yet again that he had not spoken. "What do you want from us?"

There had to be a way around her reluctance to share. "Why should I answer your questions when you refuse to answer mine?" Excellent. Soliciting her sense of fair play.

A heavy pause. A grind of her teeth. "My name is . . . Macy."

Macy. It was a lovely name, as stunning as the woman herself—whichever face she happened to don (even his)—but it didn't fit her. Still, it was worthy of shouting while pumping inside of her. Over and over again. "I am Breean, and I'm here to make a new home for myself and my men." He'd been searching forever, it seemed, but he'd finally found the perfect place to relocate.

They'd spent the last several months coming and going, preparing. Earth had everything they needed: water, technology beyond their comprehension, medical supplies, and warm female bodies. More than that, the people here knew how to survive. If plague struck, they most likely had a cure. If not, they could create one.

Never again did he want to watch those he loved die of debilitating sickness, helpless as a craving for living flesh bloomed inside them. Never again did he want to feel powerless as others died and he remained strong.

"Earth might play host to all manner of alien races, but its people are in no way welcoming," she said, and she sounded bitter about it.

Did she have firsthand knowledge of that lack of welcome? "Humans will have no choice but to accept us."

"Oh, really? Just like that?"

"Just like that." He hoped. "And now, this standoff is becoming tiresome, Macy." Waiting, he decided, could be done in a more pleasurable way. He approached her, his yearning intensifying— soon, he would be touching her—the scent of honey drifting from him with increasing potency.

Her nose crinkled as though she smelled something distasteful, but her nipples were already pearled for him, pretty and perfect against her clothing. "What *is* that smell?"

"Arousal," he said, seeing no reason to deny it. He hadn't smelled the lust-craze, which was far more pungent than his fight-craze, in so long he'd despaired of ever smelling it again. Right now, he reveled in it. "Do not try to pretend it displeases you." Not while he could see the rosy flush of her cheeks.

Macy's lush mouth floundered open and closed, and her hands shook. "Arousal makes a man burn, yes? Well, I'll show you something else that burns." Using her thumb, she changed the setting of the pyre-gun and fired at him. Just as before, he grinned and sidestepped the beam—a yellow beam this time, which meant she was through trying to stun him and now wanted to fry him.

Swiftly he closed the distance, stopping mere inches from the barrel. "I believe I mentioned that I'm growing tired of this."

She almost fell backward with the force of her gasp. "And I grow tired of telling you to stay back!" Another shot.

This time, close as he was, he wasn't quite fast enough to dodge. The yellow-gold flame singed his upper arm. "That *hurt*."

"Really? I thought you liked to burn."

The scent of honey should have dissipated as that small patch of skin blistered and sizzled. It didn't. In fact, it only seemed to increase. That he desired her enough to emit the telltale perfume despite being injured was baffling. Even with his two-year abstinence, which blew his "I'm just desperate" theory.

How was she drawing more desire from him than any other female ever had?

She wasn't (naturally) golden, as he would have preferred. She wasn't biddable, as he was used to. Being perplexed by her, even enchanted, he understood. She was a novelty. But this much desire? Just then Breean suspected he would have wanted her even if he were sated.

Quite simply, she tempted him on every level.

In theory—he was full of those today—he could have disarmed her, and had her on the ground, penetrated, before she even realized what was happening, the lust-scent making her want it despite everything around her. While some part of him would have enjoyed that, because God knew, he was a man, the rest of him knew that her willing, wholehearted participation would be a thousand times sweeter. The hardest battles, he'd come to learn, elicited the most gratifying victories.

"You're surrounded, Macy. Drop the weapons and admit defeat. No one is going to hurt you."

"I'll admit defeat when I'm dead. How's that?"

"I'm afraid I cannot grant your request. Your death would disrupt my plans for you."

Her cheeks drained of color, and she lost some of her bravado. "W-what plans?"

Rather than answer her, he tilted his head to the side and regarded her intently, drinking in her sparkling blue eyes with that hint of green and remembering the way she'd moved only a few minutes before. "What planet do you hail from?"

Undiluted panic flooded her expression. Breath rasped from her, so loud in the ensuing silence that the sound of it scratched at his ears.

"I'm from here." She fired. "I'm from Earth."

He ducked. The ocher stream glided straight through the top outline of his essence, which had been left behind by his swiftness. "Liar."

"I am!"

"You say that after everything I've witnessed?"

"Yes." Fire.

Duck. Finally he cut through the rest of her personal space, nothing between them but a whisper. He might not want to force her, but he would have to subdue her before she ran or injured him further. "A human could not change faces and bodies as you do."

"What I am doesn't matter." Just as before, she backed away. Her bottom lip quivered, and tears suddenly glinted in her eyes, crystalline pools of pain, sorrow, and intensified fear. "Now, let the agents go and leave this planet! Please."

Were those tears real or fake? Either way, he actually experienced a desire to wrap his arms around her and . . . comfort her? Comfort a woman shooting at him? Strangely enough, yes. Desire truly did screw with a man's common sense.

There had to be a way to stop those tears, disarm her, *and* get that sweet body under him as quickly as possible, all without using physical brawn. He'd mentioned negotiating earlier. She hadn't seemed interested, but then, they hadn't been discussing her friends.

"Do you wish to bargain for the lives of your fellow agents?"

She stilled, though she didn't lower the weapons. The tears dried, at least. "B-bargain? What is it you want from me? What do I have that you could want?"

"I thought I had made that clear. I want *you*."

For several drags of time, she did nothing. Gave no reaction to his words. No matter her response, he had no plans to kill the agents. They were to be tickets allowing his men to freely roam Earth. He would trade a life for a life. An agent for a Rakan. And if AIR proved dishonorable, attacking after agreeing to such a trade, well, they alone would be responsible for the war that erupted. All he desired was peace for his men. Peace and a new, disease-free life.

Macy couldn't know that, and he didn't mind letting her think she was the cause of his benevolence. If mercy was what she found attractive, merciful he would seem to be.

Too eager, though, he would not be. That would lessen his power. His years negotiating fair prices for his fish had taught him that. "My offer will end in three seconds," he said. "One. Two."

"Three. My answer is no. I'll free them myself."

That intense look of concentration descended over her features again. He tensed, knowing what was coming this time. As her appearance changed from woman to Breean, from humanoid to Rakan, he kicked into hyperdrive. But she quickly gained her bearings and raced to the far edge of the clearing before he could catch her.

Their eyes met in a moment of charged electricity. In challenge. Then, she disappeared again. He was standing in the exact spot she'd vacated a split second later. As his spirit caught up to his body, he looked for her. Spotted her just ahead. Cursed and leapt forward. She might actually be better at this than he was.

She was rushing around the group of agents, trying to uncuff and wake them, and when that didn't work, drag them away. He was there in the next instant, right beside her and gripping her arm, doing his best to contain her without bruising her. Gasping, she jerked from his hold and disappeared.

When he next spotted her, she was darting through the trees, racing away. "Take the prisoners to the dungeon," he flung over his shoulder to his men, then gave chase. He still didn't understand how the AIR agents had known they would be arriving this night, but it didn't really matter. He'd planned to hunt down a few after he settled in, and now he wouldn't have to. Now he could simply begin the negotiations. After he caught Macy, that is.

A few times she actually slammed into the thick trunks. She'd *humph*, shake her head, and jump back into motion. Once he clasped her jacket; rather than slowing her down, his grip merely ripped the torn material farther, revealing a shirt that was equally torn, as well as the planes and hollows of *his* back.

The second time he grabbed her, he encountered only hair. Hating himself, he yanked. She screamed, but continued to surge forward, leaving several strands in his fist.

"Stop," he commanded, moving the knife he'd confiscated from her to his boot. When he caught her, and he would, he did not want her having access to it.

"Do you really have to think about my answer?"

"You're not going to escape me. You might as well give up before I'm forced to hurt you."

"Says the man who's losing." She maneuvered around another tree.

Several vehicles loomed ahead. Was anyone inside them? If so, and they hustled away with Macy, he could lose her for good. He knew it, didn't like it, and wouldn't allow it to happen. He was tiring from the day's excess of speed, but he ground his teeth and forced his arms and legs to work faster.

Air beat against him, chilled and biting. His blood ran hot, though, hotter than ever before. He could hear the woman's hoarse pants and imagined her breath floating over his naked chest, then dipping lower, until her mouth encircled his cock in damp heat. Oh, yes.

Arousal spread and gave him strength. Again he quickened his steps, his gaze raking over her body. Or rather, *his* body. Which was weird, but didn't cool his ardor. As if sensing the fervor of his stare, Macy flicked a wild glance behind her. Whatever she saw in his expression panicked her and in less than a blink, she was average height with short red hair and dark brown eyes. Aged skin, a little too tanned.

She slowed abruptly, as if losing her ability to sustain the swift pace right along with her grip of his image, and lost her balance. Down, she tumbled.

Breean was on top of her in the next instant, flipping her over and pinning her to a bed of leaves. Allowing his weight to settle atop her, he locked her arms over her head.

"You should have stopped," he panted.

"Calm down, calm down," she chanted, squeezing her eyes tightly shut. She dragged in a deep breath, released it, and was golden, muscled, and tall in seconds.

He scowled down at her. "Change back."

"No." Her eyelids popped open, and his own golden eyes glared up at him.

"Change!" No way would he kiss himself. And oh, yes, he was going to kiss her. Nothing could prevent him from doing so, not even the voice in his head demanding he be gentle with this woman.

"No!"

He ran his tongue over his teeth. If she possessed his appearance and his abilities, surely she possessed his vulnerabilities as well. Once, during a battle with a crowd of infected Rakan females, he'd been bitten in the side. The area had never healed properly and was a liability, for any type of contact would send him to his knees. Even now, there was a twinge beneath the scarred skin.

Knowing exactly where to touch, he reached under the torn shirt she wore and pinched. She screamed in pain.

"Change."

"No," she said, but it was a whimper this time.

He could not back down. He increased the

strength of his grip. "The agony will stop the moment you change."

"Fine, okay, yes, but I have to calm down first. Okay? Calm, calm." While she chanted, her eyelids closed again, and she pushed out a shaky breath. Her body slackened. Slowly, so slowly, her face began to rearrange itself, the length of her nose shortening, her lashes becoming longer, paler, her cheeks rounding. Her hair altered from golden to pale.

Disappointed, he shook his head. "I want to see the black-haired wench."

She blinked up at him in horror. "W-what?"

"The black-haired wench with the green eyes. I want to see her."

"How do you— No. Never mind," she snarled, suddenly struggling to gain her freedom. One of her arms succeeded, and she drilled three quick jabs into his nose before he could stop her.

He howled as he snagged her wrist. The little witch. This was going to end. Now. "The time for pain is over, Macy. Now you're going to kiss me and make me better."

THREE

Calm down, calm down, calm down, Aleaha sang in her mind. Hard thing to do, though. Nearly impossible. A man was on top of her, pinning her down, and he somehow knew what *she* looked like. Not Macy. Not another identity. But Aleaha. How did he know which face truly belonged to her when she hadn't shown it to him? How?

And how could she like this position so much? *I am your master,* he had said, as if he owned her. Rather than enjoying his weight, she should be clawing his eyes out and feeding them to him, then later allowing herself a case of wine and a good cry.

A cry with dry heaves and a runny nose, because the fact that she enjoyed this man in any way scared her. Even the first time she'd accidentally become someone else—when an overweight, balding man had jerked little Aleaha into an abandoned warehouse, touching her in ways no man should touch a child, and she'd felt herself expand, lengthen, and transform, she hadn't been this scared.

That man had let her go; this man wouldn't release her until she'd given him what he wanted. She sensed it with everything inside her. That's just how warriors were, and he was every inch the warrior. She should know—she'd inhabited that hard body. But she couldn't relent. He was a killer and her enemy, and he wasn't frightened of AIR. Maybe because he'd defeated the agents so easily.

Guaranteed he wouldn't defeat Mia, who was probably on her way right now. Something she'd assured herself a thousand times already. So where the hell was the commander?

Didn't matter, really, she told herself now. In the

end, AIR would catch him. They always caught their targets. And when they caught this one, he would tell them what he'd seen her do, tell them what she truly looked like.

Oh. God. She would be ruined. Why wait until after scratching Breean's eyes to have her cry? AIR would then turn their sights on her. She would be on the run, hunted like an animal, just as she feared. And what if they found a way to prevent her from changing faces? She would never again be able to hide.

Would that be so bad? her mind suddenly piped up. *You can't take over yet another person's life.*

She'd found a sense of contentment as Macy, yes, but the guilt she'd denied, well, it was easier to deny than to admit. In truth, she battled guilt every damn day. Hell, she lost more and more of *herself* every day, causing despair to blend with that guilt. She hated that she was living a life that had been cut short for someone else. Hated that she'd done nothing to earn the blessings bestowed upon her. Hated that her friend Bride, if she still lived, couldn't find her because she didn't have the courage to live as Aleaha.

Don't think about that now. Escape!

She bucked and strained under her captor's hold, unintentionally meshing their bodies and fusing heat, breasts against chest, thigh against thigh. Sweet heaven, it felt good, which increased her need for freedom. If he could make her crave him, despite her fear *and* dislike of him, he would destroy her life.

"Get off me!"

His eyes closed and his lips curled in a slow, satisfied smile. "You're trying to push me off, yet you're also gripping my shoulders, holding on. Which do you really want, female? For me to get off? Or for me to get *you* off?"

Damn it, she *was* holding on. How long since she'd allowed herself such close contact? Such warm, delicious contact? *There you go again, becoming distracted, wanting what you can't have.* Scowling, she pried her fingers from him, all the while continuing to flail. "Off. I want you off."

"Keep moving. Don't stop fighting." His penis was hard and thick and every time she arched, it pressed deep between her legs. "I'll get off, I promise."

If they'd been naked, he would have been inside her. And she would have liked it.

Okay. She was only making things worse—for both of them. She stilled, panting, and he moaned in disappointment. That strange honey fragrance wafted all around them, as if they lounged in a summer meadow of wild honeysuckle rather than a gloomy forest of ice.

She inhaled deeply to catch her breath, and her mind fuzzed just a bit. So good. Smelled so good. Why fight him when she could kiss him, as she'd craved earlier? She could delight in those muscles, enjoy every naughty inch of him.

Argh! "Just . . . let me go." Clearly, she couldn't win physically. "Please. I've let you go. Do the same for me."

His eyelids opened, revealing the golden glow of his irises. They were bright with hungry desire. A reflection of hers? "You should not have run." His voice was husky, rich. "The warrior in me liked it."

Liked was growled, layered with challenge and savagery.

For several seconds, her heart ceased beating. And when it finally kicked back into gear, her flailing and bucking renewed with more force, but did little to dislodge him. She didn't care that her actions rubbed them together. Didn't care that they aroused her as much as they did him. She had to escape before he tried to take things further—and she was tempted to let him.

Tempted? Ha! Willing to beg, more like.

Already her blood sang and her body ached from the delicious friction. When his erection stabbed at her clitoris, she had to clench her jaw to keep from moaning in ecstasy. "Let me go!"

"Your fate was sealed the moment I spotted you." Droplets of sweat beaded on his forehead, making the skin appear like liquid gold. "Actually, it was sealed the moment you stepped into this forest."

Damn him. What would Macy do in this situation? What would a real AIR agent do?

An AIR agent would already have cut off his balls, used them as earrings, and danced around his lifeless form. She could do no less. Maybe. Fine, she wouldn't be going near his balls, but she could definitely fight harder.

"I guess your fate was sealed, too." Aleaha lifted her head and bit him, using the only weapon she had at the moment: her teeth. They sank into his chin. The taste of sugar teased her tongue just as she remembered she feared contamination. Sugar? Mmm, as good as his scent. Heady, like aged wine. Clearly addictive, because she already craved another helping. Who cared about possible contamination, really? After all, Jaxon didn't think the Rakans were infected. So . . . Dinner, come to mama.

Breean ripped free with a howl. Golden blood trickled from the tiny punctures and onto her collarbone as he glared down at her. Angry as he was, the moonlight paid him nothing but tribute, washing over him with loving strokes. Had she truly just tried to eat him? Did that mean she was a cannibal like . . . no, no. Absolutely not. She didn't want to feast on anyone else.

"You bit me," he snarled. "Are you infected?"

"With what?"

"A disease. Any disease."

"No. Are you?" *Please say no.*

That soothed him, but only somewhat. "No. But what if you are, and you don't know it?"

"I'm telling you I'm healthy."

"Still. You should not have bitten me. Bloodshed is forbidden."

Forbidden? "But you made the agents bleed."

"Not me."

"If those responsible were under your charge, it might as well have been you."

A muscle ticked below his left eye.

"Just let me go, okay," she said, doing her best to sound strong and assured this time rather than frantic. She (might have) sounded breathless. "Otherwise, I *will* bite you again." A lie, but he couldn't know that. No way did she want to lose herself to that chomping urge again.

"Do not ever, *ever* draw my blood. Do you understand? You'll not like the consequences, I swear it."

Don't apologize. Don't weaken. "Well, get off me and save us both. I can't breathe."

He rolled his eyes. "Now you are just being silly. You're talking. Therefore, you can breathe."

Smart bastard. "You have no right to hold me like this."

"As the victor of this battle, I have every right." Another of those slow, wicked grins tugged at the corners of his beautiful golden lips, and her heart skipped another beat. "Oh, the things I'm going to do to you. And I know what you're thinking. Is he open to suggestions? The answer is yes."

Gorgeous and a mind reader. But she said, "Liar. I've suggested you get off me about a thousand times." How she'd love to cut that grin off him. And maybe his clothes. *Stop thinking like that, you slut!*

"No. You commanded." He anchored her wrists to the ground with one hand and sifted the length of her still-pale hair through his fingers with the other. "I think I will like the dark strands better. Why do you hide them?"

No way she'd answer that and incriminate herself further. *Think, Aleaha.* To escape him, she needed a weapon. Besides her teeth. She'd tried to sheathe her pyre-guns at her waist while running through the trees, but the unusual velocity of her motions had made her clumsy, and she'd dropped them. But she'd also had a knife, a knife Breean had taken and secured to his back . . .

Her eyes widened. Yes. Yes! Keeping it had been very stupid of him because now she could steal it back.

"My guess?" he continued, oblivious to her plans. "You don't want anyone to know your true identity."

"Wow, detective. I'm so glad you're on the case." She hoped her sarcasm hid both her chagrin that he'd already figured her out and her excitement that this battle between them could very well be over in minutes. All she had to do was convince him to free her hands. "For the record, *this* is my identity."

"Once again, you lie. *Alien.*"

"I'm human, damn it!" Macy was human, so Aleaha was, too. That's how it had to be.

"You want to be, are trying to act like it, but you're not. AIR had to know."

A fear she harbored, no matter how much she relaxed. "Go to hell."

"Perhaps I'm already there." His gaze lowered to her mouth. "Soft," he said. "What's your real name, alien? Something that fits your real face, I'm sure."

"I *am* human. And I already told you my name." Shivering, trying to ignore the white-hot pulses hammering at every point of contact, she said, "Release my hands. Please."

"So you can hit me again? I think not."

"So I can *feeeel* you." She didn't have to force the words out; they wisped out of her mouth of their own accord.

He didn't pause to ask what had changed her mind; she was instantly freed. Her hands slid to his back, as if she meant to grab him and pull him closer. His nostrils flared at that first tentative, seemingly willing touch, and he braced himself on his elbows, pressing deeper into her body.

Automatically her knees fell open, welcoming him. She couldn't stop them. That honey scent . . . His hips surged forward, his erection sliding over her clothed but already moist folds. She gasped, unable to stifle the satisfied sound. And in that suspended moment, she almost forgot her true purpose.

"That's the way, Macy."

"Don't call me that. Call me—" The moment the words hit her ears, she sucked in a breath. Why would she want him to call her by her real name, especially when she'd refused to tell him what it was? She was Macy now, and she had to remain Macy, even with lovers. Not that she would become this guy's lover.

"Call you what, then?"

"Ale— Macy." Damn it! She'd almost told him. Again. What kind of moron was she?

A perverted moron at that, since she found the man responsible for the fall of her friends so damned sensual, erotic, and wholly masculine. A drug that overshadowed any hint of inhibition. Just looking at him, she wanted to drown in sensation. *For the sake of the others, don't lose focus.*

"Do you like it soft or do you like it rough, Ale—Macy?" he purred.

Why not both? *Knife. Get the knife.* "I—I don't know. Why don't you find out?" Inch by inch, she trekked her trembling fingers down his sides, not stopping until she reached the coarse material of the holster. Almost there . . . almost . . . Her palm found smooth material and hard muscle, but no weaponlike bulge.

"What's your real name? Tell me. Please."

Would he never give up?

"I promise not to tell," he murmured. "You have my word. But how can I kiss you properly if I don't know what to call you? Please."

She didn't want him to leave her yet. Not until she had the knife. And she feared he would indeed walk away if she refused yet again. That was the only reason she was giving in, damn it! "Aleaha," she found herself saying. She didn't trust him, but part of her did want him to know, which was why she didn't simply lie. "Happy now?" Where the hell was the knife?

"Aleaha." He closed his eyes for a moment, as though he savored the reverberation. "Much better. And now that we've got that settled . . . are you looking for this, Aleaha?" In a movement so swift she saw only the remnants of his spirit, he palmed a blade from his boot and waved the gleaming silver tip over her nose. "I moved it during our chase. Just in case. Over the past two years, I have learned to plan ahead."

With a yelp, she shrank deeper into the cold ground. Ice-covered rocks stabbed into her bared back where her jacket and T-shirt were torn. "If you cut me, I'll . . ." She'd what? Bleed all over him and ruin his clean clothes. Like he didn't know that already. She was screwed.

"I told you, there will be no bloodletting. Besides, I like the passion and concern you've shown for your friends," he said, tossing the blade out of reach. Then he baffled her by bending and sniffing her neck, his nose brushing the sensitive skin there, the thundering pulse. "I won't punish you for that."

Another shiver rushed her. *Concentrate.* Without the knife, there was no reason to remain in this position. No *intelligent* reason. "Let me up and I'll negotiate for the agents' freedom," she said, recalling his earlier attempt at bartering. "Just like you wanted."

"The time for that is over." The inflection in his voice was dark, carnal, and animalistic. His gaze lowered to her lips. "Now I believe I promised you a kiss."

"Don't you dare kiss me." The words were automatic, but there was no heat behind them. Passion, like fear, was not a good thing for her. Yet a part of her wanted him to take her mouth anyway. Take everything she had to give and demand more, forcing her to feel, to need, to crave. Finally. As she'd dreamed of for so long.

"Don't cut you, don't kiss you. Anything else I shouldn't do?" She started to tick off an entire list, but he added, "Never mind. I'm through with this conversation." And then his lips were meshed with hers, his hot tongue probing for entrance.

She flattened her palms against his chest and shoved. He didn't budge. In fact, he grabbed hold of her wrists and repinned them over her head, smashing her breasts. into his chest—mmm, good, so good—at the same time cupping her nape and forcing her jaw up, preventing her lips from moving away.

"Open," he commanded against her mouth.

She shook her head, even though denying him was one of the most difficult things she'd ever done.

"Open." He applied a hard pressure with his chin, creating the smallest of gaps.

Still she resisted. She'd lose control, and he'd find himself kissing a stranger, maybe even another man. He'd become enraged, disgusted, and she wouldn't be able to blame him.

Determined, he changed tactics. The pressure gentled, and he pulled back slightly. Soft, so softly, he traced his tongue over the seam of her lips. "Open. Please. You'll like what I do. I swear."

Don't give in, her mind beseeched, even as she recalled all the nights she'd lain in bed, aching so badly she'd wanted to die, wishing intimacy weren't so dangerous for her. Wishing a lover could please her without discovering her secrets. She'd been down that road a few times, and she couldn't allow herself to take it ever again.

The first time, she'd been regarded as a freak. The second attempt had ended in a fight for her life. The third—and final—attempt had started rocky but had ended successfully. Or so she'd thought, until she was chased down and nearly locked up.

Breean has seen you in action, so he already knows what you can do.

But he's a monster.
So are you.
I am not!

The internal debate ended with an, *Mmm, he smells better with every second that passes, like cinnamon and honey, wildflowers and sex.* Down-and-dirty, nothing-held-back sex. The kind she'd always fantasized about having while she touched herself, alone, always alone, finger dancing over her clitoris.

She must have unintentionally obeyed him and opened her mouth because suddenly his tongue was pushing past her teeth, stroking, thrusting, twining. Every nerve ending in her body leapt to instant life. Liquid heat flooded the apex of her thighs, and she trembled.

"Sweet," he praised. "So sweet."

Make him stop, she thought, dazed, even as she wound her legs around his waist and locked her ankles, arching her back. His erection rubbed the new center of her world, and she gasped, lost to sensation. As feared, she felt her appearance change, expanding from average height to a bit taller, a little more rounded.

Shockingly, he didn't seem to mind. Seemed to like it, actually, as he hissed in a breath. "Again."

She did, unable to help herself. She arched, appearance changing to someone shorter, rounder. They moaned simultaneously, then his tongue was back inside her mouth, hotter now, harder, and he was sucking her the way he might suck on a woman's clit, laving and savoring every drop of moisture. Their teeth banged together as he drew her closer. Her still-hard nipples pressed into his chest, abrading deliciously.

"M-my shirt." She wanted to tell him to rip it the rest of the way off her, but was having trouble forming the words. She ached, oh, she ached, and that ache demanded all of her attention. A touch, a glide. *Something.* Except, she felt the hair on her head shorten, her legs lengthen, and something harden between her legs—and it wasn't Breean.

There wasn't time even to gasp in horror. Because of her sudden spike of fear, the male form was quickly replaced. This time her hair grew and the color of her skin went from tanned to pale, her body from lean to lush. In a snap, however, she changed yet again. Female, still, but longer, slimmer. She clutched at Breean, relieved, needy. He hadn't erupted when she'd sprouted a penis. He hadn't even stopped kissing her.

"I knew I'd like the dark hair." His tight clamp eased on her nape and his fingers slid to the front, stopping at her voice box, fanning over her pulse, then dipping to her breast. He kneaded the soft curve.

With his acceptance came a flood of uncontrollable, undiluted desire. And holy hell, did she have pent-up desire. That touch, so tender, so innocent, wasn't enough.

More, she thought. "I need . . . I need . . ."

"Me." He jerked the material up, revealing her navel, her bra—which he moved, too—and then her breasts. Her stomach quivered as he studied her. Cold air beat around them, but she felt only heat. Only need. "Pretty," he said, sounding as if he were in some sort of trance. "Like berries. Pink, ripe. Mine."

He palmed her, skin to skin this time. Yes! When he thumbed a nipple, plucked it, she lost hold on reality, arching, writhing, ready to beg. There was only amazement, wonder, pleasure. So hot, blistering, singeing all the way to the bone. "Yes, yes!"

"I could touch you forever, I think."

"Lick," she commanded. Something was flowing through her veins, so potent she was almost drunk with it. That desire, yes, but also . . . what? His scent? It was strong, heady, dizzying, but could it have caused this sweet urgency? This sizzling desperation? No longer did she care where she was, who she was with, or how many times she shifted. Satisfaction was the only thing that mattered.

Her body was not her own. In that moment, it was his. Breean's. His to do with whatever he pleased. She had no shame, truly no goal save climax.

"Give me," she said, only then realizing he hadn't obeyed her. He was still staring down at her, tension bracketing his eyes. "Lick."

"I don't think I'll ever tire of looking at you."

"That's great. But look and touch at the same time," she said.

He chuckled.

Finally his lips settled over one of her nipples, tongue flicking against it.

Raspy gasps escaped her, and she rode his cock up and down, sliding, sliding, still desperate, so desperate. He sucked, hard. She cried out, closer to heaven in that moment than she'd been in her entire life. Happily, willingly swimming in pleasure, the need for release a constant ache between her legs.

"More," she demanded. "Harder."

This time he obeyed quickly, giving her what she wanted. She chewed on her bottom lip, tasting blood, wishing it were *his* lip she nibbled. His mouth, his tongue. Perhaps his cock, thrusting in and out, filling her, stretching her jaw. Her tongue would lave the thick head, sucking, sucking, until he was wrung dry, until—

Who are you? drifted through her mind. *Who is this sensual creature you've become?*

His fingers abandoned her breast, only to slip lower to the waist of her pants. In a few seconds, he was going to delve past her panties and sink straight to the heart of her. He'd feel her wetness. He'd work those naughty fingers into her one by one. He'd pump them in and out, driving her to the brink.

Yes, yes. That's what she wanted; there was no fighting this desire. This fog. Yes, fog. That's what it was. That's what was swimming through her veins, clouding her judgment and lighting her on fire. Blazing, delicious. And wrong.

Wrong?

"S-stop," she managed to gasp out. The madness had to stop. And if she just paused a moment, she could figure out *why* this was wrong.

Instantly, he stilled. He was panting as their gazes clashed. "You want it," he growled low in his throat. "You want me."

"No," she said, then more loudly, "No!" It

wasn't her writhing, but someone else. Someone he'd created.

Nailed it again, she thought. Somehow he was changing her, making pleasure her only concern. And okay, yeah. Some part of her suspected this was her fault. That she simply wanted him more than she had ever wanted another. But that was wrong for different reasons, so she *would* still stop him.

"I can feel the desire inside you. You need a man."

"Not you." *You, only you.* Damn it. *Stay strong.*

"*I* need a woman."

Pick me! Strong, remember? "Not me."

Desire was blended with irritation and anger, all three fiercely directed at her. He looked frightening just then, reminding her of the warrior who'd attacked and defeated AIR's best in a matter of minutes.

Now she felt shame. Now she felt guilt she would never be able to deny. What kind of woman tongued her enemy, no matter the reason, while her teammates languished?

"You deny us both, Aleaha."

Her stomach clenched, but she forced herself to say, "I don't know you, I don't like you. Of course I deny us both."

"Very well." He popped to his feet, dragging her with him. He was scowling. "In time you will learn about me, and you will like me. That's a command."

"I haven't obeyed you once." Or maybe she had. The details were as foggy as her mind. "What makes you think I'll start now?"

He peered down at her, one golden brow arched.

"I'm halfway there already. Your nipples are still hard."

"So?" Cheeks flushing, she fought the urge to cover herself. "It's still cold out here."

"You begged for me."

That was not something she needed to be reminded of; she remembered, both hating and loving herself for it. Hating because of all the baggage that came with the pleasure, and loving because, well, it had felt so damn good. But just as soon as she'd spent a few minutes alone, she'd love herself to earth-shattering completion and could hate him without this pesky need being in the way.

"Temporary insanity. I also told you to stop."

Clearly frustrated, he tangled a hand through his hair. "Do you have an answer for everything?"

"Yes."

His tongue swiped over his teeth. She'd tasted that tongue, almost bitten that tongue.

Never again, she told herself. Enough stalling. It was time to act. She pictured Macy in her mind and felt her body respond accordingly. Her hair shortened, as did her legs. Her boobs grew—a lot. Much better. This was her shield. Her armor against the world. And now against Breean.

He scowled at her but didn't comment. "Come. There is much to do and I've wasted enough time chasing you."

Yes, she'd made sure of that. But still the backup agents hadn't shown. Aleaha prayed nothing had happened to them. With the bleak turn this night had already taken, however, she doubted the prayer would be heeded.

FOUR

Breean's warriors had gathered the AIR agents, as ordered, and started for the underground holding cell they'd hurriedly constructed on one of their trips here. It had taken him fifteen minutes to catch up with them and their human cargo, Aleaha tossed over his shoulder, and then another five to reach the dilapidated house they'd confiscated on the outskirts of the city; it was the perfect hideout, since the area was seemingly forgotten by Earth's inhabitants. Maybe because there was no vegetation or animals, the air drier than dirt, stinging the nostrils as though acid were being inhaled. It was still cold here, but there was none of that beautiful white snow.

Breean left Aleaha locked up in one of the bedrooms, comfortable and fed, yet separated from her people, for an entire Earth week. She tried to escape at least twice a day, but he caught her each time, attuned to her in a way he didn't understand.

He'd hoped to develop a resistance to her while he saw to the defenses of his true home in the city. He'd hoped to develop a resistance to her while the days passed.

Despite his best efforts, Aleaha never left his mind. His only hope now was that time had softened her dislike of him, that she craved another of his kisses. The first had nearly burned him alive. No woman had ever tasted so sweet or felt so perfect against him. And, yes, others had clutched him with utter abandon, moaning their pleasure, desperate for more, but none had ever affected him like this. Why, he didn't know.

No longer could he delude himself, even slightly, into thinking that any other woman would have done. It was her he wanted. Her specifically. Aleaha. The fierce glow in her eyes, the sharpness of her wit. The challenge of winning so strong a prize. What would she look like when she smiled? How carefree would her laughter sound?

He had to know.

Finally, it was time to move everyone into the permanent home. It had better security and was in a livable location. Yes, they would be more easily spotted by AIR, which had, thank the blessed sea, failed to find his hideaway on the outskirts, but it was worth the risk. He planned to contact them soon anyway, and start the bargaining process at last.

By the time the prisoners were taken care of, night had fallen. Breean returned to the wasteland with half of his forces. He couldn't contain his eagerness as he entered the house and walked down the crumbling hallway to gather Aleaha. What would he find? The blond goddess or the dark-haired vixen? Eagerness to match his own or anger?

He was actually shaking with anticipation as he unlocked Aleaha's door. *I won't bed her until she begs for it*, he vowed. After what she'd already given him, nothing else would be acceptable. The hinges creaked open, and he stepped inside. She stood in front of the bed, watching him warily, pale hair dancing around her shoulders.

His heart thundered in his chest. In arousal, yes, but also in disappointment. He'd wanted the vixen.

She wore the T-shirt and jeans he'd brought her, and the material hugged her body nicely.

"Nothing to say?" he asked, feeling tongue-tied himself. Never had he wanted something so badly. Never had he had to tread so carefully.

She arched a brow, as stubborn as ever. "What about, and stop me if you've heard this one, let me go. Let my friends go."

So. She still meant to resist him. He revealed no hint of his frustration. "You will stay with me. Your friends . . . maybe."

"Why keep us? You're going to destroy us anyway. That's why you're here, right?"

He frowned. "What do you mean, I plan to destroy you?"

"Why else would you be here?" Every word was layered with disgust. "I've been thinking about it, since that's the only thing to do here, and I've decided you're here to prepare the way for that stupid queen."

"What are you talking about? I have no queen." Not anymore. Apparently, the Rakan queen had been one of the first females to succumb to the disease. She had killed her own husband. Her own children.

Aleaha studied him, her expression pensive. "I know you're not ill since I bit you and haven't exhibited any symptoms, and I know you're Rakan rather than Schön, but why else would you have come to Earth if not to help the Schön queen? An alien was interrogated recently and revealed that warriors would be arriving that night in the forest with the sole desire of clearing a path for the Schön queen. Then boom, you arrive. You take out AIR. What's that if not clearing a path?"

Everything inside him locked down. First in panic—not again, he couldn't put his men through that again—and then in rage. "Schön? You expected those vile Schön?"

"Yes. We'd already killed a few of them, and you and yours won't be any different."

"We would *never* help them. We hate them." Mouth suddenly dry, he pivoted on his heel, exited the room, and locked the door behind him. He was trembling again, but this time it had nothing to do with desire.

"Hey," he heard her call. "If we were mistaken about your race, it's possible we were mistaken about you following the Schön queen. Come back! I'm not saying I believe you, I'm just saying we can talk about this."

Breean quickly called together all of the men who had accompanied him. They filled the living room, spilling out into the hallway. As he told them what he had just learned, they reacted first with panic, as he had. And then the rage set in.

"Bastards."

"Murderers!"

A couple jumped up to pace, bumping into everyone around them.

"I will leave the decision up to you," he said. "If you want to leave, we will leave. If you want to stay, we will stay." Either way, Breean wasn't letting Aleaha go. He wouldn't leave her here to face the deadly Schön on her own. Because she was female, she would be one of the first to fall. But knowing her as he thought he did, she would not go easily.

The debate began.

"We've worked so hard, finally found a home. We can't just abandon it now."

"Yes, we can. We deserve peace."

"Will we ever truly know peace? We are outsiders wherever we go. Here, at least, otherworlders aren't killed on sight."

"I can't watch another home be destroyed."

"And what happens when the Schön ruin this planet?" Talon, his second in command, scrubbed a hand down his tired face. "They will move on to another, perhaps the next one we have chosen. We need to destroy them. Now. Finally."

Breean agreed. "At least here we know there are medications and technology to combat such a loathsome enemy. That's why we chose it. Besides, my female told me that AIR defeated the first diseased warriors who came here."

"Think of it. We can kill the Schön, as we've dreamed for so long," Talon added. "For what they did to us. For what they did to our loved ones."

"How are we to kill them? They can make themselves invisible. As we well know, it's impossible to fight an unseen enemy."

That cast a gloomy shadow over the men, memories consuming them.

"AIR obviously knows how to fight them, and there are ways to get the information from them. So tell me." Breean eyed them one by one. "Leave? Or stay?"

In the end, it was unanimous. They would stay. They would fight. Or try to. If they died in the process, at least they would die as the soldiers they'd become.

"I am proud of you," he told them. "Surrender is unacceptable. Once we are established in our new home, we will figure out a plan of action. As for tonight, we have much to do. Go about your duties. I will meet you outside."

As they strode off, Breean returned to Aleaha's room. This time, she was seated at the edge of the bed. Still blond. But, damn, if she didn't make his heart stop. "Come." He waved her over.

"Don't you want to talk?"

"No."

She stood on shaky legs. "Well. Are you sure you're not going to take off again, leaving me here?"

"I'm sure."

"Why did you rush off like that?"

"You mentioned my greatest enemy." He saw no

reason to lie. Not when he might gain information. "My men needed to know what they will soon be up against."

"Oh. So you really do hate the Schön?"

"Yes." Guess they would talk, after all. "Does AIR have any idea what those bastards can do? I know you told me some were killed, but I just want to make sure you understand the danger."

"Yes. They are infected with a disease that turns people into cannibals."

"That disease destroyed my planet. That disease is the reason we are here."

"Oh," she said again. "I'm—I'm sorry. You aren't . . . infected, are you? I mean, I know we've had this conversation and I know I bit you and tasted your blood and I haven't experienced any unusual symptoms, but you've got me worried."

"No, I'm not infected. You would be able to tell if I were. The skin turns gray, the eyes sink into the skull. *I* would have been the one to bite *you* that night in the forest."

She gulped, but that was her only response.

"How did your people defeat them?" he asked.

"I don't know. I wasn't working for them at the time."

He was glad. Though he wanted the information, badly, he didn't like the thought of Aleaha engaging such fierce creatures. At least there was hope, a way to win. He would like to work with AIR and increase the chance for victory, but he didn't think they'd welcome him.

"All I know," she continued, "is what I've already told you. Several warriors came here. They were crushed, and now their queen, the most powerful of them, is on her way."

Oh, yes. The queen was indeed the most powerful. She was also heartless, selfish, determined, and irresistible.

"Come," he said again. For the moment, there was nothing else to say on the subject.

"Are you taking me to my friends?"

Rather than start a debate—because no, he wasn't taking her to her friends—he remained silent as he escorted her out of the home and into the backyard, keeping her beside him with an arm draped around the feminine dip of her waist. She didn't try to escape. Perhaps she'd realized there was no place to go, nothing around them. Perhaps, as concerned as she was about her fellow agents, she didn't want to leave without them.

Or perhaps he wasn't giving her enough credit. Maybe she meant to bide her time and kill him while he slept. If he was lucky, she stayed because she wanted another kiss. Had she thought of him at all while inside that room? Dreamed of him the way he'd dreamed of her?

"The air," she said, nose wrinkling in distaste as her eyes scanned the darkness.

"Cold?" He removed his jacket and placed it around her shoulders.

"Yes, but also pungent."

"You become used to it." He peered down at her,

hungry. "Change for me. Please. No one will see."
There were no trees offering solace, but there was
a tall iron fence surrounding the barren yard. Plus,
there were no other homes nearby. They'd all collapsed.

She didn't pretend to misunderstand. "I will if
you'll tell me where the agents are. I never heard
them, and I'm trying not to go crazy, imagining them
d-dead." There at the end, her voice shook.

"They were underground, in a cell not far from
where we are standing." Truth. He didn't mind telling her since they had already been moved to the
new home. "I swear to you, they are alive and well
and will remain so. They are also angry as hell that
you are not with them."

"I-I believe you. That sounds like them. Thank
you." Her relief was palpable. "And now for my part
of the bargain." Again, she glanced around. When she
saw that they were alone, she began to grow several
inches, becoming leaner. Her long dark hair fell over
his wrist, and he basked in the silkiness of it. Her eyes
were so deep a green he would have sworn he was
standing in a lush, dewy meadow every time he peered
into them. Her skin was translucent, smooth, and, as
easily as she'd responded to him, probably sensitive.
She might be able to come with only a caress.

A man could hope, anyway.

Actually, a man could hope for a lot more. Even
now, he could taste her in his mouth, rainstorms and
passion. So much passion he'd nearly drowned in it.
Had *wanted* to drown in it. No matter which guise

she'd worn, even as the male—surprising, but something he wasn't going to question—she'd tasted the same. And he'd loved it. She could have eaten him alive with those sharp little teeth, and he would have died with a smile on his face.

"Beautiful," he said. The clothes were a bit too short for her now, though they bagged over her smaller chest and leaner waist, but, oh, did the sight of her like this please him.

A tremor slid the length of her spine, brushing her shoulder against his chest. "Thank you."

Renewed desire pounded through him, hot, readying his body for her. If he wasn't careful, his resolve to wait until she begged would snap and he'd try to seduce her. Here and now. No matter who watched. Even now that honey scent was wafting from him. . . .

"What are you going to do to me?" she asked, her voice raspy. Did she smell it? Yearn for him? "What are you going to do to the other agents?"

The doorway to the underground tunnel was thrown open, Talon climbing the makeshift steps, a metal box in his hands, barking orders in the Rakan language to the others, who were carrying large boxes of their own.

Aleaha gasped at the wide, dark pit now revealed. "Is the cell down there?" she asked, her previous questions forgotten. Then, she must have realized that someone else was seeing her true form, because the black locks began to lighten.

"Don't change. Please. I did not expect him to

appear so soon, but hiding now will do no good. Besides, he will not betray you."

A moment passed, but then her hair returned to its full, dark glory. He offered her a grateful smile and was rewarded with a hesitant twitch of her lips. One day he would make her laugh. One day he would—

Forget his purpose if he didn't look away. "Do you need more men?" he asked Talon in Rakan. There was no reason for Aleaha to have this information, and every reason for her *not* to have it. "I want us out of here as quickly as possible."

Talon's golden braids slapped his temples as he faced Breean. "No," he said. "Cain and Syler just arrived. Said they couldn't listen to the AIR agents any longer. I've got them carrying the last of the weapons."

"Were the agents still demanding their release?"

"Yes. But they also want to know what we did with their dead." Disgust dripped from Talon's voice when he uttered the word *dead*.

"When Cain and Syler return, they may explain that we buried them." It was the truth. But Breean was as disgusted as his friend that humans had died. Killing the agents so viciously and so violently had been unnecessary. They'd had things under control—a few of their own men had been stunned, yes, but no one had been injured—so there'd been no need to resort to bloodshed.

Because of that bloodshed, he'd had to command everyone to burn their clothes and bathe the moment they'd reached this dilapidated, forgotten house. No exceptions. Not even for the prisoners.

"Speaking of AIR," Talon said, "neither Cain nor Syler saw any sign of them, here or there, during their journey. You were right. There is no better time to finish our switch."

"Good."

"What shall I do with Marleon? Leave him," which meant, *kill him here,* "or take him with me?" Which meant, *kill him there.* "I didn't know what to do with him, so I kept him locked up here."

Marleon was the warrior, the traitor, who'd whisked inside several of the agents, taking over their bodies and forcing them to shoot themselves. He'd been sequestered this entire week while Breean considered his punishment. A punishment he didn't want to deliver, for he loved Marleon like a brother. But there was no way around this. He'd merely been putting off the inevitable.

"Take him. It's past time I made an example of him."

"Consider it done." Talon's gaze shifted momentarily to Aleaha. "I know that you wanted no reminder of her while she was locked away, so I didn't ask what I've been dying to ask. Now that you have her . . . did you learn how she was able to become you?"

He sighed. "Not yet, but I will find out."

"The change was amazing. You are keeping her for yourself, I gather." Talon switched to the Earth language on the last sentence, a hungry gleam in his golden eyes.

"Yes," Breean answered, a little stiff.

"No sharing?"

His hands clenched at the thought, dark possessiveness clamoring through him. Aleaha stiffened as well. "No."

"She—"

"Is mine."

A nod and a grin from Talon; a growl from Aleaha.

"I thought as much. Very well," Talon said. "We have been monitoring the headsets from the agents as you told us to do, but the female voice has stopped talking in them. And this morning, Torrence found and destroyed the cameras they used to watch."

"Oh, God." Aleaha groaned, paling. "The cameras. I had forgotten about them. They must have seen me . . . what I . . . oh, God."

"Excellent," he told his second, ignoring her outburst for the moment. Otherwise he would have drawn her into his embrace and forgotten his purpose yet again. "How much do you lack before the tunnel is empty?"

"We're down to the last."

"Finish up, then. I'll stop bothering you."

Talon returned to directing the men, and Breean's attention returned to the woman as if pulled by an unbreakable cord. Finally. Her lips were puffy, as if she'd been chewing them, and a bright, vivid red. Like blood. He should have been repulsed.

He wasn't.

Moonlight bathed her, and he would have sworn stars twinkled around her, as drawn to her loveliness as he was. Her eyes sparkled like emeralds, and strands of dark hair whipped around her face.

Obviously, her agent's mind had flipped on. She was studying the surrounding area with sharp precision, taking in every detail. He could not wait to have all that concentration directed at him.

As if sensing his perusal, she faced him. His desire must have been evident because she shivered, gulped, even inched backward, sinking deeper into night's shadows. But when she realized what she'd done, she straightened and reclaimed her position in the moon's amber rays. A true warrior, she was.

"What's inside the chests?" she asked, only the slightest catch in her voice.

He liked that voice, layered as it was with equal measures of fear, courage, and sexuality. "Weapons."

Her attention whipped back to the boxes, as if she could burn a hole through the metal with her gaze. "What kind?"

"Does it matter? They all do the same thing." Kill.

"We've got everything," Talon called.

Good. Breean didn't remove his focus from Aleaha. "Close the pit and head out." He wanted the girl to himself for a while longer. "We'll be along shortly."

"As you wish."

He couldn't stay long; in a few hours, the sun would rise. Only once had he made the mistake of coming to Earth during daybreak. The sun was simply too hot for a Rakan's golden skin, too blistering, something they weren't used to since Raka had three alternating moons and a small, sun-like orb that produced only the barest hint of light.

From the corner of his eye, he saw Talon and a few others secure the tunnel doorway, then gather their supplies and stride away. He should be helping them—he never asked his men to do something he wouldn't do himself—but again, he couldn't force himself to walk away from this moment with Aleaha.

"I thought the agents were in there. Where are you moving them?" she demanded. "*When* are you moving them? What if they're injured and need medical attention. And why did you leave me in that room so long?"

He didn't have to answer, but he found that he wanted to alleviate her concerns. "They've already been moved to a house in the city. I moved them for safety reasons. They are uninjured."

"Take me there."

Soon. "Kiss me first."

For a moment, only a moment, stark desire played over her delicate features. But it quickly disappeared, obliterated by fear. He sighed. Why did she continue to fear him? He had not hurt her, even though he'd had every opportunity.

Then that same intense look of concentration darkened her features, the one he'd seen that first night. She meant either to run or to challenge him. Sadly, there was no time to indulge her. "I would not do that, were I you. It . . . excites me." Truth. "And I will catch you, you know I will."

She scowled. But slowly, bit by bit, her body

slackened. "What I know is that you're a bastard."

"How so? I did not force you to my bed. Did not starve you. Kept the others away from you."

"Just . . . shut up. You're so annoying."

His lips twitched in amusement and his scrutiny intensified, as if he could discern everything about her simply by looking. What did she like, what did she dislike? What foods did she favor? How many men had she had?

The last had him ready to commit murder. Didn't take much these days.

Relax. She's with you. That's all that matters. Up close like this, he could see a scattering of freckles across her nose. Pretty. Unlike Rakan freckles, which were clear and sparkling like diamonds, these were tiny and brown, adorable. He reached out, intending to sift her hair through his fingers and trace the strands over those freckles.

She grabbed hold of his wrist to stop him. Where their skin met, he sizzled.

"No touching," she rasped.

"Silly girl." He increased the pressure, her strength no match for his, and tunneled his fingers to her scalp as he'd wished. The strands were thick and possessed a bit of curl. They were silky, like polished ebony. He reveled in the beauty, the luxury. "I can do anything I want."

"If that's your mind-set, I feel sorry for the women in your life."

"No reason for you to do so. They are all dead. And, no, I didn't kill them. Not with pleasure or menace. As I told you, they died of the Schön disease."

"Oh. I'm sorry," she said softly. Her expression turned pensive. "Your mother, too?"

He nodded. "And sisters."

"I'm sorry," she said again. "I wouldn't wish that kind of pain on anyone. Even you."

A sweet proclamation. One that disarmed him. For it proved that she was more than a soldier, more than a captive. She cared. She felt. Even for a man she deemed her enemy. While every part of his body already seemed to recognize her on a level he didn't understand, craving her, needing her, his mind now followed suit.

"You have lost someone yourself, I take it?"

She nodded sadly. "My friend, Bride. She was like my mother and sister rolled into one."

"How did she die?"

"I don't know." She chewed her bottom lip. "She could still be alive. *Is* alive. She has to be. I've been searching for her for years, but haven't found a trace of her."

"She could have traveled to another planet."

"No. She wouldn't have left me. Not willingly."

Perhaps he would find this Bride for her. Give her the woman as a present. As for now, he just wanted to continue basking in her. "Hiding your true hair should be a crime," he said. Soon that hair of hers would be splayed over his pillow. Her body would be draped over his bed, open and eager, spread completely. For him. Only him. She'd be wet, soaking him.

He might even watch her touch herself before he joined her. Might watch her sink her fingers between her legs, slipping inside that tight little sheath, arching into every glide, moaning, begging him to finish it. He nearly moaned himself. *Stop thinking like that.*

"People do whatever they have to do to survive." There was a trace of guilt in her words.

One of the clues to the mystery of her slipped into place. "And you would have been killed if your true identity was known? Sweet, to do whatever is needed to protect yourself is admirable, not shameful."

Her eyes narrowed, and he wasn't sure who her anger was directed at. Him. Or her. "You don't know what you're talking about. I'm—"

"No more lies, Aleaha. Please."

Her jaw clenched, the grind of her teeth loud in the surrounding silence. "You're not going to get away with this. AIR will catch you. They always do. And you'll be executed on sight as a predatory alien."

"Clearly your AIR team couldn't find their asses if I handed them over in paper bags."

A mix of fury and affront claimed her features, lending them a fiery edge. This time he had no trouble telling who had earned the bulk of her emotion. "You had the advantage that night. Somehow you knew we were there waiting."

"Not true. We knew nothing of the sort. You, however, knew we were coming. Therefore, you had the advantage. Yet I still consider that a fair fight."

"I doubt you know the meaning of *fair*."

"Of course I know the meaning. I just prefer to

fight dirty. Fairness is an idea most often touted by the defeated. I'll use any advantage I have, on anyone, at any time. That's how battles are won."

"Oh, you mean like this?" Her knee jerked up and she nailed him in the balls.

He hunched over, wishing he could vomit his intestines. Anything to stop the excruciating pain. At this point, he might even have been willing to cut off his cock. The burn was agonizing, like someone had set fire to his pants. Worse, she would have darted off if he hadn't grabbed her wrist and held on tight.

"Well?" There was satisfaction in her tone, even though there would be no escaping.

"Yes," he gasped out. "Like that." After an endless, strangled minute, he was able to drag air into his lungs, cooling that searing fire. Finally, he straightened and released her—but he was still panting. He couldn't fault her, however. She'd certainly fought dirty.

"Before you say anything," she said in that smug tone, "I refuse to kiss you there and make you feel better."

That had been an option? Hold everything. He might endure the pain again for such a kiss. "Shall I fight dirty with you now?"

Her lips twitched in amusement. "You can if you want, but I don't think a knee to my groin would have the same effect."

"I didn't say I'd knee you there, now, did I?"

At last her smugness drained away. He hated to

see that growing smile disappear, though, and cursed himself. Should have stayed silent. For her smile, he could endure anything.

"Why did you do that?" he asked, hoping to remind her of the reasons and thereby witness the return of her enjoyment.

Her chin lifted stubbornly. "Talking about the fight between AIR and your men reminded me of the agents who died. You didn't have to kill them."

Plan failed, he thought. And really, how many times would she chastise him for that? "Once again, *I* didn't kill them. But do you, as an agent, not kill aliens for a living?"

"I've never killed any . . . Well, I've never killed anyone who didn't deserve it."

Another lie? Her outrage seemed real. "How long have you worked for AIR?"

She licked her lips nervously, seeming to realize she'd admitted to something she shouldn't have. "A little over a month."

A month? She was a lethal baby, practically an innocent. "You are an alien in an organization that usually hires only humans. Are you an informant for your race, then?" That made sense.

"No! I'm not an informant."

There was enough disgust dripping from her high-pitched tone to legitimize her denial. The more she spoke, however, the more of a mystery she became, the single puzzle piece he'd slid into place seemingly insignificant.

What race was she? He still couldn't place her.

Why did she work for AIR, hunting those like herself?

"A predator is a predator," she said, as though reading his mind. "They need to be put down."

Like him?

A muted ray of light suddenly broke free of the sky and glowed around them. He glanced up, saw the purples and pinks forming, and realized he'd been standing out here far longer than he'd meant to. He needed to escort her to her new home, like, now, but found he still wasn't ready to interrupt their conversation. No matter the risk to his skin.

"How do you and your men know English?" she asked, drawing his attention back to her. "And before you ignore me, remember that I've answered plenty of your questions. It's only fair that you answer one of mine."

Her curiosity pleased him, even if it wasn't for him specifically. "We've studied the people, their words, their *everything*. Plus, we've been here before. Many times."

"That's impossible. We would have known."

He shrugged. "Even if I lied, languages are easy for my people. We have only to hear one to know its nuances." As he spoke, he traced a finger down the curve of her cheek. So smooth, so warm. So sensitive. Goose bumps broke out over her flesh.

Frowning, she stepped away from him, and he bit the inside of his cheek as his finger trembled for more. "AIR doesn't know where to find us," he added. "So if you are resisting me because you hope to be rescued . . ." She'd seemed scared of them, now that she knew they'd most likely seen her change forms.

"They'll learn your location soon enough," she said, looking anywhere but at him. "They've probably been scouring the area, closing in minute by minute."

"They can search, but it doesn't mean they'll succeed." Besides, his men had seen no sign of them.

"Maybe they're hiding, watching for the perfect opportunity, even now."

He frowned, scanning the area with a sharper eye. Those thick iron bars surrounded them, the gaps closed with boards. Pyre-fire could quickly and easily burn wood, allowing agents to slip inside undetected in seconds. "We had best go. We have a thirty-mile hike ahead of us. Now, do you prefer to walk or be carried like before?"

"Wa—" She stopped and pressed her lips together. "Carried," she said, and there was enough satisfaction in her tone to make him suspicious.

Did she hope to tire him so that AIR would more easily catch him? He *was* tired, for he hadn't yet fully recovered from the first night's fighting. Moving at such a speed always did that. Plus, the pain in his side still bothered him—and now the pain in his balls. But outshining the fatigue and the pain, was exhilaration. He'd finally crossed the galaxies, finally made a home for his men . . . finally had a woman to warm his bed. Kind of. Soon. He'd die before he allowed himself to be captured now.

"Carried it shall be," he said, bending down and pressing his shoulder into her stomach.

"Wait. What are you doing?" she gasped out.

"I'm doing as you suggested." He hefted her up, her body curling over his shoulder. He locked her legs against his chest with one hand and splayed his fingers over her ass with the other. Perfection. She hissed out a breath. He wanted that breath on his bare skin, not his shirt, heating, teasing, taunting. A wave of longing crashed through him with such potency, his muscles tightened their grip on his bones.

"Put me down, Breean! I was joking, okay? I didn't mean for you to carry me like this."

His name on her lips was paradise. "How did you mean for me to carry you, then?" On alert, he crossed the yard and pushed through the gate. Mile after mile of dirt stretched ahead. That didn't comfort him as it should have. The more he thought about it, the more he realized she was right. Fierce soldiers that they were, AIR's agents should have caught his scent by now.

Why hadn't they attacked?

"Carry me in your arms, idiot!" Her arms and legs flailed. "Don't carry me like a sack of potatoes. You'll hurt me. And we're almost friends now. Right? You should treat me better."

Friends. He wished. He also wished he could go slowly, be gentle with her, but he needed to reach the new house as quickly as possible. He'd waited too long to head out, enjoying her a little too much. Cursed ballsy woman. He could have stayed here another day, he supposed, and that way, he would have been able to take his time when night next fell. But the weapons were gone, his men were gone, and he wouldn't be able to enjoy *and* protect her.

"This didn't hurt you last time. I'll be just as careful with you this time. Any injury I can take upon myself, rather than inflict upon you, I will, I swear it."

She stopped wiggling. Her hands even settled on his back. "That's . . . sweet. Damn it! You shouldn't be so sweet. I don't like it."

Or perhaps she liked it too much. "I plan to win a kiss from you. Get used to it."

Starting forward, smiling, he said, "I had a guard at your door, and he told me that when the lights flickered out each night, you spent the time talking to yourself." Breean had been furious that he hadn't been notified until this morning. He would have gone to her, comforted her as he was learning to do. "Are you afraid of the dark, Aleaha?"

"No. I was afraid of someone sneaking up on me."

Far worse. That was not a fear she would let him cuddle all better. "I would have kept you safe."

"Hardly. To me, *you* were the monster in the closet."

Monster indeed. But at least she'd said *were.* Maybe they were indeed almost friends. With every mile he traveled, he increased his speed, the world streaking past him. He knew he left a glow behind, but no one would know what that glow was. Well, no one except AIR's agents, but as he'd already proven, they wouldn't be able to catch him.

Finally they reached the city. That lovely snow. Cars, homes, and shops, people carrying bags whizzed past him, wind rustling his hair. He stepped carefully, precisely, keeping his motions as smooth as possible for Aleaha's sake.

The shop windows, he noticed, were lit with multihued bulbs—red and green were the most prevalent colors—and there were fake trees in every corner, decorated with bows, ribbons, and dangling ornaments. Those things had not been present the other times he'd visited. He'd often wondered why they were here now.

MERRY CHRISTMAS, a sign said. "What is Christmas?" he asked.

"God's birthday. We celebrate by giving each other gifts. And do you know what I want most of all? For you to put me the hell down!"

A celebration of birth. They had done something similar on Raka. Some of his best memories were of the nights he'd spent in front of his mother's fireplace, his four sisters all around him, passing out the trinkets he'd purchased for them. That would have been his father's right, except that his father had died at sea soon after his birth.

A pang of homesickness pierced him. How he missed them. If only he'd come home sooner on that last trip out, he might have been able to save his mother and sisters. They might be with him now. But then, he would not have met Aleaha and he found that he could not regret that, which filled him with guilt. In a perfect world, he would have them all.

"No holiday spirit, I see," Aleaha grumbled.

"Do you have a man waiting for you to return home?" A man waiting to win her heart with the perfect Christmas gift.

"Does it matter?" she snapped, giving him the same words he'd given her about the weapons.

"Answer me." He wanted to kill any man who might be waiting for her, wanting to strip her and taste her and fill her. This faceless man would do all of that as his "gift," he was sure. Well, that was Breean's gift to give!

"No. I won't answer."

He'd begun to relax—no, she'd said—only to tense again. "Woman, I am not someone to taunt."

"Neither am I. So if you want the info that badly, you'll bargain for it."

And he'd thought her smart before. She was a genius. His lips curled into a smile as he dodged a building, his shoulder catching on a jagged stone and snow cascading onto his chest and her legs. She yelped; his grin widened.

"Very well," he said. "What would you like from me? A gift? Say yes, and I'll even unwrap it for you."

"If you dare tell me your penis is the gift, I'll scream."

"In pleasure?"

"Have I told you yet that you're annoying? I want the agents released."

He snorted. "Nothing you have is worth that."

He could hear her teeth grinding. He'd lied, though. He thought he might give anything and everything to have her writhing in his arms again. Willingly and without reservation.

Stupid cock. Perhaps one day he would be commander of it rather than the other way around. He just, well, he liked her spirit, her courage, her tenacity . . . and, yes, her body. He wasn't going to lie to himself and claim that the attraction was completely mental.

"Let *one* of them go, at least."

"No. That one could lead your precious AIR army to my doorstep." Those he'd captured and moved, he'd blindfolded, so that wasn't truly a risk, but she didn't need to know that, because really, his bargain, the trade-off, was the only viable option.

"What *will* you do for the information, then?" she asked, clearly frustrated.

"I'll give you a vow that they will not be killed by my hand. Or by anyone in my army," he added before she could mention Marleon again. Of course, he would see to it anyway, but still he would not tell her that.

"And how do I know you'll keep your word? You've already admitted that you fight dirty."

"As do you." He patted her bottom, strangely proud of her wit and the fact that she remembered what he'd told her. As if it meant something. Sure, he was undoubtedly deluding himself, and she'd remembered what he'd said simply because she'd smashed his balls into his throat immediately after, but that was neither here nor there. "You'll just have to trust me."

"Oh, really?" She sank her teeth into his back, past his clothing and straight into skin. He winced. Damn, but her teeth were sharp. Rather than scold her as he should have, however, he said, "I'll take this to mean you refuse to trust me."

"That's right." The words were moaned as if he were thrusting between her legs. She licked him through his shirt, sucked, murmured, "God, you taste good," then groaned in embarrassment and stopped. "There'll be no trusting," she choked out. She began kicking and slamming her fists into his back. "I won't stand for this kind of treatment. Do you hear me?"

"I believe everyone can hear you, Aleaha."

She bit him again, but her teeth quickly gentled and she released another of those moans.

His grin widened as he picked up speed.

FIVE

The diabolical bastard carried her into a dream.

From her perch on his shoulder, she scribbled mental notes, trying to memorize the path they raced and the surrounding neighborhood. But he moved in that superspeed of his, one snow-covered building blending into another, so she had trouble garnering more than a few tidbits.

The neighborhood itself was meant for New Chicago's elite. That much she knew without looking. The air just smelled cleaner, wealthier, as if everyone scrubbed their windows with pine-scented hundred-dollar bills rather than cloth.

She remembered how Bride used to drag her to neighborhoods like this. They had stared at the homes, pretending they belonged inside. Once she'd even assumed the features of someone's little boy and entered. It had been dinnertime, and a mouthwatering spread of ham and dressing had been laid out before her.

Bride was a vampire and only drank blood, so she'd waited outside. Aleaha had barely begun to eat—and to stuff morsels into her pockets for later—when she'd lost her hold on the boy's image, the ecstasy of the food too much. The parents had screamed at her, cornered her, and demanded to know what she'd done with their son. Thank God Bride had rushed in, gathered her up, voice-voodooed the couple into forgetting them, and helped her escape.

After that harrowing experience, she'd stopped visiting neighborhoods like this one. The desire to belong, however, had never faded. Even though she'd known how impossible such a dream was.

How could Breean, a Rakan and new Earth resident, afford something in an area like this? Didn't matter, she supposed. However he'd done it, he was now the kind of guy she'd wanted to date as a teen.

We're going to marry rich husbands, Bride had told her one day. *We'll never have to worry about anything ever again.*

They'll be handsome, she'd replied.

Of course. We're gorgeous, so we deserve gorgeous men. And they'll be so in love with us they'll drool every time they look at us.

They'll think we're the smartest girls ever.

And they won't care about our origins, Bride had added. *They'll just keep giving us money.*

That had been Aleaha's main concern. Not the money but her origins. Breean met that demand. Breean met *all* the demands. He was rich, handsome and ready to drool. Not that she was thinking of him in terms of a husband. But wow, he was rich. She just couldn't get over that fact. Did she like him more because of it? Um, yeah. How shallow was she?

When he reached the wraparound porch of a house on the far end of a perfectly paved street, he slowed. As if sensing his presence, one of his men opened the door and Breean sailed inside.

She gasped at her first glimpse of marble floors veined in gold. From somewhere, water trickled into several bathing pools, and mist circled through the damp air. Satin pillows in every shade of gold, from the palest yellow to the darkest amber, lined the walls. The windows were stained black, allowing no light inside. Her gaze lifted to the ceiling, and she saw crystal chandeliers flickering with hazy luminosity.

This totally wasn't the den of iniquity she'd expected. As run-down as the other home had been, she'd placed Breean in the poor and desperate category.

Breean stopped and spoke to one of the warriors, keeping her draped over his shoulder. She didn't mind—the better to eavesdrop. But what was he saying, damn it? She thought she heard the word *tree* but she couldn't be sure.

She drew in a frustrated breath, catching more of that honeysuckle scent. And smoke. Ugh. She coughed, inhaling the odor of burning material. The warriors she'd fought only a week ago bustled in every direction, bare except for underwear, and not quite meeting her gaze.

All that golden skin ... She tried not to stare, but they were huge. Everywhere. *Merry Christmas to me. Idiot.*

"Do you like?" Breean asked, squeezing her legs to let her know the question was directed at her.

Did she like the men? The mansion? "No," she lied. "How did you get so much water in here?" After the human-alien war, its use for bathing and swimming had been restricted, the supply scarce and expensive. In fact, the water had probably cost more than the house. Most people were forced to clean themselves with a dry enzyme spray.

"We brought it with us, bucket by bucket. Water abounds on Raka," he explained. "There is nothing better than hearing the rush and feeling the warmth, the decadence."

"So why do you want to make a new home for yourself *here*? There's not a lot of water left."

"As I told you, our planet was in ruins. We needed a fresh start in a place where the female population thrives."

So he hadn't just lost the women he loved. He'd lost everything and everyone. She felt a wave of pity for him, but quickly tamped it down. *Don't feel sorry for him. He's the enemy—and obviously prowling for sex!*

Still. His people had died of the Schön disease. AIR would find that interesting. Might even want to question him to find out how he'd survived, as well as what he knew about the race and their queen. Perhaps that information would save his life. Although, AIR wasn't known for its forgiving spirit. His people had killed several agents, and someone would have to pay for that.

"You can put me down now," she said. The position was uncomfortable, but it was being so close to him that disturbed her most.

"Not yet."

"Why? Payback?" She would deserve it. She'd given his dangly bits hell, after all. *All's fair to him when fighting, remember?*

"I told you how I would return that . . . favor," he said, and she couldn't tell if he was fighting amusement or anger.

Actually, no, he hadn't told her anything. He'd alluded to touching her, but nothing else. Diabolical bastard. It would have been so much easier to hate him—as well she should have, damn it!—if he'd flat out threatened her with violence. Instead, he'd practically threatened to kiss her better.

He rounded a corner, the hallways wide and spacious and leading to a multitude of rooms. There was even a staircase that wound to the second floor. He didn't take it, though he paused and stared up it for a long while. Finally, he sighed, then meandered down another hall before carting her *down*stairs, into a cold, dank basement.

Not a basement, she realized a moment later, but a dungeon. "Another prison?" In a home like this, she would not have expected a torture chamber to be a purchase option.

"Yes. You'll stay here only long enough for me to prepare your room."

That was a lie, she knew it was. He'd had all week to prepare a room for her. What was his purpose, then?

"Besides," he added, "the other agents are here, and I know you've been wanting to see them."

The other agents were here? Happy but panicked, Aleaha quickly pictured Macy. The blond hair, the shorter body, the bigger boobs. Her appearance changed in a blink, and she expelled a sigh of relief.

There were multiple cells, each with a barred front and dirt sides, and inside each of those cells was an agent. Finally. Her eyes collided with Devyn's; he was now wearing a loose black shirt and pants. He didn't speak, but his grip tightened around the metal, his already pale knuckles bleaching of color.

Despite his stressed expression, he blew her a kiss.

She spied Dallas next, and he winked. Then she saw Hector Dean, tattooed and muscular, who always left a room when she entered. The guys he joked and laughed with, but he'd never warmed toward her. Today, he nodded in acknowledgment. Where was Jaxon?

"I'm fine," she told them all. "Nothing's been done to me."

Each of them relaxed.

"We're fine, too," Hector said in that deep voice of his.

"Enough," Breean said.

"Suck it," she told him, and several of the agents laughed.

He didn't set her down until he reached a small, empty cell. Inside, he slid her down his body, the action igniting heat between them. Heat she couldn't afford. The moment her feet touched solid ground, she scampered backward, unsure what he meant to do—and unsure of her reaction. Would she have the strength to stop him again if he kissed her?

To her relief, he didn't comment about the change in her appearance. That, too, would have weakened her. And destroyed her.

Please don't let him call me Aleaha. Please, God, don't let him call me Aleaha. She should never have told him her real name.

Eyes on her, he shouted something in his own language. She wished she knew what he was saying. A few seconds later, a Rakan warrior stalked into the cell. He was holding a bundle of clothing, and he didn't look at her. Breean took the garments and said something else. The man nodded before racing out.

One heartbeat passed in silence, two.

Breean met her glare. He seemed taller and more like total, in-your-face carnality than ever before. What would he say to her next, now that they were seemingly alone and she was at his mercy? What would he demand of her? *Take my cock into your mouth,* she could almost hear him say. *You're welcome. Merry Christmas.*

Her heart galloped—but not in abhorrence and oh, she was disgusted with herself. She'd failed to escape, to get help, to free the agents. She'd failed to resist Breean when he'd kissed her, and had even begged for more.

In that one night, hell, one hour, one minute, he'd stripped her of all common sense and inhibitions. Would have stripped her of her clothing, too, if she hadn't fought her way out of that crazy lust-fog. The week had not dulled her desires. And here she was, still freaking desiring him, *after* he'd set her inside a cage next to her coworkers. It was insanity.

Remember how it was with the other three men you allowed in your life. How, after she'd spontaneously changed during sex, one had slapped her. How two had called her names. How one had thought to use her ability to his advantage. What would she do if superstrong Breean hit her? Hit him back, of course. What would she do if he called her vile names? Cry like a dumb baby, most likely. What would she do if he tried to use her? To hurt AIR, even? Curse at him, surely, before crying some more.

Did she seriously *want* him to like her?

Yep, insanity.

"They aren't the best of quarters," he finally said to her, guilt in the undertones of his voice, "but as I told you, they'll do for now."

The warrior who'd brought the clothing returned with blankets, a pillow, and some type of bag. He placed the items in the corner and left. The sweet scent of fruit and chicken wafted through the air, causing her mouth to water.

Dinner, she thought, her stomach growling. The tastes she'd had earlier of Breean's sugar-laced blood had left her hungry, for each drop had been better than, like, anything she'd ever prepared.

She was a decent cook, but Macy had apparently been a genius in the kitchen. First night her "mom" and "stepdad" had come over, they'd expected four-star treatment. As rich as they were and as superior as their expectations had been, the mac-and-cheese she'd thrown together hadn't pleased them. They hadn't liked the changes in her personality, either. Where the old Macy had been a champagne kind of girl, the new Macy's beer-loving ways had not been acceptable.

They'd accused her of being on drugs again, then yelled at her for throwing away her life as a cop when she could have gone back to modeling. And Aleaha had had to listen, try to answer. But the truth was, she didn't know why Macy had chosen such a life for herself.

At least dealing with the parents had been easier than the boyfriend. He'd had a key to her apartment—she'd since changed the locks—and had let himself in one night. He'd been high on Onadyn, the drug of choice for the wealthy, and ready for a game of "ride the pony."

On his way to the bedroom, he'd knocked down several of her—well, Macy's—things, breaking them. Thinking he was an intruder, she'd first tried to stun him, then, when that hadn't worked, to kill him. But just before pulling the trigger, she'd seen his face. She'd already studied the pictures hanging on the walls and those in Macy's holobook, so she'd recognized him.

He hadn't been happy with her refusal to play. As with Breean, she'd had to introduce him to her knee. Funny that Breean, who was supposed to hate her, had treated her better afterward.

"You must change," Breean said, drowning her musings of the past. Now his voice was husky with want.

"Uh, not just no, but hell, no." She would not reveal her true self while being this close to the AIR agents. But what a sweet man, not uttering the words "your appearance" while agents could hear.

He gave her a pointed glance. Aw. He meant her clothing.

"Why?" she asked.

"There's blood on your shirt."

Yeah, but it was his blood, from when she'd bitten him. "There's just a speck." A golden speck, at that, tasty and soul-shattering and maybe she could lick it off . . . *Stop, you idiot.* She'd actually been reaching for the hem of her shirt to bring it to her mouth.

Okay, time to regroup. He wouldn't rest until she'd changed out of her dirty clothes. He'd made her change that first night, too, she recalled, after she'd bitten him. She'd been happy to do so—when he'd left her alone. But why the anal need for spotless garments? She almost snickered. Anal.

He crossed his arms over his chest. "Are you going to be stubborn about this?"

"No. As before, I'll change when you leave."

"I need to take your clothes with me, so that they can be burned. We walked through the city, and I'm unsure what we came into contact with. More than that, I believe I mentioned that the sight of the blood offends me."

She'd been scanning for blood on *his* clothing; now her gaze snapped back up to him and she tried to read his expression. Surely he was joking. "You're a warrior."

"Yes. You know that I am."

"You *deal* in blood. How can the mere sight of it offend you?"

"Blood carries disease and death, diseases that are more painful than a knife through the gut. Now, I need the clothes you are wearing so that I may dispose of them."

The Schön disease, she realized. He feared it, and that made sense. But strangely, she didn't like that so strong a man, even her enemy, had been brought to such a point. "Sure you don't just want to watch me strip?" She'd meant the words as a taunt, hoping to soften the tenseness of the situation; they emerged as an invitation.

He gulped, every muscle in his body hardening. "To protect your modesty, I will wait outside. Toss your old clothing through the bars when you are done." He turned on his heel, his posture stiff.

She liked him better when he was trying to charm her.

And he wanted to charm her, right? To win

another kiss, right? So, why was he leaving her? Why wasn't he forcing her to do what he wished? Did he no longer desire her?

Unacceptable. *Make him want you again. He'll relax his guard. You can free the agents.* Yep, that's the only reason she was filled with such a need. "Wait," she called just as he was opening the cell door. Oh, God. Was she really going to do this?

Slowly he faced her, the most beautiful creature she'd ever seen. A man who'd had plenty of opportunity, yet hadn't hurt her. A man who'd taken pretty good care of her, all things considered.

Yes, she was going to do this. "You can watch."

"No," he said, though the word was soft, as if he didn't actually want to say it.

"Don't you want me to be happy?"

His brow furrowed, but there was hope in his eyes. "Why would my presence make you happy?"

"Just because."

"Then you know what you must first do," Breean croaked out.

Show her true appearance. He'd demanded this time and time again, yet it still managed to shock her. How could he prefer the real her? In no way did she compare to Macy. She was flatter, leaner, with more patrician features. She was way less ... stirring.

Still, she shifted back to her own image and nervously fidgeted with the ends of her hair.

"Better?"

"Much. Begin."

That had sounded like a plea, and spurred her on.

Hands shaky, she bent and unhooked her scuffed boots. She kicked them off, launching them at Breean one at a time. A girl had to preserve hints of her this-isn't-what-I-*really*-want facade. To his credit, he didn't cringe or move out of the way. He let them slam into him without a word. Because he was entranced? She hoped so.

This is for his benefit, remember?

She reached behind her head and pulled her shirt up and off. The shirt, too, she tossed at him. The material swooshed into his chest and floated to the cold, hard ground. Her too-large bra was next—it had been made for Macy's ample chest and was one of two things she'd kept when she'd handed over her AIR bodysuit—which left her small breasts bared. Her nipples immediately puckered against the cold. Or maybe from the heat of his stare.

Breean sucked in a—reverent?—breath. He even reached out, then caught himself and dropped his arm to his side. All the while, his gaze bored into her, white lightning slamming against all of her pulse points.

Why had he stopped himself?

"The rest," he said, his voice deep and husky with arousal.

Her trembling intensifying, she jerked her too-loose pants and underwear down her legs. Underwear—the second thing she'd kept. Her other prison had had an enzyme shower stall, so she and the garments had managed to remain clean.

When she stepped out of them, she stilled the urge to cover herself. She just stood there, daring him to say something about her concave stomach or the thickly puckered scars on her inner thighs.

He tore his gaze from her breasts, from her quivering navel, lingering for a few seconds on the fine tuft of hair between her legs before staring at the scars. He frowned. "What type of injury rendered those?"

Silent, she raised her chin. That was information she'd *never* offer, not even under torture.

"Ale— Macy," he said, catching himself. Thank God. There was a warning in his tone.

"I'm cold," she said, chattering her teeth for effect. "I'm going to dress now?" A question when it should have been a statement. "And please don't ever . . . you know." *Call me by that name in front of others.* "Okay?" It was a gamble, asking him such a thing. He could threaten to do so if she didn't obey him in all things. That would be fighting dirty, after all. But as hesitant as she'd been about revealing the truth, he had to know already that it was important to her.

For a long while, he didn't reply. Then he sighed and tossed the clothes at her. "You have my word. Now get dressed. Sleep. Eat. Tomorrow we will have a long talk." He turned and exited the cell, locking her inside.

As he stood outside Aleaha's chamber, Breean's blood was on fire.

Before, he'd thought he wanted her. Now that he'd seen her naked, stubborn determination in her eyes, he knew better. He *needed* her. She was exquisite, breathtaking, a fighter to her core, and it had taken all of his self-control not to launch himself at her, nipping and kissing all that white flesh. Sucking those ripe little nipples into his mouth and feasting for days. Fingering the moist heat between her legs, then licking away every drop.

He tried to calm the riotous beat of his heart and the raging inferno blooming with his every breath. No luck. *Push her from your mind. For now, at least. Until you are stronger than your desire for her, for a prisoner, an AIR agent, you can't have her.*

That's why he'd placed her in the cell, after all, when that had never been his intent. He'd meant to keep her in his room. Where she was concerned, however, he still didn't have any defenses. And he needed defenses or she would always have the upper hand.

"Breean," Talon called.

His attention veered to the right. He found Talon standing beside Marleon at the far end of the tunnel. Fury flooded him, and he welcomed it. The warrior's actions had nearly ruined him in Aleaha's eyes.

"Marleon," he snarled.

The soldier paled, the fine swell of veins under his golden skin visible. He was dirty from his time in the dungeon, and clearly worried. "My lord?" The words trembled.

He closed the distance between them with a purposeful stride. "As you know, you are charged with causing bloodshed without permission." He deliberately spoke in the Earth language, knowing Aleaha would be listening.

"Yes, but—"

"I have spent the last week pondering your case."

Not a sound did any of the agents make. "There are not many of us left, and I did not wish to destroy another of us. But you know the punishment for your crime, do you not?"

Blanching, Marleon backed into the wall. "My lord, they ambushed us. They meant to torture us."

Talon gripped his shoulder, keeping him from bolting.

"There is no excuse great enough for what you did, for you have endangered all of us. What if they had been disease carriers?"

"I . . . I . . . didn't think. I'm sorry. So sorry."

"No. You will die. As is our law. I have waited long enough to render your sentence. Know that I hate to do this, but it is necessary. Were I to be lenient, others would think such actions acceptable." Without another word, Breean walked straight into Marleon's body, melding them into one being. He could have eased into the man so there would be no pain, but didn't. He allowed his subject to feel every ounce of his possession.

Marleon screamed.

In control of the man's every movement, every breath, Breean forced his organs to shut down one by one. Marleon jerked and spasmed, still screaming, still begging, until finally growing quiet and collapsing to the ground.

Dead. Just like that. Quick, but not easy.

This would weigh Breean down for months to come.

He exited with only a thought, once more standing

in front of Talon, the body at his feet. "He knew better," Breean said with disgust. Disgust for himself as much as for the dead soldier. But as leader, it was up to him to mete out justice. He had not lied; if he'd shown Marleon mercy, others would not have thought twice about spilling blood during the next battle.

"He knew," Talon agreed. "You did what you had to do."

Would Aleaha think so, or view this as more proof of his black nature? "Burn him." As was their custom. They'd only buried the AIR agents because that's what they knew earthlings preferred. Handling the dead was abhorrent to them, but they'd done it to show their respect.

Talon nodded. "Everyone has disposed of their clothing and most are in the pools, even as we speak."

"Good." His gaze swung over his shoulder, zeroing in on Aleaha's door. Switching to Rakan, he said, "The two men she slapped in the forest, do you know which ones they are?" It was past time Breean spoke to them. Now that he was done readying this place, traveling back and forth between it and the other home, he had the time.

Again Talon nodded.

"Bring them to my office within the hour."

After bathing and changing into clean clothes, his tainted ones burning with the others', Breean left his room and sat at the desk, outlining the best defense against the Schön. He'd only seen a handful of the vile race before they'd disappeared and all but the queen had been male.

She had been . . . strange. Dainty, deceptively innocent, with a lilting voice he and the others had found themselves obeying without question. Her followers had managed to capture him and the others, and they'd been forced to watch as she seduced one after another. But Breean and those with him now, she'd sent away with a disgusted snarl. He'd never understood why. He would have welcomed her into his bed—and not just because he'd been without sex for so long. Whatever she'd spoken, he had wanted to do.

He'd thought her powers over men similar to a Rakan male's power over a Rakan female, his lust-scent like a drug. Only, they used their power for pleasure. She used hers to hurt. And hurt they had. Almost immediately the disease struck them, ravaging their bodies.

Once she'd mated with the men, they had then been given prisoners of their own. And once they'd mated with someone previously uninfected, the grayish tint had left their skin. Their hollowed cheeks had rounded out.

He'd wondered, why hadn't they worsened, weakened as the women had done? Why hadn't they become cannibals? Why had they gotten better?

The only answer he'd been able to come up with was that sex healed them. Would the women have remained strong if they, in turn, had had sex with their men rather than eating them?

If not, would those that were infected heal the moment the queen was killed?

Perhaps he could capture and destroy the queen, as

AIR had done to her brethren. Locked up, she would not be able to have sex—*if* he could do something about that magical voice of hers. Wouldn't be very productive if she ordered him to release her and he obeyed. This way, he could learn if she weakened without sex. And if so, he could leave her in there to rot to death, all without having to spill a single drop of blood.

So easy, he thought dryly, pinching the bridge of his nose. She kept guards around her at all times, and those guards could vanish and kill you before you had time to blink. But somehow, someway, there had to be a way to catch a warrior you couldn't see. AIR had done it.

He could always steal AIR's weapons, he supposed. Then they'd be even less inclined to trade with him, however. What to do, what to do. He sighed.

When he next glanced up, the two agents Aleaha had tried to awaken were stomping into the room, Talon behind them, keeping them docile by pressing their own pyre-guns into the bases of their necks.

He studied them. Both males were tall and muscled, one with the tanned skin the humans seemed to love so much, the other with pale, glittery skin. Breean preferred Aleaha's, a white rose flushed with pink. Lovely. And irrelevant. Both men had dark hair, and both could be considered handsome, he supposed, hands fisting on his notes and crinkling the precious paper.

Were they the girl's family? he wondered, jealousy easing. He did not want Aleaha seeking aid from a lover. A brother, however, was allowed.

Breean searched for similarities. One had eyes the

color of an ocean. One had eyes the color of a sunset. They weren't related to each other, and they weren't related to Aleaha. Her eyes were piercing green, her features more aristocratic. Unless they could change their appearances as she did? But no. There was no mask under either man's face. More than that, she wouldn't have minded if they saw her true self.

Breean's teeth ground together as he leaned back in his seat and scrubbed two fingers over his jaw.

"Are you human?" he asked them. Both pulsed with a strange sort of energy not inherent to the human race.

Blue Eyes nodded, features strained as if he were in deep concentration. "Yes. Now what's your plan for the girl? You will tell me. You want to tell me."

"No, I don't." Strangely, Breean felt a sudden urge to tell the agent anything and everything he wanted to know.

"Your plan," Blue Eyes insisted. "You were just about to tell me."

Yes, he thought, dazed. He wanted to tell, but he only allowed himself to say, "What is any man's plan?"

"Indeed," Glitter said with an appreciative laugh.

How odd. Amusement was not the reaction Breean would have expected.

Blue Eyes tensed to launch himself at Breean. Now, there was the reaction he'd expected. Fury. Talon cocked one of the guns and pushed the cool barrel into the agent's skull, and the man froze.

"Will she remain alive?" Blue Eyes gritted out. "Tell me."

412

That voice . . . nearly irresistible. Utterly powerful. He *had* to answer. And yet, as quickly as the feeling had hit him, it abandoned him. "Of course she will remain alive." What was going on? Mind control? Some races exhibited such a power, but he hadn't thought earthlings among their number. "I am not a monster."

Glitter popped his jaw, all traces of humor suddenly gone. "Have you hurt her? Forced her?"

"Believe me, I have forced her to do nothing."

Both men relaxed, but only slightly. "Let her stay with us," Blue Eyes said in that persuasive voice. "In one of our cells."

The thrum of jealousy returned but the urge to obey did not. Either the agent was not very good or Breean was building an immunity. "Are you related to her?"

"Do you want us to be?" Glitter asked.

Breean ran his tongue over his teeth. "Is she your woman?" The question burst from him before he could stop it.

A pause, heavy, tight.

"What if she is?" Blue Eyes flashed an evil smile.

Breean could have entered the bastard's body right then and punished him. Something, *anything* to hurt him. But he recalled the disgust on Aleaha's face when she'd spoken of Marleon doing it—and his own disgust at the punishment he'd carried out only an hour earlier.

"Are. You. Her. Man? That is a simple question."

"Hurt her, and I'll fucking murder you while you

sleep," Glitter said without any inflection of anger. He would enjoy it, too. That much was obvious. "How's that for an answer?"

"She's innocent. She's not like us. Let her go."

The thought of releasing her without knowing the full depth of her passion was abhorrent to him, and he shook his head. "She stays," he said, then arched a brow in curiosity. "Have you no care about my plans for *you*?"

"Not really."

"Nope. Can't say that I do."

"Is this conversation over? Because I like the view from my cell better."

Obviously, the irreverent men weren't going to tell him what he wanted to know. He wasn't going to beg, nor was he going to torture them. That would smack of desperation.

"No. This conversation is not over." He did, however, switch topics. "We have a common enemy, it seems. The Schön."

That got their attention. They straightened, glanced at each other, frowned.

"The Schön destroyed my home, my family. My planet. That is why we are here. We'd hoped for peace. We'd hoped to live among people who knew how to combat such an enemy. Yet we arrive only to learn that our enemy beat us here and they even plan to send their queen."

No response.

"We have decided to stay and fight them. Fierce as they are, we could use your help."

Again, no response.

Damn them, making him work for every scrap. "*You* could use *our* help. Unless, of course, you want to see your own planet destroyed, your women eyeing you like a tasty meal just before trying to gut you with their teeth."

Nothing.

"I've seen their queen. I've dealt with her."

Blue Eyes gulped.

Nearly imperceptible, but a show of interest. Finally.

"She came after the males had taken out our royal family and their guard. She's one of the most beautiful women I've ever seen, with a powerful voice very much like yours." He motioned to Blue Eyes with a tilt of his chin. "She kept a harem. They all did. But they only slept with each of their victims once. After that, the ones who weren't warriors were discarded out on the streets to fend for themselves, even as the disease began to consume them."

"How did you survive?" Glitter asked. There was no hint of mockery in his tone. Not any longer.

Sweet progress. "We aren't sure. None of us were chosen by the queen. Nearly all of us were bitten at some point as we were forced to fight our own people and loved ones, but we never sickened."

Blue Eyes and Glitter shared another of those dark looks.

"I'm willing to aid AIR against them in exchange for our freedom to roam this planet."

"To be honest, I don't think anyone will trust

you," Blue Eyes said. No hesitation. Which meant, he didn't have to think about it. He simply knew. "You came on the night the Schön were due. You killed several of our men."

That damn Marleon.

"And, let's face it, this could be a trap," Glitter said.

Blue Eyes spread his arms, an I'm-here-to-help gesture. "Let us go, and we might, *might*, be able to convince our captain that your intentions are good."

Rather than answer, he said to Talon, "Take them away." He needed to think some more, weigh the pros and cons of each avenue. Then, in his own language, he added, "I want at least one spirit walker in town at all hours of the night. Everyone else is to take shifts. Guards are to be posted here, of course, enough for every exit, but others can head into town and find females." How could he deny his men while he luxuriated in Aleaha? "Those who spirit-walk are to find out what they can about AIR and the Schön. They probably won't hear anything, but it's worth a try."

Spirit walking. Propelling your conscious mind from your body, roaming without being seen or heard or sensed in any way. It was how he had learned so much about Earth before anyone had discovered his presence.

The only problem was, when your mind left your body, your body was completely vulnerable. If someone attacked, you couldn't defend yourself. In fact, you wouldn't know you were being attacked until it was too late. Until you were dead.

Not all Rakans possessed the ability, unfortunately. Both Breean and Talon did, along with five others.

"Consider it done," Talon said with a nod.

"Those who are hunting sex know they are to hide their skin as best as they are able and be careful, I'm sure."

"Of course, but I will remind them anyway."

"Thank you."

Neither agent said a word during the exchange or even as they were led from the room.

Alone again, Breean ran a hand down his face, trying to scrub away his questions, his dark emotions, even his desires. He wanted Aleaha here, wanted to discuss all of this with her. But if he had her brought here, they wouldn't talk. She might deny it, but she wanted him. She'd stripped for him, after all. But the simple fact was, his desire for her was wild, fierce, while she seemed to have no trouble resisting him.

Perhaps he should join his men in New Chicago and find a woman to warm his bed. A woman who was meek and docile, who would delight in his every gesture. A woman who would fill the aching void that had grown each time one of his people had died. Once he'd had sex, he could do what he was supposed to do: plan.

But he could not work up a single shred of passion for anyone save Aleaha.

His body wanted *her*. Only she, with that dark hair, those piercing green eyes, that lean body, would do.

Just picturing her caused him to harden, to ready.

Damn this. He needed some relief so that he could better deal with her and his problems.

To prevent himself from changing his mind and going to her tonight, Breean pushed to his feet and stalked to his bedroom. When he was shut inside, he stripped and stepped into the waterfall he'd erected in place of the enzyme shower stall. Scowling, he slapped a hand against the cool tile to brace himself. With his other, he gripped his cock. He used the moisture beaded at the tip as lubricant and began slow, measured strokes.

He imagined Aleaha's mouth in place of his hand, her hot tongue swirling, her teeth lightly scraping. His testicles drew up tight; his strokes quickened. She'd kiss those testicles, of course, making them feel better after her earlier mistreatment of them. Her hands would grip his ass, perhaps delving where none had been before, her nails scoring deep. She might suck one of his balls into her mouth, might then lick her way up the shaft before sucking the head again. Sucking until he was dry. Until he couldn't take any more.

Breean's entire body jerked in ecstasy. With a roar, he came, hot seed spurting from him. "Aleaha," he shouted. Sweet, challenging Aleaha.

He stood there for a long while, panting, hand still circling his cock, Aleaha still in his mind. Jacking off, as the humans said, had helped, but it hadn't alleviated his need completely. He *still* wanted her with a hunger that surprised him. Still couldn't think of anything but being with her.

Damn this! he thought again. *And damn her.* He strode to the bed and fell onto the cold, empty sheets. He wished Aleaha were here. He yearned to hold her, to smell her delightful scent, feel her soft skin.

There had to be some way to win her. Some way to tear down her defenses against him. She wanted him; more than stripping a little while ago, the way she'd kissed him that first night was proof. She was just stubborn and probably scared.

What could he do? What could—

His eyes widened as an idea began to take root in his mind, growing. He grinned slowly. Oh, yes. He'd never done such a thing before, but he had fantasized. Now, he would experience.

Tomorrow, he would summon her. He would do that which he'd never allowed himself to do to another. And he would show her no mercy.

Six

"Come with me."

Ignoring the unfamiliar Rakan's command, Aleaha remained seated at the far end of the cell. She wasn't sure exactly how long she'd been inside it. At least eight hours. Probably twelve. Maybe an eternity. She'd heard the other "guests" clanging against their bars, heard the whisper of their conversations, but when she'd called out in Macy's voice—where's backup, these warriors hate the Schön as much as we do, tell me what you want me to do—no one had answered her.

"Come," the warrior said again.

He wasn't *her* warrior, Breean, so she didn't feel any urge to comply. "I'm not going anywhere with you." Surely Breean hadn't tired of her already. Surely he wasn't palming her off on one of his men. *Oh, God.* What if he was? She hadn't exactly been the nicest of captives.

Captives aren't supposed to be nice, idiot. He'd seen her naked. Maybe he'd disliked what he'd seen. *Oh, God*, she thought again.

The warrior looked like him: golden skin, golden hair, big, lovely features better suited for a woman yet somehow completely masculine. But his golden eyes didn't mesmerize her. He didn't smell of honey and cinnamon, and she had no desire to try to seduce him to kindness. She had no idea how to deal with him, actually.

"Are those . . ." His eyes widened as he spotted the trail of blood she'd accidentally created along the floor.

"Diamonds?" she finished for him, pretending to misunderstand. "Fat stacks of cash?"

Panic consumed his expression when that gaze reached the blood dried on her wrists. He backed away, probably not even aware that he did so. These men hadn't blinked at facing down the lethal members of AIR, but show them a little blood and they wanted to hide.

"Did you cut yourself?"

She saw no reason to lie. "Yes."

"What did you use? You're wearing our clothing, which means Breean checked you for weapons when you changed. And," he gazed around, "there is nothing sharp inside this cell."

She just shrugged.

"Tell me how—" He jumped away from her as if she were poison.

Jeez. She was just stretching out her legs to get more comfortable. She was all for precaution, but really, these men took their hatred and fear a little too far. What would he do if she bit her arm and dripped on his shoe?

Hey. That might actually be a good escape plan. She'd hold out her bloody arm, and the guys would beat feet, too afraid to grab her. She could walk right out of the house. But what about the rest of the agents? She could come back with help—*if* she could find it.

So much time had passed without an AIR assault, part of her now thought something nefarious had happened to Mia and her backup squad. They were good at their jobs, after all, and knew how to track and find the unfindable. The other part of her wondered whether Mia and her squad had stayed away on purpose. But why would they do that?

"Doesn't matter, I guess," the warrior before her said, reclaiming her attention. "You are not mine to deal with." Trying to hide his disgust but not quite managing it, he motioned her over with a wave of his fingers. "Come. Breean has requested your presence. But, please, maintain your distance from me."

The magic word: *Breean*. Aleaha popped to her feet, anticipation slithering through her. He hadn't tired of her, then. She ignored a sudden, intense rush of relief working through her. *Him*, she could deal with. Kind of.

Before, in the forest, Breean had craved her desire. If she hinted that she would ultimately fall into his bed, she could buy time. Time to "get to know each other" without being kissed, touched, or caressed—which she shouldn't want but couldn't stop thinking about. Time to figure this out.

"I was told not to hurt you or even to grab you. If you run, I am to alert Breean. He wants you to know that if he is forced to chase you, he will catch you. And he won't stop what was begun last week." The warrior's head tilted to the side. "What was begun last week? Sex?"

Her cheeks heated, and she told herself it was in embarrassment. *Not* arousal. "Just lead the way. I'm not going to run."

With a disappointed nod, the warrior ushered her past the other cells. As she walked, her gaze clashed with that of Dallas, whose hard expression and fierce blue eyes told her nothing. Beside him, Devyn grinned at her, eyebrows wagging. They remained silent, just as they had last night.

Upstairs, down a long hall, and around two corners, the Rakan stopped. "Here we are." He placed his palm over the ID box on the door. Azure lights scanned between his fingers and all the way to his wrist. A moment later, the entrance slid open.

She sailed past, changing her appearance as she walked. Gone were the blond hair and blue eyes. Gone were those magnificent breasts. She was herself again, just as Breean seemed to like.

The guard, who was gaping at her now, didn't enter behind her. He merely said something in that language she didn't understand and shut the door between them, locking her inside. Her heart began to hammer wildly as the scent of honey filled her nose.

Breean was here.

She gulped, trying to concentrate on something *un*exciting. The room was spacious, lovely and . . . her brow wrinkled in confusion—looked like Christmas had exploded inside it. There was a tree in the corner. A fir. A real fir. She could smell the dew on the lush green bristles.

Cutting down a tree was illegal, for every species belonged to the government. Since he was already known as a murdering outlaw, Breean probably didn't care. Red and green bows were tied to the branches. White lights dripped from the ceiling like stars.

There was no sign of Breean, but there *was* a large bed draped in soft-looking white sheets, rumpled from a night of tossing and turning. Or hardcore, sweaty sex. Her stomach quivered. *Don't think like that.* There was a lounge, a marble vanity that boasted a decanter of whiskey and a plastic mini-tree. There was a faux-bearskin rug on the floor with a green bow tied around one of its ears.

What drew her eye most, however, was the sunken tub in the center, filled with hot, steamy water. At least it was clear and not emerald or ruby.

"B-Breean?"

"I'm here." He stepped from the closet, and he was as beautiful and mesmerizing as she remembered: tall, thickly muscled, with golden angel-features and an innate animalism that couldn't be denied. Her heart picked up speed, slamming against her ribs with so much force she thought they might crack.

He wasn't wearing a shirt. His nipples glistened as if they'd been dipped in glitter and were beaded into hard little points. Rope after rope of muscle tapered to his navel . . . then deliciously lower. Black pants hung low on his waist and hugged his thighs.

"I knew it!" she said, doing her best to sound outraged. "This room is a mock Christmas party and your cock is supposed to be a present, isn't it?" Okay, yeah, maybe she preferred that to any of the presents Macy's family would have given her. That didn't mean she could accept it. "Or am *I* supposed to be *your* present?"

His gaze raked over her, his nostrils flaring in anger. "Were you hurt?" His eyes went black, opaque completely overshadowing amber. In that moment, he looked like the cold-blooded murderer she'd accused him of being. "Did someone touch you?"

"No, not at all. I'm fine. Swear. But back to the present thing . . ."

Gradually, the dark haze abandoned his eyes and he met her stare. "How, then, did you get blood on your new clothes? And under your nails?" he added, frowning. "Syler thinks you cut yourself. Did you?"

Or not. She swallowed the sudden lump in her throat. Convincing him to give her time to get to know him and grow to like him wasn't going to be as simple as she'd hoped. Obviously, the thought of her being hurt upset him, and that affected *her*, deeply and inexorably. Only Bride had cared enough about her to kiss her boo-boos and make them better. That someone else now seemed to want to do so was irresistible.

"Why would anyone in her right mind cut herself?" she asked. That way, she wasn't lying to him but wasn't admitting to the truth, either.

Of course, he didn't allow the subject to drop. "That does not answer my question."

"Well, it's all the answer you're going to get from me."

"You scratched or bit your wrists until they bled. *After* I told you of the dangers of contamination. Why? Why would you place my men at risk?"

"One, I'm not infected with anything, so they're safe. And two, why I cut myself is none of your damn business." There. She'd given him a partial answer. Yes, she'd done this to herself. But tell him why? Not going to happen. She would not say the words aloud. They could be used against her in the most painful, horrifying way.

"Did you hope I would command you to strip if your clothing was tainted?" He ran his tongue over his teeth, his anger seeming to swell despite his sensual suspicions. "Well, guess what? You get your wish. Take off the clothes. They offend me."

She'd half expected the demand, but that didn't lessen its impact. Her stomach tightened and her hands quivered. "No." Naked, she would lose all control of the situation. There would be no getting to know him, no buying time.

"We went over this yesterday, Aleaha. Take them off or I'll do it for you. You *are* going to wash."

She squared her shoulders. She wouldn't be cowed, not in this. She'd fight him if she had to, but she was staying dressed—and staying sane.

But if you fight him to stay dressed, he'll put his hands on you. And if he puts his hands on you, you'll cave. Damn it. Either way, they would have sex. She just couldn't win. Still she said, "You stay on that side of the room, and I'll stay on this side, and we'll chat." Curse his good looks. And his money. And his concern. And his smell. *Okay, you can stop now.*

He surprised her by grinning. "As you are fond of saying, no. We will not chat."

That smile . . . She lost every whiff of breath in her lungs. Maybe that was a good thing. Her every inhalation was filled with him, branding her every cell. "I don't want you," she said, more for her benefit than his.

"We shall see." Still grinning, he tugged at the waist of his pants. They immediately loosened and floated to the ground in a pool at his feet. Leaving him completely bare.

His penis was golden and hard, long and thick, and seeing it caused the moisture in her mouth to dry. Her hand fluttered over her lips to hold back her gasp of need. "I'm telling you now," she croaked, "I want this." Wait. What? "I mean, I want to talk to you, to get to know you."

Pleasure infused his eyes, but he shook his head. "That will come after," he said huskily. "But don't worry. *I'm* not going to take you. Yet."

He was in front of her in the next instant, moving so quickly she barely had time to register the fact that nothing was going as planned. He was supposed to bow to her desire to chat. He was supposed to give her time to accept him—so that she could then betray him.

The smell of honey wrapped around her, filled her, more intense than before, instantly clouding her thoughts. Sex with him wouldn't be so bad. It *did* take time, and time was all she wanted. Right? Seriously, screwing him blind should have been her plan all along.

"Don't move," he said. "I don't want to hurt you."

She forced out a sigh, even as a tremor of pleasure slid the length of her spine. "I thought men liked for women to move, but whatever. I'm your captive and you're in charge, so if you want to do this, we'll do this. For the record, I'm completely unwilling."

His smile fell away.

She almost cursed. Had she overplayed her hand? "What I meant to say was that, uh, I'm willing. But only because you're—"

"I believe I mentioned that chatting was for later." And then he was stepping inside her—*oh, God, oh, God*—just as she'd seen that soldier do in the forest.

Her skin tingled and burned, but it wasn't unpleasant. "Breean?" His name trembled from her. Her bones gave a sharp ache, but quickly settled into a pleasurable hum.

Shhh, she heard in her mind. *Almost done.*

Her body seemed to expand to accommodate him, but as she stared down at her hands, she couldn't see an outline of him. Couldn't see any hint of him, for that matter. Yet *he was inside her.* They were joined.

"Get out of me," she demanded. Another tremor hit her, and this time it had nothing to do with pleasure. Did he plan to kill her? Make her put a gun to her head?

Take off your clothes.

Her arms obeyed without hesitation. And there was nothing she could do to stop them, no matter how hard she tried. She watched, wide-eyed, as her hands pulled and jerked at her clothing until she was completely naked.

"How did you do that?"

I control your actions. Not your thoughts, not the sensations you feel, but your actions.

"Get out of me," she repeated, harsher this time. "If I spontaneously change shapes, you could—" What? Become trapped inside the new body? She didn't know. Nothing like this had ever happened to her before.

You won't change. I'm in control. Now, I know you wanted my cock as your Christmas present—

"I did not!"

He continued as if she hadn't interrupted him. — *since you mentioned it more than once, but I'm giving you something else.*

"What?" And was that . . . disappointment slithering through her?

You'll see. Walk to the tub.

Her feet were moving in the next instant, and she yelped in frustration and fury because she couldn't stop them. "Damn you! You can't know for sure what will happen if— Ah!" She stepped into the water and sat on the bench, the wet heat lapping and licking at her bare skin. She moaned in ecstasy as the water rippled, laving and caressing.

"Why are you doing this?" Her gaze locked on the scabs on her inner thighs, and she heard Breean give a soft sigh.

Tell me why you did that to yourself and perhaps I will answer your question.

"Unequal exchange. No deal."

Another sigh. *No more pain, sweet. Not for you. Only pleasure. Now, take the soap and cleanse yourself from head to toe. Be careful not to rub the sores.*

She didn't see the soap, but her hand somehow knew where it was and reached. Her fingers curled around the honey-scented bar and brought it to her body, where she massaged herself from head to toe as ordered. She even dunked under the water and came up sputtering.

"That's enough." *I want more.* The contradiction belonged to her, not him. "I'm clean." *Dirty.* "Let me out of the tub." *In an hour.*

Could he hear her naughty thoughts?

Not just yet. Nope. He couldn't. Otherwise he would have said something. *I want to make you come.*

Make her— Oh no. No, no, no. It was one thing to enjoy him. One thing to sleep with him. Maybe. One thing to come together. Again, maybe. But it was quite another to allow her enemy to give her an orgasm, while *he* felt nothing. No maybe about it.

"And I want you to. Get. *Out.*"

Let's see if I can change your mind. Knead your breasts.

A heartbeat later, she was cupping her own breasts, plumping them up and moaning at the scandalous decadence. "Stop. Don't . . . stop."

Do not worry. Stopping isn't an option. Now thumb your nipples.

She didn't even try to resist this time. It was futile, her body obeying before she even realized what he'd said. Her thumbs slid over her wet nipples as commanded, stroking and circling. Felt . . . so . . . good . . . Her mind was darkening, concentrating only on the pleasure.

"Oh, God, Breean."

I like when you say my name. I can't wait to hear you shout it.

"I won't." He forced her to pinch, then caress away the sting. "Won't, won't, wont." *Breean, Breean, Breean.*

You will. Because it's good. So, so good. Too good.

Yes, too good. Her skin was burning, tingling, her stomach quivering. The ache between her legs was growing, spreading. As he'd promised, however, she remained Aleaha, slave to Breean, not once changing into another person.

Pretend it's my tongue flicking over those pretty peaks.

That was not a command he could enforce because it wasn't physical but she found herself obeying anyway. As her fingers played with those hard, sensitive tips, she pictured him in her mind, golden head bent over her, hot tongue flicking.

Another moan slipped from her. "Breean. I don't . . . I don't understand how this is possible." Her hips were writhing in sync with her efforts, and water was pumping over the sides of the tub.

Are you aroused?

"You know I am." As if she could really deny it.

Do you want to touch yourself between your legs?

And finally assuage the ache? She could have sobbed, the anticipation was so consuming. Her knees were already open and spreading, waiting for that first heated touch.

Do you?

"Yes," she whispered. Just then she was beyond caring about the circumstances, what she'd come here for, what she'd hoped to avoid. About the shame she'd probably feel afterward. I'm so weak, she thought, but she needed to touch herself. Would die if she didn't. Since the moment their eyes had first met, they'd been building to this point. Her body had been ready, desperate, and she'd resisted. That had only made it worse. She realized that now.

There could be no more resisting.

She tried to slip one of her hands down her stomach, but it wouldn't move away from her breast. "Breean. Please."

Please what?

"Let me touch myself there."

What will you give me in return?

"Presents are—presents . . ." She was panting, having trouble getting the words out. "You aren't supposed . . . to expect anything . . . in return. Now please."

What will you give me in return? he insisted. *I can give you pleasure, and I can prevent you from changing. Isn't that what you want?*

Argh! "Yes. Fine. Fine, but what do you want in return?"

You. As my lover. My lover in truth.

"Okay. Yes. Deal. Whatever you want?" She'd meant it as a statement, but it emerged as a question. God, she was about to explode. The more she fondled her breasts, the more the ache between her legs increased with dizzying frenzy. If she didn't do something soon, her heart really was going to burst from her chest.

I want you now and, your god knows, maybe forever.

"No," she said automatically. "Not that." Her head fell against the rim of the tub, dark hair floating around her shoulders. Steam curled through the air, a sensual haze. A dream. "Breean. I'm dying. Please."

A growl. *Why won't you have me?*

"Lover, yes. Forever, no. We're enemies."

We don't have to be.

"Breean!"

We will discuss this again. Understand?

"Yes, you sadistic bastard." Anything for relief. "Yes."

Touch your clitoris.

Her hips arched upward to meet her hand, and she cried out as her finger circled the drenched bud once, twice. "Yes. Yes!"

That's enough. Touch your breast again.

"Motherfucker!" She was once again massaging her breasts, her nipples so hard they abraded her palms. "Tell me to touch between my legs again."

So you want more?

"Yes, damn you. Yes!"

Am I a sadistic bastard?

"No. You're a sweetie pie. Honest!"

Good, that's good. Because this sweetie pie wants you over and over. Hard the first time, slow the second. Who knows what will happen the third time.

"Oh, God." In her mind, she could see his naked body straining for release on top of hers, pumping, gliding, sliding. His weight would be delicious. His eyes would blaze down at her with passion. He'd shout her name the way he wanted her to shout his, her real name, not someone else's, as his shaft delved deep.

I want it to be my cock inside you, not your fingers. I want you to come because of me.

She wanted that, too. "Breean," she panted. She

was still massaging her breasts, and her clitoris was still throbbing. "One more touch between my legs. Let me touch myself one more time. Then you can have me. Then you can take me."

Pump your fingers inside yourself.

She braced her feet on the sides of the tub, spreading herself wider. She sank a finger deep inside, cried out again, pumped. Pumped. So good. She was hurtling toward release. So close. Just one more and she'd—

Stop.

Her finger froze. She screamed in frustration.

Do you have a man? The question was barked. *Give me that much, at least.*

"No. No man. And I'm not going to have you if you do this to me again, you sick fu— sweetie pie."

The two agents in the forest, the ones you slapped?

"Friends only. Swear."

He gave a satisfied purr. *I'm glad.*

She couldn't imagine doing this with Devyn or Dallas. She liked them, she did, and she even admired them, but she'd never felt as if she'd been set on fire in their presence. She'd never wanted to rip off their clothes and attack, licking and biting her way down until she'd tasted every inch.

"Command me to come, Breean. I'm begging you."

Finger yourself. Use two, then three.

Moaning as she obeyed, she filled herself with two fingers and pumped them in and out. When that wasn't enough, she added the third, stretching herself for a fuller sensation. Oh, oh. Yes. Yes! Just like that.

Next time, you'll feel my tongue there.

"Yes." She pictured Breean licking her clit, and she blessedly hurtled over the edge of completion, flying out of control, spinning toward the sky, a scream ripping from her throat.

Gradually, the sensations faded, her body relaxed, and she came back to her senses. She slumped over the side of the tub, panting. "I didn't change," she managed to get out. "I didn't change."

And you won't. I'm in control, remember? A second later, he added, *But, darling. I'm not sure why you stopped. You're not done. Come again.*

"W-what?" Even as she spoke, her fingers started working between her legs again, her core immediately readying itself for round two. So long she'd denied herself, she was unprepared for another onslaught. "No. No more."

You'll take it all.

"Yes, okay," she found herself groaning. Oh, God. The pleasure truly was building again. Steadily. Mercilessly. Her legs were falling farther and farther apart, giving her fingers more room to work.

Soon you'll take me.

"Yes." She couldn't deny that, either. She wanted him in a way she'd never wanted anything else. Even a life of her own. A life as Aleaha, without being hunted, without being different. And clearly, her body was already addicted to the pleasure he could give.

So lovely, he purred.

As her hips pumped, water sloshed back and forth, stroking her like a lover. Aleaha was very close to asking Breean to join her, to step out of her and assume control like he'd promised, like she'd told him she would accept. How much more powerful would the sensations be then? But somehow she held the words back, not yet ready to make that leap anywhere but in her mind. Soon, though. If she wasn't careful, soon.

Come.

Release hit her in the next instant. She bowed her back, pushing her fingers as deep as they would go, shuddering, rocking, shouting because this was more than an orgasm; this was a possession that lasted for eternity.

Finally she sagged, completely sated—and still shuddering. "Dear God."

I could feel it, Breean said, awed. *The vibrations were so strong I could feel them.* There was unabashed arousal in his tone. *Come for me. One more time. I want to feel it again.*

"I can't." Her limbs were like rocks.

Yes.

"Breean, I really can't."

You can.

"Too much," she panted. "It's too much."

Never enough.

"Let me . . . let me . . . catch my breath."

Come, sweet. Please, come for me.

The newest orgasm hadn't yet dissipated before another one sneaked up on her. Her clit was swollen, the water making her skin all the more sensitive, so every sensation was intensified. With one hand still at her breasts, she pinched her nipples and rode the waves of the third orgasm, shaking and quaking all over again.

Inside her head, she could hear Breean roaring, as if he, too, were coming. Somehow, that only increased her pleasure. "I . . . I . . ."

Breean was shouting her name, just as she'd craved, and then, suddenly, she was shivering, experiencing a fourth eruption—*his* pleasure becoming hers as well. Her blood sizzled and blistered through her veins, just like in the forest, and the scent of honey drifted from *her*, filling the entire room, branding her soul-deep.

Utterly replete, Aleaha slumped over the rim of the tub once more. She might never be able to move again, was more exhausted than she'd ever been in her life. She was breathless, her heartbeat racing, her bones like jelly. Yet she'd never felt better.

She hadn't slept in the cell, too keyed up, wondering what the future held. Now her eyelids closed of their own accord and stayed closed as if they'd been glued.

"I guess you liked your gift," she managed to say.

He chuckled. *I did indeed. Sleep now.*

And she did.

Breean had never, in all his years, experienced anything like that.

He exited Aleaha's body, reforming into a solid mass, then carried her to the bed and gently splayed her over the mattress. The ends of her dark hair were wet, dripping. Moisture danced along every inch of her flushed skin, her nipples were still hard, and her limbs were boneless.

She was the most erotic sight he'd ever beheld.

Naked, he crawled in beside her and pulled her into his side. He'd come inside her. His spirit had somehow experienced absolute release while inhabiting her. He'd never heard of such a thing happening, much less being possible, but it *had* happened. They'd been fused, one being.

Several times, he'd felt her body try to change images. Felt the bones trying to lengthen or shorten, even felt the pigment in her skin trying to lighten or darken. But he'd maintained a firm grip on her, on Aleaha, and she'd remained the same, just as he'd promised her. Just as she'd hoped. Surely that was a sign they were meant to be together.

Together. Yes. He wasn't going to let her go, he decided. Not ever. She was his, from this moment on. She didn't have a man, and she desired him. She might still be fighting it, but she did desire him.

His next mission: making her admit it.

SEVEN

In the wee hours of the morning, Breean left Aleaha in bed. With her cozied up to him, he'd been too keyed up and hadn't been able to sleep, and now he needed to meet with Talon. Though he desperately wanted to take her with him, she was still lost in slumber, at peace, and he was loath to wake her. He really had worn her out, he thought, grinning. He'd satisfied his woman into a stupor.

Even as grateful as she would surely be—in his dreams—he didn't trust her, and made sure to lock the door. And smart boy that he was, he'd nailed the window permanently shut before ever inviting her into his bedroom.

He nodded to the men striding through the halls, keeping guard. Nodded to those cleaning and sharpening their weapons, getting ready to stand watch. Seeing them work so diligently, a wave of guilt hit him. He'd have to take a shift soon. His army worked hard; the men deserved a break, and god knew he'd already had his. But damn if he was ready to leave Aleaha for an extended period, now that he had her where he wanted her.

Finally he reached his office, where Talon was waiting for him. As Breean claimed his chair at the desk, his friend, seated in front of him, glanced up from the book he'd been perusing.

"Who spirit-walked?" he asked, jumping right into business.

"I took the first shift," Talon said, "and Cain the second."

Breean studied the warrior. The tension that had shadowed his face for the past two years was gone. "After your shift, you found a woman, I take it."

Talon grinned slowly, revealing perfect white teeth. "Two, actually."

"And you kept your skin covered?"

"Completely. My scent drew them in, and after that I had only to unfasten my pants. They couldn't get to my cock fast enough. You know," Talon added thoughtfully, "I really like this planet. I'm glad we decided to stay."

If only Aleaha were as easy as Talon's females. Her resistance was her biggest flaw. Silly him for ever thinking the harder he had to work for a victory, the more he'd appreciate it. He would have given anything to have all of her *now*. "Did either of you learn anything?"

"I admit my attention wasn't where it should have been, and I was easily distracted. But Cain, well, you know he is a force to be reckoned with, more determined than most. He found AIR headquarters."

"How?" In all their visits here, they'd failed to locate the building that housed AIR's elite. Apparently, they'd been overrun by reporters one night and had since moved their headquarters to somewhere secret.

"He watched as an otherworlder was arrested, then slid unnoticed into the car that drove the blind-folded creature in."

Of course. So simple, so easy. Breean leaned forward, eager. This was better than he had hoped. "What did he learn?"

"AIR is run by a woman named Mia Snow. Her man is an Arcadian, a king, and he can move as swiftly as we can. He was with her that night, the night we arrived. They were waiting a mile or so away, ready to swoop in if a second line of defense was needed. But we weren't the Schön, as they'd expected."

Aleaha had told him that. Which meant, Aleaha had told him the truth. Darling girl. He should reward her with another orgasm.

"Still, they were coming after us when another solar flare erupted around them, as if it had purposefully been directed at them, and they disappeared."

Breean had learned that every planet had a way of utilizing those solar flares. Some used stones as a guide—if they carried a stone from a certain planet, that was the planet the solar flare would take them to. Some, like him, used visualization. Breean had imagined a planet with a thriving metropolis, and this was one of the places he'd ended up. Some simply knew the celestial gate those flares opened and which doors to enter.

Could some actually control the flares?

"Have the agents returned? Where did they go?"

"They have returned, yes, so Cain said. Where they went . . . I'm not sure this can be true. They claim to have traveled into the past. Into another plane or dimension, they weren't sure. A state called New Orleans, where females with pointed ears and unnatural strength reside alongside men who suck the blood from your body. The females called themselves the Nïxies. Nïxies house of pain. Nïxies house of pleasure, Nïxies house of crazy—something like that. Cain was confused, and could have gotten some of the details wrong."

How . . . odd.

Talon continued, "They didn't stay long. Just long enough for us to have left the forest."

Again, had someone controlled the flare, keeping them away? If so, that being would have been aiding Breean. But who would want to aid him?

The Schön queen? Most likely. After all, a group of her men had been destroyed by AIR. Perhaps she had thought Breean would take care of the problem for her. How had she known Breean was coming here, though? Since leaving Raka, he'd had no contact with her.

"Anything else?" he asked on a sigh.

"Yes, but you will not like it." Shifting in his seat, Talon massaged the back of his neck. "One of the agents escaped during the move here. Syler chased him but lost him."

Breean's hands fisted. "Why did no one tell me?"

"Syler told no one."

First Marleon's betrayal, and now this. He was losing control of his army! "By keeping this a secret, he has placed us all in danger."

"Yes."

"I will not kill him for the offense, but he must be punished. Ten lashes should teach him to use his tongue when necessary."

Talon nodded. "Fortunately, the agent doesn't seem to know where we are now located."

One small favor, at least. "Was nothing learned about the Schön?"

"No. AIR still has no idea when the queen will

arrive. The one Schön they have in lockup refuses to speak about her."

He straightened. "They have a Schön in lockup?"

"Yes."

A killing rage sprang to life inside of him. That bastard might very well be the one who had seduced his mother and sisters. And if not, that bastard still needed to die, for surely he had seduced someone else's mother and sisters.

"Cain did well," he said, forcing himself to calm. "Give him the day off and tell him to do as he pleases."

"He will be overjoyed."

"I will take his shift tonight, so he does not have to worry about that, either."

Talon's eyes widened, and there was a spark of delight. Breean knew the two men had spent time together throughout the years, even a few lonely nights. What they'd done, he didn't know but could guess. They might both crave females, as Talon had proven with his excess, but they must have enjoyed each other. Now that women were in plentiful supply, he'd expected their association to end. Looked like he'd been wrong.

He pushed to his feet. "As for now, I have something to attend to." Or rather, someone.

Aleaha came awake instantly, deeply asleep one moment, fully cognizant the next. Her entire body ached—and not in pleasure this time. Her blood was rushing too quickly, and there was too much of it, filling her veins at an unnatural rate.

She moaned, trying to fight the pain. Trying to stop the unfolding of events that always followed this sensation. Not now. Not after everything she'd just experienced with Breean.

Oh, God. Breean. Was he still here? *Please let him be somewhere else.*

She searched the bed with swollen eyes. She was splayed on the mattress, still naked and covered by soft white sheets. Breean was beside her—and he was awake, watching her every move. No. No! She'd fought so hard to keep this part of her life to herself. To be forced to reveal her secret now . . .

More than anyone, she didn't want *him* to witness what she was about to do. What she *had* to do. He'd no longer be caring or kind. He'd no longer seek pleasure from her.

She chewed on her bottom lip to cut off a groan. This shouldn't be happening, not for another few days.

"Are you hurt?" he asked, frowning. "Did I hurt you?"

"I need some time alone, okay?" she told him, voice a ragged mix of faux light-heartedness, pain, and desperation.

"What's going on, Aleaha? You're swelling."

"Leave. Please." Only the desperation emerged this time.

"I'm not going anywhere."

She could see the determination in his golden eyes. "*Please.*"

"No. You will tell me what's happening to you and I will help you. That's your only option."

Seeing no other choice, the agony intensifying, she said, "I—I need a knife."

He snorted, losing all hint of concern. "There are only two things I'll give you right now, and a knife isn't one of them."

"Please. A knife." Wildly she glanced around the chamber, looking for something, anything with a sharp tip. If she had to crawl to it, she would. Last night she'd used her nails, but that hadn't released enough blood. Obviously.

Her line of vision was shrinking, and she saw nothing she could use. No. Wait. In the corner by the door was a bowl filled with fruit. She could dump the food and break the bowl. Surely one of the pieces would be jagged enough to slice through skin and veins.

"I'm not letting you out of this bed," he told her, "so don't even think about getting up."

Ignoring him, she threw her leg over the side. The action nearly felled her. Sharp torment exploded through her every curve and hollow, and she whimpered. *Don't cry. Don't you dare cry.*

"Aleaha?" he said, concern returning. "Is this a game?"

"No game. Please. A knife."

"But why? Help me understand what's happening."

"I have to cut myself." Soon. Oh, God. Soon.

His eyes narrowed. "Bloodshed is forbidden, Aleaha. You know that. I will not let you spill mine."

"I don't want to spill yours," she admitted weakly. "I want to spill *mine*."

He blinked in surprise. "Again, why?"

"I just need a fucking knife! I won't use it on you, I swear." The last word left her mouth on a groan. She tried to sit up, to slap him, to force him to understand, but couldn't. Hurt. So badly. She'd waited too long.

"Aleaha?" His voice was devoid of emotion, his eyes flat.

"Breean. *Please.* I must."

"You're in pain, I can see that, but I can't aid you until you've told me what's wrong."

She wasn't given a chance to respond. He hissed in a breath and jerked away from her, as if he finally understood. "Are you sick? You told me you weren't infected. Did you lie? Did biting me—"

"No. Not sick. Breean, the knife." A tear slid down her cheek, followed quickly by another, until there was an unstoppable flood of them. With every second that passed, her pain and swelling increased.

"Tell me why you wish to do something so barbaric as cut yourself. Now!"

The words exploded from her on a desperate breath. If the truth was what he needed to propel him into aiding her, God help them both, she'd give him the truth. "I produce too much blood. I think it has something to do with the way I change forms. And I've changed a lot these past few days. Every week or so, I have to cut myself to drain the excess. I tried to drain some last night, but when we . . . in the tub . . ."

"You didn't change in the tub. I made sure of it."

"The pleasure, maybe . . . I don't know. Help me. Please, just help me." She was babbling, but couldn't stop. She expected him to leap away from her with revulsion. He continued to stare down at her, something hard in his eyes.

"What happens if you fail to cut yourself?" he asked raggedly.

"I swell. My organs will burst. Knife," she cried, doubling over. She must have squeezed her eyes shut because the next thing she knew, Breean was hovering over her, teeth bared.

Finally, though, he held a knife, hilt out. "I am giving you this because I would rather deal with the possibility of contaminated blood than watch you suffer. If you are lying . . ."

There would be hell to pay. "Not . . . lying." She tried to reach out, but her elbow locked in place, too swollen to move. Even her fingers had become unbendable. No. *No!* "Can't move. You . . . must do it."

His eyes widened, and there was the revulsion she'd expected.

That didn't stop her from continuing; it couldn't, not if she wanted to survive. "St-stab me. In the thigh. Biggest artery, will drain the most."

He shook his head violently. "Surely you are jesting. I have killed men for shedding blood, and you want me to stab *you*?"

"If you don't, I'll die." The more the blood built up, the faster she would destruct. "Hurry. Cut and leave the knife inside. Otherwise, heal too quickly."

"No."

"Bree-an. Need to bleed," she whispered. Then her eyes swelled completely shut, blocking his image. Maybe that was for the best. Now she wouldn't have to see that revulsion intensify in his golden eyes when he did what was necessary. Or watch when he finally abandoned her.

"There has to be another way."

If there were another way, she would have found it by now. "No, there's—" Her jaw clamped and her throat closed, jamming up her airway, her words. Her lungs began to burn and burn and she jerked, every muscle she possessed clenching on bone. Her stomach knotted, rolled. Her nose stung, desperate for air, and the stinging only increased when warm blood began to pour from her nostrils.

"Damn this!" In the next instant, the sheet was whipped away from her, a cool breeze was drifting over her, and a sharp, agonizing pain ripping through her thigh.

Almost immediately her jaw eased and her throat opened and a scream pushed its way free. Breean dug the knife in deep and twisted. He left the tip inside as she'd asked, allowing more and more blood to flow out. With that flow came sweet relief as the pressure inside her lessened, the swelling faded.

Suddenly she could move. Could see Breean hovering over her, his hand curled over the knife hilt. His gaze was fastened on her face, his expression unreadable. Much as he hated blood, she was kind of surprised he hadn't killed her outright. Instead, he truly had aided her.

As if he sensed her thoughts, he said, "Is this all you need?" No hint of his emotions in his voice, either.

"Yes," she rasped.

For a long while, he didn't speak, just watched that crimson liquid trickle onto the sheet. Then he nodded, as if he'd just made a very important decision. She was too afraid to ask what that decision was.

"How long do I bleed you?" he asked.

"Until I pass out." Even as she spoke, she could feel the darkness slinking into her mind. Sweet oblivion, she thought with relief and then knew nothing else.

Breean pulled the blade from Aleaha's leg and watched as the wound slowly healed itself, muscle and then flesh weaving back together. Why she still scarred when she healed so swiftly, he could only guess. The front runner: the number of times she'd been forced to do this. A close second: her curative process wasn't as thorough as it appeared. Either way, this precious female suffered.

Reeling, he cleaned up the blood then burned the rags and sheets before making the bed with Aleaha still in it. She slept through it all, a testament to the brutality of the entire ordeal.

The thought that this woman—or anyone—had to bleed to survive should have been abhorrent to Breean. *Was* abhorrent. Half of him feared causing another plague, killing the only survivors of his race, because of his actions this day. She could be a carrier for some disease he'd never heard of, never dealt with. But the other half of him didn't care about the consequences.

He would do whatever was needed to keep this woman alive.

She was his, connected to him on a level he still didn't understand. When he looked at her, he wanted only to please her. Well, and himself. Hurting her had ripped him up inside, but that had been better than watching her writhe in pain.

"My poor baby," he cooed, stroking her soft cheek. She hated what she was required to do to live. He'd realized it the moment she confessed, for there had been shame in her voice. She'd also expected him to be disgusted by her, for there had been grim acceptance in her eyes. But he hadn't been able and still couldn't work up a single spark of the emotion. Not when his actions had saved her.

From now on, he would help her. Be with her through it all. For there was no going back now. They would be together.

While she slept, he remained at her side. Even when Talon came to inform him that darkness would soon fall and his shift would begin.

"I need a few more minutes," he said.

"Very well." Rather than departing, the warrior transferred his weight from one foot to the other. "The others begged me to ask if they might have a turn in town."

"Of course," he replied. "They may go in pairs, each returning in an hour."

Talon was careful to keep his gaze away from Ale-aha. "They will be very happy to hear this. Oh, and we have finally properly installed the security system around the property. If AIR invades, you'll know."

"Excellent." When Talon pivoted to leave, he called, "Tell the men to be careful when choosing their women. They might end up with a wildcat."

His second in command laughed before disappearing into the hall.

Breean stared down at Aleaha for the rest of his remaining minutes, then stood. Her features were relaxed, the swelling completely gone. He never wanted to see her like that again, hurting so badly. *You're mine. I'll take care of you now.*

Once again, he left her sleeping. Fortunately, his shift proved uneventful and he was able to check on Aleaha multiple times. She never moved from that supine position, and that began to worry him.

When he returned to the room once and for all, he found her sitting up in bed. His relief was palpable. And so was his sudden desire. Her breasts were bare, the sheet around her waist, and her hair tumbled down her back, dark ribbons he wanted to wrap around his fists. Yawning, she rubbed the sleep from her eyes. Had she only now awakened?

"Feeling better?"

"Breean," she said on a trembling breath. "Yes. Much. Thank you."

"I'm glad and you're welcome," he told her, rushing to her side, dropping his weapons along the way. Much as he wanted her, he would be a fool to give her such easy access to his knives and guns while near—and intoxicated by—her. He also removed his shirt before caressing her arm, marveling at the smoothness. See? Intoxicated. "Now, there's something we need to finish."

Her gaze flicked to him, widened, then moved to her legs. "The blood—"

"Is gone," he assured her.

Shock curtained her entire face. "Why did you clean me instead of kill me?"

"I do not want to kill you." He crawled in beside her, then rolled on top of her. She gasped but didn't try to push him away. "I want to make love to you."

EiGHT

The feel of Breean's muscled weight pinning her into the mattress was amazing, Aleaha thought, dazed. More amazing? He still desired her. After everything he'd witnessed, after everything he'd had to do, he *still desired her.* She could feel the length of his erection, thick and hot against her thigh.

"But I'm an abomination to you," she whispered, afraid to place her hope in this enemy who wasn't really an enemy. "Aren't you disgusted by me?"

"You make me feel many things, sweetie pie, but disgust isn't one of them."

She felt herself melting, falling under his spell. Already he'd satisfied her in ways she'd never thought possible. But she couldn't let herself forget that AIR agents were locked in his dungeon. How selfish would she be to luxuriate in his arms while they merely endured? Well, to luxuriate *again*.

She'd been a little too selfish lately, taking Macy's identity, living a life she hadn't been meant to live. Yes, Macy had died before she'd taken over, and probably wouldn't care about the changes she'd made—or perhaps Macy was even now looking down (up?) at her and wishing her to everlasting hell—but those agents *had* become her friends.

"Breean," she said, pushing at his chest. She could have cried at the distance she gained.

"Aleaha," he said, not allowing the distance to last. He grabbed her wrists and pinned them over her head. A favorite position of his, obviously. Her back immediately arched, mashing her breasts into his chest. Her nipples were already hard and rubbed against him.

"This is wrong," she breathed. "We have to stop."

"You cannot stop a fire once it has been ignited." He rotated his pelvis, and she hissed in a breath when his cock slid across her clit, then anchored her legs to the mattress with his own.

Her hiss blended with his. "Actually, you can. With water."

"Then we'll stay away from the water. Now, do you want to talk or finish this?"

As she looked up at him, desire swirled in his golden eyes, almost a living entity, beckoning her to give in. *Just one time.* But one time wouldn't be enough, not for an addict like her. And, oh, was she an addict. She'd had a taste and now craved more.

"T-talk," she forced herself to say.

"Liar. But that's all right." His tongue swiped over his lips. Was he imagining tasting her? "I will talk with you, too."

"From opposite sides of the room."

He shook his head. "Just like this."

Thank God for stubborn men. If he'd left her, she might have stabbed him. "What about the agents?"

"I won't release them," he said darkly. "I told you. That would put my own men at risk."

"Well, you can't keep them locked away forever."

"I can, however, use them as bargaining tools. A life for a life."

They must do things differently on Raka, because she doubted "bargaining" would work out for him. Not favorably, at least. "You might want to rethink that. You'll go to trade and receive a death sentence."

"Maybe," he said. "Maybe not. Until something can be arranged, however, I want you to know that I will not hurt them. That was never my intention."

"*Until something can be arranged* could take forever. They should be home with their families."

"And they will be. Soon."

"Now."

"First, I must ensure AIR will keep its end of the

bargain." He didn't give her time to respond, but quickly changed the subject. "No matter what happens in this room, no matter what we say or do to each other, I want you to know that you will never have to cut yourself again. I will take care of you from now on, and I will tell no one your secrets."

She opened her mouth to return them to the agents, but his words sank in and he won a little piece of her heart. No more hiding? No more being afraid someone would find out who and what she was? Amazing. And that this man would be the one responsible for her liberation . . . "I can't ask that of you."

"You aren't asking. I'm simply doing." One of his hands moved from her wrists and curled around her nape, forcing her head to lift slightly. He bowed his back, placing her gaze on his chest, just above his nipple, all the while pulling her mouth closer. "And now we have talked," he said, voice husky, rich. "Ready for the loving to begin?"

He planned to release the agents "soon," which meant she had two choices. She could wait until he did so to be with him. Or she could be with him now, knowing she could lose him during the exchange if AIR decided not to work with him.

Actually, as she'd warned, that seemed most likely. They could very well agree to his demands, then start firing the moment the agents were free. Honor was for those who wanted to lose their loved ones, she'd heard Mia Snow say more than once.

Should she do everything in her power to convince Breean of the truth of her claim? No, she thought next. If she did, he might decide to keep the agents forever, and that she couldn't allow.

"Aleaha," he said, claiming her attention. He was watching her expectantly, desire still swirling in those golden eyes. "Decide."

He was a good man. An honorable man despite his assurances to the contrary, and his plans, if successful, would provide a happily-ever-after for everyone. Aleaha was not like Mia Snow. She respected honor. *I want to be with him now*, she thought. She would be selfish one more time. Otherwise, she might not ever know what it was like to be his woman, truly be his woman, and she *had* to know.

"I don't know." She flicked out her tongue, meeting his skin and trailing it over his thundering heartbeat. "What if I change? You're not inside me this time." Wait. That hadn't sounded right. "I mean, you're not—"

"I know what you meant. I won't mind if you change."

"Even if I become a man? Or you? I know it didn't bother you in the forest, but that was only for a second and it could surprise you, feeling dangly bits, and you could toss me—"

"Aleaha." Dark desperation rang from his tone. He rolled them over, placing her on top. "Give me a chance to prove myself before you condemn me." He smiled slowly, sheepishly as she settled against him. "Right now, I need you. You, no matter who you are or what you look like."

There went another little piece of her heart. His

words were a mix of soothing balm and white-hot embers of arousal. Being with him was no longer a need. It was a necessity. "I've decided," she said.

"And?"

"And I don't know why you're still talking." Trembling, she inched down his chest, not stopping until his navel came into view. She licked again, and his muscles clenched.

"Thank you. Yes. More." He was babbling. She liked that.

Lower . . . lower . . . she continued to move. His cock strained high and proud, drawing her full attention. *Mine.* His golden balls were drawn up tight. She tilted her head and allowed her teeth to graze his inner thigh. The cool press of his skin was an electrifying contradiction to her hot tongue.

"Shall I kiss you here?"

"Anywhere," he croaked.

"Free rein. I like that." Unable to stop herself, she curled her hand around his testicles and sank her mouth on his shaft, taking him deep, all the way to the back of her throat. Her jaw stretched wide, burned.

"Yes," Breean roared. "Yes."

She moaned, somehow feeling as if he were sinking his fingers deep inside her. Then her eyes widened as she realized that yes, she was feeling his fingers, phantom fingers, pumping in and out of her. Closing her eyes at the bliss, she sucked him up and down, writhing her hips all the while. *Don't switch bodies, don't switch bodies.*

"Don't stop." He grabbed her and swiveled her

around, keeping her mouth on his dick while placing her moist clit right over his face. With barely a pause, he licked her, first the outer shell, then inside, probing.

"Breean!" The sensations were too much, not enough, and her physical form began to lengthen. She forced herself to still, forced her mind to blank. Breath singed her lungs. "I'm changing. I—"

"Just let yourself go, sweet. You taste so good, and I know the woman underneath. I told you. I don't care who you are or what form you have."

As she gave him yet another piece of her heart, something broke inside her. Tension, guilt, fear. She simply allowed herself to fly, relaxing into whatever form her body happened to take. At first, she changed into one person after another, never maintaining a certain image for more than a few seconds. Through it all, Breean continued to kiss and caress her, not once pulling away in disgust.

Then, panting and sweating, she realized the changing had stopped. For several minutes, she simply lay there, Aleaha, only Aleaha. Perhaps she'd run out of identities, or perhaps Breean had left pieces of himself inside her, maintaining a grip on her image.

Breean . . . inside her . . . the first tremors of an approaching orgasm rocked her. Either way, she was truly free, her fear vanquished, leaving amazement, gratitude, and awe, each adding to her enjoyment.

"Yes, yes," she cried.

Breean gave one more lick and another tremor crashed through her, propelling her closer to the edge. Just a bit more and she'd—he spun her around until they were eye to eye. He grabbed her wrists and locked them behind her back with one of his hands, the action arching her forward, reading her. But he didn't enter her.

"More," she said, willing to beg. He'd given her so much already, but she had to have more.

"Remember how you felt in the tub, touching yourself, pumping yourself to orgasm? Do you want that again or do you want me?"

Her heart sped up, hammering at her ribs. "You."

"Perfect answer," he said, gently rubbing his cock against her.

Moaning, she closed her eyes again. "But I . . . we have to . . . I want to make you feel good, too."

"You do. More than any other, you do. And do you know what will make me feel as if I've reached the gates of heaven? Caressing you. Starting with your breasts, rolling the nipples between my fingers this time, making you writhe. Then I want to dip lower, sink my fingers between your legs. I want you to feel *me*. Only me, not a spirit version of me."

Her breathing became erratic, uneven. "Yes. I want that, too."

"You'll be hotter and wetter than you are now. I know you will be. Just like I know you'll be tight. Tighter than a fist."

She bit her bottom lip, drawing a single bead of blood. "I'm ready. Do it."

But he didn't. He didn't move. "And when you've drenched my hand, when you're practically screaming for release, I'll replace my fingers with my mouth. I'll lick, taste, and suck you again."

"Yes. Please, yes." She gasped in need, the sound of it like a little catch of wonder. Her hips moved toward him, seeking deeper contact, but, damn him, he twisted out of reach.

"I won't be able to help myself," he said. "I'll bite you, as you did me in the forest. Just a little sting, though, then I'll lick it away."

She moaned. Caught herself. Pressed her lips together. He was holding back, so she would, too. Only, her hips were moving consistently now and she wasn't able to hide the action. The scent of his arousal was so thick, it was almost a honey cloud enveloping her.

"You're all talk," she gritted out.

"No, I'm so hard for you." He released her hands to cup her cheeks. "I've never wanted a woman the way I want you."

"Then take me." *Take me in a way that they'll be no holding back for either of us.*

An animalistic sound escaped him, and he tangled his hands in her hair, jerking her head toward him for a bruising kiss. His tongue thrust inside her mouth, feverish, desperate. Finally. Sweetly. He was putting his mouth where his money was. Wait. That wasn't how the expression went. Oh, who cared. Delectable!

"You make me so crazy."

Brain fogging, she arched into him. "More," she breathed.

More? "All," Breean said, and deepened the kiss. They were both so wild, their teeth scraped together. Didn't help that her flavor was pure decadence. Not the honey he'd once been used to, but better. Sweeter. A rose blooming amid a tempest, he would have said if he were a poet. Caveman that his brain currently was, all he could think was *mine*.

He licked his way down her neck as his fingers explored her body. There was a fine, silky tuft of hair between her legs where he dabbled, tickling, exciting, before sinking his fingers into her already soaking folds.

She nearly shot off the bed. "That . . . that . . . right there. Yes!"

Her clitoris was swollen, eager. He circled it, and her hips followed the motion. *Beautiful*.

"Breean," she groaned.

"So wet," he praised.

"Hurt."

He'd already vowed to take care of all her hurts. This one would be his pleasure. "I'll kiss it and make it better." And he did. He pinned her on her back and inched down her body, licking along the way. She was delicious curves and sweet angles, and he hadn't gotten nearly enough of her. Would he ever?

He wanted her to come with his cock buried deep, but he had to have another sampling. Was already addicted to her feminine flavor. Besides, what kind of lover would he be if he couldn't make her come more than once?

She arched into him, writhing, head thrashing from side to side. Her hands found her breasts, and she squeezed. The sight was erotic, as foreign as she was. He hadn't seen her in the tub, but he'd wanted to. Oh, he'd wanted to. He liked that Aleaha was pushed so close to the edge right now that she was willing to do anything to find release.

"Want my tongue on you again?" he asked.

"Yes."

"Licking you?"

"Yes."

"Sucking you off?"

"Yes. God, yes."

His tongue was flicking out in the next instant. She was still hot and wet and she still tasted of passion. He thought he might fight a thousand wars if it meant being with this woman. He thought he might kill violently and without mercy for the privilege.

"I can't get enough." He moved his tongue back and forth, then tunneled it inside her, mimicking sex.

"Breean, Breean," she chanted.

His cock was so hard it could explode at any moment. Already he could feel the hot glide of seed on the tip. "Spread yourself for me."

Instantly she obeyed, reaching between her legs and opening herself for him. Pink, wet. His. He gently clamped her center between his teeth, sucking as he'd promised.

Didn't take long. In seconds, she was screaming her release. Still he didn't stop. He reached up and palmed one of her breasts just as she had done.

Trembling, she arched into his touch, riding the waves of bliss. Then, as she calmed, she grabbed his wrist and brought his fingers into her mouth, sucking two inside, deep, so deep.

At that, his blood reached the searing point, burning through his veins, blistering his organs. He pumped his free hand up and down his cock, thinking to find a little ease. That only made it worse.

"Ready?" he asked her. He was too desperate, couldn't wait any longer.

"Give me."

"Everything?"

"And more."

Beautiful female. He climbed up her body, nipping along the way. She was simply irresistible. When he was in position, just about to sink home, she gave a strong shove to his shoulders. Taken by surprise, he fell to his back, and for a moment, he thought she meant to leave him. He wanted to curse ... until she straddled him.

Grinning, she curled her fingers around his swollen length. "Hard," she praised. "Big."

"Like?"

Her head fell back, all that dark hair tickling his chest, and she breathed a sweet, "Oh, yes."

Aleaha more than liked. She loved. Temporary insanity, she was sure, because right now she was drowning in bliss, on fire, achy, so much more so than in the tub—something she wouldn't have thought possible.

She was fascinated by Breean's body, by the grunts of delight he'd emitted as he tasted between her legs. Actually, everything about him fascinated her. Maybe because he'd done nothing she'd expected. They were captor and prisoner. Master and slave, he'd once said, and she was everything he should hate. Yet he'd freely given of himself, ensuring she found satisfaction, all the while acting as if she were important to him, as if her needs mattered.

The knowledge was as heady and intoxicating as his honey scent.

When she'd lain in bed at home alone, touching herself, this was what she'd dreamed of. Craved. And now, finally, she was getting it. With her enemy. As doomed as they surely were, this might be her only chance to enjoy him and that saddened her.

"You look ready to cry," Breean said with more tension than she'd ever heard him use before. "Do you plan to stop?"

"Not even if your home is invaded."

"Then let me have you. Please."

Hearing him beg sent a shiver down her spine. Yes, oh, yes. She rose on her knees, placing her wet core over his cock. He gripped her hips, squeezed, and the round head pressed for entrance, stretching her, tantalizing her.

"Deeper," he rasped.

Another inch.

It had been so long for her, she felt a slight burn,

but the rapture exploding through her soon made her forget any discomfort.

"More," he urged, the vessels in his neck bulging.

"Yes." Another inch.

"That's the way. Take it all, sweet. Take it all."

Yet another inch, and another, though he still wasn't all the way seated. The few other men she'd been with had not been as large as Breean. Was anyone? Well, she had been, she thought with a small smile. That amusement relaxed her and she fell another inch. The stretch was more noticeable now, shoving through that rapturous haze.

"Big," she told him again.

"You can take me."

Yes, she could. Aleaha Love, wanton sex goddess, could do anything. She stopped resisting and slammed all the way down. Breean roared in approval, the sound blending with her own needy moan.

"Move for me, sweet." The words were barely audible.

Slowly, she rose; slowly, she lowered. Her head fell back, and she gazed up at the ceiling, lost, flying. A powerful warrior was under her, hers to do with as she pleased. He was enjoying her, delighted by her. Dream come true.

"Faster," he beseeched.

Yes, faster. She moved again, increasing her pace. Up, down. Perfect. So perfect.

"Faster," he repeated. His fingers, wrapped as they were around her waist, dug into muscle. There'd be a bruise, but it would be worth it. "It's been so long for me, and you feel so good. I don't know how long I can last for you."

She wouldn't last, either, was already hurtling through the stars. Faster and faster she allowed herself to go.

"That's the way," he praised.

"Give me everything," she said. "I want it. Want you."

He cupped her ass, spreading her even wider, making her take him all the deeper. Faster still they slammed together. She could actually see the outline of his spirit, glowing as if it wanted to burst free of his body and into hers.

"Aleaha," he growled.

Something was thrumming through her. Tenderness and caring, perhaps, making the climax she'd experienced before seem like a pale imitation. It consumed her with honey and cinnamon and glimmered as it washed through her. This was her man; his ecstasy was hers.

"Breean, Breean," she chanted. Just then, his name was the only word she knew.

He rolled her over, drilling into her, and her entire body erupted in a cascade of sparks and light, spasming, arching. *Must have another taste.* Lost again, forever, she gripped his hair and jerked him down for another kiss.

As his tongue plundered her mouth, he, too, erupted, spurting hot seed inside her and sending her on another tailspin.

He shuddered over and over before finally collapsing on top of her. She closed her eyes, basking, more alive than she'd ever been before because, in that moment, she was a woman. Not an agent. Not an alien. But a woman. She was Aleaha.

Nine

The next several days passed in a wondrous daze for Aleaha, dulled only by her arguments with Breean about the AIR agents. Her thought to be selfish just one more time? Completely obliterated. Breean kept her with him and they rarely left his room. The few times they had, he'd taken her to his office where he'd spoken with his second in command, Talon.

The two had used their own language, which Breean had yet to teach her and she hadn't yet figured out, so she had no idea what was said. Afterward, they would return to the bedroom and she would pester him for information—which would in turn lead to another argument. Somehow, someway, he always managed to distract her. Maybe it was the way he savored her body, praising her wit, her sweetness, even her determination to save her friends.

He made her feel special, cherished, something she'd never experienced before. But, damn it. She would have to do a better job of resisting him to get the kind of results she wanted. Like, her friends' happiness. Like, Breean's happiness. And continued good health. Surely there was a way to meet all three objectives.

Right now, she was naked (again) and snuggled into Breean's side (again), his fingers tracing her arm. And she let him gentle her. Luxuriated in him, actually. *You are in so much trouble, girl.* From enemy to lover. From hated to adored. *What are you going to do now?* She'd wondered a million times.

Macy probably wouldn't have gotten herself into this situation.

Aleaha frowned at the thought. *I'm not Macy; I never was.* Still, she was a friend to those agents locked below—if she needed to remind herself a thousand times, she would—and she couldn't leave them helpless. *More than you already have,* her mind supplied.

"Can we talk about the agents now?"

"We discuss them every day," he said, fingers stilling. "Just because they are prisoners doesn't mean they are miserable. They are well fed, given blankets. They aren't tortured."

"What if I said I wouldn't sleep with you again until they were free?"

"I'd call you a liar and kiss my way to your sweet spot."

She gritted her teeth. Clearly, resisting him wasn't going to get the job done. She was going to have to start fighting him. Truly fighting him. She might even have to hurt him. "Why haven't you tried to bargain with AIR?"

"They aren't yet ready to deal with me."

"How do you know?"

"I just do."

Frustrating! "Let me talk to them. I'll explain that you're willing to help them fight the Schön queen. Because of your skills and their desperation to defeat that woman, they might overlook your past behavior."

"No. I don't want you leaving."

"I'll call them, then."

"Calls can be traced. You know that."

Argh! "You can't hide out forever."

"I know."

Not just frustrating, but stubborn. He was making her rehash, and she hated to rehash. "If I had your men locked away, I suspect you wouldn't care how they were being treated. You would want them freed."

"You're right, but I can't simply let the agents go. I can't place my people in even more danger. And let me respond to the other objections I'm sure you're about to raise. They were blindfolded when brought here, yes, so I could blindfold them again and drop them off somewhere and they would not be able to find me. If I do that, however, I'll be without my backup plan if AIR decides not to risk working with me."

"Breean—"

"It has to be this way. I'm sorry. I wish it were otherwise, but . . ."

He felt guilty, she could tell from the tattered emotion in his tone, but she also realized there really would be no convincing him to rethink his strategy, no matter what she did or how hard she tried. His determination was as solid as hers.

That depressed and angered her, because it meant their time together was over.

Still. If she'd learned anything about him these last few days, it was that he truly wanted to make a home here and would never purposely hurt the innocent. So she tried one more time to make him see the light. "You want to destroy the Schön, yes? Well, if they were to appear today, AIR would be divided, trying to find you *and* fight the Schön. What if this planet falls because you are too stubborn to try to make something work? Please, just let the men go and—"

"Enough. I've spent the last two years fighting, searching for a new home, and making preparations for that home. Finally I'm here. Finally I have a moment's respite with a beautiful woman I—a beautiful woman I like. Why can I not enjoy that for a bit?"

"Because time is our enemy. AIR will find you. And knowing them as I do, I know that if you have failed to initiate a gesture of goodwill, they will show you no mercy."

He sighed. "I'm monitoring things, Aleaha. I promise you that. I'll know when the Schön queen arrives. I'll know when AIR has softened toward me."

She laughed bitterly. How many times had she told him that AIR was not known for softening? *You have to act now. No more stalling, waiting, hoping.*

Despite her resolve, she knew it was only a matter of time before he attempted to seduce her again and she caved. His scent was in her nose, his touch branded on her cells, and she would soon find herself begging for more. She always did.

"I hate to disappoint you, Aleaha. I do. But this is for the best, I promise you."

"Of course." Hating herself—and him—she rolled from his side, facing away from him. She would free the agents, no matter what needed to be done, and then she would . . . what? Come back for Breean? Would he even want her after that?

Probably not, but it was worth the risk. To save his life, to save her friends, it was worth the risk.

His fingers traced the line of her spine. She shivered, even as her blood heated. How could she still desire him? How could she still crave him so potently, knowing what was about to happen?

"Where are you going?" he asked.

"I'm hungry," she said, rising and walking to the bowl of fruit he had refilled every morning. Her legs shook. *Stop*, her heart shouted. Or rather, what remained of it. *Don't do this.*

This is the only way, her mind replied. As if clumsy, she knocked the bowl from the vanity, and it shattered on the floor. Pieces of fruit spilled in every direction. "I'm sorry," she said, trembling as she bent to pick them up.

Don't. Stupid heart. First, she palmed the longest, sharpest, shard. *No other way.*

Breean was by her side in the next instant, helping her.

Do you really want to do this?

No, she didn't. But she would.

"Go lie down," he said, clearly concerned for her. "I don't want you to cut yourself." Yep. Concerned.

If you do this, you are the monster you always considered yourself.

Not true. And damn it, why couldn't her heart and mind play nice? Keeping the shard hidden, she did as Breean had requested. For Devyn and Dallas and even Macy, for *Breean*, she *would* do this. She gulped back the lump forming in her throat. When the smoke cleared—and by *smoke cleared* she meant *blood dried*—she would speak to Mia and tell her what Breean had not. His purpose, how his planet had fallen, what he wanted, what he needed, how wonderful he was, and how she herself planned to aid him.

And if that got her fired, fine. If that got her imprisoned for aiding an alien, fine again. She'd find a way to escape. She'd find another way to save Breean and his people.

After he'd cleaned up the mess, Breean settled beside her, an orange in hand. He tossed it in the air, caught it. "Still hungry, sweet?" By the sensual bent of his tone, she knew he was thinking about her licking the juice off him.

Now or never. Do it, just do it. It's for his own good, after all. Aleaha rolled into him. Before he could figure out her intent, she pressed the shard into his jugular, deep enough to draw blood but not deep enough to kill. Blood trickled down his neck, thick and gold. Her hand was wobbling.

He stiffened, and the orange hit the mattress. "What are you doing?" The words were strained.

She shifted as close to him as possible, making it tougher for him to shove her away. "I'm doing what I have to do." Yet she couldn't deny a sense of wrongness. *Damn it! He didn't give me any other choice.*

"Threatening me is a *have to*?"

Her gaze swung guiltily away and landed on the Christmas tree. Only a few more days until Christmas Eve. Maybe she should have waited to do this. They could have exchanged gifts—not that she had one for him—and then—

No. No! With the holiday approaching, the agents needed to be home with their families more than ever. She'd made the right decision. "Apparently it is," she said.

Breean's tongue traced his teeth. "I thought we were past this."

"You thought wrong. As long as you're in danger, as long as my friends are captives, we will never be past it."

A pause. A slight transfer of his weight. "You do realize I could move to the door in the blink of an eye, do you not, taking the weapon with me, leaving you helpless against my fury? All you've done is proven I cannot trust you."

"You can trust me more than any other. And just so you know, I could sever your head before you moved an inch. I can move quickly, too. Don't forget."

Eyes slitting, he pushed out a shuddering breath. "It doesn't have to be this way."

"If you won't see to your future, I will do so. Afterward, I want to be with you. I want to make this thing work between us."

"You plan to make it work by cutting my throat? Funny. To Rakans, that's the fastest way to end something." The fragrance of honey began to thicken the air. "Put the shard down." Even his voice was like honey now. "I want you to be with me, too. You must trust me in this."

She hissed as her nipples hardened and her mind fogged with desire. "Stop that!" She pressed the shard deeper, and more of that golden blood trickled. Knowing how it tasted, like sugarplums plucked from a freaking rainbow, caused her mouth to water. Was no part of her safe from his appeal?

"Remove your breasts from my side if the smell offends you."

Offends? Had the situation been any different, she would have snorted. "I'm not moving." Yet. She had to make him understand why she was seemingly choosing AIR over him. "Someone has to make you *and* AIR see reason. Working together will benefit you both."

He reached up and grabbed her wrist, though he didn't try to shove her away. "I do see reason. I want to work with them, but your boss wants my head. Which you now seem perfectly willing to give her."

That touch . . . Her skin flushed, her blood pumping wildly for him. Only him. Aleaha held her breath and tried to figure out what to do next. She'd hoped he wouldn't force her to take this all the way.

"Drop your weapon and we'll pretend this never happened," he coaxed. There was a dark glint in his eye, and she knew there would be no forgetting. Not for a long while.

Still she surged ahead. "Promise to release the agents. Today."

"You would believe me?"

Would she? More than anything, she wanted to. Then she could curl back into his arms and give him time to heal from the wound in his neck, and they could make love again. "Yes."

"Even knowing I always fight dirty."

"Even knowing." With her, he'd always been honorable.

"Damn you, Aleaha. As I've told you multiple times, I would be putting everyone in this house at risk."

"As I've told *you* multiple times, they're already at risk."

His expression hardened. Had he expected her to say something else? "Either kill me or drop it." Obviously, he'd reached the end of his patience. He squeezed her wrist, and it was enough to make her bones ache, but not enough to make her release the shard.

You know what you have to do. There wasn't going to be another opportunity like this, he would make sure of it.

His grip tightened, his anger clearly overriding his promise never to hurt her. "I'm done waiting, Aleaha." Tighter . . . tighter . . .

Do it. Now! "If there'd been any other way . . ." she whispered with a sob. "I'm sorry. So sorry." Then she slashed. Hard.

He jerked in shock, and instantly blood poured, thick like syrup. His eyes were wide and accusing as they stared at her, but he was unable to speak. His hands flew to the injury, knocking her to the side.

Tears filling and burning her eyes, she next cut her own wrist. She had to push his hands away to hold it over his wound, dripping her blood into the center, mixing red with gold. "You'll heal faster this way. I know because I've done this before. Not slit some-one's throat, but shared my blood. You won't die. I won't let you die." Babble, babble. "And I promise you, you will not catch a disease because of this." But he *would* be too weak to come after her. "I'm sorry."

All he could do was gurgle. He'd bled her that day to save her, as well as a few times afterward, all of which he'd considered dangerous. Her actions now were a thousand times more so, and they were against him. He might not be able to get past them.

Wiping at her eyes with the back of her hand, she shoved to her feet. As fast as her feet would carry her, she rushed around the room, grabbing his gar-ments. She quickly dressed, unable to stop her shak-ing. Constantly her gaze roved back to Breean. He, too, was shaking.

I really am a monster. How could I have done that to him? "I'm so sorry," she choked out. He'd only given her joy, and this was how she'd repaid him. *You had to do it. There was no other way.* Except . . .

What if she freed the agents and they really did bring AIR to his doorstep as he feared, her recommendation to make peace disregarded? What if he was killed or imprisoned? What if he was tortured for information? She'd never seen an interrogation firsthand, but she'd heard the screams.

Maybe she could blindfold the agents, as he'd suggested, and lead them out. Maybe— She snorted bitterly. Yeah, right. Like they'd really wear blindfolds. *Free them, talk to Mia, and if she won't cooperate, help Breean hide.*

If he'd let her. Stomach rolling, she bent and pressed a soft kiss on his lips. They were still warm, yet stiff from the pain. "I'll come back for you. I'll help keep you and your people safe."

He glared up at her. He'd probably rather kill her than spend another moment in her presence.

A sob congealed in her throat. "Good-bye for now, Breean."

She strode to the door, forcing her body to grow, to develop muscles. Her skin became that lovely shade of gold, the power inside her humming. When the switch was complete, she pictured the house, mentally navigating her way toward the cells. Now all she had to do was walk there. Without incident.

Twice she was stopped and questioned in the Rakan language; both times she merely nodded and shooed the men away with a wave of her fingers, as if she couldn't be bothered. They regarded her strangely, but allowed her to pass. God knows what she would have done if they hadn't. She couldn't get her heartbeat under control and was sweating profusely.

Finally she reached her destination. The air was stuffier here, laden with dust, and she could hear an urgent murmur of voices. Poor guys, stuck in this dank, ugly place while she'd enjoyed the royal treatment.

In the corner were two Rakan guards. They straightened when they spotted her.

"I'm taking over tonight," she told them, praying they found nothing odd about her use of English. "You're free to do whatever you wish."

Grins split both their faces. "Even go into town?" one asked.

"Absolutely. Tell everyone else they've got permission to go as well."

Waiting only until they rushed off, she kicked back into gear. Just before she reached Devyn's cell, she summoned Macy's image. Her body shortened, the bones shrinking, and her facial features rounded. She didn't have to see herself to know her skin was now tanned and her hair pale.

I'm not this person, she wanted to scream.

The clothes might be hard to explain, since they suddenly bagged on her, but oh, well. Curling her fingers around the bars, she saw that Devyn was seated against the far wall, his knees upraised and his head in his hands. "Devyn," she said, her voice no longer her own, either. She'd just gotten used to being herself, damn it.

His head whipped up, and when he saw her, he

grinned and stood. In no way did he look like a man who'd spent several weeks in captivity. He looked ready for a party.

"Lolli, darling." His eyes were like amber fire in the murky darkness, raking over her. Other agents had been moved to his cell; a couple tried to approach the bars, but he waved them back and they obeyed. "How'd you escape the big guy?"

Nausea churned in her stomach. *Oh, I slit his throat and left him bleeding in his own bed.* "I made myself look like him and walked out." It was the truth.

"Cool." He didn't sound surprised.

Her knuckles squeezed the bars, losing their color. "You know what I can do?" Had he seen her that night in the forest? He'd been unconscious, and she'd thought she had been so careful.

Slowly he approached her. "I'm not a trained AIR agent, just their hired help, but I know drug addicts, and Macy was an Onadyn user. AIR hired her only to use her to find out who was dealing to her. I got to be the one to seduce her for info, not that she told me much. Which is why I planned to continue seeing her. But even though she and I had already had sex, you didn't recognize me the first time we met, and I didn't recognize your smell."

All this time . . . she'd lived in fear, but they'd known. They'd already freaking known.

"Anyway, AIR figured out you were different, though no one knew how or why you were there. So we all observed you instead, trying to discover if you were someone's plant." He shrugged. "But you never saw anyone outside of work and never told anyone the false stories we fed you. And then, not too long after your arrival, someone found Macy's body. We interviewed a few witnesses and figured out that her dealer went loco and killed her, that you saw an opp and took it."

"There was never a story in the news about her death." Aleaha knew. She had watched and waited for the day, knowing she'd have to switch identities yet again.

"AIR made sure of that."

Warmth drained from her, leaving only a cold shell. She'd had no idea. She'd been in danger, constantly scrutinized, and had been utterly clueless. "W-why didn't they kill me?" She wanted to release Macy's image, but didn't. Even though these agents knew what she could do, she didn't want them seeing the real her. That was for Breean. Only Breean.

"As far as I know, you're the only one of your kind. Human or alien, they still don't know. You'll be a great asset."

An asset. That's all she was good for, which wasn't comforting. But even more upsetting? They didn't know what she was either. She'd hoped *someone* had that information. Even her parents hadn't known.

Stay hidden, Aleaha love, her mom had said the last time Aleaha had seen her. She couldn't see the woman's face, for shadows surrounded them. *If anyone finds out what you are, they'll hurt you.*

We'll come back for you, her dad had said, taking her mother's hand.

But they never had. The two had walked off while she sobbed. They hadn't run as if they were being chased. They'd walked. They hadn't looked back.

She supposed they could have been killed, and that's why they'd failed to return for her, but deep down she suspected they were still out there, glad to be without the stigma of her origins. Whatever they were.

She would have died had it not been for Bride McKells, vampire extraordinaire, who had found her and taken over her care. Bride hadn't cared what she was. Bride had loved her.

What would Bride think of Breean? She would approve, surely.

Breean. Oh, God. Breean. Was he okay? *You gave him your blood. He's fine.*

"—listening to me?" Devyn asked with a chuckle. "I was saying how it's better to keep your enemies closer than your friends, so AIR kept you close. Just in case. Besides, I wanted a go at you so I cast my vote to keep you around."

He'd wanted her?

He must have read the question in her eyes, because he added, "I collect women. You know that. And I've never had a woman who can change personas. So if you're interested . . ."

"No," she said quickly.

He shrugged as if it was of no consequence. "As I said, AIR planned to use you if you proved trustworthy. The things you'll be able to do, the places you'll be able to get them, the information you'll be able to glean, will be invaluable."

"Why are you telling me this? Why now, of all times?"

His fingers curled around hers, warm, comforting. "I like you. I can't have you. Not right now," he added with an amused tilt of his chin, "but I do like you and I didn't want you to fear anyone's reaction to the truth, since you've clearly gone to a lot of trouble to help us escape."

Hello, reminder. Escape, the reason she was here. The chitchat needed to end. She leaned down and studied the ID box. "I don't know how to open your cell," she said. "I've never rewired anything."

"I'll tell you what to do just as soon as you tell me where the Rakan is."

"And *I'll* tell *you* just as soon as you tell me that you won't hurt him."

"Done. I vow it."

That easily? Why? And could she trust him? She would have to, she supposed.

"Breean is in bed, unable to move." She squeezed her eyelids closed, trying to block that last, heartbreaking image of him. "I didn't see a lot of his men on my way down here, and I hopefully sent the remaining ones on their way. Whoever stayed, I'll convince I'm Breean and lead you guys outside." She hoped.

"Macy?" she heard Dallas call from down the hall. Had they played musical cells?

"You're next," she told him. "Hold tight."

"So you escaped Stud Muffin."

Stud Muffin? "Looks like it." *And all I had to do was shred his neck.* "Now, how do I get through the ID box?"

Dallas laughed that razor-sharp laugh of his. "We shoulda known she'd do it," he said to Devyn. To Aleaha, he added, "You shouldn't be down here. If you're caught, I'm sure you'll be punished."

"I won't be caught. Now how do I open this?"

"Don't look at me," Devyn said, splaying his arms. "I don't know how to disable them."

"But you said—" She gritted her teeth. Bastard. He'd manipulated her for information.

There was a pause, then a sigh from Dallas. Why so reluctant? Were the situation reversed, she would be shouting orders until the bars were out of the way. Finally, he said, "Remove the lid." He reached a dark arm through the bars and pointed at the black case.

She had to pound at it to loosen it, but ultimately it slipped free, revealing a multitude of wires. "Which do I cut?"

"Only the red one."

"You sure?" Devyn asked. "I'd go with blue myself."

"They're all red!" she snapped. "There's not a single blue one."

With another sigh, Dallas rested his forehead against the bars. "I hoped they had the cheaper model. All right. Sort through them and try to find the thread that's woven through all of them."

Thread? She began sifting through the sea of red. "You guys ignored me that first night of captivity. Why?"

"There was a guard pacing the halls," Devyn said. "We couldn't risk him overhearing."

Wasn't like she'd asked for detailed escape plans. "You guys know Mia better than I do." She didn't remove her attention from the wires. All of them seemed to be connected to the rest, no common thread holding them together. "If Breean agrees to help her fight the Schön, will she let him do so?"

Dallas laughed.

Devyn snorted.

"What?" she demanded, finally glancing up. The wires had begun to blur together, anyway. Dallas, she noticed, was peering off to his left and mouthing something. Who was he talking to? She followed the direction of his gaze but didn't see anyone. Perhaps captivity had driven him insane.

He must have sensed her gaze, because he faced her and grinned. "Mia forgives no one, and the Rakans killed several of her men. Men she was charged with protecting."

"He's not exaggerating. Even I wouldn't bed her, and believe me," Devyn said, "I've slept with some real bad-asses."

"Hey, man," Dallas interrupted with a laugh. "She's like my sister. No talk of bedding her."

Aleaha suddenly felt like she was back in the forest, the night the Rakans had come. For the most part, Dallas and Devyn hadn't taken that seriously either, overflowing with jokes. "Well, Mia will lose even more men if she refuses this golden opportunity. And, yes, pun intended. Breean can help us defeat the Schön queen. You saw how quickly he can move. You saw how his men can step into bodies and force them to do what they want." She turned back to the box. Ugh. Red was now her least favorite color. "But what you probably didn't notice was the scent these men produce. It . . . lures women. Fogs their minds. What if a Rakan could lure the queen into a trap? AIR could be there to pounce, and her blood would never have to be spilled."

Devyn regarded her intently; she could feel his amber gaze probing the depths of her soul. "Was this Breean's idea? You coming here and talking to us?"

"No. It's mine," she said, hoping Breean would agree to such a plan. Not that she wanted him to be the one doing the luring. One of his warriors could do it. That Talon guy, maybe. He was kind of cute in a boy scout slash psycho killer way.

"I don't know, Mace. That would involve trusting the Rakans, and well—"

"AIR trusts no one," she finished for him. Exasperated, she shook her head. "One of his men killed the agents, and that was against Breean's rules. Breean punished him. You remember the guy we heard him castigating that night in the cell, right?" She paused, bit her lip. "I don't want him hurt. He's not predatory. Tell the commander to leave him alone, okay? Please. All Breean wants is a peaceful life for his men, and he *is* willing to aid AIR to find that peace."

"Tell the commander yourself," Dallas said.

"I . . . can't." Right then and there, Aleaha realized she loved Breean. She hadn't just given him pieces of her heart; she'd given him the whole thing. And temporary insanity couldn't be blamed this time. She wasn't lost in a passion-haze. She did. She loved him. He was gentle and kind, attentive and hard, passionate and determined. He was wild and savage and tender and protective. He was . . . everything.

She didn't want to live Macy's life anymore. She wanted to live her own. Now, always. She would free these agents as planned, but she wouldn't leave and come back. She'd simply stay here and do whatever it took to win Breean's forgiveness. And his heart. She would follow him to the ends of the Earth, whether he wanted her or not.

They *would* be together.

"I'm not going with you," she said. "And, damn it, I can't find a thread. Should I just start jerking wires out?"

Dallas sputtered, and her gaze lifted. He'd disappeared into his cell.

Devyn, she noticed, was frowning at her. "Little girl, that's not a decision you get to make."

What? Jerking the wires? "What does that mean?" As she spoke, something brushed her shoulder, and a honey-scented breeze quickly followed. Her blood heated—then chilled. No. Not possible. Not freaking possible.

Heart once again slamming against her ribs, she backed away from the cell.

"What are you doing?" Devyn demanded.

"He's here."

"The leader?" His gaze slid the length of the hall-way. "I don't see anyone."

"He's—" Her entire mind went black as Bree-an's essence slipped into her body, utterly consuming her.

TEN

How could she have done that to him? Breean wondered. How could she have cut his throat like that? Not a paltry wound, either, but a death wound. Delivered mere hours after he'd sated her.

Fury seethed through him. When he'd realized his body was indeed healing as swiftly as hers had the times he'd sliced into her thigh, he'd decided to spirit-walk, even though he'd left his physical being without a personal guard, something he hated to do. Anyone could stroll into his room right now and cut him—as Aleaha had done—and he would not be able to defend himself. But he had to stop her from escap-ing, and had been too weak to go after her physically.

So he'd allowed his spirit to rise from his body, detaching one from the other, and had stalked the home, unseen, unsensed, searching for her. Of course, he'd found her with the prisoners.

He shouldn't have been surprised that she'd chosen to injure him and save them. They were her friends, her coworkers, and he probably would have done the same. To anyone but her. He'd thought . . . what? That she'd come to like *him*? That she wanted a future with him? Damn this!

"Macy," the agent in front of her said. Glitter. He was reaching through the bars, trying to grasp her arm and hold her in place.

In control of her movements, Breean made her step farther away. Unlike when he'd entered her for the bath, she was not aware of him or her surroundings. That time, he'd wanted her responsive. This time, he wanted only her obedience, so he'd overtaken her completely. Her actions were his. Her thoughts were his. Even her voice was his.

"Macy?" Glitter said again.

"Do not worry for her. I will not hurt her," Breean said. A lie? He wasn't sure. Never had he been in such a murderous mood.

Without another word, he walked her up the stairs and back to his bedroom. The agents called for Macy's return, not understanding what was happening, but he paid them no heed.

She'd chosen the perfect time to escape, for many of his warriors were once again in the city. No one would have known of her—or the agents—release until morning. By then, the agents would have been safely ensconced in AIR headquarters, he was sure, and the hunt for him and his people would have begun.

What made it worse was that she'd used her ability against him, an ability she had feared but one he had accepted. Not once had he condemned her for what she could do. Yet she'd used it against him, *becoming* him. The remaining warriors would have let her do whatever she wanted, no questions asked.

Was she at all sorry? She'd claimed to be but . . . He released his hold on her thoughts and her voice filled their head. *What are you doing? Breean, stop this! Let me explain.*

No, not sorry for her actions. Only sorry she'd been caught.

Still inside her, he gathered four ties and anchored them to the bedposts. His physical self was still lying on the mattress, a slight rise and fall of his chest the only sign that he lived. Amber blood was dried to his throat, but the wound was weaving itself together and had healed considerably. He thought perhaps he would be completely normal in a few hours.

That didn't lessen his rage.

He had Aleaha strip before encasing her own ankles in the ties, spreading her naked thighs and anchoring them in place before making her lie on her stomach beside him.

Breean, let's talk about this. I wasn't going to leave. I had decided—

"Silence." He had her bind one of her wrists to a post, then had to use her teeth to secure the other.

Finally, she was tethered to the bed.

Breean.

He ignored her, tendrils of satisfaction blending with the heat of his anger.

Breean, please. I—I love you.

She—no! How dare she say that now. Now, when he couldn't be sure whether she meant it or merely wanted to soothe him. Love. It was what he'd come to want from her. To go to bed with her every night and awaken with her snuggled in his arms every morning. To talk with her, learn all that he could about her, to simply enjoy all that she was. But really. How could she love him after what she'd done?

Don't soften, he told himself. *You gave her more than you've ever given another and she tried to kill you.*

Well, she did *heal you.*

Silence. He didn't want to converse with himself either.

Sleep, he commanded Aleaha's mind, and she did, fading to quiet, to black.

Grim, Breean pushed his spirit from her, rising like a wave in the ocean, once against detaching from a solid form, before falling back into his own. Conscious mind and body connected, weaving back together like the wound in his neck until he once again had control over his own self.

Then, he waited.

As Aleaha drifted slowly into awareness, she realized four things at once. One, her face was smashed into a white silk pillow. Two, she couldn't move her arms or her legs, and cool air was stroking the wet heat of her core. Three and four, the most significant, she was naked and Breean was straddled over her hips, his knees at her sides.

How had she gotten here? She recalled being in the dungeon, trying to disable the ID box, then nothing. No, wait. That wasn't true. Breean had taken control of her and forced her to walk to his bedroom. He'd forced her to tie herself up.

The ties . . . that's why she couldn't move. Her stomach rolled and twisted, dread filling her veins. She tried to raise her head, tried to turn and face him, but each action was limited and gained her nothing. "Breean, let me explain. Let me—"

"Silence." There was no emotion in his tone.

"I did what I had to do. I didn't want to hurt you. I swear I didn't. Let me go and we'll—"

"I said, silence!" This time, his voice boomed through the room, echoing menacingly from the walls.

He was angry and hurt, and he had every right to be. But she didn't hold her tongue. "Let the agents go, and I'll run with you. Anywhere you want to go."

"I'm not running, Aleaha. *This* is my home. One home of mine was already destroyed. I will not allow the same to happen to this one."

"But—"

He moved so quickly she had no time even to blink before he was leaning down, in her face. "Not another word from you. What you did to me—" He banged a fist into the mattress beside her head.

She gulped. She didn't like this side of him, not when she knew how tender he could be. But she *was* aroused by his nearness. She couldn't deny it. "Breean," she said, then pressed her lips together.

His chest meshed into her back, hot, always a brand. "You tried to kill me, Aleaha. You have no defense."

"God, you're so unforgiving! I made sure you survived, didn't I? And hello, you would have done the same thing in my situation, and you know it." Struggling, she arched her back so that her ass was in the air. His cock glided between the two mounds, a stroke as sure as the ones from his hand. "Free me."

As furious as he was with her, he was still hard. "You don't get to make demands. I do. Do that again."

She stilled, panting. She'd liked it, yes. But . . . "No. I want it to be like before." When his every touch had been like a prayer.

"Too late." He ran his finger over the path his swollen cock had just taken, and she sucked in a breath. "I like you like this, helpless to anything but the passion. Mine to do with as I please."

"You won't hurt me." The words trembled from her.

"So sure of that, are you?" Breean asked, and, damn, she was right.

"Physically, yes, but I know you could tear me apart emotionally," she whispered, and that nearly broke his already shredded heart.

He moved his hands over her spine, riding the ridges. "Such soft skin. Perfect and pale." Even after what she'd done, he still desired her more than he'd ever desired another. It was shameful.

"Hate me if you want, but look at what you've done to free your people from disease. How can you blame me for trying to save my own?"

Don't soften. Don't you dare soften. "I would not have tried to kill you to do it. *That* is the difference."

"How many ways do I have to say it? If I'd wanted to kill you, I wouldn't have given you my blood," she gritted out.

"Blood that was forbidden for me to accept. Your actions could have damned us all."

"You've dealt with my blood before."

"That was different. That was to save you." His gaze slid over her curves, the elegant slope of her shoulders, the dip of her back, the flare of her hips. His mouth watered.

"No, it wasn't different. You're just being stubborn."

Flicking her hair out of the way, he bent and licked the base of her neck. She gasped, shivered. His hands tunneled their way to the mattress directly under her. He let one dabble with a ripe little nipple and the other drift down. He should hurt her in some way, but he couldn't seem to make himself do it. As she'd said, she trusted him with her physical well-being.

He strummed her hot center once, twice, never ceasing his play with her nipple. All the while she gasped. But when she began writhing for more, he severed contact, and her gasps became moans.

"Don't worry. I'm not done." He licked and nipped his way down her back before gripping her ass and giving it the same attention he'd given her breasts. Soon she was arching into his touch, again seeking more. Seeking something deeper.

Again, he severed the contact. "Are you wet for me?"

"Yes," she breathed, not even trying to pretend disinterest.

"Going to change bodies?"

"N-no. I've got that under control."

He knew that. The more they'd made love, the more control she'd gained, until she'd stopped changing unintentionally altogether. "Lift your hips, and I'll kiss you right"—he sank a finger inside her wet sheath—"there." But he wouldn't let her come. Would he? This had started as revenge. To get her worked up so that he could walk away as she had done, proving to them both that he could. That she meant nothing to him. The more he touched her, however, the more he needed her.

Moaning, she did as commanded.

He didn't move. Not yet, not yet. "Ask me nicely." *Want me the way I want you.*

"Breean," she groaned, waving that perfect little ass in front of his face. "Kiss."

"Ask."

A pause, a suspended heartbeat. "Will you please kiss me? *Please.*"

He'd expected her to protest. Then he could have walked away as planned, leaving her like this. That she hadn't . . . With such a sweet surrender ringing in his ears, he licked his way right into the heart of her, savoring her decadent flavor. Two of his fingers joined the play, sliding in and out of her, just as his cock yearned to do.

"Stop. I need to touch you, too," she breathed. "Let me suck you."

His blood heated another degree. Already she was close to coming, her sex swelling under his tongue. He *had* to stop. He lifted his head, delighting in her aroused flesh. She groaned in frustration and began pumping against the sheets, trying to find release without him.

"Oh, no, you don't." He crawled up and settled beside her head. He didn't have to say a word. She turned and fitted her mouth over his straining erection. "Don't you dare bite me."

"Only want you to feel good."

He gripped the back of her neck, fisting her hair. Just in case. Up and down she glided, her hot, wet tongue nearly undoing him. Those silky strands of hair pulled, and, fearing he was hurting her, he released them, reaching up, gripping the headboard and surging as deep into her throat as he could go. She took him, took all of him, and was still greedy for more, her tongue circling the head of his penis with every upward thrust.

She worked him mercilessly. Within minutes, his muscles were so strained and bunched, so desperate for release that he was transported to a torturous heaven-hell. Too much pleasure, yet not enough. And when he could take it no more, she sucked as hard as she could and he exploded into her mouth, hot seed shuddering from him.

How long passed before he fell back to Earth, he didn't know. Aleaha was still on the bed, still tied, still licking at him. Her hips were moving swiftly against the sheets, seeking the same release he'd just experienced.

Now was the time to walk away, leaving her in pain, needy. But he found that he couldn't do it.

"Breean," she practically sobbed.

He moved behind her again. Instantly she raised herself in the air.

"Take me," she said. "Please. I'll beg if you want."

"No begging," he said, the words choked. He didn't want her humbled, he realized. He just wanted her to crave him more than she craved air to breathe. He wanted to brand himself on her every cell, make her live only for him. See nothing but him, the agents forgotten the way he sometimes shamefully forgot his own people.

"Tell me. I'll do anything you want. Just please, love me."

Love her. He feared that he would, now and always. He sank two fingers into her, and she screamed. Not with release, he knew, but with the sheer relief of having something buried inside her heat.

"Like that," she panted. "More. More."

"Are you ever going to leave me again?" The question slipped from him before he could stop them.

"No. No!"

He skimmed his thumb over her slickness. Again, she screamed, and the sound of her desire brought him back to full life, his penis filling and swelling, hardening. "Spread your knees as far as they'll go."

The ties offered enough slack to allow her to bend her knees and widen them several more inches. She was completely helpless like that, completely at his mercy. He plundered inside without preamble. But then, she was so ready she didn't need more preparation. She arched her hips to meet him, coming the moment he was in to the hilt. She spasmed and spasmed and spasmed, her climax going on forever.

He pounded in and out of her, lost in the pleasure. She was as hot and tight as he remembered, a perfect fit, he thought as he leaned down to kiss her. She turned her head, eager for it, as lost as he was, and their tongues clashed. Kittenish purrs sprang from her throat, her orgasm still rocking her. Their teeth banged, and he tasted the sweetness of her flavor. Like rain and magic, slightly different than usual, but then, her taste and scent were always changing, becoming more central to *her*.

"Mine," he said, repeating the word he'd uttered the first time he'd seen her. Last time, it had been a mark, a warning for all others to stay away from her. This time he meant it as a promise. He hated himself for it, but there it was. He loved her, had to have her in his life.

"Yours," she replied. "Good. So good."

He reached in front of her and circled a fingertip over her clitoris. She came again—or rather, her climax reached another degree of satisfaction. She cried out, and he circled again.

"Breean!"

When he heard his name on her lips, *he* came. Loud, long, the most intense orgasm of his life. As he spurted inside her, they rocked together, locked in a bliss so intense they should have died from it.

For a long while afterward, he didn't move. He just remained in place, inside her, sated, not wanting to ponder what had happened and what he was feeling. Eventually, though, he did have to move. He was probably crushing her.

He unlaced the ties. As she rolled to her back, her hand fluttered over his throat, tracing the still-healing scab. He wanted to lean into her touch, but didn't allow himself the luxury. Already he'd done too much this night.

"I'm sorry," she said. "For what I did."

"Perhaps you are merely sorry you were caught." He hadn't meant to voice his fear; it slipped free of its own volition.

Her gaze clashed with his. "No, that's—"

"Stop. Please." He couldn't deal with this. Not now. Not after what they'd just done. He needed time. When had he become such a needy female? "I am not going to hold you tonight." He had on every other night, and it had only made him fall harder for her. Yes. Definitely female. Which was fitting. Aleaha could grow a penis, after all.

For a split second, he saw true hurt in her emerald eyes. But she nodded and inched to the other side of the bed, away from him. His chest ached, seeing her like that. *Don't soften any more.* How many times would he have to issue the command? He gripped the sheet and tossed it over her lower body.

"Breean—" she began again.

"Go to sleep," he told her, more harshly than he'd intended. At the very least, he should lock her up with the other agents, but he couldn't force himself to part with her, even now. He wanted her in the room with him, in his sight every moment. To prevent her from causing any more trouble, he rationalized.

So why did he want to apologize for taking her like he had, facing away from him as if she meant nothing? Why did he want to beg for forgiveness for not tucking her in beside him, warm and safe?

He stared up at the vaulted ceiling, trying to block her image. That didn't help. From the corner of his eye, he saw her curl into a ball. Another sharp lance shot through his chest.

"I don't know what to do with you," he said, more for his benefit than hers.

"You could forgive me," she said softly. "I had decided to stay, you know."

Oh, but she was killing him. "Just . . . go to sleep," he repeated. They'd finish this in the morning, when they had regained their strength.

"And if I don't?" she said, some of her bravado returning. "The big, bad alien will kill me?"

No. The big bad alien might do whatever she wished. She had the courage and audacity of a warrior. She would never stand behind him, but would always fight beside him.

A man could ask for nothing more.

"Your men," she said with a sigh. She rolled to her back and, like him, stared up at the ceiling. Trying to block *his* image? "I noticed that a lot of them are gone, and I maybe kinda sorta sent the others into town."

He didn't tell her to be quiet this time; he couldn't summon the will. "The house is wired to an alarm, so their absence won't cause too much of a problem."

"Well, you should know that there are microphones throughout the entire city. They record constantly and somehow only pick up alien voices. It's the frequency or something, which is different from that of humans. Anyway, when aliens are taken in for questioning, AIR records their voices and plugs them into the system.. From that point on, those aliens can be found the moment they speak."

"Were there microphones in the forest?"

"I honestly don't know. But most likely, yes. That's not public domain, but government, as most forest areas are. Trees are precious because they were nearly wiped out during the human-alien war. Anyway, I'm thinking your voices were recorded that night in the forest. I'm thinking your men can be traced if they talk while in the city."

Would he ever understand all of the nuances of this world?

Breean sighed. He could go into the city, hunt down his men, and tell them to be quiet, but they'd been making this trip for days now. AIR hadn't found them yet. That he knew of. Damn.

"Why are you telling me this?" Now, of all times.

"Because I just now thought of it. I haven't been an agent for long, you know. Just . . . tell them to be careful."

Trying to save him now. Would he ever understand *her*? He didn't think so. "Go to sleep, Aleaha. As I said, we'll talk later."

ELEVEN

A loud, piercing screech woke her.

Aleaha jolted upright, her muscles protesting at the abruptness of the movement. She grimaced. Breean sat up, too.

"What is that?" she asked.

Scowling, he burst from the bed in a lightning bolt of speed. "Get dressed," he demanded, moving through the room so quickly she couldn't see him. Not even the glowing outline of his spirit.

"What should I—" A bundle of clothing was tossed at her so abruptly she wasn't able to catch them, and they floated to the mattress around her. Heart pounding, she gathered them up and jackknifed to her feet. Her hands shook as she dressed. "Thank you. Now what's going on?" she asked over the alarm.

"What do you think?" was the grim reply.

Either agents were escaping, or AIR had finally arrived. Fear poured straight into her bloodstream. Fear for Breean. She didn't want him hurt or captured.

"Wait here," he said, his eyes fierce and golden. He'd already dressed, and even held a pyre-gun. His swiftness amazed her anew. He'd gotten that gun right in front of her, yet she hadn't seen a thing. "Do not even *think* about disobeying me."

"I can help you."

"Me?" One brow arched. "Or the agents?"

Okay, fine. She'd deserved that. "You."

He scrubbed a hand down his face. "I'm going to find out what I'm up against," he said, then lifted the gun. "Is this set to stun?" The question was growled, as if he despised himself for having to ask.

She gave it a quick glance. "Yes, but stun doesn't work on humans. Only aliens."

"Then let's just hope some of the other agents are like you, hiding who and what they are." Tension crackled between them. "If you leave this room, Aleaha—"

Before he could finish the sentence, she rose on her tiptoes and pressed her lips to his. He immediately took over, plundering his tongue into her mouth. It was a hot, wild kiss, and it was over all too soon.

Without another word, he pivoted away from her and disappeared out the door.

That quickly, she felt cold and bereft, scared. What should she do, what the hell should she do?

She hadn't felt this helpless, even in the forest. Then, at least, she hadn't really had anything to live for. Now . . . Racing through the room, she searched for a weapon. Anything to help her man.

Breean returned a short while later, and he was scowling. Bleeding. "There's a swarm of them. They must have been here awhile, because they're already spread out and your friends are free. What few of my men are here are already frozen."

Frozen was good; frozen was alive. But she heard his unspoken worry. He'd never be able to defeat AIR *and* save his people. Not on his own.

"Don't hurt the agents," she said, pulling Macy's image into her mind and forcing her body to realign, to change shape and color. "Please."

"I had no plans to do so."

"Good. Then I've got your back," she told him, raising her chin. "I need a pyre-gun of my own." As dedicated as he was to protecting his people from her, he'd clearly made sure the room was weapon-free before leaving her. She'd found nothing during her search.

He snorted, shook his head. "You, help me? Sure. Because I'm a fool. Now, I want you to hide under the bed. When the fight is over, you can come out. Until then, stay put. I don't want you caught in the crossfire."

He didn't believe her, yet he still sought to defend her. Was it any wonder she loved him? "I'd rather leave with you before they reach us, but I know you won't abandon your troops." Something else she admired about him. "Since it's too late for that anyway, I'll help. I won't harm them, but I'll do what I can to distract them so that *you* can escape. If you're free, you can spring your guys from prison. And just so you know, I realize I shouldn't have hurt you like I did, and I'm sorry for it. But I'm not sorry I was trying to take care of *my* people."

It was as if she hadn't spoken. His urgency was too great, she supposed. "You're hiding, and that's that." He grabbed hold of her and was dragging her to the bed before she could blink. "I can't risk losing you."

He couldn't risk . . . did that mean . . . surely it did. "Breean," she said, struggling against him while melting inside. He had to love her. Had to—

The door burst open, black-clad agents flooding into the room. Breean immediately released her and kicked into superspeed. He was firing his weapon, blue beams jetting from it, while maneuvering through the agents and somehow knocking them unconscious.

Even though they must have recognized her, the agents began firing at her the moment they spied her. As she dodged, she swiftly morphed into Breean's image, using his superspeed to avoid being stunned herself. She was still awkward at it, but she managed to swipe a fallen gun and fire back.

The stun ray only affected one, leaving the others, the humans, free to battle.

As many as Breean was knocking out, more were running in, closing in on them. She couldn't allow him to be taken. Tossing the gun aside, she circled through the agents. Most were wearing black masks, so she didn't know whom she was combating. Didn't matter. She was on Breean's side.

She put her self-defense lessons to use, chop-blocking throats and sending gasping agents to their knees. She even kneed a few in the balls. Always, though, she was careful to hurt them only enough to stall them, not to incapacitate them completely.

"Woman," she heard Breean shout. Even then, he was careful not to reveal her true name. "Macy!"

"Not now." She whipped behind a man and kicked the back of his legs. He stumbled forward and she doubled her fists, slamming them into his temple as he went down. "I'm busy. You should be running."

"Duck," he said, and she did.

He zipped to her side and punched the agent who had been closing in behind her. The man toppled out of the room, along the hall, and down the stairs like a plane from the sky. "I want you to leave."

"No."

"Things are about to get bloody," he growled.

He was going to cause bloodshed? Or he was about to be pulverized?

"No!" she shouted, just as Devyn stepped into her path. She jammed to a halt, fist in midair. He wasn't wearing a mask, his amber eyes were pulsing eerily, and it felt as if he were reaching phantom hands inside her, holding her hostage.

Dallas was suddenly beside him, and both wore expressions of grim resolve.

Someone knocked into her back, and she stumbled forward, losing her hold on Breean's image. Dark hair tried to sprout, but she anchored on to Macy's appearance with all her strength, her body forming into the beautiful agent's.

"I don't want to fight you two," she said as she righted, "but I won't let him be taken."

"We don't always get what we want," Devyn replied. "Do we?"

She backed away, meaning to latch onto someone and use him as a shield. But neither Devyn nor Dallas fired a weapon. Devyn simply tilted his head, and the next thing she knew, those phantom hands were once again holding her hostage.

What the hell? He hadn't stunned her, but she couldn't freaking move. She was frozen in place, her mind still active but her body unable to obey the simplest command.

She had lost, she realized, and could have sobbed.

"Noooo," Breean shouted, absolute panic filling him as Blue Eyes and Glitter lifted an unmoving Aleaha and carried her from the room. A red haze blanketed his mind. All the rage he'd experienced throughout his life combined could not compare to what he felt just then. *Mine, she's mine.*

He would kill every one of these bastards. They would know nothing but pain and suffering. Agony that lasted . . . and lasted. And if Aleaha did not awaken unharmed from whatever had immobilized her, that agony would be the least of their worries.

She'd fought with him, choosing him over AIR, and he could do nothing less than get her to safety. If he had to take her and run, just as she'd wanted, he would. He couldn't be without her; he wasn't giving her up. Even in death.

"Ale— Macy," he growled, fighting his way to the door. He kicked and elbowed and tossed men out of his way. Blood splattered over him, but he didn't care. Any man in his path, he took down mercilessly.

Only one thing mattered.

The agents who had her were standing at the end of the hall. Clearly, they'd expected him to follow, for they were smiling, waiting for him. Glitter was on one side of her and Blue Eyes on the other. Both were leaning against the wall as if they hadn't a care, their arms crossed over their chests.

Breean was huffing for breath, each drag into his lungs like inhaling fire. He forced himself to grind to a halt. He didn't think they'd hurt her, one of their own, but he couldn't know for sure. They didn't love her as Breean did and might be willing to sacrifice her life to defeat him.

"She's mine," he spat.

"I don't think so," Glitter said.

Hands clenched, he stalked forward.

"Stay where you are," Blue Eyes commanded. "My fingers are feeling twitchy." He stepped behind the still frozen Aleaha and reached around, dangling a knife in front of her throat.

Breean stilled, his heart pounding like a war drum. "Damage her in any way, and I will kill you slowly." He was afraid to use his speed to close the distance between them. If he spooked the agent and Aleaha was cut, he would never forgive himself.

"You can't kill me if you're already dead."

"What do you want from me? My head? Fine. It's yours."

Glitter's eyes widened. "Really? It would look nice as a centerpiece for my kitchen table. But can I have your skin, too? I think a golden rug is just what my bedroom needs."

Bastard. "If you will set her free, unharmed, yes."

Blue Eyes remained in place, that knife poised precariously. "A few things you should know, Rakan. The agent who escaped you, Jaxon, came back today with all of AIR. There are hundreds of us here right now. We could have slain you and yours at any time today, but we didn't."

Glitter laughed. "We were almost busted, though. When Macy showed up in the dungeon to free us, I almost had a heart attack." Another laugh.

"She almost succeeded, and would have, if I'd actually told her which ID wires to cut," Blue Eyes added.

"Why didn't you attack right away?" The knowledge that he'd been surrounded all day burned. He'd had no idea, had been too lost in his fury with Aleaha. Fury he couldn't summon now. Her friends had been in danger, and she'd wanted to save them. Now that his men were in equal danger, he realized exactly how his refusal to discuss them must have torn her in half.

Yet still she'd tried to save him this day.

"You offered to help us defeat the Schön queen," Blue Eyes said. "Right now, you're a link to her. A link we need. We've never seen her, you have. You know how she operates, and you even survived her plague."

"I've had men watching AIR, listening. Even last night, your boss threatened to decapitate me if she saw me. She wanted me and mine dead."

Blue Eyes shrugged. "Yes, and she calmed down when told you'd punished the guy who killed our men. That, and the moment she saw that we were all safe. Well, that *I* was safe. I'm all that really matters to the woman."

Glitter snorted. "That would be me, and everyone knows it."

Breean could barely believe this was happening. Everything he'd hoped for was being offered to him. "You would trust me to help you?"

Now both men snorted. "No," Blue Eyes said. "But you could have tried to kill us, and didn't. You could have tortured us, and didn't. Agents have been watching your men in town, and they haven't caused any trouble. They've only been interested in the women they can bed. Or rather, they were. Now we've got them herded into *our* cells. But my point is, you're not as much of a risk as was assumed."

"So, if I'm not to be trusted, how am I to help?"

"You'll be monitored, of course."

Monitored, as in guarded. Controlled. His hands balled into fists.

"Listen, if you aren't with us, you're against us," Blue Eyes said flatly. "The world is changing, and things get more dangerous every day. More and more aliens are coming here, their abilities unknown. A predator is a predator, and if this is to be your new home, I'd think you'd be happy to protect it."

Breean's eyes narrowed at the blatant attempt at manipulation. "How do I know I won't be shot in the back for my efforts, once the queen is dead?"

"I guess you don't." A slow grin spread over Glitter's face. "You'll have to trust us."

The way they planned to "trust" him? "If I decide to help you, I want only two things in return. Freedom for my people"—it was what he'd planned to bargain for all along, and one bargain was as good as any other—"and possession of the girl."

"I'm afraid she isn't on the table," Blue Eyes said.

"Of course she isn't on the table," he said, confused. "She's right in front of you."

Glitter flicked Blue Eyes a strange glance. "Was I ever that clueless?" With a shake of his head, he turned back to Breean. "She's not up for grabs, Goldie. You don't get her unless she wants you. But who knows? Maybe she'll be assigned as your guard."

She'd fought for him, but did that mean she wanted him? he suddenly wondered. Now and always? After the way he'd treated her? He just didn't know. He needed to talk to her, he thought with a scowl. "You're not taking her out of this house."

"Like you can stop me. You want her, you're going to have to win her." Glitter grinned, pointed a gun Breean hadn't known he'd been holding, and fired. "Oh, and come out of stun."

Before Breean could sidestep, a blue beam hit him directly in the chest, and he found himself locked in a body that refused to obey him. Fury seethed through him as the AIR agents gathered Aleaha and their fallen, as well as him and his remaining men, whistling all the while.

He could have spirit-walked—he was already helpless, after all—but he didn't want to leave Aleaha's side. So he endured. And he waited. AIR he could deal with. They wanted to monitor him, fine. They could monitor him. He'd help them since they both wanted the same thing. But if they wanted to post a guard at his side, they had damn well better chose Aleaha, as Glitter had suggested. Otherwise, they wouldn't have to worry about the Schön queen.

Breean would tear their planet apart.

When Aleaha was next able to move, she was inside AIR headquarters. She hadn't been incarcerated for aiding Breean, as she'd feared. She'd simply been placed in an empty office. Alone. To think. To agonize. To fume. Her legs were shaky, as if they'd fallen asleep, and didn't want to hold her weight, but she forced herself to lumber into the hall.

She had to reach Breean. Where had they placed him? What were they doing to him? To his men?

They'd stunned him, that much she knew. She'd heard his conversation with Devyn and Dallas, understood they now wanted his help, but had watched Devyn raise that gun and fire. Never had she felt so afraid. Or guilty. If she hadn't injured Breean earlier, he would have been at top strength and might have been able to win. Now, he was trapped.

She couldn't go back and change the past, but she could do something about the present. And the future.

Following the sound of chatter, she skirted a corner and entered the pit, where desks and agents abounded. It seemed like she'd been away forever, but the room was just as she remembered it. People meandered in every direction, while others sat in front of computer consoles, poking at their keyboards. Christmas was only a day away, so decorations were still up. A few agents had small plastic trees on their desks. Someone had even placed mistletoe over *her* desk.

"Where are they?" she demanded of the first agent she reached.

Hector Dean looked up from a file and eyed her with curiosity. Though he'd been among those imprisoned in Breean's house, he appeared no worse for wear. Well rested, well fed. "Who?"

As if he didn't know. "Devyn and Dallas. Where are they?"

He pointed to the break room before returning to his file, and she stomped forward, strength returning with every second that passed. Maybe because her determination was growing.

The door was closed, but she shouldered her way in. And there they were: Mia, Dallas, Devyn, and even Jaxon. The boys were discussing someone's boob size and Mia was sipping coffee, her black hair hanging down her back the same way Aleaha's did—when she was herself. God, she already missed being herself.

"Where is he?"

"Well, well, well." Dallas's brows rose and he grinned. "Look who Devyn freed from body-lock."

"'Cause I told him to." Mia waved her over, a sharp glint in her eyes. "There's some things we need to discuss, little girl."

Ignoring her boss, Aleaha walked right up to Devyn, morphing into Breean's image for added strength as she did so, and slammed her fist into his nose. As his head whipped to the side, she turned to Dallas and did the same before reshaping into Macy.

Though they were bleeding, both men laughed.

Mia clapped her hands, a smile of her own twitching at the corners of her lips. "Knew she had spirit."

"I need popcorn," Jaxon said.

"I told you not to hurt him," Aleaha growled to the agents.

"We didn't. We stunned him." Devyn rubbed his bleeding nose. "That doesn't even sting."

"You stunned him *after* you'd hired him! Why

couldn't you have told me that Jaxon had already sneaked inside and you guys were going to take Breean up on his offer to help? Why did you leave me in the dark? I sliced his goddamn throat to set you free."

"What?" everyone asked in unison.

Mia's mouth fell open in shock. "Yeah. What? He didn't mention you had done anything to him."

So they'd tried to talk to him. Had they interrogated him the usual way? She'd heard agents liked to stick pins under the suspect's nails, dunk their heads in water, and break their bones.

Breean was now their ace, and they had to realize that, Aleaha thought, calming slightly. Surely they wouldn't have done anything like that to him.

"You heard me. To escape, I sliced his throat." Her cheeks burned bright with shame. She might never forgive herself for that.

"Lolli doesn't fit as a nickname anymore," Devyn said. "Maybe now we should call you Slash."

Her hands fisted. "I did it for you, each of you, but you didn't need me."

"If you wanted in on the plan," Mia said, crossing her arms over her chest, "you should have trusted us with the truth about yourself and not picked your boyfriend over your coworkers."

"And I still pick him over my coworkers! Like you did your boyfriend, as I hear it. But you know why I kept silent about my own abilities? You're the freaking AIR. Lethal enemies of all things different. I did what I had to—"

"Macy!" a hard voice shouted from the pit.

Her breath caught in her throat. He was here. Breean was here! And he didn't sound as if he were in pain.

Dallas grinned slowly. "I guess Stud Muffin heard you're up and around. Before you go, though, you should know we had a chat with him, put him through a lie detector, had him show us some of the things he can do. He's not a bad guy, as far as interloping otherworlders go."

"Hey," Devyn said. "I resent that."

"Macy!"

Aleaha shifted impatiently from one foot to the other, but she stayed where she was. "So you have no plans to hurt him?"

Mia shrugged. "As long as he proves useful . . ."

"What the darling girl is trying to say," Devyn added, "is that Breean is far more useful than even she realized. In the forest that night, someone threw her and a few others into another dimension. Breean had some interesting ideas about that and offered to help discover the truth. Mia needs him like she needs Kyrin to screw her blind. And we all know she needs that desperately."

This was better than she had hoped. "I'll be his guard. I'll give you daily reports on his actions, if you want. But I'm telling you, he means us no harm."

"We know that. Now." The words grumbled out of Mia. "Still. You're not objective, so, no. You can't be his guard."

"Then I'll give the reports." Dallas tossed up his arms, the picture of exasperated male. "Not like I've got anything better to do with my free time."

Aleaha could have kissed him.

Silence filled the room, an eternity passing. Then Mia sighed. "Breean's already been warned, but I'll tell you as well." Her eyes narrowed. "If he does one thing wrong, one damn thing, I'll have him strung up without thought or hesitation. Whether I need him or not. Got me?"

Aleaha nodded. "What about his men?"

"They're being questioned one by one, but will be released once that's completed. As things stand now, they've all agreed to work for us. We'll pair them with other agents so that they're monitored, too, but it looks like we've got an army of eager new hires."

"Macy!"

Could things have turned out any better?

"Get out of here." Grinning, Mia waved her away. "Go to him. His voice is giving me a head-ache."

Grinning herself, she sprang from the room. Breean was still in the pit, looking left and right and ready to toss a few desks over his head. The agents must have been told to leave him alone, because they kept their distance, even backing away from him. A few had pyre-guns trained on him, though.

"Macy!"

"I'm here."

His gaze latched onto her. He settled in place, chest rising and falling rapidly. "I'm sorry," he choked out. "I'm sorry. I should have let your friends go. You were right. I would have done exactly as you did. I—"

Audience forgotten, she ran to him and threw herself into his arms, wrapping her legs around his waist and dropping kisses all over his face. "Don't ever refuse to snuggle me again."

That earned her a strained chuckle. "Never," he vowed. "I want to be your man, your protector."

"I don't need a protector, but I do need a man," she said, tangling her hands in his hair. "I'm sorry for what I did. I wish—"

"Speak of it no more. We both hurt each other, but we will start over. I wanted to die when they took you from me. You've become my entire reason for living, woman. I am nothing without you."

She melted into him. "Talk about the best Christmas present ever. I finally got what *I* wanted."

He grinned and squeezed her tight. "My cock?" he whispered into her ear. "I know how much you wanted me to give it to you. You hinted enough."

"That, too. God, Breean. I love you so much."

"Thank you," he said, expression softening, tenderness gleaming from him. "I love you, too. So much I ache." Never looking away from her, he called, "I'm taking her home."

"I expect you both back by eight tomorrow morning," Mia replied.

"I guess that means I'm leaving, too," Dallas said, and it was clear he was trying not to laugh. "I have to monitor the man's every move, after all. God, I hate my job sometimes."

"This sounds like a flat-out dirty mission. You'll need backup," Devyn told him with a pat on the back. "I'm going with."

They must have followed her from the break room, the perverts. "Stay where you are."

Amid cheers, Breean carried her out of the building into the twilight. "I'll lose them," he said, and then he ran, just ran, as fast as he could go. They were ensconced in his house in minutes, where he quickly undressed her, threw her on the bed, and dove on top of her. She cast Macy's image aside and donned her own.

"I meant what I said. I love you." He kissed the dark strands of her hair, then smoothed them from her brow. "I think I loved you from the first moment I saw you."

"Same here." She cupped his face and peered up at him. "We're in this together. You and me."

Slowly, he grinned. "Always. Just . . . next time you try to kill me, make sure it's with pleasure."

She returned the grin, glad that he'd truly forgiven her. That they'd made this thing work between them and even with AIR. "Kill you with pleasure, huh? Give me half an hour," she said, rolling him over and kissing her way down his body.

"Love, I think you'll only need five."

That made her laugh. "Merry Christmas, Breean."

"The sound of your laughter is the best present *I* have ever gotten. So yes. Merry Christmas, Aleaha."

Aleaha. Yes, she was. Now and always. With him.

EPILOGUE

Two weeks later . . .

Okay. So. Aleaha'd had the best Christmas ever. She'd rung in the New Year properly, meaning she'd had an orgasm last the entire countdown. Dallas treated Breean more like a friend than someone to watch closely, Mia treated him like a pet, his men were happy with their situation, and now she was snuggled in her man's arms, naked—a common occurrence—and completely sated.

The Schön queen hadn't arrived yet, and no one knew when she would finally make her way here. But AIR was prepared, and so was Aleaha and Breean. Meanwhile, when they were off the clock, he was helping her look for Bride.

Being Aleaha Love, soon to be Aleaha Nu, was pretty damn awesome.

"I've been thinking," Breean said, grip tightening around her waist.

She grinned. "You know I love it when you do

that." Always ended the same way. In bed. Oh, wait. They were already here. Maybe they'd end up on the kitchen floor this time.

"I know it bothers you, not knowing if you are human or alien, and I do not like when you are bothered. As your warrior, it is my duty, no, my privilege, to give you everything that you want, meet all of your needs, and—"

"Be my slave," she finished for him.

His lips twitched with his amusement. "Yes. So I have been thinking long and hard, and I do not think you are alien, after all. I think you are human."

"Why do you think that?" she asked, brow furrowing.

"Aliens have been here for many years, yes?"

"Yes." According to Bride, aliens had been visible for around eighty years but had snuck onto the planet long before that.

"Well, I think humans are evolving, developing abilities to help protect them from this new, possible threat."

Now that made a lot of sense. Except— "I can be stunned," she told him. "Stun never works on humans, yet it works on me."

"Stun doesn't work on the average human, no, but you aren't average. Far from it."

She rose on her elbow and peered down at him. The sight of him never failed to delight her. All that golden skin, those bedroom eyes, those plush lips. "Thank you."

"You're welcome." He reached up and traced

a fingertip along the curve of her jaw. "Either way, though, I love you."

"As I love you."

He jolted up, tossing her under him and pinning her to the mattress. She laughed, and his expression softened as it always did when she laughed. "Now, time to do what we always do when I am done thinking."

"Insatiable," she *tsk*ed as if such a thing were a curse.

"I know you are. I can barely keep up."

Another laugh escaped her, and she wound her arms around his neck. "Try."

"With pleasure."

Following in the demon's wake gave Joe a good glimpse into how the creature thought. If he'd been down there at ground level, he would have missed it. The scene would have just been too damned big to take in, but from up here, from the perspective of somebody twelve stories tall and nearly indestructible, he could tell that the demon was angry.

An alarm horn sounded. There was some shouting in Japanese. Joe had thought he was fairly fluent, but polite Japanese was different than the profanity-laced military exclamations you got when one of the techs spotted a giant demon.

Ahead, the open space was covered in black smoke, and through it, something truly *vast* moved. It froze, then swiftly turned as the demon sensed the approaching footfalls.

Four brilliant beams of red light appeared in the smoke, about even with the *Gakutensoku* robot's cockpit. Those were its *eyes*. It was watching them.

"All weapons, prepare to fire," Joe said with far more calm than he actually felt.

The smoke parted and the Summoned revealed itself. It was reptilian, with a dark, glistening hide, muscular, with a long spiked tail, two squat, powerful legs, and arms that ended in claws that looked like they could do a number on even the *Gakutensoku*'s armor. Then it snapped its razor jaws closed, spread its arms, and raised itself to its full height to meet this new challenge. It was *far* bigger than they were.

"I believe that the greater Summoned may be significantly taller than the specified fifty meters," Hikaru stated.

It didn't matter what country you were in, military intelligence was always wrong.

—from "Tokyo Raider"

BAEN BOOKS by LARRY CORREIA

Target Rich Environment, Volume 1
Target Rich Environment, Volume 2

Saga of the Forgotten Warrior
Son of the Black Sword
House of Assassins
Destroyer of Worlds

The Grimnoir Chronicles
Hard Magic
Spellbound
Warbound

Monster Hunter International
Monster Hunter International
Monster Hunter Vendetta
Monster Hunter Alpha
Monster Hunter Legion
Monster Hunter Nemesis
Monster Hunter Siege
Monster Hunter Memoirs: Grunge (with John Ringo)
Monster Hunter Memoirs: Sinners (with John Ringo)
Monster Hunter Memoirs: Saints (with John Ringo)
Monster Hunter Guardian (with Sarah A. Hoyt)

Dead Six (with Mike Kupari)
Dead Six
Swords of Exodus
Alliance of Shadows
Invisible Wars: The Collected Dead Six (omnibus)

To purchase any of these titles in e-book form, please go to
www.baen.com.

TARGET RICH ENVIRONMENT

 VOLUME 2

LARRY CORREIA

TARGET RICH ENVIRONMENT: VOLUME 2

A Baen Books Original

Baen Publishing Enterprises
P.O. Box 1403
Riverdale, NY 10471
www.baen.com

ISBN: 978-1-9821-2494-6

Cover art by Kurt Miller

First printing, December 2019
First mass market printing, December 2020

Distributed by Simon & Schuster
1230 Avenue of the Americas
New York, NY 10020

Library of Congress Control Number: 2018023358

Printed in the United States of America

10 9 8 7 6 5 4 3 2 1

ACKNOWLEDGMENTS

We had a contest on my blog, Monster Hunter Nation, to come up with a name for this collection. I want to thank Logan Guthmiller for suggesting *Target Rich Environment*. It was a great idea, and it hearkened back to the opening quote used in my first novel.

I also want to acknowledge all of the editors from the various anthologies these stories were originally published in. Gathering a bunch of authors together for an anthology is like herding cats, and editors often have a thankless job.

CONTENTS

TARGET RICH ENVIRONMENT

VOLUME
2

TOKYO RAIDER

"Tokyo Raider" originally appeared in The Baen Big Book of Monsters, *edited by Hank Davis, published by Baen Books in 2014.*

This story is set in my Grimnoir universe, where magic appeared in the 1850s and our timeline diverged from there. "Tokyo Raider" takes place about twenty years after the novel Warbound, *so if you've not read that trilogy yet you might want to skip this one because there are a few spoilers . . . and a whole lot of giant robot fights.*

Adak, Alaska
1954

"YOU WANTED TO SEE ME, sir?"
The colonel of the 2nd Raider Battalion was pouring himself a cup of coffee and looking a bit more surly than usual. He returned the salute and gestured at the chair on the other side of his desk. "Take a seat, Lieutenant."

The building was quiet. The office walls around them

3

were covered in maps of the Imperium. If—or more likely, *when*—there was war with the Japanese, this place was going to be hopping, but until then the Marines on the island of Adak had to watch and wait, train, freeze, and shoo caribou out of the barracks. The colonel was normally in a rotten mood before he had his coffee, so Joe got ready for another ass-chewing. He was the new guy, and he didn't fit in. Those made for a bad combination.

Luckily, the colonel got right down to business. "We got a priority magical transmission. Since everybody forgets about us stationed out here on the ass end of nowhere, the commo boys get excited when their window actually starts talking to them. They woke me up, telling me that the Commander in Chief of the Pacific Fleet himself had special orders for one of my butter bars."

So much for keeping his head down.

"Turns out my new junior platoon leader is some big shot back in the states. I knew you were a Heavy. File says you're really good at manipulating gravity, and you're qualified on a Heavy Suit, but nobody told me you were supposed to be some sort of genius wizard."

"I wouldn't say genius. It's all in my file. I have a degree in magical engineering from MIT and a master's from the Otis Institute."

"You went to college at what, twelve?"

"I graduated when I was nineteen, then I joined the Marine Corps, sir."

"Why the hell you ended up . . . Never mind. Whatever you've done impressed somebody. Congratulations, Lieutenant, you're going to Japan."

That was certainly unexpected. "Japan, sir?"

"Tokyo, to be exact. You'll be leaving immediately. An airship is being prepped now."

Joe took a deep breath. The ceasefire had held for a few years. There'd been some skirmishes and the usual saber rattling, but the Japanese had been too busy fighting the Soviets to cause any trouble for the American forces in the Pacific. The peace process must have broken down. If they were sending Raiders to Tokyo, that meant a full-blown war. A Marine Raider's job was to be dropped behind enemy lines to cause as much chaos as possible. Tokyo wasn't just behind their lines: it was the enemy heart. Joe wasn't sure if he was scared, eager, or a combination of both, but he'd signed up, so he'd do whatever needed to be done. "Are we jumping in?"

"I believe you'll just be landing at the air station."

Now he was really confused, but Raiders were trained to be flexible. "My platoon is ready for anything."

"No, Lieutenant, they're not. Your platoon is made up of Marines who are still trying to decide if they trust their newly assigned half-Jap officer to fight the Japanese. Frankly, I'm not sure if they'd follow you or frag you. Can you blame them? You speak the enemy's language, know their culture, and you even kind of look like one of them. I've heard of black Irish, but never yellow Irish."

"The men don't know if they should stick with rice or potato jokes, sir, but I carry on."

"Don't be a wiseass. Hell, I've been told you've got kanji brands on your body like one of their Iron Guards."

"No, sir. Those spells are a family recipe. They were inspected and approved by the War Department when I joined."

"I've been trying to decide what to do with you."

Joe appreciated the colonel's honesty. "My mother was born in the Imperium, but she was a *slave*. I may have been too young to make the last war, but I hate the Imperium as much as any man who's fought them, and I'll be here for the next."

The colonel sighed. "I believe you, but I'm not some dumb private who's going to be tempted to roll a grenade into your tent while you're sleeping because he's thinking he's doing his country a favor. I've no doubt you'll prove yourself to them eventually, but luckily, this assignment is just you."

There were limits to a Raider's flexibility, and Joe wasn't feeling up to invading the Imperium by himself. "I'm kind of hazy on the nature of my orders."

"Me, too. Per the peace treaty, you're to be a military observer. I neglected to mention that the radio man was mistaken. Turns out it wasn't the Commander in Chief of the Pacific Fleet calling, but *the* Commander in Chief."

"The president?"

"Yeah. I even voted for the man. I'll tell you, that was an unexpected way to start my day. I was a little concerned about being told to send one of my junior officers off by himself to the Imperium capital with orders to *help* those bastards, but the president spoke rather highly of your aptitude. How come you never told anybody you're buddies with President Stuyvesant?"

"Our families are acquainted."

"He said that you would be too humble, but that you were the best man for the job. That sounds fairly acquainted to me."

"Well, the First Lady does insist I call her Aunt Faye."

"Uh-huh . . ." The colonel took a drink of his coffee. "He said your presence as an observer was requested by the high commander of the entire Imperium military, General Toru Tokugawa. You know, the man in charge of our enemies, who rules over an evil empire with an iron fist. You're supposed to do him a favor for diplomacy's sake. I take it you're acquainted with him, too?"

He shrugged. "He and my father once worked together. It's complicated."

"Well, then, I can't imagine why your men don't have complete faith in you. Good luck in Japan, Lieutenant Sullivan."

Tokyo, Japan

IMMEDIATELY AFTER LANDING, Joe Sullivan had been met with a lot of ceremony by the Imperium Diplomatic Corps and then picked up by an armored car and some Iron Guard who didn't seem nearly so big on polite conversation. The Imperium elites had driven him directly to an ancient palace surrounded by cherry trees. The trip confirmed that Japan really was as pretty as Mom had made it out to be. They'd escorted him through the castle, to an ultramodern military command bunker beneath it. Then he'd stood there, waiting in his dress uniform, being eyeballed by a bunch of Japanese soldiers as they talked all sorts of shit about the *gaijin*, until somebody who'd been briefed told those idiots that he spoke Japanese, and they'd shut up.

The Imperium didn't seem to be hiding anything. The red markings on the wall maps told him that the Russians were pushing back against the Imperium in Asia. The unit markers were either true, or it was an elaborate setup for his benefit. Either way he memorized every unit and location so he could put it all in his report when he got home and let the intel types decide.

There was only one marker he didn't understand. It was shaped like a dragon, was red like the rest of the communist forces, and it had to represent something naval because it was tracking up the east coast of the island, heading for Tokyo Bay, and several Japanese naval units had been destroyed along its path, including an entire carrier battle group. Several submarines were marked as missing. The kanji on the marker identified it with the code name *Gorilla Whale*.

The Imperium were big on treating guests with respect, so the lack of respect had to be meant as an insult. After half an hour of waiting, without being offered so much as a chair, there was some shouting in the hall. Several military aides fled as a big, stocky, thickset Japanese man stomped into the bunker. He'd heard a lot about Toru Tokugawa growing up. Even though they'd been opponents, his dad had held more respect for this Imperium warrior than he did for most of the men supposedly on their side. The recent war had proven him to be one of best tacticians in the world, and in his youth he'd been one of the strongest Brutes to ever live.

Toru Tokugawa didn't disappoint in person.

"Damn those wretched Soviet pig dogs!" the general shouted as he stormed across the command center. The rest of the Imperium army staff remained quiet and polite as expected, as Tokugawa, on the other hand, was not. "Stalin has no honor!" He punched one of the bunker's walls, cracking the concrete. Tokugawa may have been in his fifties, but he still possessed an impressive connection to burn Power like that. "They fight like cowards!"

As their supreme commander flipped over a map table, the Japanese officers exchanged nervous glances. Having a visitor witness their leader acting in such a passionate manner was a loss of face. Tokugawa stood there, seething and glowering at the shower of falling papers, until one of the staffers broke the awkward silence. "Pardon me, General, the American observer you requested has arrived."

"Already? That was fast . . ." He composed himself, adjusted his uniform, then turned around and switched to English. "Present our guest."

"Second Lieutenant Joseph Sullivan of the United States Marine Corps," announced one of the Iron Guard.

"General Tokugawa." Sullivan bowed, careful to keep the gesture to the appropriate respectful level of a visiting dignitary of *equal* stature.

Tokugawa snorted. "You look more like your father than I expected. American Heavies are all so blocky and . . . corn fed . . . You're not quite so doughy as most of your fat countrymen. You could almost pass for a proper Imperium soldier, if you'd been lucky and taken a bit more after your mother, that is."

"I'd suggest leaving my parents out of this," Joe stated.

"Why would I do that? Your parents are the reason I asked for you. If I were to inadvertently insult them, what would you do about it?"

"I know you changed a lot of the Imperium's laws after the Chairman died, especially the ones about torture, slavery, and experimenting on prisoners, which all reasonable men can appreciate, but you've still got that thing where you can duel over insults, right?"

The Iron Guards shared nervous glances, but Tokugawa smiled. "Ha! Excellent. That is the defiant attitude I was hoping for. You will do. I was hoping you'd inherited your father's fearlessness, not to mention his sense of diplomacy. This will save time." Toru glanced at the assembled command staff. "All of you, leave us." They complied, rapidly shuffling out the door. The two Iron Guard escorts remained standing behind Sullivan. "You may leave as well."

"Our Finder believes he bears seven kanji, General. The Grimnoir knight is dangerous."

"They're not kanji," Joe said, as if he'd stoop to copying the spells of Imperium butchers. "And I'm not Grimnoir."

"I'm not worried," Toru stated. "Go." The Iron Guards bowed and left without another word. Toru waited for the bunker's door to be closed. "Not Grimnoir . . . Curious. You do not wish to follow in your father's footsteps?"

He'd had a bit of a disagreement with the Society, but that was none of Tokugawa's business.

"Interesting . . . An American who has barely lived there, who chose to join a military where he will never be accepted because of his half-breed race, refuses to join the one organization that must surely want him. Where do you *belong*, Sullivan?"

He was still working on that question himself. "My orders say I'm supposed to help. What do you want?"

"It pains me to admit it, but I require your assistance. In a show of mutual cooperation, your president has seen fit to grant my request. Apparently, your old friend Francis sees the Soviets as the greater threat at this time. This agreement should be beneficial to both of our nations. America and Imperium have been enemies in the past, but today we are . . . temporarily on the same side."

"Why in the world would he want me to help you? Once the Imperium finishes off the Russians, you'll go back to trying to conquer the rest of the world."

"I prefer the term *liberate*, but if you do not help, then we will be forced to use Tesla weapons to stop this threat, which will cause the deaths of hundreds of thousands of innocent civilians . . . Ah, your face betrays your emotions, young Sullivan. You'll need to work on that if you expect to make it long in this world. You might not wear the ring, but it appears you still have a Grimnoir knight's morals. I need an Active of your particular skills."

"I'm only a Gravity Spiker. We're a dime a dozen."

Tokugawa chuckled. "I believe I've heard that line before. Yet, according to my sources, despite your youth, your ability to manipulate gravity is unmatched."

"I learned from the best."

"Of course. We all stand upon the shoulders of those who came before us. Your father was self-taught. You benefit from his discoveries. We are alike in that way. I understand what is required to be the son of a great man. It is a burden, but also an incredible honor." Considering who Toru's father had been, that was probably one hell of a compliment around these parts. "There are many of your kind among the Iron Guard, some of whom are incredibly strong, far stronger than you, no doubt, but strength alone does not make a warrior great. That also requires awareness and will."

"Most folks chosen by the Power to control gravity aren't the sharpest knives in the drawer."

"I intended to be polite and say they lack nuance, but yes, most of them are stupid oxen good only for lifting things or throwing their bodies at the enemy. I've yet to find one among my army capable of the subtle manipulations of gravity your father was. Are you up to the task?"

Joe didn't actually know the answer to that. Those were some big shoes to fill. "What's the mission?"

Toru walked to the biggest wall map and pointed at the red dragon symbol. "Trust me, the monster is far more impressive in person."

As the Iron Guard moved their general and his guest across Tokyo in a convoy of armored vehicles, Toru Tokugawa had continued his briefing. "They have sent giant demons against us before, but nothing like this. The Soviets have been experimenting with increasing the abilities of their Summoners ever since they saw what happened to Washington D.C. in 1933."

"If I recall correctly, you were there for that," Joe said.

"The god of demons swatted me as if I were an annoying insect. We were only able to stop it because it was new and not yet fully formed. Luckily for all of mankind, even Stalin is not foolish enough to Summon anything that mighty. It would be too dangerous, too uncontrollable. However, they have made great strides over the last twenty years. This one is extremely resilient, far more armored than the last. The fact that they are still able to direct a demon this powerful is astounding."

"It's already destroyed a chunk of your navy."

"Correct."

"So that part was real, but I'm guessing everything else on those maps was probably wrong so I'd provide bad intel?"

"You are a perceptive man, Sullivan." Which didn't confirm or deny anything. Joe figured the temper tantrum earlier had been some sort of test as well. "The Summoned is approximately fifty meters tall and apparently still growing. Its capabilities are a mystery. It is amphibious and has been walking along the sea bed, only emerging every few days to attack. It has already damaged several cities along the coast."

"Civilian casualties?"

"I'm surprised you care."

"They didn't ask to be born under tyranny," Joe answered.

"Perhaps you may get that duel after all..."

Joe figured he would lose, but he wasn't in the mood to put up with nonsense. "I control gravity, so when we pick weapons, I vote telephone poles."

"As your people say, the apple does not fall far from the tree. Twenty years ago I would have taken you up on that duel. I'd enjoy knocking the smug off your face, but we do not have time for that. There are over one hundred thousand dead so far, but we are still pulling bodies from the rubble."

Joe gave a low whistle.

"Intelligence predicts the demon will be here within the week. Iron Guard have been unable to defeat it. Our own greater Summoned have been stepped on. Conventional weapons harm it, but then once sufficiently wounded it retreats back out to sea to hide and heal for a few days before striking again. Depth charges have done nothing. My forces have been unable to track it in the sea. Every submarine I have sent after it has been lost. Aerial bombing has stung it, but has caused more harm to the city it was attacking than the beast itself."

"Have you tried Tesla weapons?"

"Once. A low powered firing to minimize collateral damage, but it did not work as expected. The demon's hide does not react like human flesh. I destroyed an entire town only to chase it back into hiding." The Imperium was far more casual about sacrificing its people than the West, but unlike his predecessor, it seemed this Tokugawa actually cared.

The general was staring out the narrow slit of the window at his capital city. They drove into a tunnel and Tokyo disappeared. "Our defense force is prepared to intercept it. We have moved the emperor somewhere safe. Anyone who is not vital to the war effort is being evacuated from the city. The *Yamamoto* is our newest airship and carries our most powerful Tesla weapon. It is on station above us and its Peace Ray is charged. If the demon cannot be stopped I will have no choice but to fire upon it at full power."

That would obliterate a good chunk of Tokyo in the process. "So what's the plan?"

The general didn't answer. The armored car came to a

stop. The doors were opened, revealing that they'd parked inside some sort of vast hangar. Tokugawa climbed out, and Joe followed. His first thought was *Why are they building a skyscraper underground*? Then he realized they weren't actually underground, as much as they'd hollowed out an entire hill and covered the top to protect the interior from spy planes. The place was crowded with soldiers and engineers, and they began to panic when they saw who their distinguished visitor was. The Iron Guards snapped at them to get back to work. Hundreds of men were scrambling about on this level, and in the several floors of scaffolding overhead.

"There is my plan, Lieutenant Sullivan."

Directly in front of them was an armored metal rectangle, painted olive drab. His first thought was that it was a train car missing its wheels. Then he realized it was a *foot*.

"Behold, the Nishimura Super *Gakutensoku*. It has taken over a decade to build. It is the most daring feat of magical engineering ever attempted by Cog science."

He looked up, and up, and *up*. It was hard to wrap his brain around the size of the thing. "That's one *big* robot."

"Forty-six meters tall and nearly two thousand tons, it would destroy itself if it tried to move . . ."

"Galileo called it. That square-cube law is a real stickler," Joe agreed.

"Which is why it must be piloted by someone who can break the rules."

"I'm good, but I'm not that good."

"The spells bound upon it will increase an Active's connection to the Power by an order of magnitude. It has a crew of seventy Actives, and the Turing machines inside control all of the minor systems. In theory, it should be as easy to drive as a suit of Nishimura combat armor. *If the Gakutensoku* works as projected, we should be able to defeat the demon and send Stalin a message."

He couldn't figure out what kind of spells they'd carved onto that thing to get it to work. Even powered down he could feel it pulling magic from the air around him. It was hard to tell through all the scaffolding, but it was shaped like a broad-shouldered man, with two arms that were too long and two legs that were too short. He couldn't even imagine this thing moving.

Then he realized that there were craters on the concrete floor from where the thing had fallen. He glanced around the vast hangar. There were a lot of craters.

"I will speak plainly. As you can see from the dents on my giant robot, every other Heavy has lacked the will necessary to control it. We are still repairing the damage from yesterday's test. I had hope for the last test pilot, since he was very intelligent for a Heavy. Sadly Captain Nakamura lacked finesse, tripped over his own feet within two hundred meters, and the Super *Gakutensoku* fell on its head."

"I imagine it takes practice."

"Feedback from the spell caused him to have an aneurism and die."

"Great." Helping his sworn enemies work the bugs out of a super weapon sure as hell wasn't what he'd joined the Marines for. "So now that you're running out of time, you asked for me."

"Deciding between asking for American help or blowing up our capital with a Tesla weapon was a very difficult decision."

Considering the fact that Joe had less than a week to learn how to drive a mechanical man the size of a 12-story building... "Keep that Peace Ray warmed up, General, because I'm not making any promises."

"If it is any consolation, Lieutenant Sullivan, the Super *Gakutensoku* is purely a defensive weapon system," Hikaru told him. "Since you are helping us—as you Americans say—*work out the kinks,* there is no way we could bring this magnificent device to America to lay waste to your cities and crush your armies beneath its massive steel feet. How would we get it there?"

"Good point," Joe muttered, resisting the urge to drop a few extra gravities on the annoyingly helpful Cog's head. It turned out that the Japanese Actives capable of magical bursts of intellectual brilliance were just as squirrely as their Western counterparts.

Hikaru continued talking while fastening electrodes to Joe's freshly shaved head. "There is no airship that could carry it. Moving a machine of this size via sea would be too dangerous. Not to mention we've not solved the deep-water pressure problems of walking it across the ocean floor yet."

"Yet?"

"Uh...I...Never mind." The Cog spoke English better than Joe spoke Japanese, and he knew the Super *Gakutensoku* inside and out, so he'd been appointed Joe's assistant. Hikaru taped down the last wire. "There you go.

The Turing machines are now monitoring your brain. The spells have been activated. The crew is ready. We are ready to test."

Joe glanced across the control center. He knew how to fly an airplane. This was way worse. He'd spent the last twenty hours memorizing every control, and they'd skipped all the *unimportant* ones. There were four pedals beneath each foot, friction sticks directly in front of him, and half a dozen levers for each arm. Cables and pulleys were attached to bands around his abdomen, chest, biceps, and wrists. It was bad enough that he needed to tell each "muscle group" what to do physically; he had to simultaneously tell gravity what to do magically.

"It looks more complicated than it is. This should be no worse than controlling a Heavy Suit."

"Have you ever driven a Heavy Suit, Hikaru?"

"No, Lieutenant. I have not personally, but that is what it says in the manual."

"Then do me a favor and shut up." Joe looked out the armored portholes. Cranes were lifting away the scaffolding to the front, and the workers were taking cover. The row of gauges told him that all twenty of their diesel engines were running. The indicator board was all green lights. There were Fixers on board making sure everything was working, Torches for damage control and weapons systems, Iceboxes making sure nothing overheated and taking care of the ridiculous amount of friction generated by their movement, Brutes to manhandle shells and guns, and other Gravity Spikers just to help channel enough magic into the machine's spells to keep them balanced.

Joe checked his own connection to the Power. The magic was gathered up in his chest, waiting to be directed. He used a bit of it to test the world around him. Spells had been carved all over the interior of the Super *Gakutensoku*. They magnified his connection but also distorted it. It was like looking through a microscope that was just a little bit out of focus. Maybe it was because he was running on coffee and determination at this point, but it was already starting to give him a headache. No wonder the last guy had a stroke.

He put his right foot down on a pedal while simultaneously pushing forward with the right friction stick. At the same time he called upon his magic, imagining the pull of the earth against his own leg, and easing that *just* enough. He'd never tried to change gravity over such a gigantic space. It was like magic was being ripped from the Power and channeled through his body out into the great machine. Joe ground his teeth and held on.

A hundred tons of foot scraped along the concrete before rising a few dozen feet and then slamming back down with an impact that shook the whole world.

There were ten other men in the *Gakutensoku*'s head. They began rattling off readings and stats from their CRTs and gauges. This was requiring such focus that Joe only barely heard them. He pushed down with his left foot and repeated the process. The robot lurched forward, but stayed balanced and upright. The crew let up a cheer. They'd gone *two* whole steps.

"How are you feeling, Lieutenant?" Hikaru asked.

In actuality he felt like he'd just been mule-kicked in

the head. The Power draw made his teeth hurt, and he wanted to vomit. "Are you asking because you've bought into that propaganda about how soft Westerners are?"

"Quite the contrary. On our first test, at this point blood shot from the test pilot's ears. I just wanted to make sure I had the spells calibrated correctly."

It was taking effort simply to keep from sinking into the floor. Joe lifted one hand to wipe the sweat that had instantly formed on his brow. The unconscious movement caused one giant robot arm to rise up and crash through the scaffolding, tearing it all to pieces. Luckily he froze before swatting the cockpit and decapitating them. The noise of cascading, crashing metal could barely be heard through their thick armor, but it still went on for several painful seconds. Joe slowly lowered the arm, then pushed the disconnect button so he could turn enough to look out the side porthole. Yep. The scaffolding was just gone. Hopefully they'd had the sense to get everybody off of it before starting the test.

"Perhaps that is enough for your first day?" Hikaru asked hesitantly. "The physical and magical strain is considerable."

Iron Guard weren't the only ones around here taught to never show weakness. "I'm just getting warmed up." Joe looked up at the bank of CRT screens. Since the robot couldn't turn its head and their footprint took up a city block, those cameras were as close as he was going to get to peripheral vision. He found the exit out of the hillside. "Buckle up, Hikaru. Let's see what this baby can do."

❖ ❖ ❖

Five days later, the second biggest demon to ever walk the earth attacked Tokyo.

General Toru Tokugawa stood on the observation deck of the tallest building in the city, watching out the window with his hands folded behind his back. He'd moved his command center here temporarily for this very view. It was a beautiful, clear day. Twenty miles to the southwest he could see buildings falling and smoke rising.

One of his aides entered the room in a hurry. "General, the demon is crossing Yokohama."

"I am aware," Toru stated.

"We have begun the mass evacuation as instructed. The coastal defense cannons were engaging before we lost contact with them. The Iron Guard are moving into position now. The air force is scrambling. The *Yamamoto* is awaiting your orders."

Nearly ten million people lived in the wards that would be directly affected by the Peace Ray. Those who would be instantly incinerated were the lucky ones. The burns and radiation sickness were far more painful ways to die. "And the Super *Gakutensoku*?"

"It is in the hills to the west. A message has been sent." From his aide's tone, Toru could tell the officer had very little faith in that option working.

He'd understated the danger to the American, Sullivan. This demon's presence and constant raids were crippling his country and endangering the entire war effort. Demons could be banished from this world, but they were not as easy to kill as a mortal being. Their bodies were artificial magical constructs. They had no internal organs to wound or bones to break. They were filled with magical substances that best resembled ink and smoke, and the only way to end one this powerful was to bleed it dry. That took time.

"Tell the *Yamamoto* to hold its fire for now. The Iron Guard must fall back. Draw it in, farther onto land, and then we will strike. Wait for the demon to be distracted by the *Gakutensoku*, then we will hit it with every conventional weapon at our disposal. If we cannot fell it, only then will we fire the Peace Ray. Better to raze the greatest city in the world than to endanger the whole Imperium." It would either be a scalpel or a *tetsubo*, but one way or the other, Stalin's demon died today.

"We should get you to the *Yamamoto* immediately, General."

"No." Toru looked back toward the growing pillars of black smoke. If this city died, then he deserved to die with it. "I believe that I'd like to watch the fight from here."

They were making excellent time. The robot's legs were too short to call it a run, but when you covered this much ground with each stride, a shuffling jog still got them to fifty miles an hour. The fact that there wasn't much they had to go around meant they could travel in a straight line. Joe had gotten good enough that he even managed to step *over* individual houses. Mostly.

Hikaru was giving him directions based upon roads, power lines, and compass directions. They'd quickly discovered that when you were twelve stories up you couldn't give directions based on street signs, and local landmarks meant nothing when your pilot had never been here before. Joe's entire knowledge of Japan's geography came from stories his mother had told him and maps he'd studied in the off chance the Marines got to invade the place.

"The demon is tracking north. To the east is an orchard, after you cross it there is a railway. Follow that toward the city," Hikaru told him.

"Got it." He couldn't see the Cog or the rest of the crew sitting behind him. Joe had learned the hard way not to turn his head enough to look back over his shoulder because the Turing machines read that the wrong way. The first time he'd done it they'd face-planted in a field. On the bright side, that had been a few days ago, and it had taught him how to stand this thing back up without waiting for multiple construction cranes to come save them.

Moving was fairly instinctive at this point. There was a rhythm to it. *Clomp. Clomp. Clomp.* It made sense that the cockpit was where the robot's head should have been, since that was how the human body's control center was wired, and once you were magically connected, he was the brain and it was all a matter of scale. He'd spent the last few days learning to move about with a modicum of grace, and slugging boulders, and it really wasn't that much different than working a punching bag with his own fists . . . except for the part where he could punch through mountains.

The buildings were getting taller and the neighborhoods more populated. Joe had to step carefully to keep from landing on any moving cars. He was burning a lot of magic trying to keep a light step, but they still weighed so much that each footstep left an impact crater, so he wasn't sure how many of those automobiles unwittingly drove into the suddenly created holes they'd left in the roads.

One armored foot clipped the edge of a warehouse, but it was enough to rip one wall off. "I wish you people would've built wider streets!"

"I'll have you know Tokyo is the most advanced city in the world," Hikaru snapped.

"Horseshit. We've got an interstate highway system in America you could drive an aircraft carrier down. Hang on, I see smoke." The buildings here were already smashed flat or knocked over. A giant lizard-shaped footprint was clear as day in the middle of a park. "I've got the demon's trail." Joe guided the robot toward the path of carnage. Since everything here was already destroyed, he might as well take it up a notch. Joe pushed both friction sticks forward. "Hang on!"

ClompClompClomp!

The trail was easy to follow, what with all the spreading fires and collapsed buildings. Hundreds of civilians were down there. He could lie to himself and say they looked like bugs from up here, but they still looked like people, and he tried his best not to land on any of them. They might have just had a war, but that was no excuse to be an asshole.

Following in the demon's wake gave him a good glimpse into how the creature thought. If he'd been down there at ground level, he would have missed it. The scene would have just been too damned big to take in, but from up here, from the perspective of somebody twelve stories tall and nearly indestructible, he could tell that the demon was angry. It was heading toward the capital, but it was meandering about, swatting down anything that stood out along the way. A temple had been kicked over. Ornate wooden arches had been stepped on. It had gone three blocks out of its way to chase down a bus. It had picked up a passenger train and tossed it out into the ocean. The miles went by, showing an ever-increasing amount of spite. This Summoned was an engine of destruction.

It was enjoying itself.

"I can't believe this," Hikaru whispered as he looked out over the devastation. "This is nearly as bad as when the Americans firebombed the city."

"That was different," Joe snapped.

"How?"

"You started it. Now zip your lip. I'm concentrating."

An alarm horn sounded. There was some shouting in Japanese. Joe had thought he was fairly fluent, but polite Japanese was different than the profanity-laced military exclamations you got when one of the techs spotted a giant demon. Joe eased back on the sticks to slow them down.

They were in an open campus of large, ornate buildings, probably a university. The opposite end of the space was covered in black smoke, and through it, something truly *vast* moved. Long spines appeared, cutting ripples through the smoke, and there was a tremendous crash as a clock tower was knocked off its foundations to topple to the ground. The spines froze, then swiftly turned and disappeared, as the demon sensed the approaching footfalls.

Four brilliant beams of red light appeared in the

smoke, about even with the *Gakutensoku's* cockpit. Those were its *eyes*. It was watching them.

"All weapons, prepare to fire," Joe said with far more calm than he actually felt. Hikaru relayed the order. The gravitational magic lurched as a dozen other forms of Power were channeled through the spells carved on the great machine. "Let's hit this son of a bitch with everything we've got."

The wind shifted. The smoke parted and the Summoned revealed itself. It was reptilian, with a dark, glistening hide perforated by random shards of black bone. It was thick-set, muscular, with a long spiked tail, two squat, powerful legs, and arms that ended in claws that looked like they could do a number on even the *Gakutensoku's* armor. The demon stepped full into view, lowered its dragon-shaped head, and roared. It was so loud that it vibrated through their hull. Humans on the ground probably had their eardrums ruptured from the blast. The screech dragged on until it threatened to blot out the world. Then it snapped its razor jaws closed, spread its arms, and raised itself to its full height to meet this new challenge.

It was *far* bigger than they were.

"I believe that the greater Summoned may be significantly taller than the specified fifty meters," Hikaru stated.

It didn't matter what country you were in, military intelligence was always wrong.

"Put that record I gave you on the player, Hikaru. I want it blasting at full volume over the PA system."

"Lieutenant, despite your intentions, I truly do not

believe that music really soothes the savage beast. That is just a colloquialism."

"Put my record on the player or I'm getting out of this chair." He waited until he heard the scratch of the record and the whine of the intercom. "That's better." Joe flipped open the safety cover and put his finger on the trigger. "Fire on my command."

Toru watched as the two titans faced each other. To the north was the Summoned, a horrible alien creature, its spirit torn from another realm and given form here. On the bony plates of its chest the Soviet Cogs had engraved a hammer and sickle, and then filled it in with molten bronze so that it would never heal. To the south was the Super *Gakutensoku*. It was rather impressive, though not nearly as intimidating as the demon. Though it made no sense to camouflage a walking mountain, they'd painted it brown and olive drab, except for the glorious rising sun painted on its shoulder plates. Both sides of this duel were proud to claim their champions, each one representing their mighty nation. There was a certain dignity to this event.

A deadly silence covered the city after the demon's roar. It had been loud enough to break windows a mile away, and Toru could smell the smoke through the open wound in the building's side. There was a new sound, tinny, and much quieter than the demon's bellow. It was coming from the Super *Gakutensoku*. The machine had been equipped with a bank of loudspeakers for psychological warfare purposes. Now it was playing a song.

"What is that noise?" asked one of his aides.

So much for dignity. Toru sighed. "I believe that is the American national anthem."

Magical energy was building in the air. A bolt of lightning erupted from the clear blue sky and struck the *Gakutensoku*. Thunder rolled across the city. The mighty robot lifted one arm. Brilliant orange fire danced along that hand. Then the other arm came up, shimmering with reflected light as ice formed along that limb. Hatches opened on the giant robot's torso as cannon barrels extended outward.

Toru stuck his fingers in his ears. This was going to be very loud.

"Open fire!" Joe shouted. A dozen 120mm anti-tank cannons went off simultaneously. Expanding gray clouds appeared across the demon's body.

"Spells are charged," Hikaru said.

"Magic up!" The Actives released their magic, and Joe hurled it at the enemy. He slammed the far right stick forward. Normally a Torch could direct a stream of magical fire or cause small objects to combust, but, magically augmented by the *Gakutensoku*'s spells, that same magic now caused a super-heated ball of plasma the size of an automobile to shoot across the campus, melting everything beneath it, before crashing into the demon in a shower of sparks and smoking demon flesh.

The demon charged. He'd been expecting that. That's what an aggressive beast would do when confronted by a seeming equal rather than being stung by hundreds of ants.

Joe cranked on the left stick. A wave of magical cold shot forth. It was absolute zero at the release point, and not a whole lot warmer when the wave struck the demon's hide. It shuddered as molecules slowed, tissues became inflexible and cracked. Then Joe activated one of the right sticks to throw a punch. The *Gakutensoku* responded a second later by slamming its steel knuckles into the monster's side. The frozen layers of hide shattered. Flaming ink ruptured from the hole.

There was an impact that shook the entire *Gakutensoku*. The shift in gravity told him that they'd been hit low, in the legs. *The tail!* Joe directed gravity to pull them back from tripping while he worked the foot pedals. They slid across the campus, through a four-story building and out the other side, but they didn't fall.

"Damage to the secondary servos and the port accumulator," Hikaru reported.

"I don't even know what those things are," Joe said, trying to concentrate on not killing them all while the Power surging through him felt like it was going to yank his heart out of his chest.

The forest of spines was visible through the portholes, and then it was gone. The demon was circling to the side faster than they could turn. One of the CRTs had gone black, the camera lens covered in demon sludge. The others told him that it was about to grab hold of them. There was a lot to keep track of, especially on a system this complex that he hadn't had time to properly learn, but Joe was a Sullivan, and Sullivans didn't get rattled.

"Cracklers. Release on my signal," Joe ordered, and Hikaru repeated it to their Actives who could direct electricity. The *Gakutensoku* shuddered and metal groaned as the demon collided with them. "Now!"

The stored energy leapt between the two huge bodies, and a billion volts blasted the demon off of them. It flew back, across the street, through several apartments, and disappeared in a cloud of dust at the base of a large office building.

There was a terrible burning smell inside the cockpit. Smoke drifted in front of his face.

"That's horrible!" Then Hikaru began to gag. "One of our electricians is on fire. The augmented spell was too much."

Joe couldn't turn to see right now, he was trying to turn the robot to keep track of the demon. "Have one of the Torches put him out. I'm busy," Joe snarled. The magical strain was really getting to him. "Get another Crackler in that chair. Charge our magic. Get those guns reloaded. I want them to fire every time they've got a shot. Pour it on!"

The demon lifted itself off the ground. The *Gakutensoku* covered the distance in a few strides and caught it on the way up. As the big fist came down, Joe threw as much extra gravity as possible to haul it down faster. The blow hit so hard that it blew demon ink out of one of the demon's eye sockets.

It hit them around the midsection, wrapping its arms around their center of mass and squeezing. Cannon shells fired at point-blank range. A few floors below, one of their Brutes died screaming as flaming demon ink poured through the gun hatch, and then the noise stopped as it washed him away.

Joe acted on instinct, the robot an extension of his own body, as he pummeled the demon. There was an awful grinding noise, and the stick wouldn't pull back. That arm wouldn't retract; it was stuck. It took a moment to find the right CRT screen to see that their wrist was stuck on a horn. So Joe reached across with their other hand, grabbed that horn, and squeezed. The diesels powering those hydraulics redlined and it still wouldn't break, so Joe changed gravity's direction to the side and basically hung tons of extra weight on that horn. It tore free with a sick crack that they probably heard back in China.

The Summoned lurched away, spraying flaming blood everywhere. Joe still had the horn, and it was pretty stout, so he went about beating the beast about the head with it. Their movements were powerful, but slow. The demon was organic, fluid, and far faster. It caught the descending horn with one hand, turned it aside, and then bit down on their shoulder.

It was distant and down a floor, but he could hear the grinding of metal, breaking of welds, and the scream of men as they were torn from their seats and flung to their deaths. More smoke filled the air, and this time it smelled like burning wires. More CRTs had gone black. Half the lights on the warning panel had gone red. He tried to hit it with the horn again, but couldn't tell if it worked. Feedback through the electrodes told him that hand was now empty.

"Torch magic is charged," Hikaru said.

Joe drove their right fist deep into the monster's side. "Fire!"

The contact point between them was briefly hotter

than the surface of the sun. The explosion rocked them. A wave of heat flashed through the robot.

"Right arm is not responding," Hikaru warned. "Repeat, right arm down!"

Joe could have told him that by the way the control had frozen up. "Get the Fixers on it, now." The demon lurched away, so Joe lowered their uninjured shoulder and pushed both of the friction sticks all the way forward.

ClompClompClompClomp!

They collided, a wall of steel meeting a wall of meat. One of the armored portholes shattered. A thick chunk of glass spun over and hit Joe in the jaw. It hurt; he could feel the cut leaking blood, but he sure as hell didn't have time to check it. He jerked back on both sticks, stomped on the pedals to plant their feet, and even let gravity return to normal for an instant to drag them down into the ground to stop their forward momentum. Their feet dug a hundred-foot-long trench through the road, tearing up water mains, but they came to a full stop.

The demon wasn't so lucky. It hit the next building, a big twenty-story affair, and went *through* it, to crash across the next street, trip on a bridge, and then roll over to shatter a canal.

Joe drove them around the collapsing building. The demon was already getting up. Cannon shells were falling around it like rain. "Where's my ice magic? Come on!"

"Still charging. Two of our Iceboxes were in the shoulder. They are not responding."

There were more explosions around the demon than could be accounted for with just the *Gakutensoku*'s 120mms. Tanks were rolling down the street. Several fast-moving aircraft buzzed by just overhead, strafing cannon shells into the monster before veering off. Tokugawa had sent in the cavalry.

Black demon ink was pouring from its wounds, down the gutters, pooling on top of the canals to shimmer like oil, but it charged them anyway. It leapt across the distance, and the only thing he could see through the portholes was a forest of spines. "Brace for impac—"

BOOM!

No amount of gravity manipulation was going to keep them on their feet this time.

They hit a building, and then another building, and another. Joe couldn't tell what was going on. They were changing direction too fast. The demon had ahold of them, and was swinging them back and forth. It was hitting them over and over again. Magical energy was flowing back through the electrodes, and each impact was like getting hit directly in the brain with a hammer. Every warning light on the panel was red, and then the panel disappeared entirely as the demon ripped the *Gakutensoku*'s face off.

The black, slimy claw, big as a bulldozer blade, was thrashing back and forth, only a foot in front of him. It should have been terrifying, but all Joe could think of at the time was that it smelled like the ocean. And then the claw vanished as fast as it had come, and they were falling forward.

The view through the hole was of rapidly approaching ground. Joe slammed the main left arm stick forward and mashed the button to open their hand. He called upon all his magic at once, reversing gravity, trying to pull them upwards, but even the spells on this thing couldn't reverse two thousand tons once it was in motion.

Their hand hit, and that took most of the impact. They froze in place for a moment, leaving Joe hanging by the straps on his chair, staring down into a pile of debris and squirting pipes. Somebody had unbuckled their harness and fell past him, screaming, to disappear out the face hole. He hoped that hadn't been Hikaru, because he needed the little guy to relay orders.

Then a big hydraulic cylinder in the arm burst, and they were falling. Joe stomped on the pedals to kick out, pushing them so they'd land on their shoulder rather than flat. Facedown—assuming he didn't just get impaled on some rebar or smashed like a mouse beneath a boot heel—they wouldn't be able to get back up as easily, especially with one working arm. Besides, everybody in that shoulder was probably already dead.

On the upside, they landed like he'd hoped. On the downside, he smashed his head against the controls hard enough to knock himself stupid. Joe came back to reality a moment later dangling sideways about thirty feet over a ruined street. The moisture on his face was from a broken fire hydrant spraying upward.

It hurt to think. Talking was worse. "Hikaru, you still alive?"

"Yes, Lieutenant."

"Good, because we're not done yet." His voice was ragged. He didn't know if it was because he was breathing in clouds of dust, or if all the magic he was burning had damaged his vocal cords somehow. They were at a really awkward angle and looking out a jagged hole, but from the noise and shadows, it appeared the demon was trying to get away. If Tokugawa thought it was going to make it back to the ocean to heal, he'd light it up with the Peace Ray. "Get those Fixers to work. I want my arm and my ice magic, and I want them now."

"I'll do my best."

"If you don't, we're going to get flash-fried." Joe very gently tested the pedals. He'd gotten this thing stood up before, but he'd had both arms and a whole bunch of monitors to keep him informed then. This was going to take some finesse and a whole lot of screwing with gravity. "On that thought, get me a radio. This might take a minute."

"The *Gakutensoku* appears to be disabled, General. The beast is severely wounded, but it is merely fleeing back toward the bay. They have failed to stop it." The aide presented him with a radio. "The *Yamamoto* awaits your orders."

Toru took the radio with a heavy heart. He grieved for his nation, and gave no thought to his own life. The greater Summoned had to be stopped. If not now, then it would simply heal in the depths and then return to finish the job, even stronger than before. "This is General Tokugawa granting permission to fire the Peace Ray. Authorization code one five three tw—"

"General!" Another staff officer rushed forward. "Please wait."

Normally Toru was very unforgiving of rude interruptions, but since he was about to obliterate them all, he was allowed to hope for a bit of good news. "Hold on that authorization . . . What is it?" He was handed another radio.

"It is the Super *Gakutensoku!*"

"—*hear me, Tokugawa, you son of a bitch! Don't you dare touch that thing off. I can still do this.*"

Toru keyed the radio. "This is General Tokugawa."

The young Sullivan sounded exhausted. "*We're not out of the fight yet. We're getting back up. I can still stop it before it gets back to the ocean.*"

One of his aides warned, "Time is of the essence, sir. It will be at Minato soon. Once it is out to sea, we will lose it."

"What is your status, Sullivan?"

"*Just peachy.*" There was something that sounded like a groan of metal and a loud clang. "*Couldn't be better.*"

"There! The *Gakutensoku* rises." A spotter was pointing at the financial district.

Broken glass crunching underfoot, he moved over to see. In the distance the mighty mechanical man was swaying, badly charred on one side, and missing an arm . . . but *standing*. The men began to cheer.

"There is no time, General!" the aide shouted.

"*Give us one more shot.*"

Toru had once trusted this man's father and he'd not been disappointed. He keyed the radio. "Sullivan, go southeast as fast as possible. You can cut it off at the port."

"*Got it. Sullivan out.*"

The *Gakutensoku* began an awkward limping jog through the city.

"That is our only chance. Do everything we can to slow the monster down. When it reaches the ocean, we will have no choice." He handed back the radio that offered hope and took up the one that could only dispense doom. "*Yamamoto*, await my signal."

Joe didn't worry about the landscape now. It was better to bounce off a building to keep up speed than to move carefully if the whole place was minutes from being vaporized anyway. Since the robot was missing half of its head, wind was blowing freely through the cockpit. He'd not thought he'd need to wear goggles. On the bright side, now that they had a convertible, they all had a lot better view.

"Demon sighted!" Hikaru shouted.

The forest of spines was visible on the other side of some buildings to their left. It had gotten turned around and slowed down while being harassed by the Imperium military and not taken the most direct route to the bay. So they'd caught up before reaching the ocean, and judging by the numerous cargo cranes in front of them, just in the nick of time.

"Radio your air force to back off for a minute." With them all hanging in the breeze, one unlucky hit and shrapnel would kill them all. Then what good was their fancy robot? Joe had both friction sticks all the way forward and was running the foot pedals as fast as he could. He veered them to the side and tracked directly toward the demon.

The magic draw was intense. His personal Power had long since been exhausted. He was only a conduit now, a circuit between the Power itself and the hungry spells on this machine. The other Gravity Spikers aboard had either been killed or incapacitated, because it felt like he was on his own. He knew he was probably going to die here, but that just made him want to make sure this thing didn't get away even more.

The demon heard them coming. It had to be severely weakened, because rather than turn to meet them, it kept on moving toward the ocean. The demon was stumbling as bombs kept going off around it, leaving a smoking trail of lost tissue. They were almost on top of it.

"Cold magic ready." Hikaru had to shout to be heard over the wind.

"About damned time. I've got an idea. Hold on."

They were both in the open, smashing their way through stacks of cargo containers and trucks. He realized what was really slowing down the demon. The horn that he'd ripped off earlier had wound up impaled through one of its legs, causing it to limp. *So I did stick it. Nice.* Joe pulled back on the friction sticks, slowing them just a bit, allowing the demon to reach the water first.

"What're you doing?" Hikaru probably thought Joe had decided to throw in the towel.

"Trust me."

The demon reached a moored freighter and began clambering over it. Waves crashed as the ship capsized and the beast hit the water. Joe lifted their remaining arm. The crosshairs used for aiming earlier were long gone, but he wasn't shooting at the monster: he was shooting at the ocean around it. "Release the ice magic now!"

He'd not realized how well insulated they'd been before. The cold that blasted through the cockpit was a shock to the system, but it was far, far worse on the receiving end. The ocean around the monster turned solid instantly. Partially submerged, the creature could no longer move its legs or tail, and fell forward. Its snout smashed into the suddenly hard surface, and it flailed about through the slush and breaking ice.

Joe plowed ahead, only there was no longer ground ahead of him, only man-made dock facilities, and those came apart beneath their weight. It took all of his skill and concentration to keep them from falling over in the mud, but below that was bedrock, and that was solid enough to get some gravity-assisted purchase on. Waist deep, they slogged forward as water came rushing through the fresh holes in their robot.

The demon was sliding, trying to gain purchase. The loss of smoke and ink was shrinking it. The thing was no longer so massive and imposing, and Joe drove straight into the monster, crushing it back into another ship. Once he was sure they were partially on top of it, and there was solid rock beneath, Joe cut his Power and let gravity return to normal.

There was an unholy screech as the giant monster's legs were crushed, but demons didn't have bones to break, so there was still work to be done.

Its head was far beneath them, jaws snapping, so Joe lifted their remaining arm, pushed the button to form a fist, and then let the thing have it right in the teeth. He kept hitting it, arm rising and falling like a jackhammer. Each blow caused the head to deform further, spraying burning ink in every direction. The second of its four eyes went out, and then a third, and Joe just kept on hitting it.

The monster was shrieking and thrashing, A claw

caught the rest of their cockpit and tore that away, but the controls were still connected, so Joe just kept on plugging away. There was so much black floating on the waves that it looked like the ship they'd rolled over had been an oil tanker, but that was just demon ink.

There was a gleam of bronze through the churning salt water. It was the giant hammer and sickle embedded on the demon's chest. Joe opened the palm and reached down, plunging the robot's fingers through the thick hide until they were around the symbol. Then he hit the button to make a fist. Satisfied that the crunch meant he'd caught it, he yanked back on the controls, ripping it from the demon's body.

The demon opened its mouth to screech one last time, and this time Joe slammed the hammer and sickle right down its throat and through the back of its head.

The vast Summoned body began to dissolve, but so did Joe's consciousness. The pain was making it hard to think. He was leaning forward, and as he lost it, so did the robot.

The dark ocean rushed up to meet him.

Joe woke up in a hospital bed. General Tokugawa was sitting in a chair next to him.

"You know, if I ran this Imperium the same way my father did, I would simply notify your president that you perished in the battle and your body was lost in the harbor. Even his best spies would not be able to discern the truth. I have thousands of witnesses who saw the ruined Super *Gakutensoku* sink into the bay. Then you would be experimented upon, your will broken, and your impressive Power utilized for the greater good."

"Lucky for me you're not like your father," Joe croaked.

"And lucky for my city, you are very much like yours ... I have named you an honorary Iron Guard and awarded you the Order of the Golden Kite. Wear the medal with pride."

"The Marine Corps is gonna *love* that."

"You may stay here if you wish, and I will gladly change that from honorary to official ... From your expression I shall take that as a no? Oh well ... My Healers have repaired your wounds. All that remains is the exhaustion. Soon, you will be returned to your country, whether to a hero's welcome or to the shame of having aided an enemy, I do not know. Your people are fickle and unpredictable."

"Yep, but they're *my* people."

"Indeed." Tokugawa smiled. "It is good for a warrior to know where he belongs."

One of my favorite things about short story collections are the little extra bits the author puts in explaining how the story came to be and the process behind it.

In this case, "Tokyo Raider" was kind of an experiment. The original Grimnoir trilogy (Hard Magic, Spellbound, and Warbound) *began in 1932, in a world that diverged from ours when magical abilities started appearing among the populace in the 1850s. It was inspired by noir, pulp, and hardboiled detective stories. It often gets labeled as "diesel punk."*

But for the second trilogy I thought it would be fun to jump ahead a bit so I could get more into the golden age of sci-fi—basically I wanted to write wizards in space—and since technology is moving faster in the Grimnoir universe than our own, that meant the 1950s. So I jumped ahead a couple of decades to take a look at the son of two of the previous trilogy's heroes doing a favor for one of the previous trilogy's antagonists.

Plus, I'm a sucker for giant robots.

One fun thing about this series that fans of old monster movies will catch, in Spellbound I had a giant monster climb a building swatting biplanes in the same year King Kong came out in real life, and "Tokyo Raider" is set the same year as the original Godzilla. That's where the code name Gorilla Whale came from.

That 1950s Grimnoir trilogy is currently in the works.

THE TESTIMONY
OF THE TRAITOR RATUL

*"The Testimony of the Traitor Ratul" first appeared on
Baen.com in 2019. It is set in my epic fantasy Saga of the
Forgotten Warrior universe. The first book in this series
is* Son of the Black Sword, *which was nominated for the
David Gemmell Award, and won the 2016 Dragon Award
for Best Fantasy.*

I HAVE BEEN CALLED MANY THINGS, like Ratul
the Swift, or Ratul Without Mercy, and much later I was
known as Ratul the Mad, or Ratul the Traitor. I have held
many offices, most notably the rank of Master within the
Protector Order, a title reserved for only the fiercest
defenders of the Law. Yet that mighty office paled in
importance to my illicit calling, when the Forgotten
appointed me the Keeper of Names. I gave up one of the
mightiest stations in the land to become a fugitive, and
did so gladly, for I truly believe the gods are real.

Some say I am a fool, and all say that I am a criminal.

Religion is illegal; preaching, as I have done, is punishable by death. My time will come. I embrace my fate, for they are the fools, not I. It is the world which has forgotten the truth. Soon they will be forced to remember, and it will be a most painful event.

Yes, I have been called a great many things, from heroic leader and master swordsman to fanatical rebel and despicable murderer, but young Ratul Memon dar Sarnobat was a kind-hearted child, nothing at all like the jaded killer I would become.

Those years are long distant now. I was born on the moors south of Warun, second son of a vassal house, and second sons of the first caste are commonly obligated to serve the Capitol for a period of time. It is said the houses keep their eldest close to prepare them to inherit and rule, but offer the rest of their children to the Capitol to demonstrate their total commitment to the Law. In truth, it is in the hope we can secure offices of importance within the various orders to siphon wealth and favors back to our families, but I was naïve then, and did not yet understand the hypocrisy and rot within our system.

Young Ratul dreamed of being obligated to the Historians Order to maintain the relics in the Capitol Museum, or perhaps the Archivists Order, to spend my days organizing the stacks of the Great Library, for young Ratul loved stories and books. I also had a great talent for music and dance, as did all in my house, but I was the most graceful child. Perhaps I would be best obligated to an artisan's school, and go on to compose great plays? Maybe I would be an Architect, raising mighty monuments to the Law, or something odd and secretive like the Astronomer, tracking the moons and cataloging the sky? Regardless of where I was obligated, I looked forward to living in the magnificent Capitol, where it was said all the women were beautiful, the food was rich, and the waters pure and free of demons.

As a gangly boy with thin arms, a narrow chest, and a sensitive disposition, it never even entered my mind that I might be obligated to one of the militant orders. Only upon the flag of Great House Sarnobat is the wolf, and such a cunning predator is a fitting symbol for the family which mine was vassal to. I shall not delve into the petty house politics which resulted in my obligation going to the Protector Order, but basically, my father had given some inadvertent insult to our Thakoor. Thus it amused our leader to give me to the most infamous order of all, the brutal enforcers of the Law, where it was common for their young obligations to die in their unforgiving training program.

I recall my mother sobbing as I left our house, because she knew in her heart that her soft summer-born child would fail and die miserably.

At fourteen years old—which, by the way, is a little old to become a Protector acolyte—I traveled, not to the glorious and wealthy Capitol, but to the austere and miserable Hall of the Protectors, near the top of the world, high in the unforgiving mountains of Devakula, in the distant frozen south. I was despondent the entire journey there. All I knew of the Protectors were that they did nothing but pursue and execute lawbreakers.... That, and they were one of the few orders whose members were not allowed to wed until their obligation was fulfilled, so they lived a life of stoic solitude. At that age I was a silly romantic, so the idea of being bereft of female companionship until my obligation was done filled me with dread. My service was to last for a period of no less than ten years. And let us be honest, the odds of me surviving ten years of murderous village-burning butchery were slim as my waist.

We crossed a great many narrow bridges over deep chasms on the way to the Hall in Devakula, and I contemplated hurling myself off of every single one. Those I travelled with would surely tell my family it was an accident, for slipping on ice and falling to your doom— though ignominious—was a more honorable end than suicide. Hitting the sharp rocks would've been a much faster end . . .

Except it was during this journey that I found I possessed a great stubbornness, for I would not give my Thakoor the satisfaction of expiring so quickly. To the ocean with him.

Though he was the focus of my great hate at the time, honestly, I can no longer even remember my Thakoor's face—he is as forgotten by me as the gods are to man— but that initial spark of defiance which flickered into being on a swaying bridge high in those mountains has remained with me ever since.

Decades later, that tiny spark would grow into a great roaring fire.

Later that fire would help ignite a conflagration which would threaten to burn the entire world . . . but I get ahead of myself. Gather close my children. I must tell you how I believed in those days, for I still had much to learn.

The Law required there to be three great divisions within our society: the caste that rules, the caste that wars, and the caste that works. Every man has a place. Some said that there was a fourth division, meaning those without caste, but such speech could be considered subversive, for the Law declares that the casteless are not really people at all.

The first caste is the smallest, yet obviously the most important of all whole men. They are the judges and the arbiters of the Law, the members of the various Orders of the Capitol, and the Great House families.

Each Great House has an army to defend its interests. These are the warrior caste. They are more numerous than the first, yet far fewer than the third. I thought of them as a bloodthirsty, boisterous lot, with their own odd customs and a peculiar code of honor, but they were kept in check by the Law and the will of their Great House.

The worker caste was the greatest in number, yet the simplest in direction. They exist to labor. The structure provided by the Law and the wisdom of my caste had shaped Lok into a land of industry and wealth. It was the worker who dug the coal, weaved the cloth, and grew the crops. They paid taxes to the first caste, and paid again for the warriors to defend them, but in turn they required payment for their toil and their goods, for the callous worker is often more motivated by greed than allegiance to the Law.

The castes are the great division, but there are many—perhaps innumerable—lesser divisions beyond that, for each caste had a multitude of offices and ranks, and only members of that particular caste could hope to decipher where they all stood in relation to each other. Every duty or achievement bestowed status upon the individual who held it, and status determined everything else. A miner and a banker were of the same caste, only one could sleep in a mansion and the other in a hovel, yet both would bow their head in deference to the lowliest vassal house arbiter, for he was closer to the Law.

Usually caste was determined by birth, but on rare occasions the Law might require a man to be assigned to a new caste. I'd heard of a particular worker who'd shown great strength, who the warriors had claimed, and in the opposite direction, of an inept and cowardly warrior who'd been ordered to trade his sword for a shovel. A particularly brilliant man could be promoted into the first, but a member of the first would cut his wrists in shame rather than accept the humiliation of leaving his caste.

It turned out my new Order was one such place where warriors could become members of the first, albeit temporarily, for when their obligations ended they would return to their place. It was during my induction ceremony that I stood among children of the warrior caste for the first time. Every one of them, even the ones who were two or more years younger, were far bigger and stronger than I. To the Protectors, the new acolytes were all equally nothing. For the first time in my life, the status I had been born with had become utterly meaningless.

Our training began. Previously I had thought that I understood what hardship was. That had been a delusion. The Hall was as grey and stark as my house was bright and colorful. I'd lived in a land of song, but our only song in the Hall was groans of weariness and cries of sudden pain. Our instruments were wooden swords. Our drums were our sparring partners' helms.

Over and over we were broken, physically and mentally, and constantly remade, not just with muscle and brain, but also with magic. It is said Protectors are more than man. This is true. I shall speak no further about this, for there are some vows which even the vilest traitor still holds dear.

I know now that the program is a thing of beauty. It is so cruel not because the Protectors hate their acolytes, but because we love them. Great suffering prepared us to overcome any obstacle, to face any challenge without flinching, even unto death.

The Order is not so different from the gods in that respect.

As I'd been warned, many of the acolytes perished. However, I would not be among them. For despite being the weakest of the acolytes, I was also the angriest, and in my heart was a great capacity for hate. Hate fueled me. It kept me warm through the cold nights, and every night in Devakula is cold.

At first my hate was directed at that now forgotten Thakoor, who had robbed me of my dreams of idle comfort. Then my hate shifted to the few acolytes who saw in my frail form a victim to be bullied. Tormenting me provided them a temporary distraction from their own torment. But the stupid and morally weak do not last long in the program, so after I outlived those, I needed a new outlet for my hate.

Thus I began to hate the enemies of the Law.

It was the reasoning of a bitter young man. If criminals did not exist, then there would be no need for the Protector Order. If every man kept to his assigned place and did as he was told, then those of us obligated to the militant orders would be free. When it came time for the acolytes to be given lessons in the application of the Law, I excelled, as I always pronounced unhesitating condemnation upon every infraction, and I unfailingly recommended the harshest sentence allowed.

My teachers thought it was because I was smart enough to grasp the nuances of the Law, that I was impartial and calculating as a Protector should be. This was not the case. I was filled with hate. Luckily for me, so was the Law.

It is curious that it is the softest ore which can be forged into the hardest steel. After three years of training my long limbs had turned wiry strong and my already quick mind became sharper. Most beneficially I discovered that the unconscious rhythm and grace of the dancer was not so different from the timing and agility required to master the sword.

Upon obtaining the rank of Senior Protector I went forth into the world to dispense cruel justice.

It turned out that I was rather good at it.

This was the era in which I became widely known as Ratul Without Mercy. None were as devoted as I. Wherever I was assigned, criminals became afraid. From the jungles of Gujara to the plains of Akershan, I spilled blood. I shall spare you the litany of the many sins I committed in the name of the Law. It is a long list, and we have not the hours left before dawn.

Upon my tenth year, my mandatory obligation expired. I had the choice: retire and return to the house where my service had brought them great honor, to do any of the many artistic or intellectual things I had once aspired to, have a marriage arranged for me, create my own house, and raise my heirs . . . or voluntarily continue as a Protector.

Strangely enough, this was not a difficult decision, and I remained with the Order. I'd never have a wife to love me. I would make do with the loveless company of vapid pleasure women whose names and faces were forgotten the next day. I would never have heirs. There would be no sons to carry my name. I would never have a house of my own. The only symphonies I composed were the sounds of battle and my instrument was my sword. I had forgotten how to dream, but I had not forgotten how to hate. I knew that for every criminal I'd executed there was another still in hiding, and I would not be able to rest until every last lawbreaker was dead.

For a righteous hate can be addictive as the poppy.

It was as Protector of the Law, Eleventh Year Senior, that I Ratul encountered the lawbreaker who would start me on my path of rebellion. Of the many types of criminals Protectors hunted—rebels, rapists, murderers, unlicensed wizards, smugglers of bone and black steel, and so forth—none were more hated than religious fanatics, for it was those who practiced illegal religions who were the most nefarious. The others were motivated by things most of us could understand because we'd felt glimmerings of them in our weakest moments, like greed, lust, or jealousy. But the fanatic was motivated by something inscrutable, a belief in invisible forces and imaginary beings. Such foolishness was infuriating to the Law-abiding man.

For many weeks I had searched for this particular fanatic in the hill country of Harban. There had been reports of a nameless man—probably of the worker caste—going about and preaching of gods and prophecies, trying to rouse the people to rebel. As was usual with these types he'd found some success among the casteless. I thought of the non-people as gullible, and a few of them had risen up and struck down their overseer, proclaiming their actions as "the will of the Forgotten" even as the hangman's noose had been put around their necks.

I'd killed many such fanatics. I expected this one to be cut from the same cloth. A raving lunatic, bug-eyed and foaming at the mouth, filthy and unkempt, leaping about and cursing me with the wrath of his unseen gods, but when I finally tracked down my prey, I found a calm, soft-spoken scholar instead. Not of the worker caste as alleged, but like me, born of the first. He didn't live in a muddy cave, or a hollowed-out tree. He lived in a small but sturdy cottage, on a hill overlooking the city of Lahkshan.

Unlike most—guilty or innocent—who answer a knock at their door and discover a Protector waiting, this man showed no fear. If anything, he seemed resigned, as if weary from his labor. He was just old enough to be a grandfather, no more. There was a sadness in his eyes. I remember this clearly.

"Come in, Protector," said he without preamble.

I had no time for foolishness or a fanatic's tricks. The cottage was humble, but big enough to conceal several enemies. He made no comment upon my drawing my sword as I followed him inside.

There was no rebel ambush waiting therein, just a cot, a pair of comfortable-looking chairs, a kettle warming on the small stove, and a shelf *full* of actual books. That, I marveled at, because it would still be another year before the Order of Technology and Innovation approved the sale of printing presses. Only men of the wealth and status could obtain such a library in those days, and those were usually prominently displayed in a Great House, not a one-room abode in the hills.

I had not even declared the charges against him, when the fanatic declared, "I am guilty of all the crimes you suspect, and probably more. I will not resist, and I accept my punishment without protest."

"The penalty for proselytizing is death."

He simply nodded. Even though I was about to slay him, this fanatic was so polite that I almost felt bad for not taking off my shoes before entering his home.

Curious, I went to the shelf and started checking the books. Some of them were new, approved volumes purchased from the Great Library of the Capitol, but others appeared to be ancient. I opened one of those, gently, for its binding felt as if it might crumble to dust. I skimmed a few pages, at first thinking it was a history of some kind, and instead discovered the most heinous of crimes. These were religious tomes.

They were *scriptures*. There was nothing more illegal in the world.

I dropped the book as if it had burned my fingers. "Saltwater!"

"Though still forbidden, these are not originals, Protector. Those rotted away long ago. These are copies of copies, handed down in secret."

"Why would you keep such terrible things?"

"To learn about our past and our nature. The people of Lok had many different religions before the demons fell from the sky, each believing different things. I have gathered the holy books of several of those over my travels. The books disagree on more things than they agree, but all are fascinating in their own way."

I'd seen the various rough-hewn idols of the fanatics scattered about Lok; the four-armed man, the elephant-headed man and his mouse, the smiling fat man, and I'd broken each one I'd found, but I'd never before seen one of their books, because the Order of Inquisition had burned most of them long ago.

"I am curious, Protector. You've not yet set my home to the torch."

"Oh, I will."

"I know, but you hesitate. I have a feeling that you are a student of history."

He had guessed well. "As much as the Law allows."

"Then that is why you wait. May I ask of what house you were before joining your Order?"

I do not know why I answered truthfully, but I had never before engaged a madman in a conversation. "Sarnobat. Of the vassal house Memon."

"Ah!" The fanatic went to the shelf and picked out a particular book. "Your people were a rare minority in old Lok. This was the holy book your ancestors used." Upon its cover was a crescent moon and a star. I'd seen such a symbol before, in my childhood, when a farmer had unearthed an old stone, and the Inquisitors had come and smashed it to dust with hammers. He held the book out to me, like he was offering a gift, but I did not take it. Seemingly disappointed, he put the illegal tome back on the shelf. "Of course, you would not want that one anyway, Protector. That is not why you are here."

"I'm here to execute you for violations of the Law."

"You are here because the Forgotten wanted you to be. There were many religions before, but only one that mattered after the demons came." He picked out a different book, bound in grey, narrower than the others. I did not accept it either, but he left it standing alone. "This one is a copy of a book written during the Age of Kings, from after the demons were driven back into the sea. The Forgotten wants you to have it."

Genuinely baffled, I asked, "All these gods are forgotten now, so why speak of this one as if it's special?"

"I did not choose him. He chose me. And now he has chosen you."

I grew tired of this talk. The time had come. He did not so much as cringe as I raised my sword.

I could not help but ask, "Why are you not afraid?"

"Because in a dream the Forgotten showed me the man who would claim my burden and my life. Farewell, Ratul."

I had never told the fanatic my name.

Strangely enough, I did not hate this man. I stabbed him in the heart because it was expected of me, but I did not hate him.

I would have returned quickly to my duties, but the

hour was late, and a cold rain had begun to fall, so I decided to spend the night in the fanatic's cottage and return to Lahkshan in the morning. I ate the fanatic's dinner of curried goat, and sat in his comfortable chair, as he lay dead on his floor.

My sleep was plagued with strange dreams. I awoke with a great unease.

My eyes kept drifting back to the shelf, and that book. Not the one of my ancestors, but the strange grey one which had come after. A sick curiosity gnawed at the back of my mind. Part of me desired to read this lurid tale from the Age of Kings, an era whose records were declared mostly off limits to us. The Law was clear that I should not so much as let my eyes touch those pages, but I have already established that I was not a being of Law, but rather a being of hate.

I'd dealt with fanatics before, but I had never once been tempted to understand their superstitions beyond what I needed to know to better kill them. The Law said I should not, but my defiance said I should. I've fought many battles, but none were more difficult than the one I faced that night as I tried to decide between looking inside and placing it in the stove. Eventually I decided I would look briefly, and *then* I would burn it, so it could tempt me no more.

I lit an oil lamp and retrieved the book.

The brief glance I allowed myself stretched into hours as I read all through the night.

It was the forbidden history of our people, and all that came before. It did not read like the ramblings of madmen, or the lies of charlatans. I was pulled along, seemingly against my will, as I read of things strange, yet somehow familiar.

It struck me as true, and that was troublesome.

The book told of what had been, what was, and what would be. How we would rise, and fall, and rise, and fall again. It was in that last section, filled with dire prophecies, that I stopped, suddenly afraid, as I realized that centuries ago, this writer had been *writing about me*.

I speak not of generalities, or vague mumbling that could be about anyone if you squinted hard enough, but of a man without mercy, enforcer of an unjust code, who would stab a faithful servant in the heart and then read this very book while sitting next to his cooling corpse.

Suddenly furious, I threw the book on the floor. Then I dashed the oil lamp against the wall, setting the cottage ablaze. I stormed outside . . . only to be tempted to rush back in to try and save that damnable book. But I did not, and instead watched the cottage burn to the ground. Once I was satisfied all was ash, I walked back to Lahkshan in the dark and rain.

In the days that followed I devoted myself to the Law, and did my best to forget all that I had read. Ratul Without Mercy was the scourge of criminals everywhere. Rebels and fanatics fell to my sword.

Yet no matter how hard I worked, or how many criminals I killed, I could not shake the feeling that book had imparted to me. My dreams were haunted. If they were visions from forgotten gods, or figments of my imagination, I could not tell. I told no one, not even my closest friends in the Order, about what was troubling me.

As the years went on, I saw more distressing things,

events which could be taken as signs of dire prophecies, indicators of a looming apocalypse. *If* the book was true, and *if* the prophecies were true, then drastic action had to be taken soon or man was doomed.

I had been taught that before the Law, there was only madness. That it had been created by the first judges to save Lok from the chaos that was the Age of Kings. The Law was all-encompassing. All things are subject to the Law. Even the demons of hell must obey. They remain in the sea and man stays upon the land. Those who violate are guilty of trespass and will be punished.

But the Law could give me no answer. Merely voicing my concerns would have resulted in me being hung upon the Inquisitor's Dome to cook to death beneath the sun, my flesh devoured by vultures, and my bones swept into a hole. Though my faith in the Law was shaken, my loyalty to my Order remained strong, for I loved my brothers. There is a kinship that can only be found in hardship. Yet even among them, there was none whom I could confide in. To do so was to condemn them as I was condemned.

I began to question my assumptions and everything I believed. I required knowledge. Using my status as a Protector I was able to access parts of the Museum and the Great Library which were off limits to all but a select few. In secret I studied the black steel artifacts which had survived the Age of Kings. I consulted with the Historians. I learned what the Astronomers were really watching for. My desperate search across the Capitol was a grotesque version of the dreams once held by Young Ratul.

My sustaining hatred did not die, but once again shifted its aim. My fixation became the judges who had kept us from the truth for hundreds of years. I began to despise the Capitol for the things it had me and my brothers do. As I lost respect for those who wrote and interpreted the Laws, I began to delve into more forbidden areas of research.

It was in a cavern, deep beneath the world, that I met a giant. I speak not of a large man, like Protector Karno who stands a head above most, but of a true giant. Ten feet tall, with skin blue as a Dasa, who'd slept through the centuries, but had been born when kings still ruled.

The giant told me of a place in the steaming jungles of Gujara. There I sought out a legendary temple with carvings upon the wall where the last oracle of the Forgotten had prophesied of those who would be gathered to once again lead the Sons of Ramrowan in the final battle against the demons. There were three old symbols—the Priest, the Voice, and the General—representing those who must be found. Then more symbols, vague warning of some of those who would stand against the Forgotten's chosen, such as the Crown, and the Mask, and then the Demon, the last of which surely represented the entire host of hell.

In the distant south, in the coldest winter, I waited until the ice froze enough for me to walk across the ocean without being eaten by sea demons, so that I could knock upon the impenetrable gates of Fortress. They tried to blast me to pieces with their terrible magic before I convinced them that I too was a seeker of truth. I spoke with the guru and discovered that I was not alone in preparing for the end.

Yet, doubts remained.

Despite all my quests for forbidden wisdom into the darkest corners of Lok, the truth was finally revealed to me, not by a wall in a distant jungle temple or a fantastical being, but by one of my fellow Protectors. For it was I, Ratul, twenty-five-year Master of the Protector Order, who discovered the secret identity of one of our acolytes. A secret which would shake the very foundations of our society should it be revealed, for a lowly casteless had been chosen to bear the most powerful magic in the world.

It took this clear fulfillment of prophecy to finally convince me, and through conviction at last came my conversion.

The prophecies were real. *The gods were real.*

It took more research before I was certain that this boy was meant to be the Forgotten's warrior. I could never tell him who he really was. To do so would be to destroy him. And selfishly, in the meantime, I did not wish to deprive the Protectors of this powerful weapon which had revitalized and strengthened our waning order.

As I tell you that tonight, I know it seems senseless that even after being converted I would still try to help the very Order which has done so much harm to the faithful. They may be misguided by the Law, but the Protectors are the best of men. They do more good than harm. Though they despise me now, and they will surely take my life soon, they remain my brothers.

After that, I lived two lives simultaneously, Lord Protector beneath the eyes of the Law, and rebellious criminal in the shadows. While I still have faith the gods would show the General his path, it was my duty to search for the Voice and the Priest. I carefully checked every report from my Protectors involving religious fanatics. I did everything I could short of revealing my treachery to save what worshippers I could, ordering my men elsewhere, giving faulty intelligence, or even sneaking messages to the faithful to run.

That was how I found the genealogy and secretly became the Keeper of Names.

It was twelve long years after my conversion before I found the Voice in Makao. Yes, children, a true prophet walks amongst us once again. For their safety, I will not speak here of this person's identity, but the Voice lives, and I give you my word that the Voice is real. The Forgotten speaks to us, and he requires great things of us before we may have our reward.

Unfortunately there were witnesses to my discovery. Word of that event spread to my Order. I was required to explain my actions. Why had Ratul Without Mercy spared the life of an illegal wizard? I told the closest friend I've ever had the truth.

He turned his back on me.

My treachery was at last revealed, and I had to flee.

My name is worth saltwater. I am the most hated man in the history of the Protectors . . . for now.

I have hidden among the casteless and continued my search. It is here, in the borders of Great House Uttara, that I believe I have finally found the Forgotten's High Priest. He is clever, but driven by anger and bitterness, like I once was. Yet it is his ambition which will finally free our people.

We are out of time.

❖ ❖ ❖

Ratul had suddenly looked to the south, eyes narrowed dangerously. She knew that Ratul's senses—augmented by the magic of the Protector Order—were far superior to anyone else present. Maybe he had smelled the smoke of the burning barracks, or the blood of warriors being shed. Perhaps he heard the screams of the dying as the casteless attacked the warriors.

"That damned fool," Ratul muttered, sounding now like the tired old man that he was. "I must go and save his life. Farewell."

He said that not to the mob of dirty casteless who had been clustered around him, listening intently to his story, but to her. His testimony was really intended for her alone. These casteless did not know it yet, but they would probably all be dead by morning, caught up in the bloody purge which would follow Keta's inevitably failed rebellion.

She would live, as she always did.

Ratul rushed out the door of the shack. She got up and followed. There was a faint orange glow in the distance as the arson fires spread.

"There is a Protector there," she warned him.

"I know. I can sense the magic in his blood."

"Does it tell you which one?"

"No, but I suspect who it will be . . ." Ratul turned back to face her, grim. "Since my treachery was revealed, each night as I have dreamed, the Forgotten has shown me the same vision. I am wading through waist-deep snow, in the mountains of Devakula, and I know that I am being pursued by a mighty predator. It is one of the great southern bears, white as the snow, powerful and proud.

In the dream, there is no escape. And every night, the bear gets closer and closer. Last night, it was so near I could feel the hot breath upon my neck, and when I looked up, it had a bloody scar across its face."

"Devedas." She knew of him, but she knew a great many things, more even than Ratul. "Then if you go, you will surely die."

"There was one thing I did not speak of tonight. The last prophecy in that book I read in that dead man's cottage all those years ago, that enraged me so. It foretold my death, cut down by a man I'd love as a son, who would love me more than his own father . . . That knowledge . . . comforts me." The condemned man smiled. "I have no hate left."

"May the gods lift you, Ratul of many names."

"Thank you for all of your help, Mother Dawn."

Then Ratul went to seal his testimony with his blood.

❖ ❖ ❖

This story was released to come out about the same time as the second book in the series, House of Assassins, *and it was a chance for me to write about a character who had not shown up very much in the books, yet who had been extremely important in the lives of a few of the main characters.*

With "The Testimony of the Traitor Ratul," I used a style that was different than the main series. In this case I wanted Ratul to just tell his story in his own way. I had been listening to a few different Robert E. Howard collections on Audible at the time, and he used that tough guy sitting by the fire telling his tale method really well. I'm a big Howard fan, so I thought it would be fun to try that here.

The third novel in this series, Destroyer of Worlds, *will be out in 2020.*

SHOOTER READY

This story originally appeared in Galactic Games, *an anthology of science fiction stories with a sports theme, edited by Bryan Thomas Schmidt, and published by Baen Books in 2016.*

A GOOD SHOOTER does all his thinking before stepping into the box. Survey the course, plan your strategy, check your gear one last time, get that out of the way while you're on deck, because if you take the time to think after that, you lose. Shooting needs to come as natural as breathing. When it's your turn and you're there, waiting for that buzzer, hands raised to the surrender position, pistol in your holster, you don't think.

You just act.

Clear your head and shoot. It isn't draw stroke, move to the firing position, target, front sight focus, trigger squeeze, repeat a few hundred times until the course is done and you collect your trophy and your prize money and head to the after-party to bang the hot groupies. That works for local circuits on your home world, but there's nothing normal about this level of competition. When the difference between the first-place winner and hundredth-place loser is separated by a grand total of a second over eight or ten stages, there's no time for this step A, step B, step C bullshit. That's too slow.

I'm the last pure flesh-and-blood human practical shooting champion for a reason. I'm beating cyborgs with laser range finders in their eyeballs, and vat babies literally born to shoot. I'm beating robots that were designed to be one-man SWAT teams.

You know why I win? It's because in my head I go to this place where I see everything, time means nothing. It's Zen, man. I'm just shooting, five, six aimed shots a second, moving and manipulating as efficiently as I can, but never thinking about what I'm doing. Stimulus, response. After the match me and my coaches can watch the videos and see what I could have done better for next time, but I never think during the stage.

Pure action, time ceases to exist. It feels slow, but it's really fucking fast. I'm talking some Miyamoto Musashi-state-of-being shit here, you get me?

Of course you don't get it. If you got it, you'd have my job and I'd be the sports reporter.

The Zen state . . . Well, your body knows what to do because you've already trained it. Millions of rounds over thousands of hours, shooting and shooting and shooting until your hands bleed. I've loaded so many mags that there are dead spots where my fingers can't feel anything. I spent so much time at the range that my wife left me and I didn't notice she was gone for a week. I've shot so many *rounds that my sinuses are permanently filled with carbon. No, seriously, flowers and perfume smell like smoke. I fired six hundred rounds this morning before coming to this interview.*

By the time you get to this level, you've performed so damned many repetitions that the actions are burned into the pathways of your brain. It knows what to do to win, even if you consciously don't.

If you waver for even a fraction of a second, you're too slow. That's how the robots beat most of us. People blame it on them being so much faster and stronger. Robots don't get tired. Robots don't have muscle tremors. They don't have a heart that's pounding too hard to make that two-thousand-yard shot after running up Puke Hill at the Ironman. That's bullshit. That's a cop-out.

The robots win because they're programmed to win.

See this? This was the body I was born with. I'm not genetically engineered. I'm not augmented. I'm not on stims. There's no Hampson device plugged into my brain downloading techniques right into my memory. I'm just a man with a gun.

I win because I've programmed myself to win.

That's why I'm the last human champion, and that's why I'm the best there has ever been.

As he watched the old interview play, it made him smile. *I sure was a cocky little bastard.* He'd been so confident and full of himself back then, but nothing taught humility quite like a decade of getting your ass kicked.

"Could I get your autograph, Mr. Blackburn?" the fan held out the projector. "You were a legend. On New

Hebron we've got these nasty carnivorous whistle spiders. I watched your lesson on snap shooting, and it's saved my ass a few times."

"Glad to hear it, kid." He used his fingertip to sign the hologram. That made the fan happy. There weren't as many fans as there used to be, but he was still enough of a draw that gun companies kept hiring him to sit in their booths during arms expos. "Why don't you grab some swag?" He looked around for the marketing guy. "Hey, Frank, hook this young man up with a T-shirt. Here you go. Keep practicing, and don't forget to check out the"— he had to look at the logo on the T-shirt in his hands to remember which minor company he was shilling for today—"Krasnov. When you think directed energy weapons, think Krasnov."

The crowd moved on. People played with disabled guns, shouldering them, flipping switches, and looking through sights. Most of them were polite enough to keep them pointed in a safe direction. Salesmen cut deals, money was exchanged, and purchase orders placed. The off-world dealers just bought the schematics so they could pay royalties to print the guns in their own shops, which was way cheaper than shipping them across space. There were a lot of big money types wandering around, buyers from different militaries, government agencies, and large corporations, but most of the crowd were regular gun nuts who just wanted to play with cool new things and score free stuff. Arms expos always felt the same, even on backwater colony planets.

Since being a minor celebrity at this sort of thing paid his bills now, he knew them very well.

The next man to enter the booth was obviously one of the big fish. He didn't bother to look at the merchandise. He was wearing a gold VIP badge and one of those super-expensive suits with the light-transmitting fibers that made the wearer seem to glow. The man didn't care about the free pens, buttons, and probably wasn't a T-shirt type. Passing the salesmen, he went right to the minor celebrity guest. "Are you Scott Blackburn?"

"Yes, sir." He tried to read the man's badge, but the name and company weren't lit. "How can I help you?"

Now that he was closer, it was obvious the man was Human 2.1, maybe even higher. He towered over everyone else in the booth, and was just too obnoxiously ageless and perfect. It was like looking up to a god. "Are you the Scott Blackburn who won the tri-systems practical shooting championship from '78 to '81?"

"That's me." But the post-human already knew that. Their brains were wired with facial recognition programs.

"You were the best competitor?"

He couldn't tell if that was a question or a statement. "Briefly?"

"Forgive me if I am unclear. I only downloaded English a few minutes ago. I am Mr. Lee. May I buy you lunch?"

"Well, I'm working..." but apparently the Krasnov marketing manager knew who Mr. Lee was, and was making shooing motions to get Scott out of the booth. This Mr. Lee must have been in position to buy a shitload of guns. "What's this about?"

"It is about being the best, Mr. Blackburn. Ultimately, everything is about that."

❖ ❖ ❖

This is it, folks. We're here at the first stage of the Grand Halifax Open Class Invitational. As you can see, our reigning champ, Scott Blackburn, is stepping into the box. There's been a lot of talk on the circuit this year about the threat posed by the new Diomedes 5 competition robots. After last year's narrow victory over the Diomedes 4, which the Diomedes Corporation blamed on a last-minute programming error, the pressure is on Blackburn. They claim that this new generation is significantly faster than last year's model. The question on everyone's mind, can the human champ hold on one more year? What do you think, Jess?

My money is on Blackburn still, Javier. The kid's got heart. This stage will follow the highlighted route, with the shooter engaging holographic moving targets from five to five hundred meters. They'll be starting with pistols, and then switching to long guns once they clear the obstacles. Grand Halifax scoring is brutal, anything other than an X-zone hit adds half a second to your overall time. A miss adds a whopping two whole seconds. To put that in perspective, the X-zone on a Grand Halifax hologram is ten centimeters wide, and the whole hologram is only thirty centimeters across.

Pure accuracy will go to the machine, but it remains to be seen if it's got the programming to pay the bills... They're ready. We're switching live now to Blackburn.

"Shooter ready?"

"Shooter ready."

BEEP.

And he's off.

Damn, that's fast. Blackburn is already at the first

array. I don't think I've ever seen anybody clear a star that quick. He's in top form today.

You can see him dodging through the obstacles. He's not even slowing down as he shoots on the move. Blackburn's running a 6mm 3011 set on three-round burst. As you're watching, keep in mind he's still experiencing some recoil there. That's no energy weapon, and the 6mm loads still make major power factor . . . Did you see that, Jess?

Holy moly, that was quick!

Blackburn's reloading on the move. Remember, the Diomedes has an autoloader in its wrist and performs half-second mag changes.

Transitioning to the long gun, now Blackburn's got to slow down enough to nail the longer-range targets.

He's not slowing down much.

Grand Halifax is at .7 standard gravity and has zero wind, so all that training on Mars is probably coming in handy for Blackburn right now.

Remarkably, he's still down zero points. Not a single miss. He's switching to the shotgun barrel for the final speed run. And . . . the stop plate is down.

55.64 seconds clean! Down zero points. That is the fastest that anyone has ever run this stage at Grand Halifax. He burned it down.

Starting the day by setting a new stage record? Team Blackburn has got to be feeling pretty good about keeping the championship in human hands for one more year. We're going to the pit to try and catch a word with Scott Blackburn. He's unloading and showing clear to the safety officer, and it looks like Tom has caught up with our champ for a word—

Hang on. Switch back. Diomedes has already started its run.

Transcript note: Period of stunned silence. Transmission resumes.

Jesus . . .

Diomedes 4 just ran the course in 38.08.

I've never seen anything like it.

I think we've just witnessed the end of an era, Javier.

Or maybe the beginning of a new one, Jess.

From the team of security guards surrounding them, and the way every local vendor in the place bowed nearly to the floor as they passed, Mr. Lee was a big fucking deal. Despite that, they just went to the convention center food court to eat.

The glowing post-human man-god ordered chicken fingers. "Let me begin by saying the history of your sport fascinates me. To succeed requires a combination of grace, fine motor coordination, and skill. It is not about pure accuracy, like some other sports, but accurate enough, while going extremely fast. Engaging multiple targets from different positions and on the move, from conversational distance to long range, switching between different weapon systems as you go, it is all very exhilarating to watch. It is no wonder it has become one of the most popular sports on many planets."

Mr. Lee just sounded so damned earnest about it that Scott had to chuckle. "Yeah, we used to say that it was the most fun you could have with your pants on."

"Tell me about why you got into competitive shooting, Mr. Blackburn."

"Are you a sports reporter or something?"

"I am not, but I own several sports reporters."

"Oh . . ." Scott wasn't sure which system Mr. Lee was from, so he wasn't sure if that was the language download glitching or if he actually owned slaves. "Well, my grandfather started long-range shooting competitions on Mars, and my father was the champ for years. Hell, my great-grandfather shot USPSA back when there was still a United States. So I guess you can say it's in my blood."

"But you have said yourself that good competitors are not born, they are made. Raw talent and physical gifts are no match for a developed mindset." Mr. Lee tapped the side of his head for dramatic effect. "I have downloaded all your interviews."

"If you already know my answers, why ask the question?"

Mr. Lee shrugged. It was a remarkably human gesture from someone who was beyond humanity. "I have spoken with many washed-up athletes. I've found that answers provided in interviews are often different than the truth."

"I'm not *washed up*. I still shoot and I still win."

"My apologies. That was a poor choice of phrase. I meant to say that you are no longer at the top of your game. You still win, but in front of a much smaller audience, and only against other unaugmented humans in Limited Class."

The box containing Scott's lunch slid out of the dispenser chute. At least he was getting a free meal out of this bullshit. "What do you want?"

"I am what you would call a *sports fan*."

❖ ❖ ❖

It's been a hell of a ride for former champ Scott Blackburn. From the height of the sport to several losing seasons in a row, we caught up with him after his humiliating defeat at Garnier Station.

Scott, what happened out there?

Shooting in zero g is always a challenge. When you're using projectile weapons, every shot is going to propel you along. You've got to be not just aware of where you are, but where you're going to be after you start spinning and plan your angles accordingly. It's the toughest environment to shoot in. I made a bad call and misjudged the ranges going in.

But, Scott, the winner had four arms and clung to the walls with a prehensile tail. He was bred to live in space. How could you possibly hope to beat him?

I know the winner. Grez is a hell of a nice guy. He's a good competitor and a good shooter. This is a big win for him.

But wouldn't you say his genetic modification gave him an unfair advantage?

Are you looking to get me to spout off some pure human supremacy nonsense? No. Grez is a good dude. I lost, he won. That's competition. End of story. Open Class means anything goes.

Some are saying that it is time for you to get out of Open and move down to Limited Class.

I know I've lost some sponsors this year, but that's how these things go. I'll train hard during the off season and come back and try again next year.

But, Scott, some say that you've hit a physical plateau. You're as good as a normal human can ever hope to be. Have you thought about getting yourself modified?

This interview is over.

As their conversation had gone on, Scott had realized that Mr. Lee wasn't just a fan, he was one of those dreaded *super fans*, a geeky walking encyclopedia of sports trivia. Memorizing stats wasn't particularly impressive when you'd been genetically engineered to have a super brain, but it was obvious Mr. Lee was passionate about this stuff.

"I'm betting you've got one hell of a collection of sports memorabilia."

"Yes. It is impressive. The centerpiece is Madison Square Garden. I had it dismantled brick by brick, and reassembled on my home planet."

Scott didn't know what a Madison Square Garden was. "That's nice."

"History fascinates me. Did you know that though practical shooting has been around for centuries, it has only been in the last hundred years your sport has become huge? It was held back from going mainstream on Earth due to logistical, cultural, and political reasons."

Scott ticked off reasons on his fingers. "Some politicians hated people having access to guns. You needed a big area to fling lead around. Some cultures were scared of regular folks with weapons."

"Indeed. The proliferation of 3D printing destroyed the concept of gun control forever. And as mankind rapidly spread across the stars, many habitable colonies had to deal with primitive aliens."

Nothing put the practical into practical shooting like

having the local life forms constantly trying to kill you. You were hard pressed nowadays to find a colony world where people weren't armed to the teeth. Scott took a drink of his soda, thankful that at least he was way past the point of his career where he needed to hire out as *pest control*.

"Shooting clubs proliferated. The introduction of holographic and robot targets added a new element of spectator enjoyment." Mr. Lee seemed really pleased about that. "As they say, the rest is history."

"Which would make me a historical footnote."

"Exactly!" Mr. Lee laughed, only Scott hadn't been trying to be funny. "You know, they made a movie about the first robot that took your championship. Diomedes was portrayed as a modern day Jackie Robinson. You were the villain."

"I haven't seen it," Scott lied.

"I love sports movies. It is all about narrative." He said it like he was savoring the word. "Practical shooting is a throwback, the rare Olympic sport celebrating combative skills, which are now obsolete, like wrestling, or throwing the javelin. Did you know that shooting was the second-to-last sport where unassisted humans reigned supreme?"

"What was the last holdout? Golf?"

"Surprisingly enough, bowling."

He wouldn't have guessed that, but then again, he hadn't bowled in fifty years, and most of that had been futilely chucking balls down the gutter. "Go figure."

"It was easy for science to make men stronger, but it took longer to replace pure humans in games that required more finesse."

"Makes sense." Scott picked at his food with his

chopsticks but wasn't feeling particularly hungry. Talking with super fans always ended up depressing.

On the other hand, Mr. Lee seemed to be having a grand time talking about his love. "Do you remember football, Mr. Scott? The American style football? The one you throw. Not the kind you kick."

"Sure." Scott had even watched it as a kid. He'd been born on Mars, but his ancestors had come from Texas, so granddad had declared their compound to be Cowboys fans. "It's still popular on some worlds."

"It was once the biggest sport on Earth. The National Football League held an event called the Super Bowl, which for many years was the most lucrative sporting event on the planet. It was a celebration of the greatest athletes, and most of humanity tuned in to watch the struggle. Have you ever watched a Super Bowl, Mr. Blackburn?"

The last one of those had been long before he'd been born. "Can't say that I have."

"There is a reason it went away. When scientists invented performance-enhancing drugs, the NFL banned them, because that would be *cheating*. They would create an *unfair* advantage." Mr. Lee banged one fist on the plastic table for emphasis. "Can you imagine such backwards thinking?"

Several of the security guards glanced his way. Scott just gave them an apologetic look. It was the rich post-human who was getting spun up, not him.

"When the first true cyborg limbs were invented, they were also banned. When drastically improved organs were grown in vats, banned. Genetic modification and splicing, banned. Every scientific improvement for the betterment and improvement of mankind, all banned." This really seemed to bother Mr. Lee, and as a post-human himself, it made sense why. "They said this was for fairness, for equality, to level the playing field. Do you know what killed the NFL, Mr. Blackburn?"

"No."

"Boredom. People do not watch sports for *equality*. It is the quest for excellence. It is to celebrate the best, and to *be* the best. Other leagues were created which were not burdened by such racist, old-fashioned rules, or blocked by arbitrary and capricious laws. Until one day most viewers realized that instead of watching the same old limited humans playing the same limited old game, they could watch a defense made up of eight-foot-tall, six-hundred-pound titans, trying to stop a running back with a cybernetic lower body sprinting at sixty miles an hour."

"That isn't sport anymore. That's just seeing who is willing to graft more crap onto their body, replacing skill with software and muscles with hardware." Scott shook his head. "Some of us weren't in it for the spectacle."

"Too bad your audience was. Limited Class has a tiny fraction of the viewership of Open Class now. Your division has slightly higher ratings than the one where people dress up as cowboys and compete with old-timey six-shooters."

"You're right. Nobody wants to watch us boring, limited humans anymore." Scott was tired and annoyed. "Look, I might just be some washed-up nobody now, working here one step up from a booth babe, but I was pretty damned good once." Scott put his chopsticks on the table and quickly stood up. The guards tensed. "Now if you'll excuse me, I'm going to go back to degrading myself for money."

"Please wait, Mr. Blackburn."

"No." He made it another five feet before his temper got the better of him and he turned back. "You wait. I was the best. I trained my ass off. Back in my day it was about your heart and your work ethic, not your DNA or your CPU. I won because I earned it."

"I know. That's why I sought you out."

He hesitated. "What exactly is it that you want then, Mr. Lee?"

"To give you another shot at the title."

Matt,

I'm really sorry, but I'm not going to be able to see you this month. I got a slot in the Manzanita System division championship match. It was a last-minute thing. One of the Open shooters dropped out and the network needed a replacement. I've not gotten an Open slot for years. By the time you watch this recording, I'll be through the wormhole.

You're probably sick of explanations and excuses. I know, you're thinking "Oh great, Dad's missing another birthday because he's off losing again. He must care more about his game than he does about me." But it isn't like that. When I was your age, my dad was always gone, too. When he came home he was distracted and bored, just killing time until the next match. He had the bug. So I know how you feel. I really do.

I didn't get him then, but I get him now. If you're not

*competing you're not living, you're just existing. I wish I
could explain it better, but I can't. I couldn't explain it to
your mom, which is probably why she left me. And I really
can't blame her.*

*I've only ever been good at one thing, but the universe
kept progressing and left me behind. Now I'm a joke to
them. The only reason I got this slot was because watching
me fail amuses the audience. They get to feel smug and
say, wow, look how far we've come in so little time. Isn't
technology wonderful?*

*Sorry, Matt, it's never been about beating the other
guys, or entertaining the crowds, it's been about beating
myself. There's a feeling you get when you achieve
something nobody else can do. It makes you feel alive. It's
about one last chance at being the best.*

*I know I can't be the best anymore. But I still have to
try.*

Be good for your mom. I love you, son.

"Please, sit down." Mr. Lee gestured at the abandoned
chair.

Scott reluctantly returned to the table.

"I know everything about you, Mr. Blackburn. I know
that your body chemistry won't accept cybernetic
enhancements because you've already tried repeatedly.
You're too old to try manipulating your genetic code, but
you paid a fortune to black market biohackers to try
anyway and nearly died in the process."

"It hurt like you can't imagine," he muttered.

"Oh, I can. One of my many companies designed most
of the drugs involved. I've seen the pain involved break

the will of the strongest specimens. Yet you still tried *four* times. That is dedication. You were willing to destroy your body in an attempt to be a little better. To what lengths will someone like you go to win?"

Scott had no answer.

"Even if you'd succeeded, it wouldn't have mattered very long anyway." Mr. Lee opened his hand and a hologram appeared over his palm. "This is Diomedes 7. It is predicted to run the first stage at Grand Halifax under thirty seconds next season. It has an AI which would have been worthy of a starship ten years ago, and a thorium reactor meant for a hover tank. Every limb is a different, maximized weapon system, projectile, beam, plasma, and nano. In a tenth of a second, it sees every target on the course and paints them with a laser that analyzes the movement of every air molecule in its path. And after it annihilates its competition, it will put on a very realistic flesh mask and provide compelling interviews."

"I'm sure its sponsors will love that."

"No. We won't. It lacks *heart*. Test audiences like it when their heroes have to struggle." Mr. Lee moved his fingers slightly and the hologram of the robot changed to a machine even more advanced. "Which is why I want to put your brain inside of this."

Scott read the stats flashing past. It was a monster.

"Those are conservative estimates based upon our existing test subjects. Using you as the biological core, I think we can make it even faster."

"My brain would only slow that thing down."

"On the contrary, the decisions are processed in advance based on hypothetical scenarios and extrapolations, then stored. When the decision is triggered, there is only instantaneous action." Mr. Lee said patiently.

"That's how I shoot . . ."

"Exactly. Which is why you were chosen for this project. You would be surprised what the human brain can accomplish when freed from its fleshy tethers."

He spoke like he'd removed a lot of brains. "What do you do for a living anyway?"

"I own several planets, Mr. Blackburn. It is easier to ask what do I not do."

"But why are you doing *this*?"

Mr. Lee gave him a benevolent, godlike smile. "I believe sports to be about the quest for excellence. It is about pushing the boundaries of achievement. You were willing to die for this game. Instead, I ask you to live for it." He changed the hologram again, this time to a contract. "I have just sent a copy of this to your agent and your attorney."

The contract was for more money than Scott had ever imagined, but that wasn't what mattered.

"As I said before, a good sports story is all about narrative, and everyone loves a comeback. Sign here to be the champion again, Mr. Blackburn."

He didn't think. He just acted.

We're here at the final stage of the Manzanita System division championship with Scott Blackburn. He's been called the last man standing, the final human contender in a sport now dominated by robots and post-humans. How're you doing today, Scott?

It's been a hell of a match, Wendy. The high gravity and

fire winds always make shooting Manzanita a real challenge. I'd like to thank my sponsor, Krasnov Multinational, for sending me with quality gear that holds up even in these tough conditions.

Scott, you're currently forty-eighth out of fifty shooters on the board. That's a long way down from your peak showings—

The competition has gotten better.

Yes, exactly. Fans are wondering if this will be the last time you ever compete in Open Class, and if that's the case, could this be the last time that any unaugmented human competes at this level? Is this the end of an era?

Not if I can help it.

When Bryan Thomas Schmidt approached me about a sci-fi sports story for *Galactic Games*, it was really easy for me to decide I was going to write about competition shooting. I'm not particularly athletic, and that was the only sport I've ever actually been really good at. I did well, especially at three gun competition. That's where you use a rifle, shotgun, and pistol to shoot a wide variety of targets over a timed course at various distances. It takes a lot of time and effort to stay really competitive. For a while I was spending every weekend at the range, and a couple nights a week were spent reloading ammunition, but it was fun and the competitors in that sport are a great bunch of people.

However, once my writing career started taking off I had to choose how I was going to spend my limited free *time. It was either shoot at that level, or write more books. Writing won. I was never anywhere as committed as the main character in "Shooter Ready," but I've known guys like Scott. Competition is addictive. They're not living unless they're giving 100%.*

THREE SPARKS

This story first appeared in Predator: If It Bleeds, *published in 2017 by Titan Books, edited by Bryan Thomas Schmidt.*

I love the Predator movies. When I was offered a chance to write a 30th anniversary Predator story I jumped at it. Since this anthology was about Predators stalking their prey through the ages, I had a lot of options of where I could set it, but as you've seen from a bunch of my other short stories, I kind of love samurai drama. So samurai versus Predator? Hell yeah. How could I not write that?

THEY FOUND THE FIRST BODIES around noon, suspended from a branch high above them, arms dangling. Samurai? They could not tell. It was hard to know someone's social status after they had been skinned.

From the bloat and the stink, combined with the heat, Hiroto guessed they had been dead for three days. He had skinned a lot of game, so even in their sorry state he could tell that this oni was very skilled at butchery. Hiroto was impressed. There were no signs of rope. It would take an incredible amount of strength and balance to haul corpses all the way up there. He had seen great cats cache their kills in trees, but this felt different, as if staged for their benefit. Was it to send a message? Marking territory? He tried not to let his appreciation show. A regular porter should be frightened, so he tried to act that way.

The others, however, didn't have to act.

"Captain Nasu Hiroto, hero of the Battle of Dan-no-ura, hero of the Battle of Kurikara, master swordsman, and champion archer of the Minamoto Clan. Some say the finest archer in our history, if not, second only to his father. Yet after the war, there would be no peace for him. No. Hiroto took one of *my* ships, and was carried about wherever the waves would take him, always searching for a new battle, for new beasts to slay. Over the years, I heard he was hunting tigers in the jungles of Tenjiku or great white bears in the desolate lands north of Joseon. It is widely believed Nasu Hiroto is the greatest hunter in the world."

There were some exaggerations there but Hiroto did not correct the Shogun's inaccuracies. When the most powerful man in Nippon wanted to ramble, you let him. So Hiroto simply knelt and waited for Minamoto Yoritomo to pronounce his judgment.

"You were one of my most trusted warriors, Hiroto. Why did you leave? After our victory over the Taira Clan, I would have given you great responsibilities."

"I left because you would have given me great responsibilities."

"Your life was mine to spend, Hiroto."

"Spending it teaching children how to use a bow would have been a waste. I am not trying to be facetious, my Lord, but I would have died of boredom. I am not very good at peace."

"Then you picked a fortuitous time to return."

The castle was stifling. It was a miserable day in what had to be the hottest summer in generations. A servant was fanning the red-faced and sweating Shogun. Nobody was fanning Hiroto. He did not rate a fan.

"I should have you executed for your disobedience, you impudent ronin bastard. Yet curiosity gets the better of me. After all these years you returned to Kamakura. Why?"

"I received word that the Shogunate has need of my services."

Minamoto Yoritomo chuckled. "I should have known that the Oni of Aokigahara would bring you out of hiding. Summer began with it murdering a score of my warriors, picking them off, one by one, and leaving them hanging from trees, skinned. Since then, samurai have been rushing there in order to defeat it and win my favor. All have failed. Witnesses whisper of an invisible demon, stronger than any man, which kills by spear, claw, or even bolts of lightning, before vanishing as quickly as it appeared."

"You can see how such stories would catch my interest, my Lord."

"Sometimes, three glowing embers appear upon its

chosen victim," The Shogun held up three fingers, then put them against his forehead, fingertips making the points of a triangle. "Being marked by these fire kami are the only warning before it strikes. So many samurai have perished that they believe the oni cannot be defeated by mortal hand. I seem to recall they said the same thing about the Great Sea Beast, before your father killed it with a single arrow through the eye."

"A truly heroic moment."

"I know. I was there. No man has ever equaled his feat ... including the man who has hunted every dangerous beast beneath the sun. Hmmm ... Perhaps if you were to defeat the Oni of Aokigahara, you could finally match his legend?"

It might have been in his blood, but that wasn't why Hiroto followed his path. The Shogun may have been a brilliant general, but he did not understand the compulsion to constantly seek out new dangers. "You are wise, my Lord, but what is one little forest demon when compared to a mighty kaiju?"

"You could never resist a challenge, could you, Hiroto?"

He had never fought a demon before. "No, my Lord. I could not."

It was a few days' ride to Aokigahara, the dense forest to the north of Mount Fuji. Despite the blistering sun, Hiroto enjoyed seeing the land of his birth again. He felt eager and alive. Each morning the mountain was a bit closer and so was his next great challenge.

Unfortunately, he was not making the journey alone.

The Shogunate had sent a representative, a young warrior born of high status, named Ashikaga Motokane, and his retinue of five bodyguards. Though Hiroto had helped their Lord rise to power, that had been a long time ago. Now, the Shogun's samurai looked upon him as a dishonorable outcast, a wild man, an anomaly in their orderly world.

Worst case scenario, Hiroto would use them as bait.

The map provided by the Shogunate had shown a small village at the edge of the forest, so Hiroto had picked that as their destination. Upon arrival it had proven even more pathetic than expected, simply a collection of rotten huts and stinking pig pens, yet it would provide a final opportunity to restock their provisions. Hiroto also hoped for firsthand information.

The villagers saw the warriors approaching and abandoned their fields to hide in their huts. That was not surprising. Villages like this were often menaced by one conquering army or another, and during times of peace there were always bandits. One farmer remained in the center of the village to greet them. That would be their appointed headman, the presenter of taxes and hospitality.

"The rest of you hang back for a moment. There is no need to spook them further." Of course the Shogun's representative did not listen. When Hiroto dismounted and began walking into the village, Ashikaga Motokane followed, swaggering in the most intimidating way possible.

"I need to ask these farmers some questions."

"Why bother? They'll know nothing."

"You might be surprised."

Motokane looked upon the village with disgust. "They're beneath us. We're authorized to take whatever supplies we require. Let's do it and get on with it." It was no wonder the poor farmers saw little difference between bandits and samurai.

The headman had seen their banner bore the Shogunate's mon, and as they approached, had already launched into a rapid speech telling them how wonderful they were, but that his poor village had paid its taxes, and for them to please have mercy because the terrible heat had caused their crops to wilt and their well to run dry, so on and so forth.

Hiroto didn't have patience for such frivolous things when there were monsters about, so he cut the headman off. "I am Nasu Hiroto. We've come to kill the Oni of Aokigahara."

"You are not the first. The stories are true. Our land is cursed! It is a terrible scourge. We are so thankful more brave samurai came to fight the demon." Only the headman didn't actually sound relieved; if anything he was annoyed. "Many of you have come through here this summer, eating our food, putting our men to work as guides—"

"Yes, I know." The village had probably seen a parade of warriors by this point, but he needed information. "Have you seen it yourself?"

"No, but I have felt it watching. Many have, though. Young Hagi saw it first, perched high in the trees, shaped like a man, but bigger, with a head like an ox. She thought it was an angry ghost and ran away. Old Genzo saw it too.

He heard the thunder when it killed the first samurai. It put the three sparks on him too, but Genzo fled before more lightning came! Lucky it didn't chase him because it is swift as a horse!"

Any creature capable of effortlessly slaughtering samurai would have an easy time with a place this defenseless. "How many of your people has the demon killed?"

"Who cares?" Motokane said. "They're just peasants."

The headman looked nervously between the two imposing warriors, unsure whether he was still supposed to speak or not. Hiroto wished that Motokane would keep his idiot mouth shut. These farmers were probably as frightened by hungry soldiers as the demon plaguing their woods.

"I must know, how many of you have died?"

"It is hard to believe, but none, noble samurai. He has only attacked mighty warriors such as you. Our village has not been troubled by Three Sparks."

That name would suffice. "All of those men beheaded or skinned nearby, yet this Three Sparks has not harmed a single person in this humble village . . . Curious."

"Perhaps they're in league with the oni!" Motokane snarled. "Why else would it leave them be?"

The headman immediately threw himself into the dust and began begging for mercy which, with a hothead like Motokane, was certainly the wisest thing possible. "No! Please! We would never! After the killing started some of us left offerings at the shrine to appease it at most!"

"You gave gifts to a demon that was killing my brothers?" Motokane bellowed as he reached for his sword.

Hiroto sighed. Clan officials always made his job more complicated. He wasn't going to get any answers if Motokane started slaughtering villagers. "Please, calm yourself."

"The Shogun will abide no treachery!"

"And I will not abide you interrupting me again." The official may have outranked him, but Hiroto was the one handpicked for this assignment, and his patience was wearing thin. "You said it yourself, peasants are beneath your notice. You and Three Sparks have that in common. Now walk away and let me finish."

Motokane was quarrelsome, but he wasn't stupid. Rank had privileges, but they were a long way from Kamakura. The young man gave the headman one last threatening glare, then let go of his sword and went back to join his troops. *Good.* Hiroto didn't particularly want to murder him, but he would if necessary, and then simply tell the Shogun that the demon had gotten him. "Now where were we?"

"I'm sorry, great and noble—"

"Enough groveling, and stand already. I'm no tax collector." He waited for the farmer to get up. "I'm simply a hunter, and you're going to tell me everything you know about this demon so that I can kill it."

It was hard to tell over the clanking and huffing of Motokane's bodyguards, but beyond them the forest was unnaturally quiet. The wind did not penetrate far into the Sea of Trees. There were no birds singing, no insects buzzing, just the occasional tap of collected humidity falling on leaves.

It was no wonder the place had been considered haunted even before an oni had moved in.

That morning the others had dressed for war. Motokane's retinue were wearing their armor and helmets, with bows strung, spears held high, and their swords at their sides. The Shogun's finest looked like fearsome combatants, a worthy challenge for any demon.

Meanwhile, Hiroto lagged behind them, unarmed and stripped to the waist, with a bamboo pole balanced across his shoulder with a bundle hanging from each end. He had even gone and rolled about in the fields to complete the act. The other samurai thought he'd gone mad when he had left his swords behind, but Hiroto looked and even smelled like a local farmer.

Hiroto tried to appear inconsequential, head down, tired and stumbling from rock to rock beneath his clumsy burden. He would be no threat, especially to a mighty oni. He was simply a porter, conscripted from the village to carry his betters' supplies because the forest was too rugged for their horses. The headman had told him that some of the other would-be demon hunters had done the same, and each time their porter had come running back alone, terrified, sometimes covered in blood, but alive.

In his experience, most beasts targeted the weakest prey. This oni was different. It attacked the strong. He would use that to his advantage.

They walked for hours. It was slow going across such rough terrain. Thick roots waited to trip them. Each warrior was drenched in sweat. The air felt heavy and smelled of moss. The soil was dark and littered with black volcanic rocks. Between the heat and the uneven ground, the samurai were surely regretting wearing their armor, but they were all too proud to show it. Each of them thought that they would be the one to take the trophy back to their Lord, and they passed the time by boasting of what they would do with their reward.

Hiroto just kept his head down, appearing meek and subservient. He reasoned it did not do much good to use his eyes to hunt a creature which was supposedly invisible. Instead, he listened.

In a forest without sound, the faintest things became audible. The oni was quiet, but not as quiet as a tiger. In trees packed too tight for the wind to rustle through, the smallest movement was a clue. Occasionally he'd hear flesh scrape against bark, or the creak of a branch as weight settled on it. There was another sound beneath as well, barely audible, but unnatural, like the chittering of an insect combined with the slithering of a snake across sand. It made the hair on his arms stand up. All of that information would have been lost amongst the noise of a living place, but in the haunted stillness of Aokigahara, it told a story.

They were being followed.

It was somewhere above them and to the right. He tried not to let his excitement show.

"Over here," Kaneto called from the edge of a nearby stream. "There's another."

This body had been there for a few days, and was missing its head, but from his fine clothing and the broken katana lying in the water, he had clearly been a samurai.

Motokane knelt next to the corpse and pointed at the emblem embroidered on the sleeve. "I recognize this from court. This is the personal mon of Hojo Murashige!"

Hiroto had no idea who that was, but the Hojo were a family of some importance. The corpse's identity seemed to shake the others.

"He was a fearsome swordsman," Zensuke whispered. "The best of us."

"It didn't just take his head. It ripped out his *spine*." Motokane stood up and glanced around nervously. A full day of nerves and stress had worn him thin. He suddenly raised his voice and bellowed. "Show yourself, demon! Show yourself so I can kill you like the wretched cowardly dog you are!"

Hiroto took a few steps away from the angry samurai. The peasants had spoken of it throwing lightning bolts, and he didn't think it wise to stand so close to the most tempting target. He listened, but if the demon was still watching, it was being especially quiet, or at least quiet enough he couldn't hear it over the shouting. So while Motokane continued to rant and threaten the trees, Hiroto looked for tracks. Sign always told a story.

The black ground was too hard to leave good prints, but the moss, once smashed, grew differently than what was around it. There were the marks of normal sandals, and then much larger footfalls, heavy enough to crush the moss flat. The two had fought back and forth for quite some time, covering a lot of distance. He examined a cut on a tree. From the height and angle, it had come from someone extremely tall. Deep cuts. *Incredible strength.* Twin blades . . . *An odd weapon.* There were other cuts in the barks. The oni fought with a wild and ferocious style. Then he found the dried blood where the oni had finally struck true. He followed the trail. These rocks had been stained green. *Paint?* He touched it. No... It had the consistency of dried sap... *So oni bleed green. Curious.* The smell was completely alien. He spied something else lying on the rocks, something out of place. He picked it up.

And then Kaneto's chest exploded.

There was a *whoosh-crack* and a flash of light. Motokane's shouting was suddenly interrupted as the bodyguard's blood sprayed him in the face. Bits of meat and armor rained out of the sky, making ripples across the stream. Kaneto dropped to his knees, lifeless, and then flopped forward with a splash.

The wound on his chest must have been incredibly hot because it boiled the stream around it. Steam rose through the giant hole in Kaneto's back.

The samurai's reaction was near instant. Spears were lifted, arrows were nocked, only they had no target for their wrath.

"Where'd that come from?" Motokane shouted.

Hiroto had dropped his bundles, crouched behind a tangle of roots, and was listening carefully. The lightning strike had made his ears ring, but besides the warrior's heavy breathing, he caught a rapid series of *thumps* as the oni danced from tree to tree. It was pulling back to watch from a position of safety... toying with them.

That meant they had some time before the killing would resume. The odd item he had found was still clenched in his fist, so Hiroto opened his hand to study it.

The thing was too big, it ended in an obsidian claw, and the exposed meat was bright green instead of decaying red, but from the joints and knuckles, it was clearly a finger.

So Hojo Murashige must have challenged the oni to a duel, it had accepted, and lost a finger in the process... No wonder it preferred to attack from ambush.

"Why won't this damned thing come out and fight us like a proper warrior?" Motokane grumbled as they trudged through the forest.

"Because it isn't stupid," Hiroto muttered from the back of the line.

"What was that?" he demanded.

They were going back along the same trail they had come in on. Ostensibly to *find better ground to fight on*— or so the official declared. Hiroto assumed it was because Motokane had realized he was in over his head, but he didn't want to lose face by outright calling it a retreat.

Hiroto kept his voice down. It wasn't a low-born porter's place to offer tactical advice to samurai, but he did not feel that the demon was near enough to eavesdrop. "A clever hunter pits his strengths against his prey's weakness. He does not pit his weakness against his prey's strengths."

"Nonsense," Motokane spat. "He's just dishonest like you! Now shut up and keep moving!"

They continued walking, but a few moments later the nearest samurai whispered to Hiroto, "What did you mean by that, hunter?"

"It knows we are strong in close combat. The Hojo was

a good swordsman. The demon fought him, katana against some odd manner of dual blade. It won, but left behind a finger. A costly mistake. It will not be so foolish to face one of us head on again."

"Ah . . . I see . . ." The samurai was carrying a tetsubo, a heavy war club, a fearsome weapon which wouldn't do him much good when the invisible oni returned and blasted them with lightning bolts from the treetops. "Unfortunate."

Since Hiroto had assumed most of them would die poorly, he had not bothered to learn all their names, but this one did not seem as dense as the others. "What do they call you again?"

"Nobuo."

His attention had been elsewhere during the attack. "Did you see the fire kami mark your companion? The three sparks?"

"Yes, but I did not react in time. I saw light flickering on his breastplate, but the heat made me slow. At first I thought it was a trick of the eyes. Then it was too late. Kaneto's death is my fault."

He was still not sure what purpose the sparks served. "How long did they linger before the lightning struck?"

"They were already there when I looked over, for how long before that I don't know. Then only the space of a few heartbeats before I was nearly blinded by the flash."

"Hmmm . . ." At first he'd suspected the sparks held some spiritual significance, but now . . . Nipponese archers trained to see their target, then draw and release in one smooth movement, but the archers of the Song Dynasty he had trained with always drew, then paused to sight down the shaft before release. "It sounds as if the demon uses the fire kami to *aim*. This knowledge may prove useful."

They continued on for a time in silence. Hiroto could not currently hear the demon stalking them. He assumed that was because it had waited for them to leave the stream, and now it was skinning and hanging Kaneto from a tree. He had been tempted to stay and wait in ambush, but Motokane had ordered his men to move out. Faced with the choice, Hiroto had decided that live bait was more valuable than dead.

"Hunter, another question."

"Please do not call me that. The oni might be listening."

"Apologies."

Hiroto sighed, because samurai apologized to low-born laborers *so very often*. "What is it, Nobuo?"

"We have seen this hunter's strengths. What are yours?"

"I am a fast learner."

The next attack came at sundown.

Hiroto saw a single leaf fall from a tree fifty paces to their side, then a few moments later a branch vibrated high in a tree thirty paces ahead. The blessing of Hachiman—god of warriors—was upon him, because if they were anywhere other than the unnatural stillness of Aokigahara, he would not have sensed it.

"The oni is here," he whispered.

Nobuo quietly repeated that to the next samurai in line, who repeated it to Motokane, who immediately ruined any chance of an effective response by shouting, "Halt!"

Spears and arrows were readied. The warriors watched the thick undergrowth, wary. Hiroto acted the frightened porter and ducked behind a tree. Several tense seconds passed.

Three flickering sparks appeared on Zensuke's helmet.

"Look out!" Nobuo shouted as he hurled himself against his companion. As they collided there was another whip crack of sound and a brilliant flash. The two samurai fell in a shower of sparks.

Hiroto had seen exactly where that bolt had come from. He quickly dumped the satchels from the bamboo shaft he'd been carrying. His real cargo had been hidden inside all along.

One of the samurai—he had not bothered to remember this one's name—launched an arrow into the branches. To his credit, he was close, yet not close enough. The oni must have felt rushed, because the three sparks did not linger this time, and the bolt struck the warrior low. The resulting blast still sent him flipping through the air. One of his legs flew in the opposite direction.

Careful not to cut himself on one of the specially prepared arrowheads, Hiroto retrieved his bow. He had it strung and had taken up one of his poisoned arrows before the crippled samurai landed.

The oni was hurling lightning down upon the samurai like he was Raijin the thunder god. Another warrior drew his katana and screamed a challenge, but the oni had learned the hard way what happened when you duel a samurai, so it blew his arm off instead. As Motokane ran away, a tree exploded next to him, and the official was lost from view in a cloud of splinters.

Hiroto had guessed right. The oni concentrated on the warriors and ignored the supposed peasant. Like him, it only enjoyed hunting dangerous game.

That had been a terrible mistake.

Focusing on the source of the lightning, Hiroto raised his bow and brought it down as he drew. The instant his thumb touched his jaw he let fly. The oni was still invisible, but its angry roar told him that he had struck true.

Yet Hiroto did not let up. He had once pierced a great northern bear six times and it had still retained the strength to charge him. Surely a demon would be tougher. In the blink of an eye he launched another arrow, and then another. This time when the oni moved, he saw it. Light seemed to twist and reflect, like staring into a diamond, and for the first time, he saw it was truly shaped as a man.

Another arrow went into its chest. The oni dropped from the tree. Hiroto could not see if it landed on its feet or its back. He would hope for the best and expect the worst.

Zensuke was screaming in pain. Because of Nobuo's quick reactions his sode had been hit instead of his helmet, but there was a glowing molten hole through the iron shoulder plate and the lacquer had caught on fire. Nobuo had taken out his tanto and was slicing through the cords before his friend cooked to death in his own armor.

He could only hide so many of his own arrows inside the bamboo pole, so he picked up Zensuke's quiver as he ran past them. "It is wounded. Follow when you can."

Hiroto leapt through the bushes, arrow nocked, ready

to draw the instant he saw light bend. There were insects and lizards which could become the same color as the ground around them; apparently this oni's magic worked far better, but in a similar manner. Cautiously, he approached the spot where the oni had fallen.

There was more of the green blood splattered across the rocks. It turned out that when it was fresh, the oni's blood glowed like a smashed firefly. There was a lot of blood, but considering he thought he had struck it with four arrows, not enough. The light was fading quickly, which would make the glowing blood trail easier to follow.

The other samurai caught up a moment later. Nobuo had gotten Zensuke's burning armor removed in time, but the other samurai's shoulder was a bloody, charred mess. His right arm hung useless. He had to be in terrible pain, but he hid it behind a mask of grim determination, and carried his katana in his left hand.

"That's its blood?" Nobuo gestured with his war club. "Then we can track it!"

"Wait," Hiroto said as he knelt and picked up a broken arrow shaft. It was slick with the green slime. "I coated these arrowheads in a concentrated poison made from the venom of a jellyfish some pearl divers introduced me to. Its sting causes weakness, paralysis, and usually death. I do not know what it will do to a demon, but we will give the poison a moment to work."

Samurai considered poison a cowardly and dishonorable way to kill, but Nobuo and Zensuke did not protest. At this point they only wanted to survive. Surprisingly, Motokane found them a minute later. Hiroto wasn't surprised to see he was still alive—officials were more survivable than rats—but rather, that he wasn't in the process of running back to Kamakura.

"Everyone else is dead."

Hiroto had assumed that by the way it had violently blasted their limbs off. He gave a noncommittal grunt in response to the news. It was time. Hiroto began following the spilled blood.

The poison did not kill it, but either it or the arrow wounds were having some effect. Earlier the demon had been effortlessly leaping from treetop to treetop. Now it was sticking to the ground, and from the relative strength of the glow, it felt like they were catching up.

The ghostly forest was eerie in the dark. There was a full moon, which was enough to keep them from breaking their necks, but not much beyond that. It made the trail extremely easy to follow ... Perhaps a little too easy. If he were wounded, and a hunting party was following his blood trail, he would use that to his advantage to set an ambush, or lead them straight into some prepared traps.

"Motokane, you should take the lead."

"What? Why?"

"From all this blood, the oni appears to be weakening and dying. It should be a man of your status who gets the honor of striking the killing blow on behalf of the Shogun."

Sadly, Motokane wasn't that gullible. "I don't feel like catching the first lightning bolt, hunter. Nobuo! Follow that trail."

Like a good dutiful samurai, Nobuo did as he was told. That was a waste. Hiroto thought the lad had potential.

The trail led them steadily downhill. The footing was treacherous. Nobuo tried to listen for danger over the clumsy crashing and slipping of the exhausted samurai. The demon staying on solid ground rather than shifting branches made it harder to hear. He thought he caught the hissing insect noise a few times, but could not be sure.

Nobuo signaled for them to stop. "Hunter, come look at this."

He left Zensuke and Motokane and crept forward. Nobuo had followed the blood to a narrow path with stagnant pond water to both sides. Trudging through that mud would make for slow going. It was a splendid place for an ambush. When Hiroto reached him, Nobuo was pointing at something ahead. There was quite a bit of glowing firefly splatter on the land bridge, as if the demon had stopped for a bit. Even as keen as Hiroto's vision was, it took him a moment to spot the danger. There was a tiny reflection of blood light against something metallic hidden among the roots.

It had to be some manner of trap. "Good eye."

But then Hiroto noticed something the less experienced warrior had not. After setting the trap, the blood continued across the land, and then turned sharply to the side as the demon had doubled back through the pond, where its dripping blood would be swallowed from view.

It was circling behind them.

When the trap was sprung—probably a snare or a spring noose—against the lead man, the sound would draw their attention forward, and then it would assault the rear. There were only four of them left. It could take half of them in one move. Hiroto grabbed Nobuo by one of the horns on his helmet, dragged him close, and whispered, "Count to thirty. Then set off the trap." He picked up a rock and shoved it toward him. "Throw this at it."

Then he began creeping back toward Zensuke and Motokane. With luck, he would be in position to put an arrow into the demon as soon as it moved. As soon as he could make out the other two in the dark, he hunkered down, wiped the sweat from his eyes, and waited for Nobuo to finish his count.

There was a thunk as the rock was tossed . . . The whole forest erupted with yellow light.

That was most unexpected.

The demon hadn't set a normal trap. He had summoned the fires of Jigoku. Nobuo had been hurled through the air. Sparks were falling from the sky like rain. It was like being beneath an erupting volcano. Rocks big enough to split a skull crashed through the branches. Hiroto covered his head as fiery debris fell all around him.

Rather than fear, he felt a pang of jealousy. *If I had weapons such as this, there is nothing I could not hunt!*

Hiroto could barely see, but the three red dots climbing up his arm were clear as day, but he lost them as they crawled onto his chest. Instinctively, he flung his body to the side.

The tree he'd been leaning against came apart. Splinters pierced his skin.

He was the one who had hurt the oni so now he was its greatest threat. Somehow it had picked him out . . . The oni could see in the dark!

Hiroto rolled to his feet and ran, trying to put more trees between his body and the oni's fury. Lightning struck. Branches came crashing down. Rocks shattered into a million stinging pieces. Bushes burst into flame. Hiroto dove behind a boulder. When the boulder wasn't immediately cleaved in two, Hiroto risked a peek over the top.

The oni's trap had set some of the treetops ablaze. It was still using its magical trickery, somehow forcing the air to obscure its form, but that did not work so well near a flickering fire. It looked like pieces of broken glass, piled in the shape of a tall man, each bit reflecting the fire in slightly the wrong direction.

Zensuke had seen it, too. He lifted his katana in one hand and charged, screaming a battle cry. The light twisted around where the oni's head must be, facing the new threat. A refracting glow that could only be an arm rose, and two gleaming blades leapt from the end of it.

Hiroto rose, drew back the bow string, and let fly.

The arrow sped across the forest and disappeared into the demon's unnatural form. He heard it sink deep into flesh.

Dead center. A man would perish in seconds, but not this damnable oni. The pile of broken glass and flames remained standing. But everything had a weak spot. Like his father had taught him, *the arrow knows the way*. As it prepared to meet Zensuke, Hiroto nocked another arrow. The long bow creaked, power gathering in his hands. *Find the way*. Hiroto set the arrow free.

This time he had been focused on the arm. If it had no heart, then he would cripple its limbs.

The arrow sailed across the forest. It struck in a flash of blue.

Yet the arm still came down, slicing Zensuke in half.

As the samurai went sailing past both sides of the demon, Hiroto truly saw it for the first time. His last arrow had broken the evil spell! Grey beneath the fire and moon, it was truly a giant, easily two feet taller than the biggest samurai, with a too-large head made of shining metal, hair like a sadhu monk, and a body covered in a fisherman's net.

When it realized Hiroto was staring right at it, the oni reached for its wrist, clawed fingers dancing—probably casting a spell—only there was an arrow shaft blocking the way.

"Enough of your tricks, demon!" Hiroto shouted as he sent another arrow across the forest. That one punctured the demon's stomach. The next struck it in the leg.

The boulder in front of him disintegrated and Hiroto found himself hurled through the air. It turned out the demon didn't need to use the three sparks to aim its lightning after all, though it did help the accuracy.

He hit the ground so hard it knocked the wind out of him. Worse, he lost his bow. From the burning bushes he could see that he was near the edge of the pond. Twenty paces away, Nobuo was lying in the mud, breathing, but knocked unconscious, his helmet visibly dented by the demon's incredible trap.

The oni was coming. It had completely given up on stealth, and its heavy footfalls could be heard crashing against the rocks, getting closer and closer. Hiroto had no weapons. Nobuo's swords were too far. His only hope was to hide and perhaps surprise it . . . He was an excellent fighter with just his hands, but his opponents weren't usually as big as a horse.

Gasping for breath, Hiroto crawled into the reeds. As he tried desperately to fill his lungs with air, he found himself wishing he had a hollow reed to breathe through. Now that would have been handy for hiding. As the demon got closer, he held his breath and sunk beneath the muck.

He was trying so very hard not to move to avoid ripples, not even daring to exhale because it would make bubbles. Even with his eyes open he could see nothing through the thick silt, but he felt the water vibrate as the demon stomped right past him. Either it hadn't seen him, or it was going to finish off Nobuo first instead.

Hiroto's hand bumped into something. Wooden, but sanded smooth. His fingers drifted along it until touching the first embedded metal spike . . . Hachiman had smiled upon him once again.

As he slowly, painfully, silently lifted himself from the murk, he saw that the oni was looming over Nobuo. Arrow shafts were embedded across its body, each wound leaking green. The oni may have been an unnatural being, but its emotions were as clear as any performer telling a story with only a dance. The oni was *furious*. Nobuo wasn't the warrior who had filled its body with painful arrows! It lifted its arm blades to kill him anyway.

Hiroto had been trying to rise as quietly as possible, but something gave him away, maybe it was the pond water dripping from the spikes of Nobuo's war club, or the sucking sound of his body leaving the mud, but regardless, the oni heard. It spun about, braids whipping, drawing itself up, so that it towered overhead.

He never understood why it didn't strike him down in that moment, but the oni paused, just for a heartbeat, confused, as if Hiroto was the invisible one.

Hiroto smashed it with the tetsubo.

He'd been aiming for its metal head, but its sudden movement caused him to strike it in the shoulder instead. Glowing blood flew as flesh was pulverized.

The solid blow would have shattered human bones. The oni lurched to the side, but stayed upright. With a roar he hit it with another overhand strike. The pressure caused blood to squirt from the various arrow holes. Then Hiroto swung the heavy weapon in an arc, striking the oni's extended leg. Something snapped deep within and it went to its knees.

Except kneeling, it was still as tall as Hiroto. The twin blades lashed out. He blocked it with the tetsubo but the demon metal cut right through the wood as if it wasn't there, and still retained the power to slice cleanly through his face.

It was the worst pain he had ever experienced, worst he had ever *imagined*. He fell. The blow had rattled his brain. The world was spinning. All Hiroto could do was hold on. But something else was wrong. Desperate, sick, he reached up, felt along the two burning cuts to the empty socket where his left eye had once been, and screamed.

Through his remaining eye, he watched the oni try to stand, but its broken leg buckled. In his life he had seen thousands of things die. Something about the way the oni was moving told him that it was done for. Hiroto would perish, smug in the knowledge that his killer would follow soon after. The oni began crawling toward him. Hiroto tried to stand, but his body would not cooperate, all he could do was scoot backwards.

"Hunter!" Nobuo had woken up. He was too far to get there in time, but he threw something.

It was a good thing Nobuo's sword was still sheathed, because it landed right in Hiroto's lap.

The oni was bearing down on him. It pulled back its fist, blades aimed at his heart. Hiroto drew and slashed in one smooth movement.

The katana went through half the demon's chest. Green blood flew across the forest in a long arc. The two of them remained there a moment, mangled face to metal face. The demon twitched. The twin blades slowly dropped. He twisted the blade free, and Three Sparks, the Oni of Aokigahara, was no more.

Hiroto was in terrible pain, but he laughed anyway. The summer of death was over. It had been a fine hunt.

As they limped out of the forest, they came upon Ashikaga Motokane, hiding inside the trunk of a hollow tree.

"You're still alive! Is it done?" the official asked as he slowly climbed out.

Hiroto's face was being held together with stitches and dried blood, and his newfound lack of depth perception was making him nauseous. He was not in the mood, so continued walking.

"Were you hiding in there all night?" Nobuo asked.

"Yes. And I was all alone! Because some bodyguard you are!"

Hiroto didn't even look back when he heard Nobuo's sword clear its sheath. There was a gurgle, and then the sound of a head bouncing down the rocks. The young samurai rejoined Hiroto a moment later, cleaning his katana on his filthy sleeve. "When we report to the Shogun, it was a shame there were no other survivors."

"Yes, a terrible shame."

Nasu Hiroto knelt before the Shogun. Their report had been delivered. The magnificent trophy he had presented to Minamoto Yoritomo was on the floor between them. Now they were alone. The Shogun had dismissed everyone else from the room so that the two of them could speak privately.

"The eye patch suits you, Hiroto. What do you intend to do now?"

"If you aren't going to execute me for deserting all those years ago, then I'm unsure."

"When we last spoke, I came to understand something about you. Other samurai try their whole lives to make a mask that never shows fear, that declares they live for battle, hiding their true weakness beneath. For you, there is no mask. You only feel alive when you are hunting something capable of taking your life. Nothing else will do."

Hiroto nodded. The Shogun was truly a wise man.

"Your report has inspired me. I think it has given me the answer to a problem which I have struggled with for the last few years." The Shogun leaned forward and picked up the oni's mask. "We could learn much from the Oni of Aokigahara. Invisible. Calculating. Hiding in plain sight, then attacking with ruthless efficiency, leaving his enemies filled with dread . . . The ultimate assassin."

"To be stalked by such would bring nightmares to even the bravest samurai."

"Indeed. What if I offered you the opportunity to never be bored again? A hunt which never ends?"

"I am intrigued."

"The Shogunate has many enemies, dangerous men. Often politics make it so that I cannot deal with them directly. The oni has shown me the answer. I have need of invisible killers, inspired by this beast, who make its way theirs. Men who will engage in irregular warfare which most samurai would find distasteful." The Shogun stared into the blank eyes of the mask. "In short, I require men who can fight like *demons*."

Hiroto was becoming excited. "Such an endeavor would have to be done with the utmost secrecy."

"They would be the hidden men, *shinobi-no-mono*, emulating the Oni of Aokigahara to bring ruin upon the enemies of Nippon. Would you build this organization for me, Nasu Hiroto?"

"It would be an honor."

The first ninja bowed to the first shogun.

That's right. It was the Predator who inspired the creation of ninjas. That's my theory, but I'm pretty sure it is historically accurate.

One fun note, I managed to put a shout out to my other samurai versus monster story in here. Though it is completely unofficial because these stories were from entirely different publishers and not in the same universe, if you read "Great Sea Beast" in Target Rich Environment Volume 1, note that both of these main characters have the same last name, and Three Sparks takes place one generation later. That's because Monster Hunting is a family business.

RECKONING DAY

This flash-fiction-sized short originally appeared in the Monster Hunter International Employee Handbook and Role Playing Game *from Hero Games in 2013. It was just a brief little look into the daily life of some of the Monster Hunter International series' most popular characters. Shelly the Orc shows up again in* Monster Hunter Guardian.

IT WAS GOOD to be chief.

The noble orc, Skull Crushing Battle Hand of Fury, or Skippy as his human friends called him, was pleased, and for the record, he did not mind being called Skippy. The humans' ways were abrupt and strange, but their oddly short names did save time.

The Tribe was at peace. The scars of their last battle against the evil dead of the foolish human necromancer, Hood, had healed. Word of their righteous revenge had spread across the world and orcs from other tribes had journeyed far to join with their number. The Tribe's warriors were volunteering to go forth into the human world in ever increasing numbers to join the war bands of MHI. The Harb Anger was very pleased by the Tribe's warriors and much honor and respect was given, Harb Anger paid them moneys too, though Skippy didn't really know what to use that for, so they mostly kept it in a big pile which his wives then used to occasionally purchase important items, like new heavy metal albums from iTunes or flea shampoo for their mighty Wargs.

However, Skippy was far too busy to concern himself with such things as human moneys or Warg care, for today was a young warrior's Reckoning Day. Because the gods loved the orcs more than they loved all of their other children, each orc was born blessed with a special talent. These talents varied wildly, but all of them were somehow valuable to ensure a great future for the Tribe. Some orc talent's usefulness were obvious to understand, such as his younger brother's supreme skill in bladed combat, or his own mastery of the human flying machines and his unmatched knowledge of the Air Spirits. Other talents' uses were not so easy to discern, such as his cousin *Rufschertzls'* amazing ability to solve any of the humans' "crossword puzzles," but who was Skippy to question the god's choice for Rufus? Perhaps someday Rufus' ability to make letters fit into small squares would bring great honor to the tribe . . . Naw, who was he kidding? Rufus was a moron.

But regardless, today was another orc's Reckoning Day, which meant that the elders and teachers had finally been able to discern the path chosen by their gods. The young orc would be brought before the chieftain, and his talents displayed. The Old Ways required the chieftain to execute the young orc should his talents be insufficient, but Skippy considered himself a very reasonable and *modern* orc, maybe it was because he lived in America and the Hunters' strange sense of mercy had influenced him, so he'd never executed anyone on their Reckoning Day. He'd even spared Rufus, though he'd been *so* very tempted... Like most orc holidays, Reckoning Day was mostly a chance to throw an awesome party, and since Gretchen had already baked a cake, Skippy certainly hoped that today wouldn't be his first Reckoning Day summary execution.

Skippy stood in the center of the village, attended by his wives and his advisors, while the young orc was brought forward. It turned out to be a female, recently arrived with her family, refugees from another tribe. She was squat and dumpy, with misshapen tusks, and one crazy eyeball which kept looking in different directions, and despite the ceremonial fur robes, colorful feathers, and small animal bones which they had decorated her with, she certainly would never get a husband on looks alone, so for her sake, Skippy hoped she'd been blessed with a good talent. Somebody who could cook would be nice. The village could use another cook, because no offense to Gretchen, her cake tasted like ashes in his mouth, not that he would ever tell her that, because even the chieftain couldn't talk bad about his first wife's cooking.

The girl was introduced by his brother *Exszrsd*. That was intriguing. Normally Edward, as their strongest combatant, wouldn't involve himself in a Reckoning Day unless the child had displayed a particularly strong warrior's gift... or it was a really crappy talent, since he was their default executioner. Either way, this should be interesting.

Edward addressed the gathering, extremely excited crowd. The girl's parents looked very nervous. The girl seemed ambivalent, which was a proper orc war face. "This is *Slschschlee*."

Skippy snorted. Foreign orc tribes had such silly names. "For our human masters, she will be known to them as Shelly." Everybody bowed at his wisdom. Shelly shrugged. "Let the Reckoning begin."

Edward, being an orc of few words even in Orcish, looked at Shelly and grunted. She nodded, her googly eye squinting in determination. "Her talent did not show for a long time. The gods did not speak to her until she watched the Hunters through the Great Chain Link Fence of Separation and witnessed their preparations for glorious war."

Interesting. So that meant it probably wasn't cooking. Disappointing that, but Skippy nodded for them to continue their demonstration.

His brother snapped his fingers and several of the younger orcs ran forward holding empty beer bottles in their hands. There were six of them, with two bottles each. They cocked their arms back as if ready to throw them into the forest. Curious, Skippy wondered why Edward had just stuck his fingers into his ears.

The orcs hurled their bottles into the air, and a split second later, threw their second. Shelly flung open her fur robe, revealing a leather gun belt with a holster on each side. Two big revolvers appeared in her hands as if by magic. Skippy knew enough about guns to know that these were .44 Magnum Redhawks. There was a continuous roar as she fired them both from the hip, and every single one of the flying bottles exploded before reaching the trees.

Skippy's mouth fell open. The Tribe began to cheer. "By the violent tusks of *Gnrlwz*! That was so metal!" And Skippy threw the horns.

Shelly had both smoking revolvers reloaded from speed loaders and put back into their holsters before Skippy had finished his pronouncement. She looked right at him with her good eye, then her googly eye, and then she bowed. Skippy returned the bow, extra low.

"The gods must be pleased with this orc. Now it is time for cake!" *Such dry, ashy cake . . .*

And another Reckoning Day was complete.

WEAPONIZED HELL

This story first appeared in the anthology Urban Allies, *edited by Joseph Nassie, published in 2016 by Harper Voyager.*

Urban Allies *was a really interesting idea, where twenty urban fantasy authors paired off, each of us taking one of our popular characters and having them team up with another author's existing characters for a story. Like one of those crossover episodes where two TV shows collide.*

I'm a fan of Jonathan Maberry's work and really enjoy his Joe Ledger series (in fact, a story that I wrote for him for that universe appears later in this collection). When I saw that he was involved I asked if he'd want to team up. He said he'd write Ledger if I wrote Agent Franks. That sounded badass.

❖ 1 ❖

Captain Joe Ledger
Department of Military Sciences
Iraqi Desert near Mosul

THEY SAY THAT IN TIMES of mortal peril your life flashes through your mind. Ideally, those memories are not accompanied by shrapnel or bullets.

For me it isn't usually my childhood or images of my family or my ex-girlfriends. I don't have flashes of chances taken and chances missed. None of that stuff. When my life is about to fall apart, what flashes through my head are the details of how in the wide blue fuck I got into this mess in the first place.

Case in point . . .

First, you have to know that the ideal combat mission starts with solid and very detailed intel, with time for training your team, for putting boots on the ground with all of the equipment you need, and to have local assets on hand to smooth the way. An ideal mission has close-range and long-range tactical support, and the cavalry is cocked and locked and ready to ride over the hill to save your ass if things go south.

Yeah, that would be nice.

So nice.

Never fucking going to happen, though. At least not for guys like me.

I run the Special Projects Office for the Department of Military Sciences. Sounds like a bunch of nerds sitting around dreaming up cool gizmos. It's not. The name is boring and there's some misdirection built into it. And, sure, we have geeks and nerds working for us, but they're support. The truth is that the DMS is a covert rapid-response group. We run a couple-of-dozen small teams of first-chair shooters. We go after terrorists or criminal groups who are using bleeding-edge bioweapons. We are a zero red-tape outfit. If they've sent us in then the shit has already hit the fan.

The tricky thing is that this means we have to start

running the moment we hear the first rumble of that avalanche. Prep time is what you can manage on the fly. Field support is usually a voice in the earbud I wear: real-time intel that the science and tactical teams are scrambling to acquire while we're running headlong into the valley of the shadow.

I'm sure I mixed a couple of metaphors there, but I actually don't give a cold shit.

I was in Iraq, in a twenty-year-old Humvee going bump-thumpity over a road that was pocked with wagon ruts and blast holes from IEDs. My driver, Rizgar, was a friendly, a Kurd with knife scars on his face. Four of his buddies were in the back. My own crew, Echo Team, was in a fast plane somewhere over the ocean. Too far away. Rizgar drove like his lifelong dream was to die in a fiery crash. My balls had climbed up inside my chest cavity and I'd found religion five separate times during near misses with boulders, craters, and the burned-out shell of an old Bradley. Rizgar had to swerve to keep from hitting a goat and—still at high speed—leaned his head all the way out the window and yelled at the animal who was now fading in the dust behind us.

"Kerim bimzha, heez!"

I understand enough Sorani to know that it was a vile thing to say, even to a goat.

I was yelling, too, trying to have a conversation with my boss, Mr. Church. He'd snatched me away from the mission he'd sent me over here to handle—taking down a black-marketer named Ohan who was selling recovered Soviet chemical weapons left over from the Afghan war in the eighties. Church said he'd catch up to me in motion. I was, in fact, in motion.

"What's the damn op?" I demanded. "My guy in Baghdad said he could put me in a room with Ohan and—"

"We've been following a false lead," said Mr. Church. "Ohan is not in Baghdad. We have reliable intel that he is in a village outside of Mosul."

"It was reliable intel that said he was in Baghdad."

"Nature of the game, Captain," said Church. "We have very high confidence in this sighting."

"What's the source of that intel? Our friends in the Agency? Another of those hotshot Delta gunslingers? Everybody's seeing Ohan lately."

"The identity of our source is classified."

Even though Rizgar could hear my end of the conversation, the feed into my earbud was filtered through a 128-bit cyclical encryption system that God couldn't hack.

"Declassify it," I growled.

Church—being Church—ignored that request. He said, "Operatives on the ground have confirmed the presence of Ohan heading into the village. We believe he is going to meet an ISIL team to hand off a bio agent recovered from an excavated burial site."

"Whoa, wait . . . repeat that? Someone's using a burial site as a lab—?"

"No," said Church. "Sketchy reports indicate that a biological weapon has been harvested from the burial site."

"What kind of bioweapon? Are we talking mycotoxins or bacteria?"

Graves and tombs were famous for all kinds of

dangerous spores, molds, fungi and similar microscopic monsters. The whole Curse of King Tut's Tomb was a prime example. Lord Carnovan, the Englishman who backed Howard Carter's expedition to find Tutankhamen, died of a mysterious illness after entering the tomb and being exposed to a fungus that had been dormant in the tomb for thousands of years and reactivated by fresh air. Other recently opened tombs in different parts of the world revealed pathogenic bacteria of the *Staphylococcus* and *Pseudomonas* genera, and the molds *Aspergillus niger* and *Aspergillus flavus*. Very nasty stuff. Obtaining and weaponizing diseases so old that modern humans have no acquired immunity for them is a popular hobby for the world's mad-fucking-scientists. Of which there are way too many.

"The nature of the threat is unknown at this time," said Church. "I need you to make an assessment and to keep it out of the hands of the ISIL team operating in that area."

I was still dressed for plainclothes infiltration of the Baghdad hotel where I was supposed to intercept Ohan. My cover was that of a South African mercenary acting as a go-between for a party wanting to buy some of Ohan's nasty toys. I had my Sig Sauer and a Wilson rapid-release folding knife, but I was not in full combat rig. I was dressed in khaki trousers and one of those canvas shirt-jackets with lots of pockets. No helmet, no long-gun, no grenades. None of my favorite toys. And not nearly enough body armor. And, more to the point, no hazmat suit or even a Saratoga Hammer suit. Nothing to protect me if this was an active biological agent, particularly an airborne one.

"Sure," I said, "I'm on it."

I hate my job.

Rizgar pointed to a small cluster of buildings visible through the heat shimmer a couple of miles up the road. Even from that distance we could see that things had already gone to shit. A fireball suddenly leapt up from amid a group of parked vehicles, lifting them, tossing them away with fists made of superheated gasses. Over the roar of the Humvee's engine we could hear the rattle of gunfire.

❖ 2 ❖

Special Agent Franks
United States Monster Control Bureau
Iraqi Desert near Mosul

SPECIAL AGENT FRANKS of the United States Monster Control Bureau was not known for his patience— especially when he had a mission to complete—but having random terrorist assholes flip his armored vehicle with an IED really put him in an even fouler mood than usual. His driver and interpreter, assigned to him from the Iraqi Army, had been killed on impact. From the noise of gunfire and bullets striking metal, the rest of the convoy was taking fire. Annoyed, Franks had crawled out of the upside-down flaming MRAP in order to vent his frustrations on whoever had been stupid enough to ambush him.

Quickly assessing the situation, Franks realized it had been a really big bomb. It took quite a few buried artillery shells to toss an 18-ton vehicle on its roof. The explosion had flattened several of the houses at the front of the village. There was a blackened crater where the road had been. The enemy appeared to be a bunch of goons wearing ridiculous black pajamas, armed with AKs and looted M-4s. It was an L-shaped ambush. They were firing from prepared positions in the village and from a ravine that ran parallel to the road. Their Iraqi drivers, rather than push through the ambush zone, had hit the brakes. Now they were taking heavy fire. It was another example of why Franks preferred never to work with locals, but he'd been overruled. His superiors didn't like his idea of diplomacy.

Four hostiles, one armed with an RPG, had moved up on Franks' vehicle to get a better angle on the rest of the stopped convoy. The hostiles hadn't been expecting survivors, let alone a giant killing machine who was completely unfazed by the blast. Franks killed the first hostile before they'd even realized he was there, another two before they could react, and the last one as he was trying to run away.

And Franks hadn't used a weapon yet.

The rest of his convoy was made up of MCB personnel and their Iraqi Army escorts. It appeared that most of their vehicles were hit, though none as badly as his had been. Intel had said this area was under ISIS control, but they'd not been expecting resistance away from the dig site. As usual, their intel was wrong. He had to act fast or his strike team would be rendered combat ineffective, and they still had a mission to complete. His men would clear the ravine. His rifle had been crushed in the wreck, so

Franks took the rocket-propelled grenade launcher and an AK-47 from the men he'd beaten to death and went into the village.

They'd set up a PK machinegun on the second floor of a mosque and were raking it over the convoy. There had been something in the briefing over the rules of engagement about not damaging religious buildings and blah, blah, blah, but Franks never bothered to read those things. So he blew it up with the RPG. Then he went house to house, shooting every hostile he saw. Since Franks had reaction times that made most normal humans look like sloths, clearing out their firing positions was a piece of cake. He only had to gun down a dozen of them or so before the ambush broke and the remaining scumbags were running for their lives.

His radio had been broken in the crash, but from the noise, it sounded like his men had the road and ravine under control. Franks had seen a lot of casual barbarity in his life, but he knew ISIS were overachievers. Chasing them down was not his mission, but Franks really didn't like them. Sure. He liked hardly anyone, but these assholes were special. So he picked up another weapon and went looking for trouble.

He found it.

The ISIS fighters regrouped in a small market. Their leader was rallying the troops, shouting in Arabic—one of the many Earthly languages Franks had never bothered to learn—so the motivational speech wouldn't have been noteworthy except this human had the stink of demons all over him.

So their intel had gotten one thing right. The

insurgents had made a pact with demons. *Now this is more like it*, Franks thought as he flipped the Kalashnikov's selector to full auto and hosed down the market.

❖ 3 ❖

Captain Joe Ledger

I MADE A PUSHING MOTION with my hand. Rizgar grinned and obliged by pushing the pedal all the way down to the floor. He steered with one hand and beat on the roof of the car with the other—the signal for his team to get ready.

We were driving straight into the heart of a full-blown battle, and it was going south on the good guys really damn fast. I could see a knot of men in American BDUs hunkered down behind a shattered convoy of bullet-pocked vehicles. They were taking heavy fire, but they were still in the game. Bloody bodies littered the ground around the vehicles, most with weapons still clutched in dead hands.

All around the convoy, crouched down behind cars, using broken stone walls for cover, stretched out on rooftops, and even kneeling in the street were fighters in the distinctive black of the Islamic State of Iraq and the Levant. ISIS, ISIL, call them what you want. Sons of bitches who seemed to come out of nowhere and were cutting a bloody swath across the Middle East. Well armed, well provisioned, and dishearteningly well trained.

Maybe thirty of them alive and twice that number dead or wounded. This battle had been clearly raging for a while. The contractors in the convoy had fought like heroes, but there simply weren't enough of them left to win this.

Rizgar, his four shooters, and Mama Ledger's firstborn didn't seem like a big enough crowd to make a difference. But let me tell you, shock and awe comes in all shapes and sizes.

Rizgar had picked the right angle for our approach. The contractors could see us but we wouldn't be in their direct line of fire. The ISIL fighters had to turn to fight us on their quarter, which decreased the suppressing fire on the convoy. Distract and weaken. Rizgar slewed around to allow the maximum number of our guns to fire at once and we hit them real damn hard. Two of Rizgar's men came out of the Humvee with RPGs on their shoulders. One targeted a building on the corner of the square, a spot where half a dozen of the black-clothed figures were grouped. They saw the grenade coming at them, they tried to move, but feet don't move fast enough to dodge rocket-propelled explosives fired from fifty yards. The explosion killed four of them, tearing them to rags; and it turned the building into deadly debris. Every man inside the blast radius went down. Some dead, some dazed.

The second RPG struck an old Ford Falcon behind which three shooters knelt. The blast lifted the car and dropped it on them. And that left a clear line of approach for me. I ran up the middle like an offensive fullback, my Sig Sauer held in a two-handed grip. I am a very good shot because SpecOps soldiers who are bad shots get killed. I hit everything I aimed at. Might not have been the highest scores on a gun range, but men went down.

Rizgar and the others fanned out, firing automatic weapons at the ISIL team. As soon as the contractors saw what was happening they shifted their focus from defensive fire to a fresh assault. Clearing the way for us. One of them came out of an open door firing a Kalashnikov. He was a brute, a bull. Six-eight if he was an inch, and he looked like Frankenstein. But the son of a bitch could shoot. ISIL fighters spun away, blood exploding from faces and throats and chests.

They say war is hell. Sure. It absolutely is. Even if you like combat. Even when the sound of gunfire is your lullaby—which, for the record, it isn't to me. But there is a part of me—my shrink and I call him the Killer—who shares my head and my soul with my other aspects, the Modern Man and the Cop. And the Killer loves it. In times like this he is fully alive. And maybe so am I.

I hate that it's true, but it is true.

When I burned through all three of the magazines I had for the Sig, I drew my rapid-release knife and took the fight to close quarters. Using the men I killed as shields while I cut them apart, shoving them into their comrades, taking the long reach to do short, ugly cuts, going for effect rather than finesse. Slashing and slicing because stabbing will get your knife stuck and get you killed. There is a balletic quality to knife fighting when you do it right. You cruise on that edge between total awareness and a kind of Zen zero mind.

The ISIL team fell apart. Rizgar's men were brilliant,

savage, and merciless. The Kurds have old scores to settle with the kind of men who join ISIL. And the contractors, buoyed by our arrival, took the fight to the bad guys in terrible ways.

We won the fight.

Until . . .

Until the whole day changed.

I cut the throat of one of the last ISIL fighters and saw that there was a teenage girl crouched down between two of their vehicles. Not armed, not dangerous-looking. I moved in close, hoping to grab her and pull her to safety. She cringed back from me, arms wrapped around her head, and at first I thought she was a captive, maybe someone from the village being used as a hostage, or one of the unfortunate ones who would be dragged off and used savagely until her mind or body snapped.

Then I saw her eyes.

They were dark and filled with madness. Total, absolute madness.

And then they weren't.

The brown irises changed as I watched. The brown swirled like paint being stirred. Dark brown, then a medium brown flecked with gold, then sparks of red, and then they turned completely yellow. Cat yellow. Fire yellow. Her face, which had been contorted in terror at the madness and destruction around her, twisted, reshaped, became something else. Not another expression . . . it became another face.

Another *kind* of face.

Still a woman's face . . . but not a human woman's face.

It's impossible to describe, even now, even thinking back on it. There are things the human mind cannot process. Or refuses to accept.

The girl rose to her feet and in doing so stopped being a girl at all. Her spine curved into a monstrous hump, almost like a camel's hump; her leg bones broke with gunshot sounds and then re-formed, taking on the knobbed angles of a goat's legs. And her arms grew long, the fingers splaying and stretching, the nails extending as they tore through the nail beds in splashes of bright blood, then thickened into black talons.

But her face.

Good god, her face . . .

The nostrils flattened and flared, her eyes sunk into shadowy pits so that the hellish light burned like real fire. Her cheekbones cracked and shifted, forming sharp ledges, and her jaw stretched as she smiled at me. Smiled. So incorrect and stupid a word for what was happening. The mouth grinned wide as row upon row of new teeth ripped their way from her gums until she had the dripping maw of a shark.

All of this in a few seconds.

All of this as the last pocks of gunfire tore the air.

I stumbled backward from her—from it.

One of the ISIL fighters lay dead at her feet, his throat sliced open by the knife held limply in my hand. The woman seized his wrist and with a jerk like someone cracking a whip, snapped the arm loose and then tore it from its socket. Blood and bits of tendon splashed on me, and in a moment of truly bottomless horror I watched the woman raise the severed arm to her mouth and bite.

Bones crushed between those rows of teeth. Meat burst and blood ran down her chin.

"Jesus Christ," I breathed, and for a moment I was frozen in absolute horror.

❖ **4** ❖

Special Agent Franks

FRANKS DIDN'T KNOW who the new arrivals were, but one particular man could certainly fight. He'd been doing pretty good slicing up black pajama-clad assholes until he ran into a possessed woman. When she shed her face, he froze. It wasn't a surprise. Most humans choked when they saw real demonic possession for the first time. Franks would have stepped in to save the man, but he had to duck to avoid getting shot in the head by a terrorist. A 7.62×39 rifle bullet at close range had a decent chance of penetrating his armored skull and might have rendered him temporarily combat ineffective, and thus unable to complete his mission. In other words, getting his brains blown out would have been inconvenient.

Drawing his Glock 20, Franks put a controlled pair into the shooter's chest, then turned back to face his demonic target. Franks figured the newcomer would have been torn limb from limb already, but surprisingly, the man had snapped out of it and gotten right back in the fight. He was staying ahead of the claws, and even managed to counterattack and slash the creature.

Not bad, Franks thought as he went over, grabbed the

demon by her hair, swung her around in a blur, and hurled her through a mud brick wall. Bones splintered and the wall collapsed in a spreading cloud of stinking dust.

"What the fuck was that?" the man shouted.

"Demon."

From the accent, he was an American. From his skillset, he might be useful. He looked up, and up, at Franks. "Who the fuck are you?"

"Special Agent Franks. MCB."

The man scowled like he'd never heard of the MCB before, but they were both Americans getting shot at in northern Iraq, so it was obvious they were on the same team. "Captain Joe Ledger. DMS."

Department of Military Sciences personnel were probably cleared high enough to get read in on this one. He'd do.

"That's nice," Franks stated as he walked toward the pile of rubble. The bricks were shifting as the demon struggled free. This was a tougher strain than expected—

THWACK!

The rifle bullet smacked into Franks' leg. It punched a neat .30 caliber entrance hole, deformed as it struck his hardened femur, and burst back out the side. Blood sprayed everywhere. Franks immediately picked out the shooter who had appeared on a nearby rooftop, aimed, and shot him before he could get off another round.

"You're hit. Get to cover!"

But Franks just looked down at the fist-sized exit wound in his thigh and frowned. That was what he deserved for stopping to have such a lengthy conversation with Ledger. He lifted the dangling flap of skin and meat and shoved it back into the hole. "Just a scratch."

Ledger seemed a little put off by that.

That wound was going to drastically slow him down, and he'd probably need a replacement leg when he got home, but worst of all, getting shot had cost him several precious seconds he could have used killing things. The demon shook itself free from the rubble. It took one look at Franks and Ledger standing there, realized it was outmatched, and fled.

Without any hesitation and armed only with a knife, Ledger went after the monster.

This one has style, Franks thought as he limped after them.

❖ 5 ❖

Captain Joe Ledger

SO, OKAY, this is me running through the Iraqi desert with a guy I am pretty goddamn sure isn't human, chasing something I'm absolutely positive is a demon. Yeah. Actual demon. Psychologically speaking, I am seriously fucked. I mean . . . demons!

Shit.

The thing fled from us, running like the wind out of the village and onto the sands. Franks ran well for a guy built like a bridge support. Well, but not fast. I ran faster, outpacing him. I'm over six feet and I go about two-twenty, but I'm built like a ball-player. If I had even a smidge of talent I could have played third base. I can run my ass off, and I pulled ahead.

Here's the thing. Running faster meant that I was going to reach the apparently unkillable desert demon sooner than the definitely unkillable guy who actually stood a chance against this thing. As plans go, that sucks ass. But the Killer was in gear and he didn't give much of a fuck what the odds were. He'd tasted blood and he wanted more.

So I ran.

The woman—thing, whatever—cut right behind a ruined wall and fled into the open desert, heading for a clump of palms clustered around a goat pen. The goats screamed and panicked, crashing into the rickety slats of the corral, leaping over the bars as they fell, jumping on each other to escape what was coming. The demon leapt the fence with ease and crashed among them, slashing right and left to clear her path. I saw heads and legs and red chunks fly into the air. It was as if the goats had run into a threshing machine. Their screams sounded like the terrified shrieks of children.

I was five paces behind her. Even though she tore through the goats it still slowed her. When she raced to leap over the rear wall of the corral, I was there. My Wilson has a 3.75-inch blade, which is great for fighting people—the weapon was so lightweight that it allowed my hand to move at full speed. But when cutting at a fleeing target it was inadequate. The tip of the blade drew a seven-inch line across her upper back, but the cut didn't go deep enough to destroy the muscles. Droplets of red-black blood spattered me and all my cut accomplished was to make her stumble. Her left foot caught the upper fence rail and the demon fell face forward into the dust on the other side.

Fell . . . and rebounded, rising into a crouch, spinning around to hiss at me, eyes bright with madness and bloodlust, claws slashing the air. I launched myself into the air for a diving, slashing tackle.

And then something hit me like a thunderbolt, slamming into my side, driving me at a right angle to the demon. I fell hard and badly, smashing into the fence post, spinning amid a cloud of splinters, feeling fire explode on my side as something tore at me. Then I was down, rolling over and over with a second woman.

A second demon.

❖ **6** ❖

Special Agent Franks

ANOTHER POSSESSED WOMAN was on top of Ledger, trying to gouge his eyes out. The two of them were rolling through the mud and shit, trying to kill each other. As entertaining as that was, Franks wasn't in the mood to dick around, so he aimed carefully and shot the creature square between the shoulder blades. The silver 10mm blew a hole through her heart, but rather than die, she screeched and reared back. Ledger reached up with his blade and slashed her throat wide open, half a second before Franks shot her through the side of the head. The demon rolled off of Ledger, thrashing and spraying.

Well, these things were proving to be obnoxiously tough. Franks grabbed one of the kicking legs and dragged the monster away from Ledger while the first demon circled back through the pile of dead goats. Ledger would just have to deal with that one while Franks figured out just how much of a hellacious beating he had to administer to finish an Alghul for good.

❖ **7** ❖

Captain Joe Ledger

I FOUGHT THE DEMON the way I'd fight a wild animal. I've had some experience there. Wild animals and genetically-modified animals. Years ago I faced down mastiffs that had been transgenically altered to give them scorpion tails. I've faced genetically-engineered vampire assassins and some other rude and nasty shit. This was my first encounter with something supernatural, but if it existed and if it could bleed, then some of the laws of nature had to apply. That was useful, that gave me a firm piece of ground in this shit storm where I could stand. And Franks had bought me a moment. So I used it.

The demon tried to end it fast by rushing at me with those claws.

Fool me once, motherfucker...

As she darted in I twisted and marked her from wrist to shoulder with picks—short, hard taps with the wicked point of my knife that opened bleeders and ripped apart nerves—and with quick, circular slashes to the muscles for reaching and grabbing. The demon howled in pain and darted back. Tried again, got cut again, and darted back once more. Blood the color of red bricks flowed from a dozen cuts.

If this was a person, I might have used the effect of a pick or slash to close to killing distance, but the wounds were hurting it—just not enough. Those arms still reached, still moved with obvious speed and power.

"Stop fucking around," growled Franks.

"I'm. Not. Fucking. Around," I snapped as I dodged a series of vicious slashes.

"Don't you have a big boy knife?"

"Fuck you."

He laughed a cold, heartless, mocking laugh and tossed something to me. A knife. A Ka-Bar USMC Mark 2 combat knife whose blade flashed in the sunlight. I faked left and lunged for the blade, snatched the handle, dove into a roll to give myself time to grip it properly, rose and spun. I did a fast swap so the Wilson was in my left and the much bigger Ka-Bar was in my right.

"Silver," barked Franks, then he had to concentrate on his own battle.

Silver. Did that work on demons? I had no fucking idea. What do I know about any of this shit?

The demon, though, she stared at the blade and hissed. She knew.

Yeah. She absolutely knew.

I felt myself smile.

The Ka-Bar was bigger and heavier, but I've fought with them many times. You lose a fraction of your speed, but when you reach out and touch someone they get the message. I switched my grips on both knives so that I held them with the blades spiked down from my fists like the claws of a praying mantis.

"Come on, beautiful," I said to the demon. "Let's dance."

Okay, it was corny but I was having a moment.

So was she.

With a banshee howl the demon flung herself at me.

❖ 8 ❖

Special Agent Franks

HE HATED WHEN DEMONS were strong enough to warp the flesh of the possessed. They always seemed to sprout claws and fangs, just to be pricks about it. This one had scratched him and tried to bite a hole through his armor before he'd slugged her in the head enough times to crack her skull and turn her brains to mush. Franks hoisted the dazed demon high overhead, and with a roar, flung her down, through the fence, and against the packed earth so hard that the snapping bones could probably be heard back at the convoy.

The Alghul lay there twitching, beaten, glaring at him with eyes filled with hatred. She opened her mouth and hissed at him in the Old Tongue. *"Traitor."*

"Yeah, whatever," Franks said as he reached down, got a handful of blood-soaked hair, and cranked the demon's head brutally to the side. He'd been planning on twisting her head clean off to shut her up, but simply snapping the neck seemed to do the trick, and he felt the ancient malignant spirit driven from the possessed flesh.

❖ **9** ❖

Captain Joe Ledger

THE DEMON tried to end it by driving all ten claws into me like a storm of daggers. I pivoted and parried, using the little Wilson to push the outside of her left arm to one side while also hooking and trapping her wrist. I used the Ka-Bar in a hard, sweeping overhand slash that sliced through scalp, ear, left eye, cheek and mouth. I put muscle into it, using my inverse grip so that it hit like a heavy punch as well as a slash.

It drove her to the ground. Hard. Dark blood exploded upward, and everywhere a drop struck my exposed skin, I could feel it burn.

Even hurt she tried to turn, but I stepped on her elbow, pinning it and her to the ground to spoil the turn. I stabbed down into the base of her skull to sever the spinal cord. The silver-coated knife bit deep and hard.

The demon screamed so loud that it knocked me back. She screamed so hard that blood burst from my nose as I lay there, hands clamped to my ears. The scream made the palm trees shiver and tore fronds off of them. Debris rained down on me as the scream rose and rose and...

The silence was immediate and intense.

For a terrified moment I wondered if my eardrums had simply burst.

But, no.

No.

I got shakily to my knees and immediately vomited into the dust. Then I sagged back onto my heels, pawing blood from my lips and chin, blinking past pain-tears in my eyes.

Franks stood there, wide-legged, chest heaving only slightly, sweat glistening on his skin, eyes dark and intense and amused.

"What," I said, "the fuck was that?"

His expression was ugly and unfriendly. "I told you, Ledger. Demons."

"First—and don't take this the wrong way—but fuck you and your demons."

He shrugged.

"Second—since when are demons an actual thing?"

"I thought DMS knew all this stuff."

"No, we goddamn well don't."

There was a twinkle in Franks' eyes. "Your boss does. What's he call himself now? Mr. Church? You should ask him."

I tried to get to my feet, failed, and he caught me under the arm and jerked me upright. I slapped his hand away and stepped back.

"Who are you? How do you know about Church? How do you know about demons, for Christ's sake? And, just in general, what the fuck?"

"The fuck," said Franks, "is that ISIS has gone old school."

"Meaning what?"

He pointed into the desert. "The answers are out there. If you want in, you need to come with me now."

"No, first I get answers." I stepped away from him and tapped my earbud to get the channel for the tactical operations center. "Cowboy to Deacon."

"Go for Deacon," said Church.

"Two words," I said. "Franks and demons."

He said, "Ah."

He gave it to me in bullet points, but they hit like real bullets. Agent Franks. Monster Control Bureau. A group that responded to supernatural threats in the same way that the Department of Military Sciences responds to terrorists with high-tech science weapons.

Real.

All real.

If there was a note of apology in Church's voice for not having read me in on this earlier, I sure couldn't hear it. As I listened, Franks stood apart, checking his weapons and trying to look as casual as a towering freak of a monster killer could look.

"Franks is in the family," said Church. "You can trust him. He's one of us."

"One of us? Is he even human?"

Church paused. "At this point, Captain, would that even matter?"

❖ 10 ❖

Special Agent Franks

"HOW DO YOU KNOW Mr. Church?" asked Ledger.

"We've met," Franks said. "He offered me a cookie."

"Yeah. He does love his vanilla wafers. We have a pool going that there's some kind of code in that whole cookie thing. What he eats, how he eats them, what he offers to other people."

"You're overthinking it."

"Pretty good chance," said Ledger. "Equal chance we're not. He's a spooky bastard."

They walked. The sun was an open furnace.

"Most soldiers, even SpecOps, would have died," Franks told him.

Ledger cut him a look, but only shook his head.

"You fight okay." By Franks' standards, that was a huge compliment.

"I intend to go home and cry into my pillow," said Ledger. "Maybe wear sweats and eat a whole thing of Ben and Jerry's. Or get drunk. Drunk is a real contender for how I intend to process this shit."

❖ 11 ❖

Captain Joe Ledger

I'M A BIG, tough, manly man, but there are times I just want to go and hide. Like when I'm in the middle of the Iraqi desert, having just waded through a brutal fire fight and some Frankenstein-looking cocksucker tells me that demons are real and we have to go chase one of them.

It doesn't help one little bit for me to remind myself that no one drafted me. I signed on for this stuff. Well . . .

maybe not *this* stuff, but a good soldier doesn't get to choose his wars.

But, really, man . . . demons?

There is not enough bourbon in all of Kentucky to make that fit into my head.

Franks asked, "Have you heard of Alghul?"

"Sure," I said. "It's a monster from Arabian folklore."

"They're more than that."

I glanced over my shoulder in the direction we'd come. "Oh," I said. "Shit."

"*One Thousand and One Nights* has some truths. Alghul exist. They're mostly female demons who haunt graveyards, digging up fresh corpses to feed on. They lure men to remote spots and attack them. Like mermaids." He cut me a look. "Yes. Mermaids are real. They love human flesh."

"Jesus. Disney got that wrong."

"Alghul are ferocious, but rare. Most were imprisoned. Until now."

"So . . . ISIL is doing what? Recruiting desert demons?"

"Of course." He said it so matter-of-factly that it jolted me. I studied his brutish face, looking for some trace of humor or even irony. Nothing. He was as frank as his name.

"Okay, okay, so they *are* recruiting desert demons. How, though? If these Alghul are so vicious that they were imprisoned, why don't they chomp on the ISIL dickheads? I'm sure they're every bit as tasty."

"I don't do cultural evaluations," he stated. "Dark magic probably."

"And they can shape-shift? When I saw the first one

she was an ordinary girl. Sixteen, seventeen, maybe. Then suddenly she wasn't a girl."

He nodded. "They prefer to use virgins as hosts. Demons enjoy corrupting the pure."

There had been a lot in the papers about ISIS fighters kidnapping women, forcing them into marriages with their people, or consigning them to rape camps. As insane as it was, I could see the ugly shape of it. ISIS was fierce but it wasn't massive. It did not really have a home country. It couldn't put a million-man army in the field to oppose the growing coalition of international forces. Even though many of ISIL's leaders were former Saddam officers and the equipment they used was stolen advanced tech, they were still comparatively small. They could fight a guerilla war but there was no way they could achieve a decisive win or hope to hold their territories for very long. They needed a wild card. I was dealing with some of this stateside with ISIL teams stealing technologies like portable EMPs and drone tech. This was new, and if it was something they could repeat over and over again, then this was a game changer.

❖ 12 ❖

Special Agent Franks

THE SUN BEAT DOWN on their heads, and then the rocks beneath them radiated the heat back upwards. They were travelling cross-country to avoid being spotted. It was a brutally hot day and he was sweating profusely beneath his armor. Franks didn't mind. Discomfort was one of those mortal concepts he had never really grasped. Compared to the endless void of Hell, a little mortal suffering was a small price to pay to have a body.

Captain Ledger was human and must have been dying in the agonizing heat, but he didn't seem like a complainer. They'd set a tough pace across rugged terrain, as fast as Franks was willing to risk without further aggravating the bullet hole in his leg, but Ledger had kept up. In fact, he seemed to enjoy the challenge.

So Ledger could fight extremely well, hadn't been scared of an Alghul, and was tough. It was too bad he was with a different agency, because Franks found himself thinking that he could use a man like this ... But unfortunately, it turned out Ledger was also a smartass.

"So, Franks," said Ledger, "my people tell me you saved the world once."

"I heard the same thing about you."

Ledger shrugged. "Hasn't everybody?"

"No," Franks stated flatly.

But Ledger was undeterred. "That sea monster off the California coast with the nuclear sub. That was one of yours, wasn't it?"

"Classified." Franks had been working with tough guy secret agents of the US government since Benjamin Franklin had performed his first exorcism, so Franks was used to the inevitable dick measuring to see if an agent's rep was legit. "How'd you like the Red Order?"

"No comment."

"Thought so."

They made it less than half a kilometer before Ledger

tried to make conversation again. What was it with mortals and their need to break perfectly good silences?

He was a little out of breath from the climb, but he kept pace. Ledger tapped his earbud. "I'm getting a lot of nice backstory on you, Franks. Here's a fun fact. My intel guy says that people who work with you have a tendency to die horribly."

Franks snorted. If Ledger wanted to talk, they might as well talk about the mission. They would be there by sundown. "We're only a few klicks from the target. The ancient Assyrian city of Nimrud."

"I heard ISIL bulldozed it. I guess that's the sort of thing psychopaths do." Ledger snorted, seemingly disgusted by the thought. "They're destroying priceless historical relics because they think it's an insult to their skewed view of their religion. The word 'fucktard' comes to mind." He paused. "Though, I suppose something out there raised a flag, otherwise my boss wouldn't have sent me here."

Franks thought that Ledger was probably talking about intel pinged by the DMS' fancy secret super computer, MindReader. The DMS used it to predict problems by looking for patterns in the massive information streams gathered by the various covert intelligence networks. Franks wasn't sure how well that actually worked for them, but it had brought Ledger here, so maybe there was something to it.

"MCB got a tip. Terrorists found the lost Prison of Shalmaneser. It was built in 1240 A.D. to house the king's enemies." Franks snorted. The mortal ones had turned to dust a long time ago. It was the immortal ones he was worried about.

"Which is why you're here, I suppose. Church tells me he intercepted communications from an ISIL tactician who'd cut a deal with someone at Nimrud for a new super weapon. You know, man, we gunslingers in the post 9-11 federal agencies are supposed to share information about stuff like this."

Franks just grunted. He'd never been good at sharing.

"Let me guess," Ledger persisted, "this lost prison holds more of those Alghul. How many are we talking about?"

Fourteen thousand corpses of the desolate plains, an unholy army that was legend among all the jealous Fallen, until King Shalmaneser had found a way to cast them from their physical bodies and entomb them in the Earth, but Franks couldn't tell Ledger that or how he knew about it, because there was classified, and then there was *classified*.

"A lot," said Franks.

"So much fun hanging out with Chatty Cathy." Ledger sighed.

❖ **13** ❖

Captain Joe Ledger

WE REACHED the ancient Prison of Shalmaneser just as the sun began sliding toward the western horizon. Long fingers of darkness seemed to reach out toward us from the shattered rock walls, broken trees and parked vehicles. Our approach was cautious and circumspect. I reached

Bug at the TOC and asked for whatever an eye-in-the-sky could tell us.

"Read forty heat signatures, Cowboy," he said, using my combat callsign. "Thirty-four are steady, six are variable. One minute they're normal, then they shift from low-temp to really hot. Not sure how to read that. Maybe they're underground and thermals can't get a solid lock."

I told Franks and he shook his head. "As the Alghul takes over, they burn hotter. The variations in thermal signature mean that the demons haven't fully taken hold. Human spirits are hard to destroy. Even assholes like these."

I had the impression that an explanation that long caused him actual physical pain. Getting trapped in an elevator for six hours with this guy would be a hoot.

We made maximum use of ground cover and came in on a line the satellites said was as close to a dead zone as we'd get. Franks never seemed to tire as we crawled over rocks and through dry washes and up sandy slopes. I felt like I was melting.

There was a small camp built inside the remnants of a medieval building that had collapsed centuries ago. The ISIL vehicles were hidden under desert camo tarps, but we saw a half-dozen empty slots where the vehicles from the fight in town had been parked. We hunkered down to study the layout while Bug fed me what intel he could grab from the satellite.

"How many sites are there like this?" I asked, nodding to the Assyrian ruins.

"Too many," Franks grimaced, or maybe it was a smile. Really hard to tell with a face like his. "Most stay lost."

"So why haven't we heard about the Alghul until now?"

"We have. MCB find stray Alghul, we put them down. They're here. Somebody hears a woman calling at night. Goes to look . . . The bodies are torn apart. Blame it on war. Nobody looks at a corpse over here and thinks 'demon.'"

"Um," I said, but I had nowhere to go with that.

"A few days ago a girl taken captive by ISIS returned to her village as a monster and slaughtered everyone. MCB found out. Intel says this is the source."

"We shut this place down, and we shut down the threat?"

Franks shrugged.

"And here we are," I said. The shadows were lengthening and the heat of the day was already beginning to shift. Once the sun was down it would get very cold very fast. "So, what's the plan? Soft infil? Gather some data and call in an air strike?"

"No. Explosives only kill the body. We need to kill the demons."

"Shit. Let me guess, only silver does the trick."

"It varies, demon to demon," he said. "With the Alghul, it is silver or the hands of a true warrior."

"Isn't that just peachy. What if there are a lot of them?"

Franks shrugged again.

"Okay," I said, "there are forty hostiles in there and my team is hours out. We're two guys. So again I say, what's the plan?"

Frank handed me a Glock and two spare magazines. I

still had the silver-coated Ka-Bar. Franks had taken enough firepower from his convoy to launch a frontal assault on the gates of Hell. He pointed to a pair of guards walking sentry outside of the opening to the ruins.

"Kill everything. How much more plan do you need?"

<h1>❖ 14 ❖</h1>

Special Agent Franks

FRANKS GAVE LEDGER a few minutes to get into position before he started walking right up to the front of the dig site. The site was a haphazard maze of crumbling ancient buildings, twisted rock, modern prefabs, and heavy equipment. It was crawling with insurgents and absolutely reeked of demon stink. He didn't know how many humans had already been possessed by Alghul, but it looked like they'd practically formed a line to wait their turn to go down into the prison. The tactician was smart, only letting one volunteer descend into the depths at a time, because possession wasn't pretty, and it might make the others lose their nerve.

Idiots.

Construction spotlights kept most of the area well lit, but there were plenty of shadows for Ledger to work in. Franks had thought about taking out the generator first, since he could see in the dark, but so could the Alghul.

There was a Toyota pickup truck with a machinegun mounted in back blocking the road. The man on the gun saw the darkened shape of Franks approaching, pointed, and began shouting something. Franks shouldered the SCAR, put the ACOG scope's glowing green triangle on the man's chest, and launched a .308 round through his heart. The guard spun around and toppled from the bed of the truck. Franks kept walking.

The sudden noise had gotten everyone's attention. Another man had been sleeping in the cab of the truck, and he bolted upright, glancing around, confused, until Franks' second bullet went through the driver's window and blew his brains all over the passenger's side. A man in black pajamas and white sneakers ran around the truck. He had just enough time to fire a wild burst from his AK before Franks shot him once in the chest. He tumbled forward, skidding to a stop on his face.

There was movement all over the front of the camp now. *Excellent.* If they were all paying attention to him, then Ledger could get a shot at the ISIS tactician before he could create any more Alghul. Just in case Ledger needed more time, Franks slung his rifle, hopped into the back of the pickup, worked the charging handle on the big 12.7mm DShK machinegun, and turned it on the camp. Franks was really good at being distracting.

❖ 15 ❖

Captain Joe Ledger

THERE ARE TIMES you have to nut up and say "fuck it."

So I nutted up and said fuck it.

❖ 16 ❖

Special Agent Franks

THUMP THUMP *THUMP THUMP THUMP*

The massive bullets tore right through the sheet metal of the prefab buildings. Lights shattered. Men died. Orange muzzle flashes rippled across the camp as they returned fire. Franks methodically swiveled the heavy machinegun toward each one and mashed the trigger, ripping apart bodies and cover. An insurgent ran from the ruins with an RPG over one shoulder and took a knee. Franks tore him in half and the rocket streaked off into the darkness.

As the last of the belt of heavy rounds cycled through the gun, Franks heard a new sound over the pounding. The screams were unnatural, like a sandstorm processed through tearing human vocal cords. *Alghuls incoming*, Franks thought as he saw the twisted figures loping across the camp on all fours toward him. *About damned time*.

❖ 17 ❖

Captain Joe Ledger

I MOVED IN, low and fast, running with small, quick steps to keep my aim level, firing the borrowed Glock in a two-handed grip. The ISIL tactician ducked backward grabbed the shoulder of one of his guards and hurled him at me. Part shield, part weapon.

I put two center mass and dodged around him to get to the tactician, but there were more of the fighters. So many more.

They screamed at me in half a dozen dialects and began firing their AK-47s, filling the tomb with thunder. But they were panicking, too. In surprise attacks panic is the sword and shield of the attacker and it bares the breast and throat of the attacked. The swarm of bullets burned the air around me. I did not panic. I closed on them and fired, taking them in turn, shifting to interpose one in front of the other, making them pay for their fear that made them miss when I did not.

I could hear carnage and destruction behind me. Franks was a goddamn tank. I think he scared me more than what we were fighting. If he was an example of the MCB operators, then what the fuck *else* could they put in the field? I mean, I'm top of my game for what I am—a black ops gunslinger—but I'm flesh and blood. I couldn't shake off the kinds of damage he was wading through. Even so, I heard him grunt, saw out of the corner of my eye as some of the enemy fire hit him hard enough to tear chunks away, to slow his advance. Could he die?

Probably.

I damn well could.

And so could the fighters in this tomb.

Franks and I had proved that.

In one of those moments of combat improbability
that the gods of war are perverse sons of

bitches, a heavy caliber round hit the side of my gun. The force tore the gun from my hand and nearly took my trigger finger with it.

The tactician had two burly guards with him and they were all eight feet from me. Their guns were swinging toward me.

I had no time at all, and I gave them none. Eight feet is a long step and a jump. I leapt into the air, slapping the barrel of the closest AK aside a microsecond before he fired, and at the same time I hooked the shooter around the back of the neck, shoving him sideways. He crashed into the second shooter and I landed on the balls of my feet, pivoted, snapped out a low flat-footed kick to the second man's knee. The joint splintered audibly and it tore a shriek from him. I gave him a double-tap with my elbow, one very fast and very light hit to the eye socket to knock his head backward and a second much harder shot to the Adam's apple. He fell gagging and trying to drag air in through a throatful of junk.

The first shooter tried to slam me across the face with his rifle, but he wasn't set for it. I slapped the swing high and ducked low, chop-punching him in the groin, then rising fast and hitting him in the throat, too, this time with the stiffened Y formed by index finger and thumb.

That left the tactician facing me.

He did something cute. He pulled a knife.

So, what the hell, I pulled mine.

He was pretty good. Fast, strong, knew some moves.

Pretty good is great if you're fighting in a back alley or in the dojo using rubber knives. Not when you're fighting for your life.

He tried to drive the point of his knife into my chest, maybe hoping to end it right there. I clubbed the knife down and away with a fist and used the Ka-Bar to draw a bright red line beneath his chin. I whirled away to avoid the spray of blood.

❖ **18** ❖

Special Agent Franks

FRANKS CRASHED through the camp, keeping up a steady stream of fire on the charging Alghuls. The contorted bodies were nearly as fast as he was, and it was taking several solid hits to put them down.

Beneath their tearing uniforms, their skin quickly dried and cracked apart, and unholy yellow light poured through the gaps. Bones twisted into points and ripped through their fingertips. As the possessed around them shed their humanity, the mortal ISIS fighters lost their nerve and fled into the desert. Not all of them made it as, overcome with bloodlust, the Alghul fell on them, tearing them limb from limb, and painting the stone walls with blood. Franks would have shot the survivors in the back as they ran away, but he couldn't spare the ammunition.

There was a ripping noise as an Alghul tore through a canvas tent to get at him. When it appeared, the yellow leaking through its tearing visage reminded him of a jack-o'-lantern. But when he knocked mped its chest flat with one big combat boot, what came squirting out wasn't much very pumpkinlike at all.

"Franks! Over here!" He turned to see Ledger standing in a doorway to an ancient stone building. He no longer had Franks' Glock and instead held a Russian Stechkin automatic pistol he'd picked up from one of the dead ISIS fighters. Behind him, stairs led down into the darkness. Ledger glanced up as a shadow crossed him. An Alghul was spider-climbing up the rock above him. Ledger calmly raised his Stechkin and fired several rounds through its face. "I found the prison," he said as the Alghul landed next to him with a sick thud.

And the rest of the Alghul must have realized it too, because they'd quit tearing the terrorists' guts out and shoving them into their mouths long enough to all focus on the American intruders. There were at least a dozen of them left, and they all ran shrieking toward the doorway.

"Whatever you're going to do, do it fast." Ledger grimaced as an Alghul swiped at his eyes with its claws. He shot the creature repeatedly as it stumbled away. Then Ledger darted forward and punctuated the attack with a deep slash from the silver Ka-Bar. The demon shrieked and crumpled to the stone floor.

Franks shoulder-checked another Alghul into the ground and then dumped the rest of his rifle's magazine into its body, sending up gouts of blood and sand. "Don't let anything past this point," he told Ledger as he shoved by him.

"I sure hope Church was wrong about your allies tending to die horribly," Ledger muttered as he got ready to hold off a horde of demons on his own.

"Not really," Franks said as he went down the stairs.

"That's not helping," Ledger shouted as he kept shooting.

❖ 19 ❖

Captain Joe Ledger

I SWAPPED OUT a spent magazine for a fresh one just as a wave of Alghuls rushed at me.

The Modern Man inside my head more or less screamed and passed out. The Cop backpedaled because this wasn't his kind of fight.

But the Killer . . . ?

Well, hell, I think he was waiting for the right moment to take the wheel and drive us all to crazy town.

And I liked it. They rushed at me. And I . . . fuck it. I rushed at them.

I let the gun barrel lead the way but I chased the bullets into the crowd. The heavy rounds punched holes in foreheads and burst eyeballs and painted the walls with dark gore. If we'd been in a wider space they could have circled me and cut me apart. This was a narrow stairwell and it worked for the kind of close-range fighting I do best. When the slide locked back, I simply rammed the barrel into the screaming mouth of one of the Alghuls and then slashed her across the throat. As she twisted down to the ground I reached past and quick-stabbed the next one in the right eye and then the left. One-two shallow thrusts with the sharpened clip of the Ka-Bar. The demon staggered back, clawing at its face with black talons, and I knee-kicked it into the others, jamming and crowding them even more. I grabbed a fistful of hair and drove the knife into the socket of a throat, gave the blade a quarter turn and ripped it free.

The dead and dying monsters toppled against the others, pressing them backward, transforming their savage attack into a clumsy rout. I jumped onto them, riding the falling, tumbling, bone-snapping avalanche down the stairs. Claws tore at me, the stone walls and the stone steps pummeled me, teeth snapped at me, but I rode a magic carpet of destruction down to the bottom. This was my moment and although they were demons from some twisted corner of hell, I was the red king and the knife was my scepter.

Then something massive crashed past me, striking the last of the demons like a runaway truck.

Franks.

He was splashed with blood and there was a wild light in his eyes that was no more human than the monsters we fought. He smashed them with fists the size of gallon pails; he stomped on them. I saw him tear an arm from its socket in exactly the same way the first Alghul had done back at the village.

It was all red madness.

I was the only one down there who was human.

If you could call the Killer human. He was like a demon howling inside my head, and through my mouth and with my voice.

But I was wrong.

I wasn't the only human down there.

I saw a man standing at the rear of the chamber.

He was dressed in strange clothes, all of gold and jewels and leather, like someone who had stepped from a history book. In a flash of insight I realized that he was probably dressed as a shaman or sorcerer from the courts of King Shalmaneser, emulating everything down to his garb so that there was no chance of getting his horrible ritual wrong.

He was the one responsible for all this death. He was the one who had taken all of these innocent girls and turned them into monsters. He had participated in a kind of spiritual rape by opening them to the demons who destroyed their souls while stealing their flesh. The depth of this crime—this *sin*—was bottomless. If he lived, if he escaped, then all of this destruction, all of this pain, was for nothing. He would start it up again somewhere else. He would ruin more lives, and by doing it, hand ISIL a weapon more dangerous than any nuke.

Behind the sorcerer was a doorway in the living rock of the cavern. It was open and beyond it I could see flames. Maybe there was a bonfire in there, but I don't think so.

I think I was looking straight into the mouth of Hell itself.

One after another of the Alghul came running from the flames to join the fight.

"*Franks*!" I screamed, pointing.

The brute had three Alghuls tearing at him and he bled from at least fifty deep cuts, but he turned, saw me, saw where I was pointing. Saw the sorcerer.

I saw him stiffen. I saw the moment when he understood what we were seeing.

Franks reached up and ripped one of the Alghul from him and used her body as a club to beat the other two into shattered ruin. Then he lowered his head, balled his fists, and charged toward the sorcerer.

Leaving the other ten Alghuls to swarm at me.

But I kicked myself backward and stepped on something that turned under my foot. It was one of Franks' guns. A mate to the Glock he'd given me. I snatched it up, vaulted the rail and dropped fifteen feet to the floor. My knees buckled under the impact, but I tucked and rolled as best I could. The Alghul shrieked like crows and swarmed down the steps toward me. The sorcerer pointed at me with a ceremonial dagger and at Franks with a scepter.

"*Kill them!*"

The demons closed around me like a fist.

I raised the pistol and took the shot.

One bullet.

There was only one round left and the slide locked back.

The sorcerer stared at me. All the Alghul froze. The world and the moment froze.

The sorcerer had three eyes. Two brown ones and a new black one between them. Two of the Alghul stood behind him, their faces splashed with blood that was redder than theirs.

We all lived inside that frozen moment for what seemed like an hour. Or a century.

And then the sorcerer fell.

❖ 20 ❖

Special Agent Franks

IT REALLY PISSED HIM OFF when stupid mortals fucked around with things beyond their comprehension. This idiot had probably pieced the spell together out of some forbidden tome. He'd gotten the costume right but the actual magic words written in blood on the walls were the equivalent quality of crayon scribbles. The workmanship was so shoddy they were lucky he hadn't sucked northern Iraq into another dimension with this half-assed summoning spell.

Ledger drilling a hole through the summoner's brain had stopped the ritual. No more would cross over. However, they were still up to their eyeballs in Alghul, but since the path was still open, Franks had a solution to that little problem.

This next part wasn't in any of the MCB's manuals.

Franks walked to the shimmering portal, and placed his hands against the edges. His gloves immediately burst into flames. Even though they were all around them, the humans couldn't sense the disembodied, but Franks could. He saw that the Alghul's spirits were still tethered to this prison. In this place of power he could apply the might of his will against theirs.

"Your invitation has been revoked," Franks declared in the Old Tongue. A hot desert wind ripped through the ruins, sand blasting the bloody marks from the ancient

walls. The demons shrieked as the void ripped them from their newfound flesh and sent them hurtling back into the darkness.

And then he shut the door.

The flaming portal disappeared in a flash. Every possessed body instantly collapsed into a limp, wet heap.

Well, that worked better than he'd expected.

Ledger was panting, covered in blood, and surrounded by corpses. He looked to Franks, incredulous. "What the fuck just happened, Franks?"

"Mission accomplished."

❖ 21 ❖

Captain Joe Ledger

I WANT TO SAY that it was an easy wrap. I want to say that Franks did his magic mumbo jumbo and the world became all shiny and new and cartoon animals frolicked around us.

I'd love to say that. Just once.

The truth was that there were still some possessed ISIL foot soldiers out there.

Franks and I are alive right now because we earned it.

I'm telling you this now as I sit on an equipment box in Camp Baharia in Fallujah. There are a lot of U.S. military around me. Echo Team finally arrived, so I have my own people there. In that place, with that much muscle around me I should feel secure, should be able to take a deep breath.

But I think it's finally hit me.

There are demons. Real demons.

There are monsters. Real monsters.

We stopped a threat unlike anything I'd ever imagined could be real in this world. The gateway to Hell, or to wherever those demons came from, is closed thanks to a monster that stands alongside ordinary humans like me.

That doorway is sealed, but when I asked Franks if that meant that demons could no longer come into our world, he did something that I didn't think he could do.

He laughed.

And, brother, it was not the kind of laugh you ever want to hear.

No, it was not.

So I sat here, waiting for my ride out of this place, for my ride home. The night is heavy and vast. I used to think the shadows were nothing more than lightless air, that nothing lived in them, that nothing could.

Now I know different.

Holy God, now I know different.

"Weaponized Hell" is one of the two collaborations in this collection, and because writers are a weird bunch, every collaboration works out differently. But to give you an illustration of what a consummate professional Jonathan Maberry is, that entire story you just read was written over just a few days. We had agreed to do this story and then had done a bit of brainstorming together, but we are both really busy with lots of active projects

so the deadline for this one kind of snuck up on both of us.

When the editor reached out to see how it was going, it was like, uh oh. Crunch time! Of the two of us, Jonathan had the more pressing schedule that week, so I hurried and wrote a rough of each of Franks' scenes, leaving gaps where I thought Ledger bits would make sense. That night Jonathan took it, wrote his scenes, inserted a few new cool bits I hadn't thought of, and kicked it back to me. Then we spent the last day sending it back and forth, polishing and tweaking each of our characters' dialog and actions when they appeared in the other writer's scenes.

I think it came out really good.

Agent Franks is one of my most popular characters, and Jonathan gets him. In fact a year after this story came out, I got Jonathan to write an Agent Franks point of view story for The Monster Hunter Files anthology, and he gave me a World War Two Agent Franks vs. Nazis story that was great.

SON OF FIRE, SON OF THUNDER

The other collaboration in this collection is "Son of Fire, Son of Thunder," written by me and Steve Diamond, for the Crimson Pact *anthology in 2011, which was edited by Paul Genesse, and published by Alliteration Ink.*

This is one of my very first short stories, and only the second piece of fiction Steve ever wrote. I did the scenes from Diego Santos, Freelance Exorcist. Steve wrote Lazarus Tombs, FBI.

Staff Sergeant Diego Santos
Behavioral Health Department, Main Clinic,
Marine Corps Base Quantico

IN TWO YEARS, fifty-six days, fourteen hours, and ten minutes I will be brutally killed by a demon.

I've watched my own death in my dreams nearly every night since I was eight. I'm used to waking up because of teeth breaking my skin.

You might think that sounds like a tough break, but

don't shed any tears on my behalf. The rest of you poor saps have to live with doubt and worry and fear. You have to think about finding a career, marrying the right woman, raising kids, working hard, planning your retirement, getting cancer, and shit like that. Me? I know the exact minute when I'll be ripped to bits.

Just lucky, I guess.

There's only one downside to knowing the exact moment when your life will end horribly.

I hate when people waste my fucking time.

The psychologist had been asking me questions for fifty-two precious minutes. I'd finished telling him about kicking doors and fighting house to house in Fallujah, and one particular story where I'd shot a guy in the neck right when he was about to light me up with an AK, when the doctor asked, "And so how did that make you feel?"

How was it supposed to feel? How should a normal person answer? I did my job. How's it supposed to feel when you do a good job? I am a United States Marine and I have been trained to close with, engage, and utterly destroy the enemy, and I am *extremely* good at my job. I've deployed to Iraq three times, Afghanistan twice. As soon as I get home I volunteer for the next open billet. Better me than anyone else, I've got nothing better to do to prepare myself until the appointed time, and mostly because I can't die until I've fulfilled the holy mission assigned to me by Almighty God.

But that wasn't the answer this man was looking for. He wasn't worthy enough to understand the truth. I needed him to think that I *wasn't* crazy. I had to keep the demons secret. It wasn't time for the apocalypse yet.

"It was very frightening, sir."

I watched the doctor's face as he glanced down to scribble a note on his legal pad. *Just write that I'm normal and quit screwing around.* I'd always assumed that a psychologist's office would have a couch for the patient to lay down on, but I just had a stuffed chair and he sat behind a desk. He looked up at me and it was obvious he knew I was full of it. I've always hated lying. It's easier to just not say anything at all than to make shit up. "I've read your file."

They say that if a shrink declared a Marine sane, he'd be unfit for duty, but I had a reputation for crazy even by our standards. My last CO had decided that I must have a death wish, and that was how I'd ended up here, off to see the wizard. Mandatory Evaluation Time. "I would expect so, sir."

"An impressive list of commendations and fitness reports, but these After Action Reports . . . a complete disregard for personal safety, placing yourself in harm's way, not just volunteering for every dangerous assignment possible but making up new ones. There are serious worries about your stability. Did I even read that last one right? Attempting to draw sniper fire?"

"It makes them easier to spot and neutralize, sir."

"And the most recent incident?"

I scowled. It would have been certain death for anyone else . . . I couldn't tell him that one of the Afghans had been possessed. "An opportunity presented itself. I acted."

"You acted alone against an entrenched, numerically superior foe, after your rifle platoon had been ordered to wait for reinforcements." He looked me right in the eyes. "Are you trying to get yourself killed, Staff Sergeant?"

"No, sir." My answer was completely truthful this time. I'd accepted the hour of my death. It would be blasphemous, not to mention impossible, to thwart His will.

The doctor's BlackBerry buzzed. He picked it up and read the display. Our time was up. "That's it for today, but I want to schedule another session for tomorrow. Same time. We'll pick up where we left off."

More wasted time. But I was stuck here, spinning my wheels until it was decided that I wasn't a danger to myself or the Corps. "Of course, sir."

I didn't wake up screaming. Oh no. I knew how to keep the screams inside. The trapped screams turn into heat, and I simply lay there uncomfortable and twitchy. I'd learned how to do that a long time ago. You didn't want to get the reputation as the guy that woke up screaming from nightmares every single night. You might get sent in for a Mandatory Evaluation or something.

Her apartment was close to the freeway so a lot of ugly light snuck around the edges of the curtains. Flat on my back, sweating, breathing hard, I stared at the ceiling for a while, remembering the feeling of razor teeth in my neck, of claws digging through my guts, the crack of my breaking bones still vibrating in my ears. It was always the same. Sometimes there were new bits, unusual clues that I'd never noticed before, small things, but there was nothing new tonight. Just me dying while a few familiar faces watched helplessly at the ragged edge of the apocalypse. I didn't know those witnesses' names, and I'd never met any of them in real life yet, but I knew them so well that they were truthfully my oldest friends.

The girl stirred next to me, lifted one hand and sleepily stroked my chest. She bumped my crucifix, my dog tags, and ended up touching the Eagle, Globe, & Anchor tattoo over my heart.

The reason I'd enlisted was because I'd seen that tattoo in my Vision. Apparently God wanted me to be a Marine, and since I had a destiny to fulfill, I'd gotten inked the day after I'd gotten out of boot camp.

"You're hot," she mumbled. Her hand went flat and her palm was cold on my fevered chest as she drifted back to sleep. I couldn't for the life of me remember her name, though she'd said she was a dental hygienist. We'd met in a bar a few hours ago, she was lonely and alive, so I'd followed her back to her apartment. It didn't matter that I couldn't remember her name. When you've got so little time, there's no point.

Man's got to pass the time somehow.

Special Agent Jarvis "Lazarus" Tombs
FBI National Academy, Quantico

THE CHILDREN.

I still see them every night in my nightmares. Truthfully, I'm lucky if I have a nightmare where all I see are monsters and demons running around killing everyone. I would rather see that type of death and destruction than the eyes of those children again, haunting me.

Tonight was the fifteenth night in a row that I got to relive a grotesque dream version of the day six months ago when I found the house of the thing—the demon—that had abducted my son. It takes no effort to recall the feeling of walking into that house and seeing the walls covered from floor to ceiling in portraits and photographs of children. There were thousands of them. The children, still alive, trapped within their own personal "still life."

My son was included among them.

But my nightmare doesn't follow the reality of the memory.

I stand in the entryway, feeling the heat of the fire as it consumes the house. Flames spring up where the walls meet the floors. This time, the photos on the walls are utterly alive. The captured children pound on the photos from the inside, screaming silently to be let out. In the dream tears stream down my cheeks because I know I can do nothing to save them. Those tears will be on my face when I wake up. It's the same every time.

In my hands I hold the picture of my son on a backyard swing set. His picture too is animated, and he swings back and forth, laughing. As chilling as the screaming faces in the other pictures in the home are—in my nightmare I can somehow see every single one throughout the house—they are nothing compared to the laughter of my son. It is mocking and demonic, like the thing that trapped him in the picture.

The flames get hotter. They now cover the walls, burning and melting the pictures of thousands of children. Impossibly, I see each child catch on fire within their pictures, dying in agony. I can hear them all saying over and over, "Lazarus Tombs has made his choice!"

And over it all I hear my son laughing harder and harder.

I look back down at the picture in my hands. My hands catch fire, and I know the rest of me is burning too. The picture of my son is unyielding. Nothing can free him from the photo except me.

But I won't free him.

Tonight my nightmare ends the same way it always does. All the children are dead, the ashes of their pictures heaped around me in piles. Before my own body crumbles to ash, my son stops laughing and speaks to me from the photo.

"Dad, will you set me free so I can kill everything?"

Special Agent Lazarus Tombs
Personal Dormitory, FBI National Academy,
Quantico

I WOKE UP gasping for breath.

The horrifying feeling from that nightmare never dulls, no matter how many times I experience it. Wiping the tears from my cheeks, I swung my legs off the side of my bed. On the nightstand, I keep that picture of my son. I looked so hard and long for him after he was abducted, but never thought that finding him would leave me feeling like a failure. He was right there in the photo, held there by the power of an incredibly powerful demon.

I had two choices. I could say a specific phrase given to me by the demon and set my son free. But if I did, all the power that demon held would take over my son. He would lose his identity and become that demon reincarnated. And then I would have to hunt him down and kill him.

Or, I could leave him in the picture until I came upon a solution that would allow me to free him without consequences. The reality is that I constantly question whether or not the demon was telling me the whole truth. Why should it? What if its threat was nothing more than a bluff? A way to torture me with doubt and temptation?

And tempted I am. Every minute of every day.

The hope of a solution was what brought me to one of the dorms of the FBI National Academy in Quantico, Virginia. Usually I taught classes here every other year, but this time I was here as a counselor for the classes of cops and deputies that were invited to the National Academy. As a counselor I ate with the attendees, went to classes with them, shot with them, and watched for the ones that had potential. Every cop sees weird and scary stuff out there in the world, but these days the weird and scary were getting worse and worse. My division at the FBI, the Paranormal Sciences Division—or PSD—kept track of all paranormal activity, which was on the rise. Significantly. We needed recruits who could deal with the paranormal, and at the very least we needed eyes and ears out in the world that could keep us updated. The FBI National Academy was a perfect cover. We invited those that had some promise or who had actual paranormal experiences.

I reached over and picked up my son's photo. Six months and no real leads. I'd hoped that some of the attendees this year might have something, but I knew I was grasping at straws. A deputy from Sacramento had called me with a rumor about phoenix ashes. But how do you find a phoenix, if one even exists?

It would take a miracle to save my son from his current fate, but believing in miracles isn't out of the ordinary for a guy like me. How can I not believe in them considering I've died and come back from the dead twice already?

My thoughts cut out as the photo warmed unnaturally in my hand. This happened every now and again. What did it mean? Was I running out of time?

I put the picture back down, more than a bit unnerved. I needed a distraction. My clock read 8:00 A.M. As my father always said, it was never too early to get some shooting in. It would get my mind off the nightmare, and it would be a good time to get some time in with some of the cops and deputies. One had hesitantly mentioned encountering a sandman before. Another potential recruit who was here at the Academy, a girlie cop from Chicago, killed a demon in a meth house. Her hair and nails threw me at first, but Detective Cynthia Weber was one of my top prospects of the year.

I was out the door before my clock read 8:05 A.M.

Staff Sergeant Diego Santos
Rifle Range, Marine Corps Base Quantico

"GOOD MORNING, Staff Sergeant Santos."

"And a good morning to you, Gunnery Sergeant Moss."

Moss was a solid, tough, bald, mean bastard with a lazy eye. I was rather fond of him. Fleet Assistance Program had put me working for him while I was under Mandatory Evaluation. We got along because Moss liked anybody that had a reputation for being good at shooting people, and I helped him keep the range squared away. Moss was a no BS, get-the-job-done sort of Marine. I wished I could tell him what was out there, waiting, but God hadn't picked me to be a prophet. He wanted me to be a warrior.

"You look shittier than usual, Santos. Late night?"

"Of course, Gunny."

"Was she pretty?"

I shrugged. "Enough."

"Are you *trying* to be a stereotype? You know it isn't mandatory for you young guys to have every bad habit. With the diseases that's out there, that sort of behavior will kill you one of these days." Moss was happily married with half a dozen kids. I just enjoyed the crappy range coffee and finished off my morning cigar. "If smoking don't get you first."

PT studs like Moss always frowned on the smokers, which was understandable, but it wasn't like I cared about my long term health. "What's today?"

"Training wheels, baby steps, hurt feelings. The short bus should arrive soon." That meant we would be working with the newly minted officers. To be fair, by the point the butter bars got to Moss' range, they were usually disciplined enough not to do anything stupid. There were bound to be some prior service Marines in the mix to make my job easier. Range work was nothing like combat. We both knew that, but you had to start somewhere. "Watch the city boys. They're usually the worst. Don't know shit about shooting."

"I grew up in a city."

"Yeah, but you're from East LA. I bet you got lots of fam fire hanging out the window of a lowrider spraying down the hood with an Uzi." Moss grinned. He loved jerking my chain.

"I was an altar boy." That much was true. I'd hoped that maybe I could've learned something useful about how demons worked from the priests, but they'd been blind as everyone else. It had always been frustrating keeping my knowledge secret. I'd mostly wanted somebody to talk to that *got* it.

"Uh huh . . . Sure you were, Santos." He looked around to make sure we were alone. "They should just let me write up your psych eval and save everyone some time. I recognize your condition. You suffer from an acute case of *does not give a shit*. You were born to fight. Combat is where you belong. Some officers just can't wrap their little minds around the fact that men like you exist."

That was a hell of a compliment.

"Doesn't help that you're a scary little motherfucker. You always got this disturbing look on your face, all shifty, like you're deciding if somebody is worth stabbing. You should try to smile once in a while."

I tried.

"Jesus . . . Okay, don't do that ever again."

"Ooh-rah, Gunnery Sergeant."

"Let's get the lockers open. Gonna be a busy day."

It might seem odd that they'd FAP somebody they were worried about being suicidal to work on a range with live ammunition, but this was the military. I knew of a guy in the Army that was being counseled for clinical depression and they'd assigned him to be a parachute rigger.

❖ ❖ ❖

Demons have a smell. It is hard to describe, and it's been different each time I've found one. Sometimes like burning plastic, or dried blood, or the sickness in an old folks home . . . I think they had different species and each one had their own nasty fragrance, but there was always something underneath that just cried demon.

This time it was like old road kill.

It took me a moment to pick it up. Firing ranges have a strong smell to them anyway. Sweat, oil, dust, and the overpowering carbon stink from thousands of rounds of 5.56. Even on an outdoor range, if there wasn't a breeze, it would collect and hang around you like a cloud. But even then, I could smell the demon stink.

I'd been coaching a trainee when I took a step off the line. It was close. And then there was another, slightly different scent, and then a third, and then more. "It can't be . . ." I'd never encountered more than a single demon at once.

"Staff Sergeant?" the recruit asked.

We still had two years and fifty-five days until the battle for the end of the world kicked off. This couldn't be right. "Cease fire! Cease fire!" I shouted.

Immediately the command was relayed and repeated down the line. Moss shouted it into his bullhorn. One last round went off a split second after the command went out, and in any normal circumstances that Marine would've been chewed a new asshole.

I took my headphones off and ran down the concrete slab. The smell . . . Where was it coming from? It was so close I could taste the rot in my mouth. It was coming from the FBI side of the range.

Moss appeared at my side. "What is it?"

I couldn't just say that the forces of hell were loose in Quantico, but I had to do something. "Listen . . . You hear that?"

"What?"

There wasn't any yet, but I knew there would be soon enough. "Screaming."

Special Agent Lazarus Tombs
Indoor Shooting Range, FBI National Academy,
Quantico

I STOOD IN ONE OF THE ACADEMY'S indoor ranges, arms folded, watching members of my class put round after round into paper targets at twenty-five feet. Ten of my class of twenty-seven were here, each of them having been personally targeted and recruited to attend this session. There should have been eleven with me, but Deputy Helen Collins from El Paso had just discovered she was expecting. My boss, Frank Shields, had passed down the mandate that starting today Collins wouldn't be visiting a shooting range until after she was a new mother.

Regardless, I was pleased. The world was taking the straight road to ruin, and no one seemed to really care or even notice. The Bureau needed help. Hell, the whole world needed help. Most of the Academy sessions only would net one or two cops and deputies who could take the stress of dealing with the supernatural.

I had ten in the room with me. *Ten.* That meant that potentially ten more cities and towns would have a slight extra bit of help when real-life monsters began running around in their neighborhood.

It was also potentially ten more people that could keep an eye out for ways to fix my son's . . . situation.

On the far left Sergeant Tim Danielson—Reno PD—was burning through magazines at twice the speed of everyone else. He'd just been promoted for "exceptional bravery in the line of duty." His superiors didn't know the half of it. Danielson had responded to a domestic dispute that had turned into stopping a possessed couple on a killing spree. I was going to try to properly recruit him to work with me. Next to him was Cynthia Weber. She was trying out a smaller caliber Glock 17 and seemed to be subconsciously competing with Danielson. It was close. I wanted her for the PSD, but had a feeling she had too much love for Chicago. But that didn't mean I couldn't try.

The rest were probably going to be sent back home after receiving some specialized training from myself and a few other experts at the PSD. They'd each have my direct line with instructions to call with any questions or concerns.

I felt The Itch.

Stiffening, I felt the hairs on the back of my neck stand on end. I only felt The Itch around supernatural creatures or paranormal hot spots, and it usually meant things were going to get bad.

The muffled popping of ten sidearms was suddenly accompanied by a dull thudding behind us.

At the door.

The others began hearing it too, and soon they had all stopped firing and were watching the door with me.

I took one step towards the door then froze as a portion of it bulged inward. I pulled my Glock from my holster and took aim. Something was coming through, and The Itch in my head was maddeningly intense. There was no way this was going to end well.

The door flew inward, and a demon followed.

Demons come in all shapes and sizes. Some were intelligent and some were dumb as bricks, but they were all killing machines. This one had a long snout like a mutated dog with red-stained teeth bristling from its maw, with skin that was red like it had just crawled out of Hell the way they describe it in church. It was also the biggest demon I'd ever seen. At least three times my own mass, and seven or eight feet tall.

The demon smiled, then charged us.

A continuous roar of gunfire greeted the demon's sudden movement. The rounds—a mixture of .40 and .45—pounded into the creature, slowing its momentum, but it wasn't enough. Bullets thudded into the demon's black hide but didn't cause any visible harm. The demon shielded its face, keeping me from hitting it in any of its vulnerable areas, and leapt into the line of police officers to my left.

A cute, petite blonde—Lieutenant Alice Thompson from the NYPD—was the first to go down, ripped open groin to neck. Blood sprayed into the air and splashed onto the two deputies next to her. One froze in shock at the blood—Captain Carson from Minnesota—and had his head taken off by a casual swipe of the demon's clawed hand. The other deputy—Blinds, from Miami—stepped forward and emptied a full magazine into the creature's chest from three feet away. As he thumbed the magazine release, the demon grabbed him by the neck and flung him against the far wall of the indoor range. He was dead when he hit the steel trap. The demon slashed at another of the cops in the room, and the officer went down, clutching his belly to keep his insides from spilling out.

One officer—by the name of Jorge Castilla—ran for the door. Weber screamed after him, calling him a coward as she reloaded, but I could hardly blame Castilla. Some people just couldn't handle the up-close violence these kind of creatures could dish out.

The demon was slowing down. Inky, black blood was dribbling out mostly from the rounds Blinds had shot at close range. If this went on for much longer we'd all be dead. I shoved another magazine into my Glock as the demon leapt onto a cop from New Jersey, tearing out his throat with its powerful jaws. The demon jerked its head to the side and snapped the man's neck for good measure.

It turned its head and made a deep, guttural sound.

Laughter.

I extended my gun and put two shots through its left eye.

It collapsed like a puppet that had its strings cut.

Danielson and the other living rushed to the side of the cop holding his internal organs and tried keeping him alive. I reached up and pulled off my ear protection. Sounds of screaming through the open door to the range assaulted my ears. The scent of blood, gunpowder and sulfur were making me lightheaded and nauseous. I ran to my duffle bag and pulled out three loaded magazines— the rounds were all hollow-points and would have difficulty penetrating the hide of any demon that was more than a few yards away.

I left the officers behind and walked out into the bright late-morning light. To my left two more demons were playing tug-of-war with Jorge Castilla. A small mercy was that he was already dead from a dozen slashes and bites. I leveled my gun and fired in one motion. The rounds thudded into the left demon's torso, and I was rewarded with a shriek of pain. The two monsters dropped Castilla's corpse and started in my direction, smiling.

"Tombs! Tombs! Tombs!" the one on the right rasped. It sounded...*delighted*.

They *knew* me.

Staff Sergeant Diego Santos
Rifle Range, Marine Corps Base Quantico

I'M A STAFF SERGEANT. It isn't like I can order around very many Marines in the grand scheme of thing, but luckily for me, the chaotic noise of battle coming from the FBI side of the range was unmistakable. I reacted first, but the others caught on pretty quick. Moss got back on his bullhorn. NCOs dragged their men off the line, and one sharp lieutenant decided that somebody needed to go investigate.

Since I'd already taken a vest in my size off the range display, thrown it on, and was shoving loaded magazines into the pouches, I must have looked like the logical choice. Once again, just lucky I guess, because I was going anyway. Moss, God bless his ready-for-violence soul, had done the same thing, though surely he was thinking it was a terrorist attack or something. Two other vets were just as on the ball and the four of us were ready to go within a minute of the first inhuman bellow drifting across the fence from the FBI side.

Armed with range loaner M-16A4s and M-4 carbines, we took off. Even the PT stud had a hard time keeping up with me. I always seem to move faster when demons are around. Just motivated, I suppose.

We were scouts, but I already knew what we would find.

This was the only part of the base where the Marines bumped up against the FBI Academy grounds. It made sense to share a backstop. The smell was stronger here. Men and women were shouting and there were random bursts of gunfire. We crouched behind a concrete bulwark at the boundary.

Moss about had a heart attack when he saw his first hell spawn. This one was seven feet tall, red, with muscles that seemed to be constructed out of living strands of barbed wire. It was too busy yanking some poor dude's entrails out to notice the four men in MARPAT watching it. Moss ducked back down. He actually turned grey for a second and I thought the hardened Marine was going to puke. No matter how tough you are, demons always had that effect on people their first time. "Easy, Gunny. They feed on fear. Makes them stronger."

"What the fucking fuck—What is that?"

"Demon."

"Demon?"

I risked a quick peek. I'd seen one like that back in LA

on leave last winter. God had shown me where it slept so I'd beaten that one to death with a pipe wrench. "Shoot for their eyes, mouths, soft bits. Try to engage from a distance. They're super fast and their claws are nasty."

Moss was shaking his head, but not in disbelief. There was no way he could delude himself about what he'd seen. There's something about the sight of a demon that slugs you deep in your primal instincts. There was no denying the sheer, unearthly wrongness of them.

"Take it out," Moss ordered.

We rose and opened fire. I'd zeroed the Trijicon on the loaner M-16A4 myself. The chevron landed on the red beast's head and I stroked the trigger. The scope bobbled a bit, then settled back down, and I popped another 5.56 into its face. It took a several more hits before black sludge erupted from between the strands of fleshy wire. The demon took two awkward steps on its goat legs, and fell over. One of the lance corporals put a few extra into it to be safe before we ducked down.

"They're not so tough!" the lance corporal shouted.

I changed mags and stowed the partially spent one. "That was the weakest kind I know of. They're quick, but not durable. The others will be worse. Especially if they've got any of the ones that can look like people . . . You know, these feel like they just got here. They're disoriented. If we can pop the son of a bitch that brought them in, we can stop this fast."

"How can you tell who that is?" Moss hissed.

God will show me. "I just will. He'll be close."

"Damn it, Santos . . ." Moss looked at the two hyperventilating lance corporals. I had to hand it to them, they were doing okay. I'd peed my pants the first time I'd seen a demon, but then again, there's a lot of difference between a scrawny eight-year-old and a Devil Dog. "Kerchek, Whitney, haul ass back. Tell the LT everything Santos said..." and when he realized how strange the report would sound, he added, "*Convince* him." He looked at me next. "Your crazy ass is with me."

The other two got up and ran.

Moss' hands were shaking, but he was a Marine, which meant that no matter how awful or terrifying it was about to get, he was programmed to kick serious ass. "How do you know—"

"Altar boy. Remember?"

"Now you smile? Stop. You're freaking me out."

We moved out, crouched but quick, weapons shouldered. Combat waddle they call it, but it's normal for your body to crouch when it thinks it is about to get hit by something. One of the mottled green bastards with a head like a triceratops came out from behind a cinderblock wall. I swiveled at the hips, the Trijicon moved over and I blasted the fucker. *POP. POP. POP.* Moss moved up beside me. *POP. POP.* Sludge splattered all over the wall and the dinosaur-headed thing went down hard.

I could feel the source up ahead. I knew from His holy wisdom that these were just slaves. Their master was here, whipping them on. I'd run into assholes like this before. How any human being could heed the call of the darkness, I would never know. "This way, Guns." He looked up from blasting one of the red ones long enough to grunt an affirmative.

Terrified men and women ran past us, wearing the khaki pants and blue polos of the FBI Academy trainees. Some were fighting, and most of those were being torn apart. Arms, legs, heads, organs... body parts were everywhere. There was so much blood that my Danners were leaving tracks in it. It was a slaughterhouse. "That way. Go that way!" Moss waved the survivors toward the Marine line.

We kept on dropping monsters. The movements were practiced and mechanical, moving and shooting, dropping mags and reloading while the other Marine provided cover. Heat waves shimmered over the barrel of my rifle, but they just kept on coming. We'd picked up a few armed FBI on the way, and the knot of us made our way forward.

Twenty yards away, two of the big, gangly dog-faced demons had just got done pulling some poor bastard in half, and now they were loping toward another Fed. He was shooting a pistol at them, but they were shrugging it off. I'd never heard one of the inhuman looking ones speak before, but one of these was repeating the word *"Tombs"* over and over again.

The Fed looked familiar... *"Dios mio!"* He was in my Vision! He was one of the witnesses to my death. I recognized him easily. I'd known that face for twenty years. The demon was almost on him. There was no time. "Guide my hand," I whispered as I fired, and He did. The demon tilted its hideous dog face just in time to catch a 5.56 up one nostril. The bullet must have fragmented perfectly because half its skull disintegrated into a cloud of rapidly expanding fragments.

The second one looked right at me, dodged to the side

as I fired again, then turned tail and ran. Surely going to its master, probably to warn it that a Vengeful Sword of the Lord had arrived to send them all back to the festering pit. The Fed went after the demon. Of course he did. He was like me. He couldn't fall until his appointed hour.

Moss on the other hand, far as I knew, was imminently mortal . . . "Gunny!"

"Yeah?"

"Could you stay here and wait for the others?" He outranked me and you do not tell a Gunnery Sergeant what to do. "Please?"

Moss growled at me. "You seem to know what the fuck's going on here, Staff Sergeant."

"I do."

"Go and fix it then!"

I went after the Fed. He disappeared around a concrete wall and I followed. I was more excited than I had been in years. I'd found one of the witnesses! I was making progress. This was proof that I was following the Lord's path.

Special Agent Lazarus Tombs
FBI National Academy, Quantico

THE DEMON on the left cocked his head as if hearing something. Then its head exploded.

I don't think I'd even seen a demon with a look of shock on its face before, but I guess there was a first time for everything. The demon wiped away its companion's brain matter that had splattered everywhere then looked toward the origin of the shot. I followed its gaze to the far left where a Marine was sighting down a rifle. The demon threw itself to the side as the rifle boomed, then turned and sprinted in the opposite direction.

I threw a quick wave of thanks to the Marine and sprinted after the fleeing demon.

The demon loped away from me heading south. It was an odd feeling chasing it, since usually the demons were the ones doing the chasing. I had thirty rounds left for my Glock spread between two full mags in my pocket—not the ideal place to be carrying them—and the half-full mag in the gun. Hopefully I wouldn't need any more than that for one demon.

I sprinted through the campus noticing sickening patches of red decorating the sidewalks and walls of the buildings I was passing. A mangled leg stuck out from some bushes to my right. In the distance I could hear screams of terror and pain from people around the campus, and growls and howls from more demons.

Where had they all come from? One person couldn't have summoned this many, which told me this was a coordinated effort.

I caught a flash of another demon ahead. Behind me I heard the sounds of running, so I shot a quick glance over my shoulder. It was the Marine.

At least I had some sort of backup. There were at least two demons ahead of me now. Maybe more.

What were they after?

The so-called experts in the field said that demons were mindless predators that lived to hunt and kill. I knew demons could have far more intelligence. All demons were dangerous, but it was the intelligent ones that were scary.

And these knew my name.

I couldn't have been running for more than a few minutes when I came around a bend and saw one of the FBI's research buildings. Most people knew that we conducted all sorts of tests on materials, biological agents, and weaponry here. There was also an area at the back where we held most of our information on the supernatural.

Fifty yards from the building, I slowed to a stop. There were no screams around this part of the campus, and the silence was just as eerie. The main research building ahead was two floors above ground, but I knew there was subterranean storage and laboratories as well. On a typical day there could be upwards of a hundred people inside.

One hundred people that had likely never actually seen a demon. All their work was controlled. *Theoretical. Safe.*

The double doors at the entrance were a pile of shattered glass, on top of which was the unmoving body of an agent in standard HRT gear. *Geez.* Even those guys hadn't been ready for this. I ejected the half-full magazine and replaced it with a full one.

The sound of footsteps came to halt beside me. The Marine. "I'll take left," he said. He actually sounded eager. *Psycho.* But he was a well-armed psycho, and I found myself wishing for a rifle like his—an M16 from the brief glance of it I got before he began moving quickly to the left side of the wrecked door.

My Glock 23 felt a bit underpowered at the moment, but what could I do? I moved to the position on the right. As I got to the door I shifted to a left-handed grip on my gun and peered around the corner. There wasn't just one guy from HRT dead in the doorway.

There were eight.

They were cast about like broken dolls, necks and limbs bent at impossible angles. I've seen my share of bloody scenes, and this wasn't even the worst, but somehow being on the FBI Academy's campus made it far worse psychologically. The walls of the entryway were painted in blood. The frightening thing was the lack of damage from gunfire . . . and the quiet.

Practically at my feet was the trailing HRT member's discarded weapon, an M4. It was a little shorter than the Marine's own rifle, which I hoped would give me a slight bit more maneuverability if it got to close-quarters fighting.

Of course if it came to that I might already be dead.

Again.

I checked the magazine. Completely full. I motioned for the Marine to cover me so I could pull the extra magazines from the corpse. I'd worry about feeling like a grave robber later. For now I needed more ammunition.

We entered the building, leapfrogging one another for covering positions. Glass crunching under our feet was the only sound. The entire area looked as though explosives had been set off. Cubical walls were shredded, and sparks still flew from the exposed wires of shattered computers and other electronics. Bloody bodies and bloodier body parts littered the wreckage.

The lack of natural sound was unnerving, but it didn't seem to have any effect on the Marine. His eyes were constantly scanning. There was something about him that was different. It was like The Itch in my head wanted to have a reaction to him, but couldn't because of all the supernatural interference in the room.

I guided us toward the back of the building where the secure access to the Supernatural Development Studies rooms—always abbreviated SDS in the acronym-friendly FBI.

The entry to the SDS was a gaping hole. Inside, the place was a total loss. Any information not backed up to hard drives was gone. All physical material was destroyed. Was this the reason for the attack?

Then we heard the demons' howls.

And they were close.

Staff Sergeant Diego Santos
SDS Research Building, FBI National Academy, Quantico

IT WAS AN AMBUSH.

And there was only one thing to do in an ambush.

Fight your way through it.

The demons spilled out of every doorway. They came out from behind desks and filing cabinets. They pushed over cubicle walls and charged. It was an unstoppable force of demonic fury. A normal response would have been to give in to despair, curl up, and die. However, I was not normal. I was on a mission from God and had been trained by the United States Marine Corps. Fuck these stupid demons. They didn't have a chance.

I had been born for this.

Special Agent Lazarus Tombs
SDS Research Building, FBI National Academy,
Quantico

THERE WERE DEMONS everywhere. Dozens of them. They'd lured us into a kill box, but we were holding our own. The Marine seemed to know the demons' weak spots and was exploiting them with deadly accuracy. He was obviously the superior shot, so I took neck and body shots to slow them down, then he would finish them. Heads erupted in geysers of gore. The stench of sulfur and blood was enough to make me gag. I focused on breathing through my mouth, and pulling the trigger in three-shot bursts.

Then they started coming through the ceiling.

I swung my rifle and caught a demon through the armpit as it dropped three feet behind the Marine. It crumpled to the floor whimpering. Two more dropped down in front of the Marine, one of which he smashed in the face with the stock of his rifle, and the other he shot through the eye from six inches away. I used the final burst from my own rifle to put down the creature the Marine had stunned.

Pushing my last magazine into the rifle, I opened up on the remaining demons.

They were getting closer and closer. I shot one through the mouth as it launched itself at me. Its black blood sprayed onto my face and into my eyes. I screamed as it burned my eyelids. I squinted through the liquid and continued firing at the now hazy shapes of demons. They were fewer now. Much fewer.

We were actually winning.

I pulled the trigger and nothing happened. Empty.

The rifle dropped from my hands and I drew the Glock in time to shoot one of the last demons five times in the face.

And then there was pain.

I looked down at my chest and saw a clawed hand stuck into it. *Huh. Those are huge claws.*

My gun slid uselessly from my grip. My vision seemed to get even weirder. Couldn't focus. The Marine was shooting everything that still moved.

And now there was a guy walking toward us. My boss, Frank Shields. Finally we had a little backup. I was on the ground, on my side. Numbness was spreading through my chest. What was Shields doing? Even at the point of blacking out, The Itch grabbed my attention and made me focus on my boss. Shields raised his gun, and I saw the muzzle flash over and over as he shot the Marine.

I couldn't see the result. My vision tunneled until all I saw was a hazy blackness. I knew this feeling.

I was dying.

Again.

Third time's the charm.

I took one last breath, then nothing.

Staff Sergeant Diego Santos
SDS Research Building, FBI National Academy, Quantico

EVEN IF TOMBS had been wearing a soft vest, those

needle-tip claws would still have slid right through. The demon's hand came out, red and dripping. The Fed took a couple of faltering steps, looked back at me seemingly surprised, mouth hanging open, eyes wide. The demon chuckled then shoved the Fed down.

He couldn't die. It wasn't his time. I had faith. I lifted the M16A4 as the demon charged and took it apart, walking 5.56 rounds through it until it spilled over and slid to a wet stop at my feet. My rifle was empty and I reached for another magazine as I hit the release button.

Somebody shot me.

The bullet hit me in the MTV and the vest stopped it. Then a second bullet struck my rifle and knocked it from my hands. Several more bullets whipped past as I fell on my ass.

I looked up to see another blue and khaki Fed at the end of the room, and the stink on him told me that this was the asshole that had summoned these demons. He had a Glock in his hands and was walking toward me, covering me like he was going to arrest me or something. Old habits were hard to break.

The man from my dream was down. His eyes were open, flat and empty. Those were dead eyes. I'd seen it hundreds of times. He was gone.

It couldn't be.

I struggled to my feet as the summoner closed on me. He seemed surprised that we'd torn apart his monsters. The room was littered with bullet-riddled, discolored demon bodies. He flicked a cold glance at the body of the Fed. "Tombs is dead? Will wonders never cease? The mistress will be displeased. We needed him still."

"Your mistress can go fuck herself. He's not dead."

The pistol moved back to me. The summoner was old, a senior agent, probably just another dumb shit cultist seduced by lies and pride. Probably a plant by the other side, trying to sneak one of their own into a position of authority. Up close I could see the name "Shields" embroidered on his polo. "They talked about your kind!" he said when he finally got a better look at me. The cockiness was replaced with nervousness. They always reacted like that when they realized what I was.

"He's not dead," I repeated. "This is a test of faith." I took a step forward. "This is a test of my dedication."

The asshole shot me again. The bullet slammed into the Kevlar weave covering my shoulder. I grunted, swayed back, then righted myself and took another angry step forward. The gun was shaking. I was unnerving him.

"*B'nai regesh!*" Shields snarled in what I recognized as Hebrew.

"I've been called that before." I took one more step. "Among other things. The last asshole I met like you called me *Boanerges*." Ten feet away, the Glock went off. He missed. The bullet tore up carpet between my boots. His rapidly blinking eyes betrayed his terror. His grip and stance were sloppy. "It means 'son of thunder.'" One of the triceratops-looking demons was dead nearby. I put my boot on its bony neck shield, grabbed one of its horns, and wrenched hard on it until it cracked and broke free. I stepped off the demon's corpse and held the wicked horn low at my side. It was dense and cold. "I am a faithful servant. I am your earthly judge."

He took a clumsy step back. "Your god is young and weak!"

"Keep telling yourself that." Another step closer. "You think you idiots are the first to try to move in on His turf?"

"I'm going to kill you!"

"I've seen the thing that kills me, and you ain't shit compared to it."

He jerked the trigger. The bullet grazed my left forearm, just above my watch. I looked down at the nasty crease as blood ran down my hand. It hurt like a son of a bitch, but then I realized where I'd been struck. I started to laugh. "Fuckin' A!" It was a sign.

"What!" The summoner cringed. "What?"

"I've seen that scar in my Vision for years! I've been wondering when I was going to get it. About damn time." I nodded respectfully. "Thank you."

Now terrified, Shields tried to keep the gun up as he kept walking backwards. I followed. His back hit the far wall. "Stop! We've already got what we came for." We were so close now that there was no way he could miss. The end of the .40 was a gaping hole aimed right between my eyes. "The vessel has been prepared. The end is near. Your god can't protect you."

"Let's find out."

CLICK.

The demon summoner actually squealed like a little girl, but his training took over and he executed a malfunction clearance drill. He thumped the base of the magazine, grabbed the slide and racked it back to clear the dud round, but it was already too late. I knocked the muzzle aside and slammed the demon horn through his neck. I twisted the horn back and forth, widening the wound. Hot blood struck me in the face. Shields' Glock hit the carpet as he sagged against the wall.

I held him there and peered into his eyes, trying to understand what would cause a mortal man to believe the lies of the Rusted Vale. Those eyes were filled with terror and doubt, emotions I could no longer comprehend. "Told you so." He tried to respond, but his mouth was too full of blood and it just spilled past his teeth and down his chin. "When you get to Hell, let your masters know they can't win here. He won't let them."

Shields slid down the wall, still staring at me with a fanatic's fervor. I waited for him to die, just to make sure there were no other tricks.

I could hear sirens outside, but no more gunfire. Gunnery Sergeant Moss had come up behind me while I'd been distracted. He joined me, standing over the corpse, but didn't say anything.

"So, how much of that did you catch, Guns?"

"Enough to know that I don't want to know." He bent over and picked up the .40 cartridge that had been ejected from the Glock. He looked at it and then handed it over. The primer had been solidly dented by the firing pin. "About that psych evaluation . . ."

It wasn't anything to worry about anymore. "My enlistment is up soon. I've got a feeling I'm supposed to go do something else for a while." I looked back at Tombs, who was still obviously dead. This was turning out to be more complicated than expected, but I had faith that everything would work out in the end.

Special Agent Lazarus Tombs
Personal Dormitory, FBI National Academy,
Quantico

I OPENED MY EYES to a view of a ceiling, and my brain reminded me that I should be dead. I instantly panicked and tried to sit up. This situation wasn't anything new to me, but just because I've been dead before doesn't mean I enjoy revisiting. The last time I'd died I had woken up on a surgical table with half my chest sliced open.

Three months of therapy followed.

My body screamed in protest, and if felt like a cleansing fire was coursing through my veins. The fire was familiar, the same as it had been the last two times I'd woken up from the dead. It hurt more than anything, but at the same time felt absolutely wonderful. I knew where the wound was that the demon has inflicted on me, but I was more than a little afraid to look down. I didn't really know if my mind could cope with seeing massive surgical cuts or another huge Y-incision. There was no putting it off. I looked down at my chest.

A clean white bandage was wrapped around my middle. No blood was soaked through. Confused, I looked around and realized I was in my room.

I also noticed the Marine I'd seen earlier lounging in one of my chairs. He had a cigar in one hand and a glass of amber liquid sitting on the table by him.

"You do this?" I asked pointing at the bandage.

"Yep."

"Thanks."

"No worries," he said taking a puff on the cigar. "I figured saving you the bullshit of waking up all cut on would save you some sanity. And a trip to a shrink. What a waste of time that is."

I nodded in agreement. "While I do appreciate it, how'd you know I wasn't totally dead?"

He cocked an eyebrow at me. "You *were* totally dead. I just knew it wouldn't take."

"Oh?"

"Dreamed it." As if that were the only answer possible.

I looked at him a little closer and felt just the faintest hint of The Itch. He was touched by the supernatural. Barely, but touched even still. Who—or *what*—was he?

"I also saved this for you," he said. He reached forward and pulled an ID wallet off the table and tossed it to me. It was mine. "Came out of your pocket when you got killed. Says your name is Jarvis Tombs. I'm Diego Santos. Nice to meet you."

"Call me Lazarus. Or just Tombs. No one calls me Jarvis. And thanks again."

"Lazarus?" he asked with a smirk. "This 'death' thing happen before?"

"Twice." That wiped the smirk off his face. "Really, though, how'd you know I'd come back?"

"Told you. I dreamed it. Don't like repeating myself."

"Then clarify it for me," I said laying back down.

"Look, I know when I'm gonna die. To the minute. I've seen it coming in my dreams—a Vision—for years. And you're in my dream. You're there when I die. Good enough?"

He wasn't big on explanations, and I could think of one

hundred follow-up questions. I didn't bother even trying to ask them. I sighed and rubbed my face. I should just be happy that Santos had spared me the therapy.

"I gotta say though," he continued, "that's pretty crazy you not being able to stay dead. You're not a zombie, are you? That'd be some messed-up shit, and I'd probably have to shoot you in the head or something."

"Not a zombie," I said chuckling. It hurt, but in a good way that reminded me I was alive. I turned my head left to look at my son's picture.

The frame was there, but the picture was gone.

I jolted back up, hissing in pain, and grabbed the frame. I blinked a few times just to make sure I wasn't hallucinating. There were two black marks on the front of the frame, one on each side. Fingerprints burned into the frame. I flipped the frame over and saw corresponding marks for the rest of a person's hands. I lifted it closer to my face and sniffed the prints.

Sulfur.

Demon. Or someone that had summoned the demons.

"What's going on?" Santos asked.

"Someone—a demon or something—stole the picture of my son," I said. This was unbelievable. What if he was accidentally freed?

What if that was the reason why the picture had been stolen in the first place? To free my son. How powerful would he be?

"There was a girl who came out of your room when I was bringing you here," Santos said. "She had a picture in her hand. Thought she was your girl or something." He described her to me.

Helen Collins. She must have been one of the summoners. The pregnancy had just been a cover. When I investigated some more—and I'd go room by room if needed—I was sure I'd find one or two more of the bastards. I had a sudden vision of Frank Shields lifting a gun and shooting Santos. He must have been a summoner too.

"That was Helen Collins," I said, shaking my head. "She was one of the summoners along with the agent who shot at you. What did you do to him?"

Santos smiled. It was almost as frightening as the demons we'd killed. "Oh, you mean Shields? Didn't have my rifle. Had to improvise with a demon horn. Too bad you missed it."

"Yeah," I said. "Too bad." *Psycho*.

"I need to make a few calls," I said trying to stand. "My bosses need to know what went down here, and that they've been infiltrated. Who knows what else has been compromised?" I rubbed my eyes, exhausted. "And then I *need* to get that picture back." I was fuming inside. My son had been taken again. I'd *failed* him again.

The people that took my son were going to die for this.

All of them.

"I'd like to know what went down here too. Those were the same kind of demons from my Vision. In fact, they kill me in"—he looked at his watch—"two years, fifty-five days, twelve hours, and forty-two minutes. Give me the detailed version."

"It will take a while, and we'll have to talk on the move."

He smiled. "Tombs, for you, I have time."

I wanted to include this story because it was written really early in my career. Despite us both being total newbies, I think it came out pretty good. Steve and I ended up writing several Tombs and Santos stories over the next couple of years.

Earlier I talked about collaborations and how each one is different. Steve is super easy to work with. I originally met him when all I had published was my first novel, Monster Hunter International, and he interviewed me for his site Elitist Book Reviews. Back when I still had a day job, we ended up working together as accountants at the same defense contractor. Since then Steve has written several more shorts and the YA horror novel, Residue.

Currently, the two of us are collaborating on a new novel for Baen Books. Think WWI Eastern Front, in a world with dark fairy tale magic, so it's sort of a Trench Warfare Fantasy, where we are telling the story of a crew that goes into battle in a suit of magical power armor made out of dead golems.

EPISODE 22

This story originally appeared in Aliens: Bug Hunt, *edited by Jonathan Maberry, published by Titan Books, in 2017.*

This is set in the Aliens universe—which I've been a fan of since I was a little kid—and is about the adventures of the Colonial Marines. So in this collection I've already got an official story that I wrote for Predator, and now Aliens. If I ever write something for the Terminator franchise then I'll hit the ultimate 1980s trifecta. Since becoming a writer I've gotten to mess around with everything I thought was awesome from my childhood.

Considering there's actually a GI Joe character based on me—Spreadsheet, GI Joe's accountant—that's probably accurate!

I was the oddball writer in this particular anthology. Everybody else wanted to write about the Colonial Marines kicking ass and taking names, but as a gun nut I wanted to write about the real hero of the movie Aliens, *every gun guy's favorite sci-fi movie prop, the M41 Pulse Rifle. Having been a guest on a couple seasons of* Joe Mantegna's Gun Stories *on the Outdoor Channel, I had the perfect idea for how to tell that story too.*

Saga of the Weapon, Season 1, Episode 22
The M41A Pulse Rifle

THE M41A is one of the most successful combat rifles in history, and has become a potent symbol of American military might, not just on Earth, but into the furthest reaches of space. It has seen battle on every continent and dozens of worlds. It is beloved by those who use it, and feared by their enemies.

However the adoption of the Pulse Rifle was controversial, and the story of its evolution is filled with tragic errors that cost many Colonial Marines their lives.

Join us now as we discuss the history of the legendary M41A Pulse Rifle, on *Saga of the Weapon*.

There's nothing like the sound of a Pulse Rifle. It's like a maniac is running a jackhammer on a steel drum. That's the sound of freedom.

—Lance Corporal Chris Johnson, USCM

Today's Colonial Marine takes having a reliable and potent rifle for granted, but it wasn't always so. When the USCM was formed in 2101, their standard issue infantry weapon was the Harrington Automatic Rifle, with one Weyland Storm issued per squad.

Marines now don't realize how good they have it. Back in my day, you had basically two choices. Have a handy little rifle that ran slicker than snot—the HAR—but bounced its feeble little bullets off your enemies' body armor, or have a rifle that would put them down no matter what, but only when that complex hunk of junk wasn't broken down or hopelessly jammed because a speck of dirt got into the action. You ever pull the side plate off a Storm? It looks like an old-fashioned clock in there. When Marines talked about something working like clockwork, we sure as hell didn't mean the Storm.

—*Staff Sergeant Mike Willis, USCM*

Personally, back in the '60s I carried a HAR, because I'd rather know it would go bang every time I pulled the trigger, than have this super advanced killing machine that could track enemies across the battlefield from a satellite feed, but was so fickle that if you looked at it funny it would crash. Nothing sucks more than waiting for your rifle's operating system to reboot while a thousand Swedish insurgents are shooting at you.

—*Corporal Cheryl Clark, USCM*

After the battle of Kochan and the long campaign on Miehm, there was a clear need for a next-generation infantry weapon to arm the United States Colonial Marines. It needed to be rugged enough to survive the rigors of combat in a wide variety of planetary ecosystems, and fire a potent enough round that it could defeat newer forms of advanced body armor. The 6.8mm armor piercing round of the beloved HAR was simply too anemic, and the Storm was just too fragile. After many campaigns with inadequate equipment, the USCM put their foot down. Enough was enough.

I was there when General Phillips threw a fit in front of Space Command. He said that if his men were going to fight against the insurgents, what did he expect us to do?

Tickle them to death? Watching a bunch of four stars yell at each other was way over my pay grade, but it was a hell of a show.

 —Captain Trent Miller, USASF

The Marine 70 Program shook up everything, and small arms procurement was no exception. The commission that was created to study the need for new replacement weapon systems immediately met fierce resistance. The Weyland-Yutani Corporation filed a lawsuit, alleging that the Colonial Marines were simply misusing their Storm rifles, and it was their lack of following the proper maintenance guidelines that was causing the reliability issues.

Yeah ... Those pogues actually blamed us. Can you believe that? Abuse and neglect, they said. Guess what, you corpo-monkeys, this isn't a clean room at your factory. Proper maintenance kind of goes out the window when you've flown halfway across the galaxy, to be neck deep in blood and mud and guts for weeks, and have to beat a man to death with the butt of your rifle—seriously, who puts circuitry in a stock?—and the unit armorer is a little indisposed because he stepped on a land mine that morning. Well excuse me that I didn't have the proper factory-approved widget to fix it! At that point if a Marine can't fix it with a hammer and duct tape, it ain't going to get fixed.

 —Sergeant Mario Cordova, USCM

Ultimately, amid allegations of bribery, corruption, and blackmail, Weyland-Yutani dropped the lawsuit, and the new small arms appropriation committee got to work.

You know what they say about things designed by

committees, right? Well, that's where we were heading. You should have seen the original list of requirements. It was ridiculous. The specs weren't written by combatants. They were mostly wish lists from staff officers who'd never seen the inside of a drop ship unless it was parked at an air show, and specs inserted by lobbyists requiring gizmos that only their company happened to make. There were so many suggested bells and whistles screwed on that you'd need a wheelbarrow to carry the rifle.

—Construction Mechanic 1st Class Mike Raulston, USASF

It was a time for bold concepts. Many of the more advanced technological aspects proposed by the committee would later be incorporated into other weapon systems, such as the stabilization mechanism of the M56 Smart Gun, but it threatened to bog down the current rifle project in red tape.

However, there was a ray of hope. While various mega corporations were preparing their new weapon systems for trials, a retired Colonial Marine, Jonathan LaForce, was working on the prototype of the rifle that would become the legendary M41. By day he made ends meet running a food truck, but his nights were spent in his humble workshop. A distant cousin of legendary gun designer John Moses Browning (see *Saga of the Weapon*, episodes one, four, fifteen, and twenty) Corporal LaForce had served with distinction at Miehm, and knew firsthand the needs of the modern warfighter.

If you're a Marine, when you're saying your prayers, you better tell whoever it is you're talking to that you're thankful for LaForce. That man was a mechanical genius.

We're lucky he was a gun nut, and not into space ships or something. Sure . . . We'd have some awesome space ships, but my Pulse Rifle has saved my life more times than I can count. Thank Odin for Corporal LaForce.

—Gunnery Sergeant Aimee Morgan, USCM

LaForce started with the familiar layout of the HAR, utilizing an integrated pump-action grenade launcher, but the similarities end there. The sonic "shaker" burst weapons used by the rebels on Miehm to disable the Marines' HARs had shown the need for a firing mechanism that couldn't be disrupted by outside sources. So his new design started with a unique electronic pulse ignition.

This feature would go on to cause the M41As infamous nickname.

Pulse rifle isn't in the official designation, we all know that, but since it was a pulse that ignited the primer, the name just kind of stuck. Marines do that kind of thing. My great-great-whatever grandfather carried a Pig and his dad carried a Tommy Gun. It sounds cool, it works, it sticks. The problem with calling the M41 that name though is always some dumb boot hears we get issued pulse rifles and gets all excited thinking it's going to be shooting laser beams or something. What do they think this is? Sci-fi?

—Lance Corporal Tripp Dorsett, USCM

The specifications required the new weapon to use caseless ammunition, but this presented several challenges. LaForce believed that standard ammunition was a better choice, because sustained fire of caseless ammunition causes a rapid buildup of heat, which could cause stoppages or even premature parts breakage. In a rifle using standard brass-cased ammunition, the ejecting cartridge case serves as a heat sink, and some heat escapes through the ejection port. However, the committee specified all submissions had to be totally sealed from the elements. LaForce's solution to the overheating problem was using advanced materials for the internal mechanism, and ultramodern, cooler burning propellants for the ammunition.

LaForce was issued several new patents. Among them was the visionary rotating breach design, which not only cut felt recoil in half, but allowed the use of his new U Bend Conveyor magazines. This brilliant system made his weapon far more controllable than competing designs, even while using more powerful ammunition.

We had the best engineers in the business all competing to come up with a new gun, and some retired Marine, who doesn't even have an engineering degree, shows up to the trials with this cobbled-together piece of junk that looked like it got built in his garage. I found out later it literally was built in his garage. Here we were, the sharpest designers in the military industrial complex, all representing corporations with millions budgeted for R&D and marketing, and he walks up to the line like he belongs there, and pulls this ugly thing out of a case, and goes to town.

Phase one was just a demo shoot for some of the officers. No big deal. Until LaForce opens up with that beast. Everybody knows what a pulse rifle sounds like now, but this was new back then and we'd never heard anything like it before. Nothing gets your attention like the noise a pulse rifle makes. Every head on the range swiveled in that direction.

He'd chambered it in 12mm Darnall, a monster of an old caseless hunting round that can shoot through a genetically modified rhino, just to prove that he could. Show-off. This thing was shooting bigger bullets and more of them, with less recoil and still shooting better groups than every million dollar prototype on the line ... It blew our socks off.

The competitors found out later that LaForce hadn't been invited by the committee at all, but had snuck into the initial test firing. He'd saved the life of one of the Marine testers during the battle of Kochan and had called in a favor to get onto the range as an "observer." I had gone to MIT and spent thirty years designing firearms on the most advanced CAD programs in the Solar System, and there were twenty others like me there, but we all got our butts kicked by a hobbyist whose day job was selling barbeque.

—Michael Ankenbrandt, Daihotai Engineering

LaForce had the clearly superior design, but no ability to manufacture it. After a demonstration where the prototype was frozen in mud, and then fired six thousand rounds without a single malfunction, LaForce received an official invitation to the competition. He was also approached by several of the competing arms manufacturers and offered huge sums of money for his patents. Surprisingly, he refused them all, declaring at the time that he was in it to help his brother Marines, not to get rich. At the time there were even rumors of an attempted break-in at LaForce's workshop to steal the prototype, followed by an attempt at deliberate sabotage, all of which was blamed on—and vehemently denied by— Weyland-Yutani.

With a working prototype in hand, and USCM interest in his design, LaForce approached Armat. The once-respected company had fallen on hard financial times, yet retained a reputation for never skimping on quality, and always doing its best to support the soldiers it supplied. Luckily for LaForce, Armat, and America, this would prove to be a match made in heaven.

If you look at the history of small arms development, what came first, cartridge or rifle, is usually a chicken or the egg kind of proposal. Sometimes you design a platform to fire an existing cartridge to spec, other times you have the weapon system and you shoehorn in the best round you can fit. This time we got lucky. As LaForce was designing his Pulse Rifle, Armat had been making some real breakthroughs in chemical engineering and projectile materials. This allowed us to really push the boundaries of terminal ballistics.

Our new experimental 10mm × 24 caseless approximated the ballistics of the old .300 Winchester Magnum sniper round in a far shorter and lighter package, with a bullet that could penetrate most modern body armor, and an explosive payload inside that would absolutely wreck whatever was hit. The issue was that it produced too much recoil energy to control on full auto in an assault weapon-sized package, so we were primarily marketing it for crew-served weaponry. When LaForce came to us with a light rifle platform that could easily handle the recoil of our new experimental 10mm round, our executives bet the

*future of the company on manufacturing the Pulse Rifle.
The rest is history.*

—Mordechai Yitzhak, Armat Technician

Armat was able to utilize more advanced materials for
the next prototypes, which drastically lowered the weight,
while also increasing the already impressive durability.
Their new propellant compounds were able to decisively
solve the LaForce prototype's greatest weakness—heat
dissipation. The Armat rifle easily won the rest of the
competition, passing all tests with flying colors. The newly
designated M41 was put into production, and entered
service with the Colonial Marines in 2171.

However, all was not well. Some of the early batches
of 10mm ammunition were subcontracted out to other
manufacturers. It is unknown who changed the propellant
design, and later congressional inquiries never discovered
the culprit, but regardless of who was at fault, this mistake
cost Colonial Marines their lives, and gave the early
production M41s a bad reputation.

(Warning, the following footage from LV-832 is
intended for mature audiences only. Viewer discretion is
advised.)

*It was a nightmare. All of the wild life on LV-832 is gross,
mean, and cranky, but the colonists there were hard as
nails. You had to be to survive that shithole. There is only
one thing they ever needed to call in Marine support to deal
with, and that was a swarm. There's this one species,
imagine a carnivorous moose-sized critter with tentacles
instead of antlers. Individually, not so dangerous. Only it
turns out that every seven years they have a population
explosion, swarm, and eat everything like locusts.*

My platoon was supposed to protect this one settlement on LV-832 during the swarm. No problem. We're in a fortified position. We've got these fancy new Pulse Rifles. Just stupid alien animals. Nothing we can't handle. Right?

Then we heard the thunder. It was like ten million hooves on the rock, and this ... wave. That's the only word. Just a wave of angry green flesh comes rolling down the mountain at us. It was far worse than the projections. Corporal Richards was our forward observer. He died horribly, trampled into bloody chunks in seconds.

We opened up with everything. Our only hope was to carve a hole in that wave of meat, to pile up enough dead to make a wall.

But then our Pulse Rifles started to choke. Only the swarm kept coming.

—1st Lieutenant Hank Reynolds, USCM

The horrific incident on LV-832 was not isolated. Wherever the improperly formulated ammunition was shipped, problems occurred. As the weapons would begin to heat up, the propellant would expand and stick, causing malfunctions. Or worse, cook off prematurely and detonate inside the conveyor magazines, often with catastrophic results.

You ever see what a 10mm explosive round does to a man? It penetrates a bit then explodes. The secondary wound channels are nasty. You can stick a softball into the hole. Yeah ... Real nasty. Oh, we love them now. But back in '71, imagine having that same explosive round cook off inside your rifle, right next to your face. Or worse, I heard about one dude where his Pulse Rifle cooked off, and it caused a sympathetic detonation with his grenade launcher. Marines were scared of their own rifles. Some of the guys took to carrying short-barreled shotguns on them for when things got close.

—*Lance Corporal Daniel Walker, USCM*

Rumors began to swirl of Colonial Marines found dead on the battlefield, with their Pulse Rifles disassembled, killed while desperately trying to clear a stoppage.

To their credit, Armat did not try to pass the buck. Instead, they sprang into action, discovered the cause, alerted Space Command, and tried to track down the bad lots of ammunition. By the time the hearings began, the M41 was working as intended. However, the bad reputation lingered in line units for quite some time, and the topic is still hotly debated among gun enthusiasts today.

Design changes were immediately instituted to make the M41 less ammunition-sensitive and more cooling vents were added to the shell. The integrated digital ammo counter was given a dimmer switch, because Marines had taken to covering the early versions with masking tape to avoid giving away their position during low light maneuvers. This variant was designated the M41A, which remains the standard issue rifle of the US Army and Colonial Marines to this day.

With the bugs worked out, the M41A began to earn a different kind of reputation.

Our Cheyenne hit the hot LZ like a meteor. There were so many missiles and so much flak that the night sky was lit up like the Fourth of July. Before the skids had touched ground we already had tracers coming in from three directions. We lost two men before we could even unass the transport. Our APC ate a rocket and we lost our lieutenant. The DeLorme rebels were ready for us, dug in, and itching for a fight.

My platoon's orders were to take and hold the main plaza on the coastal platform. We encountered fierce resistance every step of the way. They were well funded. Most of the rebels were wearing top of the line carbon-weave armor, but our Pulse Rifles punched them anyway. Then the DeLorme Corporate Security Teams were wearing these heavy, servo assisted, armor suits. Tank boys we called them. Right hard bastards, every one of them. Except, even when our 10mm bullets failed to penetrate the plates, the impact and micro-explosions were enough to throw them off long enough for my Marines to close and finish them off through the rubberized gaps at their joints. The muzzle doesn't climb much, and the M41 is so acute, we'd just hammer the tank boys until we pierced something vulnerable and they dropped.

It was street to street, house to house. We'd catch sniper fire from a window, launch a grenade through it, and keep moving. We reached the plaza, and found out that we were it. Nobody else had made it through the drop. We had to hold that position or the whole mission would fold.

The battle went on all night, and the rebels kept throwing everything they had at us. We shot our Pulse Rifles until the muzzles were glowing orange, and they never stopped, never jammed, not so much as a hiccup. Cheyennes were doing high-speed flybys and dropping crates of U Mags and grenades on us so we could stay in the fight.

That was the first time I used an M41A. It didn't let me

down then, and it has never let me down since. After DeLorme, I've taken a Pulse Rifle to every godforsaken planetoid, orbital, moon, backwater colony, and bug hunt you can think of. I've used it in zero G. I've used it underwater. Polar wastes to burning sands, abuse it, drop it, burn it, and the M41A won't ever quit on you.

The Pulse Rifle is the only rifle tough enough for a Colonial Marine.

—Staff Sergeant Michael Newman, USCM

The M41A has gone on to earn the respect of every warrior who has used it ... or faced it. This mechanical marvel has taken its place in history as one of the finest combat rifles ever fielded. The Pulse Rifle is known for going anywhere, doing anything, and accomplishing the impossible. Seldom has a weapon so encapsulated the bold, unstoppable nature of the men it is issued to, as the M41A Pulse Rifle.

This has been *Saga of the Weapon*.

V-WARS: ABSENCE OF LIGHT

This story first appeared in the anthology V-Wars: Night Terrors, *edited by Jonathan Maberry, published by IDW Publishing in 2016.*

The V-Wars series is about a virus which reappears and spreads across the world, reawakening latent DNA and turning people into vampires, and the resulting war between mankind and the vampires. It is currently being filmed for a show on Netflix. This is the second story that I wrote in that series. The first appears in Target Rich Environment Volume 1.

THE MOB PUSHED and screamed and chanted their slogans, stinking of sweat, adrenaline, and excitement. The air was moist from recent rain evaporating off of sweatshirts and hoodies, and hot from hundreds of packed-in bodies. Marko and his vampires passed between the protestors, and the hardest thing in the world was not killing them all.

These humans are nominally on our side. These are the useful idiots. Killing them—now—would be a waste of resources. Marko had ordered his men to hurt as few of the protestors during the op as possible. He'd had to beat that lesson into his soldiers. Some of his men were more feral than others, so in a few cases, the beating had been literal. Some of his recruits struggled with the concept of discipline.

The street was absolutely full of bodies. Most of them were young, impressionable and passionate. The ones who were showing their faces thought they could make a difference, naively believing their slogans, hash tags, and painted cardboard signs were going to change the world. The protestors hiding their identities were just eager to break shit. From the smell he could tell that some of their backpacks contained all the fixings to make Molotov cocktails. So far the masked hooligans were behaving themselves. The broken glass and burning cars would come later. The day belonged to the activists. The looters believed the night belonged to them . . . In reality it belonged to the vampires, and as tempting as it was to show these idiots who was really in charge, a riot made one hell of a good distraction.

The other side of the street was a sea of flashing red and blue lights. Seattle PD had learned their lesson about protests a few times over the last decade, and that was before I1V1 kicked societal order in the balls. The cops were ready behind batons and shields, tear gas launcher and pepper balls. If it weren't for all of the news crews recording the *peaceful protest* the street would already be filled with gas. The cops and the looters both knew what was coming next, but there were *rules* to the fall of an empire. If the forces of law and order jumped the gun, morons would rant on Twitter, politicians would feign outrage, and a bureaucrat somewhere might be inconvenienced. Pretenses had to be kept up. So the street-level decision makers would be forced to coddle the mob until the situation spiraled out of control, turned into a complete cluster fuck, and then overreact to contain it. That was the yin and yang of riot control.

All those years the government had spent training him how to overthrow governments, and Marko had never realized just how entertaining it would be to screw with his own. Before he had turned, Marko had been Army Special Forces. His job had been to train and lead indigenous forces behind enemy lines. *Force multiplication*, they called it. Now he was training vampires. He'd collected these individual predators and molded them into a real unit. Same tactics, new war.

One of his vampires appeared at his side. Even with the bandanna covering his face, he could tell it was Basco just from how smoothly he moved between the humans. Basco had been a tough bastard when he was still human. Making him bloodthirsty and fast as lightning had only made him an even better soldier. "In my country, we'd run a belt-fed across a mob like this. A hundred rounds and problem solved."

"Where's the fun in that?"

His vampires were wired, tense and ready. They were hungry. Not just for blood—he'd kept their feeding to a minimum so as to not tip off the local authorities—but for action. They'd been planning this op for weeks, ever since word of the vaccine experiments had leaked. The news conference this morning had simply bumped up their timeline. The protestors had already been here anyway. His men had already been working the locals and stirring up the radical elements, so it hadn't taken much of a push to get the riot kiddies fired up. His people had been bussing them in all day.

Marko was wearing a black hoodie and a plastic Guy Fawkes mask. The irony of a bunch of lefty atheists using a Catholic fanatic as their symbol caused him no end of amusement, but he was guessing there weren't a lot of War College grads in this bunch. He needed the mask because the NSA was certain to be running facial recognition programs against the footage. As a bonus the hood hid his radio headset. "Target is in sight."

The Iwashiro building didn't look that impressive. It was just another plain old office cube. The real prize was inside. There were a hundred medical research companies looking for the Holy Grail but if the rumors were true, Iwashiro Biomedical had been making real progress on understanding the vampire virus—mostly because they had zero ethics—and according to this morning's press conference, they'd made a real breakthrough.

"Sniper is in position."

"Breaching team is in position."

Every mutation was different. Some of his best soldiers couldn't operate well in the sunlight, so they'd move once the sun was safely behind the buildings to the west. At the same time his kill teams would start taking out vital employees who hadn't come to work today because of the

protests. If everything went according to plan, by the end
of the night the technology to produce a screener would
be in vampire hands, and every human who understood
how to make more would be dead. "Assault team, blend
in and wait for my signal. We've got sundown in thirty."

The angry mob was here because Iwashiro had been
caught doing illegal experiments on vampire *volunteers*.
Some girls wearing duct tape over their mouths—
symbolic of who knew what—went marching past, waving
signs that declared *VAMPIRES ARE PEOPLE TOO*.

Marko smiled behind his mask. *No . . . We're so much
better.*

"Look at all those hippies."

"Just try not to run any of them over, Solo," Matt Kovac
told their driver.

"General May hates when I run over civilians. Look at
all that flannel. I can't tell if they're homeless or college
students." He honked the horn as twenty people
jaywalked in front of them. Somebody threw a beer can
at their car and it bounced off the hood. "You little son of
a bitch!"

"Be cool, man. It's a rental. It's on the company card."

"It's the principle of the thing," Solo muttered as the
kids flipped them the bird, but eventually they meandered
out of the way so he could keep driving. "Big Dog's team
gets to pop tangos while we have to grade rent-a-cops.
Fantastic. Hang on, police checkpoint ahead."

Toolbox was in the backseat. He leaned forward to see
better. "Cops are diverting traffic like it's a parade or
something. Can you believe this nonsense, Show?"

Kovac didn't like his call sign, but Showdown had stuck. Get in one Mexican standoff with a crazy vampire, and pretty soon everybody in V-8 was telling exaggerated stories about it, but as a new team leader, it had helped establish cred with the vets. It usually got shortened to Show for brevity's sake.

V-8 was the military's elite special response unit for vampire problems. Their personnel were some of the finest operators available, recruited from every branch of the service. Kovac had been Army SF himself, following in his deceased father's footprints. It wasn't until after he'd been with V-8 for a while that he'd learned his father wasn't exactly *deceased*.

"Pull over there."

The four of them were out of uniform—rocking the business casual as Solo put it—and driving a Honda. Normally when V-8 rolled up on a site, they were hard to miss—what with the armored vehicles and top-end military gear—but the General had told them to be discreet today. If Kovac had realized that the streets were going to be filled with cops in helmets, face shields, and vests, they'd have brought their fun stuff. It was a sad comment on the state of the world that they wouldn't have stuck out that much.

Kovac rolled his window down and showed his ID to the police officers on the corner. "How's it going, Officer?"

"Mostly vandalism and graffiti so far but they're just getting warmed up," the cop said as he read the card. Behind him, a stoned white guy dressed in tie-dyed clothing and sporting dreadlocks was trying to put a peace sign bumper sticker on the cop car's windshield. "Aw, stop that! You guys go through. My boss said to expect you. Head that way."

The cops moved a wooden barricade and waved them through. Solo drove between a SWAT van and an MRAP, honking so that the riot squad would get out of his way. They got some surly glances from the other side of those Lexan face shields. They could see a lot more of the protestors now, and Kovac was surprised to see how damned many of them there were.

"Glad that's not our problem," Kovac muttered.

People were milling around in groups and the atmosphere was charged. The rumble of crowd noise was overwhelming. Iwashiro Biomedical had been working on a vaccine for I1V1, which just about every sane person would agree was a good thing, but if people could throw a fit about animal testing, they got downright pissed when a company got caught illegally testing drugs on vampires.

"Today's lesson is if you're going to do stupid shit, don't get caught!" Solo exclaimed.

"Like these assholes care about the civil rights of vampires. Okay, maybe the chicks do, but there are two kinds of guys who come to things like this," Toolbox explained. "The ones who are trying to impress the activist girls so they can get laid, and the ones who want to break a window and get a free TV . . . Mute here was an observer in Libya with me. Those protests were sure different than this, huh?"

Mute spoke for the first time since they'd left the airport. "More AK-47s."

"Yeah, and not so many pussies sporting anarchy symbols."

Since it was the focal point of the protestors' outrage, the cops had formed around the front of the Iwashiro building. The police here didn't know who they were, but their car had been let through, so that was good enough to make a hole for them to pass.

"Weak-ass metal fence around the perimeter. Couple of decorative concrete planters would stop a car bomb from getting right under the facing," Solo said as he gave the place the once-over. "Not exactly impressed on first glance. A little bit of creative landscaping would make this place a lot harder to crash . . . and make it look nicer too. My dad's a landscaper. I should give them his card."

Inside the visitor parking lot was a little guard shack manned by rent-a-cops. The glass wasn't even thick enough to be bullet resistant. The guards inside looked nervous and distracted, which was understandable since there were a few thousand people a couple hundred yards away who thought their employer was the capitalist antichrist. "What's your business here?"

He held up his ID. "Captain Matthew Kovac, Vampire Counterinsurgency and Counterterrorism Field Team. You should be expecting us."

"The Army guys?"

"I'm Navy, but I let them hang out with me," Toolbox said quietly enough the guard wouldn't hear.

"That's us."

The guard pushed a button and the flimsy bar lifted. It was the kind of thing kids could push out of the way when they didn't want to pay for parking. Solo drove up to the front of the building and parked. "Can you believe that? A laminated ID card I could make at Kinko's gets us right in without question. The General was smart to send us to review their security, because this place sucks."

"Be diplomatic," Kovac warned as he stepped out of the car. The four of them started toward the entrance. "It's their invention. We just need to make sure they're smart about keeping it safe until it's ready for release. The military isn't officially here. This is a completely civil matter. We're only supposed to assess."

"If they've actually got a working V screener somebody should declare the whole place a national security risk and take it over," Toolbox suggested. "Nobody else has gotten a test to work yet. Can't we just say it's a public health emergency or something?"

"That's over my pay grade. Once the government gets its shit together I'm sure they'll buy the thing, and if not, it'll go to court and the lawyers can fight. General May told me these guys are big donors with lots of Congress friends, so play it cool. He offered to protect it, but the best he could talk them into without a court order was allowing some advisors."

Two men in suits were waiting to greet them at the entrance. Kovac took one last glance back at the protestors. Most of them looked like they were attending a concert, but there were a few knots of them that made his instincts tingle. He'd often felt like that back in Afghanistan, rolling through a village, getting the eyeball from some of the locals that said *you are not wanted here*, and as soon as you were out of the way those were the ones who were planting IEDs. Some of those kids were giving him that exact same vibe now.

Three men in white masks and black hoods were

standing toward the front of the mob, arms folded, watching, too still compared to the excitement swirling around them, and Kovac felt the hairs on his arms stand up. A group moved between them, waving red flags, and when they passed, the men in the white masks were gone.

"You can tell that's your son. He looks just like you," Gregor said.

"Yeah, regular chip off the old block." It wasn't a surprise. He'd figured V-8 would get involved, and he'd known Matthew was working in this area. Marko keyed his radio as he moved smoothly through the masses. "We've got pros in the building. At least four. Plainclothes."

May's elite V-8 troops were no joke. They were recruited from the best, and his old friend had done a good job staffing his special unit with the type of get-the-job-done hard asses who wouldn't get unnerved by little things like fighting creatures straight out of nightmares. It hadn't exactly been a shock to find out that his son had gone to work as a vampire killer. He'd always been a pretty straightforward good-versus-evil, protect-the-innocent type idealist, even as a little boy.

Now, somebody with even a scrap of human empathy would have kicked Matthew from his anti-vampire unit once he discovered his father had turned vampire, but General May wasn't the type to let some little thing like personal bonds or family history stand in the way of using the right trigger puller for the job.

"You want to abort the mission?"

If they could steal the screener technology it would be

a powerful recruiting tool for their new army. He'd heard that the Red Court had already paid to get backdoor access to every DNA database in the world just in case. Far more importantly, the humans couldn't be allowed to have such a weapon. If they could know for certain who among them was destined to become a vampire, there would be no more recruits. The vampires who could still pass as humans would all get caught. They would lose their spies and insiders. Their race would be driven to extinction once again.

"Negative. Stick to the plan." He checked his watch. Sundown was in twenty-five minutes.

Gregor was following him. The big vampire was eyeing some of the pretty girls hungrily. He'd not fed for a while, and his kind had an insatiable appetite. "With May's people here, you think it's a trap?"

"If it is, we'll make them regret it."

"What about your kid?"

That was a good question. Ever since his transformation, when Marko looked for that place where his feelings used to be, there was only a dark empty hole. He had loved his boy. Hell, he'd doted on him. Matthew had emulated his father and tried to follow in his footsteps. Seeing his son wearing the same uniform had been the proudest moment of his life. At the end of his mortal existence when he'd been chained and beaten, and the Syrians had begun to saw off his head, the last thing he'd thought of was his family. Only instead of dying, he'd turned, and never looked back.

When Marko thought of his family now there was *nothing*.

"The mission comes first."

The review wasn't going well.

"You're a security expert? Have you ever fought vampires, Mr. Cook?"

The head of security for Iwashiro Biomedical hadn't been expecting to get grilled this hard this fast, and was stumbling badly. "We had five volunteers here during the early testing phase and I was in charge of managing—"

"Not managed. I'm sure you're a fantastic zookeeper. I said *fought*."

"Well, no. I haven't, though one of our subjects did become unruly as a result of the drugs and caused some trouble, but as you can see outside, we're working in close conjunction with local law enforcement. Between the police presence and our employees, we have a very secure facility."

Kovac had only been talking to this corporate goon for a few minutes and he was already running dangerously low on patience. He could have stormed this facility with a crack team of Girl Scouts. "I don't think you realize that as of this morning's press conference, your company declared it has something that every vampire supremacist in the world wants. You've dealt with volunteers desperate enough for a cure that they'll let you do all sorts of things to them, but trust me, there are plenty of vampires out there who see your research as the effective end of their species, and they'll do whatever it takes to stop it."

"I've been doing this for years and think we're—"

Kovac cut him off. Tagging in Solo was dangerous, because he tended to be colorful in his descriptions, but it needed to be said. "Sergeant Gonzalez, what do you do for a living?"

"I kill motherfucking vampires, sir."

"And what did you do before that?"

"I went to places that supposedly had good security, killed the people there and took their stuff on behalf of the United States Army. I was extremely good at it, sir."

"In your professional opinion, are vampires much like regular security risks?"

"No, sir."

"How would you assess Iwashiro Biomedical's security against a potential organized vampire threat?"

"Woefully fucking inadequate."

"Well, there you go." Kovac leaned back in his chair. "That's pretty close to the assessment I'm going to give to General May, which he'll pass along to the President."

They hadn't even gotten a real tour. They'd been taken right past the entrance to the labs holding the sensitive goodies and upstairs to a conference room where they'd sat down with the CEO and his right-hand man. Cook was obviously proud of his handful of low paid, barely trained, just-over-minimum-wage security guards with their .38 Specials in nylon flap holsters and Fisher-Price My First Walkie Talkie level communication system, but Kovac's standards were a bit higher when it came to protecting one of the most important discoveries in history.

The conference room probably would have had a good view of the street, but they'd pulled the curtains. It was dark out there, light in here, and some chump in the crowd might have been tempted to pop off a few rounds at the enemy. Other than the security guards, the place was nearly deserted. Everyone who could stay home to avoid the protests had done so, except the CEO had proudly told them that the scientists vital to the screener and vaccine projects were still downstairs, bravely working away for the good of mankind, despite the danger outside. That might have sounded great on a press release, but Kovac didn't like having all of their vulnerable eggs in one basket.

Dr. Iwashiro was younger than expected for a CEO, probably only in his mid-thirties. Kovac had watched the morning's press conference on YouTube on the ride over. During that, Iwashiro had mentioned inheriting the company from his father. The CEO had struck him as somebody who was trying to overcompensate to get out of his father's shadow. Being the son of a legend and working in the same field was tough—Kovac got that better than anyone—but that didn't justify taking stupid risks. A few hours ago this man had rocked the world, yet now Iwashiro was listening intently as his security chief was being eviscerated. So far he was playing it close to the vest, and Kovac couldn't tell what he was thinking.

"If you won't accept our protection, at least let us provide a full security workup, Dr. Iwashiro. We understand the potential threats you face. We all come from special operations backgrounds."

"What did you do before becoming vampire experts?"

Vampires were so damned new and odd that he didn't think anyone actually qualified as an *expert*. Luther Swann maybe, as that dude was a walking encyclopedia of vampire trivia, but even then he was wrong half the time. "Gonzalez and I are both Army Special Forces and Morris is a SEAL."

"What's he?" the CEO nodded toward where Mute was sitting. The tall, thin man hadn't bothered to pull up a chair at the conference table, but instead was sitting on a couch by the windows, surfing the internet on a tablet.

"It's so classified you don't even want to know," Kovac said.

"James Bond-level shit," Solo suggested.

"We can also bring in information security experts to prevent outside sabotage." Iwashiro Biomedical had a good IT department. He knew that because General May already had his guys at the NSA working on breaking into their files. But they'd be more interested in stopping corporate espionage. Kovac was worried about the research being destroyed rather than stolen. As a man who'd seen firsthand the horrors of vampirism, he'd love to see the screener technology leaked far and wide. Screw Iwashiro's bottom line, he wanted vampirism eradicated like smallpox.

"I truly appreciate your offer, gentlemen, but this is *my* company. General May was rather demanding on the phone. I believe in cooperation, but you can see why I'd be hesitant to accept your help. Some of my advisors think that V-8 is overstating the danger of some sort of threat in order to gain access to my company's research."

"We've got ninety-nine bombings that disagree with your advisors," Toolbox said. "And that's just the stuff you've seen on TV."

"Yes, of course. Coordinated vampire terrorism, and stopping that, justifies *everything*."

Kovac made an honest plea. "I can't share details about national security risks, but there are groups of vampires out there who are far more organized than anyone in the media suspects. Some extremely knowledgeable people have turned." As he said that, Solo and Toolbox gave him a curious look. Everybody on the Field Teams knew about Showdown's dad, but none of them liked to talk about him. "Some of these have been organizing and training cells. Their skillset makes them extremely dangerous."

Iwashiro gave him a patronizing smile. "Oh, I'm sure they are, but since we're on the topic of vampires, there's that old bit of folklore about how they can't come into your home unless invited. Today, we know that's a myth for vampires, but it has been my experience that it is true for the government. This is my house, gentlemen. Not General May's."

The CEO sure was a smug little bastard.

"Look, I'll level with you. I hope you make billions off your screener. I hope you spend the rest of your life sleeping on a giant pile of money in a house made out of gold bars. I just want to make sure the screener is kept safe. I can have the rest of my team here in a few hours and we can get this place locked down."

The head of security came back for more. "We've already got a secure facility. No one is going to try anything when there are hundreds of cops right outside."

"And in a few days when the protestors get bored and go home, the cops will go away, and then a vampire could walk right in here."

"You can't enter without scanning a badge!" Cook was getting upset. It was a good indicator of a man's lack of professionalism when every pointed-out flaw was taken as a personal insult.

"They aren't exactly vault doors!" Solo exclaimed.

Toolbox grinned. "If it was me, I'd just follow an employee up to the door, let them swipe it with their badge, then shoot them."

Solo wasn't about to be outdone. "Or, hell, take out an employee at home and steal their badge!"

"Our employees' personal information is kept private," Cook retorted.

Mute cleared his throat and held up his tablet. It was easy to forget he was even in the room. "Yeah, about that, I just got all of your employees' names and home addresses while we've been sitting here. Your HR director really needs to do something about his Wi-Fi settings."

"Holy shit, you people suck at this," Solo muttered.

Marko watched the sun disappear. It was remarkable how few vampires were actually light sensitive. *The movies got everything wrong.* "Execute phase one."

Bringing in agitators to rile up crowds and incite riots had been part of asymmetrical warfare since they'd invented the concept. Marko had agents placed throughout the crowd, some vampires, but most were easily duped or paid-off humans. It started simply enough, with windows shattering across several blocks and greedy morons rushing into stores to steal things. The smarter humans in the herd realized that the channel had just been flipped to a different station and tried to get the hell out of the way. The stupid got stuck in the middle, but even the panicked ones were useful meat shields and noisemakers. By the time the rocks and bottles started raining on the cops, the riot had begun in earnest.

Killing the power had been a no-brainer, and any big city grid had its exploitable vulnerabilities. Remote detonation took out a few choice lines and five minutes after the first cop needed stitches from a brick to the face, half the lights in downtown Seattle were out. They could still see though, because by then some cars had been helpfully set on fire, and the flickering orange light and spreading smoke really added to the ambiance.

All around them, angry youths rushed forward, hurling things at the cops. No Molotovs yet though. That was a downer. Marko had paid good money to have Molotovs here. The cops formed up in ranks, shoulder to shoulder, a wall of Kevlar and muscle, and they started forward, like a comparatively gentle, politically-correct Roman legion.

Brave or drugged-up rioters rushed the line, kicking at the shields. Screaming and taunting, dancing around and hurling balloons filled with piss.

And they said vampires were savage . . .

"I love this stuff," Marko told Gregor and Basco. He could tell that both of his lieutenants were feeling the bloodlust too. They wanted to jump in there and start taking heads and drinking from necks like fountains. "Easy, boys. We'll feast tonight."

The cops turtled their way up, shields raised against the falling debris. He could hear the *thunk-thunk* of projectiles bouncing off of plastic. They were wearing their gas masks but they'd not started firing canisters yet. They were probably hoping for a quick clash and break to arrest the troublemakers, and then everybody could go home without any exciting news footage of downtown being gassed.

The main bodies clashed. The Seattle PD must have been drilling a lot, because they kept their formations and did a great job of rotating men in and out as their arms got tired. Groups of cops would part ranks, allowing another squad to rush through, surround some of the really unruly troublemakers, drag them down, cuff them, and drag them out of the fray. They must have had some good leaders in there keeping order. Marko picked out the guy calling the shots and keyed his radio. "These cops are too calm. Sniper team, up the fear. Your target is the tall black guy giving orders at the front of the MRAP. Don't kill him though. I want some screaming."

"Roger that."

Their shooters were hidden in the surrounding buildings, sitting back inside the rooms a bit so they wouldn't be spotted by the police snipers on the opposite rooftops, just like he'd taught them. The suppressed rifle was so quiet that there was no way anyone would hear it over the chaos in the street, but the cop fell over, blood spraying, as the .308 round tore through his knee. Marko had seen plenty of limb hits like that. The bone blew up like a grenade, fragments making all sorts of secondary wound channels. It would probably need to be amputated, but Marko had to hand it to the cop. Other than one quick bellow of shock, he stayed calm, put pressure on it, and began calling for a medic, probably a fellow combat vet. Luckily some of the cops around him weren't as cool, and they started freaking out. By the time they'd dragged the wounded cop behind the armored vehicle, the SWAT cops were looking to blast the shooter, and somebody else had given the order to fire tear gas.

Then flaming bottles of gasoline were tossed toward the line, most shattering in the street, but a couple hit the cops. Those who'd come prepared had melted Styrofoam packing peanuts into the gasoline until it had gained the consistency of jelly. It was poor man's napalm, and that stuff stuck to riot shields and flesh, melting either rather easily.

"About damned time. Breaching team, you have one minute. Move. Assault team, kit up and execute on my signal." Marko and his men unslung their packs, knelt, and began getting their gear ready.

The 37mm tear gas rounds hit the pavement, bouncing, sparking, and spitting. A noxious haze drifted through the street. The stupid humans who hadn't got out of the way in time really began to panic when they suddenly couldn't see or breathe right. A few fools were knocked down and trampled. By the time the gas washed over the hidden vampires, those who were still vulnerable to such things had already pulled on their own gas masks. The rest were taking out firearms, unfolding stocks, and racking charging handles.

Between the flickering fire, the spreading smoke, and the fog of gas, visibility was awful. A constant roar of shouting, screaming, and cursing filled the street. Nobody would see or hear them make their move, and if they did, by the time a response was organized they'd already be gone.

"Breaching team is in the truck."

He knew he couldn't bring up his own vehicle to ram the door with a protest in the way, so he'd had his stealthiest troops sneak into the Iwashiro parking lot last week to check the vehicles that were already there. They'd had plenty of time to make their own keys. The nice thing about being prepared was that even when your timeline got moved up, a professional was ready to handle it.

The cops were pushing forward too fast now. Those that heard one of their own had just taken a bullet had started cracking skulls. The rioters reciprocated and now they had a good old-fashioned slugfest on their hands. The law was pulling away from the target building and leaving gaps in their lines. *Wait for it* . . . Marko watched the whole beautiful thing unfold until all of the angles were right.

"Execute, execute, execute."

Ten vampires set out toward their target and no one even saw them coming.

When the lights had gone out, Mute had pulled back the curtains to take a look outside. His voice was eerily calm as he warned them, "We've got incoming."

There was a crash below them that shook the whole building.

"What was that?" Iwashiro shouted as the four men from V-8 drew their guns. Cook fell out of his chair and hid under the desk. When normal people hear a big bang, their first reaction is surprise, and then puzzlement. In Kovac's line of work it was assess and prepare to return fire.

Mute had his forehead to the glass and was peering down. "They rammed the front door with a truck."

Toolbox looked at Solo, as if embarrassed that he'd not mentioned that method of getting in. "I guess that works too!"

If it had been a car bomb, they'd already be dead. That meant they were about to raid the lab. "Box, call it in, then you and Mute take the north stairs. Me and Solo will take south." They had to counterattack, break the momentum. Time was of the essence. Any delay and the attackers would have to retreat because there were a whole lot of reinforcements nearby. He turned to Iwashiro. "Have your security protect the lab and get the civilians out of here. Let's move."

"Told you so," Solo spat at Iwashiro as they left. The lights came back on within seconds. It made sense that a building that did sensitive medical research had a good backup power generator. They rushed past a handful of confused employees, to the stairs and down, taking whole sets at a time. It was hell on the ankles, but riding an elevator into a potential gunfight was a great way to make yourself the proverbial fish in a barrel. They reached the main floor and headed toward the entrance.

Kovac took cover at a corner and risked a quick peek down the hall. A single headlight was visible through the dust swirling around the broken wall. The guards who'd been posted there had been hit and were lying on the ground, partially crushed by the debris. Solo moved up behind him. "If we're really lucky, that was just a stupid car accident and we'll all laugh at it over beers later." Someone began screaming and it took a moment for Kovac to realize that there was a guard stuck beneath the truck. Solo started to move up, but Kovac signaled for him to hold.

There was a *chuff* of a suppressed gunshot, and the screaming stopped.

"So much for beers," Solo whispered.

There was a lot of movement around the wreck. A man moved in front of the headlight, crouched with a stubby rifle at his shoulder. Before he could ID him as friend or foe, the man put a round into one of the unconscious bodies lying on the floor. *That would be foe.* Kovac leaned out, centered the front sight of the Sig M11 on the man's chest and pulled the trigger. Solo fired a split second later. The man went sideways, hit the wall, but stayed up. He saw them, opened a mouth full of jagged shark teeth and screeched something incomprehensible. They opened up, striking him repeatedly, but he didn't go down.

"Vest!" Kovac warned, but by the time he could sight on his head, Solo had blown the vampire's brains out. That did the trick.

More vampires around the truck began flinging rounds their way. Solo hung his M9 around the corner and cranked off several more shots. The headlight went out. Then Kovac took a turn just as a vampire moved up behind the reception desk. He put a couple 9mm rounds into the wood and was rewarded with a surprised yelp from the other side. That slowed them for a second, but then the vampires came back shooting. Their heavier rounds zipped right through the walls. One of them was on full auto and Kovac had to pull back as several rounds pulverized his corner into dust and splinters.

He heard crashing, fearful cries, and more suppressed shooting. Some attackers must have entered before they'd gotten here. They'd been too slow to establish a bottleneck. There was a flash of movement and Kovac fired at a vampire sprinting across the lobby. That one dove behind cover before he could put a round into him. Some vampires were just too damned fast. They were going to get flanked here. "Fall back."

"Cover me, Show."

He leaned out and started shooting, forcing the vampires to keep their heads down while Solo crossed the hallway. Then he followed. The two of them rushed back into the offices. Employees were running past them, and every bit of movement was making his nerves twitch. "Get out the back! Get out of here!" Kovac held up one hand as they approached a glass partition. He'd seen a dark reflection in it. Someone was moving up the other side, and this one wasn't dressed in a lab coat or a suit. They both took aim and the split second a vampire with a hoodie and a gun came around the side, they lit him up. The glass shattered. One eye socket turned into a gaping red hole and the vampire collapsed in a heap.

The slide was locked back on the Sig. "Reloading." He had two more mags his belt, but they had not come here expecting a firefight. By the time Kovac had shoved a fresh mag into the gun, Solo had moved up on the dead vampire, taken his Tavor rifle, and lifted its bloody clothing to reveal that he was wearing a plate carrier and mag pouches beneath. "Bastards came loaded for a fight."

"Grab it and go. We've got to protect that lab."

There was more unsuppressed gunfire from that direction. Mute and Box had gotten in on the action. They'd dropped two but had no idea how many more there were. From the noise coming through the building, there were several, and from the dead bodies they passed, some of the vampires had gotten ahead of them. Most of the staff had been shot, but a few looked like they'd been ripped apart by wild animals and spread across the cubicles.

The men of V-8 had gotten really good at tuning out that sort of thing while in the zone. You dealt with the images later, once the job was done.

They reached the entrance to the lab just in time to see a grey, twisted, hunched-over *thing* rip a security guard's heart through his ribs. They both shot at it, and Kovac was positive he hit it, but it lurched across the carpet lightning fast and disappeared into the lab. A split second later it came back, cranking off a bunch of rounds on full auto their way. Bullets tore through the desks around them, but Kovac stayed up and shot it in the face that time. There was a splash of blood and teeth, but the thing just shrieked and pulled back, still annoyingly alive.

"I'm hit." Solo said, perfectly calm.

Kovac jerked his head over to see his partner sinking down as his leg slid out from under him. Blood was pumping out of Solo's thigh. "Damn it." He slunk over, trying to stay low behind the desks, until he reached Solo. "How bad?"

"Bad." Solo was pulling his belt off. "Help me tourniquet this before I pass out."

Kovac did. Solo roared in pain when he cinched it up tight. His hands came away slick and red. "Take it easy." He kept risking quick peeks over the desk to make sure the grey vampire wasn't sneaking up while he pulled off his dress shirt to use it as a makeshift bandage. "Keep pressure on that."

"What the hell was that thing?" Solo asked through gritted teeth.

"One of the Indonesian types." He couldn't remember the name but he'd read about one in another team's report. "They're one of the fastest we've seen."

"What do you want to do, Show?"

"Carry you out the back."

"Hell no. That screener can ruin these suckers once and for all." Solo shoved the stolen rifle toward him. "Don't let them take it."

Solo was right. Judging by the continuous gunfire, the rest of his team was occupied at the far end of the building. "Okay. Cover the hall and call Mute and Box. I'll hit the lab."

Marko checked his watch. It had been three minutes since they'd rammed the door. They were running out of time. He glanced around the laboratory. He'd memorized the blueprints, but it still felt like he was in the wrong place. It was far plainer than he'd expected. Laboratories were supposed to have all sorts of interesting devices— Tesla coils and bubbling vats, that sort of thing. This was mostly computers and all of the fancy medical equipment looked like white or beige boxes. *Disappointing.*

He'd shot a few of the staff to make the point that he was in control. From the noise coming through the walls, the V-8 soldiers were being a pain in the ass and refusing to die. A couple of his assault team hadn't checked in, which meant they were probably dead. The breachers were holding the front door. Basco was watching one entrance to the lab and Gregor had the other. Meeker was off running an errand, and Doroshanko—who actually understood all this egghead stuff—was screwing around with their computers.

"Sniper team. Status outside?"

"I don't think the cops have made you yet. The riot is going crazy."

That had been money well spent. "Doroshanko, what've you got?"

He'd pulled his gloves off so he could type better. Marko could see the bones of his fingers through his weird, translucent skin. Some mutations were stranger than others. "I've taken most of their research, but there are a few files that have extra password protection."

Marko glanced at the scientists. He'd made them all kneel on the floor in a line. "Which one of you has the password?" They all looked at the floor. "Nobody?" He tore off his mask, went to the nearest idiot in a lab coat and picked her up by the hair. There was a hot pressure in his face as the fangs grew, and then he sank them into her neck. His jaws clamped shut, slicing through the flesh. She kicked and thrashed and screamed as the wonderful blood filled his mouth and painted the walls. He unclenched his jaw, ripped his teeth out, and hurled her across the room. She slammed into a machine hard enough to smash a huge dent in the sheet metal and send sparks flying from it. Droplets of blood sprayed from his mouth as he shouted, "How about now? Anybody got the password now?"

"Market, the number forty-two, underscore, the number twenty, blue!" shouted a young man. "All lowercase!"

"Thank you," Marko said as Doroshanko typed it in.

The Moldovan vampire nodded when he was in. "Keep being helpful like that and you might just live through the next few minutes."

Gregor came in, dragging an Asian man by the tie. "Look what Meeker found hiding in a janitor's closet upstairs."

"That boy has a nose like a hound. Ah, Mr. Iwashiro. Just the man I've been looking for. I really enjoyed your press conference."

"Why are you doing this? We're trying to cure you!"

"Cure us?" Marko laughed. "You've got that backwards, Doc. Vampires *are* the cure. I'm preventing genocide here. I'm the good guy."

"Go to hell!"

The CEO had balls, Marko would give him that. He knew he was rather intimidating when he was covered in blood with fangs sticking out and eyeballs filled red, and he'd get the truth out of the doctor eventually, but he didn't have time to screw around. "Gregor, bite off one of his fingers."

"What? No!" Iwashiro cried out as Gregor grabbed his hand. He strained and fought, but Gregor's mutation had turned him into an *asasabonsam,* and that bloodline was ridiculously strong. It was like watching a kid wrestle an adult. Gregor dragged the hand up, pried out a pinky, and smiled, revealing grey, flat teeth. "No! No!" And then Gregor chomped down and bit the finger clean off. Iwashiro screamed.

Gregor spit the severed pinky out. He saw that Marko was scowling at him. "What?"

"I thought you were hungry."

"I don't eat the *bones*, man."

Marko turned back to the weeping CEO. "We've got a problem. You said you had a prototype screener. I can't find it. Your people deny knowing where it is, and I'm pretty sure they're telling the truth." He glanced theatrically at the corpses. "So where is it?"

"I don't have it!"

"Another finger."

Gregor dragged the twitching, bleeding hand back up and shoved the ring finger between his iron teeth. *Chomp.* Iwashiro screamed again.

"Damn. Someone just experienced a drastic reduction in typing speed. Where is it?"

"I'm telling you! There is no screener! It isn't real!"

"Another."

Iwashiro screeched and babbled and fought. *Chomp.*

Gregor spit it at his feet. "I feel like I should be saving these. Make a necklace or something."

"Now you can't flip anyone off. Tell me what I want to know while you can still point."

"There's no screener. I lied! The press conference was a lie! I swear!" Iwashiro was desperate. Gregor clamped the last finger between his teeth, but didn't bite down yet.

"Explain."

"We're stuck, just like all our competitors. We can't get it to work right. We got so much bad publicity from the trials that our stock was in the toilet. I needed to do something or I was going to lose the company. Claiming to have a working screener was just to buy us time."

"You lied to boost your stock prices?" Marko had wasted his time, his resources, and lost some vampires over a PR stunt? He didn't even need to tell Gregor anything that time.

Chomp.

With a stubby bullpup rifle on his shoulder, Kovac swept into the lab.

There wasn't a vampire in sight. Moving quick and crouched, Kovac saw lots of blood, footprints tracking blood, and shell casings, but no vampires. There was a spatter trail from where he'd nailed the Indonesian in the face, and that blood had a purple tint to it, but after a few meters the trail disappeared, and he'd either healed or got the bleeding to stop.

Room after room, nothing. His nerves were spiked. He was ready to react. A fraction of a second after he picked up a target, it would catch a 5.56 round. He'd been fighting vampires for a year, so Kovac knew to keep scanning, not just side to side, but also up and down, because some of these bastards liked to climb walls or stick to ceilings. Some could only be seen in your peripheral vision when they were holding still. Kovac listened, but it would be hard to pick up the stealthiest predator sneaking up on him with all that gunfire-related ringing in his ears. The worst part about operating by yourself was that no matter how good you were, you could only look in one direction at a time.

It had all happened too fast. In minutes the vampires had swept through and killed everyone, and they'd done it with an army of cops outside. It was too brazen, too slick. There was a gnawing feeling in his gut about who was behind this.

Kovac reached a closed door. There was a headless security guard sprawled in front of it. No sign of the head. He kicked the door in.

This room was a mess. It hardly seemed possible but there was even more blood everywhere. There was a pile of dead in white lab coats now dyed red. Judging by the splatter and the waist-high line of bullet holes in the wall, it looked like the scientists had been lined up, put on their knees, and then machinegunned down.

There was so much blood that it was hard not to slip in it. He moved around a table and found Dr. Iwashiro flat on his back, staring at the ceiling, with his chest so torn open that his ribs were visible and his intestines were hanging out. Kovac swore under his breath. The vampires had fled.

Surprisingly, Iwashiro was still alive. On the other side of the red ribs, he could see purple lungs inflate. "I'm sorry."

It was such an odd thing to say when you were laying there disemboweled that Kovac didn't know what to say. He knelt next to the doctor and had to lower his head to hear the whispers.

"This is my fault. I lied. There was never a screener. My . . . fault . . . All a lie." He coughed up blood and went out.

"You son of a bitch." Kovac's phone buzzed. He pulled it out. The screen read *Toolbox*. "Are you guys okay?"

"Yeah, looks like the vamps are retreating."

"Listen. Solo's injured. He's in the hall by—"

"We're with him now. Where are you?"

"In the lab." There were footprints through the blood leading away. Three sets of them. "Iwashiro and all the

scientists are dead. He just told me there was no screener.
I think it was a scam. I've got three vamps on the move.
I'm going after them." He stood up and followed the red
path down the tile.

"Wait, Showdown. I'm coming to back you up."

"There's no time. They'll get away."

*"You just said there was no screener. There's no reason
not to wait. You go by yourself you're liable to get killed."*
They all knew that was true. Only a fool ever went after a
vampire by himself, let alone multiple vampires. Solo had
gotten his call sign by being stupid enough to do that once.
"Wait just a damned a minute."

"I can't do that, Box."

*"You can't because you think it was your dad that did
this. This feels like one of his ops. I know you want to put
him down—"*

"More than you can ever understand! He's gone evil,
Box. I've got to stop him."

"Don't let your anger cloud your judgment, Captain."

"Catch up," Kovac ordered, then ended the call. He
needed to concentrate.

They'd only been inside for a few minutes, but the riot
had changed dramatically during that time. Maybe they'd
been unconsciously spurred on by all the blood-spilling
going on right under their noses, but the rioters were
really charged up now. Maybe it was all the pent-up
aggression and worry since ancient horrors had started
rearing their ugly heads again. Maybe the cattle were tired
of getting bled and had begun to stampede—Marko didn't
know, but shit had gotten real in the street. A bunch of

kids had knocked one of the cops out of formation and were beating him like a piñata. A rioter was lying facedown in a gutter, skull cracked open. There were wounded on both sides, and some of the cops looked ready to call it a night and open fire with real guns. It looked more like a battle than a riot and the protestors had transformed into wannabe berserkers.

Into that mess, Marko Kovac melted. He pulled the plastic mask back on, put up the hood, and simply walked away. The rest of his vampires spread out, each of them taking a different route to the rally point and then they'd get out of town. The hungry among them would certainly feed along the way, and they'd earned it. Three of his new recruits hadn't checked in, which meant they were most likely dead or lost. But that's why he'd sent the inexperienced ones to roam the building to cause trouble so his elite could focus on the mission. *What a waste.*

Basco had caught a bullet in the face. It would take weeks for the shattered bones around his mouth to heal, but luckily for him, his kind fed through a spike in their tongue so he wouldn't go hungry. Gregor gave one last nod to his boss, and then his two lieutenants veered off. The last he saw of them was two shadows climbing up the side of a building to take to the rooftops. Gregor had picked up the scent of the college girls he'd fancied earlier and the two of them were going to track those girls down and have a little party. They'd earned it.

As for Marko, he savored the chaos as he strolled through the riot. There was a lot of fear stink over on the cop side. Their carefully drilled formations had fallen apart once they'd got word that one of their own had gotten shot, but there had been no more shots and no sign of the shooter. SWAT cops were spread out behind cover, rifles pointed at the surrounding buildings, scanning for threats. Now that they'd just found out that there'd been a massacre inside the building they were supposed to be protecting, they were really going to freak out.

He didn't know how it worked, but one of the abilities he'd picked up since he'd turned was being able to sense when he was being watched. It was more of an instinct really, a certain knowledge of where humans were looking, and how to avoid being there. In that one instant, he knew there were eyes on him, but this time it was different. Normally he used the instinct to avoid the eyes of his prey, but this wasn't food, this was another predator stalking him. Marko kept his head down and kept walking until the feeling lessened just a bit and the other predator kept scanning.

"Marko, you've got company," his sniper warned. *"One of the V-8 guys is moving your way."*

He froze in place, surrounded by fools and animals, in a fog of blinding gas and choking smoke, between the burning cars and the angry law, and took stock. The whole city was filled with anger tonight, but it was unfocused, cruel, lashing out stupidly, but piercing through that haze was another feeling, only this anger was the righteous wrath of a warrior, focused like a laser beam, and sharper than any sword.

Marko slowly turned until he saw his son.

Across the mob, Matthew Kovac was searching for him. He was wearing a bloodstained white T-shirt and had an assault weapon hidden under one arm, concealed in one of the protestor's discarded red flags. The tattered bits were whipping in the hot wind behind him. The image made Marko think of a crusader for some reason. His boy was certainly dedicated enough. Brave too.

"I've got him in my sights. Want me to take the shot?"

Matthew hadn't made him yet. He didn't have the senses of a vampire. He was a strong man—a better man that Marko had been when he was still human, for sure—but he was still only a man, so he was out of his league, and he couldn't pick out his target through this chaos, but he sure as hell wasn't going to give up. The boy had never been a quitter.

Marko's instincts had evolved. He'd been blessed to become something more. Vampires had existed before, but they'd failed because they had not had officers like him to lead them. His people, his *true people* needed Marko to survive, to continue training the others, until the day the vampire army was strong enough to rise up and take what was rightfully theirs. Matthew was one of the humans who would end that dream.

"Marko, I've got the shot. Say the word."

Marko knew that if he let Matthew walk away tonight, his son would hunt him for the rest of his life. The smart thing to do was to end this here and now.

Except Marko had found an emotion in that pit he'd thought was empty.

Fatherly pride.

He let Matthew follow him into the darkness. The best would win and the other would die.

"Hold your fire."

Marko Kovac faded back into the night.

PSYCH EVAL

This story first appeared in Joe Ledger: Unstoppable, *published in 2017 by Griffin, and edited by Jonathan Maberry.*

The bestselling Joe Ledger series is a lot of fun, and it is also a lot of books, so when I had a chance to write a story set in that universe I asked Jonathan what were some of the crazy urban fantasy things he'd not touched on much yet. Demons had shown up in "Weaponized Hell," but he'd not really done anything involving them or anything like possession.

Say no more.

And yes, this story was written to a David Bowie soundtrack.

"WHY AM I BEING INTERROGATED?" she snapped as soon as Rudy walked through the door.

"Relax. It's just an interview."

"Then why does the sign say 'Interrogation Room'?"

Rudy pulled out a chair and sat down across the metal

table from one of the survivors of Bowie Team. She was obviously suspicious and frightened, but his goal was to help, not make this adversarial. Lieutenant Carver had been through enough already. Rudy's plan was to be his normal, good-humored self, and help this brave soldier through the aftermath of her ordeal.

Unless Mr. Church's suspicion was right, and she was a murderous traitor, because then her fate was out of his hands.

"This room is what the Army had available on short notice. Believe me. I'd much rather be having this conversation in a nice office." As usual, he wanted to make his patient feel safe and comfortable. Only it was summer in Texas, the building's air conditioner was dying, and it was muggy enough in these stuffy windowless rooms that sweat rings were already forming on his shirt. So comfort was out, but Rudy could still try to make her feel safe.

"We've not spoken before, Lieutenant Carver. I'm Dr. Sanchez. You can call me Rudy."

"The Department of Military Sciences' number one shrink. I know who you are, so I know why you're here. But I'm not crazy."

"Nobody said you were."

"I'm not a liar. I know what I saw. I gave my report."

She was clearly agitated. Rudy had read her file on the way over. The DMS mission was so sensitive that every team member's background had been gone over with a fine-toothed comb. Her record wasn't just clean, it was spotless. Her service record was exemplary. Carver's previous psych evaluation had made her sound as a rock, solid under pressure, but the poor young woman in front of him today had been reduced to an emotional wreck.

He'd watched her through the one-way glass before coming in. She'd spent the whole time staring off into space and occasionally muttering something incomprehensible to herself. Now that there was another person for her to focus on, she was demonstrating bad tremors in her hands. Her eyes kept flicking nervously from side to side. By all accounts Carver had been fine before leaving on this mission, but she'd developed several severe nervous tics in the last forty-eight hours.

"I've read your report, Lieutenant. Do you mind if I call you Olivia?" She didn't respond, so he went with it. "Believe me, Olivia, I'm on your side. After some of the things I've heard from other teams over the years, I never assume anybody in this outfit is lying, regardless of what they say they ran into."

"Do you believe in the devil, Rudy?"

Considering what she'd just been through, with most of her team murdered, and the only other survivors in critical condition, it wasn't such an odd question. "I believe in good and evil. My small part in that struggle is helping good people deal with traumatic events and the horrors they've faced. I'm just here to help you."

Carver stared at him for a long time. It was the first time her tremors had stopped. She responded like she hadn't even heard his words. "I believe in him now."

"You hungry? Want some coffee or something?"

The survivor lifted her arm to show that her wrist was handcuffed to the metal table.

"Yeah, well. Sorry. That's not my call," Rudy explained.

"No. It's his." She looked over at the mirrored wall and raised her voice. "Hello, Mr. Church."

Rudy just shook his head, but he didn't deny who was on the other side of the glass. He'd asked about the necessity of the restraints already—it was hard to make somebody feel safe enough to open up while they were chained like a prisoner—but he had been shot down. Apparently it wasn't clear yet who had done *all* of the killing. Lieutenant Carver could be the survivor of some kind of new chemical hallucinatory attack, or could have been the victim of an unknown terrorist bioweapon, or she could have just had a psychotic break, or even be a traitor who had simply murdered her teammates in cold blood and lied to cover it up. The fact was they didn't even yet know what they didn't know.

Say what you will about working for the DMS, it was never predictable.

"Let's just talk. Tell me about the mission. Tell me about what happened in Mexico."

This part of Sonora looked a lot like Arizona. She was born and raised in Phoenix, so it seemed weird to be rolling hot in an area of operation that looked suspiciously like her hometown. Only back home she hadn't been worried about car bombs or cartel gunfights growing up, common threats the poor folks stuck here had to deal with on a daily basis.

Their convoy moved fast. The black government Suburbans barely slowed as they left the paved road and hit gravel. Carver was at the wheel of the second vehicle in line. The view out the window was creosote bushes and sun-baked rocks as far as the eye could see, just like it had been for the last hour. The only difference was now the ride got bumpier, and she began to taste dust in the air conditioning.

Captain Quinn got on the radio. He said something in Spanish, and the last three vehicles in their convoy broke off. Those were white and green pickups filled with *Federales*. They would be setting up a roadblock to keep anyone from getting in or out of the AO. From here on in, the DMS was on its own. The Mexican government and the US State Department had come to an agreement that all parties were cool with. This was DMS' show. Everybody official was just going to deny that this op ever happened anyway.

Their commanding officer was in the vehicle behind them. Satisfied that they were now speeding toward the target by themselves, the captain switched to the encrypted DMS channels and addressed Bowie Team.

"We're ten minutes out. You know the drill."

There would be silence between their vehicles the rest of the way in. Intercepting even garbled radio transmissions could warn the bad guys something was up. Carver just concentrated on driving. The loose gravel turned to washboard, which threatened to rattle their armored vehicle to death. These pigs didn't have the smoothest ride in the best situations.

Sandbag was riding shotgun. Gator and Corvus were in the back seat. Louie was serving as trunk monkey, ready to pop open the back window and open fire with a SAW.

"You really think there's something to this intel, LT?" Sandbag asked.

"We know Hezbollah has an exchange program going with the cartels for years," she answered. "One side has expertise, the other has more money than it knows what to do with. Smuggling people and weapons across the border is a piece of cake to the cartel, and terrorists get an easy way into the US. It's a match made in heaven."

"Yeah, nothing like sharing your cultural traditions with others, like beheading, or car bombings," Gator interjected.

"Well, now DMS thinks they're sharing something else. Word is a few days ago an unknown weapon was shipped from an undisclosed location in the Middle East to this little town. Once it is ready, they'll send it north. We just don't know what it is yet. Which is why we're going to nab these bastards and find out," Carver stated. She was trying to stay right behind the truck ahead of her without rear-ending it while blinded by its plume of dust. At least the dust was obscuring the view of cactus and endless nothing. "It's one thing to look at this area on the map, another to see it in person. They picked a village so isolated that it's making me worried they're playing with something really nasty."

Her teammates readied their weapons. They were pumped. They'd done this sort of thing many times before, but it was always exhilarating. When they were only a few minutes out, Carver hit play on the sound system. This song was pre-raid tradition for them. Captain Quinn was a proud Texan, so when the DMS had set up a team out of Fort Hood, he had christened it Bowie Team. Of course, his boys had immediately decided that meant David rather than Jim.

"I'm afraid of Americans" began playing over the Suburban's speakers.

Carver grinned. *Good.* The terrorist assholes they were hunting should be.

The Suburban ahead of them was slowing down. That didn't make any sense—the village was still a mile away—but she slammed on the brakes fast enough to keep from rear-ending them.

"Get ready." Something was up. It could be an ambush. It could be a barricade. Regardless, speed was their ally. Getting bogged down out here meant the cartel was more likely to see them coming and get ready. "What the hell, Zeke?" she muttered. He was driving the lead vehicle, and wasn't the type to hesitate.

But nothing happened. The point vehicle maintained radio silence, only lollygagging for a few seconds before speeding up again.

"Yo, LT. Check it out." It was Sandbag who first saw what had caused the point vehicle to hesitate. He tapped the bulletproof glass of the passenger side window. "There's a—good lord..."

There were telephone lines running alongside the road. The poles were the tallest thing for miles, and so constant flashing by every couple hundred feet that she'd begun to tune them out. Only this one was different. Somebody had been *nailed* to it.

There wasn't much time to assess. Hanging ten feet up...adult male, Mexican, mid-thirties, jeans and a flannel shirt, coated in dried blood. Arms extended above his head, dangling with multiple nails—no, spikes— through his hands and wrists.

Then it flashed by. She looked in her mirror, but the body was already obscured by the dust.

Since Louie was in back he'd gotten the best look. "I know the cartel leaves some brutal warnings, but crucifixion? Damn. Fucking barbarians."

Then they passed another pole, and there was another body stuck to it. Female. Twenties. Vultures were perched on the crossbeam above her. There was more swearing and muttering. And then she too was swallowed by the dust.

The next telephone pole had another body hung on it. This one was elderly. Had she been somebody's *abuelita*? And the next. And the next. Every couple hundred feet the spectacle repeated. Men, women, children. The soldiers quit talking. This wasn't a warning. This was a massacre.

Numb, Carver concentrated on the road.

"All the way to the village?" Rudy asked.

"All the way," she confirmed. "Every single pole."

He swallowed hard. "That wasn't in your initial report."

Carver shook her head. "Considering what else we saw, it wasn't that noteworthy."

Bowie Team rolled into the village ready for a fight.

It was dead.

She'd been ready for the sound of gunfire, but there was nothing. There should have at least been a dog barking. There was no movement, no sound other than the wind. There were a few dozen small houses and other assorted buildings, but not so much as a curtain parted for the locals to spy on them. No matter how scared they were, nobody kept their heads down that well.

Ten seconds after dismounting, they stacked up on the little grocery market that their intel had said housed their targets, tossed bangs through the windows, breached the doors, and rushed inside.

"Clear!" Carver shouted after she swept through the back storage room. The smell of death assaulted her nostrils. There were dried blood puddles on the uneven wooden floor, big enough that it looked like they'd butchered a cow in here, but no bodies, and certainly no living terrorists or cartel members.

Somebody had set up a shrine inside the storeroom. She'd seen the painted skull faces in the briefings, *Santa Muerte*, popular with the cartel assassins. Corvus walked over to the shrine and started shoving around the flowers, papers, and dolls with the muzzle of his SCAR, checking if there was anything interesting. All of the crucifixes had been turned upside down. He found a plastic dog bowl. Corvus gagged and backed away from the shrine. There was a pile of glistening, white spheres inside.

"I think those are human eyeballs, LT."

A bunch of little devotional candles were still lit around the shrine. So the occupants couldn't have been gone long.

"They must have bolted," Sandbag said. "Did they see us coming?"

She shook her head. There was only one road out, and nobody had passed them. The terrain was rugged enough that they could have escaped on foot, horseback, or four wheelers, but she wasn't getting that vibe at all. "My gut's telling me nobody got out of this place."

"Yo, LT. I've got something weird here. It looks really old." Gator had picked up an odd-looking silver amulet. He was scowling at it. "Is that Arabic?"

She looked at the antique. It was the head of a goat, with ruby eyes. An unconscious shiver of revulsion went through her and she had no idea why. "Greek maybe? I don't know what language that is."

Gator was holding it in his glove. Suddenly, red droplets of blood appeared on the silver. She looked up to see that it was coming from Gator's nose. He was just staring at it, and didn't seem to notice the rivulet of blood running down his chin. It was like he was in a daze.

"Gator, you're bleeding."

It took him a long second to focus. He slowly looked up from the amulet. "Huh?"

"Did you hit your head or something?"

Gator seemed to snap out of it. He wiped the blood away with a sleeve, and looked at it in surprise. "Naw. Damned dry heat."

Captain Quinn came over the radio. *"Target's in the wind. We're splitting into teams and searching the town. Zeke, take the cantina. Carver, you've got the church."*

"Roger that. We're on the church." She let go of the transmit button. "Bag that necklace and let's go."

"What did you find in the church?" Rudy asked softly.

"He found us." The lieutenant's trembling had gotten worse. He was inclined to give her a sedative, but Mr. Church had been adamant they needed answers now.

"Who is *he*?"

Rudy waited for her to elaborate, but this interview was like pulling teeth. "Tell me about what happened in the church, Olivia."

Abruptly her trembling stopped. The change in manner was so complete, so chilling, that it brought to mind patients he'd worked with suffering from Dissociative Identity Disorder. In the blink of an eye, there was a different person sitting across from him. Only this one was utterly calm.

"Are you okay, Olivia?"

Seemingly curious, Carver tilted her head to the side, a bit too far. "I like eyes. Your eyes are broken, Rudy. I can only see through one of them."

The shift was so sudden, and the question so unexpected, that it put him off his game. "I was injured. I have a glass eye."

Carver nodded slowly. "Your world is flat."

"You mean I have no depth perception. Correct."

She stared at him for a long time. "It makes me sad you're broken."

Despite being summer in Texas, Rudy felt a sudden chill. There was a knock on the other side of the glass. It made him jump.

He tried to hide his relief at having an interruption. "Excuse me a minute." Rudy got up and went to the door. He had to wait for them to unlock it.

There were four MPs waiting in the hall. Mr. Church was by himself in the observation room. He was simply standing there in the dark, watching Lieutenant Carver through the one-way glass, inscrutable as ever.

"What do you think, Doctor?"

"It's too early to tell. She's a severely traumatized young woman who has been through a lot, but beyond that I'm going to need more time to reach her."

"I've received a call from another agency. They are sending a specialist. He'll be here soon."

"What kind of specialist?" Rudy asked suspiciously. "From what agency?"

"The kind you don't ask questions about. His name is Franks. I've worked with him before." Considering how broad and mysterious Church's background was, that was incredibly unhelpful. "Agent Franks is a thoroughly unpleasant individual, but very good at what he does. You'll want to stay out of his way. He's not big on conversation."

"It's unlike you to turn over DMS jurisdiction to someone else. Carver is one of us."

"Is she?"

"What do you mean by that?"

Church glanced at the wall clock. "He should arrive in an hour."

"Then let me keep talking to her until this specialist shows up."

"I wouldn't advise that . . . However, I will admit I'm curious to hear what she has to say. Carry on."

"Okay then," Rudy started walking away.

Church called after him, "By the way, Doctor, we got the preliminary results back on her dead teammates. No toxins, drugs, or biological agents were present in their systems. The causes of death were all straightforward— gunshot wounds, stabbings, strangulation, blunt force trauma, that sort of thing."

"Okay. Anything else?"

"It might be a sticky subject, but I would suggest asking her about the cannibalism."

"*What*?"

"Human tissue was found in some of their stomachs. We have not had the time to get the DNA results yet, but considering some of the bite patterns on the survivors, it probably came from their teammates."

Rudy blanched.

"Do you still want to continue?"

Like he'd told Carver, his small part was helping put the good people back together. Until proven otherwise, he was going to assume good whenever possible. "Yeah, I've got this."

"Very well. Can I help you with anything else, Doctor?"

"Sure, tell the Army to turn down the air conditioner. It's freezing in that little room."

"Really? They were just apologizing to me for the ac-commodations. According to the thermometer it is over eighty degrees in here."

"Shit." Rudy put his head down, plowed through the hall, past the MPs, and back into the oddest psych eval he'd done in quite some time.

Carver had gone back to shaking and mumbling. It was sad, but that sign of human frailty made him far more comfortable than the creepy mood swing from a few minutes before. Rudy sat back down. She gave him a weak smile.

"Okay, Olivia. Tell me about what happened inside that church."

❖ ❖ ❖

Corvus kicked the door open and her men swept inside. They had trained so constantly that their movement was like clockwork. Each one covered a sector.

"Clear!"

A minute later the small Catholic church was secured. There was still no sign of the tangos, or any of the locals for that matter. There should have been something.

The church was old, and humble. The wooden walls had been painted white a long time ago, but they were faded and chipped now. Heavily lacquered wooden saints looked down on them. The pews were polished smooth from decades of use.

"Where is everybody?" Louie wondered aloud.

"Nailed to the telephone poles," Sandbag muttered.

"No, this town held more people than that." But that didn't mean she had a clue where they'd gone. Carver had her men take up defensive positions on the doors and got on her radio to contact Captain Quinn. She got nothing but static. *Weird.* "This place is giving me a bad vibe."

Carver turned around and nearly jumped out of her skin when she saw a little Mexican boy sitting on the altar. Sensing her reaction, her men spun around, lifting their weapons.

"Hold on!" she shouted before fingers could reach the triggers. "It's just a kid." He was probably only seven or eight years old, wearing a T-shirt, shorts, and barefoot. "Whose section was that? Damn it, Corvus! Why didn't you clear that?"

"I did, LT. He wasn't there a second ago."

It didn't matter now. They'd found *somebody*. Carver swung her carbine around behind her back and let it dangle by the sling. She lifted both hands to show they were empty. "*Hola.*" She spoke three languages fluently, but Spanish wasn't among them. Sandbag was fluent though. "Tell him we're friends."

Sandbag started talking. He was a big scary dude, but he kept his voice nice and soothing. Only the little boy kept staring at her instead. She found it odd that he was sitting cross-legged on the altar. She wasn't religious, but that seemed really disrespectful. "Ask him what's going on."

Sandbag did. The boy smirked as he answered.

"He says he just got up from a long nap."

"Huh? Where?"

"In the ground, I think. No. A tomb." Sandbag shrugged. "He's not making a lot of sense, LT."

"Ask him where everybody is."

The little boy finally looked at Sandbag and rattled off a dismissive answer. Sandbag seemed really confused by it.

"He says that he forced them to walk across the desert."

"Who did?"

"Him." Sandbag nodded at the kid. "He's talking about himself. He said he did it."

The little boy had an annoyed expression on his face. He said something else, like he was correcting the translator. He spoke for a long time. Sandbag's eyes kept getting wide.

"He says he made them take their shoes off so their feet would bleed on the rocks and thorns, and to not stop until they fell. They're probably dead from thirst by now." Sandbag was distressed. He'd never struck Carver as the religious type, so when he unconsciously crossed himself, it unnerved her. "That was only for the ones who pray. The rest he nailed to the poles."

"Little fucker would need a ladder," Corvus muttered. "He's gone mental."

"He says they brought him here, but they didn't understand what they dug up. He's insulted they thought he was just some mere weapon."

The kid smiled at them.

Then he began weeping blood.

That was when everything went horribly wrong.

Rudy realized he was gripping the edge of the table so hard that his knuckles had turned white.

"What's wrong, Rudy?" Lieutenant Carver asked him with unnerving calm. "You seem frightened."

"I'm fine."

"No. You are broken. You are an unworthy vessel."

All the hair on his arms stood up. "You mean my eye?"

"Among other things." She smiled, but it wasn't a real smile. It was more like something was wearing Carver's face as a mask, and pulled the strings to make the face muscles perform the motions it assumed were appropriate. "I've been hidden away so long. The world above has changed. I do not understand it anymore. I was supposed to rest until the final days. Only the Canaanites opened my tomb. By the time I was fully awake, they had brought me to the hot lands below."

"Canaanites?"

"I don't care what you name them now. I was weak, without purpose. I have found one again. I will seek out my old enemy, and begin our war anew."

Rudy didn't know where his next question came from. "Why did you come *here*?"

"I heard this one's song. I had to come and see for myself if it was true. Is my enemy here?"

"Who?" It was now so cold his breath came out as steam.

She leaned close and whispered to him.

Rudy bolted upright and headed for the door. He pounded on it. Thankfully the MPs opened it right away. "Keep that locked. Nobody else goes in or out." He didn't have the authority to order them around, but it wasn't a suggestion.

Church was waiting for him in the observation area. "She really seems to be opening up to you, Doctor."

Rudy raised one hand to stop Church. He wasn't in the mood. He was silent for a long time, breathing hard, staring through the glass at the woman on the other side. She'd gone back to trembling, knees nervously bouncing, just a poor, traumatized woman, who had seen her squad turn on each other and rip themselves to pieces.

"Clinically, on the record, I'd say she's severely delusional."

"And off the record?"

"I'm not going back in there without a priest."

Then the lights went out.

"Stay calm." Church's voice was flat.

The logical part of his mind immediately rationalized the power outage. The overworked air conditioner had caused the building to blow a fuse. But the part of him that had just been laid bare and terrified by an alien presence that should not be, knew that wasn't the case.

The lights came back on.

She had left two bloody red handprints on the other side of the glass for them.

"Carver's gone."

The interrogation room was empty. The handcuffs were on the table, still closed, like she just tore her hands right out of them. The door was closed.

Church moved to the hall. The MPs were still there, oblivious but unharmed. He threw open the door, and despite Rudy's admonition to the contrary, they knew not to mess with Mr. Church. He came back out. "Sound the alarm. Find her, but do not engage." The soldiers rushed off. Church returned a moment later, glowering. "She's escaped."

Nothing ever seemed to shake Church, but Rudy was sick to his stomach. "That specialist who's on the way . . . He's an exorcist, isn't he?"

"I don't know if Agent Franks puts that on his business cards, but I suppose that might be among his many qualifications," Church replied. "This is important, Doctor. I couldn't make it out over the speaker, but the last thing she said to you, when you asked her about this old enemy, about why she'd come here, what did she say to you?"

"The song said 'God is an American.'"

MUSINGS OF A HERMIT

This story first appeared in the Forged in Blood *anthology set in Michael Z. Williamson's Freehold universe, edited by Michael Z. Williamson, and published by Baen Books in 2017.*

The idea behind Forged in Blood *is really interesting. Every story features the same sword, as it is handed down to different users, starting in ancient Japan, through WWII, through modern times, into the future and out into space (where it eventually belonged to the main character in the novel* Freehold*).*

Sometimes the author picks the setting, and other times the author gets picked because he can write a particular setting. In this case I already had a rep for writing samurai drama, and Mike approached me because he needed some stories set in that era.

If you are familiar with this series, it has a very strong theme about freedom and liberty running through it, so I wanted to write about one of the sword's wielders who could never really have those things, yet yearned for them. I wanted to write about a man who had been born in the wrong time.

WHEN YOU HIT A MAN with a sword, it can go clean or ugly. A clean hit and you barely even feel the impact. Oh, your opponent feels it. Trust me. But for the swordsman, your blade travels through skin and muscle as if it is parting water. Arms can come right off. Legs are tougher, but a good strike will cut clear to the bone and leave them crippled. A katana will shear a rib like paper, and their guts will fall out like a butchered pig. Then, with a snap of the wrist, the blade has returned and the swordsman is prepared to strike again. Simple. Effective. *Clean.* I'll spare you all the flowery talk the perfumed sensei spout about rhythm and footwork that inevitably make killing sound like a formal court dance, but when you do everything just right, I swear to you that I've killed men so smoothly that their heads have remained sitting upon their necks long enough to blink twice before falling off.

However, an ugly hit means you pulled it wrong, or he moved unexpectedly. The littlest things, a slight change in angle, a tiny bit of hesitation, upon impact you feel that pop in your wrists, and then your sword is stuck in their bone, they're screaming in your face, flinging blood everywhere, and you have to practically wrestle your steel out of them. Whatever bone you struck is a splintered mess. Usually the meat is dangling off in ghastly strips. Some men will take that as a sign to lie down and die, but a dedicated samurai will take that ugly hit and still try to take you with him, just because, in principle, if a samurai is dying then, damn it, he shouldn't have to do it alone. It can be a very nasty affair.

The tax collector died very ugly.

I only wanted to be left alone.

Kanemori was sitting by the stove, absorbing the warmth, debating over whether it was too early in the afternoon to get drunk, when there was a great commotion in his yard. Someone was calling his name. It wouldn't be the first time in his long life that someone with a grudge had turned up looking for him, but this sounded like a girl. He rose and peeked out one of the gaps in the wall that he'd been meaning to repair, to see that it was the village headman's daughter trudging through the snow with determination.

"Go away!" he shouted.

"Kanemori! The village needs your help."

The headman always wanted his help with something, the lazy bastard. A tree fell on old lady Haru's hut. Or Den's ox is stuck in the river. Or please save us from these bandits, Kanemori-sama! And then he'd have to go saw wood, or pull on a stupid ox, or cut down some pathetic bandit rabble. He knew it was usually just the headman trying to be social, but it was a waste of his time. He didn't belong to the village. He'd simply had the misfortune of building his shack near it.

"What now?" he bellowed through the wall.

"The new Kura-Bugyo is going to execute my father!"

"What did your imbecile father do to make the tax collector angry this time?"

"The last official was honest, but the officials this year are corrupt. They take more than they're supposed to. They take the lord's share, and then they take more to sell for themselves! Father refused to give up the last of our stores. If we do we'll perish during the winter."

Of course the officials were corrupt. That's what officials were for.

The girl was about ten, but already bossy enough to be a magistrate. When she reached the shack, she began pounding on his door. "Let me in, Kanemori!"

"Go away."

"No! I will stay out here and cry until I freeze to death! Your lack of mercy will cause my angry ghost to haunt you forever. And then you will feel very sorry!"

Kanemori sighed. Peasants were stupid and stubborn. He opened the door. "What do you expect me to do about it?"

"You are samurai! Make them stop."

"Oh?" He looked around his humble shack theatrically. "Do I look like Oda Nobunaga to you? I am without clan, status, or even basic dignity. Officials aren't going to listen to me. Do you think I moved to the frozen north because I am so popular?"

"You are the worst samurai ever!"

In defense of the clumsy butchery that passed for a battle against the corrupt tax collector and his men, my soldiering days were over. It had been many seasons since I'd last hit a man with a sword, so I was rusty. When your joints ache every morning, the last thing you want to do is practice your forms, so my daily training consisted of the minimum a retired swordsman must do in order to avoid feeling guilty. Why do more? I had no lord to command me, no general to bark orders at me—the only person who'd done so recently was my second wife, and I'd buried her two winters ago—and if I spent all my energy swinging a sword, who was going to feed all these damnable chickens?

It isn't that peasants can't fight. It is that they're too tired from working all day to learn to fight. A long time ago some clever sort figured that out, traded his hoe for a sword, started bossing around the local farmers, said, you give me food and in exchange I'll protect you from assholes who will kill you, but if you don't, I'll kill you myself, and the samurai class was born. From then on, by accident of one's birth, it determined if you'd be well fed until you got stabbed to death, or hungry and laboring until you starved . . . or got stabbed to death.

Spare me the history lectures. I actually do know where samurai come from. I was born *buke*. I slept through the finest history lessons in Kyoto. You would not know it to look at me now, but I was once a promising young warrior. It was said that handsome Hatsu Kanemori was a scholar, a poet, and the veritable pride of my clan, and high-ranking officials were lining up to offer me marriages to their daughters . . . until one day I finally told my lord I was sick of his shit. Then I promptly ran away before he could decorate his castle wall with my head.

Now, the life of a ronin is a different sort of thing entirely. Samurai live well, but they're expected to die on behalf of their lord. Ronin live slightly better than dogs, and are expected to die on behalf of whichever lord scraped up enough coin to hire us. Being a wave man retains all of the joys of getting stabbed to death, but with the added enticement of being as miserable and hungry as a peasant, up until when you get stabbed to death.

But at least you are your own master.

After he closed his door in her face, the headman's daughter had sat down in the snow, started wailing, and seemed petulantly prepared to freeze to death in his yard in protest. He'd known mighty warriors who had committed seppuku to protest a superior's decision, but this was a new form of protest to Kanemori. He thought about throwing rocks at her until she left, but even a curmudgeon has his limits. So he put a blanket over his head to muffle the noise and took a long nap instead.

When he woke up, the girl was still there. Kanemori was surrounded by stubborn idiots.

"Does your family know you walked all the way here?" he shouted through the hole in the wall.

"No! I snuck out. They will think that I was devoured by wolves. They will perish with sadness! You are so cruel, Kanemori! My ghost will wail like this forever!"

He opened his door. When the orange light of the stove hit the girl, she quit her fake crying.

"You will save our village?" she asked.

"The Kura-Bugyo is an important man. If I report him, it is his word against mine, and I am without status in this district. There isn't much I can do." Before she could start crying again, he hurried to add, "But I suppose I could try."

"Thank you, noble samurai!"

It was a very long walk to the city, and the local governor's representatives would probably just turn him away, but he'd traded with these villagers, at times he'd chosen to help them, and they'd chosen to help him. It was remarkable how well folks got along without being ordered around.

"I will leave in the morning and travel to the city. I can request an audience with the Mokudai about this corrupt tax collector and—"

"There's no time. They're coming for father tomorrow morning. If we walk all night we can get back in time to save him."

Well, that complicated matters. That meant engaging with the tax collector personally, and since Kanemori had no place in this province, the petty official would probably take an interruption as an insult, and the girl's father wouldn't be the only one executed in the morning.

But she had started crying again, and as far as Kanemori could tell, it looked real. Those tears were probably going to freeze her eyelids shut, and then he wouldn't have to just walk all the way down to the village, but carry a blind girl too.

Kanemori sighed. "Stop that awful noise. Fine. I'll try to save your stupid village. Let me get my sword."

I have never been good at taking orders. Petty authority annoys me. I have always had a surly, contrarian disposition. These are not desirable traits in a samurai. A good warrior is supposed to have unquestioning loyalty to his lord, no matter how ridiculous he might be. My problem was that I always questioned everything. When

I was a boy, my individualistic attitude helped me collect an inordinate number of beatings. That was good. It made me tough. Because if you are going to make it on your own, wandering a world that is all about surviving as part of a group, you'd better be tough.

Luckily, by the time my family sent me off to training, I'd learned when to keep my mouth shut . . . mostly. I had enough natural talent with a sword that my sensei usually overlooked my flippant attitude. It turns out you can afford to give some inadvertent insults when everyone else is scared to duel you. But that only applies to equals—insult a superior, and you had better have a fast horse nearby.

In this world, every man has his place. You know it, you live it, and you pretend to love it. A good samurai would rather let his superior make a foolish decision unchallenged than bring dishonor to his name. Yes, your leader could be an imbecile giving orders that are sure to lead to ignominious defeat, but you'd better take those orders and die with a smile on your face. That is the way of things. So when you slip up and anger your betters, you need to be very valuable on the battlefield—which I was—for them to overlook it. Sadly, when peace finally came to my home province, my painful honesty outweighed my value with a sword.

Stupid peace.

I remember the day when my father gave me my sword. It had belonged to him, and his father, and his father's father's father, so on and so forth, back to tales of glorious battles long ago, and a family legend of a one-handed matriarch, all accompanied with a proud genealogy that was probably half forgery, and half wishful thinking. But regardless, it was an excellent sword.

I suspect he knew I was unworthy of such a legacy, but every father hopes for the best.

At sunrise the village headman ran down the steps of the storehouse, slipped through the packed snow, scooped up his little girl, and swung her around in his arms before holding her tight. "Iyo! You're alive! We woke up this morning and you were gone. Where have you been? We were so worried about you."

"I went to fetch the samurai so he can save you from the officials," the little girl declared proudly.

"What?"

"Defiant Kanemori! Hero of Sekigahara!"

Kanemori cleared his throat so the headman would notice him. Personally, he hated those titles, but bored peasants like to tell stories. The little girl's head had been filled with nonsense exaggerations about his exploits. During their journey down the mountain, she'd asked him about *all* of them.

Kanemori had walked all night, in the dark, in the miserable cold, lucky he hadn't fallen off a narrow trail to his death, and now he was tired, hungry, and annoyed, and probably about to anger another official who could order him killed with so much as a nod. At least it had been a clear night, and he'd always enjoyed gazing at the stars. His father used to say he was too much of a dreamer in that respect.

"You?" The headman was shocked to see him there. He quickly regained his composure, and went into a deep bow. "Apologies for my daughter disturbing you, noble samurai." Then he realized he probably wasn't showing enough deference to his better and began to grovel. "So many apologies for this inconvenience."

"Stop it. Just..." Kanemori waved his hand. "Stop all that." He'd never been much for etiquette or social niceties.

"It was not Iyo's place to—"

"She says you're about to get executed for not paying your taxes and you need help. This isn't any different than when you needed an extra man to drag that dumb ox out of the river. Today you're the ox. Where are these officials? I'll try and talk some sense into them."

"Thank you! Thank you, samurai!"

"I can't promise anything." Over the years he'd found that any given official's reasonableness and mercy was in direct proportionate opposition to their inflated sense of importance and level of corruption. Since they'd been assigned to administer a northern pig hole like this, he wasn't expecting much.

"The Kura-Bugyo should be here soon. I am willing to be executed. It is better they take out their wrath on me, than steal the last of our rice from the mouths of our children." Again, a good man was prepared to lay down his life for others. Too bad he was so poor nobody would bother to write a poem about it. He looked up, hopeful. "I would rather not die. They will listen to you."

"Maybe. More likely they'll still kill you, then take the rice anyway. Either way, that means you have time to make me breakfast first."

❖ ❖ ❖

When I was young, they called me a dreamer. I suppose that is true. I imagined a world different from this one. Where a man could be free to do as he wanted, without legions of officials standing in his way. Where a man could own things without his superiors taking them away on a whim. A world where someone bold enough to make his own way could do so, and not be bound by the status of his birth. Where you could decide for yourself how to live, rather than be spent on a bloody field by a shogun.

I still imagine a world where a man could marry the woman he loved, rather than having her lord give her to another man for political expediency. A world where a samurai could protest this unfair decision, but not lose face and be condemned for his emotional outburst, and have to run away in shame . . . only to find out years later that she cut her own throat in protest, rather than be wed to a cruel, barbaric man instead of him.

These are silly ramblings. That is not the world we live in. Not at all.

The four men rode into the village not long after breakfast. Only Kanemori and the headman walked outside to meet them. The officials seemed amused that the rest of the peasants were hiding from them. Their haughty attitude was not so different from bandits.

Unfortunately, the Kura-Bugyo was a young man. An older, wiser official might have let the slight pass. The callousness of noble youth, coupled with the unrivaled arrogance of a tax collector, meant that Kanemori had his work cut out for him. The official also had three samurai escorting him, who were acting more like friends than guards. That was another bad sign. An official would feel no need to show off for soldiers, their opinions would be beneath contempt, but the same official would strut like a rooster to save face in front of his friends.

"Where is my rice, headman?" the official shouted, not bothering to give any introduction. "I said to have it waiting. There is a wagon not far behind. Why do you waste my time?" His friends snickered.

The headman bowed so hard he nearly buried himself in the snow. Kanemori was ashamed for him. This wasn't the emperor. This was probably some minor noble's third or fourth son, given a job intended for a clerk, probably to get him out from underfoot, but having power over these poor people had clearly gone to his head.

Only Kanemori had promised little Iyo that he would try, so he needed to speak up before the headman's blubbering caused this pack of dogs to get too riled up. When a deer ran, a dog's instincts were to chase it down. Likewise, a peasant's weakness would make a bully eager for violence.

"Greetings, honored officials." Kanemori gave a very proper bow, showing the right amount of deference, and for the correct amount of time. He hadn't slept through *every* lesson.

They didn't even bother to get off their horses. Sitting up there must have made them feel tall.

"Who are you supposed to be?" the tax collector sneered.

"I am Kanemori. I am merely a humble friend of this village, and have come to beg for leniency for them today."

The officials exchanged confused glances. "Who?"

"These kind people have called on me in the hopes that I might be able to appeal to your mercy. Their harvest this year was not very good, purely due to weather beyond their control and not from laziness, yet they still met their obligations. If you examine their stores, you will see that if they meet your new demands, they will not have enough food to survive the winter. They're already eating millet only fit for livestock."

"That's a sad story, only it isn't my problem," the tax collector said.

"But if these villagers sicken and die, then next year there will be no harvest at all." Thus far Kanemori had kept his face neutral and his voice polite, but he could feel that starting to slip. What was it with shortsighted fools? Officials who had nothing personal at stake could never see beyond their immediate gratification. "Please think of the next season, honored representative. Will your lord not be disappointed?"

"Next year I will have a better appointment."

"You talk like a samurai, but you wear no mon," said one of the young men. His own family signal was proudly embroidered on his sleeve with golden thread. "I think I've heard of this old man. He's that ronin hermit that lives up on the mountain."

"Ha! From his ratty clothing, I took him for another peasant!" said one of the other fine young examples of Bushido. "Have you been rolling around in the dirt to look like that?"

"He has dirt under his nails. He's more farmer than samurai."

"You are obviously a long way from home, old man. Step aside. You have no say here. Now where is my rice, headman?"

This was not his place. Kanemori had done all that he could. He had no further legal recourse. It was his duty to step aside. This was the world they lived in.

Enough.

They'd started calling him Kanemori the Defiant for a reason. Nobody had ever accused him of being Kanemori the Eloquent.

"It isn't *your* rice, boy."

"How dare you, old man?"

"Did you grow it? Did you harvest it? No. These people did. I didn't see your pampered ass sweating in the fields."

It was plain the bullies were not used to that kind of response.

"This land belongs to your lord, and he appointed you to administer and defend it. From the look of you songbirds, you've never defended a thing. The last few times these poor saps have been menaced by bandits, they didn't even bother calling for you. They came and got me instead. Your lord has already collected his taxes. This is about your greed. Spare me the sanctimony. I know how it works. That wagon coming down the road is probably some merchant paying you on the side."

"Such impudence! I'll burn this whole place down!" the tax collector bellowed.

The headman squeaked in fear, but the sound was still muffled by the snow. "Please no, young master! Have mercy." Kanemori had forgotten about him there.

"I was feeling merciful until you got some ronin fool involved. Now you will discover what happens when you disobey your betters."

Kanemori was old, tired, and too damned grouchy to get out of the way. His order-taking days were over. "The only difference between the government and bandits is that the bandits are at least honest about it."

"Kill him, Shingen," ordered the tax collector. One of them kicked his horse and it started forward. Kanemori watched him rapidly approach. It was obvious the young man wasn't a trained cavalryman, and that was certainly no warhorse, but the animal seemed used to the idea of running down peasants.

Kanemori reached for his sword. Out of practice or not, a soldier kept his instincts, and not getting pulverized by hooves was among them. He drew his blade as he smoothly stepped aside, and the cut went very deep. The animal's front leg collapsed, the other hooves slipped, and the unseated rider flew over its head to land in the snow.

The tax collector was obviously shocked. This wasn't what normally happened when you rode down a peasant at all. His friend was thrashing about in the suddenly red snow, trying to figure out how he'd gotten there. The horse was screaming. The other horses began bucking, terrified at the sudden smell of hot blood, which just went to show the value of a horse properly trained for war.

There is nothing in the world quite so unnerving as the scream of a horse. Kanemori had killed a lot of men in his day, and none of them really kept him up at night, but the wide-eyed thrashing of a terrified wounded horse always bothered him, so he struck again. This time at the neck. *Clean*. It died quickly.

Worst-case scenario, once this was over, the hungry villagers could eat the horse. Peasants were efficient like that.

It was not so much a battle as a slaughter.

If any of those young samurai had a brain in his head, he would have stayed on his mount and ridden for help. The authorities would have come, and I would have died a criminal. But no. Fury made them dumb and pride demanded that they had to put me in my place. They were better than me. That's just how it was. That's how it always has been, and always must be. They don't understand any other way. That's how it is with these people. It's like they're compelled to meddle.

Such is the nature of man. We must join together to survive, but then somebody has to be in charge. Somebody always has to be in charge. And we let them. At first because we need them, but even when we really don't anymore, they're still there. And their power grows, and grows, and grows, until it consumes everything.

I dream of a world where a man can make his own way, but I suppose there will always be samurai and peasants.

I just wanted to be left alone.

The horse was the only clean death that morning. The rest were ugly. Damned ugly.

No honorable samurai would ever sink to the level of doing manual labor, but Kanemori had often lowered himself to help the local peasants, whether it was cutting trees, or dragging an obstinate ox from the river or, in this case, digging a shallow grave in the frozen ground.

"This must never be spoken of," the headman told the handful of peasants who were standing around their hastily filled hole. The ground was so hard that it had taken a long time, and they'd broken a few valuable shovels in the process, but if there was one thing peasants knew how to do, it was work. By the time the sun had gone down, there was no sign the tax collector, his friends, or their merchant crony had ever come to the village at all.

"If the governor was ever to discover what happened here today, our village would be razed, and every single one of us would be beheaded as criminals." The village headman really wanted to keep his. "We never saw our tax collector. He simply never arrived. Is that understood?"

All of the peasants agreed. Even though none of them had lifted a finger against the tax collector, those in power would never tolerate even the hint of rebellion. If there was something else peasants understood, it was how to keep a secret.

"It is unfortunate, but such things happen when there are so many bandits in these mountains," Kanemori stated flatly. "Perhaps they will send more officials to protect you better in the future."

Of the peasants, only young Iyo was truly glad he'd done what he had. To the rest, he'd simply complicated their already difficult lives. That's because, like him, Iyo was a dreamer. She was still naïve enough to think that one person could change things.

After the somber and terrified villagers returned to

their huts, Kanemori had remained standing by the grave. Men of such stature were due a proper funeral ceremony, and a small shrine. Instead, they got a shallow pit that no one would ever speak of. Some of the villagers had thanked Kanemori, but it had been a dishonest thanks. Those who were incapable of defending themselves were often frightened of those who fought on their behalf. He saw there was fear in their eyes, directed at him, and he did not like it one bit. If he had enjoyed such things, he probably would have made a fine tax collector.

It was time to move on, to find a new place, to try and make a new home again where he could just be left alone. Where he could be free.

But there was no place like that in this world.

Kanemori gazed up at the stars, and wished for another way.

Far up the hill, past an old hut, three villagers built a pyre for the body of an old man. The corpse had mummified, and the wiry muscles of the man underneath showed through the shrunken skin.

The youngest said, "Shouldn't we just put him in a hole? He was only an old hermit. This is costing the village money."

"No, we must do it this way."

"Why? He was a ronin."

"But his kami was that of a samurai. It deserves this. You do not know what he has done for us before."

The boy looked at the stone which was to become a discreet monument over the urn. "It's a lot of work."

"Just make the carving neat."

The inscription was simple.
The Defiant.

Even a ronin could fight with honor. Preventing peasants from being abused and starved was not a grand act, but it was still a great act. While she wished for more action, his life was a worthy one she was proud of.

She understood why she was hidden away. Peasants were not allowed swords, and the chief's daughter was no warrior. She waited in her saya, inside a silk case, in a trunk while time ebbed endlessly past. The samurai themselves faded away. That saddened her, and she hoped there would be another culture that respected her, not let her age away for naught. Eventually, the red blight of rust bloomed on her skin.

Then one day, she was taken from the trunk, and hands passed her to another.

INSTRUMENTS OF WAR

This novella was originally published by Skull Island Expeditions in 2013, edited by Scott Taylor and Doug Seacat. It is set in the universe of the Warmachine *and* Hordes *tabletop war games. If I recall correctly, this is the first thing that I ever wrote set in someone else's already existing universe. It is the origin story of one of their main faction leaders in the game. However, anytime I write a story set in someone else's IP, I always try to do it in a way that everything is self-explanatory enough that you don't need to already be familiar with the setting in order to enjoy it. This is about a fantasy race of vicious desert warriors known as the Skorne, who are just so hard-core and mean that I had a blast writing it. There were some challenges though, in that I had to take an alien culture based on dominance, slavery, and continual warfare, then make them the heroes of their story.*

❖ PART ONE ❖

"WHAT IS IT that you whisper to yourself, child, when the pain becomes too much?"

Makeda wiped the blood from her split lip. Her head was spinning, and her body ached from the savage beating. "I recite the code."

"Why must a warrior recite the code of hoksune?" Archdominar Vaactash asked rhetorically.

"The code shows me the way to exaltation. Only through combat may one understand the way." She studied the blood on the back of her shaking hand as she spoke. All of it was hers . . . so far. She would have to remedy that. Akkad had beaten her mercilessly, but Makeda could still fight. The tremors slowed and then stopped. "Suffering cleanses the weakness from my being. Adhere to the code and I will become worthy."

"Correct. You have learned much for one so young," her grandfather stated without inflection. It was as close to a compliment as the archdominar had ever paid her. "Take up your swords, Makeda of House Balaash. Your lessons are not yet through today."

The practice swords lay in the sand near where she'd been thrown down. They were made of hard wood, their edges dented and cracked from hundreds of impacts, their hilts worn smooth by sweat and callus. She had begun learning their use as soon as she was strong enough to lift them. She may have been a child, but she was skorne, and thus she did not question, she endured. Makeda reached out and took the pair of wooden swords from where they had fallen. They mimicked the heft and balance of true Praetorian blades. They felt comfortable in her grip.

"Rise," Vaactash commanded.

Makeda struggled to her feet, muscles aching in protest.

Her laminate armor had been crafted for an adult, and was far too big for her slim body, but it had kept her intact during Akkad's last merciless assault. She had yet to begin her studies in the art of mortitheurgy, but she did not need to be a master reader of the energy that dwelled within the blood and sinews to understand that her body was in danger of failing her. Her opponent was simply too strong.

Akkad was waiting for her to stand, obviously excited to prove his worth to their grandfather. There were only three present within the gigantic training arena of House Balaash, but one of them was Archdominar Vaactash himself, master of their house, and a warrior so great that he had already secured exaltation for his deeds. It did not matter that the stands were not filled with spectators, since the opinion of Vaactash alone mattered more than several cohorts of troops.

"What lesson would you have me teach her next, Archdominar?" Akkad asked. As the eldest of the two children of Telkesh, first son and heir of mighty Vaactash, Akkad would someday lead House Balaash. The code of hoksune dictated that the eldest, unless unfit for war, must lead. It was vital that Akkad display his martial superiority before his grandfather, and so far he had. "She is still but a tiny thing."

Vaactash's expression was unreadable. "Then why have you had to work so hard to defeat her?"

Makeda took some pleasure in seeing the anger flash across Akkad's face as he sputtered out a response. "I merely wished to provide you with an amusing show."

"Watching a paingiver flay a captured enemy is amusing," Vaactash snapped. "I am here to make sure my grandchildren are being properly prepared to bring glory to my house. Demonstrate to me that you are ready to fight in the name of Balaash."

Akkad dipped his head submissively. "Of course." Her brother was ten years older, far larger, and had already received advanced training under the tutelage of their father's veteran Cataphract. Akkad walked to the nearest rack of weapons and removed a war spear, the heavy pole arm of the Cetrati. It was longer than Makeda was tall, and even though the blade had been replaced with a block of shaped wood, she knew that it would still hit like a titan's tusk. Akkad tested the balance of the heavy weapon before grunting in approval. He spun it effortlessly before pointing it at Makeda's chest. "I will finish her swiftly this time."

"See that you do. Hold nothing back. Demonstrate your conviction."

For the skorne, life consisted of either making war or preparing for it. It was a harsh, brutal, and unyielding existence. That was especially true for those blessed enough to be born into House Balaash, the greatest of all houses. There was no doubt they would fight their hardest until physically unable to continue or were commanded to stop by their superior. Other, lesser houses may have done it differently, perhaps not risked the lives of their heirs so flagrantly, but that was why they were weak and House Balaash was strong.

Makeda welcomed the challenge. She crossed her swords and saluted her brother.

Their grandfather studied the combatants intently, his white eyes unblinking. Though bent with age, his mere presence seemed to fill the arena. This was a warrior who had led tens of thousands into battle and conquered more houses than any other dominar in several generations, earning himself the extremely rare title of archdominar. He was a master mortitheurge capable of commanding the mightiest beasts and rending unbelievable magic from the flesh. Makeda wished that she could have a fraction of his understanding, but promised herself that one day she would. Vaactash was the epitome of what it meant to be skorne.

After a long moment of consideration, Vaactash stepped aside, gathered up his red robes, and took a seat on the first tier of the training arena. He gestured dismissively. "Continue."

"Come, sister. Let us end this."

Akkad swung the spear in a wide arc. Makeda raised both blades to intercept, but the impact was so great that it nearly tore them from her grasp. Her arms were already exhausted and quivering. She grimaced and pushed back, but her boots slid through the sand of the arena as Akkad overpowered her. The pressure released, the heavy pole moved back, and Makeda lurched aside as Akkad stabbed at her. He followed, relentless, eyes narrowed, looking for an opportunity to finish her.

He was stronger, but she was faster. Stepping in to the threat, Makeda slashed at Akkad's face with her right, narrowly missing. *Show your foe one blade. Kill him with the other.* She stabbed with her left sword, and clipped the edge of his breastplate. Akkad didn't seem to notice. The spear hummed through the air again, and this time Makeda was unable to stop it.

She crashed hard against the arena wall.

The code of hoksune declared that the eldest was the default heir, but every child of the highest caste was a valuable war asset, and thus not to be wasted frivolously. Yet, when Makeda looked into Akkad's maddened eyes, she wondered if her brother really did intend to kill her. She narrowly rolled aside as the wall was pulverized into splinters. Vaactash said nothing.

Her brother was relentless. The war spear covered vast swaths of the arena with each attack. The muscles of Makeda's arms clenched in agony as her practice swords bounced harmlessly away. Sweat poured down the inside of her cursed, cumbersome armor. She was struck in the ribs, and then in the leg. Flesh bruised and swelling, Makeda continued fighting. She would fight until her archdominar said it was time to stop or she was dead, for that was the code. Another massive strike knocked one of her blades away. It spun through the air and landed in the stands with a clatter.

Makeda knew she was losing, but the words of the code played through her mind. *Only by conflict can the code be understood. Embrace your suffering and gain clarity.*

Time seemed to slow. His moves were too fierce, too uncontrollable. He had underestimated her resolve. Akkad lifted his spear high overhead before bringing it down in a crashing arc. Makeda barely moved aside in time. The mighty hit threw a cloud of sand into the air, but before Akkad could lift it, Makeda planted one boot on top of the war spear's blade. Though slight, the extra weight was enough to cause his grip to slip as he tried to tug the spear away. The momentary surprise was just enough to allow Makeda one clean strike.

"*Balaash!*"

The tip of her practice sword caught Akkad in the side of the head. Blood flew as skin split wide. The spear was pulled from beneath her boot and the siblings stumbled away from each other.

Makeda gathered herself, but there was a lull in the fighting. Akkad was glaring at her as if stunned, one gauntlet pressed to his head to staunch the flow of red. She had struck him hard. His ear appeared to be mangled, and the tip was broken and hanging by only a small bit of skin. Surely, he had felt that one.

"I have seen enough."

Gasping for breath, barely able to stand, Makeda looked to their archdominar. Vaactash nodded once. Her heart swelled.

"Both of you have improved since last I watched you spar. It pleases me that the blood of House Balaash does not run thin in this generation. One day I will die and your father, Telkesh, will lead my House, and you will serve him. In time, Akkad, you will take his place. When you learn to temper your ambition with wisdom, you will bring great honor to our house. Your sister will make a fine Tyrant in your service, and I have no doubt that multitudes will be conquered to feed our slave pits. Until then, you have much to learn."

"Yes, Archdominar."

"The more you bleed in training, the less you will bleed in war. Learn from every fight, Akkad. Do you know why Makeda defeated you this time?"

"She did not defeat me!" Akkad snarled.

"Silence!" The entire arena seemed to flex at Vaactash's

displeasure. That one stern word caused Akkad to fall to his knees and bow. "Do not ever disagree with the ruler of your house. If that had been an actual Praetorian blade, the contents of your thick skull would have been emptied into the sand. Fool. How dare you question my decree?"

The siblings shrank back. The archdominar's legendary temper was a thing only spoken of in hushed whispers.

"For that you will not have this wound repaired. Have the end cut off and cauterized. You will wear that scar as a reminder of your impertinence."

"Yes, Archdominar." Akkad kept his head down as droplets of blood painted a pattern in the sand. He was trying not to sound sullen. "It will be as you command."

"Again I ask, do you know why a tiny child capable of hiding in your shadow managed to beat you?"

"Forgive my ignorance. I . . . I do not know the answer, Grandfather." Akkad risked a quick glance toward Makeda. She could feel the malice in his gaze. Makeda did not gloat. She had merely done her best, as was required. "Please, enlighten me."

"You only understand the concept of victory. Makeda does not comprehend the concept of defeat."

A generation had passed, but the lessons of Vaactash would never leave her. His words were as ingrained into Makeda as the code of hoksune itself. It had been a year since her grandfather's death under the tusks of a great beast of the plains, but she still found herself calling upon his wisdom during times of struggle. She was a mature, yet unproven warrior now. The Swords of Balaash were sheathed at her side. Slivers of her grandfather's sacral stone were among those empowering the mighty blades, and though only an extoller could contact the exalted dead, Makeda always felt as though Vaactash was there to guide her with his wisdom.

Makeda would need that wisdom if she were to survive the day.

The atmosphere inside the command tent was as heated as the drought-scourged plains. The officers of her decurium were in disagreement over what to do next.

"Tyrant Makeda, House Muzkaar's forces are nearly upon us."

"Akkad's reinforcements have not arrived yet. We are badly outnumbered. If we do not fall back now, we die here." Urkesh was the dakar of her taberna of Venators. Of course a warrior who specialized in engaging the enemy from a distance with reiver fire would choose the pragmatic, if somewhat cowardly, approach.

"We have been commanded to hold this hill! So we dig in and hold!" Dakar Barkal was the leader of her Praetorian karax. Of course, the karax would choose to die like that, in a perfect xenka formation, each of their great shields being used to protect themselves and their fellow Praetorians at their side as they impaled their enemies on their long pikes. "Honor demands it."

"Muzkaar outnumbers us five to one," Urkesh insisted. "Your honor will not beat those odds."

"Do you question the strength of the karax?" Barkal shouted.

Makeda let them debate. She knew that they would follow her final decision, no matter what. Perhaps in the meantime one of them would surprise her with a solution.

"Your mighty shields won't matter when a wall of titans stampede over you." Venators were the lowest of the warrior caste, but Urkesh was young and hotheaded. Makeda doubted that he realized how close he was treading to simply having Barkal strike him down in anger. "We cannot hold anything if we are all dead and howling in the Void. I say we retreat from this trap, move to the plains, where we can maneuver and harass these Muzkaar dogs until Akkad's forces arrive."

Barkal looked to Makeda, his narrow face pinched with rage. She needed every warrior, even a Venator whose devotion to dying by the hoksune code was questionable at best. Makeda shook her head in the negative. She would approve no duels of slighted honor until after their battle was through. She could not spare any warriors. Deprived of his chance to gut Urkesh for his insolence, Barkal went back to defending his position. "Our duty requires us to hold," he snapped.

Deep in thought, Makeda listened to the words of her subordinates as they argued. She was glad to see that none of them feared death, only the possibility of failure. Skorne lived to serve and die, but there was no honor in dying pointlessly. This was her first command, and she would not lose it so easily.

Primus Zabalam stepped forward and placed his body between the two shouting warriors. Both dakars stepped back out of respect for their senior officer. "Regardless of which decision is best, we must give the order soon. We will be cut off by Tyrant Naram's beasts within the hour, and then it will not matter either way." It was the first time the veteran leader of her Praetorian swordsmen had spoken. Zabalam was the oldest warrior present, and had even served as one of Vaactash's personal guard. As usual, he spoke with the wisdom that could only be gained from countless battles. "Our commander must choose now, or the decision will be made for her."

The map was open on the table, but she was staring through it, rather than at it. The map was irrelevant. She had already memorized every brush stroke and line of ink. *Fail in their orders, retreat and live to rejoin the rest of the army, or hold their ground in the vain hope that her brother would arrive in time, and more than likely die as nothing more than a temporary distraction*... Ultimately, the choice was hers alone to make.

The situation was dire. The honor of House Balaash lay heavy on her shoulders. It was times like this that tested a warrior's dedication to the code.

Grandfather, what would you have me do?

Having only recently reached the age sufficient to go through the rites of passage necessary to be considered a full member of the warrior caste, this was the first time Makeda had led a cohort into battle on behalf of House Balaash. Archdominar Telkesh had ordered her to hold this position, a small hill on the plains south of Kalos, but no one had predicted this level of resistance. Their spies had reported that the bulk of the enemy had been camped much closer to the city, nowhere near here. So the main army of House Balaash was marching unopposed, while Makeda's cohort was badly outnumbered against the entirety of the forces of House Muzkaar.

If somehow she did live through the day, Makeda intended to have those spies tortured for a very long time.

That, however, did not solve her current dilemma. The enemy army was led by Naram, a Tyrant legendary for both his skill with beasts and the cruelty he used in breaking them. She had learned what she could of Naram's exploits, and had come to respect him for his brutal and unflinching victories. He was truly an adversary worthy of her father and his mighty army, not nearly as appropriate a foe for an inexperienced commander and one small cohort, but the ancestors had placed Naram against her, not her father. This battle was hers.

Makeda knew it was not her ever-increasing skills in the art of mortitheurgy, nor her considerable natural talent with the blade that made her valuable to her house. It was her certainty in the truthfulness of the code of hoksune. Her grandfather had recognized that. So as she always did, Makeda searched the code for an answer.

Combat favors the aggressor. There is a time for both defense and mobility, but every tactic is merely a tool enabling your inevitable attack. To draw with and kill your enemy is the true path toward exaltation.

She said a silent thank you to the shards of her grandfather's essence resting in her swords.

Makeda held up one hand. Her officers were immediately silent, waiting. "We will not retreat..." Regardless of whether they agreed or not, they immediately snapped to and began to move out to spread the word. "Nor will we hold this position."

The men froze, uncertain. They looked to each other, none daring to question their new commander. Though she was the youngest in the room, she was their superior both by birth and by appointment. Finally, Barkal of the karax dared speak. "What would you have us do then, Second Born?"

Makeda smiled. "We strike."

The sound of the reivers firing reminded Makeda of a swarm of angry buzzing insects, only this swarm was made up of thousands of razor-sharp projectiles. A House Muzkaar titan bellowed in agony as its hide was shredded. The gigantic warbeast took a few halting steps, showering bright blood from a plethora of wounds. Several Muzkaar beast handlers lashed the beast, urging it forward through the steel cloud. Driven mad with pain, the titan lumbered onward.

"Reload!" Urkesh shouted at his Venators. There was only a single datha of ten armigers, but they acted quickly, unscrewing the spent gas cylinders from their awkward reiver weapons. Makeda sized up the distances. The armigers were quick, but not quick enough. The titan would trample right over Urkesh's warriors and she would lose her ranged advantage.

House Muzkaar had brought no ranged capability of their own, and dozens of Muzkaar corpses littered the road from where they had been scythed down by her Venators while trying to cross. Makeda did not wish to give up that advantage.

Makeda had few warbeasts of her own to spare. Since her cohort had been marching quickly in order to seize their objective, she had only been given a pair of cyclops savages. The tougher, but slower, beasts had been left with Akkad. She reached out with her mind, using her mortitheurge powers to find the lump of muscle and hate that was the nearest cyclops. She took hold of its mind and steered it into the path of the enemy titan.

The cyclops hoisted its great sword and stalked forward, towering several feet over even the tallest warriors in its path. What the cyclops lacked in intelligence it made up for in violent cunning. The beast's single eye flicked back and forth, seeing the battlefield as only a cyclops could, a few seconds into the future, and Makeda wondered idly if the cyclops could see its own death coming.

The earth shook as the wounded titan charged. Each footfall was like an earthquake. As large as the cyclops was, it was dwarfed by the titan. Armored tusks crashed into the cyclops' armor with a clang that could be heard over all the chaos of the battle. The cyclops went rolling away, and the wounded titan followed, swinging wildly with its massive gauntlets. Instinct demanded the cyclops flee, and it screeched in protest as Makeda overcame its mind and forced it to stand its ground.

Their weapons ready, Urkesh shouted at his taberna. "Concentrate fire on that titan!" The Reivers rose from the ditch they'd taken cover in, aimed, and let loose a stream of razor needles. Hundreds of projectiles ricocheted off of armor plates and ivory tusks, whining into the distance, but hundreds more found their mark. Hide puckered and bled as the titan roared and crashed into the dust.

Somehow, her cyclops had survived the mighty charge. Barely alive, it was struggling to stand, using its sword to lever itself up. Makeda used her magic, feeling the precious blood pumping out of the cyclops' damaged body, and then she reached deep within the beast and spurred its fury to whole new heights. The new anger gave her beast unnatural strength, and before the enemy could recover, Makeda's cyclops cleaved one of the titan's four arms off at the shoulder.

The titan's death bellow was like music across the plains. Its suffering would probably be heard all the way to the city of Kalos. Truly this was a great day for House Balaash.

The Muzkaar beast handlers that had been driving that titan were fleeing back across a ravine. "Urkesh." Makeda's voice was calm. "Make sure this is the last time those beast handlers annoy me."

The order was given, and the whine of razor needles filled the air, but Makeda had already moved on to survey the next part of the battle.

House Muzkaar had not expected her furious attack, and Makeda had stacked their corpses deep as a result. Tyrant Naram's army had been confident of their victory, but Makeda had struck so hard and so fast that House Muzkaar had been thrown into disarray. A wild charge by her swordsmen and karax had bloodied Muzkaar. They'd pushed back, but it had been disorganized, panicked, and it was only through their vastly superior numbers that Muzkaar had survived at all. She'd drawn most of her melee troops away, letting her karax set up a defensive line, allowing her Venators time to bleed the enemy. The proud swordsmen were eager to return to glory, but she ordered them to be patient. Let Muzkaar think they'd been used up...

As the sun had climbed and the hot morning had turned into blistering afternoon, House Muzkaar had counterattacked, and though it had been sloppy and hurried, Makeda was drastically outnumbered. She could not win a war of attrition against a Tyrant with a stable worth of titans.

Despite heavy casualties, the line of Praetorian karax was standing firm. They stood shoulder to shoulder, a wall of steel and wood, shields absorbing blows and their pikes thrusting continuously, spilling Muzkaar blood. The karax were methodical, plodding forward, always stabbing.

The code of hoksune taught that the purest combat was individual, warrior on warrior. She could see now why it was so much more difficult for a member of the karax to gain exaltation than a swordsman. This was not the battle she knew, the calculation of offense and defense, and the sudden flash of a sword . . . this was mechanical. This was more like watching the lower castes harvest grain from the fields. The karax would stab, block, stab, block, and whenever Barkal saw an opening he would order an advance through the bloodstained plains, and then, as one, they would begin their harvest again. It was hypnotic to watch.

Zabalam was waiting for her at the ridge overlooking their remaining karax. His taberna of elite Praetorian swordsman were ready there, crouched in the tall golden grass, hidden, as per her orders, until the time was right.

"Second Born Makeda." Zabalam bowed.

"A fine afternoon for war, Primus," Makeda greeted him respectfully. Though she outranked him by birth and command, Zabalam had been her primary instructor in the art of the two swords. Truly, he was a credit to their house. She thanked the ancestors that her father had seen fit to send Zabalam with her cohort. "How goes it here?"

"The swordsmen chafe at being told to hide in the grass like mere Hestatians."

"They are elite warriors, proud . . ." Makeda noted. "It is understandable."

"They will do as they are told . . . I do not think your brother will relieve us in time."

"Akkad will come." Makeda had her doubts, but she did not speak them aloud.

"The karax have fought past the point of exhaustion. They will fall soon, and when they do, we will be overrun by these wretched Muzkaar *belek*."

"Good." A belek was a thick-skulled herd animal, strong but notorious for blundering stupidly into wallows and getting stuck. Makeda did not think Zabalam realized what a fitting insult that was.

"Good?" Since Zabalam's face had been split nearly in half with a sword many years before, only half of his mouth moved when he frowned. The other side was permanently frozen in a straight line. "I'm unsure how that is a good thing?"

"We cannot outlast a force this size. Our only hope to defeat them is by killing their Tyrant. Without Naram, Muzkaar will quickly fall. What do you know of Naram?"

"He is renowned for his skill, but your grandfather defeated him once and took many slaves from one of his cities."

"Yes. It is said he retains a rather passionate hatred of House Balaash, and he is still a warrior without peer. My ancestor shamed him, so he will come for revenge. He knows I am here, so Naram will want to give the killing blow himself."

"Or maybe he will capture you and turn you over to his Paingivers."

Makeda shrugged. "Either way, Naram is coming, and when he does, I will kill him first."

"You remind me of your grandfather sometimes . . . But what of the karax?"

"Hopefully Akkad's reinforcements will have an extoller with them." Only a member of the extoller caste or the much rarer ancestral guardians could save a warrior's spiritual essence in a sacral stone so they could live on as a revered companion to the exalted. "Look at how many they have slaughtered. Surely some of them will be worth saving."

"And if Akkad has none of their caste amongst his reinforcements?"

She thought it over for a moment. Though no extoller had arrived, the warriors below did not know that, so she signaled for a message runner. "Tell Dakar Barkal that I am personally observing the battle, watching for any who are worthy of exaltation. Tell him to spread the word to his troops." The messenger did not seem disturbed in the least that he was to relay something which would raise an impossible hope. He merely bowed and ran down the hill. Makeda turned back to Zabalam. "That will make them fight that much harder."

Zabalam's half face twisted up in the other direction. "You *definitely* remind me of your grandfather."

The temperature continued to climb as the sun beat

down on her armor. Droplets of sweat rolled freely from under her helmet and into her eyes. Makeda welcomed the sting. The cries of the dead and dying were all around her. The cohort of House Muzkaar seemed to be an endless thing stretching across the plains. She passed the time mentally steering her cyclopes toward the weakest points of the Balaash lines. She stood there, her back banner whipping in the wind. Makeda wanted all of the enemy army to see her, defiant. Let them tell their Tyrant that a scion of House Balaash was waiting for him.

Makeda felt the pang of loss as the cyclops that had been injured earlier was dragged down and killed. She drained the last bits of vitality that had been dwelling in the cyclops tissues and gathered that strength to herself. She would need it shortly.

The line of karax faltered, broke, and were swept away before the swords of House Muzkaar. Their center had fallen.

A trumpet blew, and then another. A black banner was raised on the other side of the road and waved back and forth. The entire Muzkaar host seemed to hesitate, then their lines parted as a small escort of warriors and beasts advanced through the army.

"That is a lot of titans . . ." Zabalam muttered.

There were only two of the great grey beasts lumbering along behind Naram's personal banner, but one titan was a lot of titan.

"On my signal, rally your men and charge that banner. All that matters is that Naram dies. I shall use my power to give you speed," she ordered. Zabalam conveyed that order to his swordsmen who were waiting in cover. She mentally summoned her remaining cyclops closer. "Runner." Another messenger appeared at her side. "Tell Urkesh that when I draw my swords, his Venators must clear for me a path to that banner."

The knot of Muzkaar elite had advanced to the front of the army. The squat, powerfully built skorne in the lead had to be Naram. With a mighty spiked club resting on one shoulder, and his black armor gleaming in the sun, Naram appeared a formidable foe. She could sense his mortitheurge power, churning and hungry.

"I remember when you were teaching me the way of the two swords, Primus . . ." Makeda said.

"You were my finest student."

"I recall now one lesson in particular. Show your enemy one sword, and when they are focused upon that, kill them with the other. I am the first sword . . . Await my signal."

Makeda walked down the hill to where Naram and his army were waiting. She ran her hands across the tops of the thick grass. It was sharp enough to draw blood. The fury taken from her beasts was like a hot lump of power within her chest. She stepped through puddles of blood, and over the mangled bodies of her warriors.

Naram was striding toward her, with a great wall of titan muscle on each side. "Makeda of House Balaash!" he challenged. The two beasts were obviously well controlled, as they took a few extra steps forward to shield their master.

She stopped just within range of his voice. "Tyrant Naram." She placed her hands on the hilts of her sheathed swords. Part of her grandfather was within those swords. She would never let them fall into the hands of someone so unworthy. "It has been a fine battle so far. Have you come to surrender personally?"

The enemy Tyrant gave a hearty laugh. "I must admit, your tenacity impresses me. It has been a generation since I've seen someone so outnumbered account for themselves so well." He had to shout to be heard over the hot wind. "Order your remaining warriors to lay down their arms. Swear fealty to me, and you may retain your caste. There is room in House Muzkaar for such as you. A political marriage will be arranged to one of my sons. Your father will have to withdraw from Kalos, but this will be best for both our houses." Naram waved his free hand dismissively. "Or you can fight, and once you are defeated and shamed, you can join your men as slaves to my house. Choose quickly."

Naram's words, though certainly filled with truth, did not sway her. He did not understand just how powerful Makeda's mortitheurgy really was ... Few among their people could. Their dark magic took decades of devotion to master, but no one was more devoted than a child of House Balaash. She closed her eyes and felt the world around her. Living tissue and pumping blood ... She could sense Naram and his army before her, and then her few remaining warriors behind, each and every one of them reduced to their component bits of muscle, bone, and sinew, cloaked in steel and laminate armor, powered by blood and spirit, all of it there waiting to be manipulated by her superior will. Gathering up the energy she'd gleaned from her fallen beast, she awoke the power residing within Zabalam's waiting Praetorian swordsmen ... In her mind's eye, their blood turned to molten, pulsing fire.

She opened her eyes. Zabalam's standard bearer rose from the grass and waved the flag of the Praetorian swordsmen. They leapt from their hiding place and moved with impossible speed. Makeda drew the twin swords and charged.

"So be it," Naram stated. His titans both took another great step forward, completely shielding him from view.

Urkesh had received her message, and his Venators fired. Makeda heard the high-pitched screech before she felt the passage through the air all around her, buzzing through the tops of the grass like angry bees. Razor needles exploded into the titans, and then Makeda was within the rain of blood.

The titan's leg was as big around as a tree, and the first sword of Balaash cleaved a chunk of meat sufficient for a feast from its thigh. She sidestepped as a massive gauntlet was swung past. Makeda was faster than any mortal had a right to be, and then she was behind the first titan. The second studied her, giant head tilting to the side in confusion, tiny black eyes blinking, before Naram drove it toward her like a great, flesh-covered weapon.

A hand, palm as big as Makeda's torso, reached for her, hoping to crush the life from her, but Makeda lashed out, the supernatural edge barely slowed, and the titan's thumb went flipping off into the grass. Makeda dove and rolled, armor clanking, and she came up behind the second titan before it could even begin to bellow in pain.

Naram was in front of her, surprised, but already invoking his own mortitheurgy.

But then they were surrounded in swordsmen, and most of them were not his.

The fight was brutal. It was a swirling mass of chaos as swordsmen clashed beneath the thunder of titan feet. She beheaded a Muzkaar swordsman that crossed her path. Naram crushed the skull of a Balaash warrior with his club. The two leaders met in the middle of the melee, and Makeda knew that this was the perfect moment spoken of in the code of hoksune.

Her blades met the spiked club. Naram was incredibly strong, surely driven by his own magic. She had to cross her swords and use both to block at once. The impact would have broken a normal blade, but the Swords of Balaash were anything but normal. Naram shoved her back, and Makeda moved gracefully away, ducking beneath a wild swing from a Muzkaar guard. She returned the favor by removing that swordsman's face.

As his essence fled, Makeda could feel herself growing stronger. *Let this dance continue forever, for surely, this is exaltation.* She had never felt so good.

The nearest titan picked up one of her swordsmen in two vast hands and pulled the screaming warrior in half. Then another barrage of reiver fire put out the titan's eyes. Makeda's remaining cyclops was chopping away at the other titan.

The Tyrant swung at her, but she was able to skip aside. Naram's mortitheurgy surged outward in a wave of force and swordsmen, both black and red clad, were knocked down. Makeda felt the hot energy pass over her, but she resisted it by sheer force of will, and leapt right back into the fray.

Naram looked down in surprise as the tip of a sword burst from his abdomen. He swung his club in a mighty back arc, and the Balaash swordsman that had struck the Tyrant from behind disappeared in spray of red. Naram grimaced and pressed one gauntlet to his stomach. The nearest titan roared in agony as Naram used his power to afflict the terrible wound onto the flesh of the beast in his stead.

Already severely injured, the titan toppled. Makeda jumped back as the beast blotted out the sun. She narrowly made it out of the way as the concussive impact blew the tall grass flat. Makeda found herself on her back. She rolled and sprang up, trying to get back into the fight, but then there was a black flash as Naram's club filled her vision.

She was falling. Turning through the air. The golden grass rushed up to meet her.

Much as Naram had a moment before, Makeda desperately called upon her power, instinctively seeking out her mental connection to her remaining warbeast. She could feel the damage, the all consuming agony, and the gasping blackness of the void, and instead of welcoming it, Makeda took all of that and shoved it off on her cyclops.

The cyclops absorbed all of the damage it could, snuffing out its life like a candle, but even then, that wasn't enough. The impact still left Makeda stunned and bleeding. The cyclops' body collapsed into the waiting arms of the Muzkaar titan, and not even realizing it was dead, the titan violently attacked the corpse, pummeling it beneath its great fists. Even disoriented, Makeda was far too practiced to let any vital life energy go to waste, and she instinctively gathered up the last of the cyclops' dying rage to fuel her magic.

The world was spinning. Makeda got to her hands and

knees. All around her, the Balaash swordsmen were falling. Muzkaar soldiers were swarming in from every direction. Naram was walking toward her, spiked club dripping red.

Before he had died, Archdominar Vaactash had taught Makeda everything he knew about the thin line between life and death. Her people were a stubborn, hardy lot, and they did not give up their mortal shells easily. She was surrounded by the bodies of dead and dying members of House Balaash, but House Balaash still had need of their services. Makeda drew upon the well of power within her own blood. It was the greatest feat she had ever attempted, far beyond what she should have been able to accomplish as a novice mortitheurge.

She was a scion of House Balaash, granddaughter of the greatest warrior the world had ever known, and daughter of Archdominar Telkesh . . . Makeda did not comprehend defeat.

"You are not done yet. Rise and fight for House Balaash!"

Her power spun outward, blowing the tall grass almost as if another titan had fallen. Naram froze as he sensed the sudden shift in the battlefield. The wind died and the air hung unnaturally still. "What have you done?" the Tyrant of Muzkaar demanded.

And then the fallen soldiers of House Balaash stood up and returned to the fight.

"What have you done!" Blades pierced Naram's armor. His remaining titan bellowed and died, and then there were no beasts left for him to shift his wounds to. Hearts stopped, eyes blank, bodies broken, the spirits of the soldiers of House Balaash pushed onward. A sword took a piece of Naram's arm, another pierced his leg, and a third knocked his helmet off. "What have you done!" He clubbed them down, shattering limbs left and right.

Makeda was on her feet, striding forward, both swords raised. She called upon all the fury left inside and used it to give strength to her arms. Bleeding, barely standing, Naram turned to meet her . . .

But it was too late.

They were eye to eye. Naram's gaze slowly lowered toward his chest. Both of the Swords of Balaash had been driven cleanly through armor and between his ribs. Two separate shafts of red steel protruded from his back. The heavy club fell from nerveless fingers.

The army of House Muzkaar was frozen, staring at their Tyrant in shocked disbelief. They slowly lowered their weapons to their sides. The battlefield was strangely silent as the fallen swordsmen of Balaash sank back to the ground, their obligations fulfilled. Only a handful of Zabalam's swordsmen had survived, and all of them were painted red, panting, and exhausted.

"You are victorious?" Naram whispered.

Makeda nodded. "Yes." She could feel the strength leaving Naram's body. He was only still standing because he was leaning against her. Makeda knew the instant she removed her swords, Naram would perish. She slowly lowered him to the grass.

"Heh . . . Today was a good day. Best battle . . . in a very long time . . ." He trailed off, and Makeda could no longer hear his words. His eyes were wide, but not with fear. She pressed her ear in close. Makeda could feel his dying breath on her skin.

"The code shows me the way to exaltation. Only through combat may one understand the way." Naram gasped. "Suffering cleanses the weakness from my being... Adhere to the code... and I will become..."

"*Worthy,*" she finished the verse.

What is it that you whisper to yourself, child, when the pain becomes too much?

This was a great and worthy leader of skorne. This one did not deserve to be lost in the Void. Makeda looked to the nearest Muzkaar soldier. "Do you have extollers amongst you?" The swordsman nodded quickly. "Summon one. Now."

They did not look the part of a victorious force as they marched along the road northward. There was no parade of slaves, no baggage train of looted treasure, no trophy heads raised on poles. No, Makeda thought to herself, they looked more like the losers. Only one third of her warriors had survived, and many of them were injured. They limped down the road, reeking of death, and covered in dried blood and bandages. They had no warbeasts. They'd been forced to leave their dead behind without ceremony. Their weapons and armor, much of it broken, was piled upon a wagon.

Yet, her single decurium had somehow defeated the combined might of a great house cohort.

This was not a pure victory however. Normally when a Tyrant is thrown down and a house conquered, then that house would be absorbed by the victors. That had not been an option here. Makeda was both relieved and bitter about the results. The Muzkaar army had them completely surrounded, and her ragged survivors would not have stood a chance. Akkad and his reinforcements had never arrived, because if they had, then all of House Muzkaar would have been in chains . . .

Instead, she had received a message from Naram's heir. It had simply read, *As you have spared the essence of my father, I will spare you.*

The sun was bloated and red as it set over the golden plains. Only two of her officers had lived through the battle. Dakar Urkesh, who stank of the caustic gasses used to drive his reivers, and the seemingly unkillable Primus Zabalam marched beside her. Dakar Barkal had perished, as had the vast majority of his karax.

"Tell me, Zabalam . . ." It was a sign of weakness, but she struggled to keep the weariness from her voice. "This was the first battle I have commanded. Does victory always taste so bitter?"

"Sometimes . . ." His ruined face was expressionless. "This was a great victory. Glory will be positively heaped upon your name when word gets back to our house."

She was unsure if Zabalam was capable of sarcasm. "Do you mock me, Primus?"

"I am incapable of mockery. If you believe I do so, say the word and I will cut out my own heart and hand it to you by way of apology." He looked her in the eye. "The bitterness is only because you were denied your rightful spoils."

"We should have crushed all of Muzkaar and looted Kalos, if only Akkad had brought his cohort like he was supposed to," Urkesh spat.

"That is what troubles me," Zabalam said.

An entire army had not troubled Zabalam earlier, why would the lack of one? "What disturbs you, Primus?"

"Just a feeling. Forgive an old swordsman for his nerves." Zabalam looked at the ground, not wanting to meet her gaze. "I am sure it is nothing."

"Where was One Ear anyway?" Urkesh muttered.

Makeda instantly backhanded the Venator in the mouth. The steel of her gauntlet split his lip. Urkesh crashed into the dirt, and before he could even begin to sit up, the tip of her blade was pressed against his throat. She twisted the hilt slightly, letting the edge of the sword of Balaash rest against the artery. Makeda could feel his pulse through the steel. All she had to do was relax a muscle and he would die.

Urkesh averted his eyes and did not speak. It was the not speaking that saved his life.

"Heed my words, Urkesh," Makeda hissed. "You killed many today. Your *taberna* was essential to achieve victory. You may prove useful for me again. For that reason, and that reason alone, I will spare your life. However, you will never speak ill of anyone above your caste again, or I will have the paingivers flay you. Do you understand?"

"Yes, Second Born."

"You do not truly understand hoksune. You kill from a distance. You have not looked into another warrior's eyes as they drown in their own blood. Hoksune is not real to you as it is to Akkad, who has felt a thousand deaths at his hands. Lay there in shame and think upon your transgression." She sheathed the sword in one quick motion and walked away. "Come with me, Zabalam."

The old Praetorian left the young Venator in the road

and followed his commander. "What would you have of me?"

Makeda did not need deference, she needed honesty. "I have no patience for speaking around the truth. You know that. I never have."

Zabalam nodded. "Which is exactly why I asked to be assigned to your cohort rather than your brother's."

"So speak plainly and tell me what is on your mind, elder teacher."

"Our lack of reinforcements was suspicious. We should be dead." Zabalam took his time, choosing his words carefully. "Akkad has always desired glory. Abandoning you in a battle is as sure a murder as a knife in the back, and it is not unheard of for siblings to murder each other in order to rule a house."

Makeda shook her head. "But Akkad is the eldest. He is already Telkesh's heir. Ancient tradition declares that the eldest must rule." Despite any of her personal opinions about her brother, she would never go against the traditions of her caste, for to do otherwise would cause chaos and weaken their house. "The order of succession has been decreed. Telkesh rules and has declared it so. If I believed him unfit to lead, then I would declare a challenge. Anything else would be dishonorable."

"Ah, Makeda, but not everyone shares your devotion. They do not follow the old ways so closely. They merely talk of it while having no real devotion in their hearts. They assume all are like them. So they whisper and talk. They are not like us. They lurk in the shadows and play politics with their birthright." Zabalam spit on the ground. "Their words are like poison, and it would not surprise me if one such as that would whisper to your brother that you are a threat to his eventual rule."

There had to be another explanation. She knew that Akkad was extremely ambitious, and he was a fine warrior. She had no doubt he would make a decent archdominar when the time came. Violating the wishes of their father Telkesh was simply unimaginable, and she did not know which idea she found more disturbing: that her brother would leave her to die, or that anyone would doubt her honor so much.

"Incoming riders!" the shout went up along the column. "They fly the colors of Balaash."

Scouts for the army. They would be reunited soon enough. "Do not worry, Zabalam. I will speak to my father about today's events. I'm sure there is an explanation for Akkad's delay."

"As you wish." The Primus bowed.

She could see the cavalry now. The scouts tore down the road, heading straight for Makeda's tattered banner. The first rider came right up to Makeda, riding upon a ferox, one of the swiftest predators of the plains. The messenger wore the insignia of a dakar, and her mount foamed from the journey. The creature snarled at Makeda, so the rider punched it in the back of the head. It wheeled about and snapped at her legs with is long razor teeth, but she simply struck it again harder. Dominance established, that finally settled it down.

"Second Born Makeda," the messenger dipped her helmet. It was as close as could be approximated to a bow while on the back of an enraged ferox. "You are alive?"

"Obviously," she answered. "Where is the army?"

"Encamped a few miles to the north," the rider seemed rattled. "We were told your cohort had been destroyed by Tyrant Naram."

"He tried. It was an excellent battle, but Naram was the one who was destroyed. Who told you such lies?"

"Forgive me. It was all over the camp. Ancestors! You have not heard?"

"Spit it out, Praetorian!"

The rider was obviously terrified. Her mount sensed the unusual fear, and turned back curious and sniffing. "Your father—Archdominar Telkesh is dead."

The ferox was unbelievably swift. The powerfully muscled beast moved in great leaping bounds, its talons ripping up tufts of grass and dirt as they moved across the plains. A sudden plunge down a ravine forced Makeda to place one hand against the reptilian skin before her saddle. It was softer than expected. The ferox turned one curious eye back toward her. Perhaps, if it had been any other unfamiliar rider, the vicious thing may have attempted something, but it could sense the danger in Makeda, and simply did as it was told.

Her mount jumped high into the air, taking them over the edge of the ravine and into the open dusk. A large encampment stretched before them, hundreds of tents, all flying the proud banner of House Balaash. Housing thousands of soldiers, thousands of slaves, and dozens of beasts, it was more of a mobile city than an encampment. Makeda roughly kneed the ferox in the ribs, pointing it toward the nearest set of lanterns.

The guards rose immediately to challenge her approach. Just because she was flying the banner of Balaash did not necessarily make her an ally, especially here in Muzkaar land.

"Who goes there?"

"Makeda, Second Born of Telkesh."

The nearest guard shifted the grip on his spear. "Makeda is dead."

Makeda reached up and removed her helmet as the ferox padded closer to the lantern light. The sudden wind felt cool on her scalp. "Silence, imbecile. Take me to my father."

The guards were stunned. "She lives!" One of the soldiers, probably unfamiliar with the violent nature of the ferox, nearly lost a hand when he tried to gesture a direction. The beast snapped at him, and the daggerlike teeth missed his wrist by less than an inch.

A smarter guard pointed with his spear. "Forgive us. The archdominar's tent is over there."

Makeda looked at the tent. That was not her father's tent. That was Akkad's tent. There was a sudden pain in her heart, an altogether unfamiliar feeling. "Ha!" She kicked the ferox hard. It reached Akkad's tent within three bounds. Makeda slid off of the saddle and walked quickly inside. These soldiers recognized her and immediately bowed and moved out of her way.

Despite being a huge affair which needed several of its own pack animals to move anywhere, the inside of Akkad's tent was crowded with warriors of rank and lineage. Makeda recognized many of her father's advisors and officers. They all wore solemn expressions which turned to shock when they saw her. Whispers radiated outward as all eyes turned to see.

"Where is my father?" Makeda demanded, but already knowing the answer.

Heads were bowed. Feet were studied. A scribe hurried to the rear of the tent and disappeared beneath a flap into the sleeping quarters.

Abaish was the first to speak. He was of the paingiver caste, but was one of father's closest advisors. Only his narrow chin was visible beneath the traditional mask worn by all paingivers. "Forgive our surprise, Tyrant Makeda. We were told that your cohort had perished in battle today."

"Not today. Perhaps next time. Now where is my father?"

Abaish shook his head with exaggerated sorrow. "I am afraid mighty Telkesh is dead."

Makeda's knees turned to water. She tried not to let her emotions show. Telkesh had not been archdominar for long. Vaactash had only been dead a year. This was inconceivable. "How?"

"A sudden illness," said one of the Cataphracts. "He was overcome with fever."

It seemed impossible, a skilled mortitheurge, a house leader with mastery over energies which controlled the flesh or could withstand death, to be taken by a simple fever.

"The chirurgeons could not find a cure in time," Abaish added apologetically. "For that failure, Akkad had them executed."

It was as if saying his name had summoned him, but it had more than likely been the scribe because the same flap opened and Akkad entered. Tall, broad and powerful of build, his features were sharp and strong, his eyes narrow and intelligent. When the artisan caste attempted to capture skorne perfection in a work of sculpture, it usually looked something like Akkad, except of course, for the one ruined stump of an ear.

He surveyed the room expectantly. All of the assembled officers and functionaries went to one knee and dipped their heads. The act should not have surprised her. Akkad was after all, now the archdominar of House Balaash.

"Sister," Akkad seemed as surprised to see her alive as she had been to find out their father was dead. However, he was better at concealing his emotions than she was. The paingiver Abaish rose from his knees and placed himself at Akkad's right hand. Akkad's smile seemed forced. "It is good to see you. My scouts had told me that your cohort had been surrounded and wiped out on the plains. It is good to see you escaped Naram."

"I did not escape Tyrant Naram, I killed him." The tent was suddenly filled with excited whispers, some more incredulous than others. She could not hear the words, but she could imagine them. *How did this inexperienced girl defeat the great Naram?* She would deal with them later. Yet many of the warrior caste seemed rather pleased. This news seemed to upset Akkad, but she could not dwell on that. "Please, Brother, tell me of Father."

"Yes. Poor Father. He fell ill during our march. Mighty Telkesh brought low by a disease only yesterday. I rushed to his side as soon as I heard. I was with him as he was consumed by fever."

"A tragedy." Abaish agreed.

"Indeed. He was in terrible pain, robbed of all his dignity. A death that was in no way fitting—"

"Wait!" Makeda could not help herself. She looked toward the council extoller. They were all watching her. All of their highly specialized caste ceremonially plucked out one of their mortal eyes and replaced it with a crystal that allowed them to see into the spirit realm. Her reflection was visible in the extoller's crystal oculus. "He did not die in battle . . . Are you saying his essence was not preserved?"

The extoller shook his head sadly.

Makeda gasped. "No." Telkesh had not been given the opportunity to be proven worthy. *Her father had been consigned to the Void.*

Akkad folded his arms as he studied his council. Abaish leaned over and whispered in Akkad's good ear, and it reminded her of Primus Zabalam and his warning about those that lurked in the shadows. Akkad frowned. "Why do you not bow before your archdominar, Makeda? Do you intend to disrespect me?"

Makeda was shaken from her thoughts by the accusation. "Why—"

"You are not kneeling. Why do you disrespect House Balaash by failing to honor your archdominar?"

And in that moment, Makeda knew . . .

Akkad had known Father was dying this morning. He had abandoned her entire cohort, knowing that Naram would kill them.

She could see the truth in the faces of many of the warriors in the room. They had figured it out as well.

"Kneel," Akkad commanded.

Her brother had consigned her to death. *Why?* Did he truly consider her a threat to his rule? Her mind was still fatigued from combat. Many of the warriors were staring at her expectantly. She could feel anger boiling up within her, yet the traditions of their caste were clear on this matter. It was the responsibility of the eldest to rule. Makeda forced the anger back, then went to one knee and lowered her head. "I am sorry . . . Archdominar."

Akkad had no idea that her sense of honor had just saved his life.

❖ PART TWO ❖

THE HALL OF ANCESTORS was a sacred place, and the only sound was their footfalls upon the stone. At this late hour the stonemasons of the worker caste were gone and only a few extollers scurried about in the shadows. Archdominar Vaactash lit their way with a single lantern. The pale light illuminated row upon row of statues as they passed. Makeda thought that the Ancestral Guardians towered over her, much as her grandfather did.

"Do not shrink before them, child. These are your exalted ancestors and their revered companions. They lived for House Balaash. We are the culmination of their great works," Vaactash said softly. "Each one of them has a story."

"Yes. Father ordered the servants to give us summaries," Makeda answered.

"And of course, when the summaries were not enough, you read everything in the library..." It was not a question.

Makeda was suddenly nervous. Was that why she had been summoned to the Hall? In a society based upon strength and born into a caste bred for war, scholarly pursuits were frowned upon. Time spent on lesser arts could easily have been spent on more important things. Yet one did not disagree with the archdominar. Akkad's missing half ear was a constant reminder of that fact. "Yes, Grandfather. I have read the histories. In truth, I find them..." she trailed off.

Vaactash paused. The lantern cast deep shadows around his gaunt features, his eyes nothing more than white dots in a black pit. "Finish your words."

"I have read all of the histories of my ancestors, and I am *inspired* by them."

"How?"

"I wish to emulate their successes..." She glanced at the statues. Inside each of them was a sacral stone, and within each of those stones rested the spiritual essence of a hero, fallen for the honor of House Balaash. She did not wish to give offense, but the truth was required. "...yet avoid their mistakes."

Vaactash nodded once, his expression unreadable. "This answer is acceptable." Then the light turned away and the old warrior continued on his way down the hall. Despite an ancient injury that had left Vaactash with a severe limp, Makeda had to hurry to keep up with her much shorter legs.

A moment later they came to the center of the Hall.

Vaactash stopped before the largest statue of all. He turned back to her, the lantern again casting odd shadows on his features. "Do you know why this statue is special?"

Makeda nodded. "It is because there is not yet an essence stored within it." The stoneworkers had been toiling away on this project for years, for what seemed like most of her short life. It was the finest example of the artisan caste's craft in the entire Hall. It was a stylized rendition of her grandfather, only a much younger version, a version which she had never seen herself, and frankly had a difficult time imagining. "This is to be your exalted resting place, Grandfather."

Vaactash turned back to the statue and stared at it for a very long time. Makeda stood silently, still not knowing why she had been summoned in the middle of the night. "We are still so devout in our worship . . ." Vaactash spoke slowly, choosing each word carefully, "for a people who have no gods."

Makeda knew what the ancestral teachings said about the subject. "The skorne do not need gods. Through hardship we forged our own path. Only the weak need gods."

"So it is written . . . Where there was only a wasteland, we built our world. We forced crops from the sand, subjugated the beasts of the plains, and taught ourselves the power that dwells within blood and pain." The greatest living warrior remained fixated on his great statue. "And what happens to those of us who die without achieving exaltation?"

Was she being tested? "There is only the Void." It was a place of black infinity, a boundless eternal suffering that even the most creative of paingivers could never hope to emulate. Except for the exalted few or their revered companions, all skorne were destined for eternal torment.

"Long ago, there was no exaltation . . . All of us were consigned to the Void. It was only through the wisdom of Voskune, Ishoul, and Kaleed that we learned the way to preserve our essence. Rather than being cast into the Void, our spirits could be kept safe in a sacred stone. Our wisdom could be saved to be shared with our descendants, and in times of dire need, our honored ancestors could even return to fight for their house."

"It is a great blessing," Makeda agreed.

"Yet, even after the revelation, so very few could be saved. Choices had to be made. Who would live on and who would be cast into the eternal death? There must be order. It was Dominar Vuxoris who would become the First Exalted. It was his teachings which would become hoksune, the code which governs the conduct of all warriors. Thus it was declared that only through adherence to the tenets of hoksune could we prove our worthiness. Only the greatest of warriors can earn exaltation. For everyone else, there is the Void."

"But, Grandfather, you have earned your place amongst our ancestors. In time, Father Telkesh will as well. I will do the same."

"When I'd heard you were neglecting your mortitheurgy in order to read the histories, I was angered—Balaash blood is not thin scholar's blood—but I can see now that there was no need. There is a place for such knowledge amongst the warrior caste."

It was a tremendous relief to finally know why she had

been summoned, and even better to know that she had passed the archdominar's test. "My ancestors will guide me as I defeat the enemies of our house."

"And there must always be enemies . . . I do not think you yet understand the true burden of the warrior caste. You are old enough now. I will tell you a story." Vaactash leaned against his statue, taking the weight off of his crippled leg. It was a rare show of weakness from the aging archdominar. "Two generations ago, I visited the islands south of Kademe. That was the first time I have seen the sea. It is far bigger than Mirketh Lake. It seemed to stretch further than the eye could see, further even than the wastes."

That much water sounded inconceivable, but Makeda did not dare question the archdominar's truthfulness. She preferred her ears properly shaped and pointy, not mangled into scar tissue.

"There are mighty predators that live beneath the sea. Those that fished those deep waters spoke of a fearsome beast that would eat anything in its path, so I sought out one of the local beast handlers to learn more."

Makeda nodded. Of course, anyone skilled in the art of mortitheurgy would be interested in a fascinating new beast. Those that could be broken could be useful weapons or tools, and those that could not still provided useful lessons in anatomy.

"The beast handlers told me much about this mighty fish. It had more teeth than a ferox, and was the ultimate killer in its realm. It could sense the spilling of blood, even from miles away, and never hesitated to destroy the weak."

"It sounds wonderful."

"Indeed. Yet that was not what fascinated me the most. You see, this sea beast must constantly be in motion, hunting, seeking prey, or it will *die*. It cannot be restrained. It cannot stop, for to stop moving is to perish. It was not its might, or its savagery that impressed me. No . . . It was this constant need of struggle that reminded me so much of the warrior caste."

Makeda was perplexed. "I do not understand, Grandfather."

"Like the sea predator must perpetually hunt, so we must perpetually have strife. We are instruments of war. Only through war can we achieve exaltation. If that opportunity is removed, then we cease to be skorne."

"The houses would never stop fighting! That would be madness."

Vaactash chuckled. "Perhaps . . . Perhaps I am just an old warrior in his waning days and my mind tends to wander toward abstract thoughts. You have learned of *how* our ancestors fought, but now you must truly understand *why*." His voice grew dangerously low. "Only through conflict can we become pure, and only the pure can be exalted. This is why we fight. This is why we always *must* fight. Strife is our only opportunity to avoid being cast into the Void. Our entire society is based upon this."

Makeda bowed, thankful for the wisdom which had just been shared.

"Do you know what the foulest, most evil idea in the world is, Makeda?"

She shook her head. She had never heard her grandfather speak like this before.

"Peace." Vaactash spat the word out, as if it tasted foul on his tongue.

She knew the word, but peace was a difficult, abstract concept to her. "That is not our way."

"Correct, but it is a tempting one. I know you do not understand this now, but you may when you are older. Those of the lower castes can seldom achieve exaltation, so the ideal appeals to many of them. Sometimes, the idea of *peace* may even corrupt some of our own caste."

"I cannot conceive of this."

"Of course there are times when a house is not making war. There are consolations after conquest, or when a house bides its time waiting for a better opportunity to strike, and during those such, there is a lack of conflict, but it is certainly not *peace*. No. There is always another rising power, or a strong leader who becomes weak and must be cast down, or even the old being toppled by the young. You see, our caste must have something to strive against. It betters us. It completes us. Strife must be embraced."

He had never spoken so freely before, and Makeda tried her best to absorb her grandfather's wisdom.

"For every house I have imposed my dominion upon, I must constantly prove my worth, or I will be replaced by someone better. Ultimately, it is possible for a mighty enough conqueror to unite all of our caste beneath one banner. Even then, there would be strife among our caste, for we are like the great sea beast, and to cease striving is to perish."

"I understand, Grandfather."

"Do you, Makeda? Fools often mistake this tempting concept of peace with the similar concept of surrender.

They would live without strife. There are many who feel as if being born into the warrior caste should be enough to earn exaltation. They would see an end to war so they could grow fat and soft, and yet still somehow escape the Void. So few of us can be exalted, it is vital that only the greatest achieve this."

"That is what the code dictates. It would not be right for anyone to achieve exaltation without sufficient struggle!" The blasphemous idea shocked Makeda and filled her with anger. "Why, then the weak would be saved while superior warriors would be cast into the Void!"

"Indeed. You must ponder on these things." Vaactash regarded her solemnly. "A warrior's thoughts must remain open to ideas beyond what they have been taught. Akkad is cunning, and his mind is quick, but it is dangerous to entertain new ideas without governing them against principles of honor. If only I could combine your adherence to hoksune with your brother's ambitious pragmatism, then House Balaash would be unstoppable. The mind reels at the possibilities."

"I will serve House Balaash, as the code dictates, and when he is archdominar, I will serve Akkad. I promise."

"A warrior does not need to promise, Makeda. The mere act of saying a thing will be done means that it will. To our caste, the act of saying and doing are the same. I have no doubt as to your loyalty to our house, and for that, I am glad that you were Second Born." Vaactash smiled. It was a rare expression. "Enough of an old warrior's ramblings. That will be all." He turned and went back to admiring his soon-to-be tomb. "You are dismissed."

❖ ❖ ❖

"You are dismissed."

Makeda bowed low. "Yes, Archdominar Akkad."

She stood. Only a few of the warriors assembled in the great tent met her gaze, and those were warriors that she had trained with or who had served under her grandfather. There were far too many new faces already amongst the leaders of House Balaash. Makeda turned and walked quickly for the flap. More than anything, she wanted to be outside, away from the whispering nest of razor worms. Her brother seemed pleased at the show of subservience, but Makeda noted that Abaish of the paingivers was already whispering secrets into his ear before she had even made it outside.

The night was cool. Makeda took a deep breath and savored being alive.

Grandfather, what would you have me do?

The surviving remnants of her own decurium had not yet arrived. It would take them hours to catch up to the nimble ferox that had carried her here. Despite their great victory, she already knew there would be no conquerors' welcome for them. They had been a sacrifice sufficient to avoid suspicion, for why would an archdominar throw away troops? Surely, Akkad had meant for her and her token army to die on the plains, killed by Muzkaar hands and not of his treachery.

Her body still ached from the day's battle. Though she had been able to stave off serious injury by shoving it off to her cyclops, the pain remained. Makeda remembered her training and welcomed the pain. Morkaash, the first of the paingivers, had learned that suffering could lead to enlightenment. She accepted this truth. Once pain was understood, even welcomed, it could provide clarity of thought.

And Makeda needed clarity right then.

The night was far too quiet. The encampment was too somber. With thousands of warriors present, it was unnaturally still. The sudden, dishonorable death of Telkesh hung like a fog over the warriors. The only noise came from the nearby pens, as the enslaved warbeasts shuffled and grunted and fed. This encampment had been set up while she had been marching to her intended execution, so it took her a few minutes to find the tent of Telkesh. The archdominar's banners were missing, surely taken down sent to adorn Akkad's own. Telkesh's tent was dark.

A few of her father's long-time slaves were still there, kneeling in the sand, wailing and gnashing their teeth at the loss of their master. Makeda stepped around their prostrate forms. There was a great pile of ash where they had burned Telkesh and a few of his servants in a mighty funeral pyre.

"It is already done?" Makeda whispered.

One of the slaves looked up at the sound of her voice. He squinted in the dark. "Makeda lives?"

"It is I." She recognized the slave but had never bothered to learn the name of someone from such a low caste. "Why was my father burned so quickly?" she demanded.

The slave looked away in fear. "The new archdominar declared that the disease could spread through the camp."

Makeda gritted her teeth. This was an added insult to the memory of her ancestor. "Tell me of this mystery illness. What were the symptoms?"

"It was as sudden as lightning on the wastes. We had just broken camp and set out on the day's march when the master felt a pain in his stomach. It radiated out to his limbs and he complained of tingling and weakness. Soon, he was unable to march or even stay in a saddle. He was overcome with fever, and then madness and seizures. I was there. He twitched and jerked so much that I could not even get water past his lips."

The description reminded Makeda of something she had once read in the family histories...."And the chirurgeons?"

The slave pointed to a nearby pile of rocks that she had not before noticed. It was an accepted form of execution. Place the condemned beneath a board, and then slowly pile rocks upon it all day until they were eventually crushed flat. It was an agonizing and slow method of execution, and thus one of the favorites of her people. "Tormentor Abaish was displeased with their failure."

"I see. Did the chirurgeons speak with anyone before their execution? Did they speak with any of Father's retainers?"

"Besides Abaish and the new archdominar?" the slave shook his head. "A few, but all of them were given the honor of going into the fire to accompany Telkesh on his journey into the Void." He was trembling in fear. Makeda realized that she had unconsciously placed her hand on her sword as if she were about to draw it. She let go of the hilt.

"What is your name, slave?"

"Kuthsheth, personal servant of Telkesh, and Vaactash before him."

"Bring me the servants that prepared Telkesh's meal that morning."

"I'm sorry. I cannot. They too were cast into the fire."

Makeda's hands curled into fists. She remembered now exactly what she had read all of those years ago in the family histories about one particularly dishonorable ancestor, a Tyrant who had used poison to remove threats to his rule.

Murder was not unknown amongst her caste, but it was frowned upon. Being caught at it would bring shame to your house, but that did not mean that it did not happen anyway. A people that lived in a state of constant warfare had to find a balance between honor and the more pragmatic matters of house politics, but even then, a house lord deserved to die by the blade. It was possible Akkad had been impatient to assume his mantle and poisoned their father. However, Telkesh was of the warrior caste, and had already proven himself as a mighty Cataphract over and over again in Vaactash's armies. Poison was meant for sick animals and slaves who had ceased to be useful, not for house lords. Poison was a terrible, shameful way to die, and the most dishonorable way to kill.

Makeda had one final question, but it was not one that could be answered here.

"I speak out of turn, but your father will be missed." Kuthsheth said. "I was a soldier once. When Telkesh defeated my village and I was taken prisoner, I believed my life to be through, but Telkesh was an honorable master. I am consigned to whatever fate you would have of me, but I am thankful that my children will have the opportunity to rise to a higher caste in the greatest house of all—Balaash."

Telkesh had been a strict devotee of the code of hoksune. Surely, he had proven his worthiness, so why had he been robbed of his exaltation? Having no doubt that she was being watched by Akkad's spies, Makeda knelt as if she was paying her respects to the pile of ash. She kept her voice low. "Kuthsheth, I have two tasks of you. You will take word to my cohort. Seek out Primus Zabalam. Tell him my orders are to stop where they are now. They are not to enter this encampment. But first you will go now in secret and find the extoller Haradum. Tell her, and only her, that I have need of her, and that she will speak to no one about this. She must meet me…" Makeda needed someplace within in the camp where she would not be easily spotted or overheard. "Tell her to be at the beast pens at midnight."

The titans were nervous.

Something was in the air, and it was not just the stink of the massive warbeasts.

Makeda had wrapped herself in a cloak and was sitting in the shadows. The encampment's beast pens were a hurried affair of boards and serrated wire, in no way sufficient to hold an excited titan. But these beasts had been subjugated and broken. They would do as the barbed whips of the beast handlers demanded. The fences were mostly to keep a distracted beast from wandering too far. Titans were relatively smart animals, but they were still animals.

The titans were herbivores, and would often graze

along the march, but it was too dangerous to let them graze on the open plains while in enemy territory. A titan was a considerable investment of a house's resources, so at night they were kept inside the encampments. Slaves had brought in tons of feed for the beasts, so Makeda had hidden herself between a haystack and the fence.

They did not look so dangerous without all of their armor, but Makeda knew better. In the distance, the camp's lone bronzeback scratched itself against a nearby post. The post was thick and had been set deep into the ground by slaves just for that purpose. The alpha titan's rough grey hide turned the post into splinters within a few minutes. Born in the wild, there was no such thing as a tame bronzeback, only one that was temporarily compliant because of an exhaustive regimen of carefully regulated abuse. There were paingivers watching it even now, because a single enraged bronzeback could cause unspeakable damage.

In the morning the beasts would be dressed in armor, and the pain compliance hooks would be driven into the most sensitive parts of their flesh, all in order to make them more efficient weapons and stores of mortitheurgeal energy. But for tonight, the itch finally satisfied, that particular beast lay down to sleep, surely to dream of grass and cows.

Makeda reached out and touched the great bronzeback's mind with her own. "Sleep well, great one. For tomorrow House Balaash may have need of your might."

A keening wail caused Makeda to shudder. The titans looked up from their chewing. A nearby Agonizer had begun its piteous mewling. Thankfully, it fell silent after a few moments, and the titans returned to their hay. That was lucky. Nobody wanted to listen to an Agonizer all night. She continued to scan for threats, but could see nothing. The occasional guard passed by, but she remained unseen.

Makeda had gone into Telkesh's tent and found a dark cloak. She had then slipped out the back. Hopefully, if Akkad was having her watched, then the spies would still be watching the tent. The warrior caste did not waste time mourning, but it was not unheard of to spend time meditating upon the deeds of the deceased.

However, Makeda needed to focus on the problems of the present, not dwell on the past.

Her stomach growled. Quite some time had passed since she had last eaten, but warriors were used to fasting. Makeda simply ignored it and went back to her vigil. She spotted a hunched form entering the beast area a short time later. There was a small glow coming from the other's hood, a sure sign of the extoller's crystal gaze. Haradum had arrived. Makeda had known that she would come, for it had been the elder Haradum that had taught her about the traditions of their people since Makeda had been but a small child.

The extoller caste was supposed to be separate and distinct from the politics of the houses. They were the isolated guardians of exaltation and the only ones who could communicate with the deceased. Haradum was utterly devoted to the extoller's path, and Makeda had no doubt that she could be trusted to be honest, but even then, Makeda watched for a time for any sign of a trap.

When she was confident that Haradum was alone, Makeda rose.

Aptimus Haradum approached immediately. Of course she had seen Makeda hiding in the darkness. The crystal eye could discern the essence which was inside all living things. She was an ancient, alive for at least six generations, her face a mass of wrinkles and folds dangling loose over a skull. The only smooth part of Haradum was the crystal that had replaced her right eye.

"Second Born Makeda. It pleases me to no end to discover that you are still among us," the extoller wheezed. "I rejoice at this good fortune."

"Time is short, Elder." Makeda kept her voice low. Nobody would be able to hear them over the heavy breathing of the nearby titans. "I must know. Why was the spirit of Telkesh not preserved?"

Haradum did not seem moved by Makeda's intensity. "A difficult decision. It was not mine to make. Shuruppak was the extoller present at Telkesh's deathbed. I did not hear until afterward. I was busy working on my research. Did you know that beetles have a spiritual essence as well?"

Shuruppak had been raised as a warrior, and been a companion of Akkad's before deciding to pluck out his eye in order to join the extoller caste.

"Tiny, tiny, little things . . ." Haradum put her bony hands together at the wrist and quickly wiggled her fingers back and forth, like scurrying legs. "Yes. But their essence does not go to the Void, no. Are there beetle gods then, I wonder?"

Had Haradum's mind finally broken? It happened

occasionally to the few among their people who managed to die of old age. "Telkesh has killed hundreds in battle. Like Vaactash before him, Telkesh was all that it means to be skorne. My father lived by the code. That cannot all be washed away by one day of fevered madness. Why would Shuruppak choose not to save him?"

The ancient extoller's mortal eye narrowed and she leaned in conspiratorially. "When a spirit is pulled, screaming, into the Void, it can tell no stories. So much knowledge is lost that way."

"Answer me, Haradum."

Haradum smiled. She had no teeth. "I just did. What stories would Telkesh have been able to tell, I wonder? Would he be able to tell of plots and lies? Would he be able to tell of conspiracies between houses? Perhaps of allegiances between castes which are supposed to remain neutral?"

"Tell me these stories, Elder."

"I would not know. I am nothing. I wish only to be left alone to continue my research. Yet, an extoller hears things . . . Yes, yes we do. It is easy sometimes to forget we are there, always watching, always judging. Telkesh judged too. He judged wisely. When presented with two paths by his advisors, he always chose the warrior's path, never the plotter's path. Perhaps those advisors tired of being denied? Maybe they decided they needed a new archdominar, someone willing to listen to their strange new ideas, one not so bound up in the traditions of old? Akkad would be such a one, yes?"

"He would," Makeda agreed. Akkad cared far more for personal glory than he did for tradition.

"These same plotters, after deciding to go so very far, would surely not risk having yet another honorable warrior of Balaash only a heartbeat away from becoming archdominar. Surely, once this honorable scion discovered the truth, she would raise an army from all of the honorable warriors of her house, and wage war against the plotters."

So there had been a conspiracy to kill Telkesh and replace him with her brother. Akkad's actions were cowardly, and depriving Telkesh of exaltation was blasphemous. "Thank you, Elder. But there will be no army raised. I will not weaken my house through civil war." Makeda placed a hand on Haradum's shoulder. She was surprised at how fragile the extoller felt beneath her robes. "Even if Akkad murdered my father...He is archdominar of House Balaash. The code declares that he is to rule. It is my place to serve, unless I believe he is a danger to the house, and then I must bring a formal challenge."

"We both know you are no match for Akkad in single combat. You will surely die."

"I cannot go against the traditions of my caste, Elder."

Haradum's laughter was like the rustle of dusty paper. "Child, those without honor assume that everyone is like them. There is no way he will ever accept a formal challenge to his rule. He will send assassins for you."

"How do you know this, Haradum?"

The crystal eye flickered across the beast pens. "Because they are already here."

Makeda spun in time to see the shapes running between the haystacks. There was a flash of crimson and steel and someone leapt effortlessly over a serrated fence only to disappear back into the darkness. *Bloodrunners!*

Bloodrunners were the elite killers of the paingiver caste, students of the magic released at the moment of death. Their presence confirmed the extoller's tale. "Flee, Haradum." The Swords of Balaash appeared in Makeda's hands. "Return to your beetles."

A titan startled and snorted as something brushed past one of its column-sized legs. There was movement all around them, a single careless footstep on gravel, the hiss of a dagger leaving its sheath, and then the bloodrunners attacked.

The first came seemingly out of nowhere, leading with a wickedly curved blade. Makeda deflected the attack with one sword, spun, and drove the second deep into the attacker's bowels. He gasped as she ripped the sword free, but did not cry out. She marveled at the mastery of pain, but only for a moment, because then she was fighting for her life.

A female stabbed at her throat, but Makeda ducked and slashed, cutting the bloodrunner nearly in half. They were all armed with the strange daggers, hooked and jagged, tools designed to incapacitate and torture. Makeda struck aside another attack, and then another. That bloodrunner had been a bit too slow, and a sword of Balaash removed his arm at the elbow. That one made no sound either, he merely stepped to the side, struggling to staunch the flow of blood.

The assassins were all around her, blades humming through the air. The clang of steel on steel caused the nearest titans to stir and grunt themselves awake. Those that had been eating looked up from their hay, confused and wondering if it was time for battle.

A handful of sand was thrown at her eyes, but she turned away just in time. Another kicked a cloud of straw between them, and feinted, all in an effort to distract her from another bloodrunner who was trying to stab her in the back. These assassins certainly did not follow hoksune, but Makeda relished a new challenge. She spun one sword, reversed her grip, and stabbed behind her, driving the point clean through the lightly armored torso of a bloodrunner. "Who sent you?" She sidestepped, and chopped another one to the ground. The spilled blood was fueling her strength. "Who?"

They did not answer. More of the assassins materialized from the shadows. Makeda was forced to dodge aside before she was completely surrounded. The terrain was not to her advantage. "Akkad?" A dagger clipped the edge of her armor. It stung and she felt the warmth of blood trickling out. Makeda circled around the nearest haystack. "Abaish? Who?"

Crack. There was a flash of pain as something hit her in the back. She turned to see another bloodrunner, this one was lifting a long, bone-studded whip for another swing. Makeda wheeled about, shrugging out of the cloak. *Crack.* The whip snapped through the fabric and was entangled. With a frustrated snarl, the bloodrunner shook his whip, trying to free it.

Two more attacks left Makeda with two more small cuts and two more dying bloodrunners. They were masters of anatomical precision, guiding their attacks past her armor. There were at least a dozen more assassins moving around the pens, and she would bleed to death long before she took them all. She kicked the knees out from under a bloodrunner and he fell, impaling himself on his own blade. *I must escape.*

One of the slave's hayforks was hurled at her from out of the shadows. She knocked it aside, turned, and vaulted over the fence into the titan enclosure. Her boots slipped in the muck of the wallow, but she did not fall. Two bloodrunners were right behind. One dove between the wires, rolled, and came up standing. One simply leapt smoothly over the top in a rustle of cloth. She struck at them simultaneously, but they both parried with their daggers.

Agitated, the nearest titan opened its mouth and bellowed a challenge, bits of ground hay flying everywhere. Makeda had trained her entire life, learning how to master warbeasts and forcing them to obey her will, and she recognized an opportunity when it presented itself. It would take a second of concentration, but it was worth the risk. *I am your master. Obey me.*

The two bloodrunners pressed their attack as their brothers followed. The one with the whip appeared to be the leader. He was silently communicating through a series of rapid hand gestures at the bloodrunners still hidden in the shadows. An alarm horn blew as the Balaash guards overseeing the pens realized something was wrong.

Obey!

The titan blinked stupidly for a moment, but then its tiny black eyes narrowed in understanding.

Destroy.

Makeda parried another attack and kicked that

bloodrunner hard in the stomach. His mouth twisted beneath his mask, but he remained focused on his mission. It only mattered for a split second though, since the titan's fist hit him so hard it left a pink cloud hanging suspended in the air.

The titan lifted itself to its full height and roared its battle cry. If the alarm horn hadn't already sounded, *that* would have certainly woken up the entire encampment. The second bloodrunner turned in surprise, so Makeda used the chance to slice his head off. It landed in the muck of the wallow at her feet, so Makeda kicked the severed head at the other remaining bloodrunners. "*Balaash!*"

The bloodrunners tried to avoid the titan, but it was too late. One had gotten caught on the barbwire of the fence, and the titan closed its hands around the assassin. This was the first one that had lost his composure and he started shouting. This seemed to annoy the titan, since it simply lifted the bloodrunner overhead and then hurled him screaming out into the night.

There were still bloodrunners everywhere, but they seemed to be fading back into the darkness, aware that their mission of a quiet assassination had failed. The titan easily stomped the fence flat and went after them. Light and shadows bounced along the fence posts nearby as the guards came running.

CRACK!

Makeda nearly blacked out as something wrapped hard around her neck. She was jerked from her feet and landed sprawled in the mud.

The one with the whip had not given up yet.

Her armor had saved her life, but bone shards had pierced her neck. The whip was pulled and the noose tightened. Makeda slid through the wet ooze. The cuts deepened, yet she was calm. *No arteries severed . . . yet.*

A quick slash of her sword cut the whip in half. The pressure ended and she could breathe again. The guards were closer and she could hear their angry cries over the ringing in her ears.

"Capture the traitor Makeda!"

"The archdominar says his sister has betrayed us!"

Curse you, Akkad. She did not need to be a mortitheurge to know that she was losing far too much blood. She would not be able to face the guards. She would be captured and executed as a traitor. Her name would be stricken from the histories.

The last bloodrunner was not content to let her die under a board and a pile of rocks however. He was intent on doing the job himself, and had dropped his ruined whip and drawn a paingiver's blade. He was charging across the pen, and Makeda knew she would not be able to stand in time.

He was upon her, dagger raised, mouth twisted into a snarl, but then the paingiver seemed to come *apart*. He jerked and spasmed as blood flew into the air, and then fell onto his face, forward momentum sliding him through the mud to stop at Makeda's feet, his back shredded so badly that she could see the white of his spine. He had been dead before Makeda had even heard the whine of the reiver.

A ferox landed next to her with a splash. She looked up to see that the predator was laboring under a pair of riders. Primus Zabalam and Dakar Urkesh both dismounted. She tried to speak, but no sounds would form in her damaged throat. "Makeda!" Zabalam grabbed her by the armor and hoisted her up with surprising strength while Urkesh loaded a fresh needle cone on his reiver.

"You must flee, Makeda," Zabalam hissed at her. "Akkad has declared you an outcast. Your life is forfeit. Go. Your cohort is waiting." The guards were almost upon them. The titan she'd enraged was still chasing blood-runners and crushing tents underfoot. There was no time. Zabalam was right. She tried to climb into the saddle, but she was weaker than she thought, and struggled to do so. Zabalam pushed her roughly upward. The ferox shifted beneath her, but understood this was not the time to fight against its handlers.

There was a horrendous whine as Urkesh spotted another bloodrunner and cut him to bits. Zabalam grabbed him by the arm. "Go with Makeda. I charge you to protect her." He drew his swords.

"What are you doing?" Urkesh shouted.

"This ferox can't run fast enough to get away if there are three of us on it. I'll buy you time. Protect her with your life. She is the future of Balaash, not that wretched dishonorable belek, Akkad." Zabalam looked to Makeda, the half of his damaged face that still worked turned up in a grin. "My apologies for insulting your family."

Makeda still could not speak. She put one bloody hand on Zabalam's head. It left a red print once she took it away. Urkesh climbed up behind her.

"You always were my best student. Now go!" He stuck the ferox on the rump with the hilt of a sword. The predator lurched away in an ungainly run.

Makeda looked back to see Zabalam striding toward the rushing host of guards, arms extended, displaying his swords proudly. "I am Primus Zabalam of the Praetorian, swordmaster of House Balaash, student of exalted Vaactash, and I fight to defend Makeda, the *true* heir of Telkesh! Who among you is stupid enough to contend with me?"

About half the guards froze, torn and unsure, but the other half attacked.

"Come then!" There was a flurry of motion as Zabalam struck back against overwhelming odds.

It was a single perfect moment of all that it meant to follow the code of hoksune, but then the ferox was around a tent and Zabalam was lost from sight.

"Ride! That way." Urkesh pointed with his reiver. The Venator had obviously never ridden a ferox before and was doing his best to hold on. Makeda kicked the predator in the ribs and turned it with her knees. There was a huge crash as the enraged titan slammed through a tent and appeared in front of them, a bloodrunner stuck on one of its tusks. Urkesh shouted in surprise right in her ear. The ferox bounded around the titan in two leaps, narrowly avoiding the desperate beast handlers who were trying to bring the titan under control.

More horns were sounding. Officers were standing at the corners, waving torches and repeating Akkad's proclamation that Makeda was a traitor to House Balaash and that she had to be captured. Yet as the ferox loped through the camp, many soldiers clearly saw her, but did not move to intercept. Enough others did, however, that escape did not look likely.

Cataphracts moved ahead of her, war spears leveled.

She struck the ferox and it turned, sliding through the grass, only seconds away from being impaled upon a wall of spears. A brief sprint and another corner took them into more swordsmen. One tried to stab the ferox, but it simply lunged forward, sank its huge teeth into a shoulder, and shook him to death. Another soldier came from behind but Urkesh shredded him with a reiver burst.

Soldiers loyal to Akkad were moving throughout the camp, shouting for the traitor Makeda's blood. "We're not going to make it," Urkesh stated.

The Venator was correct. They would be surrounded, cut off, and brought down. Unless...

The titan she'd bonded with was occupied, so Makeda reached out for the spirit of the great titan bronzeback she had connected with so briefly earlier. He was still there, snoring peacefully through the pandemonium now engulfing the encampment. The petty games of the skorne didn't matter to the mighty bronzeback. He existed only for the next challenge or the next cow. Makeda tapped into her power and awoke the bronzeback from its slumber. Bonding to such a potent beast, especially after such a fleeting contact, would be a great challenge. It took all of her effort, but Makeda pushed hard against his mind. His spirit was great, but simple, and she awoke its natural rage; in fact, she ignited it and set it free.

A terrible roar shook the entire encampment. Every skorne for miles all looked in the same direction at the same time. The ferox slid to a trembling halt. "What in the name of the ancestors was *that*?"

Our escape, Makeda thought, but it was still too difficult to speak.

The enraged bronzeback let its feelings be known by picking up another titan and throwing it across the encampment. The vast animal blotted out one of the moons for a moment as it passed overhead. The titan's landing shook the foundations of the world and nearly knocked over their ferox. Makeda did not even need to kick the ferox in order to make it run this time.

They bounded past Akkad's soldiers, knocking down a distracted Cataphract, as the bronzeback rampaged through the camp. Then they were out on the open plains and fleeing into the unknown.

The pain began in her ribs and then radiated out from there. At first it was a tingling in her nerves, and then a tightness of the muscles, and then an arcing lightning through the veins and arteries. Her mortitheurgy identified the cause quickly. The bloodrunners' daggers had been treated with some manner of strong poison, but she was overcome so quickly that there was nothing she could do but scream.

Every move of the ferox caused pain to ripple through her body. Every jolt and bounce caused joints to grind as if filled with broken glass. The air that filled her lungs was like bubbling acid, eating away at her flesh.

The midnight plains faded into complete darkness as she was robbed of her sight. She could no longer control their steed. Her limbs would not respond to her commands, and every effort at making them work merely caused the pain to grow.

This was not poison. This was a living thing, born only to cause suffering.

At one point she slipped from the saddle and crashed into the dirt. It was almost cushioned compared to the pain that was now cascading through her entire body, but even then, the poison discovered this small bit of cool relief and extinguished it. The ground seemed to become hotter and hotter until every bit of clinging dirt burned like lava. Urkesh had lifted her back onto the ferox. He was saying something about pursuers, but it was hard to hear over the hurricane in her ears. The pain was causing her to hallucinate and his fingers pierced her skin like the needles of his reiver.

The pain had gone on and on. Time lost all meaning. Reality was taken away and replaced with a world that was nothing but agony, and somehow Makeda knew that she was dangling by a thread over the Void. All she had to do was cut that tiny string of life and she could be plunged into the Void. It was cold in the Void, but the cold would extinguish the fire which was consuming her. She could see her father within the Void. The poison, the evil, sentient *thing* had done the same to him, until he had cut that thread and welcomed the nothing.

Somehow the pain became worse, and through it all, the only bit of the real world that remained with her was the presence of the Swords of Balaash, and the tiny sliver of her grandfather's spirit which powered them. Despite the agony, her exalted ancestors were still there. They helped her understand.

This poison was designed to kill mortitheurges, brewed to unravel bodies, corrupt wills, and break minds. Normal poison was useless against someone who could stall death or manipulate blood and tissue. How could she fight such an enemy? She reached for her power, but it was swept aside by the crashing waves of agony. The harder she tried, the more pain it inflicted on her as punishment. It whispered that only the cool Void could save her.

Suddenly a gigantic black stone statue was towering over her, offering a path away from the Void. The stylized face of Vaactash did not move as the thought hammered its way through her mind. "What is it that you whisper to yourself, child, when the pain becomes too much?"

And then the words were there.

Suffering cleanses the weakness from my being. Adhere to the code and I will become worthy.

The suffering was the key. She could not reach her power because she was weak.

Her power was still there, still ready to be utilized, she only needed to be strong enough to take it. She had to go through the pain, through the unraveling of mind and spirit. Let death come. Let her heart stop, but in that brief time while hurtling toward the Void, she would take what was rightfully hers.

Makeda welcomed the poison and told it to do its worst, for she was skorne, and she would *never* break.

The pain was gone. Now there was only the memory of pain.

Where am I?

The walls were made of rock, chipped and chiseled until it was in the semblance of a room. A single feeble lantern hung from a brass fitting sunk into the wall, leaving most of the space hidden in darkness.

Is this a dungeon? Have I been captured?

Yet when she moved, she discovered that she was not in chains. She felt the cold stone floor beneath her palm before realizing that her body was resting on a pile of dark furs. Her armor was missing and she was only wearing a thin grey robe. A bloodstained cloth was nearby, and resting upon it was a multitude of tools, tiny blades, pliers, hooks and barbs, needles and thread, bottles of potions, and bags of herbs. Though similar, these were not the injury-causing tools of a tormentor, but rather the injury-repairing tools of a chirurgeon. Bandages pulled as she tried to sit up. Clearly someone had tended to her many wounds.

Where are my swords? There was a brief flash of panic before she spotted them, sheathed and leaning against the wall. Makeda breathed a sigh of relief. Death was far preferable to losing her family swords. *Thank the ancestors.*

Something stirred in the darkness. There was a shape there, and it took Makeda a moment to make out the silhouette of a skorne in the light armor of the Venator, with a reiver resting on his lap.

Her throat ached. "Where am I?" The words came out so raspy that Makeda did not recognize her own voice. It did not feel like just the whip, but rather that her throat was raw and parched, as if she had been yelling for hours.

The warrior in the shadows stood quickly. "She is awake," he spoke loudly, his voice seeming to echo through the chamber. "Makeda is alive."

"I tire of hearing that said as if it is some sort of surprise." Speaking hurt. She welcomed the minor pain as it helped clear the sleep from her mind. She had seen real agony; from now on, minor pain would merely be another tool. "What is going on?" Makeda pushed herself up, but the effort made her head swim.

The figure in the dark had been Urkesh, and he rushed over to her side. "Do not struggle." He caught her by the shoulders and lowered her back to the furs. It was an insult to have someone of a lower caste touch her without permission, but it was obvious no offense was intended, plus she was not in any shape to do much about the slight regardless. "Those assassins' blades were poisoned. You nearly died."

Poison . . . a weapon of cowards and traitors. "Akkad. He poisoned Telkesh."

There were other voices inside the cavern. Armored footsteps echoed. More figures appeared. She should have been able to recognize them, but her vision seemed blurry, however they were wearing the colors of House Balaash. Some of them were bearing their own lanterns, and now she could see that the room was larger than expected, with windows covered in thick brown curtains. A small hunched figure moved between the much larger skorne. "They are aware. I told them. Most even believed."

Haradum? "So you survived the assassins, elder teacher. Good."

"I followed your cohort for days, even after Akkad's loyalists gave up the chase."

"Days?" Her body felt weak, but she did not feel like she had been asleep for days. "How long have I been ill?"

"Ten days and ten nights. I believe it was the same poison which felled mighty Telkesh. The others thought you had died." The old extoller came closer and placed one freezing-cold hand on Makeda's forehead. The crystal oculus stared down at her. "But I could see that your essence had not yet left your body. You would not allow death to claim you . . . it seems the last of the fever has passed. You must rest. The flesh needs time to heal."

"The flesh will do as I tell it to." Makeda rubbed her eyes. Her vision was improving. Now she could recognize many of the other figures as officers of her father's army. Their faces were grim, their white eyes reflective in the glow of the lanterns. "Where am I?"

"The Shroudfall Mountains," Urkesh answered. "We were fleeing Akkad's army and needed a place to hide."

"This is an old fortress. The mountain passes are extremely difficult to cross," stated one of the warriors, whom Makeda recognized as a veteran Cataphract of her father's cohort. "Your army is safe here until you decide it is time for us to mobilize."

My army? All that had remained of her small cohort had been a few battered taberna, and many wounded. This time Makeda focused through the dizziness and forced herself to sit up. Urkesh was there, ready to help, but she ignored him. She placed her hands on the stone and forced herself upright. Her knees nearly buckled, but she would not show weakness before these warriors. "What army do you speak of?"

The Cataphract nodded to the side. One of his soldiers rushed to the nearest curtain and drew it back. Cold night air flooded into the room. "While you were taken with the fever, they gathered."

Though curious, Makeda first walked slowly to the

side and retrieved the Swords of Balaash. The scabbards felt good in her hands. Only then did she go to the window. Her steps were slow, unsteady. Her muscles quivered with weakness, but she would not show it. The cold air cut right through her thin robes and she began to shiver uncontrollably. She had lost a lot of weight and knew she had to look like a spirit that had escaped from the Void.

Outside the window was the ruined courtyard of a once great castle. They were so high in the mountains that the clouds had come down to gather around the towers like fog. Those clouds were glowing, reflecting the flickering light of hundreds of campfires.

"I do not understand..." Makeda whispered.

"We were few at first. Just your cohort and a handful of slaves," Urkesh said. "But then word spread of your sickness. Others had to come and see."

"It was a few individuals at first," the veteran Cataphract said. "Warriors loyal to Telkesh and Vaactash, then maddened cultists of Xaavaax, and even soldiers of proud vassal houses such as Bashek and Kophar. Akkad executed many as an example, but soon whole taberna and even decurium had deserted in order to come here and keep watch over you. More gather every day."

Makeda was stunned, her mind unable to estimate the number of troops assembled here. Even if there was but a single datha around each of those fires, it had to represent a mighty host, surely more warriors than most houses could boast, possibly even enough to rival Balaash's combined sabaoth.

One of the warriors saw her standing in the window.

There was a shout, and then another and another, until the entire camp erupted in one long incomprehensible roar. It was a battle cry.

She was nearly overcome. "But I was sick with fever. I was helpless." The events in the encampment came rushing back. "I have been cast out of my house and declared a traitor. Why would they risk everything to follow such a weak leader?"

"It was anything but weakness." It was a new arrival who answered. Makeda turned to see a young paingiver whom she had never met before. "When I heard of these events, I had to come and see for myself. This poison is an extraordinary invention, a curse that would make even great Morkaash proud. It is a marvel of the paingiver's art. Never before have I seen a mixture capable of causing such pure agony and suffering. It felled even the great Telkesh and drove him insane within a single day. Even as strong as he was, his flesh could not withstand that level of purification before it broke his mind."

The pain. It was only half recalled, like a bad dream. Yet, she had not broken. She did not follow the way of the paingivers so she did not feel as if she had reached any sort of enlightenment, but she had endured. That was what mattered.

"Your cohort told others of this terrible agony you were experiencing," Haradum said. "So they had to come to hear for themselves."

"Hear what, elder teacher?" Makeda rasped. "Hear me descend into gibbering madness?"

"No," the paingiver answered. "Despite being rent apart by the most delicious agonies possible, you rose above it. As your body was wracked with unfathomable pain and seizures, you transcended it all. These warriors came to hear the way to enlightenment."

Haradum sounded reverent, "Every day for ten days and every night for ten nights, you recited the entirety of the code of hoksune."

As if of one mind, every warrior in the room went to their knees and bowed.

❖ PART THREE ❖

THE TWIN SWORDS OF BALAASH had been placed reverently on the stone floor before her as Makeda had knelt in meditation. At times she was envious of the extollers and their ability to commune with the exalted dead, because the swords were silent to her ears. Hours had passed, but still the answers eluded her. If only she could truly know the wisdom of her ancestors, perhaps then, choosing between the demands of honor and the potential future of her house would not be so difficult.

They were high in the Shroudfall Mountains, and the air in the uppermost chamber of the tallest tower of the old fortress seemed permanently chilled. Makeda's measured breathing left clouds of steam in the air. The sun would rise soon, and when it did, her army would need direction.

There was a sound from behind her, a shuffling and wheezing on the stairs. Makeda did not need to look to know that it was Aptimus Haradum. The aged extoller had made it a habit to check on her. "Archdomina Makeda?" she called out.

"That is not my title, Haradum."

"Your warriors seem to think it is."

Makeda stared at her swords. "They believe me to be more than I am."

Haradum wheezed and shuffled her way into the upper chamber. "So many stairs, and it is so cold here. This place must have been built by nihilators wishing to suffer. I am lucky our young dakar with the reiver allowed me to pass. I believe he has appointed himself to be your personal guard."

"Urkesh?" Makeda asked. She had not been aware that the Venator had been following.

"Yes, yes. He took the final order of Primus Zabalam most seriously. I collected Zabalam's soul by the way. He killed twenty warriors before catching a spear in the throat." She patted a glowing stone chained to her apron. "He will make a fine revered companion to Vaactash."

Makeda was surprised by the sudden feeling in her chest. She hid the physical reaction, and merely nodded in approval. "A wise choice."

"As for the young Venator, after you were overcome with poison, he lost control of the ferox. Wily beasts have no patience for untrained masters. He carried you on his back for miles until reaching your decurium. He never left your side the entire time you were consumed with fever."

"I was unaware." Urkesh's commitment to duty was commendable. Perhaps it was possible to honor hoksune even without looking into a warrior's eyes as you killed them.

"What troubles you, Makeda?"

"I have a decision to make, but the code does not provide me with clarity on this issue. I do not like being uncertain."

"You always were one for clarity. As Vaactash used to say, when a titan is chasing, do not dither, pick a direction and run!"

That really did not sound like something her grandfather would have said at all. "I would ask a favor of you, Aptimus."

"I am already aware of what you seek, and I already have an answer for you. While you were battling the fever, I attempted to commune with the essence of your grandfather's spirit which dwells within your swords. Such a task is onerous and difficult, and sometimes our exalted ancestors do not deign to answer. Sometimes they know that the living must seek out wisdom for themselves. There was only the briefest communication."

"What did he say?"

"*The true heir of House Balaash has already won.*"

Makeda was not surprised. It was not like Vaactash to provide an easy way out. "Akkad is the eldest, thus it is his legal right to rule. However, should an heir be deemed unfit, and I believe his dishonorable and cowardly murders—"

"Do not forget the blasphemy!"

"Of course." Makeda had to suppress a small smile. "That too. These things prove he is unworthy to lead House Balaash. So it falls to me to issue a challenge. It is my duty to defeat him in single combat and assume the mantle of archdomina."

"Assuming of course you could defeat the finest warrior of his generation in a duel, but that doesn't matter now, does it?"

"Akkad will ignore my challenge and merely have me killed. Someone so dishonorable will not risk his throne. Akkad declared me an outcast. Officially, I am of lower status than a newly captured slave."

"Most slaves do not have their own armies."

"Yes. And if I march this army south, then somewhere on the plains north of Halaak we will clash against the rest of House Balaash. Thousands upon thousands will die."

"It will be glorious." Haradum shook one of her bony fists in the air. "To war! To war! The blood will flow like rivers!"

Makeda sighed. "The problem with a civil war is that whoever wins, House Balaash loses. Akkad or I, the victor is irrelevant. We will rule over a house that is weakened and ripe to be conquered by our neighbors. House Balaash has far too many enemies to gut our army and expect to survive."

"Yes, yes." Haradum was nodding along. "Perhaps you should accept your title of outcast and wander the wastes the rest of your days. I hear the Abyss is quite the sight to see." Haradum's laugh sounded like old bones being shaken in a dried-out leather bag.

"My fate does not matter, Aptimus, only that of my house. Is it better that a blasphemous fiend rule than I start a war that ends House Balaash? Will my house rot under the rule of a dishonorable archdominar? I am of the warrior caste. I must fight for the good of my house."

"Is that why you fight?"

Makeda paused. It was such a simple question with such a complicated answer. Why did she fight? Why did the skorne have to fight? She thought back to the very first time in her life when she had come to understand the reasoning behind that question, in a hall filled with silent ancestors . . .

And then Makeda had her answer. *Thank you, Grandfather.*

"Do you know what the foulest of all words is, Haradum?"

"Surely something involving rhinodons. They are obnoxious things with disgusting reproductive habits!"

"The foulest of all words is *peace.*" Makeda took up her swords and rose. "Come. I must prepare the warriors. We march."

The ancient extoller squealed with delight. "Many will be exalted, I am sure!" Haradum cackled and patted one of the many empty sacral stones she wore like jewelry, knowing that it would soon be filled. "To war! To war!"

During the journey south, her body healed, but her mind was at turmoil. At night, sleep would not come, and when it did, it brought uneasy dreams of disapproving ancestors and House Balaash in flames.

Her cohort grew. New warriors joined her daily. From simple Hestatians from the plains wearing basic armor stitched together from titan hide, to proud Cataphracts so large of stature and wearing so much steel and laminate armor that they looked more like ancestral guardians than mortals, to nihilators obsessed with death and with barbed pain hooks embedded in their flesh, to Venators armed with nothing more than slings and vials filled with corrosive acid, to other rich and powerful tyrants with their own stables of warbeasts.

Veterans knelt before her. Great leaders presented their swords or their mortitheurgy and swore to fight in her name. She formed new datha and taberna, and promoted warriors to lead them, gave battle orders, and saw to their logistical needs. They travelled fast and lean, often making do with innate toughness rather than sufficient rations. By day Makeda had to learn to balance the politics, bickering, and petty ambitions of so many competing warriors, and by night she dreamed of war.

The warriors came for various reasons. Some because of old loyalties to Telkesh, or belief in the code, or disgust over the dishonor of losing an archdominar to poison, or vassals who decided to support one heir over another, to others who simply wished for a battle worthy of their skills. But whatever the reason, they continued to join, and the further south they went, the stronger her army became.

Within a week of leaving the Shroudfall, her army had grown large enough to pose a real threat to House Balaash. She estimated that nearly a quarter of House Balaash's total sabaoth was under her command. A host so numerous, in fact, that even if they were to go down in defeat, it would be a great enough battle that it would surely ruin the entire army of House Balaash in the process.

And for one of the only times in her life, Makeda understood what it was to fear.

She feared not for herself. If she was to be found wanting, let her be cast into the Void with the rest of the failures. That did not matter. Makeda feared only for the future of her house.

Ancestors, if I am to be defeated, let it happen swiftly, so that my house may be spared.

Each night she would counsel with her officers and listen as the tacticians made their plans. Far too many of those plans ended with a slaughter that would lead to the eventual destruction of her house. She spoke with each of the officers individually, searching for ideas that would accomplish her mission, yet leave the great army of Balaash relatively intact.

Yet it was not one of the mighty war leaders that had finally proposed a possible solution to her dilemma.

It had been a slave.

"I do not see Akkad's personal banner among the horde," Urkesh said as he slowly moved his eyes from side to side, searching carefully for targets. "He did not bother to come himself."

The Venator had proven to have the most acute vision of any of her officers so Makeda was inclined to believe him. "I should not be surprised." It was difficult to keep the disgust from her voice. "But I am disappointed."

The morning mist had risen from the lake and a low fog hung over the plains. Makeda had spent most of her life in this region. She knew it well. Within a few hours the sun would rise enough to cut through the knee-high fog, but until then the air would be still. To the east was what seemed like a never-ending sea of red and gold marching through the churning grey. The majority of the great army of House Balaash was arrayed before her, thousands strong. A few miles behind that army was House Balaash itself, once her home, and now her target. At her back was a much smaller army, made up of warriors who still believed that honor meant something. To their north was the long crystal-blue expanse of Mirketh Lake. To the south was nothing but miles of open plains until the great city of Halaak.

It was a fine place for a civil war.

Makeda and Urkesh had stopped on top of a small rise to survey the opposition. The rest of her command staff was making their way up the hill for a hasty council before the battle commenced. It had taken a month to march south from the Shroudfall Mountains. During that time they had been met by a few small cohorts of Akkad's loyalists, but had faced no serious combat. Judging by the great force waiting for them, that was all about to change.

It did not matter. Makeda had looked upon these officers and judged them worthy. The warriors of House Balaash who believed in hoksune and the traditions of their ancestors had flocked to her banner. Despite being outnumbered three to one, victory would be hers. The real question was whether House Balaash would survive for long after the slaughter necessary to achieve such a victory.

It was the potential fall of her house which had kept her awake each night during the journey. "I was afraid of this. I had hoped he would show himself. Curse Akkad. This complicates matters, Urkesh."

"I understand."

"Do you?" Makeda glanced at her subordinate. The Venator had barely left her side since their march had begun. "You assume much, Dakar. I know what I must do, but in order to succeed, I fear I must behave as dishonorably as my brother."

"A Venator spends so much time looking at targets in the distance that often we cannot focus on things that are near." Urkesh studied her for a moment. "I know what vexes you. The burden can be seen in your countenance, Archdomina."

"That is not yet my title."

"It would not be my place to disagree with you, but if it was, I would tell you that you are wrong. You are nothing like your brother. He would burn your house in order to rule it, but you would kill yourself in order to save it. This army follows you because to them you embody the code of hoksune. You are more the true heir of House Balaash than your brother could ever hope to be, and these warriors know it."

Her caste did not display their emotions openly, so Makeda gave the Venator a small, respectful nod. "They follow me because they follow the code. So why are you here, Urkesh?"

He shrugged. "The code means different things to different warriors. Just because I am not good at it, doesn't mean that I don't believe it."

"You are wiser than you look."

"Thank you, Archdomina." Urkesh went back to surveying the opposing army. "Now where are you hiding, One Ear?" Urkesh looked over at her and grinned. "I didn't think you would mind me calling him that now."

Makeda sighed. "Do not tempt me. Beheading you could still boost morale."

The incorrigible Venator chuckled. The other officers had reached them, so Urkesh put on a much more serious face. "Since Akkad is telling everyone that our army is only a minor rebellion that needs to be squashed, apparently he decided we're not nearly worthy of his attentions, and has failed to honor us with his presence."

Her officers took in the great horde awaiting them. "Leading from the rear? That is not how Akkad was taught," muttered Primus Tushhan of the Cataphracts. "I served Telkesh and Vaactash before him. They would never have done such a cowardly thing."

Aptimus Haradum had shuffled her way up the hill along with the officers. "Not cowardly—cunning," she interjected. "Akkad is a shrewd one. He knows that his sister will take the honorable and direct path, thus his absence is the most politically expedient choice." At times Makeda suspected that the ancient extoller was not nearly as mad as she liked everyone to think, but then she cackled with glee and removed all doubt. "House Balaash will be emptied of blood before you crack him from that shell. Extollers will have gathered from all across the land! So many will die! Everyone will die! It will be *glorious!*"

Makeda ignored the crazed extoller and addressed her officers. "I cannot challenge Akkad if he's not present. If he were here, he would either have to accept and risk potential defeat, or decline and be dishonored. I was hoping he had retained enough honor to come out and face me."

The gigantic young Cataphract from the vassal house of Kophar had a deep, hearty laugh. "Be careful what you wish for. I have trained against Akkad. He is a mighty warrior, the finest of our generation. I do not mean to question your skill with the blade and offer no offence, but know that Akkad is one of the greatest combatants I have ever seen."

There were solemn nods of agreement from every officer who had ever served with Akkad in combat. Even her most loyal warriors understood that honor alone would not carry her through that duel, yet they followed anyway.

"Not that I wouldn't enjoy watching you two duel." Only a small contingent of House Kophar volunteers had joined her forces, but they were renowned for their size, ferocity, and strength. "But I did not come all the way from Halaak to leave without a proper battle."

"Do not worry, First Born Xerxis. You will get your fight, but it is better to spill my own blood than leave our house without an army to defend it. I intend to finish this quickly." The time had come to share her plan. It would be controversial, but it was necessary. "Tell me, noble Cataphract. Does your house still speak of how my grandfather conquered you?"

Xerxis frowned, obviously not liking having to admit his family had ever been bested. "Of course we do. Each of us studies the battles in great detail." He folded his thick arms. "There is no dishonor in losing against the greatest tactician of all time."

"Of course not. When Vaactash went to war against House Kophar, your warriors impressed him greatly, so much in fact that he decided it was a waste to kill them. I remember him telling me the story, *Why kill these warriors who would be able to fight so capably in my name*? So instead Vaactash concentrated his strength against your dominar, defeated him, and added the proud Cataphracts of Kophar to his own army, strengthening us all."

That seemed to placate the heir of Kophar. The rest of her officers were nodding. "What do you propose then?" Xerxis asked.

"There was great wisdom in what Vaactash did to House Kophar. I will not see House Balaash destroyed. I will not satisfy my honor only to see House Muzkaar or Telarr sitting upon our throne within a year. As Vaactash said, 'Why kill those who would be able to fight so capably in my name?' Yes, you will fight here today, but seek your exaltation quickly, because you will only fight long enough for me to reach Akkad."

"There is the matter of a very large army standing between the two of you," Tushhan pointed out.

"Indeed, but Haradum spoke the truth. Akkad will expect me to do the honorable and direct thing. He knows that honor demands that my place be here, leading this cohort. Yet, I remember the lessons of my sword master. Show your foe one blade, and kill him with the other." Makeda looked toward the waters of Mirketh Lake. "Today you will be the first sword. I will be the second."

Ancestors communed with, blades sharpened, and armor readied, the battle of House Balaash commenced.

Hundreds of eager extollers looked on, seeking those worthy of exaltation from the masses.

It began simply enough, as affairs of such historical magnitude often did, but every veteran on the field knew that by the time the sun crawled to the middle of the sky, thousands upon thousands of House Balaash's warriors would be dead.

Venator catapults hurled balls packed with explosives and steel shards high into the air to hurtle down into the opposing ranks. The mechanical whine of millions of needles filled the plains as thousands of reivers fired simultaneously. Beasts bellowed and shrieked, whipped into frenzies by the beast handlers, before being released on paths of destruction.

And despite this great conflict, the army of Makeda fought on, completely unaware that their leader was not even there.

If only I could combine your adherence to hoksune with your brother's ambitious pragmatism, then House Balaash would be unstoppable. The mind reels at the possibilities.

The words of Vaactash gave her hope. Makeda's hand was resting on the hilt of one of the Swords of Balaash. If victory required her to be pragmatic, then she would do so, no matter how much it pained her. She knew that her grandfather was watching over her now, but she could only hope that he approved of her decisions.

Kuthsheth the slave worked the oars, and the small rowboat made steady progress along the shores of Mirketh Lake. The morning fog had not yet burned off, and it still provided some measure of cover.

Makeda could not see the battle begin, but she could hear it. The clash of sword and spear, the whine of reivers, the thud of catapults, the screams as acid ate flesh, and the thunder as warbeasts clashed. It was the sound of two forces testing each other. Soon the melee would become general. Her army would fight and die all without her there to lead it, and Makeda cursed fate and begged her ancestors to forgive her dereliction of duty.

She wore a rough cloak of woven hair, ratty and filthy. The garb of a slave hid her proud armor. Her banner, bearing the noble glyph of House Balaash, had been left flying with the army she had abandoned. It was not even the indignity of it all that bothered her, it was that she was being robbed of her chance to lead her warriors into glorious combat. Perhaps if she was lucky, one of the great underwater beasts of Mirketh Lake would do everyone a favor, rise from the depths, and devour her to hide the dishonor.

Makeda had never truly hated Akkad before. She had merely done her duty as honor dictated. She was warrior caste and thus lived only to bring glory to her house. However, now as the great battle commenced without her, Makeda understood what it was to hate. She despised Akkad.

And she pitied him as well. How empty would a life be without hoksune to fill it?

"We are nearly there," Kuthsheth said. "The docks are not—" He cringed as a black shadow passed overhead. The massive beating of leathery wings rocked the tiny boat with blasts of wind, but then the Archidon was past. The flying warbeast paid no attention to their tiny boat.

It had been summoned to the battle by some powerful mortitheurge. It roared, and dove, plunging out of sight behind the dunes along the shore.

"The docks are what, Kuthsheth?" Makeda asked calmly.

"They are not well guarded. The slaves use the docks mostly to bring fish to the kitchens. There are always a few warriors, but I am certain they will be the most inexperienced."

Of course. The most capable would have gotten themselves placed into the battle. No capable warrior would volunteer to guard a dock when such a great opportunity for exaltation presented itself. At worst they would be facing Hestatians, little more than militia. "The problem will be Akkad's personal guard. They are all veteran Cataphracts."

"Also the bloodrunners who prowl the corridors," Kuthsheth said, and seemed surprised when Makeda did not appear to understand what he was speaking of. "Noble Telkesh kept a few on retainer to watch out for assassination attempts against his heirs. They skulk about the house, answering only to Tormentor Abaish."

"I was not aware of them."

"That is because they are very good at skulking . . ."

Makeda had learned that there was much she had not known about the inner workings of her household. There was a world beneath the surface, populated entirely by workers, slaves and servants, members of the lower castes which she had never bothered to pay attention to. The warriors and leaders of a great house did not wish to look upon their lessers all day, so they remained hidden as they fulfilled their purpose, hurrying through their world of mazes.

Kuthsheth was laboring against the oars, but he still did his best to compose himself. "Once I get you into the central keep, I believe I can distract the bloodrunners. They pay no attention to mere house slaves. I have overheard them speaking about what they perceive to be vulnerabilities. Once you are inside the servants' tunnels, I will cause a disturbance in Abaish's laboratory. That should attract the bloodrunners like a moth to a flame."

"What do you intend to do?"

"Make lots of flames."

To attract the attention of the bloodrunners was to die. "Why do you do this?"

"Because I was a warrior once, a swordsman of the Praetorian, long ago before my village was taken. As is our way, I lost my caste and was placed among the slaves of House Balaash. Because Telkesh was an honorable master, my children will be given the chance to be warriors. If not them, then their children, or their children's children will have a chance at achieving exaltation. That is the way."

It had been this particular slave who had broached this idea to her during their march south. He had overheard her speaking with her officers, and had later spoken on the subject of this little-known passage through the great fortress that was House Balaash. At first she had been annoyed by Kuthsheth's impertinence, but the more she had thought about it, the more she could see the possibilities. If Akkad was trying to avoid their duel, then she would simply bring the duel to Akkad.

There was an explosion in the distance. Makeda turned to see the ball of fire rolling into the sky. The battle had truly been joined.

"We are nearly there. Do not worry, Archdomina."

Makeda did not correct the slave's terminology.

The last dying warrior fell into Mirketh Lake with a splash. The water billowed red around him, and then he sank from view. Makeda lowered the Swords of Balaash and let them disappear beneath the slave cloak. The docks were clear. She had eliminated all of the guards before the alarm could be raised. "Come, Kuthsheth. Show me these tunnels of yours."

The slave finished rolling the last corpse into the lake before rushing past her, his sandals slapping against the weathered wood. They passed barrels of salted fish and sacks of grain. In all the years she had lived here, Makeda had never seen this part of her great house. Kuthsheth opened a door and led her inside.

There were a few slaves there, working away, chopping fish with cleavers, blissfully unaware that they were being invaded. What did it matter to a slave if they were being invaded? The work would continue regardless of who was their master tomorrow.

Kuthsheth knew right where to go, so she followed, keeping her head down and her face covered. He took a lantern from the wall to light their path. They went up a flight of stairs, down a long tunnel, and then up another circle of stairs. Kuthsheth took her through a multitude of passages and alcoves. The great house had been grown and added to for twenty generations, until the interior truly was a warren that would confound any invader, but her guide knew these passages well. The stone around her began to feel familiar and comfortable. The lantern oil smelled of home.

They entered a hall that Makeda knew well. She had gazed from these windows, admired this artwork. Her sleeping quarters were not far away. It was an odd sensation, being an invader in your own home. "We are nearly there." Kuthsheth rounded a corner and disappeared from view.

"You, slave! Where are you going?" a voice demanded. "Did you not heed your overseer?"

"Forgive me, Praetorian. I meant no—"

"Silence!" There was the sound of a gauntlet striking flesh. "This area is off limits while the council meets."

Makeda walked around the corner. A swordsman stood over the fallen Kuthsheth. He looked up at Makeda and snarled. "You slaves will get the lash for—" and then his head went bouncing down the hall. Makeda had time to wipe her sword clean with the slave cloak before his body realized it was dead and fell, dumping blood down the polished floor. She frowned. Killing an honorable Praetorian was such a waste . . .

Kuthsheth stood, rubbing the spreading bruise on his cheek. "Thank you, Archdomina." He pointed at a nearby tapestry detailing the life of Vuxoris. "Behind that is a passage which will lead you directly to the council chambers. Please allow me a few minutes to set fire to Abaish's laboratory, otherwise you will surely encounter bloodrunners on the way."

"One moment, Kuthsheth. If you are to die for me,

then you should do it as a member of the caste you were born into." The headless Praetorian was bleeding on her boots. Makeda reached down and picked up the dead warrior's swords. She presented them, hilt first toward the slave. "I hereby proclaim you to be of the warrior caste of House Balaash. Here are your swords, Praetorian."

"My lady...I...I..." His eyes were wide, his mouth agape.

"Wield these in my name."

Kuthsheth took the swords from her with trembling hands. "I will." Now armed, Kuthsheth moved like a changed skorne. With renewed purpose, he quickly lifted the tapestry, revealing the passage. "There is an alcove around the first corner. You should be able to see when the bloodrunners leave, but they should not be able to see you. Go straight on after that, up three more levels of stairs, and you will come out near the council room."

Makeda had spent many hours in the council room, watching and learning as her grandfather, and then her father had ruled over their house. It would be a fitting place to face Akkad.

"I have been a slave of your family for two generations now. I know the soul of Vaactash favors you." Kuthsheth, still reeling from Makeda's generosity, bowed with great humility. "May he guide your steel."

Makeda threw off the slave's cloak and entered the passage.

There had been six guards in the hall leading to the council chamber, but they had not mattered. The last of them crashed through the double doors of the council chambers and rolled down the stairs in a clanking, bloody heap.

The assembled leadership of House Balaash leapt to their feet and reached for their weapons. Akkad was standing at the great window which looked toward the west, watching the distant battle. He turned to see the guard spill out the last of his life down the marble stairs. "What is the meaning of this?"

Makeda paused in the doorway and surveyed the council chambers. The room had always reminded her of the arena, only this sunken floor was meant to be occupied by house leaders rather than gladiators, and the stone benches were filled with those petitioning the council as opposed to bloodthirsty spectators.

There were thirty present: assorted leaders of House Balaash and their vassal houses, as well as representatives of other castes, such as the extoller Shuruppak, the wretch who had denied her father's exaltation, and of course, Abaish, who represented the paingivers, and then many scribes and scholars. There were gasps or curses from all present. Akkad's personal guard lowered their spears and rushed forward in a rattling armored mass to place themselves between their lord and the threat.

Makeda turned slowly, looking everyone present in the eye. Many shirked and looked away, others met her gaze, surely knowing that a reckoning had come. Those were the ones torn between honor and duty. They retained some measure of her respect. *Excellent.* She needed witnesses. She would kill all of the others later, and she made careful note of who fell on each side.

"I am Makeda of House Balaash." She kept her voice

cold and level. "Second Born of murdered Telkesh, granddaughter of mighty Vaactash, and I have come to take back what is mine."

Akkad seemed speechless, but Tormentor Abaish rose from where he had been seated at his left hand. "How dare you enter this house! You are an outcast, a criminal! You have been exiled!"

"So now the whispering servant finds his voice? Do not worry, Paingiver. I will get to you." Makeda stated. Abaish seemed to shrink and tried to hide behind her brother. "So, Akkad, why did you bother to wear your armor if you are too much of a coward to lead your army?"

Her brother's lip curled back in a snarl. "I am afraid of no one."

"You should be . . ."

"Kill the traitor!" Abaish shrieked. "Kill her!"

The elite Cataphracts of Akkad's personal guard hesitated. The order had not come from their archdominar, and for this Makeda was thankful. She would not be able to fight an entire datha of Cataphracts. "Only a coward would send his warriors to do something he lacked the spine to do himself." She pointed the Swords of Balaash at Akkad's heart. "Akkad murdered Archdominar Telkesh with poison, denying him a proper warrior's death. Akkad is a coward and a usurper. His dishonorable behavior has brought shame to House Balaash. Shuruppak of the extoller caste is a heretic, denying murdered Telkesh his rightful exaltation in order to hide Akkad's blasphemous crimes."

"Lies!" Abaish was desperate. Even if Makeda was to be killed, the words had been spoken, the accusation made, and it could never be taken back. "No more of your lies."

"Search your hearts and know I tell the truth." Makeda looked about the crowd as she walked down the stairs. "You are the leaders of House Balaash. I am disgusted that the honorable few among you would tolerate this filth in your midst. You would have a coward take up space in our Hall of Ancestors?"

More eyes were averted. Makeda vowed that those would weep bitter, repentant tears before this day was through.

Akkad pushed between his Cataphracts, roughly shoving them aside. "You dare threaten the archdominar with his own family's blades?" One of his retainers ran forward, presenting the archdominar with his personal war spear. It was a mighty weapon that also bore slivers of their ancestors' souls, and its wicked blade glowed with a pale light. "I will not tolerate this insolence. Surrender *my* family's swords, and I will have you executed painlessly. Resist and you will suffer—"

Makeda laughed hard. "You think to threaten me with pain, brother? I know pain."

"You know *nothing*!" Akkad bellowed.

"I survived the same poison you used to kill Father. Tell me what I don't know then, Brother, because I would like to understand this treachery of yours before I send you into the Void."

"You threaten me? For half a generation I fought for Vaactash. I won battle after battle in his name. I crushed our enemies and drove them before me. I burned cities and took hundreds of slaves. Yet they never listened to me. For a year I fought for Father, but he preferred you. I was the heir! Me! You are a child. You play at war. You speak of lessons that no longer matter and stories of dead heroes, but they are not your words. You have not earned them! You are weak, pathetic, tiny!"

"My lord! Say no more, please." Abaish cried out.

She continued slowly down the stairs until she reached the sunken floor. "Is that all? Because while you talk, our army kills itself. Think of the future of our house."

"You don't understand that it doesn't matter. Just like Telkesh, you lack vision."

"Enough," Makeda ordered. The council chamber was suddenly deadly silent. "Stand aside," she ordered the Cataphracts, and shockingly enough, they did.

Now it was only brother and sister, nothing between them but two philosophies that could never be reconciled. The glyph of House Balaash had been engraved deep into the marble beneath their feet. Akkad stood at the top. Makeda stood at the base.

"You speak of dangerous new ways. They are not *our* way. Demonstrate your conviction, Akkad. I challenge you to a trial of individual combat."

"To the death." Akkad lifted the war spear and spun it effortlessly. "Come, Sister. Let us end this."

They met in the center of the glyph.

The war spear hissed through the air in a blur. Makeda blocked with one sword. The impact sent electricity through her joints. She slashed with the other sword, but Akkad spun and knocked it aside with the shaft. Specks of light, like dust motes in the sun, floated as the two magical weapons hammered against each other.

Akkad moved with frightening speed. He was still bigger, still stronger, and Makeda barely danced aside as the war spear tore a chunk of stone from the floor. He lunged, stabbing, and Makeda rolled aside at the last instant. The spear pierced the chest of a scribe. Akkad lifted the screaming worker and flung him off the blade. The lesser caste members pushed back, scrambling over each other to get to the higher seats. Contemptuous warriors shoved them aside so they could better watch the duel.

Makeda attacked, furious, her blades descended, hacking away, one after the other. One would strike while the other rose in a continuous rain of soul-hardened steel. Akkad retreated smoothly, the massive war spear effortlessly diverting every attack. He backed against the far wall, but then placed one boot against it and launched himself at her.

She was able to avoid the blade, but his armored shoulder caught her in the chest and knocked her back. Ribs cracked. Akkad swung the war spear along the ground, but she was able to jump over it. Akkad quickly followed, extending one hand and pointing at her. Makeda was unprepared for the bolt of power which leapt between them. It hit her in the side. Sickening energy crackled through her bones, causing her muscles to contract in clenching agony. She was flung back, but managed to stay on her feet. *His mortitheurgy is strong.*

Akkad rushed forward, eager to finish her, but Makeda focused through the crackling pain, and forced her arms to respond. The dark powers were gathered up from her body, channeled through her, and pushed away. Akkad gasped as his spell was broken. Makeda quickly counterattacked. One sword diverted his spear, while the other one struck armor, then flesh, and finally bone.

They separated, the full length of the Balaash glyph between them. Akkad glanced down at the strap severed and dangling loose below his shoulder plate, and then blood began to drip slowly down his armor. He pressed one hand against the wound, and grimaced as he probed the hole. It was not fatal, not nearly so, but the message had been sent, and Akkad had felt the sting of Balaash steel.

Makeda stood, waiting, her armored breastplate scorched and smoking. Akkad's attack had hurt her, but this pain was *nothing*.

Wary now, Akkad took his bloody hand from the wound and placed it upon the shaft of his spear. He shifted slowly, his boots sliding across the marble as he took up a ready stance, the spear point angled low toward the floor, ready to sweep up and eviscerate. Makeda lifted her swords, one protectively before her, the other low and ready at her side, in a stance taught to her long ago by Primus Zabalam.

They waited, unmoving, studying each other, watching for any sign of weakness, any opportunity to strike. Two warriors, both masters of their respective martial traditions were coiled, ready.

A minute passed. Another.

No one in the council chambers made a noise. All knew that a single movement would end the duel and decide the fate of House Balaash.

The loudest noise in the room was the *drip-drip-drip* of Akkad's blood sluggishly decorating the floor.

It was that splattering of life that would force Akkad to move first. Such was the danger of having such an understanding of the anatomy and the power that dwelled within. Time was no longer on his side, and every heartbeat that passed would leave him that much weaker. Makeda shifted, ever so slightly, and her grip tightened on her sword. The tiniest bit of a smile split her face.

The siblings struck.

They looked into each other's eyes. This should have been one of those moments of perfect enlightenment spoken of in the code, only achievable at that razor-sharp moment between life and death, but as Makeda saw into Akkad's soul, she saw only the turmoil, the lack of conviction, the doubt in the true ways of their people, of their family . . .

She judged him unworthy.

The spear blade had grazed her, barely turned away by one sword as she'd stepped inside her brother's reach. The tip of her other sword was *in* Akkad's neck.

Makeda spoke slowly to her dying brother. "I would have followed you. It was your place to rule. I would have done whatever duty required of me. I would have followed you into the Void if necessary."

Akkad tried to speak, but sound would not form through the blood running down his throat. She could tell he still understood her words though, and that was what mattered.

"But you thought I was weak, malleable like you. You misjudged me. So now you must go into the Void alone." Makeda twisted the sword and drove it upward, deep into Akkad's brain.

The true heir of House Balaash has already won.

The new archdomina of House Balaash pulled her

sword from her brother's skull and stepped away from the falling corpse. Akkad collapsed, and lay there in a crumpled heap, deprived of all his glory, his blood slowly coloring the crevices of the house glyph engraved in the floor.

Makeda looked up from the body and around the council chambers. None dared question. She would deal with the traitors soon enough, but there were more pressing matters at hand. She turned to the nearest military officer. "Order the cohorts to stand down. Tell them that Makeda rules House Balaash now and has declared this battle to be through. No more of my soldiers will be wasted today." Several warriors ran up the stairs to spread the word. One of the Cataphracts opened the great window to the west, while another brought forth a green signal flag, the color which would order a full halt. He shoved it out into the wind, and began waving it side to side.

Extoller Shuruppak gathered up his voluminous robes and rushed down the steps, grasping wildly for an empty sacral stone at his belt. Makeda looked at the extoller with mild disbelief as he knelt next to Akkad. "What are you doing?"

"Akkad was one of the greatest warriors of his generation. I must keep his soul—"

"Silence." Reaching down, Makeda gathered up a handful of the extoller's robes. "You would betray the ideals of your caste?" She hauled Shuruppak roughly to his feet. Makeda raised her voice, but she was no longer addressing the extoller. "Let the dishonorable name of Akkad never be spoken again in the halls of House Balaash."

"But Akkad was—"

"I must have not made myself clear." Makeda dragged

the extoller past the Cataphract with the signal flag, and hurled Shuruppak out the window. His scream could be heard for several seconds, but they were too high up to hear the impact.

Turning back to the council, Makeda raised her voice. "My brother's name will be stricken from all of the histories." Several scribes immediately opened their scrolls, inked their quills, and began furiously blotting out names. "And as for his fellow conspirators . . ." Makeda glanced at Abaish, who was crouched fearfully on a stone bench, looking like he might be contemplating jumping out the window himself. "Fetch *my* tormentors. Fetch *all* of my tormentors. They are going to be very busy."

Makeda went to the window. In the distance, horns were sounding. The green flag had been seen. The fighting would cease, and hopefully before enough of Balaash blood had been spilled to leave them weakened before the other great houses.

Smoke rose in pillars across the battlefield. From this great distance individuals were nothing more than tiny specks of movement; only mighty warbeasts could be distinguished as what they really were. It was nothing more than a swirling mass of color, red and gold, death and life, all beneath a spreading tower of black.

She watched the smoke climb into the clear sky and wondered if she could see as the extollers did with their crystal eye . . . would the flow of souls into the Void look at all like that smoke drifting into nothingness? When the worker caste refined the impurities from metal, they had to torture it with fire. The weakness was burned away, but what was left was refined.

Saved.

"This is why I fight," the Archdomina of House Balaash whispered to herself.

Grandfather said a warrior did not promise. House Balaash would not fall today, nor would it fall as long as she lived, and as long as House Balaash stood as the greatest of all houses, the skorne would continue as unceasing instruments of war.

Archdominar Vaactash had imparted great wisdom to the child Makeda that night in the Hall of Ancestors. He had taught her, even praised her for her devotion to hoksune, and cautioned her as to her place within the hierarchy of their house. It had been a blessed evening, one that she would always remember, and now she had been dismissed.

Makeda stood perfectly still, unsure, staring up at the seemingly giant Vaactash and the even bigger statue behind him. She was not quite ready to navigate her way back through the darkened Hall of Ancestors, and there remained one thing that the archdominar had mentioned which she had always wondered about. She built up her courage to speak. "Grandfather, I have a question."

Vaactash turned away from the great statue that would someday hold his soul, and toward her, seemingly curious as to why she had not simply fled when given the chance. "Yes. I will allow this question. Speak."

"Tell me about the gods we don't have?"

The greatest warrior of their people folded his arms. "You ask difficult questions, child."

"Yes."

"Lyoss had gods . . ." Vaactash stroked his long chin as he contemplated his answer. "There are lands beyond that sea, lands beyond the Abyss, beyond the Stormlands, even lands past where the giants dwell. We live in a land free of meddling gods, but are there still gods in those other dark lands? I do not know. And if there are gods there, do they have people who worship them still?"

"Only exiles have gone beyond those places, Grandfather. They are a mystery to us." It was an odd thought, but she was clever enough to see it through to a logical conclusion. "But if there are others, and they still had their own gods, then they would be soft, probably used to relying on divine help. Not like the skorne at all."

"Indeed. Ponder on this then, child. We must always make war because our salvation depends on it . . . But should the opportunity present itself, what if we could make war on *someone else*?"

Makeda mulled it over carefully, and the sudden answer struck her like a war spear to the heart. "If there was a foreign house, we could have a whole new adversary. There would be no need for our people to make war on each other. Making war against a new enemy would surely provide opportunities for exaltation to all our houses!" The idea nearly stole her breath away.

"This idea is only a fantasy, but imagine it with me, Makeda. All skorne, all of the warrior caste, all of the houses, united in one glorious conquest. It is *beautiful* . . . May your dreams be of war, Makeda."

"May your dreams be of war, Grandfather."

Two generations had passed, but the lessons of

Vaactash would never leave her. His words were as ingrained into Makeda as the code itself. It had been ten years since her grandfather's death under the tusks of a great beast of the plains, but she still found herself calling upon his wisdom during times of struggle. She was the archdomina now and had led her house through countless battles. The Swords of Balaash were sheathed at her side. Slivers of her grandfather's sacral stone were among those empowering the mighty blades, and though only an extoller could contact the exalted dead, Makeda always felt as though Vaactash was there to guide her with his wisdom.

"Archdomina, I fear the news is grim. Three more western houses have fallen before the invader from the west. Two of the southern houses have bent their knee and offered fealty rather than fight. The ranks of the invader's army have swollen with troops."

"The invader is like nothing we have ever seen before. He has crushed every cohort that has stood in his way."

The council chamber of House Balaash was silent as the words sunk in. Makeda walked away from her advisors and across the Balaash glyph that adorned the floor. The stain had been scrubbed clean over a generation before, but she could still sense a chill on the spot where her nameless brother had died so long before.

The word from the western tors had been troubling, but this new information was even worse. The divided houses were being systematically conquered. It was as Vaactash had spoken of so long ago: there were lands beyond theirs, and now a warrior of incomprehensible power had come from those lands, and was systematically subjugating her people.

"We are the last great house standing in his way..." one of her Tyrants said.

And should we fall, all our people will be dominated.

"What is the name of this *conqueror*?"

"They say he is called Vinter Raelthorne."

Walking slowly, Makeda went to the window and looked toward the west. Ominous clouds had gathered over the plains. The honor of House Balaash—the honor of all skorne—lay heavy on her shoulders. It was times like this that tested a warrior's dedication to the code.

Grandfather, what would you have me do?

A MURDER OF MANATEES
The Further Adventures of Tom Stranger, Interdimensional Insurance Agent

This is the first time this story has appeared in print. It was originally an Audible exclusive audiobook in 2018, narrated by Adam Baldwin, and edited by Steve Feldberg.

The Adventures of Tom Stranger are a comedy series about an Interdimensional Insurance Agent and his bumbling intern. Adam Baldwin (Firefly, Chuck) is so talented that every single character has a distinct voice. Since this was originally written for audio, there are going to be a few parts where you see something like INSERT X NOISE here. Being able to add sound effects is a nice perk.

❖ CHAPTER ONE ❖
Tom's 8 AM Customer Service Response Panel

Miami, Florida
Earth #984-A-3256

IT WAS TIME for the press conference to begin. Tom

Stranger—an unremarkable-looking man in an unremarkable-looking suit—walked onto the stage and surveyed the audience. The room was crowded with reporters and concerned citizens from across the Multiverse. Once again Tom's company had been embroiled in controversy and its good name besmirched. He knew from experience the best way to deal with spurious allegations was to meet them head on, with honesty, integrity, and superior customer service.

"Hello, I am Tom Stranger, of Stranger & Stranger Insurance. As an Interdimensional Insurance Agent I often travel across the multiverse caring for my clients' needs. My job takes me to many alternate realities, where I deal with a variety of insurance-related, sometime apocalyptic crises. Many would consider this..." Tom paused to make quote marks with his finger "...*adventure*. However, what unaugmented beings think of as adventure is merely a normal day here at Stranger & Stranger. I do not understand why anyone would chronicle such mundane events, but recently I was informed that a client of mine documented one of my average work days and created an '*audiobook*' about it. For those of you perplexed by this term, on some worlds that is a *book that you listen to.* Though this '*audiobook*' about my life has been extremely popular on Earth #169-J-00561, the customer satisfaction rating for this product has averaged less than four and a half stars out of five. I always strive for perfect scores in customer service. That half a star is...*troubling*. Thus I have called upon this panel of experts so that we may address these customers' legitimate concerns."

"We're number one! Whooo!" somebody shouted from off stage. "Bestselling audiobook in the world, baby!"

"Correction, Jimmy. *The Adventures of Tom Stranger, Interdimensional Insurance Agent*, written by Larry Correia and narrated by Adam Baldwin, was briefly number one on one particular world. On most civilized worlds it came in a distant second place after the eighth *Game of Thrones* novel."

"Whatever, dude! Number one! Hear that, Mr. Chang? *Number one!*"

"Who is Mr. Chang?" asked one of the reporters.

"Please, let us hold questions until the end."

But Jimmy the Intern answered anyway. "My high school guidance counselor, man. He said I'd never amount to anything. Suck it, Mr. Chang! I starred in the number one audiobook in the world! Woot woot!"

"Calm your wooting, young Intern." Tom Stranger shook his head sadly at Jimmy's display of wanton unprofessionalism. "Such frivolity is an example of why I arranged this Customer Service Response Panel."

"Sorry, Mr. Stranger."

"You might as well come out now. Allow me to introduce our panelists. You have already heard from my intern, Jimmy, whom I brought along today because he was present during the chronicled events."

"S'up, homies." Since today was such an important day, Tom had asked Jimmy to act and look his best. So Jimmy was less unkempt than usual, only partially hungover—a remarkable achievement—and was wearing a shirt and tie instead of one of his usual Chico State T-shirts. However, since Jimmy's default state was *disheveled mess,* he had already dropped a salsa-covered breakfast burrito down his shirt during the drive to the press conference.

"Also joining us is Larry Correia of Earth #169-J-00561, who authored the work in question."

"Hi." Larry the Author waved as he came out on stage and took his seat. There was a little bit of sporadic, polite clapping from the audience.

"And last, but certainly not least, a very special guest, representing one of Stranger & Stranger's most-valued clients, renowned expert on customer relations, Wendell T. Manatee, Chief Financial Officer of CorreiaTech, the most powerful megacorporation in the Multiverse."

A giant fish tank was rolled out on a dolly. Wendell the Manatee floated peacefully inside. "Mehwooooo," Wendell shook his ponderous bulk in greeting. The audience immediately went wild, cheering and chanting his name. *Wendell. Wendell. Wendell.* A woman even threw her panties at Wendell's tank.

Tom waited until the enthusiastic standing ovation for the popular manatee tapered off. Having a public figure of such eloquence and gravitas on his side was certain to help his case. Wendell had agreed to appear as a personal favor. They had picked this location because it was Wendell's home reality, and only one hyperspace jump from Home Office World.

"Let us begin. Mr. Correia, as an accountant—it is good you have retained those skills by the way, in case this writing thing does not work out for you—do you have the statistics?"

"Yes, Tom. We currently have 4,237 five-star reviews on Audible.com, where *The Adventures of Tom Stranger,*

Interdimensional Insurance Agent can still be downloaded."

"Of course. The consumers of your home reality would be fools not to purchase this fine entertainment product. But that is not why we are here. How many one-star reviews are there?"

Larry the Author hung his head in shame. "Two hundred seventy-three."

"Tsk, tsk. I always strive for tens on all customer satisfaction surveys. Or fives, when a world's rating system is based upon stars, smiley faces, or stickers. Now, we shall address these customer complaints directly."

Larry the Author had a stack of 3×5 cards with all the negative reviews written on them. He began flipping through. "Okay, let's see ... 'I'm offended,' 'I'm offended,' 'I'm super offended,' 'This was offensive.' It's about ten 'That was funny' to every one 'I'm offended,' but that guy is *really* offended."

"I see. I believe I know what the problem is," Tom nodded thoughtfully. He turned to address the audience directly. "I accept full responsibility for causing this offense. At this time, I would like to issue a formal apology to all of those whom I inadvertently upset. Humor can be subjective, and what one person finds amusing, others may not. However some things are *never okay* to joke about. So, at this time, I would like to offer my sincerest apology ... to dolphins."

"Wait. What?"

"Yes, Mr. Correia. During the events chronicled in the previous audiobook, I referred to aquatic mammals as 'flippant.' I inadvertently implied that dolphins were not meticulous about paying their insurance premiums or filling out their claim paperwork on time. That is a hurtful negative stereotype, and for that I am truly sorry to the dolphin people."

"Actually, Tom, I'm pretty sure these were mostly humans, offended that I poked fun at their political beliefs, and they took it personal."

Tom scowled. "That makes no sense. Does your world not have *Saturday Night Live*, stand-up comedy, skit shows, *South Park*, Jon Stewart, Tina Fey, Seth Rogan, John Oliver, *That's My Bush*, Judd Apatow movies, the rest of Comedy Central's programming, Patton Oswalt, Bill Maher, Lewis Black, Stephen Colbert, Janeane Garofalo, or any episodes of *The Simpsons* featuring Lisa?"

"Flooooooo," Wendell explained.

"You are telling me that on Larry the Author's home planet it is only acceptable to make fun of *some* beliefs, yet the predominant belief system held within their entertainment industry is sacrosanct?" Tom thought the manatee had to be pulling his leg. "Good one, Wendell. No. It has to be dolphins. Moving on to our next complaint."

Larry the Author read from the next card. "'It was vulgar.'"

"All things considered, I found R. Lee Ermey to be remarkably restrained," Tom stated.

"Fleeeeeeerrp," Wendell agreed. He was a huge *Full Metal Jacket* fan and could practically recite the opening boot camp scene from memory. The manatee showed them his War Face. "Hoooon."

"A fantastic impersonation, Wendell. Regardless, I

will pass this concern onto Secretary of Defense Ermey. Next card."

"Some of the humor was dated, and made jokes relating to pop culture as far back in ancient history as the 1980s."

"Hope that dude never watches *Family Guy*," Jimmy muttered.

"Silence, Jimmy. The customer is always right, even when they are being absurd. Also, he will want to skip the *Guardians of the Galaxy* movies. Next card, Mr. Correia."

"'There was too much profanity.' Now this one is interesting, Tom, and I've got the numbers here. We used no F-bombs. Twice we used the word **BEEP**." Larry paused, confused. "Is the panel being bleeped if we use bad words now?"

"Yes. I thought it best not to cause further customer anguish. Do not worry. I will shut it off after the conclusion of this press conference."

"Hang on. I gotta test this," Jimmy interjected. "**BEEP BEEP** mother**BEEP BEEP** sheep dip! Man, that was awesome!"

Larry the Author looked at his cards. "That's going to make reading these complaints a challenge. Okay, we used **BEEP** six times, uh... That's the naughty word for a butt."

"What kind of lame**BEEP BEEP** is that?" Jimmy asked.

"We used crap eleven times... Wait, no beep? Okay, apparently crap is cool. H E double hockey sticks, a whopping *seventeen* times, but in our defense that was an actual geographic location in the story. There you go, Tom."

"You must explain this one, Mr. Correia. Your sad customer service failings are not upon my head this time."

"Well, as a writer, language is art, and words are your tools. You choose the best tool based upon the impact you are trying to achieve. Sometimes bad words are funny." There was a scattering of half-hearted applause from a few members of the audience.

"Meewhoo**BEEP**ooo**BEEP**eeeer**BEEPBEEP**floooB **EEP**"

The audience laughed uproariously at Wendell's profanity-laced, George Carlin-like rant. The manatee was killing it.

"There you have it. I don't think anyone can argue with such keen observational humor. Next one-star complaint."

"Well, Tom, there's accusations that you are some sort of *idealized libertarian superman.*"

"Preposterous. As an insurance agent, I am above petty partisan politics and only care about providing quality customer service. You must be mistaken. That customer was probably referring to President Adam Baldwin."

"Yeah, that guy is pretty awesome," Jimmy agreed.

"Fleeeeeerp," Wendell added, because he mostly knew Adam Baldwin as Animal Mother. "Mooo."

"You heard the manatee, Mr. Correia. Next card."

The author had a perplexed look on his face as he read from the stack. "It is apparent that Larry Correia hates people like me. I'm triggered."

"Sheesh, friggin' dolphins," Jimmy said. "Let it go, already! You guys need to chillax."

"Okay, this one is a direct quote: *The story lacks in every dimension.*"

"Hmmm..." Tom was puzzled. "Do you think they meant that literally, or was it an attempt at humor regarding the existence of multiple dimensions? Regardless, the customer is always right. Bad writer. Bad."

"Sorry, Tom. Up next, we have a few about what awful ego-stroking it is for an author to insert himself into a story. That's kind of a funny one since I didn't exactly cover myself in glory back there. I spent most of my time getting my **BEEP** kicked."

"It does not matter. The customer has spoken. An author putting himself into the narrative is never okay. In the future you should strive to be more professional, like Stephen King or Clive Cussler. Is that all of the negative comments?"

"It appears so, Tom."

"Well, there you have it, news media and gentle-customers. Thank you for attending this Customer Service Response Panel. Are there any questions? Yes...there in the back."

"This question is for Larry the Author. Despite your virulent anti-dolphin hatemongery, do you intend to write about any more of the adventures of Tom Stranger?"

"Okay, first off, I don't even know any dolphins."

"That just makes it worse, sir."

"Second, sure. I'd be up to writing another story about Tom and company."

Because of Larry's ham-fisted, clumsy, pulpy writing style, it meant Tom probably had more of these awkward press conferences to look forward to in the future. "Next question, please."

"This question is for Mr. Manatee. Would you care to

comment about your megacorporation's controversial move to perform a hostile takeover of many of the most evil companies in the Multiverse, thus creating one super giant megacorp legion of doom ensuring galactic domination?"

There were murmurs from the audience. Tom had not even been aware of these events, and he read the Drudge Report.

"Floorp." And when Wendell the Manatee put his flipper down and said no further questions, he meant it. His handlers immediately came out and wheeled his tank off stage.

"Well, I am afraid that is all the time we have today. We apologize for this utter failure of customer service, and I will personally endeavor to make up that half a star in the future. Thank you for coming."

❖ CHAPTER TWO ❖
Stranger & Stranger's Quarterly Employee Evaluations

Home Office World

AFTER THE PRESS CONFERENCE Tom had returned to the office, looking forward to another productive workday. There was a Multiverse in constant turmoil, clients in need, and quality customer service wouldn't supply itself. Plus, it was nice to turn off that annoying profanity beeper.

The Stranger & Stranger Home Office was a bustling,

upbeat place, where the finest office staff in the Multiverse efficiently processed claims and sold policies using the most advanced technology available from a hundred worlds. Tom's personal executive office was very plain and businesslike. There were no personal mementos or knickknacks to distract him from his duties. It was his happy place.

And today was a very important day on Home Office World.

An Interdimensional Insurance Agent was only as good as his team, so it was company policy that every quarter Tom would assess his Junior Associates to make sure that they were operating as a well-honed insurance unit should. Each member would be tested in a variety of grueling simulations, pushing their mental and physical limits to the ragged edge, and then Tom would personally grade their performances.

Interns came from many different realities, but only a handful survived long enough to make the leap to Junior Associate. That position required genius intellect, Olympian physicality, and a courageous dedication to customer satisfaction. After years of experience, the greatest among them would step into the Insurance Crucible and overcome the Final Claim in order to be certified a full-fledged Interdimensional Insurance Agent. Those elite few would get their own franchises and the circle of life would continue.

Until his employees faced the Crucible, it was Tom's solemn duty to mentor them in the Path of Customer Service. Luckily, as the evaluations came in, it turned out that most of his staff was excellent as usual. Tom only had one evaluation left to go over, and he *had* been putting it off for last. He did not rejoice in the failure of others, and it was with heavy heart that Tom ever let anyone go. Alas, Tom could procrastinate no more, so he pushed a button on his desk.

"Ms. Wappler, could you bring me Jimmy the Intern's evaluation, please?"

His secretary entered a moment later, loudly chewing her gum. Muffy "Sparkles" Wappler was part Jersey girl, part android killing machine, and all insurance professional.

"I kinda been dreading this one too, Mr. Stranger. I know you've taken Jimmy under your wing and all, but . . . Well, here you go. See for yourself."

Tom looked over Jimmy's performance records. The results were not pretty, like anal polyps-level *not pretty*. "This is possibly the most dismal score I have ever seen from anyone in the Interdimensional Insurance Business."

Muffy had blown a rather magnificent pink bubble while he'd been reading. She popped it and went back to chewing. "Yeah, I thought so, too, so I checked with the Licensing Board to see if scores that low were some sort of record. Like an anti-achievement. I thought no way could Jimmy be the worst intern ever. Remember, there was that period back in the nineties where some other companies tried to save money by hiring sign language gorillas."

"At least Jimmy is not last place then."

"Sorry. I didn't mean to imply Jimmy beat out the gorilla. That Amy could really hustle. For the record, Jimmy isn't dead last. Just the lowest-scoring carbon-based life form. One year Conundrum & Company hired a See 'n Say as a customer service rep. You know the toy you pull the string and the little arrow spins and *the cow goes moo*? It was close, but Jimmy edged it out."

"That is . . . something." Tom had been doing his best to help Jimmy discover his inner insurance agent, but they had faced some serious hurdles. "We must remember that Jimmy is from a very backwards Earth. It's the one reality so statistically improbable that their Cubs actually won their World Series."

"Also, I think that's one of those weirdo oddball universes where Donald Trump got elected president, Mr. Stranger. Back on my planet, that guy owns a chain of all-you-can-eat buffets slash strip clubs."

"Before my home planet was obliterated, our Donald Trump was a professional wrestling villain. Jimmy's home reality is truly an oddity," Tom agreed. "By the way, who won the recent presidential election on your home world?"

"Adam Baldwin's two magnificent terms were up, but the Libertarian Space Cowboy Revolution Party won it again, and former Labor Secretary Mike Rowe is president now."

"It's a dirty job, but someone has to do it." That was enough workplace-appropriate small talk. "Now, back to Jimmy's evaluation. Test scores are valuable, but real world performance is where it counts. How has he been integrating with our corporate culture?"

Muffy shrugged. "Jimmy's the reason I had to send out that employee newsletter about why licking toads is a terrible idea. He routinely burns popcorn in the break room microwave. That new sign on the copier saying that it is not okay to photocopy your own butt? Jimmy."

"Surely there is some way to get him up to speed."

Tom's body had been extensively enhanced and genetically modified with every groundbreaking combat and customer service-related technology possible. Muffy's robot arm could bench-press a truck. "Perhaps we could have him cybernetically augmented?"

"We tried implanting an infolink chip directly into his brain so he could automatically access the Galactic Data Sphere. But then I had to disconnect it a few days later because Jimmy was downloading so much that he was eating up all the company's bandwidth."

"Let me guess. Pornography?"

"Surprisingly, no. It was something called Ozzy Man Reviews."

"I see." Though providing quality customer service to their existing clients was an Interdimensional Insurance Agent's greatest calling, it was always important to find new clients. The thought of some poor potential customer out there somewhere in the Multiverse, insufficiently insured, was a terrible one. "How does Jimmy do at developing new business?"

"To put it bluntly," which went without saying because that was the only manner Muffy ever put anything, "Jimmy kinda sucks at selling policies, too."

"That is most unfortunate, but let us remember that we all struggled with sales at first." Back when he'd been an intern at Mifune & Eastwood, Tom had once been submerged in acid by an enraged Burgundian Hive Queen for forgetting to give her a free rate quote. It had been a teachable moment. *Good times.*

"Seriously, just in case you think I'm exaggerating, Mr. Stranger, watch this."

She transmitted a file to Tom's desktop holo projector. The image showed a very nervous Jimmy seated in their conference room, and resting on the table in front of him was what appeared to be an ordinary head of cabbage.

"Hmmm . . . curious. Why is Jimmy speaking to a leafy vegetable, Ms. Wappler?"

"I didn't trust him not to scare off any real prospective paying customers, and I was cleaning out the break room fridge and found that. It had gone a little wilty. I didn't think whoever brought it in would miss it. So I told Jimmy that it came from a universe run by sentient vegetables."

"And Jimmy believed this ludicrous ruse?"

"Sir, Jimmy still believes all the spambots sending him friend requests on Facebook really are lonely beautiful women. He answers every email from Nigerian princes trying to move money out of the country. Jimmy didn't even question it when I introduced him to Cabgar, Chief Ambassador of Cabbage Land."

Muffy hit play.

"So insurance, you know? Well, Mr. Cabgar, 'round here that's like our dealio. It's where you pay money for stuff that hasn't happened yet, so when it happens we fix it and you don't get screwed. Because there's like this thing, where there's these different dimensions, but what's normal on one planet isn't normal on another planet. And sometimes they bump into each other, and like stuff happens, and then more stuff. Cool, right? No way. Sometimes it's totally uncool. Anyways, that's what we're here for."

Tom winced. "At least he is enthusiastic."

"Oh, don't worry. It gets worse." Muffy fast-forwarded through Jimmy's rambling, incoherent sales pitch.

Jimmy's tie was now undone and he was looking rather flustered. "*So, uh, you're like the strong silent type. Fine, whatever, dude. If you don't want insurance, that's on you, man. Don't come crying to us when a portal opens and vegetarians attack and make your planet into a salad bar! And you're all like ahhh nooo I'm getting chewed! Some dude's eating my face!*"

"Not the most diplomatic approach, but young Jimmy does raise a valid concern." Militant Space Vegans really were a terrible menace, so gassy and self-righteous, as they roamed the galaxy in their eco-friendly battle cruisers.

"There's more," Muffy assured him.

When the hologram returned to normal speed, giant sweat rings had appeared in the armpits of Jimmy's dress shirt. He had taken his necktie off and was wearing it as a bandana as he shouted at the hapless cabbage. "*You just keep staring at me! Why you got to be so judgmental, man? You think because you're all full of vitamins and minerals and antioxidants and shit you're better than me? Huh? Well you're not! You're not!*"

"Ah, I think I see your point, Ms. Wappler."

"Uh-huh." Muffy just nodded as she skipped forward again. Now Jimmy was out of view of the camera, but it was obvious from the sound that he was beneath the table, crying.

"It would appear that Ambassador Cabgar won that round."

"That whole video was only four and a half minutes long, Mr. Stranger. Look, I know you like the kid because he took a bullet for you, and I'm not saying that he's *totally* useless, just mostly useless."

"What use *would* you suggest for him then?"

"Uh . . ." Muffy was temporarily stumped, but like a true insurance professional she always managed to find the bright side of every situation. "Some planets still use Soylent Green. Jimmy is mostly made out of valuable proteins and fats."

He had been hoping Jimmy had some prospects better than being rendered down into an edible paste. "Thank you, Ms. Wappler. That will be all."

"Sorry to be the bearer of bad tidings, Mr. Stranger." Muffy got up to leave.

Normally, anyone who was enough of a warrior and scholar to survive an Interdimensional Insurance Internship would be offered a Junior Associate position upon graduation. Despite Tom's initial assessment that Jimmy would be a miserable failure—for heaven's sake, he was getting a degree in *Gender Studies*—Tom had still hoped the young man would make the cut. Miraculously, Jimmy had survived for a bit, but in so doing he had brought dishonor upon their company. Unfortunately, in a business where the smallest error could lead to horrifying painful death or, worse, dissatisfied customers, there was no room for a Jimmy.

"Would you please send Jimmy in to speak with me? I'm afraid I'm going to have to make some cuts."

Muffy clapped her hands gleefully. "Yes, sir! Should I fetch your decapitating axe and a tarp?"

"What? Why?"

"To protect the new carpet obviously."

"Oh." That failure of clear office communication was upon Tom. Jimmy's use of slang had rubbed off on him.

Yet another example of reckless unprofessionalism. The intern was a force of chaos. "Sorry, I meant I was going to terminate him. His employment I mean ... Not his life. That would probably be wrong."

"Well, shucks." Muffy seemed a little dejected. "I'll go get Jimmy."

When Muffy told him that Mr. Stranger needed to speak with him in private, Jimmy was super pumped. He'd been totally rocking it as the new hotness at Stranger & Stranger. He was probably going to get an epic raise, probably a promotion too, a big office with windows, and his own giant fighting robot.

"S'up, Mr. Stranger?"

"What is that thing on your head?"

"Oh, this?" Jimmy touched the awesome bundle of hair he'd tied up on top. "It's called a *man bun*. It's the hot new look on my planet. Pretty badass, huh?"

Jimmy saw Mr. Stranger pause, scowling as he checked the internet thingy implanted in his brain. "Apparently the latest 'hipster' fashion trends on your home world require looking like an effeminate lumberjack in a romper. *What an odd dimension*... Please, have a seat, Jimmy." He gestured at the chair in front of his desk. "We need to talk about your future with the company."

"Cool." Jimmy sat down. As usual, Mr. Stranger's desk was super organized. There was a cup with pencils in it and they were all exactly the same length and uniformly sharp. Even the papers in his inbox were perfectly lined up. "When I get my own giant fighting robot, I want it to look like a ninja turtle. Not Donatello though. Who wants a friggin' pole? But everybody always wants to be Leonardo with the sword. That's cliché. So I'm thinking nunchucks."

"I'm afraid discussing the relative merits of various turtle-based weapon systems is not why I have summoned you. Now please, I am attempting to show an appropriate amount of sensitivity. Because you once saved my life—"

"I sure did! That Jeff Conundrum guy is such a douche! He's like the worst insurance agent ever, like how way back he let your home planet get blown up. He's our competition but his company is a total rip-off. It was pretty awesome how you left him trapped in Hell."

"Indeed. That was rewarding. Now please, stop interrupting..." Mr. Stranger cleared his throat and tried again. "I had high hopes that you would develop the skills necessary to provide quality customer service. With this internship completed, you will be graduating soon—"

"With a degree in Gender Studies I'll be making the big bucks!"

His boss sighed. "Yes...*Gender Studies*."

"I just got to say, Mr. Stranger, these last few months have been the best time of my whole life. I've gotten to fly around outer space, blow up monsters with lasers, and meet all sorts of hot alien chicks, and they're all like, whoa, *you're with Tom Stranger? Whaaaaat?* And I'm all like, yeah baby, I'm his right-hand man. And they're all swooning and stuff. You know what I'm saying?"

"As usual, not really."

"Before this internship I didn't really know what to do with my life, man. You can only go to so many protests before you get tired of catching scabies, and all the ladies are bossy with dreadlocks and smell funny, and blocking freeway traffic with your body isn't nearly as fun as it sounds. Insurance is James Bond super cool. I love being an insurance agent. This job is like the best thing ever!"

Tom Stranger took a deep breath. "Then I'm afraid that I have some unfortunate news. It is with great sadness that I must inform you that you are being term—"

Suddenly the Claim Alarm sounded. "AWWW-WOOOOOGA! CODE RED! CODE RED! ALL ASSOCIATES ON DECK! THIS IS NOT A DRILL!"

The announcement was so loud that Jimmy fell backwards in his chair. With catlike reflexes honed over months of hard core insurancing, Jimmy rolled to the side and tried to take cover behind a potted plant.

"What's going on, man?" he screamed, trying to be heard over the shrieking noise.

Mr. Stranger had leapt to his feet. "That alert only sounds when one of our Premium Comprehensive Platinum Policy holders files a Level Ten Claim."

"That sounds bad! Is that bad?"

"Exceedingly." Mr. Stranger calmly walked to a big case mounted on the wall, which read *In Case of Armageddon Break Glass,* and shattered it with his fist. He reached inside and pulled out an unremarkable leather briefcase. "I must get to the conference room."

It was crazy out in the office. The lights were flashing red. Junior Associates were ducking and covering beneath their desks. Someone had taken a bunch of files, dumped them into a wastepaper basket, and set it on fire. Jimmy had never seen his coworkers wig out like this before.

Another intern ran by wearing nothing but football pads with spikes on them.

"I'm scared!"

"That's just the customary dress of Fred's people. I should have never allowed the implementation of *Casual Friday*. That decision also allowed such travesties as your *man bun*," Mr. Stranger explained as they hurried down the hallway. "Oh, wait, you are remarking upon the general atmosphere of pandemonium and terror. That is to be expected with a Level Ten Claim. The last time we had one of these, hundreds died."

That totally sucked, but from what Jimmy knew about Interdimensional Insurance, that sort of thing happened all the time. "Compared to whole planets blowing up, hundreds doesn't seem too bad."

"I meant hundreds *in this office*. The death toll across the Multiverse was incalculable. Many brave Junior Associates gave their lives. It was a dark day for insurance. Our entire HR department was vaporized. We even had to replace the carpet."

"Whoa. So what were you about to tell me when that siren went off, Mr. Stranger?"

"It will have to wait. If we do not all perish, we will speak again later."

"Cool, cool." Mr. Stranger was a busy dude, he'd get around to Jimmy's promotion later. They had reached the conference room and it was filled with nervous employees loading guns and checking spreadsheets. Jimmy would just have to wait until after this Level Ten thingy was cleared up before he got his fat raise and some sweet nunchucks.

❖ ❖ ❖

Tom had dealt with several Level Ten claims over his career and he knew that they always required the utmost care. To qualify as a Level Ten, the potential damages had to be staggering, the likely outcomes catastrophic. Previous events of such magnitude had caused the fall of empires, the extinction of species, the destruction of worlds, and a great deal of customer dissatisfaction.

Muffy had already prepared the conference room, put a pot of coffee on, and even had time to apply her war paint. She had gone with a festive blue *Braveheart* theme. "We're all ready, Mr. Stranger."

"Excellent. Which Platinum Policy is it, Ms. Wappler?"

"The *big one*," she whispered.

"CorreiaTech Prime?"

"The Interdimensional Lord of Hate *himself* is on the line."

The room fell deadly silent. A few of the weaker-willed Junior Associates fainted.

Not only was this their biggest account, but this particular claim was coming from the merciless CEO of the most powerful megacorporation in the Multiverse, a man whose hobbies included collecting vintage antique atomic bombs, who subsisted on a diet of endangered unicorn steaks, who was so rich that when he shot trap and skeet, he used Fabergé eggs instead of clay pigeons.

That guy . . .

"Put him through, Ms. Wappler."

The ruggedly handsome, totally ripped CEO appeared on the screen, smoking a cigar.

"Greetings, sir. How can we serve your insurance needs today?"

The Interdimensional Lord of Hate ran one massive hand through his thick, luxurious, heavy metal-quality hair in a very frustrated manner. "Damn it, Tom! Where's my manatee?"

"I do not understand."

"Wendell volunteered to help you at that panel thing this morning, with you, your idiot sidekick—"

"Hey!"

Tom shushed Jimmy.

"And that bald fat clone version of me who writes fantasy books or some crap."

"Technically, the author is not a clone, merely another version of you from an alternative reality, who is, comparatively speaking, an utter failure."

"Lame. Whatever. Anyways, my CFO went missing after your presser. I'd leave it up to my private army, but our scans show another dimension was involved, so his abduction should be covered."

There were gasps from the Junior Associates. Wendell the Manatee had been kidnapped! This was terrible news.

"That is most unfortunate. I can assure you that Stranger & Stranger will not rest until we find him and your claim is settled."

"That's what I'm paying you for, Tom. I don't know who took him, but you'd better shake the trees until something falls out, or there's gonna be hell to pay."

Tom made a solemn vow. "I will not rest until Wendell sleeps with the fishes."

Only Jimmy was confused. "We're going to kill him in a mob hit?"

"What is *wrong* with you?" Muffy whispered.

"What?" Now it was Tom's turn to be puzzled. "No, Jimmy. He lives in the ocean. We are going to return him to his home."

"Oh, okay. But I still don't get what's so important about one manatee?"

All of the other Junior Associates stared at Jimmy like he was insane. Then they quickly stepped away from him, clearing a circle like he was about to get struck by lightning. Which he probably was, since the Interdimensional Lord of Hate had snarled and raised his mighty finger and thumb, poised to snap.

"Please forgive him, your Hateyness. Jimmy is but a lowly intern, ignorant in the ways of the Multiverse. I assume you are aiming a satellite death ray or some such device at him as we speak. I would politely ask you to refrain from disintegrating any of my staff."

"Fine." The Interdimensional Lord of Hate lowered his fingers. "But I'll elaborate for your village's idiot. Wendell may be my accountant, and we've roped him into playing the cleric in our monthly company D&D night, but it isn't me you have to worry about. When his people find out, they're going to be torqued. They will call for a *hooning*."

Tom was proficient in six hundred and eighty-five languages so he explained it for his staff who weren't as knowledgeable. "The word is rather nuanced, but *hoon* is the battle cry of the Manatee. They are slow to anger, but when it comes, it is terrible to behold."

"Damned skippy. There isn't anything scarier than a herd of vigilante sea cows on a rampage. They tend to nuke first and ask questions later."

It was a race against time. "Understood, sir. Consider it done."

"Good. Contrary to what my critics might say, I don't like when whole planets get slaughtered. Losing that many customers sucks. CorreiaTech Prime out." The screen went dark.

"Okay, am I the only one who is really super confused?" Jimmy asked. "The manatees on my Earth are pretty chill."

"That's what they want you to think!" Muffy said. "Does your home world have legends of the sunken continent of Atlantis?"

"Yeah, sure, I think so."

"Who do you think sunk it?"

"Enough," Tom ordered. "Muffy is correct. Manatees are known for two things: their fiscal responsibility, and their unrelenting thirst for vengeance once provoked. Wendell is a hero to his herd. His kidnapping will surely rouse their fiery Florida-Man tempers. Their justice will be swift, unflinching, and indiscriminate. If we do not retrieve him quickly, the Multiverse will face *a murder of manatees*."

❖ CHAPTER THREE ❖
The Big 10 AM Shakedown

Miami, Florida
Earth #984-A-3256

FOR CLAIMS LIKE THIS, Tom knew it was best to

start at the scene of the incident. He quickly assembled a crack team of forensic insurance investigators and they traveled through the Thorne Gate back to the press conference center. The parking lot was quickly filled with Stranger & Stranger battlemechs and hover tanks from across the Multiverse.

After interviewing the witnesses and watching the security camera video, Tom had a good idea what had happened. After concluding the panel, Wendell's handlers had wheeled his giant fish tank back to his signature monster truck. Of course, Wendell had been given the VIP parking space. While loading they had been set upon by invisible attackers (good invisibility cloaks, too, genuine Predator brand, not the chintzy knock-off invisibility cloaks you could pick up at Walmart on any half-decent world).

The handlers had been stunned with phasers and had not seen a thing. Wendell was a fearsome warrior, usually armed with several advanced CorreiaTech weapons but, alas, had been distracted looking at his phone, having a political debate on Twitter (where the popular manatee had more than ten billion followers) and had never seen them coming. His fish tank had been shot with a freeze ray, instantly solidifying the water and placing the noble sea cow into cryostasis. Then the whole thing had been rolled into a suspicious black van with out-of-universe plates which had been waiting nearby. The kidnappers were gone in seconds.

This was the work of professionals. The only DNA found at the scene was aquatic mammal. The kidnappers had left no tracks, and according to Miss Cleo, no psychic residue. They were well trained, well armed, and highly motivated. This was shaping up to be quite the challenge.

"All right, listen up Junior Associates, our manatee has been missing for 90 minutes. Average rocket-boost-assisted hover van speed is 400,000 miles an hour. That gives us a radius of 600,000 miles. What I want from each and every one of you is a hard-target search of every gas station, residence, warehouse, farmhouse, henhouse, outhouse, and doghouse in that area. Checkpoints go up at the edge of the solar system. Your manatee's name is Wendell. Go get him."

"Whoa! I love that movie too, Mr. Stranger!"

"What movie?" Tom was momentarily puzzled why Jimmy the Former Intern was present at all, but then he remembered that in the heat of the moment he had neglected to finish firing him. "Oh, I'm sorry, Jimmy. I forgot to tell you that you're fired."

It took Jimmy a moment to process that. "Huh?"

"Fired. Terminated. You are no longer employed by Stranger & Stranger. It was due to your terrible performance review. I should have told you back at the office and saved you the drive. I would be happy to discuss this with you later so that you may learn from your mistakes, but right now I must focus on staving off the Sea Cow Apocalypse."

Tom did not enjoy rudeness, but he had no choice but to leave Jimmy befuddled and stammering in the parking lot. He had much work to do. The rest of his team were running back to their vehicles. There was a series of sonic booms as mechs blasted off. He found that Muffy was busy consulting the Galactic Data Sphere, searching for any individual or group which might hold a grudge against the manatee, either professional or personal. Professionally, the Chief Financial Officer of an ultra-powerful, Multiverse-spanning megacorporation tended to make enemies. The personal list was far longer, but mostly because Wendell tended to talk a lot of trash while playing *Call of Duty* online multiplayer.

"Ms. Wappler, this morning a reporter asked a pointed question about a hostile takeover. Do you have any further information concerning that?"

"I sure do. CorreiaTech wants to merge a whole bunch of super evil companies together, and really corner the market on evil products."

"Sounds evil, yet efficient. Do you have a list?"

"A bunch of our clients are already on there: Weyland-Yutani, Cyberdyne Systems, LexCorp, Umbrella, Kentucky Fried Velociraptor, and United Airlines." Muffy sent the data directly to his infolink. "You got a hunch, Mr. Stranger?"

"A good agent must follow his instincts," Tom said as he picked up his Doomsday Briefcase and headed for his mech.

As Tom strapped into the pilot's seat and prepared for takeoff, he noticed poor Jimmy still wandering the parking lot, lost and forlorn, dreams shattered, forever deprived of the opportunity to provide quality customer service. Perhaps Muffy had been right, and it would have been more merciful to put him out of his misery. Just not on the new carpet.

"This sucks," Jimmy muttered as the last of the groovy

space tanks and giant robots blasted off, leaving him all by himself. There was a conveniently located can for him to angrily kick down the road.

It wasn't fair. Jimmy had been awesome as an insurance intern. He'd made copies, fetched coffee, and only ate an appropriate amount of doughnuts when Muffy brought them in. Where did Mr. Stranger get off with his fancy *evaluations*? That cabbage dude had been stone cold. Nobody could have sold that heartless bastard insurance.

He had never really been good at much. Sure, he had a whole bunch of participation trophies, but now he was beginning to suspect those weren't as meaningful as he'd always thought. But he'd worked super hard to get good at insurance, harder than he'd ever worked before. He'd even been pumping iron. Heck, he'd gone from a .07 on the Grylls Survivability Scale to a .09. A 1.0 was how much trauma it took to kill a single Bear Grylls, and Jimmy had a ways to go before that, but he'd started out equivalent to a standard Earth chicken, and now the GSS ranked him as survivable as a ficus plant. Though Jimmy didn't know what a ficus plant was, he was certain it had to be pretty badass.

He'd come too far to give up now! He was going to show Mr. Stranger that he had what it took to be an insurance agent! He knew he could do it if he believed in himself hard enough. Only, unlike college, Mr. Stranger had standards. Begging wouldn't work. Mr. Stranger only cared about customer service and results.

That gave Jimmy an idea. Everybody else was out trying to find their missing client, but if Jimmy could find that manatee first, he'd be golden. He wouldn't just get his job back, he'd be Employee of the Month! All he had to do was figure out the Crime of the Century before all of the trained, competent people did.

Only he had something those guys didn't. Most Junior Associates came from super tough worlds, where every day was a fight for survival, so they didn't watch a lot of TV, but Jimmy had mastered the art of binge streaming and most of that had been cop shows. He'd had to keep his love of cop shows a dirty little secret from the other Gender Studies majors because they mostly watched *Girls* on HBO and if they found out, they would've yelled at him about *cisnormative fascism* or some other big words he didn't really understand.

If all those cop shows had taught Jimmy anything, it was that it was always the rogue, loose-cannon detective who didn't give a damn about "authority" and "rules" who got the job done. That sounded like Jimmy to a T because, let's face it, Jimmy knew he was pretty much a real-life cross between Luthor and Raylan Givens.

Sure, the average Junior Associate at Stranger & Stranger had been a Navy SEAL Astronaut Lawyer or something before getting into insurance, but right now they'd be bogged down with "logic" and "facts" while Jimmy was going to follow his gut. And on TV cop shows, whenever they didn't know what to do next, they would go roust some shady characters until somebody talked, and somebody always talked.

This version of Florida was way more high-tech and swoopy than Jimmy's home world, but it also had kind of a cool cyberpunk *Blade Runner* vibe. That meant there was bound to be a seedy criminal underworld.

Since he had tankpooled over to the conference center and his Prius was back on Home Office World, Jimmy had to call for an Uber. He told the driver to take him to the sleaziest cesspool of shifty lying dirtbags on the whole planet. But, sadly, by the time they got to London it would be after work hours so there wouldn't be anybody at *The Guardian* to shake down. It was those newspaper dorks' lucky day.

So they picked the next best sleazy local thing.

The Faceless Mook Bar & Grill was supposed to be a wretched hive of scum and villainy. Jimmy's driver said this was where all the bad dudes hung out. Not the top tier really bad guys, but more like the low- and mid-level threatenable bad guys who would rat out their bosses. Man, Uber drivers were super helpful in this dimension!

The bouncer at the door was a five-hundred-pound cyborg gorilla. "Greetings. Human females drink free on Fridays."

"Sweet. Maybe I'll meet some ladies."

The gorilla looked at Jimmy's ID. "Oh, my bad. You are a human male."

"Whoa." He'd heard about this all the time in Gender Studies but had never had it happen to him personally before. "Did you just assume my *gender*?"

"Yes. You are very puny with delicate bones." The gorilla plucked a tick from his own pelt and ate it.

"I can't wait to post about this on Tumblr!" Misgendering was worth like ten thousand victim points!

"I must warn you, frail human. Inside this establishment the sick and weak are usually killed and eaten. But you are over twenty-one, so go on in." The gorilla opened the door.

On the other side was truly the scariest bar Jimmy had ever seen. It was all bikers, roughnecks, Yakuza, killer robots, pirates—both space and the old-fashioned, time-travelling kind—and assorted monstrous aliens from across the Multiverse. He'd heard Wendell's home Earth was truly cosmopolitan, which was a word they'd used a lot in college though Jimmy wasn't sure what three-flavored ice cream had to do with anything. All he knew was this place was so nasty Patrick Swayze from *Road House* would have walked in, took one look around, and said, nope, screw this, I'm out of here.

Jimmy swallowed hard, called upon his inner insurance agent, and stepped inside. The music was so loud it punched him in the ear holes. It was a good thing they'd shut off that profanity filter, because otherwise the gangster rap soundtrack would be nothing but a string of beeps. Jimmy thought because he'd watched every episode of *Burn Notice* and *Dexter* he would be prepared for the Miami criminal underworld, but this was a bit overwhelming. There were exotic dancers in cages suspended from the ceiling, several burly men were engaged in a bloody knife fight, and Jon Taffer from *Bar Rescue* was loudly berating the owner about how the buffalo wings had not been cooked to a safe temperature in order to prevent salmonella.

He went up to the bar. The bartender looked suspiciously like Danny Trejo. Jimmy ordered a mojito because that seemed a very Miami thing to do. This place wasn't messing around, and it came out in a Super Big

Gulp-sized cup, which Jimmy immediately chugged. Then he thought better of it, and ordered four more, because his courage could use a little boost.

"You think you can handle all that, little man?"

Jimmy snorted. He might not be as skilled as some of the other interns, but he'd gone to Chico State. Jimmy could function with a blood alcohol level of *half*. "Just keep 'em coming, Machete."

"Okay, but don't blame me for your poor life choices. What brings you here anyway?"

Jimmy leaned over the bar and looked on the other side, just in case there was a manatee tied up behind it. *Nope.* That would've been super convenient.

"I'm looking for information."

"You a cop?"

"Do I look like a cop?"

"Not really. They've usually got some department-mandated physical fitness and grooming standards. What is going on with your hair?"

"It's my man bun."

"So you're like a special-needs samurai or something?"

"Nope." He pulled out a business card and slid it across the grimy bar. "Jimmy Duquesne, Interdimensional Insurance Agent . . . Intern . . . Former. Whatever. Maybe you've heard of me?"

"No way, homeboy!" The bartender stared at the card in shock. "You're *the* Jimmy the Intern?"

"Wait . . . Seriously. You have heard of me?"

"Sure. We all loved that audiobook, *esè*! Adam Baldwin is the bomb!" the bartender shouted so everyone could hear. "Guys, guys, it's Jimmy the Intern!"

Suddenly Jimmy was surrounded by a crowd of terrifying meat heads, asking things like, "Is Muffy super hot?," "Can I get your autograph?" and "What's Tom Stranger really like?"

Jimmy was starting to feel his 64-ounce mojito so he answered truthfully. "Muffy looks like the movie version of Harley Quinn, only less slutty, more classy. Sure, I'll sign stuff. And Mr. Stranger is super badass at customer service, but he can be kind of insensitive. He fired me today!"

There was a chorus of "No way, man!" and "That's bullshit!"

"I know, right? Us interns have feelings too!"

The room of hoodlums seemed moved by his plight. "Yeah, nobody ever stops to think about how us minor supporting villains feel. We're always getting beaten up and we never get no credit!"

"John Wick shot me seventeen times," one giant with a handlebar mustache sniffed, "and my boss didn't even send me a get-well card."

This was going way better than expected. "Groovy. So like I'm here to kick some ass until somebody tells me who kidnapped Wendell so I can get my job back. So consider this a shakedown!"

"Yay!" Thugs loved a good shakedown.

Jimmy downed his third mojito. It was getting a little blurry since he couldn't remember drinking the second one. "Okay then!" He stood up on his stool. "I need information and I ain't leaving until somebody talks! So how do we do this? Do I just like grab a pool cue and start whacking dudes over the head or what?"

Immediately, several of the patrons shattered their beer bottles so they could stab Jimmy with the pointy ends.

"Damn it! I have to clean this place!" the bartender shouted.

"Sorry. Reflex," said an embarrassed thug.

"Every night I've got to spend an hour sweeping up broken glass and eyeballs and nobody ever says so much as a thank you. Now listen, Jimmy, you don't have to solve all your problems with violence. I suppose you could just ask nicely."

It turned out stereotypical criminal bar bartenders really were wise. "That works too, I guess. Okay, help me out guys, what kind of sick bastard would steal a manatee?"

The thugs pondered on it for a moment and then began shouting answers.

"Sea World!"

"Manatee collectors!"

"No! You can't just guess! Somebody has to know the right answer so I can get to the bad guys and file a claim before Mr. Stranger does. Think!"

"Uh ... Petco?"

"Not helping!" Jimmy was getting frustrated. And also a little dizzy, so he got down off the stool before he fell off.

"Psst ..." The bartender leaned in conspiratorially. "I think I know which *pendejos* stole your famous manatee. They're the baddest of the bad. They hang out at this rival bar down on the waterfront. It's even meaner and tougher than this place."

Well, knowing that would have saved him a bunch of time! "Damn it, Uber!" Jimmy shook his fist at the ceiling. "Sorry, everybody, but it looks like I've got to take my shakedown business elsewhere!"

The assorted scumbags were all like "awwww, man . . ." and "bummer, dude."

"Hey, everybody, I know what to do!" the bartender shouted. "Let's go riot and burn things to help Jimmy the Intern get his manatee back!" *That was a great idea*! The rest of them immediately began to cheer as they pulled out a wide assortment of guns and knives.

Jimmy led his newly formed angry mob out into the street. This was gonna be sweet! As Mr. Stranger would say, things were going *splendidly*.

❖ CHAPTER FOUR ❖
Tom's 11:00 AM March for Science

Louisville, Kentucky
Earth #587-F-2288

THINGS WERE NOT going splendidly for Tom Stranger at all. It looked like he would have to work through his lunch hour again *and* he was being pursued through the jungle by a pack of vicious, genetically-modified, plus-size velociraptors.

A velociraptor leapt from the shadows. Tom slugged it in the teeth, sending the eight-foot-tall dinosaur flying back through the leaves.

"Bad dinosaur. Stay." Only like most husky velociraptors it was exceedingly disobedient, so it hopped back up and tried to disembowel him with its deadly hook toe. Dodging aside in a blur, Tom let the superefficient predator pass by, and then grabbed it in a choke hold.

It began rolling and crashing through the underbrush, trying to dislodge him. This was not the first time that he'd had to choke out a dinosaur—this week—but their colorful feathers got all over his suit, which was a very unprofessional look, and he'd left his lint brush back in his office. Tree trunks shattered into splinters as his body was driven into them, but Tom held on as its struggles gradually became weaker.

Once he had rendered the dinosaur unconscious, Tom got up and tried to dust off his charcoal three-button Men's Wearhouse suit only to discover there were feathers stuck to him *everywhere*. "Tsk tsk." Then he realized that he had been surrounded by the rest of the pack, and they were creeping slowly forward in order to rip him into pieces. Tom was opposed to being devoured by hungry dinosaurs on general principle, but getting killed while he was trying to take care of an important claim was especially vexing.

"I really do not have time for this nonsense." Tom drew the ultra-lethal CorreiaTech Combat Wombat from the holster on his belt and declared, "Unless you wish me to obliterate your entire flock, show yourself, Colonel."

Someone blew a whistle. Immediately all the velociraptors fled in terror. A moment later Tom heard the high-pitched whine of a jet pack as a portly, white-haired gentleman in a white suit descended through the treetop canopy. The Colonel stopped and hovered above the clearing. "Surprise! So what did you think of our exciting new dining experience?"

"I'm not sure I see the appeal, sir," Tom said as he holstered his Combat Wombat.

"Great googly moogly, Tom, the adrenaline rush makes the meat taste better!"

"The customer's meat or the dinosaur's?"

"Both! Don't you get it? It's man versus his dinner! Only the strong will survive. It's primal supper!"

"Hmmm ... I believe I will stick with original recipe."

"That's because you're a traditional sort. Popeyes came along and then everybody wanted spicy! Well I'll show them spicy! There's nothing spicier than fighting your food to the death. Will the tables turn? Will the hunter become the hunted? I call it the Most Dangerous Meal Deal. We drop you off in the jungle with nothing but a sharpened spork and a bucket of mashed potatoes, biscuits, and a medium soda for $7.99. It's even all-you-can-eat, if you're man enough."

"That does sound like an excellent value."

"And the best part, so many customers will get eaten, I'll save a bundle on velociraptor feed. I'll still come out ahead!"

It was unfortunate when his clients descended into murderous insanity, but Tom did not discriminate. As long as the Colonel's premiums were paid on time, Tom would continue to render the finest customer service possible.

"If I may be so bold as to offer a suggestion, Colonel,

if you will be advertising this *meal deal* across dimensions, have them sign a waiver first. It will prevent many claims. In most realities dinosaurs went extinct."

"They're so finger-licking good those poor saps don't even know what they're missing. I do declare I was surprised to see you show up here, Tom. I saw the news. I figured you'd be keeping your head down because of all those angry dolphin protestors."

"That was all a misunderstanding, Colonel. I hold no animosity toward dolphins and was wrong to use a hurtful stereotype."

"*Sure,*" the Colonel said as he gave a big obvious wink.

Tom sighed.

The Colonel paused to wipe his brow with a handkerchief. It was very humid in the primordial jungles of Kentucky. "Anyways, what brings you all the way out to my dimension?"

"There are rumors that CorreiaTech is attempting to take over all of the . . . I will call them *alignment challenged* companies in the Multiverse. You are among their number. I was curious if you knew if any in particular would go after Wendell."

"That sea cow is a financial genius. Without him the whole deal falls apart. So any of them might want him dead. I'd have taken him myself and fed him to my flock, but manatees are fatty, and raptors get sluggish after a big meal like that."

"Fortunately, I believe you." If it turned out the claim was against another one of his clients, it would require some finesse to come to an equitable solution. He'd never be voted Number One in Customer Service for the fourth year in a row if he started shooting his own clients. "Do any of them in particular stand out to you?"

"Now that you mention it, there's one shady type who holds a grudge. Personally, I'd check out Bill Nye."

"The Science Guy?"

"More like the megalomaniacal science jerk."

Tom knew of him, and did not care for Bill Nye at all. As a children's television show host, he had been okay once, but he'd been driven mad with power, and now he was giving all bow tie wearers a bad name. "I did not think Bill Nye would be into Grand Theft Manatee."

"Those two got into a heated argument recently. Bill Nye hates rising sea levels. Manatees think they're great. Really opens up new real estate opportunities for them. They went at it on Twitter, until Bill blocked him because Wendell made fun of his song 'My Sex Junk.'"

"To be fair, 'My Sex Junk' is quite possibly, literally, the worst thing ever made."

"I'd agree, Tom, and if this encounter was ever recorded into another one of those newfangled audiobooks of yours, I'd encourage listeners to go plug Bill Nye 'My Sex Junk' into YouTube and listen themselves to see that we ain't exaggerating." The Colonel gestured at the unconscious velociraptor. "Anyways, you want that I should fry this one up for you?"

Tom still had important business to attend to, but it was rather difficult to provide excellent customer service on an empty stomach. "Thank you, Colonel. Please make it a to-go bucket."

❖ ❖ ❖

The Colonel waited until Tom Stranger's mech had disappeared into the atmosphere before speaking aloud.

"Alrighty then, Tom's gone. You can come out now."

There was a weird twisting of light as an invisible kidnapper floated through the jungle. As suspected, the nefarious beings had been watching the whole exchange to make sure the Colonel honored their deal.

"I did just like you asked and sent Tom off on a wild goose chase. I said the same thing to those manatee bounty hunters that came by earlier. Now pay up." A little bottle appeared as the invisible creature tossed it to him. The Colonel caught it and greedily read the label. "Ah, the rarest of my eleven herbs and spices, all the way from Arrakis." Ground-up sand worm kept the meat so tender and juicy it warped the very fabric of space and time.

Chuckling, the Colonel dropped the spice into his pocket. "Pleasure doing business with you fellows—" But suddenly another invisible creature materialized behind him and ripped a spark plug wire out of his jet pack. The engine sputtered and he fell into a giant fern. "Hey!"

The kidnappers laughed at him as they levitated away.

"You good-for-nothing, double-crossing scallywags!" the Colonel shouted. Realizing he'd been had, he pulled out the spice bottle, unscrewed the cap, and sniffed. "What? This is just *paprika*! Come back here! Nobody bamboozles the Colonel! Nobody! Mark my words, you seedy ruffians, you'll pay for this!"

Except they were already gone. Grumbling thoughts of revenge upon the tricksters, the Colonel got up, only to trail off as he realized he was surrounded by deadly velociraptors. "Stay. Bad dinosaurs." He reached for his anti-raptor whistle, only to discover the kidnappers had snagged that too. "Well, ain't this a pickle."

The Most Dangerous Meal Deal pounced.

Washington D.C.
Earth #169-J-00561

TOM STRANGER had been to this particular dimension a lot recently. It contained Jimmy's home planet, a place so odd and statistically unpredictable that it made Tom a little uncomfortable. But it was also the home of Bill Nye, alleged manatee kidnapper. On most planets Nye would merely be considered an engineer who had gotten a TV show, but apparently on this strange world that meant he had been crowned Science Pope.

On most civilized worlds science was a process involving observable data and testable hypotheses, not a religion based on feeling superior toward anyone with differing political beliefs. So it was with a great dealt of trepidation that Tom attempted to infiltrate the so-called March for Science to search for his target.

It was an exceedingly smug, yet festive event. Tom did not understand the strange local customs, so when he found an oddly shaped pink knit hat which had been recently discarded, he put it on in order to blend in better. Most of the other marchers were carrying colorful, grammatically incorrect signage having something to do with Cheetos, or pithy sayings that always boiled down to how anyone who disagreed with them were stupid idiots who could be safely dismissed without thought, analysis, or debate. This didn't seem particularly scientific to Tom, but what did he know? He was only a man with eleven advanced degrees who flew around the galaxy in a space ship. It wasn't like he knew "science."

There was no time to scan the entire crowd of self-righteous marchers, so Tom would need to gather human intel directly. Luckily he had been trained on how to build rapport with backwards, superstitious civilizations. He approached some marchers who were having a conversation.

"I read on this movie star's blog that a good juice cleanse can remove vaccines that cause autism, because I think I'm like totally allergic to gluten."

"Me, too! I just need to align my chakras so my healing crystals will fight off GMOs better."

"I'm so glad that we're smart and believe in science, unlike those nasty Republicans!"

Tom smoothly tried to mingle. "Greetings, fellow citizens of Earth 169-J-00561. I, too, pound sign f'ing love science."

One of the Science Marchers glared at Tom suspiciously. Despite Tom's new pink hat, she must have suspected he was not really of their tribe. "I wish Medicare would cover goat milk therapy, don't you?"

From his extensive knowledge of anthropology, Tom could tell this was some manner of test. He would have to tread carefully in order to be accepted as one of them. "Obviously." They did not immediately attack, so Tom pushed onward. He needed to build a relationship of trust. She was carrying a sign that said REPUBLICANS R FLAT

TEH EARTH SOCIETY. "I have been to the Flat Earth. It was mostly a tourist trap with a very underwhelming gift shop."

"Triggered!" She hissed and pointed. "Republican nazi fascist sexist!"

"Seize the climate denier!" someone else shouted.

This was not going well at all. Before Tom could be seized by the mob and burned at the stake for heresy against their unquestionable science gods, he threw down a ninja smoke bomb and escaped in the confusion.

After several more failed interactions, Tom found himself wishing that Jimmy was still employed with the firm, because at least he would be able to communicate in the mangled gibberish of made-up buzz words this particular tribe spoke. Many of these humans were also sporting man buns. Tom began wondering if perhaps he had been too harsh on the lad . . .

Then Tom caught a break. Through the meandering crowd he spotted another bow tie wearer. It was Bill Nye! *Finally.* And since Nye wasn't a client, Tom was free to deal with him however he wanted, up to and including merciless beatings. Tom was looking forward to getting this claim filed so he could return to a sensible reality. He began pushing his way through the marchers.

Only that was when Tom realized he wasn't the only one heading directly toward The Science Guy.

Like Tom, the pair of manatee bounty hunters were doing their best to blend in with the Science Marchers. They had both put on 8XL *I'm With Her* T-shirts over their power armor. One manatee was holding a sign that he'd found which boldly declared HANDS OFF MY UTERUS, only he was holding it upside down because he had probably never bothered to learn English. The other had stretched one of the odd pink hats over the glass dome of his helmet. Their disguises were perfect. Though the anti-grav propulsion units in the suits made it so that their tails were hovering inches off of the ground, none of the marchers seemed to notice. Manatees were sleek infiltrators that way.

One bounty hunter stuck a flipper beneath his Hillary shirt—probably stolen for this mission, since manatees were such big supporters of free market economics they'd never vote Democrat—and pulled out a Combat Wombat.

That was a bad sign. There was no *Less Lethal* setting on a Combat Wombat. In fact, they were advertised as *More Than Lethal*, because sometimes they even killed ghosts. CorreiaTech was so philosophically opposed to Less Than Lethal weapons that they'd once made a version that shot bean bag rounds, only the bean bags were made of depleted uranium.

So these manatees really weren't messing around.

"Hmmm." Tom was in a bit of a quandary. Even though the bounty hunters were from a different dimension, Nye wasn't one of his clients, so technically this wasn't his problem. However, if they obliterated Nye before Tom confirmed he was the kidnapper then he'd never know where to send the claim paperwork. So he pushed onward. "Excuse me. Pardon me."

Before Tom could reach The Science Guy, he received a priority call from Muffy. "I am really rather busy right now, Ms. Wappler."

"I figured, Mr. Stranger, but it'll only take a second. Remember how those initial DNA tests from the seawater spilled at the scene came back as Aquatic Mammal? Well, it wasn't Wendell's tank water at all. I'll send you over the detailed results right now."

"Very well." Tom viewed the report over his infolink as he continued to shove hippies out of the way. He was very good at multitasking. He gasped when he got to the DNA match. This wasn't just terrible news, it was the worst outcome possible! The repercussions would be awful. He'd never hear the end of it. Also, it meant that he had been set up.

"The kidnapper isn't Bill Nye after all."

"That guy who made 'My Sex Junk'?"

"Yes. And he's about to be destroyed by manatees for a crime he didn't commit."

"Ugh. Let them. That song was so bad it's like sound barfed in my ears."

"Indeed."

"Photons that touched the 'My Sex Junk' video touched my eyes, Mr. Stranger. My eyes! I had to pay to grow new eyeballs in a vat and get a transplant it was so bad."

The manatee was dramatically screwing a silencer onto the muzzle of his Combat Wombat. "Please forgive me for interrupting your tirade, Ms. Wappler, but I will have to call you back."

Bill Nye was giving a long-winded speech to his adoring worshippers. "So then Neil DeGrasse Tyson said nobody could make science more boring and pedantic than he could, so I said challenge accepted! Ha ha ha!" He noticed Tom. "Oh, hello my child, have you come to hear about how our Lord and Master Science has declared nuclear power is scary bad?"

"Everyone on this planet is insane, but no." In fact, Tom had three nuclear reactors on his body at that moment, and he used one to activate his personal energy shield because the manatees were closing fast. "Get behind me, Science Man."

"Witchcraft!" Bill Nye shrieked when he saw Tom's flickering energy shield materialize.

The manatee fired his Combat Wombat. The hypervelocity round exploded against the shield. Tom immediately responded by spin-kicking the pistol from the manatee's flipper. Though incredibly fearsome, their lack of opposable thumbs could be a real detriment in close combat.

The bounty hunters seemed surprised to see an Interdimensional Insurance Agent here, and hesitated before launching their rampage. Tom took advantage of their momentary confusion.

"Stand down, noble manatees. Though sanctimonious and annoying, this human is not your enemy."

The bounty hunters exchanged a glance. They did not give up so easily, but they knew Tom Stranger had a reputation for integrity. "*Fleeerp?*"

"Correct. Bill Nye has, as you put it, *jumped the shark,* but we have been lied to. In the colloquial terms your people are so fond of, he is a *red herring.*"

"The red herring is endangered because of fracking," Bill Nye suddenly declared. "Impeach Trump or the red herring will go extinct. Science has spoken!"

"Science has spoken!" chanted all the marchers,

even though that hypothesis had not been tested, and no data had been collected or analyzed. "We are more smarter!"

"May clean energy be upon you, my children."

"I stand in awe of how absurd this planet is." Tom turned back to the bounty hunters, because at least they were rational. "Please spare these pathetic land mammals. I will go settle this claim, and retrieve your leader."

"*Hoooon,*" said the other manatee.

"What do you mean you two are just tying up loose ends because your herd has already dispatched an armada to wage unrelenting total war across the Multiverse?"

He spread his flippers apologetically, like *whoops, shit happens.* Then since his mission was already compromised, the manatee took his ridiculous pink hat off in order to retain what little dignity he had left.

"Oh, no," Bill Nye cried once their clever disguise was revealed. "Behold! As was prophesized in my scholarly Netflix show, these peaceful sea creatures have been driven from their habitat by global warming! Hurry, my children! Roll them back into the water. They're dying!"

The marchers immediately mobbed the manatees. The bounty hunter began beating people with his UTERUS sign. It turned into a giant wrestling match between the cultists and the manatees who really didn't want to get rolled anywhere. Tom figured they could work it out without him, so he began running to his mech. He had to get back to Wendell's home world before the manatee armada indiscriminately pulverized every Florida in existence.

❖ CHAPTER FIVE ❖
Tom's 12:00 Noon Reminder
to Have Muffy Schedule Some Training
on Non-Violent Conflict Resolution

Miami, Florida
Earth #984-A-3256

THEY HAD ASSEMBLED a crack team of insurance professionals in the abandoned warehouse across the street from the building where they believed the kidnappers were holding Wendell. When Tom arrived, Muffy was already briefing the Junior Associates.

"Okay, kiddos, time is of the essence. The manatee armada is on its way to blow up this Florida as we speak. However, we can't just barge in willy-nilly and start wrecking the place."

One of the Junior Associates raised his hand. "How come?"

"Because this has potential public relations nightmare written all over it. Duh. You all saw Mr. Stranger's press conference this morning. This is super sensitive. The last thing this company needs is more controversy. One screw-up and this is going to be all over social media. The details are in your handouts . . . Oh, hey, the boss is here. It's all yours, Mr. Stranger."

"Thank you, Ms. Wappler." Tom took his place in front of his team.

They were the elite, the best of the best, the finest Junior Associates in the Multiverse, perched like falcons, ready to swoop in and deliver the finest-quality customer service possible. They all came from harsh, tough worlds. Before getting into the far more challenging field of Interdimensional Insurance, each of them had developed a respectable resume. Rip Face-Punch had been an elite hostage rescue team leader, brain surgeon, and children's book illustrator. Dirk Hardsack had been a matador, Shaolin monk, and inventor of the Fidget Spinner. And last but not least, there was professional polar bear wrangler, Iditarod champion, and cosmonaut, Beardly McSpetsnaz.

"Gentle-agents, we will strike in exactly five minutes and forty-seven seconds. I have downloaded detailed maps of the target directly to your infolinks. Using my years of experience I have formulated an exacting plan, accounting for every possible danger, which you will memorize, and then execute to the second. This will be a surgical strike."

Tom pointed at each Junior Associate as he gave their assignments. "Face-Punch, you are on over watch. McSpetsnaz, crowd control, and remember when you hand out business cards to let them know about our free rate quote. Wappler, heavy weapons."

Muffy pumped her fist in the air. "Yes!"

"And Hardsack, claims paperwork."

"Aww . . . but I brought my nunchucks."

"Do not forget the photo documentation this time. This claim could go to Arbitration and Chuck Norris has no patience for sloppy paperwork. Now, as Ms. Wappler has already so aptly explained, discretion is everything; the reputation of our company, and also the future of this Florida, are at stake. Due to the sensitive nature of the individuals involved, this could go very badly for us. We must keep this quiet. So I reiterate . . . *discretion* is of the utmost importance."

"Sir, there might be a problem." Face-Punch interrupted the briefing, but he was at the window on lookout duty, so it had to be important. "I don't think Jimmy the Intern got the memo."

"I fired Jimmy this morning. Of course, I did not CC him on the email."

Face-Punch peered through the scope of his Sniper Wombat to confirm. "Well, Jimmy's blundering down the middle of the street directly toward the target building at the head of what appears to be an angry mob."

Well, there went that plan.

Jimmy was having a great time. "Man, this is awesome!"

The bartender looked over their small army as they flipped over cars and broke windows, and nodded approvingly. "You were right, Jimmy. Taking the time to stop by Home Depot for torches and pitchforks first really set the ambiance."

Mr. Stranger was always talking about the value of being *proactive*. He was going to be so impressed that Jimmy was sure to get his old job back. Sure, there might have been *some* inadvertent property damage to the city on their way over, but it was a small price to pay for customer service or whatever.

"This is the place," the bartender declared.

It was a rough neighborhood down by the docks. There was lots of trash, stray dogs, and graffiti everywhere. The cars had already been flipped over so Jimmy's mob flipped them back right-side up.

"Where?"

The bartender pointed. "That one."

The building was extra sketchy, cinder blocks, bars over the windows, razor wire over the bars, and featuring gaudy neon signs which declared the establishment was named Bottlenose Jack's.

The mob paused because it was a little intimidating. This place had a rep.

"You sure about this, Jimmy? These guys are the baddest gang in town. There's no shame in backing down now."

"No way, man. Insurance is counting on me!" Jimmy boldly walked right up to the entrance.

A five-hundred-pound cyborg gorilla was working the door. "Hit the bricks, human."

"Hey, aren't you the same gorilla from that other bar?"

"Do I know you?"

"Dude, we talked like a couple hours ago!"

The gorilla shrugged. "You puny Homo sapiens all look the same to me. But sure, the way the economy is now, I need two jobs just to put peanut butter and grubs on the table. Not all of us gorillas can get fancy insurance jobs like Amy. Some of us got to work for a living."

"Yeah, tough story, bro."

The bartender joined them. "What's taking so long? Oh, hey, Harambe."

"'Sup, Danny."

"Second job, huh? Me, too. I teach interpretive dance at the community college."

Fascinating as this was, Jimmy really didn't have time for dicking around. That checkout line at Home Depot had taken *forever.* "Anyways, same deal. I've got to go in and rough these guys up for information. So, step aside."

"No can do, buddy." The gorilla jerked one massive thumb toward another sign. This one read DOLPHINS ONLY. "No bipeds allowed. Trust me, you don't want to go in there anyway. It's all porpoise strippers eating fish. Real snooty."

"Wait . . . This is a *dolphin bar*? Like literally dolphins? Like those humorless, easily-offended reviewers who are all angry at Mr. Stranger?"

"Dude, Jimmy, I told you on the riot over this was a dolphin bar."

"Yeah, but I thought you meant like Miami Dolphins, like the NFL team."

The gorilla snorted. "There's a football team called the Dolphins? How lame is your universe?"

"I'm a Miami Manatees fan," the bartender proclaimed. "I've even got season tickets."

"So jealous," said the gorilla.

Jimmy started freaking out. He'd read all those one-star reviews. Dolphins seemed hypersensitive and perpetually offended. After the controversy around that audiobook, Muffy had sent out a memo warning everybody to be super careful not to offend any more dolphins. If he went in there and started kicking porpoise butt, Mr. Stranger would get even more bad reviews! Jimmy would never get his job back. He'd be like . . . *extra fired.*

"Oh crap. Oh crap. What've I done? We gotta go."

Only, while Jimmy had been distracted talking to the bouncer, his mob had grown restless, stolen a city bus, and were in the process of driving it toward the front door really fast.

"Stop! Stop!" Jimmy jumped up and down, waving his arms. "Noooo!"

Only the driver couldn't hear him over the roar of the engine. "This is for you, Jimmy the Intern! *To Valhalla shiny and chrome!*"

Luckily, the gorilla had reflexes befitting a mighty silverback, and he scooped up Jimmy and the bartender, and leapt out of the way right before impact. The cinder block wall exploded into fragments as the bus flipped end over end through the dolphin bar. The mob ran through the smoking breach, eager to put boot to blowhole.

The gorilla bouncer lifted his head as debris rained down around them. "Aw, come on!"

"Trust me, dude, the version of you on my home planet got it way worse," Jimmy said.

The gorilla groaned. "I am soooo gonna get fired for this."

"You and me both!" Though, technically, he was already fired. Causing an interdimensional incident was like the cherry on top of today's poop sundae. However, Wendell was still missing, so Jimmy still had a job to do. Did rogue TV detectives ever give up just because they accidentally caused a post-apocalyptic maniac to steal a bus and crash it through a bar full of dolphins? Not that he knew of! To hell with the consequences!

"Cover me! I'm going in!" Jimmy sprang to his feet and ran for the hole.

"Cover you from what?" the bartender shouted back.

"I don't know! That's just what they always yell in the movies!"

Since these were animals who lived in the ocean, Jimmy had kind of expected the place to be filled with water. Instead, the interior of the bar was all strobe lights and techno music, conveniently perfect for a fight scene. It turned out that when dolphins wanted to party on land, all they needed to do was turn up a humidifier and it was all good.

Jimmy's army was slugging it out with a whole bunch of rowdy dolphins. It had already turned into a giant rumble. Dudes were getting tossed into mirrors, lots of kung fu, that sort of thing. Dolphins might be a bunch of easily offended prima donnas on the Internet, but it turned out in real life they could *throw down*.

He narrowly dodged a flipper. Then a tail swept his legs out from under him. Jimmy got up, only to have another dolphin shatter a chair over his head. "That was a dick move!"

But that dolphin was fresh out of pity, and it grabbed Jimmy by the shirt collar, picked him up, and slid him down the bar. Jimmy crashed face first through a bunch of bottles and fish sticks before flying off the end and onto the floor.

"I'm not leaving until somebody tells me where Wendell is!" Jimmy struggled back to his feet, only to get nailed in the head by another chair. "Oooof! What is up with all the friggin' chairs! You dudes can't even sit!"

The dolphin held up one flipper and dramatically twirled open a butterfly knife.

"Whoa, easy there! You don't want to do something you'll regret."

The dolphin looked over incredulously at the upside-down bus in the middle of their dance floor, then back to Jimmy, as if to say *are you shitting me, human?* Then it lunged for him.

Jimmy scurried back, and then grabbed a butter knife off the bar. He held it out defensively. "I'm warning you, I've played a whole lot of *Fruit Ninja!*"

Only before the dolphin could gut Jimmy like . . . well . . . a fish, a bunch of flashbangs went off, disorienting the combatants. A hole was blown through the ceiling, and a shadowy figure dropped through, landing smoothly next to the knife-wielding dolphin.

"You've made quite the mess of things, Jimmy."

"Mr. Stranger! What're you doing here?"

"I was about to ask you the same thing," Tom Stranger said as he used a sweet judo throw to toss the dolphin on its snout. "But there is no time for chitchat."

A big crew of dolphins was heading their way. Jimmy's army had gotten trounced fairly quickly and were in full retreat. Tom Stranger took up a fighting stance.

"Kick their ass, Mr. Stranger!"

"There is no need for violence, my dolphin friends. I merely seek information pertaining to the whereabouts of my client. Let us resolve this peacefully, then I will force these hooligans to leave your establishment, and I will arrange for this young man to pay for all the damages and any emotional distress he has caused."

"Wait . . . What?"

"Silence, Jimmy. Grownups are talking. Now, please, let us be reasonable."

The biggest dolphin ever swaggered up. He was wearing a bunch of gold chains and had prison tats from SeaWorld. "INSERT DOLPHIN NOISE HERE"

"That is a terribly cruel thing to say about my mother."

The dolphins charged. Having been left with no choice, Tom Stranger responded. It was flipper against fist. Only Interdimensional Insurance Agents fight like watching a Jet Li movie on fast forward, so the dolphins never had a chance. He clothes-lined one, body-slammed another, and when they inevitably threw a chair at him, Mr. Stranger caught it and flung it right back, knocking that jerky dolphin right out the front window and into the street.

There was a *cha-chunk* noise as the dolphin behind the bar racked a shotgun. Only before it could fire, Muffy appeared and stuck a giant plasma cannon against its nose.

"Drop it, you cetacean son of a bitch, before I blast you into chum."

"Ms. Wappler, please! Remember we are trying not to be so culturally insensitive."

"Sorry, Mr. Stranger."

Inappropriate or not, the dolphin put the shotgun down. The techno music had stopped. The floor was covered in moaning, semiconscious dolphins and humans. The knock-down, drag-out fight was over.

"I swept the place, Mr. Stranger. They've got a money laundering operation, and a meth lab in the basement, but no sign of Wendell anywhere."

"Drat." He looked over at Jimmy, who was busy picking

splinters out of his hair. "I know your world is remarkably odd, but are you unfamiliar with the concept of how employment works?"

"I know I got fired, but I was going to prove those evaluations wrong and take care of this claim."

"Strange . . . As statistically improbable as it sounds, even deprived of the firm's resources you still somehow figured out that this pod of criminal dolphins hired out some of their cartel assassins to a secret cabal of shady businessmen to thwart a hostile takeover, in the same amount of time it took me to come to the same conclusion."

"Uh, yeah, that's like totally what I was thinking happened."

Mr. Stranger seemed confused. He looked at Muffy, who was blowing a bubble. She shrugged.

"So do I get my job back?"

"Hmmm . . . We will revisit the accuracy of our employee evaluations later." He went over to the big boss dolphin and picked him up by his dorsal fin. "We know Wendell was taken by members of your pod. Now talk."

The prison-hardened dolphin made an extremely rude gesture. Which was saying something since it was kind of limited, not having fingers and all.

Jimmy realized that they'd been joined by some of the Junior Associates. They were all taller than he was and super buffed. Plus they were like smart and good at stuff. To be honest, they made Jimmy feel a little dumpy and inadequate.

Face-Punch went over to the Alpha Dolphin. "A tough guy, huh? Back on my planet we had a way of making dolphins talk. I'll need a hair dryer and a ShamWow."

"*Nyet*," said McSpetsnaz. "There is no time for reverse waterboarding. There is deep fryer in kitchen. We should see how much dolphin can fit."

"I respect your enthusiasm, Junior Associates, but inserting sentient beings into deep fat fryers is against company policy. Such barbarity is better suited for firms like Conundrum and Company or United Airlines." Tom Stranger sighed and released the dolphin. "Besides, if we engage in atrocities, we will be plagued with negative dolphin reviews forever."

Jimmy thought back to the profound bartender wisdom of that Danny Trejo guy. "We could just try asking him nicely."

Tom Stranger didn't seemed convinced, but Jimmy *was* on a roll. "Very well."

"Cool. I got this. Okay, Mr. Dolphin Mob Boss dude. I'm really sorry about the bus crash. With all due respect and stuff, we really need to get this manatee back, so could you like do us a solid and help us out?"

The dolphin studied Jimmy with his beady, shifty, little black eyes, and slowly nodded in agreement.

"See?" Jimmy turned around and grinned. "Told you guys—"

Then the dolphin grabbed yet another chair and broke that one over Jimmy's head, too.

"Enough of this foolishness and carrying on." Tom Stranger put the evil dolphin in a headlock and squeezed. "I tried being polite, but if I am to receive a one-star review in pursuit of my duties, so be it. Where is the manatee?"

From Jimmy's new position on the floor, he had a good view out the big hole in the wall. At first he thought he was hallucinating from all those traumatic brain injuries, but the big thing outside seemed pretty real. It looked like a gigantic spaceship was rising out of the ocean. "Uh, Mr. Stranger?"

"Where, curse you, where?" Mr. Stranger shouted as the dolphin's face turned from grey to purple. Jimmy reached over and started tugging on his pant leg. "What?"

Jimmy pointed at the big warship that was rising into the sky until it blotted out the sun. It was like a sleek, manatee version of the Space Battleship *Yamato*. It began blaring a warning through loudspeakers as it hovered over the beach.

"*FLOOOOOO.*"

Tom Stranger dropped the obstinate dolphin. "For those of you who do not speak the language, the manatees have dispatched ships like this to a hundred worlds as part of a *punitive expedition*. They just declared the land mammals have one hour to return Wendell which, all things considered, is a remarkably merciful time frame, or the perpetuators will taste their righteous vengeance."

"That doesn't sound too bad," Jimmy said hopefully. "For everybody other than the perps obviously."

"Except historically, manatees aren't very good at target identification," said Face-Punch. "Back on my home world, off the coast of Innsmouth, a manatee strike team mistook King Triton for Dagon. It was the worst friendly fire incident of the Deep War."

"Oh, man, not Ariel's dad!"

"The claims paperwork still haunts my nightmares. Dead flounders and talking crabs everywhere . . . Sorry, Jimmy. Where I'm from *The Little Mermaid* is considered a very tragic movie. We've got to do something, Mr. Stranger."

"You are correct, Junior Associate." He began dragging the evil dolphin over toward the hole. "I'll start by turning this miscreant over to the manatees."

The dolphin thrashed in terror. "INSERT DOLPHIN NOISE HERE"

"Begging for mercy will do you no good. Manatees laugh at the Geneva Convention. Now do you want to talk?"

"INSERT DOLPHIN NOISE HERE"

"See? That wasn't so hard. Thank you for your cooperation." He karate-chopped the dolphin and knocked it unconscious.

"What just happened?"

"Now I know where the kidnappers are. Sadly, I was just in that reality. Come, Junior Associates, we need to get back to Jimmy's home dimension." Scowling, he looked at the battleship looming overhead. "And we must hurry."

"Yeah, man. It's like high noon out there."

"Worse. It's *nigh hoon.*"

❖ CHAPTER SIX ❖
Tom Networks on the Golf Course

Somewhere over Florida
Earth #169-J-00561

THE STRANGER & Stranger battlemech blasted through

the dimensional rift and tore across the sky at Mach 3. Tom, Muffy, Jimmy, and the three Junior Associates were all crowded into the cockpit, making Tom glad that he had purchased a battlemech with a roomy interior.

After the dolphin crime lord had admitted that it was his crew who had been hired to kidnap Wendell, Tom had quickly figured out the entire complicated plot. Someone was trying to stop the CorreiaTech merger by pitting two of Tom's clients against each other. The damages would be astronomical. The paperwork never-ending.

Muffy was looking at a spreadsheet. "Mr. Stranger, if this incident causes an interdimensional war, we insure *both* sides! Whoever is found at fault, the payout would ruin our third quarter numbers."

"And millions of innocents would die."

"Oh, yeah, that too. Total bummer."

"I shudder to think of all the customer dissatisfaction that could cause." Tom pounded one fist against the control panel. *"Not on my watch!* Prepare yourselves, Junior Associates. We will be over the drop zone shortly. Somewhere inside that compound the dolphins have hidden Wendell. The humans there are unaware that they are being set up, but they will attempt to defend themselves, as will the manatee raiders. We will split into teams to cover more ground. You must find Wendell, secure him, and avoid harming any of our clients, human or manatee. Stun weapons only."

"What about dolphins?" asked McSpetsnaz.

"For them you may set your Wombats to *mulch*. There is our destination, the Mar-a-Lago Resort and Presidential Golf Retreat."

"All signals are being jammed," Hardsack shouted. "I can't make contact with the clients."

There was a huge manatee battleship floating ahead of them. It began firing its particle beam cannons.

"Taking evasive maneuvers." Tom's super-quick reflexes saved the day as he pulled the stick and rolled the mech between the death rays. Of course, Jimmy had unbuckled his seat belt in order to get a drumstick from the Kentucky Fried Velociraptor to-go bucket and wound up smashed against the ceiling by centrifugal force. One of the manatee's rail guns got lucky and blew a hole through their shields and shattered the window.

Muffy reached out with her robot hand and snagged Jimmy by the sleeve right before he would have gotten sucked out the hole. "Seat belts are company policy for a reason, Jimmy! Why do I even write all those safety briefings if you dipsticks never bother to read them?"

Jimmy screamed incoherently in response.

"Well I, for one, appreciate your timely emails, Ms. Wappler." Tom grimaced as one of the mech's arms was torn off. Manatees were incredibly lethal marksmen, and despite Tom's *Top Gun*-like piloting skills, the mech took several more hits.

"We are going down. Now remember, team, this America is a new client. Prior to my saving their previous vice president from Ball Sharks, they were insured with Conundrum and Company. Let's show them what proper customer service looks like."

As the flaming mech hurtled toward the ground, the Junior Associates began bailing out. Since each of them was rated fairly high on the Grylls Survivability Scale, they didn't even bother with parachutes. An impact at this velocity was only sufficient to kill four or five Bear Grylls, tops. Unfortunately, not all of his team were up for such strenuous activity. "By the way, Ms. Wappler, would you kindly stick a jet pack on Jimmy or something? I would hate for him to explode on impact."

"So does this mean that Jimmy is rehired, sir?"

Tom glanced over at the screaming intern as he flailed back and forth in the thousand-mile-an-hour fire wind over the hull breach, through which could be seen the ground rushing up to violently meet them.

"Well, it was rather sloppy, but he did provide some quality customer service to our client today. I think that perhaps Jimmy, coming from such an outlandish and silly universe, may actually turn out to be a benefit. At times it's as if his very presence alters the laws of probability. Let's give him another chance."

"*Aaaaaaaaahhhhaaaaaaahhhhaaaaaaaa!*"

"You are most welcome, Jimmy."

"Aw, that was really nice of you." Muffy shoved an anti-gravity belt into Jimmy's arms, and then let him career wildly into the atmosphere. "Let's face it, Mr. Stranger, you're really a big softie." Then Muffy unbuckled, tucked her arms to her sides, and smoothly flew through the hole.

Needing to draw the manatees' fire, Tom stayed in his crippled mech, wrestling with the controls as missiles exploded all around. He activated his personal energy shield as the cabin was engulfed in flames. He'd already gotten feathers all over this suit today; getting charred to a crisp would make him look completely unprofessional.

The mech was headed right for the golf course. Trying

to minimize casualties and maximize customer satisfaction, Tom aimed for a water feature on the fourth hole. Except a manatee photon cannon blasted his stabilizers into shrapnel and the controls seized up. The mech went into an out-of-control spin and slammed into the green at several times terminal velocity, erupting in a huge fireball.

Miles above, the manatee gunners high-flippered. Which is sort of like a high five, but you get the idea. They hadn't even known what they were shooting at, but manatees simply loved to blow shit up.

Jimmy the Intern somehow managed not to die. Luckily for him, he got the anti-gravity thingy figured out right before he would have been turned into sidewalk pizza. According to the help menu, the device created a *repellant force field*, not that Jimmy understood what those words meant. Unfortunately, he cranked it up a little too high, and ended up bouncing on impact like he was riding a giant hamster ball, through a bunch of trees, a flock of very startled ducks, and directly into a big glass window, which shattered, and then the stupid belt shorted out as he skidded through a luncheon on his face.

"Whoa." He groaned as he sat up. If it wasn't for all the bruises and the sick carpet burn on his forehead, that landing would have been *Die Hard*-level cool. Then Jimmy realized he was being stared at by a whole bunch of old guys in tuxedos and rich ladies with furs and little dogs in their purses. This place was *really* fancy. They had like monocles and stuff. He looked up and saw that he had crashed through a big banner that read WELCOME WORLD LEADERS.

They were staring at him in shocked silence. Jimmy waved. "Hey, everybody. Don't mind me."

"Where did you come from, young man?"

"He fell out of the sky!"

"Well, we started in outer space, but no biggie. I'm just your friendly neighborhood insurance guy."

"It's like the commercials!" cried Chancellor Angela Merkel. "If you say the incantation, insurance agents will suddenly materialize."

"Like a good neighbor, State Farm is there," sang the president of China. He looked around expectantly, but then got disappointed when nobody else appeared out of thin air.

"Wrong company, dudes. I'm not like Beetlejuice or something." Jimmy got up and brushed the broken glass off his clothes. He was feeling pretty awesome. Nothing builds confidence like a near-death experience and getting your job back. Super smooth, he whipped out a business card. "Stranger & Stranger, for all your interdimensional insurance needs. Call us for a free rate quote."

"This is all so very exciting!" declared the kid from *High School Musical*, or maybe it was the Prime Minister of Canada—Jimmy always got those two mixed up. "These summits have been such a drag since my real da—uh . . . I mean, Fidel Castro died. He was the life of the party."

"But anyways, we're all going to get blown up by that big floating battleship outside, unless any of you guys has seen a manatee around here?"

The world leaders all simultaneously pointed toward the buffet.

Jimmy followed all the fingers, and there, in the middle

of the table, past the organic kale gold-leaf truffles, was Wendell T. Manatee, frozen just like Han Solo in carbonite, serving as the decorative centerpiece.

"Friggin' sweet!" He'd done it! *Boom. Evaluate this performance, Muffy*! "Alright, anybody here know how to safely thaw a manatee?" But nobody did, because they were politicians, which meant they were basically useless.

"Some suspicious caterers left that there. We all just assumed the frozen sea cow was an artistic statement about the catastrophic dangers of man-made climate change."

"Okay, I got to ask, is that like actually a real thing or just something you guys made up to mess with people?"

The world leaders all had a good laugh.

There were a few golfers near the impact zone. The mech had plowed a giant crater in the green. Munitions were cooking off, creating a chain of secondary explosions. Fire leapt hundreds of feet into the sky.

"You all saw that. That thing fell right on my ball."

"Yes, Mr. Defense Secretary Mad Dog, sir," said the Secret Service agent serving as the caddy. "You get a mulligan."

"Damned right I do," the SecDef muttered as fiery debris rained down around him.

The President of the United States was sitting in the golf cart, tweeting: *Giant robots falling out of sky. SAD. Probably made in China. BUY AMERICAN!*

Tom Stranger walked out of the pillar of fire, carrying his Doomsday Briefcase, and dusting off his suit. "Pardon my interruption, gentle clients, but there are shenanigans afoot."

The SecDef gave him a polite nod. "Tom."

Tom returned the nod. "Chaos."

"Freeze, scumbag!" shouted the Secret Service agent as he pulled his pistol and aimed it at Tom.

"Damn, you kids are high strung. Relax, Carl. This is just our Interdimensional Insurance Agent." SecDef pointed his golf club at Tom's chest. "I'm assuming this has something to do with that big grey spaceship up there ruining my view."

"Correct. Did you not receive the manatees' list of demands?"

"That's what that was?" The Secretary of Defense shrugged. "Nobody speaks manatee on this planet."

Carl the Secret Service Agent was putting away his gun. "We ran *floo* through Google Translate for a threat assessment. It came back saying it was about how they *wanted to ravish our porcupines.*"

"Sadly, you typed it incorrectly. The message was *floooooo* with six o's. It is a very nuanced language."

"So majestic," agreed the SecDef.

The President had not looked up from his phone and was still busy tweeting: *Sea Cows come here. Should learn to speak English. Bigly good like we do! BAD.*

"Their message actually said you must turn over their leader or they would declare war."

The Secret Service agent didn't seem impressed. "They're just gassy herbivores. Who cares?"

But SecDef just shook his head. "You know how manatees get all those scars, Carl?"

"Sure, they just float along until they get wacked by speed boats."

"That's what they want you to think. The scarred-up ones are really veterans of the Deep War. You ever been menaced by Fish Men, Carl?"

"No."

"Then thank a manatee . . . and read a friggin' history book once in a while." SecDef turned back to Tom. "I didn't realize that was a manatee vessel. I thought it was just more of those damned obnoxious Space Vegans. But all right, I could use a good fight. Golf is dumb." He chucked his nine iron into the fire. "Waste of a good rifle range. I just snuck out here with the boss because we were sick of listening to those namby-pamby Euro-weenies. How do we best proceed, Tom?"

"They gave you a one-hour ultimatum." A laser beam lanced out of the sky and blasted a nearby tree into splinters. "And it would appear that was about an hour ago . . . Run!"

Explosions rocked the golf course as the manatees began their bombardment. The three of them piled into the golf cart next to the President, who was still tweeting: *They say manatees don't ruin golf. FAKE NEWS. BUILD A WALL!*

The golf cart took off with a fierce electric hum.

Tom looked up to see that a swarm of fighters had launched from the battleship and were headed their way. "We have incoming."

"Put the hammer down, Carl!" SecDef ordered.

"I'm going as fast as I can, sir!" he cried as they bounced wildly across the green.

The targeting implant in Tom's eye zeroed in on the fighters' weak spots. He drew his Combat Wombat. "Aim for the intakes."

"Roger that." Surprisingly, SecDef had hidden a Stinger missile in his golf bag. "What? I told you I hate this sport. I only ever used the one club for everything. Might as well put something useful in this stupid bag."

"Personally, I find golf to be rather relaxing," Tom said as he began to rapidly blast the oncoming fighters out of the sky, forcing the pilots to eject. Even floating toward the ground, suspended beneath parachutes, the manatees still managed to appear relaxed about the whole thing. As Jimmy would say, they were *pretty chill*.

There were explosions all around them. Tom threw down smoke bombs and nanite swarms for cover. Carl managed to get some serious air by jumping the golf cart over a sand trap. Fighters flashed by, billowing smoke. Chaos downed another fighter with a shrieking surface-to-air missile as tracers zipped back and forth. The President continued tweeting furiously.

Tom activated his communications uplink. "Come in, Junior Associates. Does anyone have eyes on Wendell?"

"*I found him, Mr. Stranger!*"

"Jimmy?" That was certainly improbable, but the intern had a gift, like an idiot savant of insurance. "Well done. We are on the way. Everyone converge on Jimmy's position."

"*I'm just getting him thawed out and . . . Hey. What's that? Oh, crap—*"

Then there was a *thud* noise over the line and Jimmy was suddenly silenced.

"Jimmy? Come in, Jimmy."

But Tom received a bone-chilling answer instead. "INSERT DOLPHIN NOISE HERE"

The line went dead.

"To the clubhouse! And hurry, Agent Carl. Dolphin assassins have assaulted my intern."

"I am *so* confused right now!"

"Serpentine! Serpentine!" bellowed Chaos.

The golf cart zipped wildly across the blasted golf course, narrowly dodging explosions, until they smashed through the convention center's fence and up the stairs. The wild jostling caused the President to make a typo: *Despite the constant negative press covfefe*

But it was too late. He's already hit submit. POTUS narrowed his eyes dangerously and scowled at Carl. The poor Secret Service agent gulped in fear.

"Don't worry. This should all be covered. I'll be back with the claim paperwork shortly." Tom Stranger bailed out of the golf cart and ran into Mar-a-Lago.

Inside, the resort was pandemonium. Desperate now that their plot had been exposed, the remaining dolphins had attacked to keep Jimmy from thawing Wendell. Most of the world leaders had run away or were hiding under tables, except for Bibi Netanyahu, who had gleefully Krav Maga'd one dolphin unconscious. Unfortunately, Jimmy had been taken hostage by one of the others. It was hiding behind him, one flipper around Jimmy's neck, while the other flipper held a gun to Jimmy's head.

"Sorry, Mr. Stranger. I tried my best but this *stupid fish* got the drop on me."

Jimmy's use of species slurs were the least of their problems at this point. "Remain calm, Jimmy."

"Don't worry. Do what you've got to do. I've moved way up on the Grylls Survivability Scale since I started. I could probably survive getting shot in the brain. The GSS says I'm as tough as a ficus now."

"Hmmm . . . that comparison would imply you are still vulnerable to things like low humidity, drafts, and over-watering."

"So not even a teensy bit bulletproof?"

Tom shook his head in the negative. "Not even a little bit."

"Well, crap." Jimmy suddenly looked a lot less confident. "Never mind then."

Two more dolphins uncloaked next to the buffet table and leveled their weapons at Tom. He would be able to take them easily, but not in time to save Jimmy. The lead dolphin was gibbering threats about how if Tom didn't surrender, it would blow Jimmy's head off. Tom slowly placed his Combat Wombat and Doomsday Briefcase on the carpet and then raised his hands to show he was now unarmed.

"You might as well surrender. I figured out your scheme. The only thing I do not know is who hired you mercenary scum to start this war."

The dolphin activated its infolink, and a hologram appeared between them. It was the head of a wild-haired, grinning, fat man—sort of like a low-rent Guy Fieri only with blue hair. Tom groaned when he saw his rival Interdimensional Insurance Agent, nemesis, and all around jerk face, Jeff Conundrum, appear. "Not you again."

"Heya, Stranger Things."

"You can't be behind this. I left you trapped in Hell."

"Yeah, and that place really sucked! Thanks a lot for ditching me there, by the way. It was all nightmare suffering, grumpy torture demons, and it's really humid so everybody always has swamp butt. Only Hell couldn't hold me, Tommy boy. I escaped! But while I was there, in between painful fiery pitchfork pokings, I came up with this nefarious master plan. Pretty cool, huh?"

"Why would you do all this, Jeff?"

"Easy. Conundrum and Company insures a bunch of those evil companies. If the merger went through, they'd fall under your Premium Platinum Plan and I'd lose all that business. Wendell the financial wizard had to go. So I hired these fanatical dolphin separatists to do my dirty work, knowing you'd be too PC to risk hurting their feelings after your last snafu. Then I started dropping clues that the bums on this loser planet were the guilty party. That's what they get for dumping my coverage and switching to you!"

"But why go through all the effort to rile up the manatees and frame this universe for the crime?"

"That was the best part, Strange Brew. *Revenge*! No matter how it turned out, one of your clients was going to be dissatisfied. You've won Number One in Customer Satisfaction for three years running. I was going to break your winning streak!" Jeff laughed maniacally.

"You would cause an interdimensional war just to keep me from being voted Number One in Customer Service for a fourth year in a row?" Tom whistled. Jeff Conundrum hadn't been quite right in the head for a long time, and apparently a stay in Hell hadn't improved him any. "That's evil even by your standards, Jeff."

"Yeah, psycho," Jimmy chimed in. "That's all sorts of messed up." But then the dolphin thumped Jimmy over the head with the pistol so he quit talking.

"Well, I for one thought it sounded like a perfectly clever plan," squeaked one of the world leaders from beneath a table.

"Shut up, Trudeau! Nobody ever cares what Canada thinks about anything!" Jeff Conundrum roared. "Any second now, Tom, manatee commandos will kick in the door, and when they see their hero looking like a big freeze pop next to the hors d'oeuvres, they'll be so mad they'll bust a cap on this whole planet. I'll keep my business. You'll not win Number One in Customer Satisfaction *and* you'll be dead. So I win! I win big this time, Tom!"

But Tom's keenly-honed Insurance Agent instincts had noticed something the dolphins had not. Before they had appeared, Jimmy had been chipping away at Wendell's block of ice, and a crack had formed. The crack had continued spreading while Jeff had been monologuing. *Villains never learn.*

"You'll never get away with this, Jeff."

"What're you going to do, Tom? Make a move and your intern gets it!"

"I personally do not need to do anything. Company policy says that a Level Ten claim requires a team of agents in order to render maximum customer service . . . Face-Punch, are you in position?"

"*I'm only five thousand meters away, sir,*" the Junior Associate answered over their comlink. "*Piece of cake.*"

"What does cake have to do with anything?"

Jeff Conundrum was confused, but he was only hearing

half the conversation. "Who is getting punched with cake now, huh?"

"*Sorry, Mr. Stranger. Jimmy's use of slang is contagious. I meant I am ready to dispense this claim with extreme prejudice.*"

"Then let us *earn* those one-star dolphin reviews. Fire."

BOOM!

A bullet hole appeared in the wall. The shot was so close that it cut off Jimmy's man bun before striking its intended target. The hostage-taking dolphin was sent hurtling across the buffet.

"Oh, man!" Jimmy had been drenched in dolphin puree. "Right in the blowhole!"

The other dolphins reacted, but not quickly enough.

Tom had known the sonic crack of the Junior Associate's Sniper Wombat would further weaken the block of ice. It shattered and Wendell T. Manatee fell out. The dolphins looked up in terror as they were engulfed in shadow, but it was too late. "*HOOOOON!*" And they were crushed beneath Wendell's sleek blubber.

The smoke was clearing. The dolphin terrorists were down. "Are you unharmed, Wendell and Jimmy?"

Wendell, always calm under pressure, nodded at Tom in the affirmative, but he was already busy contacting his people on his comlink to call off their armada.

"Kinda." Jimmy held up the sad ball of hair that had once been his glorious hipster topknot.

"I'm okay, too!"

"No one asked you, Justin Trudeau." Tom's home world hadn't even had a Canada. They'd just had North Idaho and French Idaho. He turned his attention back to the hologram of Jeff, who was looking rather flustered at the sudden carnage.

"Okay, I'll admit I wasn't expecting you to mulch my dolphins that hard-core."

"That is the difference between us, Jeff. I understand that being a good agent isn't about the customer satisfaction surveys or the awards. It's about doing what you know in your hearts is the best thing for your clients." He turned toward Jimmy and gave him a nod of approval. "And sometimes superior customer service requires following your instincts, no matter how stunningly bad those instincts may seem."

"Thanks, I think?" Jimmy said.

"That's touching, Walker, Texas Stranger."

"That one doesn't even make sense, Jeff."

"I'm running out of things with Strange in the title. So sue me! You may have foiled my plans this time, Tom and Jimmy, but I'll be back. You've not seen the last of Jeff Conundrum!"

"Not this time. The Multiverse has had enough of your bad attitude and lackluster customer service." Tom reached down and picked up his Doomsday Briefcase. "You have gone too far and must be stopped for good."

"What're you going to do about it, smart guy? Huh? You're talking to a hologram of my big awesome head. I'm safely like a billion miles and ten realities away in an armored bunker riding a comet made of Kryptonite."

Tom opened the briefcase. An eerie green glow and a banshee wail gushed out.

"Oooh, scary," Jeff mocked.

"Is this going to be like that part in *Indiana Jones* where ghosts come out and melt our faces off?" Jimmy asked nervously.

"Possible, but unlikely. I had the Ark of the Covenant stacked way in the back." Tom reached inside the briefcase and rummaged around for a bit. He stuck his arm in all the way up to his shoulder, revealing that the briefcase was far bigger on the inside than on the outside. It was also very cluttered with various powerful technologies and artifacts, so it took him a moment to find what he was looking for. Luckily Tom didn't have to use this thing very often. "Ah, here we go." He pulled out a tiny, struggling man, dressed all in green, with a four-leaf clover in his hat.

"Is that a friggin' leprechaun?" Jimmy asked.

"Oh no," squeaked the hologram of Jeff Conundrum, suddenly afraid.

"Which feckin' gobshites dare summon me! Oh, heya, Tom. Ye got two wishes left, then I'm free. Back to me cereal empire!"

"I am aware, Fergus." Leprechauns were a cross-dimensional menace and all-around pain in the butt, but sometimes agents had to make sacrifices.

"Who do ye want me to implode now? I still feel a wee bit badly about what I did to yer carpet and yer HR department from last time."

Wendell covered his eyes with his flippers.

"No implosions. I merely wish for you to bring Jeff Conundrum here."

"I know that Conudrum, the sap. I called his help line once. Spent two hours getting the runaround from a See 'n Say. *Dog goes woof*, me arse. This wish is on the house."

"Whoa, Tom, buddy, let's talk this out like reasonable insurance—"

The leprechaun snapped his tiny fingers and the real Jeff magically appeared in the room with them. "—professionals." Jeff looked around. "Oh, crap."

The president of China clapped his hands in delight. "It works! I did not even have to sing the song this time!"

"Now, Tom, boyo, let me tell ye of me magically delicious Lucky Charms. Ye skip the milk and soak 'em direct in whiskey—" Tom shoved the leprechaun roughly back into the briefcase. He had better things to do than listen to the crazed ramblings of a cereal-addicted marshmallow junkie.

Some manatee commandos hovered into the resort in their power armor, led by Muffy "Sparkles" Wappler, who was chewing her bubble gum in a loud and most satisfied manner. "Just like I told you guys, here's your culprit." She gestured at Jeff Conundrum. "He's all yours."

"No! Not manatee justice. Please, send me back to Hell instead."

Wendell's roughnecks grabbed Conundrum by his neon glowing suspenders and dragged him away as he kicked and struggled. "You'll still lose, Tom! Nobody's customer service is good enough to fix this mess! Mu-wha-ha-ha-ha—" but manatees have no patience for gloating super villain laughs, so they "accidentally" banged Jeff's head against the door frame on the way out.

Tom looked around. Past the cowering world leaders and flattened dolphins, through the broken window, the golf course still burned. The President had wandered in and was composing a snarky tweet. It would be all over social media. Sadly, Jeff was right. This claim was a big mess, and it would take a lot of work to satisfy these customers.

But it was moments like this which separated outstanding insurance agents from the merely great.

"It's time to roll up our sleeves, team."

❖ EPILOGUE ❖
Mandatory Overtime

SEVERAL GRUELING HOURS LATER, Tom was alone on Home Office World, putting the finishing touches on the settlement paperwork and thinking about his productive workday.

Since they were so fiscally responsible, the manatees had accepted full responsibility for all the damages they had caused against all non-dolphin actors. So they'd not even needed to go to Arbitration. Because of the exchange rate between Wendell's ultra high-tech home world and Jimmy's relatively backward Earth, it didn't even cost them much. The manatees repaired the Mar-a-Lago golf course for less than their daily lettuce budget.

But then it had gotten personal. The negotiations had almost broken down over the pain and suffering payouts. Both sides were proud, hard-headed negotiators, and both had been wronged. A respected neutral statesman had to be brought in from off world to mediate. Adam Baldwin was paid handsomely for his time.

Eventually, it was decided that the President of Earth

#169-J-00561 would be compensated for the pain and suffering caused by his infamous typo with a one-year supply of Kentucky Fried Velociraptor Extra Crispy Taco Bowls. A settlement which Tom had to admit he was a little envious of. Carl the Secret Service Agent was able to keep his job. The Secretary of Defense declared today to have been the finest round of golf he'd ever played.

Tom had no idea what happened to Justin Trudeau, but he usually did not concern himself with world leaders from any country which did not at least have its own aircraft carrier.

Harambe the Gorilla from Earth #984-A-3256 had, in fact, been fired from his bouncer job due to the bus incident, but Tom recognized talent when he saw it. After interviewing with Muffy, it was decided the gorilla would start on Monday as their new HR manager.

The dolphin home worlds disavowed the fanatical dolphin separatists hired as mercenaries by Jeff Conundrum. They also said they had no idea what Tom was talking about when he brought up all those "offended" one-star reviews. Tom remained suspicious of their denials.

Even though his evil company merger deal had fallen apart, overall CorreiaTech Prime had been very pleased with the outcome of his Level Ten claim. He ended up making a great deal of money that afternoon selling anti-human weapon systems to the manatees and anti-manatee weapon systems to the humans, in preparation for potential future conflicts. Then he'd secretly made even more money under the table selling both types of weapons to some really vengeful dolphins. The Interdimensional Lord of Hate was kind of a dick like that.

As for rogue insurance agent Jeff Conundrum, he had been taken to the dreaded manatee black-site prison known only as *Under-Gitmo*. Which, despite the name, was actually beneath a lake in Minnesota.

In order to thank his rescuers and to apologize for his followers' overly enthusiastic vigilante behavior, Wendell the Manatee had thrown a pool party and invited all the humans who had been so terribly wronged. All of the supermodels and rock stars who followed Wendell on Twitter also attended. Tom was not a fan of such frivolity, but he had excused his exhausted team to go to the celebration. *What the heck?* They had earned it, and it was the weekend.

Everyone had a fine time. Despite Conundrum's best efforts, it appeared that customer satisfaction had been brought to the Multiverse once more.

Tom had briefly joined them at the Mar-a-Lago Presidential Water Slide Park. However, he was too preoccupied with work to partake in the festivities. Jimmy, on the other hand, did not have that issue. He had already declared himself Beer Pong Champion of the Multiverse, and then gotten into a drunken slap fight when he'd accused one of Wendell's posse of "manateesplaining." (In his defense, Jimmy had been in a bad mood because it turned out all the contestants in the wet T-shirt contest were lady sea cows.) Luckily the fight had been broken up by the Swedish Bikini Team before anyone had been hurt.

Frankly, Jimmy was totally unsuited for Interdimensional Insurance. Yet, somehow, he had still managed to save the day. There was no rational or logical explanation for that. It was enough to make Tom question his earlier decision to rehire Jimmy as his intern.

But then there had been a glimmer of hope. Tom had been having a coworker-appropriate conversation with Muffy, when someone had tossed a head of cabbage to the hungry manatees loafing in the pool. Jimmy had seen this and, without hesitation, sprung into action.

"Ambassador Cabgar! NOOOO!" Jimmy leapt into the pool and begun fighting to save what he'd wrongfully assumed was a potential client. "Get your filthy snouts off him!" He tore a leaf from a manatee's mouth. "You monsters! Spit him out." He grabbed that manatee by the jowls and shook him. "Spit! Give it! Bad water cow! Bad!"

It was in that moment that Tom understood. Though Jimmy may have only had one heart, it was in the right place. He was terrible at quite literally everything else, but Jimmy really did care about their customers. So Tom decided then and there that he would do everything in his power to help Jimmy achieve his true insurance potential. Of course, the manatee commandos did not like having their dinner interrupted by a drunken human, so they began to kick the living crap out of poor Jimmy.

"You think maybe we should step in before they drown him, Mr. Stranger?"

"No. I think we shall consider this a *teachable moment*. Have a pleasant weekend, Ms. Wappler."

"See ya Monday!" Muffy said as she wandered off to try to get Adam Baldwin's autograph.

Then Tom had returned to Home Office World to wrap up their paperwork. Late that night, as he made an addendum to subsection 14, paragraph 4, appendix J of the claim, Tom Stranger smiled, because he knew he had the best job in the Multiverse.

I told the story about how Tom Stranger *came to be in the last* Target Rich Environment, *but it is kind of fun how Mike Kupari gave me an idea for some really silly blog posts, and those somehow turned into a bestselling series of audiobooks narrated by a famous actor. I recently completed* Tom Stranger 3, Apocalypse Cow.

One fun note, on all those bits where it said INSERT DOLPHIN NOISE HERE, *we used the same exact dolphin sounds for all of those dialog bits with wildly different meanings. It's a very nuanced language.*

Monster Hunter Memoirs: Sinners
9781481482875 • $7.99 US/$10.99 Can.

Monster Hunter Memoirs: Saints
9781481484114 • $7.99 US/$10.99 Can.

THE FORGOTTEN WARRIOR SAGA

Son of the Black Sword
9781476781570 • $9.99 US/$12.99 Can.

House of Assassins
9781982124458 • $8.99 US/$11.99 Can.

THE GRIMNOIR CHRONICLES

Hard Magic
9781439134344 • $15.00 US/$17.00 Can.

Warbound
9781476736525 • $7.99 US/$9.99 Can.

MILITARY ADVENTURE
with Mike Kupari

Dead Six
9781451637588 • $7.99 US/$9.99 Can.

Alliance of Shadows
9781481482912 • $7.99 US/$10.99 Can.

Invisible Wars
9781481484336 • $18.00 US/$25.00 Can.

The Hot Gate　　　(pb) 978-1-4516-3818-9 • $7.99

■ ■ ■

Von Neumann's War with Travis S. Taylor
　　　(pb) 1-4165-5530-8 • $7.99

Citizens ed. by John Ringo & Brian M. Thomsen
　　　(trade pb) 978-1-4391-3347-7 • $16.00

■ ■ ■

The Looking Glass Series

Into the Looking Glass　　　(pb) 1-4165-2105-4 • $7.99

Vorpal Blade with Travis S. Taylor　　　(pb) 1-4165-5586-2 • $7.99

Manxome Foe with Travis S. Taylor　　　(pb) 1-4165-9165-6 • $7.99

Claws That Catch with Travis S. Taylor
　　　(hc) 1-4165-5587-0 • $25.00
　　　(pb) 978-1-4391-3313-2 • $7.99

Master of Hard-Core Thrillers
The Kildar Saga

Ghost　　　(pb) 1-4165-2087-2 • $7.99

Kildar　　　(pb) 1-4165-2133-X • $7.99

Choosers of the Slain　　　(hc) 1-4165-2070-8 • $25.00

Unto the Breach　　　(hc) 1-4165-0940-2 • $26.00
　　　(pb) 1-4165-5535-8 • $7.99

A Deeper Blue　　　(pb) 1-4165-5550-1 • $7.99

Tiger by the Tail with Ryan Sear
　　　(hc) 978-1-4516-3856-1 • $25.00
　　　(pb) 978-1-4767-3615-0 • $7.99

■ ■ ■

The Last Centurion　　　(hc) 1-4165-5553-6 • $25.00
　　　(pb) 978-1-4391-3291-3 • $7.99

Master of Dark Fantasy

Princess of Wands (hc) 1-4165-0923-2 • $25.00

Queen of Wands (hc) 978-1-4516-3789-2 • $25.00
(pb) 978-1-4516-3917-9 • $7.99

Master of Bolos

The Road to Damascus with Linda Evans
(pb) 0-7434-9916-6 • $7.99

. . .

And don't miss Ringo's NY Times best-selling epic adventures written with David Weber:

March Upcountry (pb) 0-7434-3538-9 • $7.99

March to the Sea (pb) 0-7434-3580-X • $7.99

March to the Stars (pb) 0-7434-8818-0 • $7.99

Throne of Stars (omni tpb) 978-1-4767-3666-2 • $14.00
March to the Stars and *We Few* in one massive volume.